BLOOD OF GODS

The Breaking World

BY DAVID DALGLISH AND ROBERT J. DUPERRE

The Breaking World Series

Dawn of Swords
Wrath of Lions
Blood of Gods

ALSO BY DAVID DALGLISH

The Shadowdance Series

A Dance of Cloaks
A Dance of Blades
A Dance of Mirrors
A Dance of Shadows
A Dance of Ghosts

The Half-Orcs

The Weight of Blood
The Cost of Betrayal
The Death of Promises
The Shadows of Grace
A Sliver of Redemption
The Prison of Angels

The Paladins

Night of Wolves
Clash of Faiths
The Old Ways
The Broken Pieces

Others

A Land of Ash (compilation)

ALSO BY ROBERT J. DUPERRE

The Rift

Volume 1: The Fall & Dead of Winter
Volume 2: Death Springs Eternal & The Summer Son

Others

Silas
The Gate: 13 Dark and Odd Tales (compilation)
The Gate 2: 13 Tales of Isolation and Despair (compilation)

BLOOD OF GODS

The Breaking World

David Dalglish
Robert J. Duperre

47NORTH

This is a work of fiction. Names, characters, organizations, places, events, and incidents are either products of the author's imagination or are used fictitiously.

Text copyright © 2014 by David Dalglish and Robert J. Duperre
All rights reserved.

No part of this book may be reproduced, or stored in a retrieval system, or transmitted in any form or by any means, electronic, mechanical, photocopying, recording, or otherwise, without express written permission of the publisher.

Published by 47North, Seattle

www.apub.com

Amazon, the Amazon logo, and 47North are trademarks of Amazon.com, Inc., or its affiliates.

ISBN-13: 9781477824986
ISBN-10: 1477824987

Cover design by Kerrie Robertson Illustration, Inc.
Illustrated by Alejandro Colucci

Library of Congress Control Number: 2014936354

Printed in the United States of America

To all our dear readers,
this book is for you.

ASHHUR'S PARADISE

NELDAR

Mt. Hailen
NORTHERN PLAINS
Rigon River
Jelwood
CRESTWELL MOUNTAINS
Sully Lake
Riverrun
Thettletown
Veldaren
Erznia
Beaver Lake
Brent
Omnmount
CLUBFOOT MOUNTAINS
Karak's Bridge
Temple of the Flesh
Port Laneaster
Quellasar
Ghostwood
HAVEN
THULON OCEAN

CAST OF CHARACTERS

ASHHUR'S PARADISE

ASHHUR, God of Justice, creator of ASHHUR'S PARADISE

—AHAESARUS, Master Warden of the west

—JUDARIUS, a Warden of the west

—AZARIAH, a Warden of the west, brother of JUDARIUS

—ROLAND NORSMAN, his confidant, deceased

—JUDAH, a Warden of the west

—GRENDEL, a Warden of the west

MORDEINA

BENJAMIN MARYLL, first king of ASHHUR'S PARADISE, 16 years old

HOUSE DUTAUREAU

ISABEL DUTAUREAU, first child of ASHHUR

—RICHARD, her created husband

—ABIGAIL ESCHETON, their first daughter, 72 years old

—TUROCK ESCHETON, her husband, 40 years old

—their children:

LAURIA DAGEESH, daughter, 25 years old, wife of UULON

CETHLYNN, daughter, 23 years old

DOREK, son, 20 years old

BYRON, son, 19 years old

JARAK, son, 17 years old

PENDET, son, 9 years old

—PATRICK, their only son, 67 years old

—BRIGID FRONIN, their second daughter, 64 years old, wife of BAYEN

—CARA, their third daughter, 63 years old

—KEELA NEFRAM, their fourth daughter, 60 years old, wife of DANIEL

—NESSA, their fifth daughter, deceased

—HOWARD PHILIP BAEDAN, master steward of the house

THE TURNCLOAKS

—PRESTON ENDER, brother of CORTON, leader of the TURNCLOAKS

—EDWARD, his son, 18 years old

—RAGNAR, his son, 17 years old

—BRICK MULLIN, a boy from NELDAR, deceased

—TRISTAN VALESON, a boy from NELDAR, 15 years old

—JOFFREY GOLDENROD, a boy from NELDAR, 14 years old

—RYANN MATHESON, a boy from NELDAR, 17 years old

—BIG FLICK, a boy from NELDAR, 18 years old

—LITTLE FLICK, a boy from NELDAR, 16 years old

KER

HOUSE GOROGOROS

BESSUS GORGOROS, second child of ASHHUR, deceased

—DAMASPIA, his created wife, deceased

—BARDIYA, their only son, 88 years old

—KI-NAN RENALD, his friend and confidante

—GORDO HEMPSMAN, a man of KER

—TULANI, his wife

—KEISHA, their daughter, 8 years old

—ONNA LENSBROUGH, a man of KER

NELDAR

KARAK, God of Order, Divinity of the East, creator of NELDAR

VELIXAR (formerly JACOB EVENINGSTAR), first man of DEZREL, High Prophet of KARAK

—MALCOLM GREGORIAN, Lord Commander of THE ARMY OF KARAK

HOUSE CRESTWELL

CLOVIS CRESTWELL, first child of KARAK

—LANIKE, his created wife, deceased

—LORD COMMANDER AVILA, their first daughter, deceased

—JOSEPH, their first son, deceased

—THESSALY, their second daughter, deceased

—MOIRA ELREN, their exiled third daughter, 54 years old

—UTHER, their second son, deceased

—CRIAN, their third son, deceased

HOUSE MORI

SOLEH MORI, second child of KARAK, deceased

—IBIS, her created husband, deceased

—VULFRAM, their first son, deceased

—YENGE, his wife, 35 years old

—their children:

ALEXANDER, son, 20 years old

LYANA, daughter, 18 years old

CALEIGH, daughter, 14 years old

—ORIS, their second son, 68 years old

—EBBE, his wife, 28 years old

—their children:

CONATA, daughter, 11 years old

ZEPPA, daughter, 9 years old

—ADELINE PALING, their first daughter, deceased

—ULRIC, their third son, deceased

—DIMONA, his wife, 43 years old

—their children:

TITON, son, 22 years old

APHREDES, son, 21 years old

JULIAN, son, 18 years old

—RACHIDA GEMCROFT, wife of PEYTR, 53 years old

VELDAREN

KING ELDRICH VAELOR THE FIRST, second king of NELDAR, 39 years old

—KARL DOGON, the king's bodyguard

—PULO JENATT, captain of the Palace Guard

—JONN TREMMEN, Palace Guard

—RODDALIN HARLAN, Palace Guard

—JOBEN TUSTLEWHITE, priest of KARAK

—LAUREL LAWRENCE, councilwoman, 23 years old

—GUSTER HALFHORN, elder councilman, deceased

—ZEBEDIAH ZANE, councilman

—DIRK COLDMINE, councilman, deceased

—WALTER OLLERAY, councilman

—MARIUS TRUFONT, elder councilman

—LENROY MOTT, councilman

THE MERCHANTS

—ROMEO CONNINGTON, high merchant of RIVERRUN

—CLEO CONNINGTON, high merchant of RIVERRUN

—QUESTER BILLINGS, Crimson Sword of RIVERRUN

—MATTHEW BRENNAN, high merchant of PORT LANCASTER, deceased

—CATHERINE, his widow, regent of PORT LANCASTER

—their children:

MARGERY, daughter, 15 years old

ELLA, daughter, 13 years old

RHODA, daughter, 10 years old

CATTIA, daughter, 5 years old

RYAN, son, 3 years old

—BREN TORRANT, bodyguard of CATHERINE

—URSULA, housemaid

—PENETTA, housemaid

—LORI, housemaid

—PEYTR GEMCROFT, high merchant of HAVEN, husband of RACHIDA

—TRENTON BLACKBARD, high merchant of BRENT

—TOD GARLAND, high merchant of THETTLETOWN

—TOMAS MUDRAKER, high merchant of GRONSWIK

THE ELVES

THE DEZREN

STONEWOOD

—CLEOTIS MELN, former Lord of STONEWOOD, deceased

—AUDRIANNA, his wife

—their children:

CARSKEL, their banished son, 183 years old

AUBRIENNA, daughter, deceased

AULLIENNA, daughter, 14 years old, betrothed to KINDREN THYNE

—AAROMAR KULN, protector of LADY AUDRIANNA

—NONI CLANSHAW, nursemaid of AULLIENNA

—DETRICK MELN, brother of CLEOTIS, acting Lord of STONEWOOD

—ETHIR AYERS, confidante of DETRICK

—DAVISHON HINSBREW, confidante of DETRICK

DEZEREA

—ORDEN THYNE, Lord of DEZEREA

—PHYRRA, his wife

—KINDREN, son, 18 years old, betrothed to AULLIENNA MELN

THE QUELLAN

—RUVEN SINISTEL, Neyvar (King) of QUELLASAR

—JEADRA, his wife

—CEREDON, their son, 97 years old

—IOLAS SINISTEL, cousin of RUVEN, member of the TRIAD

—CONALL SINISTEL, cousin of RUVEN, member of the TRIAD, deceased

—AESON SINISTEL, cousin of RUVEN, member of the TRIAD, deceased

—AERLAND SHEN, chief of the EKREISSAR

PROLOGUE

The skies burned red as men fell bleeding from above, and Ashhur watched it all with a shard of fear in his heart. His city of Allaketh was protected by a massive circular wall, the homes within dwarfed by a mountain of marble. Yet that mattered not when Thulos's soldiers flew on crimson wings, their bronze armor glistening in the twilight of a fading sun as the light of a thousand fires consuming his beloved city.

"Trust our archers," Karak said beside him, the two overlooking the battle from the steps of the Golden Castle. Ashhur glanced to his brother, bedecked in fine dark steel plate and resting an enormous ethereal sword across his broad shoulders. He looked confident, but Ashhur knew it for the lie it was. They could hold no confidence in their creations, for they were weak compared to Thulos. The humans had trusted in Justice and Order to prevail, for their allies in Love and Creation to hold back the tide, but against the God of War, they were all inferior. Humankind sought power, and the easiest way to achieve it was through their vengeful brother.

Giant balls of flaming pitch soared over the walls, accompanied by another wave of winged soldiers. The pitch smashed atop homes, setting them ablaze as Allaketh's archers fired in vain from along the walls, downing foes with their deadly aim, yet unable to stem the tide. Ashhur drew his own sword as battle began atop those ramparts, their men quickly falling.

"We have no choice," Ashhur said. "The gates will soon fall, and the footmen of Thulos will make their charge. We must meet them head on."

Karak pulled the sword from his back and ran his other hand through his dark brown hair, for not a single strand would he allow to remain out of place.

"So be it," he said. "If our followers cannot find victory, let us give it to them."

The red haze blackened as the fire spread throughout the city. The two brother gods walked side by side down the road, leaving the castle behind them, listening to the screams of the dying. Every whisper, every groan was perfectly clear to their ears. For Ashhur, it was nearly overwhelming. There was no justice in what they witnessed, only betrayal and murder. He wished he could grant them comfort, even in their dying breaths, but there would be no time for that. The God of War came to their gates, and strength alone would defy him.

Ashhur readied his blade, its fine edge shimmering white and gold. Thirty of the winged soldiers—war demons, as Thulos had named them—approached from above in a diamond formation. Letting out a cry to their god, the demons dove with near suicidal speed. They'd give their lives for Thulos, if only to bring him a drop of blood closer to victory. Such devotion. Such loyalty. Ashhur wondered where he and his brother had gone so very wrong.

"Your very forms reek of chaos!" Karak shouted to them as they dove. "Come die and be cleansed."

Fire wreathed his sword, and he swung in wide arcs, unafraid of the charge. Ashhur stepped aside, giving himself room to fight, and he met the assault with his own twirling blade of light. With each swing they cut down several demons at once, blasting through their bronze armor, shattering their wings so that both blood and feathers rained down from above.

Three demons flew past, slashing out with long halberds. Ashhur twisted, let his armor absorb the glancing hits, and then spun with sword raised high. As the third demon curved about, a great flash shone from the metal, blinding in its power. Unable to see, the three banked upward, failing to react in time. Into one of the tall marble homes they slammed. Ashhur heard every bone break, heard the drip of their blood, the crunch of their armor as the force of their impact bent its shape. A single step left, a pivot, and his sword swung through the air, the arc perfect, slicing in twain the first demon and removing the head of the second following behind. Their bodies crashed against Ashhur, but his feet remained planted, their weight bouncing off him as if he were made of stone.

"Chaos!" Karak screamed, seemingly overwhelmed by fury. Fire blasted from his sword, lashing into the air in great waves. Those demons unfortunate enough to be in its way were pulverized, screaming and plummeting, their skin blackening to ash, their armor melting. Around and around danced Karak's sword, filling the sky with fire, until the last of the demons fled toward the outer wall to rejoin their god.

Their departure did little to calm Ashhur's brother.

"Everywhere, chaos!" Karak roared. "The fields, the rivers, our cities and forests! Only the graveyards know peace."

The ground rumbled, and from the far wall they both heard a loud *crack*.

"Blame our brother," Ashhur said. "And save your fury. The siege engines roll forth."

They ran faster, taking giant strides with their long legs. At either side cowered the women and children of Allaketh, taking to the streets to cry out their fear and grief to their gods. Ashhur did his best to ignore them, to focus on the task at hand. It was they he sought to defend, those powerless before the war machines of Thulos, his demons ruling the air, his paladins overwhelming the ground. At least the archers had done much to whittle down the fliers so that they were but a nuisance to Allaketh's ground troops as they massed before the great double doors protecting the city. But without men on the walls, there was nothing to slow the battering rams, and with another great tremble the doors shook.

"They will not last," Ashhur said.

"Thulos will lead their charge," said Karak. "Let us meet him and end this now. This world has no need for a God of War. Let Order and Justice be all that reigns."

"We'll reign over only corpses," Ashhur said, thinking of the conquest Thulos had waged across the continent, devastating city after city.

Karak's sword lifted higher.

"I can imagine worse fates," he said. "Stand tall before our soldiers. We are their gods, their source of strength and courage. Do not fail them."

Toward the crumbling gate they dashed, and their soldiers moved aside so their path remained unblocked. Rumble after rumble, *crack* after *crack*, multiple battering rams hammered into the steel-reinforced wood. Ashhur felt his focus narrowing, saw the sheen across his sword reach blinding levels. All his rage he focused into his weapon. With it, he could cleave stone and steel like warm butter. With it, he could even pierce the flesh of a god. A great bellowing cry left his throat, drowning out the cacophony unleashed by the shattering of the gates. Ashhur led the way, Karak a mere footstep behind, as Thulos's paladins came surging forth. They held their radiant weapons, hammers and swords and axes, and their armor was the finest in the land, bronze-tinted steel that shimmered red with the power of their faith.

Against the rage of gods, that armor meant nothing.

Karak and Ashhur waded into them, and if the onslaught of paladins was a river, they were the dam. Blood soaked their armor, and every swing of their weapons brought down dozens. At either side were Allaketh's defenders, forming an enclosing ring so that any who somehow survived were quickly cut down. Soon the door was sealed with the bodies of the dead. His weapon heavy in his hand, Ashhur took a step back to survey all they'd done. Hundreds of paladins, Thulos's finest, broken by their fury.

But Thulos was not there.

"We have been played for fools," Karak said, and Ashhur heard the trace of fear buried in his anger.

To the far west came a new rumble, deeper, longer. With it came an ear-splitting *snap*, and there was no doubt as to what Ashhur heard. The very wall itself was crumbling.

"Let none pass!" Ashhur ordered the defenders before running back up the road, needing to get higher, to climb the hill of the Golden Castle if he must. It didn't take long to find a vantage point, a sturdily built house of marble that, with his long arms and legs, he climbed with ease. Once atop it, he towered over the homes, and with dread growing in his heart, he watched the western wall crumble, fire and stone exploding in all directions. Ashhur could only guess as to what weapon his brother wielded, but in the end it didn't matter. Their wall was breached, and there were no defenders there to protect the gap, to stem the tide of millions pledged to Thulos's banner.

And in the heart of those millions of swords and shields, their brother would walk, towering over the humans, soaking in the power of their faith.

"Brother . . . " Ashhur said, but the words of surrender, of hopelessness, seemed impossible to form on his tongue.

"No," Karak said. "Follow me to the castle. All is not lost."

As they ran, the ground shook beneath their feet, vibrating from the river of flesh and armor that poured in from the west. Screams of fear joined them, and Ashhur could hear cries of surrender, men and women kneeling and begging to be spared. None were. The time for surrender was before the walls were breached, before the demons filled the air and dumped burning pitch onto the great city.

At the door to the castle gathered the last of the defenders, a paltry hundred. There was no hiding the fear in their eyes, but they stood tall. Even at the end they had faith in him, Ashhur realized. Had faith there would be salvation for them, a way their god would protect them. But there wasn't. The end had come, for all of them, for against Thulos's blade, even gods could die.

"We need time," Karak shouted as they arrived. "Descend the hill, and hold it with your lives. Even a single heartbeat may decide our life or death!"

They saluted and rushed down the hill. Ashhur watched them run with pride. Karak, however, put his hands on the doors of the castle and closed his eyes.

"I don't understand," Ashhur said. "What is it . . . "

"Quiet," Karak said. "There is a way, but only if she hears us."

"She? Who?"

"Celestia."

Ashhur could not believe it. That was his brother's last and only plan?

"What makes you think she would aid us?" he asked. "When we were there last, we destroyed her world, nearly ripped it asunder."

"We were whole then," Karak said. "Now we are but broken pieces of Kaurthulos. She will know this. She will understand. Where else have we to go?"

"There are thousands of other worlds," Ashhur said.

"And we only know the way to one."

Karak closed his eyes again and murmured prayers loaded with magic and power. The door shimmered, turned translucent for a moment, then returned to normal.

"It matters not if she heard you," Ashhur said when his brother's prayers halted. "What creature or army could she send to us to aid in our battle?"

"I do not seek aid," Karak said. "I seek sanctuary."

With that, he pulled open the doors to the Golden Castle. Instead of the fine hall within, filled with paintings and lined with a vibrant red carpet, there stood a swirling portal of violet and shadow. In its heart Ashhur saw stars twirling, planets and moons revolving in a constant dance. A cold wind blew from the portal's center, and even through his armor he felt its chill.

"You would have us flee?" he asked.

"What other choice do we have?" Karak asked. He looked to the portal, and Ashhur joined him. From within he saw a feminine shape, a hand beckoning. Celestia would accept them even after all they had done? It seemed bewildering to him, but she was a goddess herself, and her actions were her own. But to leave their world, their people, his beloved city of Allaketh?

"We failed here," Karak insisted as Thulos's army converged from all directions. "We let humankind grow unchecked. We thought our teachings would be enough. But it will never be enough, not unless we keep a close hand. Not unless we ensure loyalty with every breath we take. Let us go. Let us make amends in a world where Order and Justice may still have a home."

Without waiting for an answer, Karak stepped into the portal and vanished.

Ashhur looked back, gazing upon his burning city. He listened to the cries of the fearful, the crackling flames, the soldiers dying at the bottom of the hill. And then he saw his brother marching through their ranks, face hidden with a great horned helm. The God of War. The conqueror of all.

"Never again," Ashhur swore. "And my people . . . please, forgive me."

With that, he turned and stepped into the portal, felt reality shift around him, slipping him through the stars, to the realm of the goddess Celestia and the land she called Dezrel.

CHAPTER

1

Karak's eyes shone with liquid fire that burned through the morning mist. The god paced across the dead brown earth covering the valley in which his army camped, his gaze constantly returning to the walled township that loomed in the distance. Velixar saw anger in his stare; anger that grew even more pronounced whenever he looked at the massive tree that had risen from the ground, sealing the gap in the wall his fireball had created. The deity's giant hands curled into fists, and the brightness of his eyes intensified. It was only when he turned his head to see his near fifteen thousand children busy at work that his stern expression softened even the tiniest bit.

The morning air was crisp, and the evening dew still lingered, causing Velixar's cloak to cling to his flesh. Though a cool wind blew, the High Prophet felt no chill. The fire burning inside him, stoked by the demon whose essence he had swallowed, was all the warmth he needed.

He had risen before sunrise along with Lord Commander Malcolm Gregorian, joining the one-eyed man in awakening more than two hundred of the soldiers who had been sleeping fitfully in their tents. There was much work to do: bark that needed to be stripped, stakes that required sharpening, sanded timber that had to be fastened together with twine and iron nails. It all filled the wide expanse of the valley with a bustle of activity as saws ripped through wood and hammers *thumped.*

Yet despite the soldiers' work, despite all the lessons Karak taught them, progress was maddeningly slow. They'd built sixty ladders, stacked neatly in twelve piles to the left of the construction site, but they had only managed to finish three meager siege engines over the eleven days since their initial attack on Mordeina's walls: two solid towers and a single catapult. The rest of the partially formed engines sat useless throughout the valley, half-formed giants awaiting the necessary materials to complete them.

It wasn't the soldiers' fault, Velixar knew; when Ashhur, Karak's brother god, had created a legion of grayhorn men to defend his people, he had stripped the land of life, which accounted for the dead grass crunching beneath their feet. The trees of the nearby forest were brittle as spent tindersticks, crumbling away in a rain of dust when struck by an ax. A weakened Karak had tried to raise more trees from deep within the soil, but it seemed Ashhur had decimated the land to such an extent that nothing could grow there any longer.

"It will be years until this earth is fertile again," Karak had told him with a growl. "I have no time for this." And so the soldiers carried their axes a mile toward the Gods' Road, chopped down the trees in the healthy forest, and lugged the trunks all the way back to the camp, where they could be stripped and quartered and assembled into tools of war.

Velixar eyed the workers, sweat dripping off their brows as they slaved away. He did not like the weariness in their expressions, or the labor in their movements. Each hammer seemed to weigh a hundred pounds; each plank lifted with a grunt as if it weighed ten times that much. The soldiers were tired and hungry, and each morning he noticed that a handful who had been working dutifully the day before had disappeared in the night. The previous evening he'd ordered the Lord Commander to have the camp watched while it slept, and Malcolm's sentries caught six soldiers attempting to tiptoe out of the valley under the cover of darkness. Those six were now fastened to a post in front of the camp, beaten and bound by throat, wrist, and ankle, pleading for mercy with any who passed within earshot.

As morning progressed and the clouds passed over the sun, the pleading of those captured intensified. Velixar stood back and watched with interest as a soldier approached the bound men, offering a cup of mulled wine. Malcolm was on the soldier a second later, yanking him backward by the hair and tossing him to the ground. The Lord Commander pressed his boot into the man's throat, his one good eye watching the young soldier struggle. None of the other soldiers came forward to aid their distressed comrade; despite the fact that his left arm was still in a sling, every soldier knew Malcolm Gregorian was not to be trifled with. Finally the soldier's protests dwindled, and Malcolm removed his foot before giving him a swift kick in the side and demanding he get back to work.

Velixar felt a heavy hand fall on his shoulder, and he gazed up at Karak's face.

"Yes, my Lord?" he asked quietly.

The god knelt beside him. "There is unrest among my children," he said.

"They are hungry, my Lord, and exhausted. Our caches of salted meats and vegetables have dwindled. We haven't enough to sustain so many men."

That was the second price of the dead land they camped on; the quest for food had become as trying as the quest for lumber, and required just as many men to retrieve, which further slowed progress. Their only other recourse was to wait for the next train of supply wagons to arrive from Neldar, but they could be waiting for those supplies for a week, if not a month. To alleviate the stresses on his god's men, Velixar had dumped the foraging duties onto the elf Aerland Shen and his band of a hundred Ekreissar, the best warriors the Quellan elves had to offer. Though proficient with bows, the elves were fighters, not hunters, and the provisions they returned with proved dissatisfying. In the end Velixar could only hope that the people of Mordeina, trapped as they were inside their walls, suffered far worse.

"They are human," Karak said. "They will persevere if their love for me is true."

"Love does not fill an empty stomach, my Lord."

Karak's glowing eyes turned to the six bound men.

"Why are the deserters tied up in view of all?"

"To strip them of their freedom, to teach the others that abandonment will be punished harshly."

Karak grunted. "You disappoint me. Losing freedom is a paltry reprimand, High Prophet. Think of a more effective method to teach my children."

"I will, my Lord," Velixar said with a bow.

Karak stood and turned away, loping back to his massive pavilion. Velixar threw open his cloak and marched through the throng of laborers, making his way toward the deserters. They saw him approach, and six sets of eyes widened in fear.

"Have mercy!" one of them begged. "We were starving and only wished to find food!"

The captive closest to the post lifted his head to the heavens. "Listen to your prophet," he said loudly. He had straight, silvery hair, copper eyes, and a firm square jaw, as if he had sprouted equally from both the Crestwell and Mori lines. "We were caught; now we pay the price like men."

The others fell silent. By then, the sounds of construction had died away behind Velixar as the working soldiers stepped forward to watch the spectacle.

Velixar tilted his head at the man. "What is your name, soldier?"

"Donnell Frost," he said, dipping his head in respect.

"And where are you from?"

"Felwood, High Prophet."

"I see." Velixar looked down the line at the pathetic, whimpering men. "And the rest of them, as well?"

The man nodded. "We all worked in the armory."

"And did your cohort speak the truth? Was your party foraging for food?"

Donnell's staid expression never changed.

"We were not, High Prophet."

"Shut up, Donnell!" shouted a captive with a scar running across his brow.

Velixar squinted, the red glow of his eyes intensifying, and the scarred captive sank back in his restraints, clutching at his throat. "Go on, soldier," Velixar told Donnell. "Tell it, and tell it true."

Donnell's eyes brimmed with tears even though his manner remained strong. "We thought the situation hopeless. With the goddess defending Ashhur, what chance is there of victory? She would strike us down the moment we tried to scale those walls."

"Is that so?" asked Velixar, his heart sinking in his chest at the words.

"It is." Donnell's eyes glanced toward his cohorts. "It's been months since we laid eyes on our families and bedded our wives, so we thought—*all of us*—that we should return home."

Velixar took a deep breath, gathering his strength. "And was this the correct choice?"

Once more, Donnell dipped his head. "It was not, High Prophet. We succumbed to weakness."

"Asshole," one of the other captives muttered out of the corner of his mouth.

Velixar took a step backward and turned to face the massive crowd gathered behind him.

"These men are guilty of blasphemy of the highest order!" he shouted. "The greatest sin we children of Karak may commit is to turn away from the one who created us. The love of your god fills your lungs with breath, your muscles with strength, your minds with knowledge. Without that love . . . " He spun back around and faced the captives.

"Without that love, you deserve none of it."

Velixar raised his hands above his head and reached down deep within himself, accessing the demon's ancient knowledge. Shadows swirled around his fingertips, black lightning sparked, and the red glow from his eyes heightened tenfold. He felt power surge through him, making his every hair stand on end. He then lowered his gaze to the deserters, imagined their bodies undone, their insides boiling, their tissue and fibers dissolving.

And then it came to pass.

The screams of the bound men were deafening before they died. All but Donnell. The copper-eyed, silver-haired man remained unharmed, though he silently shook.

This one is nearly as faithful as Malcolm, Velixar thought. *Such a shame.*

"The others were undeserving of Karak's mercy," Velixar said, addressing the bloodstained man but ensuring his voice was loud enough for those gathered to hear. "You, Donnell Frost, have shown wisdom even when facing death, and courage before fear. Your punishment shall be swift, your death painless, your soul made pure for the eternity to follow."

Despite his constraints, the man bowed low. "Thank you, High Prophet."

The heavily scarred Lord Commander Malcolm was the one to unfasten Donnell's restraints and lead him to the edge of the construction site, in the shadow of a completed siege tower. As Velixar watched, the doomed man knelt and presented his neck. A young soldier helped Malcolm out of his sling. Malcolm winced as he reached behind his back and slid Darkfall, his giant sword, from its sheath. The Lord Commander held the sword above his head with both hands. "For Karak!" he shouted. A moment later Donnell's head rolled across the dead grass, his lifeless copper eyes open, staring heavenward.

After the body was disposed of and the head was carried away to Velixar's tent, the soldiers went back to work on the engines with renewed, fear-fueled vigor. Troubled, Velixar climbed the low hill on which Karak's pavilion sat. His eyes kept turning toward Mordeina, its massive walls, and the tree Celestia had brought up from the earth to thwart them. In his mind, he heard Donnell's words endlessly looping: *"With the goddess defending Ashhur, what chance is there of victory?"*

"Have you taught my children a lesson, High Prophet?" Karak asked when Velixar stepped through the flap and entered the pavilion. The god's back was to him as he sat cross-legged in the middle of the tent's empty expanse. It was a pose Velixar often found the god in whenever he came calling.

"I have, my Lord." He hesitated before adding, "I also learned a lesson myself."

That piqued Karak's interest, and the deity turned about to face him. "Yes?"

"We seem to have a problem, my Lord. A problem of perception." Velixar's heart raced faster with every word he spoke.

Karak's glowing eyes narrowed. "Go on."

"Some of your children fear the goddess." He began pacing a circle around the deity, hesitant to look Karak in the eye. "Though Chief Shen and the Quellan try to convince them otherwise, they all witnessed Celestia raise that damn tree to protect Ashhur, as well as crush your second meteor of fire."

"They do not believe in the righteousness of my quest?"

"Your righteousness is not in question. It is that they doubt our army can be victorious if the goddess has sided with Ashhur."

"Doubt is fear's insidious brother, and much harder to defeat," said Karak, and his suddenly wistful, reflective tone eased Velixar's nerves. "Once given life, it spreads like a disease, forever growing stronger. We must crush it early and with due haste."

"I know this," Velixar said, and despite his trepidation, he voiced his own fear. "But my Lord . . . are they right? Can we find victory if Celestia fights alongside Ashhur?"

Karak shook his head. "Once more you disappoint me, High Prophet. If Celestia truly fought alongside my brother, none of us—myself, you, this entire force we have gathered—would be here any longer. She is cosmic, she is eternal. My brother and myself were like that once, when we were whole, but no longer. We shattered ourselves to pieces, thinking that if we walked among humankind our leadership would be more potent, our relationship like a father to a child. Foolish, perhaps, but there is nothing to be done about it now. Until we once again rise to the heavens, we are weaker than she. Celestia could eliminate each and every one of us in a single human heartbeat."

"But she defended Ashhur. She *protected* him."

"She did, but not for the reasons you might think," the deity said with an impatient grunt. "Celestia may love my brother, but she desires balance and carries a deep sense of fairness in her breast. Sometimes I wonder if she thinks Ashhur was unfairly pushed to war, or unprepared for this conflict. But more than anything, she will protect her world, and that is why we must be patient. We must be calm. We must show, not just to our own people but the very heavens itself, that we act in righteousness, that our war was inevitable, our victory a necessary."

"As you say, I believe," Velixar said with a bow. "But how do we know she will not interfere again? So long as our children believe the goddess is against us, their doubt will foster and grow."

Karak frowned.

"Will my word not be enough?"

Velixar shook his head. "Consider that their own failure, my Lord, but they will not. Not while that ironbark tree blocks our path."

His god let out a sigh.

"Our number of siege engines will grow, and soon Darakken will join our side. Come then, we shall assault the walls, and when we do, and Celestia stays her power so our battle may play out, all will understand."

It made sense, but something bothered Velixar. If the goddess sought fairness and balance . . .

"We should attack now," he said, suddenly snapping his eyes up from the earth to meet his god's gaze. "Before Darakken arrives."

"We have a paltry three engines. Any attack would be fruitless."

"Perhaps," said Velixar with a grin. "But as you say, our men will believe once we attack again and the goddess stays her hand. We only need to bloody Ashhur's nose to show our men that victory may still be at hand."

Karak rose to his feet, and he put a giant hand on top of Velixar's shoulder.

"You are wise," he said. "And I could not be prouder of my prophet. I sense my brother's weakness, for just as we were struck by Celestia's interference, so too was he caught in its power. Those within the walls suffer hunger, and chaos will sow among their ranks. If valor may lead to victory while our foes brace for a much later battle . . . "

He smiled.

"Ready one of the towers, and gather a battalion of two hundred. Ensure the Lord Commander holds back his greatest warriors until I give the order. Come dusk, we will demonstrate to my children that the only thing they have to fear is my wrath."

CHAPTER

2

Ashhur's eyes were closed, his pristine flesh like marble as he lay unconscious on the slab. His flesh was hot to the touch, as if an inferno burned within him that would soon break the surface and roast the whole world. Ahaesarus, the Master Warden of Paradise, dipped a cloth into a bucket of water, brought it out dripping, and then dabbed it against his god's forehead. Ashhur didn't so much as twitch as beads of water steamed off his flesh.

They were in the makeshift throne room inside Manse DuTaureau, the bastion that rested on the highest hill in the sprawling township of Mordeina. There was an empty feel to the place; whereas two weeks ago the spacious room had been constantly filled with smiling people coming to give their regards to young King Benjamin, the first king of Paradise, now only Wardens and those who called the manse home ever came calling. Ahaesarus glanced about, saw the plump young king sitting on his wicker throne. Tears streamed down Benjamin's cheeks while an annoyed-looking Howard Baedan, the master steward of the township, rubbed his shoulders. Not that Ahaesarus could blame Sir Howard, as the man liked to call himself, for being annoyed. The king was seemingly in a constant state of duress over the last eleven days, and his endless blabbering was just as irritating as it was unproductive. Not to mention that Howard's precious pallium was stained with the boy's snot.

"Your people are frightened," Howard said to the boy. "You must go outside, speak with them, ease their fears. You are the king; it is your duty . . . your *responsibility*."

In reply, King Benjamin only sniffled.

"He speaks the truth of it, boy," said Ahaesarus. "You have duties to perform."

Howard's head shot up, and he glared at the Master Warden. Ahaesarus scowled right back. The master steward hated it when anyone referred to the young king as anything but *my liege*, but Ahaesarus would sooner march out beyond the walls and present himself to Karak in a frilly surcoat than bow down to this sniveling child who could not lead a grayhorn to grass, never mind an entire fledgling nation to war. *This is what you wanted, isn't it, Jacob?* he thought. *Your final insult to the god you betrayed?*

"H-h-how can I s-s-soothe them," the young king blubbered, his eyes locked on Ashhur's unmoving body. "Our god is d-d-dead. W-w-we are h-h-hopeless!"

Ahaesarus sighed while once more running a wet cloth over Ashhur's forehead. The god had been atop the wall when Karak sent a fireball from the heavens to destroy it. Ashhur had been caught in the blast, plummeting back down to earth. He'd not moved since, though his body still burned and his immortal heart still beat.

"Ashhur is not dead," Ahaesarus told the boy.

"Then w-w-why won't he wake up?"

"Because he is gravely hurt. Because the fires within him need time to heal his outward form."

"But . . . but . . . "

That was all the king could spit out before he fell into another fit of sobbing. Howard Baedan finally ceased his scowling and rolled his eyes, again rubbing the king's shoulders. The unremitting sniffles and moans nearly drove Ahaesarus insane.

"Get him out of here," he said. "Now."

"This is *his* chamber, the king's place of rule," Howard shot back. "It is his right to remain—"

"I care not for his right," snapped Ahaesarus, flinging his wet cloth at the man. Howard backed out of the way, and the cloth slapped against the side of the young king's face, making him bawl all the harder. The master steward made to step out from behind the wicker throne, his hand on the hilt of his belted knife. In return Ahaesarus glanced to his sword, which was propped against the wall in the corner. At that look, "Sir" Howard abruptly wedged his hands beneath King Benjamin's armpits and lifted the king off his throne. He led the sniveling boy away, straightening his white pallium in the process.

The door slammed shut, leaving Ahaesarus in blessed silence with his unconscious god. The Master Warden leaned back, closed his eyes, and let out a deep breath as he snatched his mug from the table beside him. Tipping the mug back, a scant few drops of water dripped into his mouth. He glanced at the large bucket he'd been using to bathe his deity, saw that it was nearly empty as well. Sighing, he grasped the bucket by its handle and left the room.

When the door closed behind him, he felt a sort of lessening, as if the vitality were being sucked from every fiber of his being. Over the last eleven days, he had experienced a similar feeling each time he left Ashhur's side. He wondered if the others who frequented the makeshift throne room felt the same thing; if they did, that begged the question why more people didn't remain in the god's presence, whether he was conscious or not.

The hallway of Manse DuTaureau was long and straight, the carpet underfoot as red and fiery as the hair of the children of the First Family who lived within it. There was a definite gloom to the corridor; none of the candles lining the walls were lit, and the narrow windows that opened up to the outside world revealed a sky bathed with clouds and murk. *Autumn is here and it is angry.* Ahaesarus could hear traces of the untold thousands outside, but the thick stone and wood of the walls deadened the racket to a vague murmur.

Isabel DuTaureau's children and grandchildren passed him in the hall, their lithe frames draped with crumpled cotton dresses. Cara offered him a slight bow as he walked by, and Keela and her husband stopped him in the hall to ask of Ashhur's state. Brigid and her husband ushered a battalion of children, four of their own and one of their absent sister Abigail's, toward the western wing where the bedrooms resided. He even happened upon Richard DuTaureau, the created husband of Isabel, who was escorted by two more of Abigail's elder sons. Although the two young men gave him a friendly wave, Richard refused to look him in the eye. The left side of his face was swollen and covered with an ugly purple bruise, a gift from his deformed son Patrick on the very day that Karak had attacked Mordeina. Ahaesarus ignored the man and kept on walking. He had never spoken it aloud, but inside he applauded Patrick for striking his father. If any citizen of Paradise deserved to have violence heaped upon him, it was Richard DuTaureau.

The one individual he did *not* see was the lady of the house, Isabel. Ever since Patrick had told her of her youngest daughter's death, she had remained locked away inside her bedchamber, allowing visits only by her husband and children. Sometimes in the night he could hear the immortal woman wailing, a disconcerting sound to be sure, especially given the strength and stoicism Isabel had displayed for almost a century as she led her people out of their infancy. Ahaesarus found himself wondering if that strength had ever truly been real.

Finally, he reached the atrium and stepped outside. He was struck by a brisk wind that carried with it the clamor of all those who now called Mordeina home. Placing the bucket down, he gazed out over the courtyard that progressed down the high hill the manse sat upon. People covered nearly every square inch of grass, pale-skinned, dirty, and frightened, their mass stretching out as far as Ahaesarus could see. The reek of so many in such a relatively small area assaulted his keen nostrils. Warden Leviticus had guessed that two hundred and ten thousand human souls now resided within the sixteen square miles of Mordeina surrounded by the double walls. To Ahaesarus, it looked eerily similar to the pens he and his people were gathered into when the winged demons invaded his home world, albeit on a much larger scale.

He pushed aside the memory of that horror and weaved through those camping on the courtyard, stepping around lean-tos, tents, and cookfires where scared women prepared food for the evening. When he reached the large ring of stones marking the manse's well, he yanked the rope up from the depths. Water sloshed from the pail as it rose, and he dumped the contents into his bucket despite its insufferable smell. Ahaesarus sighed. The liquid inside the bucket was a murky tan color, the result of the combined piss and shit of those two hundred thousand people sinking into the earth and contaminating the ample spring that flowed beneath the settlement. The last time he had gone to retrieve water was three days ago, and though the water had been somewhat soiled then, it was far worse now. Azariah would need to purify the water again, though the solution was always a temporary fix. Ahaesarus watched scared humans drink from their own cups and wondered if they knew the danger. Humanity in Paradise had lived so long without a risk to their health, and yet now, everywhere they turned, it seemed there was danger, even from something so simple as a cup of water.

Finding Azariah should not have been difficult, for though the short Warden spent his evenings camping outside the small thatch of forest in the northwest corner of the settlement, his days were usually spent within the sacristy inside the manse, teaching both Ashhur's words of love and forgiveness and the spells he had learned during his time in Dezrel. However, as Ahaesarus wandered from room to room, the pail of stinking water swinging in his grip, he could find no trace of him. *Perhaps he decided to preach among the populace,* he thought. Ahaesarus had first been a farmer and priest, then a Warden, then a tutor to a potential king, and finally a warrior protecting an infant people from annihilation. Even though he had been blessed with Ashhur's ability to heal most all ills, the less practical study of magic had always escaped him, and curing such a massive stream deep below the earth was far beyond him. That meant his only recourse was to boil the water over the fires in the kitchens behind the throne room, a slow and irritating process.

Much to his surprise, when he entered the throne room, he found Azariah there, with Denton Noonan and his son Barclay as well as two other teen boys who had fallen under the shortest Warden's tutelage. Denton and all three youths were tall and tan, with unkempt, sandy hair, marking them with the look of the far east of Paradise, where they once had resided on the outskirts of the Kerrian Desert, near the western deity's old home of Safeway.

They were gathered around the slab on which Ashhur lay. All had their hands on the god's bare chest, their eyes pressed closed as they mouthed prayers to their unconscious creator. The hall was the largest room in the manse, nearly twenty feet tall, and their pleading voices reverberated off the vaulted ceiling. Ahaesarus watched for a few moments in silence, bathing in their pure, songlike tones, before placing his bucket down on the stone floor with a *thump*.

The prayers ceased and all eyes lifted to him. "Master Warden," said Denton, offering a bow. The other young men did the same.

"Praying with Ashhur is truly a humbling experience," Ahaesarus said. "I applaud you, Azariah, for teaching his children humility."

"We weren't praying *with* Ashhur," said Barclay.

One of the other youths smiled proudly and added, "We were praying *for* him."

Ahaesarus furrowed his brow, confused. "For him?"

Azariah stepped out from behind the prone deity, hands held out in supplication. Gone were his usual deep brown leather breeches and jerkin, replaced by a white, flowing ensemble spun from fine cotton, made for him by Denton's wife. The outfit was very similar to those the priests of Rana had worn back on the Wardens' home world before it was destroyed. It was odd that Azariah had taken to wearing such a thing, as of all the Wardens he was the most carefree and adventurous, often disregarding prayer as unnecessary. Judarius had often guessed this was because Azariah's stature was closer to that of the humans than his fellow Wardens. "Ashhur gave us his healing gifts when we were brought here," Azariah said. "And he gave it to his children as well, if they are strong enough to access it. What better way to thank the god we owe so much to than to try and mend his wounds?"

"A noble thought," said Ahaesarus, "but unnecessary."

"Unnecessary?" said Barclay.

"Ashhur is a god, boy. The talents you have were given to you by him. It is folly to think that human hands—or those of a Warden, for that matter—could ever heal one of heavenly descent with his own gifted power."

"It never hurts to try," insisted Azariah.

"It might," the Master Warden said. "Especially when such attempts make one think himself of higher importance than he truly is."

As soon as the words left his mouth, he regretted them. He watched as Azariah's calm veneer shattered, the Warden's cheeks flushing red and his fingers curling into fists. Denton, Barclay, Astin, and Yarin backed up a step, their lips pressed into tense white lines.

"I am sorry, Azariah," Ahaesarus said. "I did not mean to insult."

"Yet you did."

"I did, and again I apologize." Hoping to ease the tension in the room, he reached down and lifted the bucket of water. "And if I am to be honest, I have spent the last hour searching for you. The waters beneath the city have been fouled again and need to be purified."

Azariah chuckled and stepped toward him, waving for his four students to follow. They gathered around the Master Warden, their eyes suddenly alive with excitement. Azariah reached into the satchel hanging from the rope around his waist and pulled out a pinch of some sort of powder.

"Many spells require a physical catalyst," he told his students. "And all materials, no matter how small or seemingly useless, contain mystical properties. Take granite dust as an example. The particles are tiny and barbed, and there have been many a man and woman whose lungs the Wardens and healers have had to set right because of the bleeding sores the dust can cause. And yet the granite that forms that dust is only created through pressure and time, and represents the purity of the land on which we live. When using the correct words, it is the one element that can distill the water we might wish to drink, removing salt, sediment, bacteria, fungus . . . and animal waste."

Azariah worked his fingers together above the bucket, dropping dust particles into it while his lips mouthed the spell. Just as with every time before that Ahaesarus had seen this process carried out, he was enthralled by its simplicity; something magical made to seem ordinary. There were no bright lights, no eerie sounds carried on the wind; only the water, slowly brightening as the granite dust and Azariah's words did their work.

Soon the water was clear, the putrid odor that had infused it gone. Ahaesarus looked down at the shorter Warden, and noticed that although the expressions on the four humans were awash with wonder, Azariah did not look satisfied. Ahaesarus placed his hand on his shoulder and dismissed the others.

"I need to speak with your teacher in private," he told them. "Gather several other Wardens at the well near the manse, and have them wait for us to come purify the water."

The others bowed to him and filed out of the throne room, Astin's young eyes glancing at the empty wicker throne on his way by. Ahaesarus's frustration with Benjamin bubbled anew. The boy could be a huge help if only he would cease being a sniveling little child and become the leader he was chosen and trained to be. Picking up the discarded cloth beside the throne, Ahaesarus made his way back to Ashhur's side and resumed wetting the god's scalding flesh. All the while Azariah stood there in silence. Ahaesarus realized how silly it was that he should berate Azariah for attempting to heal Ashhur while he himself sat there and bathed him for hours on end. At least Azariah was attempting to be proactive.

"Why aren't you out on the wall with your brother?" Ahaesarus asked as the quiet stretched on. "You have never struck me as one to remain still and away from a conflict."

The Warden's shoulders slumped. "You have me confused with someone else," he replied, and he sounded so tired, so broken down. "Before our world ended, I was a quiet man. I loved books and working with wood; adventure was something that belonged to the bards who traveled and sang their tales."

Ahaesarus watched steam rise from his god's chest, the moisture from the cloth evaporating almost as soon as it touched him. "What changed?"

"Ashhur and the goddess saved us," Azariah said with a shrug. "We witnessed the end of our world and the birth of a new one. It seemed a chance to become someone new as well. My older brother was always the brave one, so why not behave as he did?"

Azariah reached out and touched his hand, and Ahaesarus released the wet cloth. The smaller Warden took over bathing the god, seeming to find catharsis in the simple act.

"The young man. Roland Norsman. You miss him."

"I do. And it makes it worse that I killed him."

Ahaesarus cocked his head and stared at him, confused. Azariah let out a bitter laugh, not taking his eyes off his god.

"Jacob Eveningstar was my friend. At least, I always thought he was. I had a chance to kill him, Ahaesarus. At the Wooden Bridge, before we crossed, we were attacked by a group of soldiers from Neldar. We all would have perished had I not sensed Ashhur's wolf-children lingering nearby and called them to our defense. During the skirmish, I struck Jacob with a maul. He was unconscious on the ground before me, and I could have ended his life right there, but I did not. Even though he swore Jacob Eveningstar was dead, even though he had tried to murder Roland, I hesitated. I couldn't kill him. Instead, I fled, taking Roland with me. That's when the arrow pierced his back. If I'd been stronger, if I'd done what needed to be done . . . "

Ahaesarus shook his head. "Life ends, it always has and always will. Think of how much of our own brethren we have lost since Karak began the march west."

"You don't have to tell me that, Ahaesarus. They died by my side. Just as Roland and Brienna did while I was unable to help. I am tired of it. I want to be *helpful*."

"You need to be strong," said Ahaesarus, taking hold of his arm. "We're needed, each and every one of us. Every morning I walk that wall and try to keep spirits high, even as death looms in the valley below. You have a gift, Azariah, an understanding of humankind surpassing mine. You know what to say, how to say it. Your presence would be much better served out there with the fighting men than in here wallowing over your loss and teaching humans religious rite. Let Daniel Nefram perform those duties. When Karak's Army finishes their siege weapons, we will need all hands to help hold them off, especially if our god remains . . . indisposed."

Azariah shook his head. "No. Absolutely not. I have lost my taste for violence, if I ever had it in the first place. This world needs healers as much as it needs warriors, perhaps even more so." His eyes glanced back down at his prone god. "I will indeed be out there with the warriors when Karak comes at us again, but I will honor Ashhur by saving lives rather than taking them. Now excuse me; I have water to purify."

With that, the short Warden tossed the cloth back into the bucket, turned, and walked away. His flowing white clothing billowed behind him like a ghost's tail. Ahaesarus wanted to call out for him to stop, but held his tongue. *He is right,* he thought, gazing at Ashhur. *Perhaps he is the most right of any of us.*

Yet despite it all, he could not shake the doubt that clung to his chest, gnawing.

CHAPTER

3

It was dusk, and Patrick DuTaureau was busy demonstrating to a group of youngsters how best to parry a sidelong chop. They practiced in a small field to the left of Celestia's giant tree, where Mordeina's outer-wall gate had been smashed by Karak's fireball from the sky. The gate on the inner wall, positioned seventy feet to the right of its demolished sister, was still intact. They'd been at it for over an hour when the muted sound of a blaring horn sounded. His students were young, greener than grass in the middle of summer, and their reaction to the horn showed just how green they were. They dropped their practice sticks to their sides and glanced around, confused.

To Patrick, though, its meaning was clear, its sound painfully familiar. Karak's Army was launching another attack.

Someone tugged on his shirtsleeve, and Patrick glanced down to see one of his students staring at him, eyes bulging with fear. The boy was no older than twelve, and stocky, with red-blond hair and dark freckles. The rough-spun shift covering him was filthy, appearing to be splotchy black in the murk of the setting sun. He was the only of his class who remained; the others had already fled away from the wall, most likely searching for someplace to hide.

"Mister Patrick, what do I do?" the boy asked, his voice quavering.

Patrick knelt down, the hump in his back sending shooting pain up his spine and his knees popping. "Vinsen," he said, "have you been practicing your archery like you were supposed to?"

The boy nodded.

"How many targets did you hit this morning?"

"Six."

"Out of how many?"

Vinsen's lips curled up, and his brow furrowed in thought, before he replied, "Thirty."

Patrick let out a deep sigh. *No way good enough, but it will have to do.*

"Go there," he said, pointing through a gap in the rushing bodies to where one of the Wardens stood behind a stone barricade at the base of a hill, handing out recently strung bows and quivers filled with crudely fletched arrows. "Grab a bow and join the others on the line. You will be our last defense. If Karak's bastards get through . . . "

"Put an arrow in them?" asked Vinsen, a blank look on his face.

"Yes, that would be better than dying. Now go."

Patrick rustled the boy's hair, and Vinsen sprinted off through the throng of dirty and scampering people. Patrick ran in the opposite direction. His every muscle ached, and his misshapen head throbbed. The burgeoning evening was cool, and without his armor on, his light clothing did little to protect him from the onset of cold, making him shiver. For the millionth time in his life, he wondered why he, the son of Ashhur's first daughter Isabel, should feel so much pain. What good was agelessness if each day was filled with physical torment? It just didn't seem fair.

Blame your father, the voice of his inner hatred said. *He made you this way, so heap that responsibility on his head.*

He shook off his impure thoughts and hurried behind a group of five Wardens climbing one of the slender stairways. The

Wardens were each a full head taller than him, and their long, elegant legs were able to scale two steps at a time. In a matter of moments, they were far above him, nearing the top of the wall, while those behind Patrick urged him to pick up the pace. At one point he nearly lost his balance and fell, but he righted himself just as he was about to slip off the edge, even as bodies collided with his backside.

Amazingly, he realized that was the first time his heart rate had risen above normal since the horn started blaring. *Falling and breaking my neck scares me, but the possibility of death by sword doesn't?* He shook his head. *Something isn't right in this head of mine.*

Once he reached the top of the wall, that fear finally came. He gazed across the valley at the army Karak had massed a mile away. The countless soldiers were like some black disease that had momentarily stagnated, hovering there atop a distant hill, seemingly still in the dimness, yet buzzing with frenetic energy. Patrick was so focused on the sight of them that he almost stepped off the plank connecting the inner wall with the outer. If not for one of the thick limbs of Celestia's tree, which extended out over the plank, he would have fallen.

When he reached the ramparts of the outer wall, all frenetic energy seemed to die, and his nerves settled. Warden and human alike were behind the parapets, with bows at the ready, peering between merlons at the valley below, a sight that even a few short days ago would have seemed impossible. Warden Judarius had joined Karak's former soldier Preston Ender in preparing the settlement's defenses, and the discipline they inspired was a sight to behold. There had to be ninety individuals on the wall, and none of them so much as breathed or shook or whimpered, even when the warhorn sounded once more. Judarius paced behind them, pleading for calm, his long black hair bouncing with every step he took. It was a display of restraint, of *order,* that would have made even Karak proud. Patrick shuddered at the thought.

He placed his hand on the shoulder of a sandy-haired teen wearing tattered breeches. The youngster glanced behind him, visibly started as he gazed at Patrick's ugliness, and then dutifully stepped aside. Patrick sighed and leaned between two merlons, peering at the dead land below him, squinting to adjust his eyes to the coming darkness. He heard the whine of wood scraping against metal as he watched a mobile mountain slowly approaching. It was more than halfway between the awaiting army and the protective wall, flanked on either side by at least a hundred armored men who marched with their curved shields raised high. The wheeled tower they guarded was nearly as high as the wall itself. Soldiers stood atop it, hiding behind shields as Karak's banners fluttered above their heads. Patrick reached over his shoulder and behind his back, but his hand grasped at nothing. He wore no armor, and he'd given his massive sword, Winterbone, to one of the new, young stable hands for safekeeping when he'd begun his lessons. *Stupid,* he thought. *Stupid, foolish Patrick.*

The warhorn blew again, and the siege tower rolled ever closer.

"I'd give my left nut for a bow and quiver," he called out, not taking his eyes off the approaching death tower, and a few moments later one was handed to him. He nocked an arrow and leveled it, feeling how unsteady the bow felt in his grip. Although he was a natural with a sword, he was a less than proficient archer, perhaps no better than even young Vinsen. He closed his eyes. *Ashhur, please let at least one of my arrows find purchase in the flesh of my enemy.* The contradiction of his prayer was not lost on him.

Someone nudged him, and Patrick glanced to his right to see Preston Ender there, grinning at him, his bowstring lax. The older man's gray eyes twinkled in the coming darkness, his peppered hair and beard trimmed and proper. In that moment he looked like a stately version of his deceased brother, Corton, who had taught Patrick how to wield a sword in the swamps of Haven. Preston's armor, which had once been black and adorned with Karak's roaring lion, was now a shade of off-white, cured in an acidic mixture and repainted to show the man's new allegiance to Ashhur. He had even stenciled a crude mountain to replace the old sigil on his breastplate. Preston and his band of seven young warriors, all formerly soldiers in Karak's Army, had been lovingly dubbed the Turncloaks by their fellow defenders on the wall.

"Something amusing about all this?" asked Patrick.

Preston chuckled. "Of course. You don't see it?"

"See what?"

"That whatever Karak has planned, it's not going to work," said a voice on the other side of him. It was Tristan, another of the Karak Turncloaks under Preston's charge. The boy was only fourteen, but the confidence with which he carried himself while in armor made him seem much older.

Patrick frowned, his insides churning.

"Why not?" he asked, trying to keep himself in the moment. Ever since Tristan had told him about the murder of his beloved sister Nessa, he found it difficult to look at the boy without feeling dismay start to darken his soul.

Thankfully, it was Preston who answered him. "They aren't ready for an attack. That single tower they're pushing toward us is nowhere near enough to overtake these walls. Ten men at most can stand atop it at once, and they'll be hampered, able to do little more than push forward. Even as raw as our defenders are, we can surely take out ten men at a time."

"So why sound the horn? Why come at us at all?"

"Boredom, maybe," Preston said with a shrug. "Or perhaps a way to test the strength of the towers they're building. Who knows?"

Patrick leaned between the merlons once more. The tower was now only a quarter-mile away, and he could hear the *clank* and *clink* of the armored men marching beside it.

"Ten men at a time we can handle," he said. "But what happens if Karak himself is one of those ten? You think we'll still hold?"

Before either Tristan or Preston could answer, a commanding voice shouted from somewhere farther down the wall: "Everyone quiet!" Patrick glanced up, saw Ahaesarus was now on the wall as well, the Master Warden pacing alongside Judarius. *The family's all here.* Patrick nodded to Preston, nudged Tristan without looking at the boy, and then hunkered down to await the inevitable.

It took a maddeningly long time for the tower to get within reach of their arrows, and by that time Patrick could hear the soldiers pushing the giant tower along, huffing and moaning as they strained against its hefty weight. Those marching chanted, "Karak! Karak!" with each step they took.

"Those to the left fix on the soldiers atop the tower; those to the right aim for the men on the ground," Ahaesarus instructed when the tower was a mere hundred feet away, looming in front of them like an obelisk from the heavens. The whisper and creak of ninety bowstrings being pulled taut came next. The two Wardens continued to pace along the wall walk.

"Hold," Judarius said, and suddenly it seemed the tower's painfully slow progress was now far, far too rapid for Patrick's liking. "Hold . . . hold . . . let loose!"

The arrows descended on the marching soldiers, slowing their approach, but those that pushed the tower were hidden behind its massive wooden frame. Arrows ricocheted off shields and armor, only a handful of the ninety or so loosed finding gaps and piercing flesh. As quickly as the first round was spent, more bolts were nocked, and at Judarius's command the next volley launched. Patrick aimed unsteadily at an older soldier, of some importance he hoped due to the man's lion-headed helm. His arrow plunked meekly into the ground just left of the man. Patrick grunted, reached into his quiver, and nocked yet another arrow.

The tower inched ever closer, now only twenty feet away and swaying. Those atop it stood from behind their shields and loosed their own arrows at the defenders. Others threw spears. Patrick and his brethren ducked behind the merlons as the bolts came flying toward them, arrows expertly crafted with sharp steel heads that flew with much greater accuracy than their own. Patrick groaned as an arrow flew through the gap and snapped against the inner wall. A spear wobbled overhead. Once more he wished he'd brought Winterbone with him.

"Archers back!" he heard Ahaesarus cry. "Spellcasters, forward! Focus on the tower!"

Patrick glanced to his rear, saw that during the confusion more defenders had gathered behind him, including a number of the spellcasters Master Warden Ahaesarus had brought back with him from Drake. Giving them room, he watched as they approached the parapet. Once there, all fifteen lifted their hands, words of magic on their lips. Small fireballs and bolts of electricity flew from their fingertips, and the *crack* and *pop* of the attacks striking the wooden structure sounded over the shouts of the soldiers below. A couple of stray arrows came flying at them, and one of the spellcasters—Bordo, if Patrick remembered his name correctly—took a bolt in the shoulder and collapsed moaning. Judarius grabbed him by his tunic and yanked him out of the way of the other defenders. The screams outside the wall intensified.

"Their archers are down! Finish them!" shouted the Master Warden, but it was difficult to hear him over the shrieking.

Patrick scampered back to his feet and nocked another arrow while the spellcasters ducked down to gather their strength. When he peered through the merlons, he saw that the tower leaned to one side, part of its base engulfed with flames. Two burning men tumbled off the side, crashing into a few of those who were foolishly attempting to put out the spreading fires. Patrick focused on them and released another arrow.

It took the spellcasters a half-minute before they were ready again, and now without fear of arrows they climbed atop the merlons and hurled their magical attacks, the dancing flames making them look like the odd beasts that were carved into the outer walls of Peytr Gemcroft's estate in Haven. Thinking of Haven brought, for the briefest of moments, a memory of Rachida, the merchant's wife, and the child he had supposedly placed in her belly. That line of thinking quickly vanished when one of his arrows finally found its mark, punching through the cheek of a burning man and dropping him to the dead and withered ground.

The burning tower collided with the wall. Patrick backed away, tossing aside his bow. Without Winterbone, he was defenseless. Soldiers scurried onto the top platform, looking frightened and angry at once. Those with pikes and swords shoved Patrick aside, rushing to the edge of the parapet just as the soldiers began vaulting over the wall. Spear tips crunched into armor, blades clanged off steel plating and chainmail. Grunts and shouts filled the air, as well as the crackle of flames. Still the soldiers rushed up to the top of the tower, attempting to leap onto the outer wall walk.

Patrick's heart raced as the throng of defenders pushed him back toward the chasm between the walls. Swiveling his head, he saw Preston and the other young Turncloaks battling the soldiers. A few of them collapsed back onto the tower as others sailed over the side of the wall and fell sixty feet to their deaths. Five of them had succeeded in avoiding death, and now they clashed with those on the wall walk, mere feet from where Patrick was standing. Patrick glanced quickly to his right and saw one of Mordeina's defenders standing there, a sword held limp in his hands while his eyes bulged with fright. The man was shaking. Without another thought, Patrick snatched the sword from the man and shoved him aside.

The blade was short and a third the weight of Winterbone, the steel not nearly as durable, but it would have to do. Finally armed, he shoved his way into the conflict. The Turncloaks and Wardens had the five who'd gotten onto the wall walk surrounded, so Patrick joined those trying to keep the soldiers on the flaming tower at bay. He jostled and thrust his way to the front of the line, the sword singing in his fists. He stepped between two merlons just as a soldier attempted to squeeze his way through, bringing the blade down on his head. The soldier's helm dented when the sword struck it with a *twang*, and the man stumbled backward, teetering off to the side, his foot missing the edge of the tower, sending him plummeting to his death. With a grunt, Patrick drove the sword forward, trying to impale the next man in line. That one fell aside, and the one behind him came down hard with a maul, striking the merlon to Patrick's left, sending chunks of stone into his face. Patrick reeled backward, grabbing hold of the merlon to keep from falling into the crush of bodies behind him. In that moment he peered up, and his heart nearly leapt into his throat.

Karak was approaching, the deity ambling across the dead valley, followed by a massive phalanx of soldiers.

"Shit."

It seemed the spellcasters from Drake saw as well, and they unleashed a fresh barrage of flame against the siege tower. The light was blinding, and amid its roar Patrick heard a loud creak, followed by a series of heavy cracks. Those atop the tower, those trying to force their way onto the wall walk, teetered along with the tall wooden construction. They dropped their weapons and held their arms out to their sides to keep their balance, but it was no use. The siege tower crumbled in an inferno of red and yellow light, swallowing those standing atop it and crushing those still lingering beneath. The remaining soldiers on the ground dropped their shields and fled the trailing barrage of arrows and magic, staggering across a dead valley that was now illuminated by the crackling flames engulfing the destroyed tower. Karak stopped his march halfway across the valley, the glow of his eyes dimming as the god squinted.

Cheers erupted from Mordeina's defenders, each and every man standing up tall and beating his chest in victory. Patrick was caught up in the moment, embracing anyone who came within reach of him, and in the thrill no one seemed put off by his deformities.

Even the normally stoic Judarius had a hint of a smile on his face as he worked his way down the line, congratulating his charges. Preston clapped Patrick on the back, and Tristan wrapped him up in a mighty hug. Though it did seem strange to feel so much elation over the deaths of nearly one hundred men, Patrick thought it beat the alternative. *We could all be dead instead.*

His delight waned when he spotted Ahaesarus standing on top of a merlon, not taking part in the celebration. The Master Warden's expression was dour, the roaring flames giving his flesh a frightening, almost demonic tint. Patrick shrugged off one of the spellcasters who was trying to embrace him. Wedging his foot into the nook between merlons, he pulled himself up until he stood next to the Warden. Night was fully upon the land now, and everything beyond the dying flames coming from the destroyed tower was a deep blackness against a slightly less black foreground. Karak had turned about and was leading his phalanx back to the camp.

"Why so glum?" he asked, hoping Ahaesarus would shudder and begin smiling. "We won."

Ahaesarus gestured toward the campfires of their enemy.

"We killed barely a hundred men and lost twenty of our own," he said. "Including a caster from Drake and a fellow Warden, Castiel. Tell me, Patrick . . . which of our armies is better trained, and which can better withstand such losses of skilled men?"

Patrick frowned, looked back across the tens of thousands of skilled soldiers arrayed against them.

"Well," he mumbled. "When you put it that way . . . "

Chapter 4

The girl entered the solarium of the Brennan estate with a baby nestled in her arms, the door closing softly behind her. While the girl waited to be noticed, Catherine Brennan sat behind her desk, dropped her quill into the inkwell, and stroked its hawk feather as she blew across the words she'd written on the wrinkly parchment. Only after it was dry did she look up.

The girl was young, seventeen at most, and the spacious solarium made her look dainty standing there. Her hair was dark and quite curly, contrasting with her crystalline blue eyes, which seemed inhumanly bright, sparkling in the sunlight streaming through the windows. She'd given birth recently; of that Catherine had no doubt. The mother's breasts looked swollen, and she retained some of her baby weight, her midsection pushing against a burlap shift that was too small for her. Despite that, Catherine could see the girl was quite attractive. In fact, she looked much like Catherine herself, with round, ruddy cheeks and thick lips. It was no surprise that her dear departed Matthew had bedded the girl.

"Sit down," Catherine said.

The girl did as she was told, moving sheepishly toward the desk and plunking herself into the chair opposite Catherine. The girl shifted uncomfortably in her seat, refusing to look Catherine in the eyes.

"Luna Glover, is it?" Catherine asked.

The girl nodded.

"Do you know why I sent for you, Luna?"

The girl shook her head.

"Come now. You might be a whore, but you aren't stupid. I repeat: Do you know why I sent for you?"

Luna finally brought up her gaze and spoke so softly it sounded like a slight breeze leaving her lips.

"I do, Miss Brennan," she said.

"And why is that?"

"Because I . . . because I was . . . with your husband."

Catherine tilted her head and pointed an accusatory finger at the girl. "You were not *with* my husband. You *fucked* my husband. For coin."

"It is just an expression," Luna mumbled. "I meant no offense."

At that response, Catherine smiled. "Of course not. Please, Luna, I need you to understand something. We are both women in a man's world, and there needs to be trust between us—that is, if you want us to remain friends. You want us to be friends, don't you?"

Luna hesitantly nodded.

"Good." Catherine sat back in her chair, pinned up her hair, and adjusted her bodice. "Now answer me this, Luna. How did you meet my poor Matthew?"

The girl's face scrunched with uncertainty before she replied. "He paid for me in a brothel in Tarrytown. Said he was stopping in on his way to Veldaren, for business."

"Tarrytown is near Felwood, is it not? A long ways away. How did you end up in Port Lancaster?"

Luna bit her lower lip as the baby squirmed in her arms.

"Luna, you can tell me," Catherine said. "Remember, there must be truth between us women."

For a moment Catherine thought she'd still remain silent, but then the words came forth in a great rush, like water pushing through a broken dam.

"The big man came, the one who brought me here today . . . he paid Madam Pritchard a bag of gold and put me on a wagon. He said Master Brennan wished to have me near. Of course, to a woman like me, it's obvious what a man means when he says something like that."

"Interesting." The big man was Bren Torrant, Matthew's old bodyguard and the one Catherine had paid to turn on her husband; he was the high merchant of Port Lancaster and the self-appointed lord of freight in all of Neldar. Of all the girls she'd questioned, this one was the first to admit Bren had a part in her coming to Matthew's bed. "And did Matthew greet you in your cottage by the wall, or did you come here?"

"Both, Miss Catherine. Sometimes he would come to me, but other times a man would take me on a boat to a tunnel and lead me to a big room with lots of beds."

"When was the last time you visited this tunnel?"

"A long time ago, Miss Catherine. Maybe two years?"

"I see. And when was the last time he took you?"

Luna didn't answer.

"Tell me, Luna. Tell me now."

The girl glanced nervously at her child, then back at Catherine. "Three months ago, just after our . . . just after my baby was born," she said softly.

"At the cottage he placed you in?"

"Yes."

Catherine stewed. Even as things were going to shit around them, even after the attempt on his life that she had secretly paid for, Matthew had still risked sneaking out on his own for a midnight tryst. There were times when Catherine regretted having him killed, but now was not one of them.

"And how old is the child?" she asked.

"Five months, Miss Catherine."

"Does it have a name?"

Luna nodded, and tears began to dribble down her cheeks. "Mattia, Miss Catherine."

Mattia. What a pathetic name. "A girl, I take it?"

"Yes," she said, unwrapping the cooing baby and lifting her up so Catherine could see the lack of male bits.

"Put it away," Catherine said, waving her off, and Luna hastily wrapped the child back up. Satisfied, Catherine rose from her chair and walked around the desk, breezed past the girl and her baby, and cracked open the door to the hall. Bren was standing there at the top of the stairwell, leaning against the wall, with his hand resting atop the hilt of his sword. It looked like he was sleeping.

"Bren," she said sharply, and his eyes popped open.

"Yeah?"

"Come in here. Now."

He kicked himself off the wall and followed her back into the solarium. Catherine walked up to Luna and held out her arms.

"Give the child to me, Luna," she said.

Luna hesitated, momentarily pressing the child tighter against her chest before offering her to the lady of the house.

"Thank you," Catherine said, gently rocking the child for a short moment. An ugly thing, but then again most babies so young were ugly. She looked at Bren and nodded. The big man let out a sigh as he drew his sword.

"Sorry, lady," he said, the only warning he gave Luna before his sword cleaved open the woman's throat. Her body dropped, not even a scream in protest, as blood poured across the fine floor. Catherine watched it flow as Bren sheathed his blade, then handed the baby over to him.

"Bring her to Ursula, and tell her to find a suitable wet nurse." She kicked Luna's corpse. "Then get back up here and get rid of this . . . thing. Have Penetta and Lori mop up the blood afterward. I don't want so much as a stain to show."

"Will do," Bren said. "Oh, thought I'd let you know, your special guest has arrived. He's waiting for you at the pier. Odd fellow."

Her heart fluttered. "Thank you. Now go."

Bren hurried out of the solarium, trying in his gruff voice to soothe the weeping infant and failing miserably. *Thank the gods you have actual talent with a sword; otherwise, you'd be useless.* Catherine snatched up the letter she'd been writing when Luna entered, rolled up the parchment, tucked it into her bodice beside the one already stowed there, and swept out of the room.

As she descended the staircase, she breathed deeply, trying to find a balance between her excitement and her guilt. Luna was the ninth, and last, of Matthew's mistresses in Port Lancaster, the sixth to have had a child by him. Luckily, the Brennan family curse—the scarcity of male offspring—had stricken Matthew as well. Catherine was thankful for that, for while she could eliminate his whores in the name of preventing future embarrassment, the prospect of murdering children did not sit well with her. The girls would be well cared for, but if he'd had a male child, under Neldar law that child could potentially challenge for the family fortune somewhere down the line. For Catherine, this was an unacceptable risk after all she'd suffered for.

Thinking of the children made her contemplate her own, and she stepped off the stairwell onto the estate's third floor. She heard laughter and walked briskly down the hall, stopping when she reached an opened door. She peeked around the doorframe, saw her four girls sitting on the floor and laughing as their nursemaid Brita read stories from an old tome. She turned away, her heart thrumming in her chest as she slipped from the bedroom and crept farther down the hall. At the next doorway she dipped inside to find little Ryan Brennan, two years old and angelic in his nakedness, sleeping soundly in his crib. Though she did not want to wake him, she couldn't help but reach down and place a hand on his small back, feeling his little lungs expanding with each breath. Ryan's flesh was warm and a shade darker than Matthew's or Catherine's. His hair was slightly different as well, his curls tighter than hers and her husband's had ever been. She smiled. Matthew wasn't the only one who'd kept secrets.

Ryan stirred, and Catherine backed away before he woke. She stole a quick glance out the window. It was approaching the high point of the day, the sun climbing into the sky. She did not have much time.

She beat a quick retreat, hurrying down the stairwell to the estate's next floor. For a moment she hesitated, thinking of heading to the pier to greet her guest as quickly as she could, but in the end she stepped off the stairwell. Best to get this regrettable business over with first.

This time when she reached a door, it was closed to her, and she paused to let down her hair and flatten the wrinkles in her finely crafted cobalt dress. After taking another deep breath, she rapped on the door.

"Who is it?" a brusque yet feminine voice asked.

"Catherine."

"Come in."

The invitation had no warmth to it, which filled Catherine with dread, but she shoved open the door nonetheless. Standing in front of her bed inside the large chamber was Moira Elren, the exiled daughter of Clovis Crestwell, Karak's first child. Moira had been in the Brennan house for over a year, given to Matthew as collateral by Peytr and Rachida Gemcroft for the Brennan estate's assistance when the merchant fled Haven for the Isles of Gold. Though Moira was certainly aging and almost a score older than Catherine's thirty-six years, she still appeared to be younger, the gift of the blood of the First Family that ran strong in her veins. She had washed the dark dyes out of her hair after helping the women of Port Lancaster slaughter the last of Karak's soldiers who remained in Neldar; her short-chopped locks were now their original silver, making her sapphire eyes seem all the paler. The woman also looked to be a waif, with the typical dainty facial features of the Crestwell line and a slender form made to appear even frailer with the tight black leathers she wore, but that appearance was deceiving. Moira more than made up for her lack of strength with incredible quickness and guile, and Catherine had never seen anyone more deadly with a sword. Even Bren, though he weighed more than two of her, feared the small woman. *Tread lightly here,* she thought, and though her heart pounded, she put on her most confident face.

Moira sat down on the featherbed in the middle of the spacious bedroom. "What do you want?" she asked. Catherine looked around, saw the room still bare save the bedding and a heavy bag resting on the floor. Moira had moved into this room a week ago, yet there was virtually no sign she lived here.

"What is that?" Catherine asked, jutting her chin at the heavy bag.

"My things, not that it's any of your business," Moira replied sharply.

"I assure you, it *is* my business, Moira. You are my hostage, my *compensation*. Your duty is to me."

Moira threw her head back and laughed. "My duty was to your husband, not you. That deal was broken the moment you had his bodyguard impale him with a sword." She scowled then and turned away. It was a look Catherine had gotten quite used to.

It had been three days after Matthew's death that Catherine finally told her hostage what truly happened in Rat Harbor. She disclosed all of it—even paying the bandits whose attempt on her husband's life had failed because of Moira's presence. Moira's reaction had been . . . unfavorable, and nothing Catherine said about Matthew's failings as a spouse and merchant improved things.

"I don't care what you think about the deal, Moira. The facts are the facts: You are a servant now, nothing more and nothing less. You will do as I say, when I say—end of discussion."

Moira swiveled around to face her. Her movements, combined with her silver hair and pale flesh, made her look like some evil specter. Quick as a cat she crouched down, her hand darting beneath the bed and withdrawing one of her light shortswords. With a single flick of her wrist the scabbard clattered across the room. Moira pointed naked steel in Catherine's direction.

"I am not your slave," she said, her voice devoid of emotion. "The next time you dare act as such, I will cut your throat."

Catherine laughed. "You could do that, yes. However, I don't think you would like the repercussions."

"Come now. You really think I fear your sellswords?"

Moira took a step forward, waggling the tip of her shortsword. It danced inches from Catherine's neck, and it took all her composure not to back away or flinch at the sight of the sharp steel.

"You won't touch me, Moira," she said. Amazingly, her voice didn't so much as quaver.

"Why shouldn't I? You'll die before you make a sound."

"Because the moment I'm discovered murdered, or even harmed in any way, fifty similar letters will be sent by bird to the Isles of Gold."

At last Moira flinched, the tip of her sword dipping ever so slightly.

"Saying what?" she asked, doing well to hide the worry in her voice.

Catherine smiled. At last she was back in control. At last this wild woman knew who was in charge. She took her time telling her, enjoying every moment, every syllable.

"Saying how *close* you and my maidservant Penetta were while you lived beneath my roof. How very close . . . and how Penetta knows things about you that I dare say only a lover should know." She smiled as she plunged her fingers into her bodice and removed the first of the two rolled-up bits of parchment. "Each letter is addressed to Rachida Gemcroft."

The sword dropped, clanking on the floor. Moira grew even paler than normal as she took the offered bit of paper, unrolled it, and read the words. The woman seemed to deflate. Her eyes were bloodshot when she tore them away from the letter's contents.

"Every one . . . "

"Yes," said Catherine. "I wonder, just how would the love of your life react to hearing of such infidelity?"

The silver-haired woman said nothing as she backed up a few steps and plopped back down on the featherbed. The letter fluttered from her hand to the floor. Her face was drawn out and dejected, her shoulders slumped. Catherine felt her confidence rise, confidence that left her once she gazed at the window on the other side of the room. She had to finish this business quickly if she was to make her next meeting, the most important one, in time.

Taking out the second parchment, already sealed with wax, she stepped forward and placed it in Moira's limp hand.

"I know you hate me, but I do what I must to protect myself and my family. Don't blame me for your own failures. Besides, you won't have to look at my face any longer. Tomorrow you leave Port Lancaster."

"Where will I go?" asked Moira without looking up.

"You are to take five sellswords of your choice and head for Omnmount. The letter I handed you is for Cornwall Lawrence, and it is for his eyes only. Make sure he reads; make sure he *understands*. Afterward, make your way to the docks outside the settlement and sabotage as many barges and skiffs as you can. Even if they are my own, destroy them. We will build more. If Karak wishes for food and supplies while he's traipsing about Paradise, he can raise them with his own godly hands. Once that is done, consider yourself free from my service. So long as you don't act against me, you will have nothing to fear."

"How do I know you'll keep your word?" asked Moira softly.

Catherine swept toward the door.

"You don't," she said. "Good travels, Moira Elren. I hope I never see you again."

Once in the hall, she exhaled deeply. It was a shame to send the woman away. Moira was more capable than anyone, better than even Bren and the sellswords at keeping her safe in a dangerous, unpredictable world. Yet Moira's fear of what Catherine held over her head meant she was the only one she could trust to complete the tasks she had given. Had she assigned one of her sellswords, he might abandon her and sell his services to a different bidder.

"Sacrifices are necessary," Catherine whispered. Just as her sacrificing Matthew had united the women of Port Lancaster to her cause.

She lifted her skirts and hastened down the stairwell, taking the steps two at a time on her way to the estate's front entrance. Her excitement grew each time her slippered foot touched ground, and soon all her worries—Matthew's legacy, Karak, the dead girls, Moira—dropped away. They were replaced by a face, one of exquisite, exotic beauty, covered with skin of the deepest brown.

A plain covered wagon awaited her outside the estate. She climbed in and ordered the driver, a girl of no more than twelve, to take her to the docks. Catherine dropped the curtains on either side of her as the horses began to clomp along Port Lancaster's cobbled streets. Her breath caught in her throat, her heart pounded in her chest. She nervously fiddled with the bottom of her skirts, fraying the hem along the way. She didn't care.

The ride seemed to take forever, and by the time the wagon stopped moving, she was so overcome with anticipation that she felt close to vomiting. She pressed her lips shut, lifted the curtain, and stepped out of the carriage. The dockhouse and the pier loomed before her, a long, sleek skiff tethered to the dock, gently rocking in the undulating waters of the Thulon Ocean. It was the only ship in the harbor. *His boat.* The young cart driver turned in her seat, facing away from her as she'd been told to do. Catherine took a deep breath, placed a hand over her breast, and slowly made her way toward the dockhouse.

The gravel street gave way to the dock's slatted struts. The soft slippers on Catherine's feet *swooshed* against the wood, kicking up bits of dust. The dockhouse itself was a sturdy but harsh-looking square construction of wood gone gray from the constant assault of sea salt. The door was propped open, and she stepped through, breathless.

"Hello?" she said.

"My love?" replied a strong, soulful voice.

Catherine followed the voice down the dockhouse's long hallway and around the corner into the main storeroom. He was there, sitting at a small table in the middle of the room, eating a blood-red orange. Fish netting, anchors, spare timber, spears, harpoons, and oaken lockboxes surrounded him. He looked up at her, his complexion nearly black in the sparse lighting the dockhouse offered, just as handsome as the first time she'd seen him. When he smiled at her, his teeth shone like polished pearls.

"Catherine," the man said, bowing slightly.

Her hands moved to her belly, rubbing it, feeling the gentle rise four months in the making. She smiled in return and took a step into the storeroom. "Reginald," she purred. "It has been too long."

"It has. It truly has. But please, my dear, call me by my true name."

Catherine smiled coyly. "Very well, Ki-Nan."

He stood from his seat and approached her, dressed in a pair of short leather breeches and a sienna vest with no tunic beneath, revealing the black hairs on his chest. She nearly ran at him, colliding with his strong body and wrapping her arms around his back. Their lips met, their tongues probing. Catherine savored the salty taste of his mouth, thrusting her pelvis against him each time their tongues intertwined. Their lips then parted, and Ki-Nan made his way down her neck, planting tiny kisses, before stopping at the swell of breast above her bodice, taking in a mouthful of flesh and sucking. Catherine felt like she would explode.

"Do you wish for me to stop?" asked Ki-Nan, breathless.

Instead of answering, Catherine leaned back, grinned, and grabbed his crotch.

"We haven't much time," he gasped. "I must be on the open water before dusk."

"I know. I don't care."

They made love, first atop the table after swiping the basket of oranges aside, then in a pile of netting, then beside a rack of fishing poles, her breasts pressed against the wall while he took her from behind. Ki-Nan was rough yet measured, never thrusting so hard as to actually hurt her, his brown skin slick with sweat. Catherine's insides were on fire, her nipples sore from being bitten, and goose pimples covered her every inch. She had to grind her teeth into her bottom lip to keep from screaming, lest anyone who might be lingering outside the dockhouse hear.

Finally, the dark-skinned man spilled his seed inside her, letting out a low, animalistic groan. They both collapsed on a pile of musty tarpaulins. They nuzzled and squirmed for a long while afterward, cherishing the wantonness they both felt. It had been much the same the six other times they'd been together. It seemed neither wanted the feeling to end nor looked forward to the coming weeks upon weeks they always spent apart.

Ki-Nan Renald was a fisherman by birth, a trader in training. He had first visited Port Lancaster nearly seven years ago, at the behest of his employers, the brothers Connington. He had happened upon her in secret one night while Matthew was away in Veldaren, coming to ask if the lord of freight would be interested in forming a truce in regard to the disagreements between the two houses. Catherine knew she should have been distrustful, but

Ki-Nan disarmed her with his direct way of speaking and his exotic beauty. He'd said he was from Ker, the unofficial southern province of Ashhur's Paradise. How a man from Paradise had come to be in the employ of merchants from Neldar was lost on her, and it was a subject Ki-Nan never broached, even when she asked.

That was fine by her, for though his voice was deep and soothing, what Catherine wanted from him had little to do with talking. They had made love that very first night, and every time they'd seen each other since. Catherine had stopped taking crim oil in the aftermath of his visits long ago, and the results of that decision now slept peacefully in the estate and showed in the puffiness of her abdomen. No one in Port Lancaster save her trustworthy maids Lori, Penetta, and Ursula, who had helped her keep the affair a secret, knew it. She had even kept Bren in the dark.

Ki-Nan's hand went to her belly. "I can feel it," he said.

She playfully slapped his cheek and nibbled his chin. "You can? So tell me . . . is it a boy or a girl?"

"I am not clairvoyant, love," he said. "But I feel much."

"Yes, you do."

Ki-Nan rolled onto his back, staring at the dockhouse ceiling while fiddling with his chest hair. "And how is my son?" he asked, frowning slightly.

"He's fine. Perfect." She leaned up on her elbow and stared at him gravely. "But Ki-Nan, you must promise that those words are not spoken by you in any company but my own. Should anyone find out that Matthew's only heir is not of his own blood . . . "

"No need to explain that to me, love. But my son is two years old, and I have never laid eyes on him."

"You will. Please believe me, you will. If everything falls into place, and I can convince the other houses to join my cause, I will no longer be simply a regent. I will be the lady of the house, in station as well as name."

"You rely too much on things beyond your control," he said, shaking his head. "And what of the war in the west? If Karak should return home, all your careful planning will be for naught."

She patted him on the shoulder. "That is what *you* are here for, isn't it?"

"Yes, it is," he sighed. He looked to the window on the western side of the room, set high on the wall, and Catherine followed his gaze. The sun shone in the cloudy glass. It must have been two hours at least since she'd entered the dockhouse. It was amazing how time seemed to have little meaning when they were together. "It is late. Is the new cargo in my skiff as I asked?" he inquired.

She nodded. "It is. Sixty extra swords, lifted off Karak's own dead soldiers. Bren nearly pitched a fit when I told him we needed to give them up, but I convinced him they served a greater purpose. Speaking of which, you *do* have the three crates my late husband gave you, correct?"

"I do. They are well hidden, and guarded by those I have pulled to my side."

"Good."

"And now seriously, my love, I must be going."

Catherine groaned as Ki-Nan gave her one last kiss on the lips, then stood up, retrieved his leather breeches, and slid them on.

"Promise me you'll come back," she said. *"Promise."*

"That I cannot do."

"If you promise, then I will promise to take you for my husband."

His lips spread into a wide, toothy grin.

"With such reward, how could I not? I promise with all my heart. Now if you will excuse me, Lady Catherine, my ship awaits. Shower my son with kisses for me. War waits for no man . . . especially when that man is a giant twelve feet tall."

CHAPTER 5

Rachida Gemcroft watched waves crash against the jagged black rocks, lapping and withdrawing, leaving behind a coat of shimmering water. Sea spray accosted her cheeks, soaking her. She shivered and pulled her fussing babe closer to her breast, making sure his head of soft red fuzz was covered by his woolen blanket. The waves crashed yet again, the seawater coming within inches of engulfing her sandaled feet. Lifting her eyes to the horizon, she saw the three dark shadows approaching through the day's stormy gloom.

"What's out there?" asked Gertrude Shrine, the only practitioner of the healing arts on the Isles of Gold.

Rachida turned to the older woman and felt her cheeks run pale. "Ships," she said.

"*Friendly* ships?"

"I doubt it."

"Why not? Perhaps Master Brennan has sent reinforcements to assist us."

Rachida shook her head. "Matthew *has* no ships, Gertrude. All but ours were conscripted by Karak's Army." She pointed toward the three rapidly approaching vessels. "Besides, those boats are *large*, far larger than any built in Paradise. What approaches is either an envoy from the Conningtons or . . . "

"Or Karak?"

She nodded.

Gertrude frowned, the lines of age around the corners of her mouth deepening. "What do we do, then?" she asked.

"*I* must go speak with my husband. You, Gertrude, are to take Patrick for me and find his wet nurse. He seems to be hungry."

"Of course, my Lady."

Rachida handed the swaddled babe over. The older woman held the child with easy familiarity, pulling him close and gently rocking him as she strolled across the rocks. Though Gertrude was obviously frightened about the coming ships, her gait showed none of it. She walked confidently, smoothly, a natural mother as she made her way up the incline toward the collection of hovels carefully hidden by a wall of glimmering volcanic stone. Rachida couldn't help but feel a tinge of resentment, for she had often found herself struggling with motherhood of late.

She began walking in the opposite direction, heading for the cliffs that bordered the island's eastern shore. Everything around her was drab; the land beneath and above were varying shades of black and brown, and even the ocean seemed more gray than blue. There were many times when Rachida wondered if the name "Isles of Gold" was given just to mock those who came to live there, as she had for the last three months.

Then again, the islands weren't named for what sat atop it.

Peytr had come across the islands during one of his many ventures around Dezrel, and discovered great veins of gold hiding inside the caverns beneath the archipelago's many cliffs and crags, waiting to be mined; hence the name he gave it. Yet despite its treasures, the Isles were a dank and dreary place. The only landmass that was hospitable was the large central isle that Peytr had dubbed "Provincia." The others were harsh and barren, the waters shallow and filled with lurking dangers to both man and ship. Each day Rachida found herself pining after Moira, the love of her life, whom she'd left behind in Port Lancaster. If not for her son, magically born from Patrick DuTaureau's seed, she might have gone insane . . . or slit her own wrists.

The cliffs blotted out the day's light when she passed beneath their overhangs. The way was treacherous here, the stones underfoot slick, but Rachida was nothing if not agile. Corton Ender, the old sellsword who had taught her to dance with blades back in Haven, had said that she and Moira were the most physically gifted students he'd ever taught. *Of course we were,* she thought. Both she and her love were the direct offspring of Karak's First Families, the purest blood in all of Dezrel. It would have been disappointing if they *weren't* immensely capable.

The darkness deepened as the outcroppings lowered. She moved along, at a slower pace, until a soft glow appeared to her right, marking the opening to Provincia's mine. Rachida entered the tunnel, lined with flickering torches, their light dancing off uneven, damp walls. Each time her boots touched ground, the sound of her footfall echoed throughout the narrow passage, combining with the muted *clink* and *clank* of metal on rock from down below. The torches made the atmosphere muggy, and she began to sweat through her heavy woolen cloak. She disrobed as she walked, heading ever deeper beneath the cliff.

The passage finally ended at a wide, artificially constructed cavern. The expanse had been turned into Peytr's study of sorts, complete with a desk, inglenook, dresser, and even a mound of blankets that served as a large bedroll. Remnants of smoke stifled the air. A second tunnel leading to the mine was cut into the opposite wall. Numerous candles of thick tallow were scattered throughout, adding their light to that of the torches and creating an oddly ominous atmosphere. The cave ceiling was high, and the light never reached there. Sometimes, when she stood in the middle of the space, it looked to Rachida as if the empty void beneath Afram was coming to swallow her. This was not a place she enjoyed visiting.

Peytr was in there, Rachida's husband in name only. His black hair, peppered with gray, was tousled as he sat atop his desk, the sounds of the workers' tools echoing around him. His lover, Bryce, was with him, twenty years Peytr's junior. Bryce was a lithe man, almost womanly in appearance, with long silvery-blond hair. Rachida was grateful for his presence. Peytr could be quite distant from her at times, but Bryce had a way of putting the man at ease. The two of them had been lovers for almost as long as she and Moira; in fact, it was their mutual affairs, and their need to hide them from those who might not understand and react harshly, that precipitated their marriage.

The couple was leaning on the desk in the center of the cave, Bryce placing kisses on Peytr's pale, powdered cheeks, when Rachida cleared her throat. They both started, their heads whipping around. When they saw her standing there, Bryce smiled sweetly while Peytr frowned.

"Darling," her husband said. "I was not expecting you."

"I feel there is quite a bit you weren't expecting," she answered.

His frown deepened. "Such as?"

"Ships, O husband of mine. Three of them."

"Oh, is that all? I thought it was something important." He grabbed Bryce by the cheeks and brought his face back to his neck.

"I would not be so glib if I were you," said Rachida sternly. "You know this is trouble."

Unexpectedly, Peytr grinned. "Well, I would assume it is representatives from our beloved god come to visit. We should greet them accordingly." He turned to Bryce, who was hastily sliding his arms into his red velvet jerkin. "My love, please go into the mine and inform our brothers that company has arrived. You should gather the . . . appropriate gifts. Our guests are early, and we must prepare for them." He then tied his breeches and strode forward, his brown eyes twinkling with excitement as his lover disappeared into the darkness.

Rachida felt awash in confusion. She began to open her mouth and ask about his apparent lack of angst, but he silenced her when he lightly brushed her cheek.

"Fear not, most beautiful wife of mine. I have expected this."

Two hours later, nearly the entire populace had gathered on the edge of their concealed township to watch as three great ships steered into the crescent bay. Only Bryce was missing. Rachida shrugged off his absence and gazed out at the gray water. She recognized the boats; they had been galleys in the Brennan fleet, sister ships to the *Free Catherine*, which was docked alongside a pair of clippers—more gifts from Matthew—on the other side of the island. These boats had not been fitted for war like the *Free Catherine*; the only thing threatening about them, other than their size, were the banners of Karak, thirty red lions roaring high above the waves. And the soldiers, of course. She thought it foolish that the *Free Catherine* was not moored closer to the mouth of the crescent. The nine spitfires on her deck would have come in handy.

The galleys quit rowing a half-mile into the deep bay, and their oars, forty apiece per ship, lifted. The stone anchors dropped. Rachida squinted, watching tiny armor-clad men scurry about the decks as large dinghies lowered into the water. Soldiers climbed down ropes and boarded the crafts before the rowers began paddling. There were fifteen of the smaller boats, each filled with at least twenty soldiers. Rachida shivered and glanced behind her, at the nearly four hundred men, women, and children who now called this depressing island chain home. They were all filthy, lean, and sore from the daunting task of creating a small township on this desolate black rock, where any food other than fish was hard to come by. Though some of the men among them had fought the forces of Karak when the god stormed into Haven to demolish the Temple of the Flesh, they now appeared sickly and feeble.

We do not stand a chance.

"Gertrude," she whispered, and the healer appeared beside her, along with the girl Trish, who acted as little Patrick's wet nurse. Rachida peered over, saw her child busily sucking on the frightened girl's breast, and felt an ill-timed tinge of jealousy; Rachida's milk had dried up only two weeks after giving birth to her precious son. It seemed a magical conception was not without drawbacks.

"Yes, my Lady?" asked Gertrude, her voice shaky.

"I've changed my mind. Bring the girl and Patrick back home. Close and bar the doors, and try not to make a sound."

"Yes, my Lady."

"I told you I wanted everyone here," Peytr said from the other side of her as Gertrude and Trish scampered away. "All our people need to be on hand."

Rachida gave her husband a dour look. "I will take my precautions as I see fit, Peytr," she snapped at him. "I do not know what game you're playing here, but my son will be safe."

"*Our* son, darling," he said. "Patrick might not be of my loins, but he is my heir. I wish for him to be safe just as much as you do."

"Then why this farce? Why stand out here and allow us to be slaughtered?"

"That's not . . . " he began, but then he snapped his mouth shut. His eyes went back to the approaching dinghies. No matter Rachida's pestering, he refused to broach the subject further. Eventually, she stopped trying.

"Nester, bring me the Twins," she called out. A moment later a scruffy man hustled toward her, two scabbards clutched in his hands. Rachida snatched the shortswords by their hilts and yanked them free, the slender blades hissing. She held them out before her, admiring the handiwork, the polished gleam of the steel, the woven silver and bronze of the hilts. Just looking at them caused a knot of guilt to form in her stomach.

The swords had been fired in Haven's very first smithy, only they weren't twins when they were forged, but quadruplets. Two had been for her, and two for Moira; blades Corton Ender had designed especially for them. Individually, they were half the weight of normal shortswords, which allowed Rachida and Moira to utilize their superior quickness while masking their lack of strength. There had been many a day when she and her love would spar with these very swords out in the soggy fields by the Temple of the Flesh, working up a sweat before they stripped down and bathed in the stream behind Moira's quaint little cottage. And yet over the past twelve months, they had been together a scant two days. She missed Moira dearly, which brought about hateful feelings for her husband. If Bryce had been the one so adept at swordplay, would Peytr have willingly parted with him? She thought not.

Speaking of Bryce, where in the underworld is he?

A hand roughly grabbed her arm, and she flinched, almost driving the blade in her free hand into Peytr's gut. Her husband stared at her, lips puffed out in impatience.

"You don't need those," he whispered, gesturing to the Twins. "Put them away."

She jerked out of his grip. "No. Not unless you tell me what is going on here."

For a moment Peytr appeared as if he might try to disarm her himself, but he obviously thought better of the idea and yielded.

"You'll see," he said. "But please, just promise me you won't do anything rash."

Rachida scowled. Peytr turned his attention back to the sea.

The first of the dinghies ran aground on Provincia's rocky coast, followed by a second, then a third. Rachida gulped down her growing fear. Their township was well hidden, positioned below sea level, in a crater surrounded by black crags. The crags acted as natural walls that could be defended with arrow and pike; yet the position the survivors from Haven watched from was the mile-wide clearing five hundred feet away from their home. The ground beneath her was cracked and uneven, with occasional tufts of sea grass sprouting in the fissures. She cursed Peytr's stupidity. They were out in the open here, vulnerable. If her husband had wanted to negotiate, he should have stowed all the people in their homes, where they stood a fighting chance should the worst happen.

Myriad soldiers stepped out of the dinghies, gathering into formation on the rocks. The captains, distinguishable with their great helms and oversized, spiked pauldrons, shouted orders. The men did not seem all that disciplined, which struck Rachida as queer. She had been there in Haven when Karak's Army descended on the Temple of the Flesh, had seen how organized her former god's forces were. Had it not been for Moira, Corton, Patrick DuTaureau, and ultimately Ashhur, all would have been lost. She wished they were all here with her now. Perhaps one look at Patrick's massive sword would convince the soldiers to climb back aboard their boats and leave them alone. The natural father of her beloved child was indeed a fearsome warrior, and frightening when provoked.

When all the dinghies were emptied and ranks were formed, the twelve captains urged the soldiers onward. Six hundred booted feet clomped over the shoreline's slippery rocks in uneven lines.

Peytr closed his eyes, took a deep breath, puffed out his chest, and then took three steps forward. For a moment Rachida thought to join his side, but she hunkered down and held her swords at the ready instead.

When the twelve captains were fifty feet away from where Peytr stood, they halted their troops. One of them stepped to the forefront and lifted his great helm, revealing the face of a hard, middle-aged man with cold, ice-blue eyes that looked very much like Moira's. The captain gave a signal and the soldiers fanned out in a single line, their armor clattering. Rachida found her view blocked by dented armor and scornful faces. The captain who had stepped forward then drew his sword.

"To what do I owe the honor?" asked Peytr with a mock bow. Amazingly, his tone sounded playful, without a hint of fear.

The captain acted as if he had never spoken. "Citizens of Haven!" he shouted, his voice carrying across the rocks. "You have been found guilty of blasphemy of the highest order. Because of your deceit, the mighty Karak, God of Order, the Divinity of the East, has sentenced you to die. But let none say Karak is without mercy! You have two options before you: Perish or submit. Those who bow, and give themselves back entirely to Karak, will be given the chance to serve the Divinity in his holy war against his bastard brother. The choice is yours."

Rachida's heart dropped when the man spoke. She remembered a time not so long ago when it had been her beloved brother Vulfram making similar proclamations. The memory brought worry crushing down on her soul. Though she had not spoken with a member of her family since she'd fled Neldar when Moira was banished by her father, they had never left her heart. Despite it all, she loved each of them dearly and hoped they had come through these trying times unscathed.

"I fear you have the wrong locale," Peytr said, drawing Rachida's attention. "This is Provincia, not Haven. I think you took a wrong turn somewhere or read the charts incorrectly. Best you be on your way."

Behind Rachida, the people shifted nervously.

"Do not play coy with us!" the captain screamed. "It is well within our rights to storm these shores and put each of you to the sword." He looked beyond Peytr, to the tired, frightened masses. "Again I will say, perish or submit. Choose wisely."

Peytr shook his head. "What if we choose the third option?" he asked.

As the captain tensed, Peytr placed his thumb and pinky finger in the corners of his mouth and whistled. A soft rumbling sounded next, and the other captains turned, hunkering down as if they expected an unseen phalanx to fall upon them. From beneath the crags to Rachida's right came Bryce, tugging along a wooden barrow covered with a thick blanket. It seemed all movement ceased as he guided his cargo across the rocky shoreline. Confounded, Rachida glanced at her husband's back, wishing she could see what kind of expression he wore.

All eyes were on Bryce as he gave the massive throng of soldiers a wide berth until he reached his lover's side. Peytr then stole a quick glance at Rachida before whipping the blanket off the barrow, revealing a shimmering mound of small yellow stones. A few dropped off the side of the barrow, tinkling on the ground. *Gold. A huge mound of gold.* Rachida's breath was stolen away.

"What is this?" shouted the blue-eyed captain.

"This is *negotiation,*" Peytr shouted back at him. "What you see here is a token of what we have extracted from the caverns *beneath* this island. An untold fortune in gold . . . "

The soldiers behind the captains began to murmur.

"Karak's faithful cannot be bought!" screamed a second captain, this one much younger than the first.

Rachida took a step forward, not able to take her disbelieving eyes off the heaping mound of gold. Lethal rage swelled in her bosom. A fortune before her, a fortune her husband had insisted they did not have when he gave Moira away as collateral . . .

"I'm not speaking to the faithful," Peytr said, grinning.

Rachida brought her gaze up to the captains. The one who had first spoken raised his sword above his head, and he looked ready to burst into laughter.

"You cannot bribe us, you damn fool. You'll die, the whole lot of you, before we take everything we desire. Men, charge!"

A great howl erupted from the soldiers, the captains striding forward with menacing steps, ready to attack, and the rest followed. Rachida sensed her people cowering behind her, bawling apologies and turning to flee as the approaching horde made their way across the uneven rocks. Only Peytr and Bryce remained unmoved. Her fury at seeing the gold abated, giving way to bone-chilling fear. She hunkered down, holding one of the Twins out before her while lifting the other above her head, prepared to take out as many men as she could before her lifeblood leaked out onto the damp earth. *I'm sorry, Moira,* she thought as she watched rage-filled eyes glowering from beneath helms. *I'm sorry, Patrick. Please, whatever gods still care, keep my son safe.*

Those prayers were unnecessary.

Rachida's body went slack, watching in confusion as soldier attacked soldier from behind. Sharpened swords and spears sliced throats, impaled through backs, and severed limbs. In a matter of moments, the charge had abated, the captains whirling around to see their forces locked in battle with one another. The sound of colliding steel and pained screeches was deafening. Peytr and Bryce fell back from their position as the fighting drew close to them; Rachida's husband snatched her forearm and lugged her along as well.

The shoreline was chaos, all flailing limbs, spurting blood, and flashing steel. Someone fell against the barrow filled with gold, knocking it over and scattering yellow stones across the ground. With everyone wearing the same sigils, it was difficult to tell who was attacker and who was prey. Blood flew into the air, carried along by the sea spray from the crashing waves in a pink mist. The captains hesitated, seemingly as confounded as Rachida, before entering the fray themselves. They fought diligently, but their efforts were futile. One captain after another fell victim to their men's blades. The blue-eyed captain who had taken the lead received a sword through the neck; the younger one who had spoken second was impaled in the groin and fell down screaming, left to be trampled by innumerable booted feet. His great helm rolled away, and a soldier stomped mercilessly on his head, crushing the young captain's skull.

As the numbers thinned, she finally saw an order to the chaos. The men who'd taken up the rear were in a tightly knit formation, advancing as one in an admirable display of discipline that ran counter to the army's initial sloppy arrival. One soldier in particular caught Rachida's eye; a man with long blond hair sprouting from beneath his half helm, whose chin was marked with an outrageous forked beard. His helm was knocked off his head by a wayward sword, revealing a youthful face that was quite beautiful for a man. He guided his circle of attackers, shuffling them left and right, shouting directions, cutting down those who would attempt to break their formation. He moved fluidly and seemingly without effort, even though the damp boiled leathers, mail, and plate covering his body was assuredly heavy. Rachida was transfixed with him, especially when she realized that through it all, the young man never once stopped grinning.

When it was over, the only sound Rachida could hear was her own breathing, the crash of waves against the cliffs, and the moans of the dying. The traitors finally broke ranks, moving among those lying on the wet rocks and spearing them through the eye to silence their dying wails. Soon even the moans ceased, and Provincia's shore was flowing red, covered with at least a hundred corpses.

The young soldier with the horned beard approached them, sheathing his bloodied sword. That knowing grin was still on his face. The others followed his lead. Rachida felt her body go tense once more, her fingers tightening around the Twins' handles. She heard soft sobs and shuffling feet behind her, the refugees from Haven moving as if in a dream toward the carnage.

Peytr stepped in front of her, smiling. The young soldier threw up a hand, and the rest of the turncoats ceased their forward march. He then dropped down on one knee in front of Peytr, his head bowed.

"Master Gemcroft," he said, "we are at your service."

Peytr laughed. "Quester, there is no need for that. I am not your god."

The young man lifted his head. Between his fingers he rolled a small nugget of gold, which he'd scooped up at some point during the fray.

"Not yet," he said, "but when the true gods are gone from this land, it will be those who possess the gold that deserve our reverence." He chuckled. "By all appearances, that man would be you."

"Could be," Peytr said with a shrug. "But until the gods are truly gone, we are all equal in our slavery. Now stand up, Quester. You're embarrassing me."

The handsome man rose to his feet, his armor clanking, his eyes turning to Rachida. He licked his lips.

"And is this your lovely wife?" he said. "The legends of her beauty do her no justice."

Rachida's grip on the Twins tightened. Quester glanced down at them and took a step back, his hands held up in surrender.

"No offense meant, milady," Quester said, still grinning.

She felt the eyes of the rest of the soldiers on her, nearly two hundred of them. She was used to it by now; ever since she'd been old enough to remember, she had been the object of constant attention from all men around her. Her mother Soleh had long said she was the most beautiful girl in all of Neldar, and none had ever stepped forward to refute that claim, not even Aprodia, the stunning priestess who had gone up in flames with the rest of the Temple of the Flesh. Though the attention they gave her was not without its uses, it still made her feel uncomfortable, even dirty, when strange eyes undressed her.

She swiped one of the Twins before her, then sheathed both swords before jutting her chin at the brash young soldier. "Who are you and why are you here?"

Quester's grin faded ever so slightly, and he cast a doubtful look at Peytr. *This one isn't used to his advances being thwarted.*

"I am Quester Billings, milady," he said. "The Crimson Sword of Riverrun, sworn shield of House Connington." He bowed to her. "Pleased to be at your service."

Rachida turned to her husband. "You have some explaining to do, *darling*."

"I do." Peytr cleared his throat. "The men you see before you are sellswords formerly in the employ of the merchant families throughout Neldar. Karak's acolytes conscripted them weeks ago, with the intention that they would march west as reinforcements to assist in the war against Ashhur." His face scrunched up as he considered Quester again. "Though I don't see Bren Torrant here or any of Matthew's other swords. Are they still on the ships?"

Quester shook his head. "They never arrived. In fact, the acolytes never returned either, nor did the regiment Karak kept in Neldar. Our brave dead captains waited for them for a week, then decided enough was enough. We set sail without them."

"Strange," said Peytr. "Without them, how many are you?"

"Six hundred," Quester answered. He glanced at the raging sea and the three galleys floating in the distance. "Those of us before you, plus an additional four hundred on the ships."

"I thought you said you were supposed to march west," Rachida said, resting her hands on the Twins' hilts. "Why are you here?"

"Ah, a stroke of genius." The smile returned to Quester's lips. "The conscription was predicted by my masters as well as your husband. After we were gathered up, I informed the magister in Omnmount that I knew precisely where the Haven deserters had fled. I also told our brave captains that we could perform double the good service to our beloved Divinity—destroy the blasphemers and attack Paradise from the other side, hemming in Ashhur and his children. It took a little persuading, but in the end, here we sailed."

"Why wait until now to turn on them, if you outnumbered them so?" Rachida asked. "It shouldn't have taken any persuading at all."

Quester winked at her.

"Turn on our captains before making sure your husband here could make good on his extravagant promises? My dear, do you think us fools?"

Rachida leapt forward, snatching the gold nugget from Quester's hand. The sellsword stumbled backward, surprised at her aggression, and almost lost his footing. She held the gold in front of Peytr's face, ignoring the oaf with the forked beard.

"And how long have *you* had this?" she snarled.

"The mines have been in operation for three years."

Rachida reared back and hurled the gold against the ground, the soft metal bouncing when it struck the rocks. She grabbed Peytr by the collar of his heavy jerkin and pulled him close. Spit lathered his cheeks when she shouted.

"All along you've had this . . . this fortune! You pled poverty to Matthew—you said we had nothing but Moira to give. You told *me* that it would take decades to mine the gold from these islands. You *gave Moira away for nothing*!"

"I had no choice," Peytr insisted.

She shoved him, sending her husband stumbling. Bryce caught him before he fell.

"No choice?" she said. "*No choice!* I should gut you for what you've done."

Peytr calmly smoothed the wrinkles in his jerkin.

"I understand your anger, darling. I do entirely. But Moira had her part to play in this game, the same as myself and you and the Conningtons and the Crimson Sword here. The gold I withheld goes to these soldiers, to pay for their services." He put his hands on his hips and stared at her with equal parts compassion and disappointment. "You have railed against Karak's duplicity for years. You have decried the way he treats his creations, and preached disobedience to our people. Do you think this defiance comes without a price? In gaining our freedom, sacrifices must be made . . . by myself, by you, by everyone."

"But Moira—"

"—is a capable woman. And though it was my instruction, she went *willingly* to Matthew, did she not? Your love understands the dangers of our time. I expect the same from you."

"You want her dead. You made me lie to her, made me hide from her during my pregnancy."

"I don't *trust* Moira. No matter your relationship, I must have a son and heir. But please, trust me, I wish her no ill will. Do you think she'd live otherwise if I did?"

Rachida's shoulders slumped. Her hatred and anger gave way to frustration. "Fine," she said.

Peytr shrugged out of Bryce's clutches and went to her, placing his hands on her shoulders. Amazingly, his every action conveyed compassion.

"I have given up my home, darling. I have given up safety and comfort and much of my fortune. If worst comes to worst, I will give up my life. But I will never give up hope, and neither should you." He looked at the handsome young sellsword. "As for Moira . . . tell me, Quester, what was the last you heard of our dear exiled Crestwell?"

"My masters say she is fine," he said. "Matthew's wife sent a letter stating as much."

"See?" said Peytr. "All is well with her; now put her from your mind. Your role in things is about to increase tenfold, and I must have you trust me if we are to succeed."

Rachida glanced up at him, confused.

"What do you mean, 'my role'?"

He squeezed her shoulder and then let her go. His compassion seemed to recede, replaced with a hunger she both feared and envied.

"As it is said throughout the Wardens' stories, every revolution requires a figurehead to lead the way, an individual of noble birth who will guide their people to glory and freedom. What better leader could there be than the lost daughter of our gods' First Families, one who is beloved and admired by her people? *You* will lead the charge, my darling. *You* will pave the way for a Dezrel free of the bonds the gods have placed on us. So smile, Rachida Gemcroft; smile and prepare to take sail, for the gold you would have used to buy Moira's freedom instead bought you an army."

CHAPTER 6

His body was covered with cuts and bruises from the beatings he'd been given, his wrists and ankles chafed and bloody from the irons that bound him, and yet for Ceredon Sinistel, dismay was the worst of his pains.

The prince of the Quellan elves had been tethered to the back of a supply wagon and marched endlessly south through Ashhur's Paradise, made subservient to all present. Quellan, Dezren, or human—it didn't matter; all who happened upon him abused him, striking him with reeds and whips, spitting in his face, shattering a few of his teeth, and some even going so far as to run their blades across his flesh, opening small wounds that would weep and sting as sweat rolled over them. He was theirs to torture, yet he didn't complain, even as he lay there in the sand beneath the light of the moon, parched and unable to sleep. His hatred would be sated in time, as would revenge for the murder of his father; the lord and lady of Dezerea; and Tantric, the rebel leader. *"Become like the mountain I love so dearly,"* his goddess Celestia had whispered to him. Mountains did not weep. They didn't scream and kick. They waited. They watched. They *endured.*

Ceredon had lost count of how many days it'd been since they left Dezerea, but it had to be at least twenty. Their march had started out quickly, the force of a hundred human soldiers, four hundred Quellan Ekreissar, and another three hundred conscripted Dezren moving across the forests and rolling hills of eastern Paradise, passing by many abandoned or decimated townships, until they reached the Gods' Road. The demarcation line was the husk of a lone, gigantic cypress tree that loomed on the south side of the dusty road, its trunk scarred, its leaves burned; an omen of the land they would soon cross. After they passed through miles and miles of scorched landscape, tall prairie grasses rose up to meet them, and the procession slowed to a crawl. They were in Ker now, the unofficial province where Ashhur's dark-skinned children resided. Ceredon had never been here, and despite his pain he could recognize the beauty of the place. In many ways Ker seemed like elven lands—the earth sparsely farmed, the wildlife free to roam wherever it wished. There were none of the fences, stone buildings, or clear-cut fields that had become common in most human lands, which made Ceredon, for the first time, feel a sort of kinship with the poor doomed souls. The settlements they came across were akin to those of his people; the land unaltered to suit their needs, with each simply built domicile nestled into the earth as if nature itself had given birth to them.

Yet despite their beauty, these settlements were the root cause of his dismay. Most whose path they crossed were abandoned, some with cookfires still burning in their large communal pits, but in others people still remained. These unfortunate souls were fallen upon in an instant, the flesh flayed from their bodies, their corpses hung upside down from the branches of the small, twisted trees that dotted the plains. It went like this for miles, a slithering militia bringing death, seeking out those who fled, to put them to the sword, even when the grassland was slowly overtaken by desert sands. At first Ceredon had counted the dead, but he stopped when he reached one hundred. It was too macabre to keep up the count.

Through it all Darakken, the demon in a human shell who led the charge, fed. Every time Ceredon saw the creature, riding high atop his palfrey like a pale courier of disease, with lumps shifting beneath his flesh, he would close his eyes and whisper a prayer to Celestia for strength. Sometimes she would answer, and renewed vigor would fill him. Most times, he heard silence. *Do not abandon me, goddess,* he silently told Celestia's star, glittering in the heavens. *I am not ready to meet you just yet.*

These were his thoughts as the prince of Quellassar drifted off to a fitful sleep. He was awoken some time later by rough hands lifting him into a sitting position. Groggy, his head lolling, he choked as liquid was poured down his throat. Ceredon coughed and struggled in his restraints, the chains clinking with his every movement. His mouth felt as if someone had stuffed it with cotton. His right hand grabbed a fistful of leather, but he hadn't the strength to push whoever it was away.

"Quiet," a kindly voice whispered. "Stop moving. He'll hear."

Ceredon ceased at once, blinking the world back into clarity. It was still night, the half-moon high in the blackened sky. The camp slept all around him. He smelled shit and sweat and charred flesh. The one standing before him was Boris Morneau, the young soldier with the diamond-shaped scar on his left cheek who had arrived to inform Darakken of Karak's orders to invade Ker. Ceredon had not seen much of the young soldier during their long march, but on occasion he spotted Boris riding at Darakken's side. Though he had not noticed the soldier taking part in the various slaughters, Ceredon knew he had played his part. On seeing him, he hacked a wad of phlegm into Boris's face.

"That was unnecessary," the young soldier said, wiping the spit away. "I was trying to help you."

"Get away from me, human," Ceredon growled in the common tongue.

Boris put a finger to his lips. "I told you to be quiet. Should anyone notice what I'm doing, we'll both be punished."

"I never asked for your help."

Boris let out a long, slow breath as he shook his head.

"You elves are impossible."

Ceredon didn't argue.

The soldier leaned forward again, holding out a wooden bowl filled with water.

"Listen, believe me or no, I do care what happens to you. I won't try to make you drink again, but if I leave the bowl here, will you take it?"

Ceredon nodded.

"Good." Boris placed the bowl down within his reach and then leaned back against the cropping of desert stones to which Ceredon was tethered. It was cold at night in the desert, a stark contrast to the day's oppressive heat. The young man shivered, let out another long sigh, and closed his eyes. "I wish it wasn't this way, you know."

"Are you tired of sucking the demon's cock?" Ceredon asked.

Boris laughed at that. "So you *do* know what he is. I'd wondered. The rest of the soldiers call him Crestwell, but they know his true nature. As for your elven brethren, well . . . I think they know *something* is wrong—how can you not? But I feel they are denying it to themselves."

"They are self-righteous and blood hungry," said Ceredon. "Bloody fools, all."

"Even the Dezren who joined the march?"

Ceredon hung his head. "No. Those are simply weak. And tired of the torture, the pain, the agony they endured for over a year. Their involvement is understandable . . . though they deserve death just the same."

"And you?"

"What about me?"

"What do *you* deserve?"

Ceredon opened his mouth, then shut it. Finally, he mimicked Boris's position, leaning against the rocks and sighing. "I allowed countless Dezren to be tortured and executed. I murdered my uncles in cold blood under the pretense of justice. I deserve death, but when it comes, I will serve my goddess."

Boris chuckled.

"What?" Ceredon asked.

"Serve your goddess," he said. "Tell me, how does one serve a goddess while imprisoned in chains?"

Ceredon felt his neck flush, and he remained silent at the mockery.

"Thought so," the man said. "All bluster, no plan. I swear, you elves are better at acting indignant than actually doing something about whatever bothers you. Let me see if I can get the wheels turning in your head. Start with this one, elf: Why has the demon kept you alive?"

"I will not pretend to guess the motives of a demon," Ceredon said. "He must seek to humiliate me. What other reason could there be?"

Boris narrowed his eyes. "My prince, you know what the beast is. Do you really think that he would keep you alive for such a petty reason? If he wanted to humiliate you, he'd eat you, shit out your corpse, and then piss on it before his army. Try again, and this time, give it some thought."

"If you are so wise, then tell me, and stop with the games."

The young man shook his head. "You're no child, and I'm no mother to spoon-feed you. Put some thought into it, elf. Stay aware. You want to serve your goddess, do it with your eyes open and your mind moving." Boris paused, and he looked to the stars. "We're close to our destination. Come tomorrow morning, we will be upon something called the Black Spire. The village of Ang is half a day's march from there. I thought you might like to know."

Ceredon thought to be snide, but he fought the reaction down. This man . . . something was different about this man. By no means was he trustworthy, but he seemed more aware than the others, more . . . mischievous.

"And why is that?" he asked.

Boris shuffled over and knelt before him. The solemn expression in his eyes only made Ceredon further concerned.

"Because Ang won't be enough," Boris whispered. "Because after Darakken destroys Ker, he'll turn his back on his promise to your people. He will fulfill the purpose he was created for: devouring elves. Stonewood will come next, then Dezerea, then Quellassar. With Ashhur preoccupied and Karak not caring, there will be nothing to stop him."

"My goddess will intervene."

Boris looked at him queerly. "Something you shouldn't hold your breath for, I think. Celestia has done little to protect your people so far."

Celestia, keep Aullienna and Kindren far away from here, he prayed. *Please, keep them safe.*

"Why are you telling me this?" he asked Boris. "Why do you not warn the others?"

Boris shrugged and then stood.

"Not my place," he said. "And besides . . . do you really think it'd matter? For an elf to listen to a lowly human soldier like me, I think I'd need to tie them up, beat them, starve them, and then drag them through a desert. But well, it's laughable to think I'd find an elf like that whose opinion would matter. An elf his people would listen to. Just laughable."

He walked away, and as much as Ceredon hated to admit it, the wheels were indeed turning in his mind.

It was midday when the strange sounds first reached Bardiya's ears. He'd been sitting on a cliff with Onna Lensbrough, overlooking the emerald-green waters of the southern Thulon Ocean, when he heard it. His first thought was that a distant storm approached from the north, but when he turned to look that way, there were blue skies and thin white clouds as far as the eye could see.

"Not thunder," he said.

"A different kind o' storm," said Onna.

Bardiya nodded at the older man, whose skin was dark and rough as leather and whose hair and beard were white as bone. "'Tis true, Onna. Remember that Ashhur loves you, no matter what occurs."

"What do we do?"

"We stay strong. We stay true to the teachings of the one who created us."

Even though he meant what he said, inside Bardiya wavered. It had been difficult to trust any of his preachings of late. His mouth would speak the virtues of love and forgiveness and decry violence, yet at night his dreams were filled with blood. From outside his body he watched himself crush the heads of his enemies with the trunks of trees, his massive hands ripping entrails from their stomachs. Over the last few weeks, he'd often lain awake beneath the stars on a bed of moss, pricking himself with a sharpened stick to stay awake. He was exhausted because of it, but he would take grogginess over those terrible dreams.

But this time, it was no dream. Karak had finally come for them all, and it'd be either the peace of his sermons or the bloody massacre of his dreams.

"You scared, my Lord?" the old man beside him asked. "You be shaking."

"I am not your lord, Onna," sighed Bardiya. "I have told you that many times. And yes, I am more frightened than I have ever been in my life."

Onna nodded severely. "That why Ki-Nan and the others left us? Because they were scared?"

Bardiya cringed. "We mustn't speak of them. Come, the God of Order approaches. Let us gather our people."

The giant slowly rose to his full twelve feet, knees popping and elbows creaking. Another wave of agony washed over him when he raised his hands over his head to adjust his spine. Of late he had taken to railing against the pain, his constant companion for eighty-eight years in his forever-growing body, but in this instance he welcomed the hurt. The pain let him ignore the name Onna had just spoken, allowed him to forget, if only a moment, that his best friend had deserted him.

Together they turned away from the shore, taking the path through the thick forest back toward Ang. Bardiya gradually loped along while Onna used his walking stick to limp beside him, taking two strides for every one of the giant's. In a matter of moments Onna was out of breath. The dark skin on his cheeks gained a reddish hue. Fearful that the older man's heart would give out, Bardiya offered to carry him, but Onna refused. Onna was a proud man, a loner for nearly all of his fifty-seven years, more content to spend his days aboard his tattered cog, *Kind Lady*, than to break bread with his fellow man. The murder of Bardiya's parents by the elves, Karak's march west, and the constant fear of a lurching death had changed that. Not that Bardiya was surprised. It seemed that *everything* changed after the brother gods clashed in the shadow of the Temple of the Flesh.

You should have stayed your course, Ashhur, the giant thought. *Had you remained true to your teachings, we would still have peace.*

He shook his head and pushed through the final copse of tall evergreens as Ang came into view. The village sprawled out before him, tiny cottages haphazardly dotting a landscape of pines, tropical broad-leafed trees, and lush green grass. His people greeted him as he walked through the settlement, the fear plain on their faces when they peered toward the north and heard the steady *thrum, thrum, thrum.*

The villagers gathered in the center square, a wide, circular thatch of grass surrounding a giant fire pit. Gordo Hempsman, Tuan Littlefoot, and Allay and Yorn Loros were leading the charge, urging the frightened citizens to stay calm as they congregated. Bardiya and Onna remained on the outskirts of the square, allowing the stragglers to scurry past. It was only when all of Ang was present that he, the spiritual leader of Ker, took his place at the head of the assembly. Onna fell into the swelling ranks of his brethren, leaning against his walking stick once he found a suitable place to rest.

A myriad of dark, alarmed faces stared up at the giant—men, women, and children alike. Bardiya gazed on them and frowned. There were at least three hundred in attendance, which seemed like a copious number, but he knew better. Ang had once been home to a thousand strong, living, breathing, praying, and breeding by the cliffs overlooking the Thulon Ocean. Yet over the past three weeks, those numbers had dwindled as frightened individuals left the village, seeking safety in the desert, the plains, and the crags and cliffs bordering the water's edge—anywhere but the one place Karak was sure to visit when he invaded their homeland. Some departed under cover of night, but most chose to leave in full display of their fellow Kerrians, words of warning on their lips and scowls on their faces.

Again Bardiya thought of Ki-Nan, and his frown deepened. The last time he'd seen his friend was on the craggy beach when the Stonewood elves had shown him the massive crates of weapons nestled between the rocks. *"Gifts from Celestia,"* as Aullienna Meln, the little princess of Stonewood, had called them. He and Ki-Nan fought about those weapons after the elves departed, and his friend stormed away in a huff. At the time Bardiya hadn't thought much of it; he and Ki-Nan had developed an adversarial relationship when it came to what they believed to be right and wrong. Despite his friend's words to the contrary, he expected to see Ki-Nan again that night at supper, sitting down and laughing off the disagreement as he always did.

But that never happened. Ki-Nan stayed away, his hateful, blasphemous words echoed by all who left after him. *It is his doing,* thought Bardiya. *He is stealing my people's hearts and minds, leading them on a path to ruin.* He closed his eyes and prayed that they would all come back into the embrace of Ashhur's love, prayed that all of Ang could share the burden of horror soon to come, but when he opened his eyes again, all he saw was the same small congregation. They fidgeted and squirmed, sniveled and hitched, nervous as a herd of antelope surrounded by a family of sandcats.

These are my people. I must comfort them.

Bardiya raised his arms above his head, casting an imposing shadow over his flock.

"Brothers and sisters," he said, his voice booming and confident. *If only they could see how frightened I am on the inside.* "Dire times have come to our land. You hear Karak's soldiers now approaching from the north. When they come, we will face them as one, with Ashhur's grace in our hearts, as our deity always intended."

"Is it really them?" shouted one voice.

"They want to kill us!" cried another.

"You said they would leave us alone!" accused a third.

Bardiya shook his head and held his arms out wide. He wished he could hold them all in a single, protective embrace.

"You are wrong, Grotto. I said Karak *may* leave us be. I do not speak in absolutes, unless I am speaking of the grace of the gods."

"But Karak's a god," said Onna. He leaned forward against his walking stick for emphasis.

"He is."

"Does he still have grace if he wants us dead?" asked little Sasha, her black curls glistening with sweat, though the air was cool.

Damn you, Ki-Nan. In a time not long passed, such concepts would never have crossed his people's minds. There was no sickness, and none of them had died before their time. Yet that all changed when the renegade elves murdered Bardiya's parents in the mangold grove, coupled with the news of Ashhur and Karak's battle after that. At first he'd tried to allay their fears, but as time went on and his relationship with his friend soured, he saw that more and more of the populace not only understood these concepts but also felt the fear and doubt they caused. Someone had been feeding it to them, preaching violence and terror just as he taught love and forgiveness. *Why could you not leave well enough alone, my friend? Why did you not trust me?*

"All gods are glorious," he told them. "All gods are mighty, the images of perfection." He swallowed hard, not wanting to say the next part. "But that perfection is *only* an image. While a god's ideals are flawless, the gods themselves are not. Gods can be wrong. Ashhur was wrong for turning his back on his flawless teachings, and Karak is wrong for marching into our lands."

A collective gasp came over the crowd.

"But if the gods are amiss, what can we do?" someone wailed.

"We turn the tables. We teach them both the glory of grace and peace."

A couple began arguing, followed by a pair of brothers. Then a group of elder women, their hair white as down, joined the fray, and soon the clamor of the throng overtook that of the approaching force. Bardiya tried to call out for them to stop, but they were deaf to him. A fist flew, striking Yorn Loros in the jaw. The violence of the display froze Bardiya. He had never seen his people like this before. He knew not how to react.

Just then he spotted Gordo Hempsman on the edge of the assembly, leaning heavily on his cane while his wife Tulani and daughter Keisha walked beside him. The family of three had been the only survivors of Ethir Ayers's attack on the mangold grove that claimed Bardiya's parents; Gordo's limp was a result of a wound he'd received there.

The three of them reached the giant's side. Keisha craned her neck to look up at him. Her eight-year-old body was tiny in contrast to his, no more than a fly that he could crush with a single hand, and yet the courage reflected in her eyes made her look as colossal as Celestia herself.

Gordo caught his eye next, then Tulani. The family nodded to him and faced the crowd. Bardiya could not hear Keisha as she began singing, but when her parents joined her, the thin vibrato of Tulani's voice broke above the din. Bardiya listened to the words, let them envelop him—a sermon of Ashhur, sung to the sweet tune of a lullaby. He began to sing with them, and soon the angst of the crowd broke. One by one, the residents of Ang turned their attention to the singers, falling silent, allowing their voices to flutter across the plains, through the trees, into their hearts. At first only a few joined them in singing while the rest watched sorrowfully, but soon nearly all of those gathered in the square had their chins lifted into the air, their mouths opening and closing as they sang Ashhur's words of love.

In that tiny space between one moment of turmoil and the next yet to come, Bardiya was happier than he had been in a very long time.

They sang for an hour, changing from one tune to another while the sun dipped lower in the west. They sang and held each other, their quarrels all but forgotten, even as the sounds of the approaching menace grew more and more present. They sang until a great horn sounded, seemingly ten times louder than a grayhorn's bleating. Then the song tapered off, and all eyes turned to the edge of the northern wood, waiting, anticipating. Little Keisha continued to hum, the sounds of heavy stomping feet and snapping branches adding a percussive yet ominous backbeat.

A trail of wispy clouds passed over the sun, turning the sky red, as the first horse appeared from within the trees. It was an elf on horseback, his skin a sleek bronze and his hair like black satin, a vest of boiled leather painted green covering a tan jerkin, a khandar dangling from his hip. Bardiya's mouth twisted in confusion. He had never seen an elf such as this before, for his only association had been with the Dezren in Stonewood, they of the pale milk-white flesh and hair with differing shades of gold. When relations between their races had been amicable, Cleotis Meln had told him tales of the Dezren's cousins who resided on the other side of the Rigon River. *The Quellan,* he remembered, and his confusion doubled. What was this one doing so far from home?

Yet it wasn't just one, for trailing after the initial elf came scores more, both Quellan and Dezren, pouring out of the trees like grains of sand through a sieve, their horses snorting and whinnying. They guided their steeds around the square, encircling the people. *There are so many,* thought Bardiya. From the trees emerged humans dressed in armor painted black and silver, carrying banners bearing the roaring lion. They lined up in front of the forest, flanked on either side by the elves, and soon the people of Ang were completely surrounded by flesh, leather, and steel.

For a long while no one moved. The elves and soldiers stared at the huddled mass, lips twisted into sneers, a burning desire to do harm showing in their eyes, and though each invader panned the crowd, it seemed their stares always settled on the giant. All sound but the noise of the horses ceased; even the crickets that usually began their sexual dance at the edge of dusk remained quiet.

Bardiya lifted his head. "Sing," he said loudly, addressing his people. "Show our guests the glory of our love, of our beauty, of our kindness."

"I truly wish you would not."

It was a slogging voice, like rocks grinding together underwater. Bardiya took another step forward, looking on as a huge black charger trotted out of formation, approaching him. The charger acted agitated, as if it hated the duty of carrying its rider. That rider was a man of odd shape, the tight black leathers covering his body revealing enormous muscles that bulged and rippled in the wrong places. The man's head was bald and warped; his chin distended; his eyes, beady red dots beneath a jutting brow. In a way the man looked like Patrick, only more monstrous.

Bardiya swallowed his fear. "Who are you that have come to visit us in our humble village?" he asked. "With whom do the people of Ang have the pleasure of making new friends?"

"Clovis Crestwell, former Highest of Karak."

Clovis Crestwell? It cannot be. Bardiya had seen Karak's first child only once, back in his youth, when his father had brought him along to a gathering of the four First Families in the swampland between the Gods' Bridges. So far as he could recall, Clovis had been a tall and slender man with crystal-blue eyes, long silver hair, and a stately posture. He saw none of that in this bulging man-toad before him.

"You do not look well," he said.

"Time changes all men," Clovis replied. There was also that grating, almost inhuman voice to consider. "The last time I laid eyes on you, you were a mere five feet tall."

"I have grown."

"Apparently. Very impressive, if I do say so."

Bardiya stretched his back, trying to appear even taller than his twelve feet.

"And may I ask you, Clovis, what your intentions are in our fair village? We are messengers of peace and love, and have no wish to fight." He dropped down on one knee, bowing before the strange man and his army. He muttered a silent prayer to himself, his blood racing through his veins, and heard the rest of his people mimicking his actions behind him. "Whatever you desire to do to us, do it. If you wish to kill us all, do so. You will find no resistance here."

"That is . . . unfortunate. And predictable," said Clovis. The man spurred his charger, and the animal bucked as it made its way around the assembly. "However, I do not wish to kill you."

More agitated murmurs sounded, only this time it was from those on horseback. Bardiya looked up to see the elves staring back and forth at one another in confusion. Only the human soldiers didn't seem surprised by the man's words.

"You do not?" Bardiya asked. "Then why have you come here?"

"Why, we came to take you on a journey," the man said, his words accompanied by the most wicked laugh Bardiya had ever heard. "Judice, get the chains and bind them. We cannot have anyone fleeing before their time."

"And where do you plan on taking us?" asked Bardiya, standing once more. Behind him, his people whimpered when armored men carrying chains approached.

"To the tall black crystal in the middle of the desert, my brown colossus."

Soldiers grabbed Bardiya's arms. He could easily have thrown them aside, could have effortlessly bashed their skulls with his bare hands, but he stayed his anger and allowed them to bind him.

"The Black Spire?" he asked. "Whatever do you want with us there?"

"To fulfill your purpose," Clovis answered with a wide, hideous smile. "I need you to bring *true* beauty back to this world."

CHAPTER

7

Sunlight shone through the tree branches, lighting up the multicolored crystals that lined the skywalk's railing. Aullienna Meln took it slow, one foot in front of the other, as she made her way across the plank. The day was certainly a bright one, and filled with joyous sound. Her people scurried about on parallel walkways, calling out to her, cheering her on, yet she felt no relief in the sound. *I must enjoy the wonder of it, of them,* the young elf told herself. *I must, I must, I must.* Even though autumn's chill rode on the wind, even though her world had fallen to shambles around her.

Ever since returning to the Stonewood Forest, nothing had gone right. Their band of elves had been surrounded, her betrothed shot with an arrow, her mother clouted in the face. Aullienna herself had been carried away in a sack, only to be dumped onto the floor of Briar Hall, the court of the Lords of Stonewood. No smiles had greeted her. Instead, she'd been welcomed by a long-lost brother she'd never met, who had been banished from Stonewood long before Aully was born.

I hope you die horribly, Carskel, she thought, hearing the elf's whisper-soft footsteps behind her. *I hope your insides catch fire and your intestines fall out your mouth.*

"Stop dawdling," she heard Carskel say. Something poked into her shoulder blades, and she peered behind her. There stood her brother, tall and slender, with a head of long white-gold hair, flowing satin blouse over gossamer breeches, and his khandar swinging from his hip. *He looks so much like father,* she thought in despair. The tip of his walking stick was pressed against her back. He smiled, baring his teeth, his eyes twinkling in the slender beams of light that infiltrated the canopy. He seemed so pleased with himself. Just seeing him like that made her hate him all the more.

I should conjure a fireball and wipe that smile off his face, she thought.

"I'm going," she said instead. She knew that somewhere nearby, Ethir Ayers and Mardrik Melannin, Carskel's loyal enforcers, held the rest of her loved ones. Should she turn against her brother, should she hurt him in any way, Mother, Kindren, Noni, Aaromar, and all the rest of those who had traveled with her would be in danger.

We should have never left Ang, the child in her complained. *Bardiya would never have allowed this to happen.*

Grow up, her new resolve answered.

Elves cheered as she circled around the skywalk, passing small home after small home nestled into the branches of the old, sturdy trees. Her people hung out of windows and from the railings of the planks above, tossing handfuls of shredded leaves down on her in celebration. The scene was eerily similar to when she'd been ushered through the courtyard of Palace Thyne on the announcement day of her betrothal to Kindren. Aully thought she should feel sadness at the memory, or even regret; instead, all she felt was anger.

The Dezren city within the trees took up a relatively small section of forest—only a two-hundred-yard area at most, consisting of a ring of forty-seven trees. What the city lacked in width, it made up for in height, with each of the thick trees containing multiple homes circling around its trunk. Although Briar Hall was one of only two structures resting atop the highest and most distant of the trees, those closer to the center of the ring were much more densely populated, with the lowest of the thirteen houses still twenty feet off ground and accessible only by rope ladders. Within the city's boundaries, there was no need to let one's feet touch the earth at all. Each tree was connected by even more ladders, along with those spiraling stairs and hanging skywalks. Back before she'd become a prisoner, the skywalks had been Aully's favorite places to be. She would stand there for hours, smelling the sweet scents of roast rabbit, blackroot stews, and cooling raspberry and boysenberry pies, in between singing with her friends and listening to wizened old elves tell stories of days long ago. She blended into the crowd then, a nondescript member of a loving and joyous community, for though her parents were the Lord and Lady of Stonewood, it had long been practiced that one elf was of no more import than another.

The odor of food was still present, but she was no longer faceless. Every set of eyes that looked at her now did so expectantly, with reverence, as if welcoming a goddess back into the fold. The attention made Aully feel dirty, but not nearly as dirty as what she was about to do.

Carskel gently nudged her onto the swaying causeway that crossed through the city's central clearing. He kept his hand firmly gripped around her forearm, squeezing once they reached the center platform. Very slowly he spun her around, and Aully gazed in wonder at the multitude of people that waved and whistled from the various walks. She caught sight of Hadrik, Mella, and Lolly standing with their respective families, the only three faces Aully could see that weren't smiling. They seemed sad. The three of them had been Aully's friends since the cradle, and it had been those three who'd found her and her ragged group as they wandered home through the forest. But they'd only been there to put them at ease before Ethir and his henchmen rounded them up.

They aren't sad, Aully thought. *They're ashamed.*

"Wave to our people," Carskel muttered out the side of his mouth. Aully looked up at him, her lips drawn tight in defiance. Her brother squeezed her arm even tighter, making her yelp, a sound that was swallowed by the raucous cheering. Aully caved, lifting her hand and fanning her fingers as she and Carskel circled in place. The cheering picked up a notch. *"We love you, Aullienna!"* someone shouted. *"Our princess has returned!"* said someone else. The platform she stood on rocked back and forth. Aully felt her insides clench.

Carskel then knelt beside her, put his arm around her shoulder, himself waving and smiling at the crowd. "Look down, to your right," he whispered into her ear. "But don't you dare react." Aully followed the jut of his chin, squinting as she gazed at the darkened area beneath the lowest walkway. At first she couldn't make out what was there, but then Kindren stumbled forward, falling to his knees at the edge of the clearing. Kindren raised his head, staring up at her with pleading eyes. His face was marked with bruises, and his left shoulder was in a sling. For a moment Aully thought about leaping over the platform's hempen rail. More than anything she wanted to call out to him, but she didn't dare. Her eyes closed.

"There is more," Carskel said in his sweetly menacing voice.

She peered through half-closed eyelids as her mother and more than two dozen other elves were shoved into the light. Aully looked on helplessly as Lady Audrianna pulled Kindren to his feet, wrapping her would-be son-in-law in a protective embrace. Kindren shuddered in her grasp, the Lady of Stonewood holding him tightly, as if squeezing the sobs from him. The rest of her troupe then gathered around, consoling him like they would their own child, until Ethir and his cohorts began to roughly separate them. Aully looked all around her, wondering why everyone was still cheering when thirty of their brethren were being mistreated in plain sight. Then she peered behind her, saw that the lower walkways on the opposite side of the clearing had been kept empty. From the vantage point of those on the upper skywalks, only the overhanging edge of the lowest domiciles would be visible.

Aully took a deep breath, stilling her nerves.

"You won't hurt them," she said.

"So long as you keep your end of the bargain, no," her brother replied, again in that sickeningly pleasant tone. "Make sure it remains that way. Your uncle is with us. It is time."

Carskel gave her shoulder a light squeeze and stood up. He was two heads taller than Aully and carried himself with an air that oozed royalty, but she knew it was nothing but a ruse. This was an elf who had brutally assaulted his own sister, violating her in the most depraved of ways. He was a monster.

The platform began to shimmy, and Aully glanced down the walk to see her Uncle Detrick striding toward them. He looked dignified in his white robe, but she could see the anger hidden behind his easy smiles. His left hand was wrapped in beige cloth, hiding the empty socket where his index finger had once been, cut off when he dared raise his voice against his nephew. Detrick was an elf beaten, resigned to the role Carskel had given him.

Detrick stopped halfway down the walk and raised his hands. The frenetically cheering crowd hushed.

"Citizens of Stonewood Forest," Detrick began. "My brothers and sisters, we have been rudderless for quite some time, but on this day we gather to welcome our royal family back into the fold. You all know Aullienna, my niece, your princess. Thirty days ago she returned to us, limping through the forest, desperate for home. This young girl has experienced horrors we can only dream of, losses that would send the best of us howling into our beds. Her father, our Lord Cleotis, is dead. Her mother, our dear Lady Audrianna, is seriously hurt, and her recovery is not certain." Aully gulped at the words and glanced down at where her mother stood, but she could not make out the expression on Lady Audrianna's face. Detrick went on: "However, she did not go through her ordeal alone. With her the entire time was one brave elf, a lost soul who has returned our princess to us, a brave warrior who saved the lives of many. He will help guide us through the trying times ahead. Are we ready to greet him?"

The crowd roared, but the sound was half as vociferous as it had been. Aully then noticed looks of disapproval painting the faces of the elder elves. *They recognize him,* she thought. *They know what he did.* She felt Carskel stiffen beside her.

Her uncle gestured to her and Carskel with an open hand. "And now," he shouted, "Princess Aullienna!"

Aully's hands twitched, her knees shook. She knew the story she was supposed to tell by heart. She had been made to recite it daily whenever her jailers came to give her soup and bread: The humans of Paradise had turned rabid, the god Ashhur attacking Dezerea and putting countless of their cousins to slaughter. Her beloved brother, Carskel, who had been wrongly accused by Lord Cleotis, had returned from his exile to save his cherished family, freeing the prisoners from their bonds and leading the dash across western Dezrel. For months they'd hidden in the desert, avoiding the ravenous humans, gradually sneaking along endless dunes until finally wending their way home.

A horrible lie, every last part of it. The truth, as she had learned during her uncle's drunken and weeping late-night visits, was that Carskel had taken refuge in Quellassar during his hundred-year exile. He was a tool of the Quellan Triad and had convinced Ethir Ayers to take control of the forest city with promises of wealth and land. Her betrothal to Kindren, as it turned out, was a ruse to get Lord and Lady Meln out of Stonewood, to supplant them. From that day forth Carskel had ruled Stonewood in secret, waiting for the day his sister returned. Evidently, the plan had been to free Aully, and only Aully, so she could return home to become betrothed to her brother, solidifying the allegiance between Dezren and Quellan.

Their escaping Palace Thyne had never been in the design, Ceredon's righteous conscience never expected. Once more Aully damned herself for ever leaving Bardiya's side. Had she never come back, her people would still be safe. Had she stayed put, Kindren's life wouldn't be in danger . . .

The cheers died down and the crowd began to murmur. Carskel again squeezed her arm. He peered down at her, his phony smile faltering.

"Go on," he said, his voice full of worry. "You are wasting time."

She nodded to him and shook out of his grip. Stepping forward, she grasped the hempen rail and stared at the many expectant faces. She cleared her throat. "My people," she said. "I have returned—"

"Louder," snapped Carskel.

"My people," she said, trying to gather strength in her throat. "After a long, harrowing journey, I have returned home. Words cannot express how joyous it makes me to see all of your faces, to once more greet friends I thought gone forever." She shot a look at Hadrik, Mella, and Lolly. "This beautiful forest I never expected to see again. It fills me with . . . with . . . "

Her whole body was shaking. "I am happy," she continued. "I am relieved. And that relief is all due to the elf you see behind me. This great elf who was framed for a crime he did not commit, a noble elf who was forced to live a hundred years away from the home and family he adored . . . an elf who will lead us into . . . into . . . "

She paused, glanced behind her at Carskel, saw him urging her to go on. Then she looked down at Kindren, Lady Audrianna, Noni, and Aaromar, flanked by their captors. Her eyes met her mother's, and Lady Audrianna lifted her head proudly, emanating strength. Kindren did the same. Aully focused on them, on their tear-streaked faces, and saw Kindren mouth, *No.* Her eyes widened. She lifted her gaze to the heavens.

Do I dare, Celestia? Please tell me what I do is right.

A gust of wind blew, rattling the branches, swaying the platform, bringing goose pimples to her flesh. In its sound she heard her answer, cruel and unforgiving.

"An elf who has spat in the face of our goddess!" she shouted. A shocked silence fell over the three thousand elves in attendance. Aully didn't think about what she needed to say, she just said it, and was stunned by the volume of her voice. It seemed to carry for miles despite her diminutive size. "Carskel Meln, my exiled brother. He's a liar, a fool, a murderer. He raped my sister, Brienna! He plotted our destruction! The goddess damn every last one of you who follows him into ruin!"

A hand closed over her mouth, an arm wrapped around her waist, and she was yanked backward. The crowd erupted, this time in a din of angry, frightened shouts. Some began to throw vegetables from the skywalks.

"Our princess is feverish!" Aully heard her uncle's voice shout close to her ear. "Tired from the journey and delusional!" She bit down as hard as she could, drawing blood. Detrick shrieked and spun around, releasing her. She stumbled forward a few steps across the platform . . . directly into Carskel's arms. Her brother spun her around and locked his hands around her waist, lifting her off the ground.

"You have been a bad girl," he murmured, his hot breath moistening her neck. "And bad girls need to be punished."

Detrick continued his pleading with the infuriated people of Stonewood Forest while Carskel spun Aully around and leaned against the thick hempen rail. The rope bowed outward so far that Aully feared it would break, sending the both of them plunging to the rock- and root-covered ground below. But the rope held.

"Look what you wrought," he said, forcing her to look to where her people were huddled in the shadows. They were being beaten by their captors, the sounds of their struggle drowned out by three thousand hollering voices. Already one lay dead: Aaromar, her mother's protector, kind, handsome, and now nothing but a corpse with an arrow pierced through the eye. Aully looked on in horror as Noni was brought to the front, her upper body bathed in darkness. Unlike the others, the ancient elf did not struggle, tight-lipped resolve on her wrinkled face. Ethir appeared behind her, grabbing her by both shoulders. Noni gazed up at the girl who had been her ward for fourteen years, and she opened her mouth to scream.

Aully never heard what her nursemaid had to say, as a moment later Ethir came down hard on the old elf's head with a dagger. Noni's eyes bulged, the dagger's tip exiting below her chin along with a spray of pinkish blood. Her eyes rolled back and she collapsed, falling into Ethir's arms like a fainting lover.

Aully's entire body went numb, and she collapsed just as Noni had. Carskel held her tightly, carrying her across the walkway, deftly avoiding flying fruit and sticks. The whole while, Detrick continued his pleading, declaring Carskel's innocence and Aully's lunacy.

"You have been bad, my darling," her brother said in a sinister whisper as they exited the walkway amid a mob of angry elves. Two of the Meln house guards appeared, shoving protesters aside. Carskel rounded the corner and began climbing the spiral stair back toward Briar Hall. "But all is not lost," he said when no one was around to hear. "The people will come around . . . *you* will come around. Once I show you the cost of betrayal, you will have no choice."

Aully stayed silent, allowing him to carry her. She had seen her father murdered right in front of her. She had suffered in a dungeon, lived as a refugee, and became a prisoner to pain. It'd have been easy to succumb to it all, but her loved ones had shown her the way, defiant even before the face of death. Because of Carskel, she'd suffered, she wept, and now she swore to the last breath in her lungs to never give the bastard what he wanted.

Not ever.

CHAPTER

8

The bombardment began at sundown.

The ground shook with the force of an earthquake, rattling Patrick's teeth. He slipped off the rock he sat on, whacking his elbow on the ground. His wineskin slipped from his grasp and spilled across the grass. Preston and the Turncloaks, who were with him around the fire, similarly lost their balance. Little Flick even teetered into the flames, scalding his meaty hand in the process. All around them, the defenders of the wall broke into panic.

"What the fuck?" Patrick shouted, turning his eyes upward, toward the wall and dark purple sky looming above him. Another massive *thud* then sounded, ringing in his ears. Bits of rock and dust misted down from the top of the wall.

"They're attacking!" said Preston's son Edward.

"They can't be!" Joffrey Goldenrod said. "They haven't finished their towers!"

"Climb the wall and see then!" shouted Tristan Valeson.

Patrick heard an odd whining sound and threw his arms around the closest man to him. "No, you dumb shits!" he said, collapsing on top of young Ragnar Ender. "Get *down*!"

A massive black shape soared over the wall, crashing against the upper parapets and sending large chunks of brick and stone careening to the earth. It was like a deadly rain pounding all around them. The black shape continued its flight, dropping ever lower until it smashed down a hundred feet away, right atop a small gathering of confused people, crushing bodies and hurling chunks of dirt into the air. Now unmoving and in the light of their fires, Patrick saw it was a boulder the size of a small hut, gray and craggy. Screams of pain erupted, filling the early evening with terror.

"The catapults!" Preston shouted. "They're using the catapults!"

Of course they are, thought Patrick. He should have known this was coming. It had been almost five weeks since the first failed assault on Mordeina's walls, and the people within were beginning to grow careless. Since that day they had done nothing but watch from afar as the besieging army busied themselves with building engines of war. By last count, they had a dozen working catapults and four siege towers. Master Warden Ahaesarus surmised they would not bring an offensive until the entirety of their force was ready. After the last failed attempt, Patrick had thought Karak would just wait them out until their depleted food stores ran out completely.

They were wrong.

Patrick rolled to the side, grabbed his discarded helm, and threw it on his head. Luckily they had just finished supping and he hadn't yet removed his mismatched armor. He hurried to his feet and spun around in search of Winterbone. The dragonglass crystal adorning its hilt sparkled in the light of the flying embers, and he snatched the huge, trusty sword in his mitts. This time, he wasn't getting caught without his blade.

He could hear wailing in the background as he slung Winterbone's scabbard over his shoulder and began to make for the wall steps, followed by the Turncloaks, the newly trained archers, and a large cadre of Wardens. The Drake spellcasters were nowhere to be found. Patrick's insides rumbled, the wine he'd drunk jostling about in his belly. The scent of rot was much stronger than it had been five weeks ago, making bile rise in the back of his throat. *It's only a reaction—I'm not truly sick,* he thought. Many had fallen ill from drinking the city's water, despite Azariah's best efforts to keep it clean. There were thousands of sick, filling each day and night with the sound of puking and shitting. It became a full-time effort for the healers, which now included Warden Azariah's ever-growing army of students, to cure their sickness. Even so, there were many who succumbed to dysentery before having the chance to be healed. Their bodies were stashed in a small space to the right of the inner gate, heaped atop those who had died during previous assaults, to keep the settlement relatively free of further rot and disease. With every square inch of space required to keep so many people housed and fed, there was nowhere to bury the corpses. They would have to wait.

Ignore it, Patrick told himself. *Think of Nessa instead of your stomach.*

He did, and anger gradually cured his ills.

Still more heavy impacts rumbled as Patrick reached the bottom of the stairwell. Ahaesarus stood there, handing out bows to those who required them. Their eyes met and Ahaesarus nodded to him, as if he could see the fury burning behind his eyes. Patrick passed him by and led the charge up the stairs, his muscles not aching this time, though he could still feel a dull throb in his knees. Even the vibrations brought on by the collisions couldn't shake him. Ever since that first assault, he'd dedicated himself to running up and down these stairs five to six times a day, getting his body used to it. Now it was easy, though his mismatched legs would always offer him at least a little discomfort.

Another boulder soared overhead while he was halfway up the stairs, this time missing the parapets and instead snapping off one of the rock-hard branches of Celestia's tree a few yards to the left. The branch thumped off stone before falling into the narrow space between the inner and outer walls. More screaming reached his ears from down below, and a moment later he heard a sickening *thud* and elongated *crunch*. He wondered how many had perished this time, how many bodies they would have to clean up in the aftermath.

Too many if you don't move your ass.

He fully scaled the stairs and dashed along the wall walk, weaving around the casks of purified water that had been placed along the wall for those whose duty it was to watch the distant army. Countless others followed on his heels. By then he had counted sixteen impacts. Patrick sprinted past the smashed merlons and ducked down, peering between the stones at the army beyond. Now at the top, with a cold wind blowing in his face, he could hear the shouts and chants coming from Karak's followers, those fifteen thousand strong separated by nothing but a mile of dead, brown earth. Another dark and spinning object cut across the purple sky, forcing Patrick to duck once more.

"Incoming!" he cried.

The new boulder struck the wall, and he heard a loud *crack*. The distant army roared.

Keeping his head down, Patrick counted to sixty before chancing to peer between the merlons again. He squinted, trying to force his eyes to adjust to the ever-deepening darkness. A strange sound came to his ears, like an infant's rattle combined with countless twigs being snapped consecutively. He braced himself and stood in the nook between the two merlons for a better vantage point, but it was no use. All he could see was a black, shadowy blur on the horizon. No more boulders careened through the air.

Something isn't right here.

The Turncloaks had taken their places to his right, three Wardens to his left. Behind him men and Wardens alike rushed about, some carrying thick lengths of rope, others lugging between them oaken barrels filled with pitch, while the archers took their places along the rear of the wall. *We could still use some spellcasters.* Patrick looked to his left and saw that the gangplank connecting the inner and outer walls was still intact. For a moment he considered dashing across it to get a better look.

A strong hand grabbed his shoulder, halting him in place. Patrick looked up into Judarius's face.

"Best not," the Warden said.

"Why? What do your fine eyes see that mine don't?"

"Glowing red eyes, a hundred feet from our wall," Judarius said. "It is the First Man. There are a great many soldiers alongside him." The Warden scowled, then pointed toward Celestia's tree. "And there, black shadows climbing along the outer wall, where tree meets stone."

Jacob. That bastard.

"Give me fire!" Patrick shouted. One of the torchbearers came over to him, panting, fear making his eyes glisten. The youngster held the torch out to him. Patrick grabbed it and hopped off the wall, heading down the line until he reached the tree, ducking beneath branches hard as iron. Judarius and the Turncloaks followed behind him.

"What's going on, DuTaureau?" asked Preston.

"The First Man is using dark magic to pulverize the weak spot in the wall," Judarius answered for him.

When he reached the side of the tree, Patrick bent over the ledge and held the torch down into the darkness between the walls. Sure enough, he saw tubes of shadow, almost like smoke, winding in and out of the new cracks that had formed in the thick masonry of the outer wall. Heavy chunks of stone fell away, creating a bevy of holes that grew wider and wider as the shadowy feelers thickened. Soon those holes combined into one large opening.

"Shit," Patrick muttered.

Tristan was at his side. "What *is* that?" the young soldier asked.

"Celestia's tree may be harder than steel, but the outer wall is already weakened at the edges where the fireball first struck," said an authoritative voice. Patrick turned to see Ahaesarus standing behind them, hands on his hips, looking godly in his own right with his impressive height and long golden hair. "The boulders chipped away at the stone, further cracking it. Now Eveningstar is using whatever new power he possesses to widen it."

"How many soldiers approach?" asked Preston.

Judarius shook his head. "Too many. Five hundred, with at least half the army trailing behind. More than enough to overpower us."

Patrick closed his eyes, and once more he saw Nessa's face, green with rot, worms crawling through her empty eye sockets, her hair a nest of red hay. He squeezed his fists together, grinding his nails into his palms until they drew blood.

"They will *not* overpower us," he growled. Rearing back, he tossed the torch into the space between the walls, the glow from seventy feet below like a lone firefly in an empty field. Yet the light was enough to show clearly the breach in the wall growing wider and wider. "They still have to destroy the inner gate . . . and they still have to pass though *there*. We have fire and weapons and height, and the breach is only wide enough for them to enter three at a time at most."

As if to answer him, the slithering shadows tore another hunk of wall away, broadening the fissure.

"Will you stop that!" Patrick screamed. His rage reached its boiling point and everyone—Ahaesarus, Judarius, the Turncloaks, the archers—gave him a wide berth as he spun around and ran toward the interior edge of the rampart. He collided with the low wall, gazing out at the carnage the two falling boulders had caused. His eyes settled on Manse DuTaureau, sitting atop its high hill like a privileged child, surrounded by flickering torches.

"Damn you, Ashhur, you miserable excuse for a deity!" he cried. "Wake up already! What are you waiting for? Have you given up? Do you wish for us all to perish here? *Tell me!*"

There was no answer from the low stone building where the God of Justice had lain unconscious for well over a month, but there was from behind him.

"They're here!" Judarius shouted, and the *clunk* and *clank* of steel and stone followed as the defenders of the wall took their position.

"Well, fuck," Patrick muttered. He turned to see Ahaesarus ordering those who carried the barrels of pitch to cross the gang-plank and douse the enemy when they drew near. Patrick watched them go, struggling as they hefted the heavy barrels over the thin slab. The rest of the men the Master Warden ordered to stand ready, to unleash all they had on the horde once they entered the breach.

Just then a strange, fluid sensation overcame him. Patrick wob-bled, having to grab tight to the low wall to keep from falling. It seemed a beam of light washed over his vision and then vanished. The sound of wailing followed, definitely Jacob's voice, splitting the night. It carried on for what seemed like forever, a raucous cry of pain. *Good. I hope you're burning.*

"Look there!" Ryann Matheson, one of the Turncloaks, exclaimed.

Patrick rushed to the wall and peered down. The bulging tubes of darkness writhed, catching fire and dissolving into the night. Jacob's distant scream intensified. The crease in the wall had grown to fifteen feet wide, bits of mortar dropping from the rough stone in a trickle. *Celestia?* thought Patrick, lifting his eyes to the spot in the heavens where the goddess's star would appear when full dark over-took the land. *Have you come to our aid when our creator will not?*

The wail died away, and the rumble of booted feet grew all the louder. Arrows flew over the outer wall, striking one of the bar-rel bearers, causing him to fall backward into the gap between the walls. The rest stooped, avoiding the flying bolts. Those standing with Patrick on the inner rampart hid behind the merlons as steel tips bounced off the stone. The attackers shouted orders, words

Patrick couldn't quite make out. But Judarius did, and the Warden raised his voice to those manning the barrels.

"Light them and toss them over! Do it now!"

Torches lit long thatches of rope attached to the tops of the barrels, and then the bearers shoved them off the parapets. A series of explosions and bright flashes came from far below, seen through the gap in the wall. Patrick poked his head out from where he'd been concealed, and heard screams as the soldiers were set ablaze outside the wall.

"Burn, you motherless twats! Burn!"

It was a matter of moments before all six barrels were lit and thrown over the side, and with the advent of screaming from those doused with flames came desperation-fueled cheers from the defenders. Another barrage of arrows came a second later, ending those cheers with blood and sinew. Three more barrel bearers died, as did four of the archers standing behind Patrick. He heard metal scrape against rock.

"More barrels!" he called out. "They're coming through!"

The remaining three barrels were hefted atop the inner wall. Down below, soldiers began to lurch through the fifteen-foot breach.

"Wait for more of them," said Patrick. "The more in the gap, the more we burn!"

The arrows continued to soar, piercing men through the thigh, the chest, the face. Now the screams atop the wall matched those coming from without. Patrick was growing more and more infuriated by the moment. An arrow clanged off his helm, jostling it to the side. He righted it and chanced a peek into the narrow pathway below. He saw shapes moving in the darkness, packed tight together like fish in a crowded barrel. *"Now!"* he shouted. "Drop the barrels now!"

Drop them the bearers did. Two of the barrels burst, the pitch spreading, sliding over the shields and giving the passageway the look of some fiery abyss. The third barrel bounced off heavy, upraised iron shields, crushing the two soldiers that held them, its fat wick snuffing out as it rolled off to the side, disappearing beneath the invasive horde of humanity. The fires began to peter out, and there were very few screams. Patrick was left to look on in horror as the soldiers edged their way through the passageway, the last of the flames fizzling atop upraised shields. The soldiers that had fallen, either choked by the smoke or burned by the fire, were trampled.

Not enough dead. Not anywhere near enough. Their damn shields saved them.

Patrick whirled on Master Warden Ahaesarus. "I thought you said this would work!" he yelled. "I thought you said the fire would stave them off!"

Ahaesarus shook his head, appearing more annoyed than afraid. "It did. It slowed them." He calmly backed out of the way of a zipping arrow and pointed down. "If their shields had been wood, it might have incinerated them all. However, iron is much more difficult to burn. But the pitch will still burn, and still bring them pain."

Patrick stared into the passageway. The soldiers were at the inner gate now, and he heard the *clang* of those in front pounding on the bars. Another arrow flew by him, grazing his unprotected elbow. An angry red line appeared between the torn folds of his tunic.

"Someone, *please* stop those arrows," he heard Ahaesarus say.

"How?" asked someone behind him.

"Return fire!" screamed the Warden.

The archers hurried across the gangplank in a crouching run. Four of them were struck with bolts, and they collapsed into the gap, bouncing off the upturned shields. Patrick took a deep breath, pleading for patience. It was only when the defending archers began returning volleys of their own that it seemed safe enough to move about. Patrick ran toward the low interior wall and peered over and to his left, where he saw men and Wardens with pikes defending the inner gate, lunging with pikes and swinging heavy stone hammers. He also saw the Drake spellcasters, all twenty-six of them, scruffy and bearded, running between the two fallen boulders and the wailing people gathered around them. They were headed for the stairwell, but still a hundred yards away. *Too far. Too damn far.*

"Preston!" Patrick exclaimed. "Preston, where are you?"

The crowd around him had thinned, and the old soldier shoved his way through those who remained, his seven underlings beside him.

"What?" Preston asked, raising his voice to be heard over the ruckus.

"How are you at fighting in close quarters?"

"Why the Abyss do you care?"

Patrick gestured below. There had to be two hundred of Karak's soldiers down there now, bottlenecked at the breach. The soldiers were intent on bashing down the gate and hadn't spread out farther along the passageway, leaving no room for their compatriots to enter.

A smile formed on Preston's lips. "Good enough . . . especially with a running start."

"That's what I like to hear."

Patrick turned to the frightened people behind him, those who carried ropes and supplies. "You all—run along the wall. Fifty feet beyond the gate, I want you to fasten the ropes and throw them over the side."

Ten young men took off, dragging their ropes behind them. The Master Warden stopped yelling instructions to the archers on the outer wall and turned his way.

"What are you planning, Patrick?"

Patrick grinned. "To stop the bastards from breaking down our gate."

"With just the nine of you?"

"Make that ten," said Judarius. The black-haired Warden lumbered from the back of the pack, holding a giant stone club in his hands. A stray arrow flew by, almost taking him in the throat.

Up stepped the Wardens Grendel and Olympus. "Eleven and twelve."

"Twelve's a good number," said Patrick.

Ahaesarus shook his head. "You cannot hope to fend off so many with only twelve."

"No, but *you* can."

"How?"

"Gather up all the casks of purified water you can. Wait until Turock's spellcasters crest the stairs. When they do, dump every single cask onto the soldiers, and then tell the casters to give them a good shock." He winced. "And please make sure we're nowhere nearby when lightning strikes."

Ahaesarus shook his head. "You are all insane."

"We do what we can. Now excuse me, Master Warden, but we have men to kill."

Patrick turned on his heels and sprinted the other way, leading Judarius, Grendel, Olympus, and the Turncloaks along the wall. They passed over the gate, and he could hear the grunts and banging and shrieks coming from both those trying to get in and those fending them off. "Help will be there soon," muttered Patrick, and he pushed his stunted legs faster.

The ten youngsters were almost done tying off the ropes when Patrick and his band of cutthroats arrived at the spot fifty feet past the gate. They backed away silently, giving the fighting men room to maneuver. Patrick, Preston, and Judarius tested the ropes, making sure they would hold. It seemed they would.

"Ready?" Patrick asked the Turncloaks.

"Ready," said Preston.

"Ready," echoed his sons with far less confidence. Of the rest of them, only Big and Little Flick seemed truly ready to dole out some punishment.

That best be enough.

Over the wall they went. Patrick descended at a rapid pace, the roar of the soldiers a deafening clamor. The passageway was almost pitch black when his feet hit the ground. He gave a quick glance down the corridor and saw the flurry of activity fifty feet away as the soldiers continued their assault on the inner gate. They were so intent on their task that none of them bothered to glance in his direction. He swore he saw one of the bars bend to the point of breaking. Drawing Winterbone from its sheath, he took in a deep breath as those around him readied their own weapons. Though it was dark he could see the gleam of violence in Judarius's green-gold eyes.

"Wardens, stay behind us," Patrick whispered to the tall, elegant creatures. "Use your height to your advantage. Let our armor take the hits."

The three of them nodded. Turning back to the fight, Patrick lifted his sword high and murmured a prayer to Ashhur.

"No better time than now, you laggard. You best keep us safe."

Useful as surprise might have been, they really wanted intimidation and shock, and with the greatest roar he could manage Patrick led the way, sword raised high as his party joined in with their own hollering. Those on the outskirts of the packed-together mass started, heads whipping in their direction, eyes wide with fear. The distance between them vanished in a heartbeat, and Patrick thrust Winterbone forward like a spear, driving into their ranks, stabbing upward, thrusting backward, and swinging his elbows to smash jaws, allowing room for those behind him to make good with their weapons. There were grunts and shrieks all around him as the soldiers tried to counterattack, but he was too strong and the space too cramped. Most couldn't even get their weapons drawn. The few that succeeded did more damage to their fellow soldiers then to him. Alongside him crashed the rest, a chaos of dying, the Wardens finding their weak spots and smashing them with their giant clubs and mauls.

Someone collided with Patrick from behind, and he felt cold steel slip beneath the armor on his back. A hollow *clang* followed, and the steel disappeared, gashing him in the process. Patrick stumbled, his wound leaking, tackling a pair of struggling soldiers in the process. Before a swinging sword could halve him, he rolled to the side. The blade buried in the face of the one of the prone soldiers, eliciting a furious cry from the attacker.

Patrick tugged on Winterbone's handle, but there was a body on top of the sword, pinning it down. He rolled from one side to another, trapped by an ever-closing wall of armored legs. In the darkness of the passageway, it was chaos. He couldn't tell friend from foe. He glanced up and saw a shadowy, sneering face press in on him before that face exploded in a rain of saliva, blood, and teeth. The soldier collapsed atop him, and Patrick saw a large figure looming above the crowd, swinging away with a club, shadowy swirls of hair dancing behind him. Never before did Patrick think Judarius could have appeared so vicious, so deadly.

Finally able to wrench Winterbone free, he plunged the blade into another belly, legs driving to give him power. He kept his legs pumping, shoving the body backward as far as he could. A sudden surge of panic hit him as he wrenched the weapon free. In the bedlam he'd lost track of where he was.

A second later came a deafening crash of thunder and a flash of light so intense he was momentarily blinded. Men screamed, flesh sizzled. Patrick fell backward, crashing into an unknown soldier and eventually slamming the back of his helmed head against something hard. A hollow *twang* rang in his ears. When the stars cleared from his vision, he glanced behind him and saw that he sat atop a bleeding Joffrey Goldenrod. Quickly he brought his eyes forward, seeing the soldiers who had been nearest to the gate stumbling about in panic while countless of their compatriots hollered and shook. Still more bolts of lightning and energy flew from above, though their flash was not quite as bright or powerful.

About damn time.

In their panic, the surviving soldiers attempted to flee back the way they came, scampering over the soaked and shuddering pile of dead soldiers in search of the chasm in the wall. They too perished, their bodies thrown into convulsions while the smallclothes beneath their armor caught fire. Those who didn't flee were cut down by the Wardens and Turncloaks. Patrick looked on in wonder, not able to believe his plan had worked. Even more surprising was just how terrifying the spellcasters could be, naked power killing without chance of defense or retaliation.

The putrid stenches of smoke and roasting meat reached Patrick's nose, and he gagged. This time he did empty his stomach . . . right on top of Joffrey.

"Had enough, old boy?" asked a hoarse, tired voice.

Patrick rolled off Joffrey, who scampered away from him, retching. He looked up at a bloodied and limping Preston. When the older man smiled, his teeth were stained red.

"I dare say I have," Patrick said.

"What do we do now?" asked Ragnar Ender, just as bloody as his father.

Patrick himself was covered with nasty cuts, and now that he'd vomited, he could feel every stab of pain that covered him.

"Now we have someone open the gate and let us in," he said, spitting out his words. His head tilted to the side, and he looked beyond the sodden bodies of the dead soldiers to the hole in the wall beside the massive trunk of Celestia's tree. Several hundred of Karak's men were dead, but how long until thousands more rushed through the gap? "Actually, strike that," he said, struggling to his feet. "First we need to get someone down here to fix that wall."

"No need," shouted Potrel Longshanks, the eldest of the spellcasters, from up on top of the wall. Frowning, Patrick looked up to where the men from Drake gathered. They were working on something, and he could see the magic flicking off them like the light of tiny stars. Then, without warning, the ground shook. The broken pieces of the wall rumbled as if alive, and then they rolled toward the gap. One atop the other they piled, groaning and shifting. Soldiers still trying to get inside were crushed by the ascending stones. It was hardly even, nor a third of the height it had originally been, but when the noise stopped, and the spellcasters lowered their arms, the breach had been sealed.

Potrel laughed down from the rampart.

"Celestia's not the only one who can fill a hole," he shouted.

"Bloody Abyss," Patrick shouted up to the wall. "Why in the name of Karak's hairy ass did you not do that earlier?"

Potrel shrugged. "I thought you wanted to kill a few of them first."

Patrick shook his head as Judarius clapped him on the shoulder, laughing.

"Damn spellcasters," Patrick muttered.

CHAPTER

9

Ahaesarus watched Karak's soldiers retreat back from the wall, clearly frustrated by the wizards' sealing of the breach. Knowing it was only a matter of time before the siege towers approached and the catapults resumed their barrage, the Warden descended into the pit. He had witnessed the carnage in the narrow corridor between the walls, seen the bloody, charred remains of the soldiers who had entered the breach, smelled their cooking flesh. He and Warden Judah took on the task of counting their dead foes while other Wardens and the human healers mended Patrick DuTaureau and his eleven brave companions who were injured but alive. In the end neither he nor Judah could come to an exact number, but they both agreed that number was greater than two hundred. *Two hundred soldiers dead, while we lost thirty. So why do I feel we came out the losers?*

Thirty was too many. After the interior gate was opened, the corpses of Mordeina's fallen were separated from those of the soldiers and carried to the ever-growing rows of dead that littered the far grove, an open mass grave that was barely hidden by a makeshift wall of twigs and bed sheets. Given the rot that was beginning to infest nearly every corner of the sixteen-square-mile settlement, he knew those bodies would have to be dealt with soon, though he also understood it would be difficult to convince Isabel and the fat young king to take action. *Mordeina buries their dead, and all that.* Ahaesarus let out a disgusted grunt at the thought.

The next order of business was to fix the damage left behind by the boulders that had crashed down inside the settlement. There were another sixty dead there, fragile bodies crushed by the immense stones, and many more injured. Broken bones healed easily enough, but for some there was no choice but to remove their mangled arms and legs. Mothers cried for their children; husbands sobbed for their wives; sons and daughters wailed for their lost parents. For Ahaesarus, trying to soothe these people was worse than the carnage of battle. There was nothing he could say that could take away their pain. He could only hold them, caress them, tell them how their loved ones were in a better place now and that there was no reason for tears.

It was an act of kindness no one had offered him after the winged demons invaded his home world of Algrahar. Though it hurt, he was happy to give it.

All of this left him exhausted, and with the sky brightening as daylight returned to the world, he eagerly anticipated lying down in his bed and getting some rest. Even if the nightmares came, he would welcome them with open arms so long as he could put up his sore feet. But that respite still had to wait until he fulfilled the last of his duties.

"What next?" asked Judarius. The black-haired, green-eyed Warden walked beside him on Mordeina's main throughway, passing between row after row of campsites packed with restless and frightened people.

"The Manse," said Ahaesarus. "I've been ordered to keep your former student abreast of what happens during my watch, and so I must obey."

"My student?" snorted Judarius. "*My* student, the one who *should* have been king, died two years ago. The whelp who wears the crown now in no way resembles the boy I trained."

"So you claim no responsibility for Benjamin's behavior?"

"I would had I been allowed to continue my tutelage. But Lady Isabel has taken him from me, molded him into whatever she wishes. As if Jacob did not soil him enough."

Ahaesarus sighed.

"He seems to have put back on all the weight you made him lose. He also is prone to crying fits, more so now that our god is indisposed." He passed his fellow Warden an inquisitive look, eyebrows raised. "Judarius, Benjamin was served rightly by your wisdom. He demonstrated potential for greatness when you mentored him."

Judarius hawked a wad of spit to the ground. "Ben Maryll was *never* destined for greatness. I tried convincing myself otherwise, but the more I trained him, the more I wondered why Jacob picked the boy. The strength he showed when under my tutelage? A farce. A mirage, brought on by fear of my wrath. Without someone strong to keep him in line, he's backslid into frailty."

"What if you resumed your tutelage?" It was an idea Ahaesarus had been contemplating for some time, and with Isabel finally seeming to have conquered her grief over Nessa DuTaureau's death, it grew stronger by the moment. Isabel was more protective of the boy king than even before, tugging him deeper and deeper into her protective bosom. Now Benjamin was so deep that he seemed to be an infant living in a body moving rapidly toward manhood.

"No, that would not do," said Judarius with a grave shake of his head. "A true leader does not need someone above him to pull his strings. A true leader learns, a true leader *leads*. Benjamin will never be that. All that I could give him is the false strength I offered him before."

"Sometimes the people need to see strength, even if it is false."

"I refuse to believe that, Ahaesarus. And to be honest, I would not take him under my wing again even if I could. For nearly ninety-five years I have been something I am not, playing a game I was ill suited to play. I was a warrior in our past life. It is time I became that again."

They paused at the base of the hill leading up to Manse DuTaureau, and Ahaesarus glanced over to see a gleam in his fellow Warden's eye, a smile playing on his lips. Strangely enough, given what had transpired that night, Judarius seemed *relieved*.

"You look quite pleased with yourself," Ahaesarus said.

"I am," the black-haired Warden replied. He waved his hand at the Manse dismissively. "You can play politics all you like, Ahaesarus. Azariah can pray and practice his spells with his students. For me, for the rest of our kind . . . we're warriors now. Protectors. Innocent lives depend on us to kill, and so we kill. Is there not purity in that simplicity? Is there not an order that even Karak could appreciate?"

Ahaesarus understood completely. Though he was not the fearless and eager warrior Judarius had proven himself to be, he still had to admit there was a certain clarity about the battlefield that made him feel alive. Much more alive than the hours he was required to spend with the king and Lady Isabel.

"You were a sight to behold tonight, my friend," he told Judarius. "Because of you, and Patrick and his Turncloaks, we can sleep this morning away, knowing we are safe."

"We're not safe," Judarius said. "Not yet. But you may sleep without fear. I dare say that's close enough."

The Warden loped off, and Ahaesarus took a deep breath, trying to clear his muddled thoughts before climbing the hill. What had once been mild irritation became full-on dread once he reached the Manse itself. Isabel DuTaureau was outside waiting for him, wearing a satin nightdress, rouge painting her cheeks, her fiery red hair set just so. He let out a sigh of frustration. Mordeina was a place of war, of heartache and pain. Yet this woman still looked as if she lived in luxury without a care in the world. Had she learned nothing from the death of her daughter?

"Lady DuTaureau," Ahaesarus said, inclining his head to her.

"We must talk, Ahaesarus," said Isabel. Her voice was cold and full of disdain. She had been this way ever since she'd reemerged from her bedchamber, refusing to call him Master Warden and treating him more like a nuisance than a friend. *She will never forgive me for releasing Geris against her will,* he thought. That was one decision that Ahaesarus would never regret, no matter how much abuse the small but influential woman heaped on him for it. Geris Felhorn was hopefully far away from Mordeina by now, safe and with the young girl he loved by his side. If anyone in Paradise deserved a chance at happiness, it was he.

"What is it?" Ahaesarus asked.

"Your presence is not required. Go home."

"Go home? I have duties to attend to. I must speak with the boy."

"No. I forbid it."

Ahaesarus felt flustered and angry. *I tire of the games as well, Judarius,* he thought. "Where is Howard?" he asked, a cruel edge to his voice.

"I gave him the morning to rest. *Sir* Howard spent the evening calming your frightened wards and taking complaints. He was quite tired."

"Yes, and we did nothing but stand around all evening," he said sarcastically. "In case it failed to wake you, our walls were attacked last night. Karak's children almost broke down our gate. If not for those of us on the wall, if not for Patrick, we—"

She snapped her fingers in his face, cutting him off. "Do *not* take that tone with me, Warden, nor mention my son in my presence again. I am not blind to what goes on in my home, to *my people.*"

"So they are *your* people now, are they?" he shot back, his anger melting away his exhaustion. "I thought they were Ashhur's—and after him, our noble King Benjamin's?"

Isabel looked as if she was about to scream, but she snapped her mouth shut. Her whole body shuddered for a moment, like she were trying to rid her body of an invading demon, and when she looked up at him once more, her manner was calm.

"I will not fight with you, Ahaesarus," she said, her tone once again devoid of emotion. "As much as I wish it weren't so, you still hold your position within our society. We must work together to cure the ills of our people. Go to them. Leave here."

She turned on her heels and stormed into the manse.

Clenching his fists, Ahaesarus followed after her.

"I told you to leave!" Isabel snapped.

"No!" he shot back at her. "You cannot stop me from speaking with the boy."

Isabel cursed and stomped along the corridor. Ahaesarus remained by her side, refusing to walk ahead of her or trail behind. He took a perverse sort of pleasure in the way that made her fume. They passed the manse's central hub in an uncomfortable silence. It was not until the double doors leading into the makeshift throne room came into view that Ahaesarus spoke.

"You do the boy a disservice, Isabel," he said calmly, breaking the silence. "He needs to be among the populace. His people—*your* people—are hurting. It would do them good to see their king among them, talking to them, helping to quell their fears. It is what a king is supposed to do. It is what Ashhur wanted of us."

Isabel smirked. "There will be no need of that," she said. Gone was her anger, replaced by the coldness Ahaesarus had come to know so well. "Young King Benjamin has no need to hear what has happened, nor does he need to see the horror of its aftermath."

Ahaesarus stopped short. "Then whatever would you have him do?"

"What a king is *supposed* to do—whatever is best for his kingdom." A sick sort of smile came over Isabel's face. "There have been many complaints coming in over the past few days that the rations are not enough to adequately feed the many families outside. King Benjamin is going to stop the rationing and allow all to have their share."

The Master Warden stepped back, his anger overtaken by horror.

"Are you insane? Our stores are almost empty! Even with rationing they will last two weeks at most. Winter is fast approaching; plants are not taking root in the soil; and there are entire communities forced to camp on much of our farmland. And you wish to give everyone what they ask for? What would you have us do when our food runs out?"

She huffed at him. "You think this war will last long enough for that to occur?" she asked. The venom had returned. "Our god, my creator, is useless. He is already defeated. Karak will overpower us, and all you see before you will be no more."

Ahaesarus couldn't respond. He didn't know how to.

"Do you not see, Warden?" Isabel continued. "We have lost. We are done for. Let the people drink and eat to their hearts' content before they die."

"You . . . you've given up." He couldn't believe how sure the woman sounded, how resolute.

"I have accepted reality. Karak is the stronger, Ashhur the weaker. If Nessa had been Karak's child, he never would have allowed her to perish the way she did. He would have put those who ended her to the sword. While Ashhur lies on a slab, doing nothing, Karak brings forth the justice our god claims to represent."

Ahaesarus's mouth dropped open. It seemed Isabel was enjoying how much horror he expressed at her words.

Isabel laughed. "Do not look so shocked, Warden. I know you have thought the same."

"I have not. I would never surrender my people to die as you have."

"We shall see. In three days, you will have your wish. Ben will exit the manse as you desire. He will walk among the people, and he will convince them to throw open the gates of Mordeina to Karak and his army. The Eastern Deity desires order? We will give it to him. All our people will bow before his grace." She huffed and turned around, storming toward the double doors.

He stepped up to her as her hands fell on the handle.

"We will stop you," he warned. "We will not let you defame Ashhur so."

Isabel's green eyes bore into his. "There is nothing your fellow Wardens can do about this, nor my monster of a son. *You* serve *us*, Warden, not the other way around. If my people demand this course of action, you will step aside. *Humans* were given free will in this land, not your kind. Now leave me and my king be."

With that, Isabel shoved open the doors. They swung wide, slamming against the walls on either side, the echo reverberating down the long hall. When she stepped into the old dining hall, Ahaesarus still kept pace with her. She was so tiny compared to him, so frail. He could snap her in two if he so desired. A strong part of him wanted to do just that.

Then he heard the sound of soft, joyous sobbing. He looked up and what he saw stole away his breath and all his vengeful thoughts.

Ashhur sat up on his slab, luster in his pearly white cheeks, his glowing eyes filling the room with light, his hair like streams of woven gold. Ben Maryll was before him, arms wrapped around the god's massive right calf. It was his wailing Ahaesarus heard, the boy king soaking the deity's shin with tears as he happily proclaimed, "You haven't abandoned us, you haven't abandoned us!"

The god was staring at the boy as he patted Ben's head, and very slowly his gaze lifted. Ashhur looked healthy, vibrant, and *angry*. Ahaesarus had never seen him that way before, and it was one of the most frightening sights he had ever gazed upon—more so than Geris slitting Ben's throat, more so than the battle in the passage, more so than the demons slaughtering his wife and children on Algrahar.

Ahaesarus fell to his knees.

"Your Grace," he said.

"Stand, Master Warden," said Ashhur. He then leveled his angry gaze at Isabel, who gawked at her creator, hands shaking, eyes wide and brimming with tears. "It is not you who should kneel."

Isabel collapsed to her knees. "Your Grace, I am sorry . . . Your Grace, I thought you were gone . . . you were gone . . . "

"Enough!" the deity shouted, and Lady DuTaureau clammed up. Ashhur stood, crossing the distance between them in two giant strides. Ahaesarus stepped aside, allowing the god room to squat down in front of his second creation.

"You have disappointed me greatly, Isabel," he said. "You would willingly sacrifice your brothers and sisters when the last breath has not exited my body?"

"I . . . your Grace, I didn't know . . . "

"You are hereby relieved of your station, Isabel. Get out of my sight, and find solace in the fact that I do not tear your body asunder for the treason you proposed."

Isabel seemed as though she would plead some more, but she thought better of it when the glow of Ashhur's eyes intensified. The woman scampered to her feet and left the room as fast as she could. King Benjamin looked on from his place on the floor, having not moved since Ashhur stood to approach them. There was a queer mixture of relief and despair in the tears that ran down his cheeks. For not the first time, Ahaesarus felt sorry for the boy . . . a thought that exited his head as soon as a giant hand wrapped around his shoulder.

"And you, Ahaesarus," Ashhur said. "Prepare your Wardens. Prepare my children. You have done your best, but a proper defense of our home begins now."

CHAPTER 10

While the thunder crashed from within Mordeina's walls, and the Lord Commander shouted for the advancing soldiers to retreat, Velixar knelt motionless in the dead brown grass, surrounded by the corpses of soldiers who'd lost their lives to arrow and raging flame no more than a hundred feet from the breach in the wall. That breach was now being covered over with rough stone, sealing it. He stared in disbelief. Where he had seen imminent success had come failure. Where he had expected glory, he'd received shame.

"My magic is strong," he'd told Malcolm. *"My bond with the demon's power grows stronger every day."* During the long weeks leading to this night he had dived deeper into the recesses of his combined soul, gaining access to new abilities, new reservoirs of magic he had not known existed. The demon that had once borne his name seemed to have been formed from the very root of magic itself; every layer he peeled back revealed greater and greater secrets.

And yet it hadn't been enough. The wall should have crumbled under his will, but still it stood, no matter how he chanted, no matter how much strength he funneled from his god—yes, Karak's power still burned inside him. He had succeeded in widening the gap, and then Velixar's shadows had simply burned and retreated, a magical ward rising around the township, thwarting his every spell. He reached inside his cloak and withdrew his pendant, that of the lion standing atop a mountain. The bas-relief vibrated, glowing a deep red around the edges. Letting the pendant dangle in front of his chest, he fumed. Who had raised the barrier against him? Celestia again? Or were the novice spellcasters inside somehow growing more powerful than he?

He shook his head. It had to be Celestia. The other option wasn't possible.

Finally, when the sun rose behind him, Velixar slapped the frail grass and stood up. He walked slowly across the valley, heading for the sprawling camp at the top of the rise. He could feel the eyes of Mordeina's defenders on his back, watching him, mocking him. He curled his hands into fists, fighting the urge to turn around and hurl a massive bolt of living shadow their way. *It would do no good. The spell will fail before it ever reaches them.*

Lord Commander Gregorian was awake and sitting tall atop his horse, his arm no longer in a sling. With tired eyes he watched the physicians tend to the wounded. At Velixar's arrival, the man met his gaze and nodded. There was no accusation in his stare, and no mockery either. *There best not be.* It was Malcolm whom Velixar had first gone to with the plan, and the Lord Commander had eagerly approved the strategy. Malcolm had also spoken of the men's angst and exhaustion, their hunger and doubt that they would succeed in their task. *"Most of these soldiers were laborers, craftsmen, and farmers,"* he'd said. *"Though their faith in their Lord is strong, they themselves are fallible. Any course of action that brings an end to this conflict quickly would be best."*

So they marched, using their twelve finished catapults to barrage the outer wall while allowing Velixar's magic to finish the job. It was a risky proposition given that none knew the proportions of the walls themselves, how large the space was between the two, how wide the ramparts, or the location of the inner gate. And none knew how many defenders the settlement truly had. Yet Velixar had laughed those questions off. *Who needs information when you have my strength at your side?*

How wrong he had been.

Velixar walked through the first cluster of tents without uttering a word. Those who had marched to the walls, nearly half the army, lingered outside their canvas enclosures, muttering. Those who had remained behind were lighting cookfires to warm their thinned-out wine and perhaps cook a few meager scraps of horsemeat before starting their day. There were still machines of war to build, after all, and every man who knew how to swing a hammer and work a saw was needed.

Had I succeeded, they would not *have been needed.*

Spiraling into dejection, Velixar came upon the Quellan camp. Chief Aerland Shen was outside, sitting before his cookfire, his thick legs crossed one over the other. His muscular back flexed, and his square chin jutted toward the rising sun. His eyes were closed. The other elven rangers, nearly a hundred of them, all held the same posture in front of their odd, triangular tents. When Velixar stepped on a twig, many of their eyes snapped open and looked in his direction. Some offered polite greetings in their native tongue; others acted as if he wasn't there, and Chief Shen scowled. Three days ago Velixar had promised the Ekreissar chief battle for his rangers, a promise that hadn't come to pass.

Velixar flipped his hood over his head, hugged his cloak tight, and gazed toward Karak's pavilion, majestic and austere, the tallest structure that could be seen within the camp. He wanted nothing more than to march up the rise, fall down on his knees, and confess his failure to his god, but he dared not. Nine days ago Karak had announced he was not to be disturbed while he went about some enigmatic godly rite. He had not exited since. Velixar sighed, turned around, and headed back for Malcolm. Though he required sleep, he refused himself the luxury. These were his soldiers that were wailing in the distance as their bones were set and their mangled limbs sliced away. He would go to them, comfort them as best he could, and then oversee the construction of the towers until nightfall. Karak would beckon him when Karak so desired.

That beckoning came two nights later when, just before dawn, Karak entered Velixar's pavilion. Velixar had been sitting at his desk, jamming a quill into the soft wooden tabletop and staring at his clothing chest, atop which the head of Donnell Frost sat, the faithful man who had been justly executed after attempting to flee. Velixar sat awestruck for a moment, too confounded to move, until he fell from his chair and dropped to his knees before the god. Karak had never entered his pavilion before.

"My Lord," he said, nearly kissing the ground. "I am unworthy of your presence."

The deity acted like he didn't hear him. Karak leaned over the chest atop which Donnell's head rested, his glowing eyes seemingly studying every crease and bump on the slowly rotting flesh.

"Why is this here?" Karak asked.

Velixar sat up and cleared his throat. "I ordered my stewards to dip it in wax and place it in my tent."

"For what reason?"

"For trials. Though Donnell Frost made a mistake, he was a faithful man, perhaps as faithful as the Lord Commander. If it is true what the elves say, that threads of a being's essence remains tied to its body even after death, I surmised the head would be where his spirit lingered strongest."

"You have been discovering further . . . talents," said Karak.

"I have, my Lord. I have been studying how to commune with the dead, how to gain their secrets, and since it is my faith in you that gives me strength, and Donnell possessed that same faith, it is only logical to use him as my first trial."

"Have you been successful?"

Velixar shrugged. "I have not attempted yet, my Lord. I have been . . . awaiting the right moment."

Karak poked at one of Donnell's jellied eyes with his giant finger. The eye burst, leaking pus over the cracked flesh of his cheeks. A worried lump formed in Velixar's throat.

"My Lord, might I ask what you were doing in your pavilion all this time?"

"I was scouring my kingdom," the god said, still not looking in his direction. "Gazing through the ether at the souls of the true and the deceitful alike. That is why I am here."

Velixar slowly rose to his feet. He didn't like Karak's tone. The deity seemed weary, almost dejected. Velixar had never heard him sound such a way.

"Something troubles you," he said.

Karak nodded. "I have seen much. I have seen our fourth regiment on a rudderless ship in the Tinderlands, with their captain gone, assaulting Turock Escheton's people and finding themselves in a stalemate. Their faith in me is faltering. I have seen ships set sail from Omnmount, the last of our fallback division departing without my knowledge or permission and sailing to the Isles of Gold along with conscripted sellswords from Neldar." Karak looked at him finally, his golden eyes severe. "The faithful were destroyed, and now the sellswords have reached Paradise, with the last surviving daughter of Soleh Mori leading them."

"Rachida? She is here in Paradise?"

"I have seen betrayal after betrayal," the god continued, ignoring him. "The Judges have taken over Veldaren, though the puppet king opposes them. Merchant families are banding together with secret pacts, and they have infiltrated my army. There has been so much failure."

Velixar dropped his head. "Speaking of failure, my Lord, I have something to confess."

"Yes, your thwarted attack on the walls. I saw that as well."

"Then you know that someone raised a magical barrier to counteract my power. Either Celestia has once more stepped into the fold, or one of the—"

"It is neither. My brother is the one who raised the barrier."

"Come again, my Lord?"

"Ashhur is awake. He rose from his slumber while your boulders cracked the wall. You were thwarted by him, no one else."

Once more Velixar dropped to his knees. "My failure knows no bounds, my Lord. I do not deserve forgiveness, I do not deserve—"

"Enough, High Prophet," said the god. "You are still only mortal. That your power paled before a god's is merely inevitable and needs no apologies. As for Ashhur, it is fortunate he has awoken, for now the two sides are balanced, and there is no need for Celestia to further intervene. No, Velixar, your failure lies elsewhere."

Karak's hand was on him a moment later, forcibly making him sit up. Those glowing eyes bore down on him, seeming to shrink his very soul. Velixar's heart pounded in his chest as he awaited the accusation.

"Have you heard word from Darakken and the elves?" the god asked.

Velixar was taken off guard by the out-of-place question.

"I have not, my Lord. I assume they encountered delays, or the Dezren were not as hospitable as we assumed they would be."

"Neither is the case," said Karak. "They are no longer in Dezerea."

"Then where are they?"

The deity leveled his gaze, his eyes shining brighter than ever. "Ker. The demon has turned his remaining soldiers, as well as the might of the Ekreissar, against my brother's darker-skinned children."

Velixar's jaw dropped open. "I . . . is it . . . is this not fortuitous, my Lord? Darakken is a simple beast, seeking only to please its creator. He most likely hopes to make you proud by dismantling those you have saved for last."

"Once more you prove how little you know," Karak said with disappointment. "And you fool yourself if you think a creature such as Darakken would seek to please *me*. The demon was given life for a single purpose: to destroy all of Celestia's creations. *That* is all it seeks, a slave to its primitive urge. Worse, it craves to become whole once more."

"That is not possible," Velixar said, shaking his head. His whole body had gone numb. "The only way he could make himself whole . . . "

Karak nodded gravely.

"My journal," said Velixar with dread.

"Yes, High Prophet. I found it. In the possession of Darakken."

Velixar's whole body went limp, and he fell back to his knees, arms dangling by his sides. "How?"

"It was given to the beast by a human soldier, one that once marched with us through Lerder. Boris Marchant. Do you recall him?"

Velixar nodded, anger churning in his gut. Boris had been a soldier he once thought might have replaced Roland Norsman as his apprentice. That the man had betrayed him . . . he was beyond words. He saw red.

"How the beast obtained the book is not relevant," Karak said. "What is relevant is that you said you could control it. The demon was to tip the scales in our favor in case Ashhur proved stronger than we assumed. Yet now, because of your carelessness, your hubris, you have let this thing run amok. If he succeeds in remaking himself, he will bring chaos to this land, and it will be up to me to banish him to the pit yet again, once my victory is secure."

"I am sorry, my Lord," Velixar whispered. "I . . . am . . . sorry."

Karak ran a hand through his short, dark hair and closed his eyes. "It is not all your doing. I am at fault as well. In my haste to bring about this conflict, I failed to do that which I had done for an epoch. I failed to *watch*. Had I kept an eye on my children, I would have known of their treachery and put a stop to it. Had I taken a moment to quell Darakken myself, instead of making plans for war, I would have him under better control. Humans are fallible; I am not supposed to be."

Velixar did his best to compose himself.

"What do we do now?"

Karak formed a fist and ground it in his opposite palm. "Now we accelerate. My brother's children must fall, and they must fall soon, while he is still weakened. If we cannot assault them with magic, we will assault them with everything else at our disposal. I will walk among my children and aid them in their construction. Once they are finished, we will attack, and this time we will know exactly when and exactly where."

"And how is that, my Lord? Have you seen something of Ashhur's children through the ether?"

"I can no more espy my brother's children than he can see mine, High Prophet. It must be you. You are the greatest of humanity—surely you can discover a way. Is your magic not powerful?"

"It is powerful, my Lord, but the walls are protected now, as you have said."

Karak glanced once more in the direction of Donnell Winter's head. "Perhaps all this power has weakened you in other ways. You are strong, you are mighty, but in many ways Jacob Eveningstar was cleverer. What would *he* have done?"

Velixar had no chance to answer before Karak bid his farewell and left the pavilion. He stood in the center of the space, perplexed and more than a little insulted. *What would Jacob Eveningstar do?* It was a question Velixar hadn't pondered since he took the name of the demon as his own. Jacob was a mere *human*, albeit an ageless one. What could he accomplish that Velixar could not?

Velixar lifted his gaze to the hanging mirror of his room and stared at his reflection, his narrow chin, his elegant nose, his high cheekbones, his satiny black hair, his glowing red eyes. Karak was right. Beneath the veneer the demon's essence had given him, he was still Jacob Eveningstar. And it was the First Man of Dezrel who had facilitated the battle in Haven, who had brought about this very war by using tools such as this dragonglass mirror before him. How would that man use the tools at his disposal . . . ?

Dragonglass.

He traced his fingers along the elegant carvings on the mirror's edge. The mirror had once belonged to Crian Crestwell, and Jacob Eveningstar had stepped through it to end the life of both the romantic dullard and his western whore. *Dragonglass.* It was an element with properties he had long ago learned how to manipulate. Jacob had used the pendant Brienna Meln had given him to commune with Clovis Crestwell, had whispered promises of power and might and glory into the egotistical bastard's head. *Dragonglass.* A rare beauty created by the breath of the last dragon in Dezrel. The only items made from it that he knew of were this mirror, his and Clovis's old pendants, and . . . and . . .

The blade. Winterbone, the sword, one of the greatest forged in the Mount Hailen armory, had a dragonglass crystal affixed to its handle. He laughed to himself, softly at first, then louder and louder until his cackle seemed as raucous as thunder. The sword was inside Mordeina's walls, in the possession of the deformed Patrick DuTaureau . . . which meant it was Velixar's tool as well. He knew how to manipulate that mutant of a man as well as he did dragonglass.

"My dear Patrick," he said into the mirror when his laughter died down, "I think your beloved little Nessa wishes to speak with you."

CHAPTER

11

Rachida Gemcroft was bored out of her drunken mind. She lay on a bed inside a drab, one-room hovel in Conch, a strange little village on the northwestern coast of Paradise, waiting for dawn to come. She was alone despite being surrounded by hundreds.

What I'd give to have Moira with me, she thought bitterly. *Nothing was ever boring when she was around.*

Rachida had been seven years old when she met her kindred spirit. Moira was a year older, more slender, and boyish, though she had a certain cuteness that could not be denied. Her silver hair was chopped short, to the obvious dismay of Lanike Crestwell, who had brought her then-youngest child to visit the secluded village of Erznia at Soleh Mori's behest.

The two girls struck up a bond almost immediately, and for the first time ever Rachida began to understand how complex people could be. Although Moira was certainly tough—being raised a Crestwell, she had no choice in the matter—there was still a sort of sensitivity, a neediness in her that melded well with Rachida's more stern and manipulative personality. The silver-haired girl was prone to daydreams, sitting by the pond behind Mori Manor and gazing at the sky while the passing clouds reflected in her eyes. The moments they spent together in the woods, running around collecting frogs, insects, or salamanders, were pure bliss.

That first visit lasted a mere four days, and after Lanike brought her daughter back to Veldaren, Rachida was crestfallen, and began writing letters to the girl. Moira always wrote back, and Rachida would find herself looking to the skies each day, waiting for the next bird to arrive. For the first time in her short life, she actually felt like the maidens from her mother's stories. Every night she would kneel by her bed and thank Karak, in her little girl voice, for bringing this wonderful creature to her.

It was a time of wonder, of beauty, of endless hope and dreams.

Now those dreams are gone, she thought.

Her parents were dead. Her sister was dead. Her brothers were dead. All of Erznia had been slaughtered, including Bracken Renson, the first man she had ever kissed, when she was thirteen. And for what?

For nothing. Because our bastard god demanded it.

Quester Billings, the so-called Crimson Sword of Riverrun, had told her of Erznia's slaughter during their two-day jaunt from the Isles of Gold to Conch. For the rest of the journey, Rachida mourned while the galley rocked and creaked. She saw her mother's face each time she closed her eyes; felt Vulfram's strong arms around her when she wrapped herself in a blanket; heard Oris's hearty laugh in the laughter of the soldiers drinking in the common room belowdecks. At times she felt close to tears and had to bite down on her lip or pinch the skin of her arm to hold them back. *I will not,* she told herself, vehemently shaking her head. Rachida Gemcroft did not cry, not since that first night Moira had been taken away so long ago.

Moira . . . that was the worst wound of all. Quester informed her that Moira had known of the death of her family since the first night of her servitude to Matthew Brennan. That she didn't tell Rachida before her departure was a stinging betrayal. She knew she shouldn't feel that way, but anger was a hard emotion to quell. Moira was still alive, if the blond sellsword was to be believed, and it was easier to cast blame on the living than weep for the dead.

You know who to blame . . . and it is not Moira.

She rolled over in her uncomfortable bed, staring at the dreary simplicity of her surroundings. This hovel had been her home for the last few weeks, and she loathed it. She wanted to move, was itching for action. She and the six hundred sellswords—her personal army—had been here for far too long already, slumbering among Ashhur's naïve children while they collected provisions for the march ahead. Surprisingly, the citizens of Conch had welcomed them with open arms, offering anything Rachida and her men wanted. They were a tender, trusting people, regaling the newcomers with stories. These people laughed and sang, and gave them whiskey and wine and food for their bellies. Their constant prayers to Ashhur were bothersome to Rachida, and though she appreciated their hospitality, she found them far too credulous. She wanted to leave. But the late fall crops they promised to share had yet to be harvested, so for the last twenty-six days the sellswords had spent hours tending the fields, yanking corn, beets, rutabagas, carrots, and beans from the fertile soil. It was work unbefitting for men of their particular skills, and not a one of them was happy about it, but they all knew it was better to be unhappy now than starving to death on the road later.

A bird cawed, and Rachida sat up. Her blankets slipped off her, and she shivered in her smallclothes. The room was cold and dark, a breeze flowing in through the window she had forgotten to shutter before she'd collapsed drunk in her bed. She wrapped the blanket back around herself, stood up, and made her way to the window. Before she closed the shutters, she caught a glimpse of crimson fingers stretching across the darkened sky. Morning already. At least she had drunk enough corn whiskey to pass out for a few hours. Sleep had not come easily as of late.

An odd sensation came over her, like tiny pinpricks working up her spine, and she whirled around. In the far corner of the room, she spotted the outline of a figure sitting cross-legged on the ground. She squinted, trying to see it clearer, and then moved to open the shutters once more.

"No need for that," said Quester's somber voice. "It is only me."

Rachida breathed out deeply, glancing to the edge of her bed, where the Twins rested against the wall. "Why are you here?" she asked. "Do you *wish* to lose your head?"

The brash young man laughed. It was a sad sound. "That would depend on which head you speak of. One of mine would gladly lose itself in you for a few hours." He sighed, then slapped his knees as he stood up. "But alas, such a desire will never be granted, so I must settle for the next best thing."

"Which is?"

"Watching you sleep, milady. You make the most pleasant of sounds."

Rachida groaned inwardly. Quester had been oppressive in his advances during the entirety of their excursion. His eyes, and the eyes of nearly every other sellsword, were constantly affixed to her rump and bosom, despite her loose-fitting clothing. Even many of the western men, in their childlike exuberance, took to staring at her as she worked the fields with them. Not that this was unusual; Rachida had grown up dealing with the constant attention of men. It was something she could handle, even understand. Having one of them sneak into her room to watch her sleep, she could not.

"Get out," she said. "Now."

Instead of moving away, Quester took a step forward. Rachida inched toward the bed, tensing her muscles in case she needed to leap for the Twins.

"It's all so strange, milady," said Quester, his tone reflective and even a bit sad. "So much to do, yet they are willing to give up so much." He looked up at her with pleading eyes, and Rachida could see red veins, hear the hint of a slur from too much drink. "I am drawn to beauty. I revel in it. I thought the red dyes I wore in my hair were beautiful, but they made me wash it out. It is . . . not . . . fair."

Quester moved away from her, approaching the window. When he entered the faint light coming in from beneath the shutters, she caught sight of a glint of steel on his hip. Rachida leapt over her bed and snatched one of the Twins. The scabbard thudded on the hovel's soft dirt floor as she whipped the blade around, anticipating his advance.

He didn't look at her, didn't seem to be paying any attention to her at all. He fell against the window, then yanked open the shutters and lifted his right hand. For a long time he simply stood there, staring at his fingers while gently swaying from side to side. She could see he was wearing his leather armor over his smallclothes.

"Quester," Rachida said, moving toward the center of the room with her sword held out before her. "What is the matter with you? What are you looking at?"

"This hand has taken so many beautiful things from the world." He turned to her, frowning. "I detest it."

He laughed. It sounded out of place given his dejected expression.

"This world is full of treachery, you know," the man said. Despite his obvious drunkenness, his voice was surprisingly steady, though deflated. "Do you remember that wreck of a ship we passed our first day on the water?"

She nodded, remembering it well. It had been a long, sleek ship, built for speed and painted black as night, half sunken just beneath a rocky precipice. Rachida had never seen its like before, and there were no discernable letters or sigils marking its cracked hull. She had suggested they investigate it, but Quester had told them not to bother. *"Our destination is all that matters,"* he'd said, *"not some sunken oddity."*

"I lied to you," the man continued. "I knew the ship. It was my masters who built it. It was crafted to appear lustrous and ominous, even though only the cheapest of materials went into its construction."

"Why?" she asked, to keep him talking. So long as he was talking, he might not do something stupid.

"Because it was a ruse," said Quester.

"Ruse? For who? You're making no sense."

"The ship was meant to be handsome, to inspire wonder and fear," he said with a sigh. "And yet its sole purpose was to carry three large crates filled with weapons from Port Lancaster to the coast of Paradise."

"To what end?"

"I don't know. Does it matter? I was never told the ship's intention, but then again intention is such a strange beast. Does anyone truly know what anyone else *intends*? Beauty . . . beauty is tangible, it is *visceral*, yet it can hide so much. That ship was beautiful, but that beauty was a lie."

Rachida let the tip of her sword drop to the ground. "What does any of this mean? What does it have to do with you sneaking into my quarters and watching me sleep, while armed no less?"

"Everything."

Quester stood from the bed, causing her to flinch. He undid his belt and let his sword drop to the ground.

"I am like that ship." He stared at his right hand again. "Outside, I am beautiful, I know that. Yet inside, I am vile. I have killed. I have captured men and women and led them to torture and bondage. I've taken joy in watching a man break down while his wife was flayed. I killed a *child* . . . "

Despite his frightening words, Rachida took a few steps toward him, and when he didn't move, she placed her own sword down on the bed and lifted his chin with her fingers. He gazed at her, his eyes clear and blue, his skin perfect but for a single scar tracing the left side of his jaw. Despite his attractiveness, she could see exactly what he spoke of, the violence that hid just behind his eyes.

"Enough memories and riddles," she said. "Tell me what all this means."

He took a deep breath. "You are so unlike me. Both inside and out, you radiate splendor. This world would be a worse place without you in it, and more than anything I detest removing beauty from this wretched world."

Rachida froze, her hand still gripping his chin. "What?"

"Before we left the Isles, Master Gemcroft promised me fifty pounds of gold if I ended your life."

She let go of him, backed toward the bed, slumped down on it.

"Why?" she asked. Her fingers touched the cold steel of her sword, and for a moment she considered driving it into Quester's gut.

"I don't know, milady," he said.

"Was this the plan all along?"

Quester shook his head. "No, not at all. My masters simply said I was to take Peytr's gold, and so long as the end goal was to make our god's life miserable, I was to do as he said."

"I was never a part of the plan? I was never supposed to *lead you to glory*?"

"No. I fear Peytr made that up to conceal his true intentions."

Rachida ground her teeth together. Her heart raced, her blood boiled. Every part of her wanted to disbelieve this man, but what he said made too much sense. Her marriage to Peytr was a convenience, a disguise to hide their true lives. Her darling husband had often said that it was her station as Soleh Mori's daughter that made their marriage worthwhile, but now that Soleh was gone, the gods were at war, and any advantage Rachida's name held had shriveled up and died. Peytr had his heir. He had no need for her any longer.

She grunted, spat on the ground, and turned to the sellsword. A ray of hope bloomed. Quester might have been lower than a common brigand, doing whatever it took to line his own pockets, but Peytr had misjudged the man. A rare mistake for her darling husband; a mistake she could use to her advantage. Nudging her sword aside, she patted the bed. Quester appeared hesitant, but eventually took a seat at her side. He smelled of stale liquor with a hint of lilac. For some reason that made her think of Moira, and her heart thudded harder in her chest.

"Swear to me, Quester. Swear to me that what you've told me is true."

"I swear, milady. On what little honor I have."

"Good." She leaned over and placed a single kiss on his cheek, then stood, lifting her sword in the process. "That is your reward . . . for now."

"For now?"

She poked her blade into his chest. "Yes, for now. Do not go getting any ideas, however. What I promise you is double what Peytr offered to kill me. My word is my bond, as any will tell you. Is that an appropriate price for your soul?"

Quester smiled sadly. "I will do anything you ask, milady."

"Anything?"

"Yes, anything."

"Good. This is the way it will be from here on out. Everything Peytr declared when we departed the Isles will remain the same. We will march, we will fight, and I will lead you. The people of this hamlet say there is a battle raging in the north? Then that is where we go. Do we have the supplies we need?"

"We have enough for a couple weeks, but it would be prudent—"

"I care not for prudence," she said, more harshly than she'd intended. "What I *do* care about is that we make this war as miserable for Karak as possible. What I care about is surviving until he and his brother destroy each other, so you can fulfill your duty to me."

"My duty to you?" he asked with a slight, expectant grin.

She smiled, and it felt good to do so. "Come the end of this war, you are going to help me find Moira, and after that, my son."

Quester nodded in silence.

"And Quester?"

"Yes?"

Her hand drifted to her sword; the thought of revenge was a sweet cure to her frustration and helplessness.

"Once we return to my beloved husband, you will not take his life," she said. "That right is mine, and mine alone."

CHAPTER

12

Ceredon lay on the cold sand inside his tent, reflecting on how quickly his situation had changed. One moment he had been an object of ridicule, harassed and tortured nearly every minute of every day; the next, he was left alone, three hundred new objects of ridicule taking his place.

The people of Ang had been forced from their home and marched through the desert for countless days. Most of the humans' skin had been dark brown to black, yet as the whips urged them onward, the shackled masses became tinged with splotches of deep red. Ceredon had thought Darakken's murderous actions in the villages they'd crossed on the way there brutal, but what he now witnessed went far beyond that. It was *evil* what was happening to these people. Men, women, and children alike were cruelly ushered onward, denied so much as a cup of water while shuffling beneath the heat of the desert sun. Only when they neared death from dehydration were they given sustenance; when they were felled by the myriad of lashes covering their bodies, they were brought before the enormous Bardiya, who would place his hands on their bodies and heal their ills. Afterward the victims were shackled once more, and the process began anew.

Having been sheltered in Quellasar for most of his life, Ceredon had seen a god only once—the day Karak and his First Children came to their forest dwelling to introduce themselves to the elves. Ceredon was four years old at the time, and to him the twelve-foot colossus that was Karak had seemed unreal, the stuff of legends and nighttime terrors. He felt the same way now, staring at this dark giant whose eyes constantly ran wet with tears and whose voice was hoarse as he sang songs of peace to the heavens. Bardiya was a living contradiction; he could have easily crushed any of the elves or human soldiers that harassed him, could have inspired his people to revolt against the beatings they suffered on a daily basis, but did not. He did nothing but cry for peace. Ceredon didn't know if he should feel awe, pity, or anger.

What he did know was that his own inner shame was growing. He found himself walking, yanked forward by his wrist irons toward the rear of the column, all but forgotten. Larstis, the Dezren elf whose horse he was tethered to, proved to be a kind jailer. Larstis would offer him water and food, and even allow him to ride in the saddle when the elf wished to stretch his legs. Ceredon was thankful for each moment of relief, though each brought rise to his shame. Here he was, thankful to the man who kept him prisoner, for showing him tiny measures of kindness. True kindness would have been releasing him. True mercy would have been standing up to the torture the humans endured.

The path Darakken forged through the desert was circuitous, and often they looped past certain trees or cliffs Ceredon recognized from days before. He concluded that the demon was dragging them endlessly just to punish the humans with the beating sun and fiery sand of the desert beneath their bare feet.

Ceredon rolled over, his chains jangling, and moaned. Outside, Bardiya was telling his people a story, something about a rat and a swamp lizard and the seductiveness of false faith. He could barely make out the words, but he swore he'd heard a story very much like that one at some point in his youth. He finally stopped trying to listen, gulped down the last swig of weak wine Larstis had given him, and tried to fall asleep to the giant's soothing tone.

A few minutes later, he heard the shuffling of feet over sand, followed by the flap of his tent being shoved aside. A tinderstick was struck, and brightness filled the tent. Ceredon opened one eye. Boris Morneau was standing there, holding a lantern in one hand and a sack in the other. The human looked down at him and smiled.

"You look better."

Ceredon nodded. The young soldier had made himself scarce since the night he'd come to Ceredon speaking words of warning about the terrors Darakken would impart on his people. He was constantly riding ahead of the procession, acting as the demon's forward scout. Now, when they came upon the occasional small village, it was empty. He couldn't help but think that was the human's doing.

"You're silent," Boris said, tilting his head. "Do you wish me to leave?"

"No," said Ceredon in the common tongue. He pulled himself up as much as he could in his fetters and drew his knees to his chest. "Please, sit with me. I am sorry I have nothing to drink, or I would offer it to you."

"I brought my own," the human said with a smile. "Besides, given our conditions, you are more my guest than the other way around."

Boris meandered across the open space, set down the lantern and sack, and then sat cross-legged across from him. He pulled a skin from his jerkin, and popping the cap, tipped it back and took a sip. When he offered up the skin, Ceredon took it without hesitation. The liquid inside tasted of cinnamon and was harsh, burning his throat as it went down. But there was also a certain sweetness to it that caused warmth to spread in his belly.

"What is this?" he asked.

"A drink my father liked to brew. Fermented potato rinds mixed with rosemary, birch sap, and cinnamon."

"It is quite good. Sweet, yet potent."

"Thank you." Boris squinted at him, shaking his head. "Prince Ceredon, I must apologize for the last time I called on you. It was presumptuous of me to think that you could trust me without my proving trustworthy. I was out of line."

"I almost broke your neck," Ceredon said, thinking it terribly funny. "It was the bowl of water you brought that saved you."

"I count myself lucky, then." Boris chuckled. "I'll make sure I carry a drink with me at all times."

Now they both laughed, and despite their exhaustion, their stress, it felt good to do so. Even then, he kept the sound quiet, for he could only guess at what ears listened in, and what Darakken might think of their nighttime meeting.

"Your question," Ceredon said, wiping tears from his eyes. "I have had an excess of time to dwell on it, and I fear I still have no worthwhile answer."

"My question?" asked Boris with a smirk.

"You asked me why Darakken has kept me alive."

"Ah, yes. That. No answer, truly? Consider me disappointed."

"Yet you appear to know," Ceredon said, shaking his head. "Which convinces me you haven't told me everything yet. What is it you know that I don't?"

Boris hesitated.

"Come now," Ceredon insisted. "If we are to play this game, we should play it fair."

The human tsk'ed and wagged a finger.

"Not just yet," he said. "You see, I brought a gift for you, one that should keep you from snapping my neck anytime soon."

"And what might that be?"

Boris squeezed his lips together, uncoiled his legs, and rose to his knees. Untying the string binding the sack at his side, he opened it and tipped it over. From within rolled a bundle with tangled white hair that sank into the sand. Ceredon's heart rose into his throat. The human leaned over the thing, positioned it in the sand, and smoothed aside the hair. Iolas's face stared up at Ceredon, his bulging eyes milky and his mouth opened wide in an eternal scream. Ceredon could do nothing but gawk.

"Know that he suffered greatly," said Boris. "Cactus needles beneath the toenails, open wounds covered with salt, that sort of thing. His cries would have awoken the dead had I not gagged him."

Ceredon sighed. "Put it back in the bag."

The human appeared surprised, hurt even, but he did as he was asked. Soon the head of the last of the Triad was safely tucked away.

"I apologize if I offended you," Boris said, "but I thought you would be happy."

"It is hard to explain," Ceredon said, looking the man in the eye. "It is good to know he is dead, but it wasn't by my hand. He didn't stare into my eyes, knowing his betrayal cost him dearly." He jabbed a finger at the sack, which was dark and sodden. "Iolas and the Triad brought so much suffering to the Dezren, and they deserved a horrible death. But forgive me—I cannot gaze upon another severed head and smile. Not when the heads of Orden and Phyrra Thyne stared back at me while Darakken kept me imprisoned in Dezerea."

"Again, Prince Ceredon, you have my apologies." Boris heaved the sack toward the tent flap, where it landed with a squishy *thud*.

"Call me 'prince' no longer. Ceredon will do."

"Very well."

"It is settled then." Ceredon sat up, pulling his fetters tight, and stretched his legs out before him. He jutted his chin toward the wayward sack. "Now you've given me your gift, so answer my question. Why am I still alive? What purpose does the demon have for me?"

Boris slowly nodded. "You must understand, the two are still linked. The knowledge I have, the reason for your continued existence, was spilled to me by Iolas while he . . . suffered. But first I must ask you . . . what do you know of Neyvar Kilidious?"

"Neyvar Kilidious?" Ceredon asked. "Why?"

"Humor me."

Ceredon rolled his eyes. "Kilidious Sinistel was the youngest Neyvar in the history of the Quellan. He was a mere nine years old when he was crowned toward the end of the Demon War, after the deaths of his father, Kardious, and brother Rentious. *Hen eterunas vi,* they call him in my tongue: 'the boy who saved us.' It is said that after the last of our defenses were shattered after the last of our winged horses were slaughtered, it was his prayers that brought Celestia down from the heavens to cast the demons into the void."

"You are a direct relation to him, no?"

"Separated by many generations, but yes."

"I see. And how many other families of the Sinistel line were alive during the time of the great war?"

Ceredon laughed at the absurdity of the question. "None, of course."

"And why is that?"

"Because it is law among my people that no child of the Neyvar shall bear children until they themselves become Neyvar. A child born of the sovereign is a child born with inherent knowledge of how to lead the people to greatness. Any child born before their father is crowned is henceforth forbidden to receive the crown."

"And the Neyvars all obeyed this edict? None had children before their crowning?"

"Obviously," Ceredon snapped. "What ruler would suffer his children to be forbidden their birthright?"

Boris held his hands up. "No need for snippiness."

Ceredon shook his head. "Then start making sense, human. What does my family history have to do with Darakken keeping me alive?"

To this, Boris grinned. "It's blood, Ceredon. It's history. And to something that is for all intents and purposes timeless, such as Darakken is, history is all that matters."

That got Ceredon's attention. "Explain."

Boris began playing with the sand by his feet, picking up handfuls and letting it trickle between his fingers. "Iolas's version of the end of the Demon War is very much the same as yours, with one significant difference. According to him, it was not Kilidious's *prayers* that called Celestia down from the heavens, but the blood that flowed in his veins. Your history says that two thousand years ago, when the elves were first created, Celestia molded a single family from each race that she loved more than all else, two families to rule the separate races for all time: the Sinistels for the Quellan, and the Thynes for the Dezren. Is that not true?"

"It is."

"All of which brings us back to Neyvar Kilidious."

"In what way?"

Boris's grin became wider. "The Dezren have always been a more . . . liberated people, unlike your Quellan, who hold tight to their rigid tenets. There is Thyne blood sprinkled all throughout Dezerea and the Stonewood Forest, and has been for centuries, while, by your own admission, *your* family is singular. When the Demon War climaxed a thousand years ago, and Neyvar Kardious and Rentious were killed, Darakken and Velixar burst into the Great Hall of Kal'droth—"

"To find young Kilidious on his knees. The goddess then came forth, swallowing the demons in a vortex and banishing them from the realm."

"Precisely. Only the goddess did this not as an answer to Kilidious's prayers, but because he was the last of his family line."

Ceredon stared at him doubtfully.

"Think on it," said Boris. "Celestia created the Sinistel family to rule the Quellan for *all time*. That was her decree, as written in your ancient scrolls. Celestia might have allowed you to fight your battles, allowed thousands of your kind to die, but if she had let Kilidious perish, her own word would have been proven false. *For all time* would not be."

"This feels wrong," said Ceredon, his breathing heavy. "Iolas insults our goddess with such a belief."

"Perhaps, but whether it is right or wrong is irrelevant, at least for the time being. *Darakken* believes this. That is why he has kept you alive. He does not do you mortal damage for fear Celestia will come down from the heavens and banish him again. And it is this fear that we will use against the demon when the time is right."

Ceredon gaped at the human. "Who are you? What is your purpose here?"

"I am but a humble servant," Boris said with a bow. "I am Boris Morneau Marchant, son of Francois Marchant and Gillea Connington, sworn to protect the house that bears my mother's maiden name." He stopped talking and glanced over his shoulder, looking suddenly cautious before leaning in close and saying, in a hushed voice, "I am a mutineer, Ceredon, a wolf among wolves. I am one of many infiltrating the army of the Eastern Divinity and spreading falsehoods, sparking desertion, and casting a seed of doubt into all who stand with Karak."

The Quellan prince found himself taken aback, frightened even by the man's proclamation. "But why? To what purpose?"

"To reach an end where no more gods walk upon Dezrel, an end where humankind is truly free. Karak and Ashhur are at war, and it is our duty to make sure that neither of them wins." The man smiled, the teardrop scar on his cheek flaring red in the light from the lantern. "We wish you no harm, Ceredon, not you or your people."

Ceredon shook his head. "Yet you handed the demon means to remake its true form."

"True, but don't think that you will stand alone should the worst come. Please trust me on this. Though we are surely different, we are very similar, humans and elves. We both love, we both hate, and eventually we both die. They are similarities we should ignore no longer. When the time is right, when it is safe, I will free you from your bonds. And when this war is done, should the gods destroy each other and leave us be, you will always have an ally in House Connington." The man cocked his head and peered once more at the tent flap. "Now, if you will excuse me, I must be going. The prisoners have gone silent, which means dawn is just around the corner. Get some sleep, Ceredon. You will need it."

Boris grabbed his lantern, stood up, and hurried to the exit. He snatched the sack containing Iolas's head on his way by.

"Wait," Ceredon called out to him before he exited.

The human paused. "What is it?"

"What should I do until that time comes?"

"Wait and watch," Boris said. "And learn."

With that, the soldier disappeared through the flap. Ceredon sat there for a long while, stunned and frightened by the conversation. Outside, he swore he heard the giant weeping. The night drew to a close, and sunlight brought a glow to the sides of his tent. With the dawn, he ceased thinking of potential, future horrors and focused on the present. His fear and doubt waned. He thought on Boris's words, on what they *meant*, and finally his lips curled into a smile. If the human was right—if Darakken believed as Iolas said—it changed *everything*. Ceredon was no longer a powerless, vulnerable whelp.

By the time the soldiers outside the tent began beating the prisoners from Ang to wake them and begin the march anew, Ceredon finally felt like the mountain he had promised his goddess he would become. *You still have your life,* Celestia had told him. *That is all that matters.* There was more truth in that statement than he had realized. And when Larstis came to retrieve him and break down the tent, he stood in the middle of the hot desert sand and stared at the bright blue sky.

"Unyielding, unmoving, forever," he said, and meant every word.

CHAPTER 13

Someone was watching. Bardiya could see figures in the distance as he sang; black dots that spread out along the desert's hazy white horizon behind the procession. He could not tell for sure who they were—if they were human, elf, or animal—but he was convinced it wasn't his eyes playing tricks. When the convoy shifted directions, so did the pursuers. When the column turned about to march back, they hastily disappeared like soldier ants retreating into a threatened anthill.

Even more interesting was that no one else seemed to notice. Even the elves, with their far superior vision, made no mention of their presence. Perhaps they knew of the pursuers and simply didn't care. Or perhaps, in their overconfidence, they never entertained the thought that they could be hunted.

His foot caught in a shallow hole in the sand, and he stumbled, the song dying on his lips. The ox harness fastened around his neck caused his back to buckle. All thoughts of Ashhur's grace or secret scouts left his mind, replaced by pain. He fell to his knees, the rear of the heavy wooden harness smacking the back of his skull. Stars burst in his vision.

"Stand up," someone commanded, followed by a *snap* and a pinprick of pain in his shoulder. Then came another crack and another small ache. The soldiers were whipping him again. Bardiya lifted his head, peering at them through squinting eyes, and saw a few of them smiling. He wondered if they would get such joy from torturing him if they knew how little it hurt. Truth be told, the ache in his soul was far worse than anything physical they could do to him.

Calloused hands were on him then, and voices shouted for the whipping to stop. Bardiya turned to see Gordo and Tulani Hempsmen grabbing his shoulders, urging him to stand.

"Please, Bardiya," Tulani said, fear in her eyes. "You must get up."

"That's right," said her husband. "If you stay down, more of us will be hurt."

They backed away from him. Bardiya nodded, dug his fingers into the sand and rose on popping knees. Keisha, Gordo and Tulani's daughter, appeared between her parents. Her rosebud lips were cracked and peeling, as was her brown skin from too long a time spent beneath the brutal desert sun. Little mute Marna came next, followed by Tuan Littlefoot and the brothers Allay and Yorn Loros, followed soon after by old Onna. Voices both human and elven shouted for the column to keep moving, but the people of Ang ignored them. Before long most of the three hundred stood before him, the chains binding their wrists hanging, their eyes solemn, their posture slumped. It was a brutal sight, one no song could hide: Their hope was gone.

"Why are we not moving?" asked that familiar, grating, inhuman voice. A massive charger approached, Clovis Crestwell sitting atop it. As had become the norm, Clovis appeared sickly, his body losing the heft it'd had when the force first rode into Ang. His neck was now slender as a reed, his eyes sunken into his skull, his lips pulled back to reveal chipped teeth and white gums. The man was wasting away before their eyes.

Clovis approached him, having to look up at Bardiya, though he was on horseback.

"Set your people to march, Gorgoros," he said, his red eyes leaking pink tears. The appalling man peered toward Bardiya's throng, who were now huddling close together, surrounded by soldiers with pikes. Clovis's gaze fell on Keisha. "Or would you prefer it if we tortured another of the children? Perhaps that one, the one with the large eyes and sweet voice?"

"No," Bardiya murmured. He bowed his head. "We will march."

"Good. Make sure they all keep pace."

He tried to do just that, but it was difficult to keep three hundred people from stumbling. At one point Onna's walking stick caught in his chains and snapped, and he collapsed. A group of the olive-skinned elves with clubs beat the man senseless, then beat a young woman named Nina who urged them to stop. Before they started moving again, five people had been sent to Bardiya to mend their broken bones, their bruises, their internal and external bleeding. But no matter how well he healed their bodily wounds, he could do nothing to repair their fractured souls.

Still they were kept walking, made to suffer lashes and still more beatings. By the time the sun began to set, Bardiya was exhausted. The amount of energy it took to heal the injured drained him, making it difficult to lift a foot off the ground. Yet he persisted. Yet he went on. *My faith in Ashhur's teachings will not waver. I will be an example to them all.*

That night, as the rest of his people slept beneath the cold desert moon, Bardiya wept.

The next day brought more of the same: lashings and insults, flying fists, rapes, and beaten men, women, and children. Bardiya swallowed it all, unwilling to lift a finger in violence. *The song will take me home,* he thought as air filled his lungs. But even that seemed not to help. As he took one step after another, closing his eyes to let the song fill his soul, what he saw behind his eyelids was the scene in the mangold grove the day his parents were butchered. He saw himself lunging with a tree limb, swatting aside the Dezren murderers as if they were flies, and pinning their leader, Ethir Ayers, to a tree trunk. For the first time since burying his parents, he dared wonder if it had been wrong to let those murderous elves live.

A shrill cry rang out, and the procession came to a halt. All singing stopped. Elf and soldier alike were thrown into a panic, the soldiers running past the cluster of prisoners, with weapons drawn. Bardiya turned about, for a moment believing their stalkers had made themselves known, but when he looked to the horizon, all he saw was an endless sea of white sand. *Perhaps it was all in my head after all.*

There was a flurry of activity toward the rear of the procession. Even standing at least three heads taller than the largest wagon, he still could not make out what was going on. Forms struggled, throwing punches, twisting and pulling on armor. Clovis galloped past on his charger, approaching the fray, his strange voice booming as he screamed for the chaos to end.

When the fracas concluded, the soldiers and elves rushed back to their positions in the now-stalled convoy. Clovis wheeled his horse around and trotted toward Bardiya. Behind him walked a young soldier with unkempt auburn hair and a small scar marring his left cheek, carrying another soldier in his arms, struggling with the weight. Behind that soldier were seven more who wore Karak's sigil and were lugging a thrashing, screaming elf.

The young soldier stopped in front of Bardiya, dropping the limp body on the ground. The young man's silver breastplate was smeared with crimson. The soldier inclined his head and stepped to the side, allowing Clovis room to approach.

"Heal him," said the twisted shell of a man, a scowl on his lips.

Bardiya knelt in the sand, trying to keep his balance despite the ox harness. He leaned over the body of the prone soldier, saw this one was just as young as the one who'd carried him. His eyes were bulging and watery, his lips quivered. Hacking breaths left his mouth and his body was thrown into a spasm. Bardiya saw a stream of blood pour out of the gash in his belly, where there was a gap in his armor. He placed a massive hand on the wound, felt the warmth and stickiness.

"Heal him," Clovis repeated.

"Do not, you craven wretch," said a strange, accented voice. Bardiya lifted his eyes to see an elf forced to his knees. Bardiya had seen this elf many times over their long march—a captive like his people, chained to a horse and kept separate from the rest. He had long russet hair and copper skin, marking him as Quellan. There were golden bruises covering his face, and his arms were covered with blood to his elbows.

"If you heal that man," the elf said in the common tongue, "you are a bigger fool than you look to be. Let . . . him . . . *die*."

"I cannot," Bardiya said softly as he placed his other hand over the soldier's wound. The young man vomited up a torrent of blood. "I am a sworn protector of life. The blood of my enemy is no different from the blood in my own veins. Ashhur has taught us this, and Ashhur's teachings are absolute."

"Then Ashhur is as great a fool as you are."

Bardiya ignored him, instead closing his eyes and offering words of entreaty to his wayward god. He felt the power surge through him, his core growing hot and expanding outward, through his chest, down his arms, into his hands. His stomach constricted, feeling the depth of the young soldier's pain. Light shot from his fingertips, entering the soldier's body. Tissue mended, torn intestines knit themselves back together, and the waste products that had leaked throughout the man's abdomen dissolved into nothingness. The flesh of the wound itself then shut, creating a thin white scar. The power retreated back into Bardiya as the prone soldier gasped, clutching his stomach tightly, filled with a burst of energy.

Bardiya collapsed onto his rump, the ox harness heavy as a boulder now that his god's strength was gone. He watched the young soldier sit up, examining the scar across his belly. His eyes were filled with tears as he looked up at Bardiya. There was still fear in his gaze, but gratitude as well. For a moment it looked as if he might lurch forward and wrap his arms around the giant, but he seemed to notice his fellow soldiers standing around him and thought better of it. Instead, he offered Bardiya a nod and stood up.

"Good," Clovis said from above.

The restrained elf spat in the sand.

"Bloody ignorant savage. You deserve all you receive."

Other elves then came forward, both Quellan and Dezren, dragging the elf to his feet. The captured elf began shouting in his native tongue, spitting at each of them as they roughly handled him. Clovis watched this all with seemingly detached interest, until one of the Quellan drew his khandar.

"No!" the malformed human shouted. "Beat him if you wish, but Ceredon is to live. That one does not even *approach* death."

"Iolas is missing and now this!" one of the elves shouted back. "He must suffer!"

"Suffer he will," Clovis said gravely, "but he is not to be killed, lest all the reward Karak promised you fall by the wayside."

The khandar was reluctantly resheathed. Bardiya looked on as the restrained elf smiled. It was a sickening thing to see, frightening even. That smile remained even when the back of a mailed hand connected with the side of Ceredon's face, even when a whip struck his back, tearing his tattered tunic further.

Such hatred, thought Bardiya. Though he tried to be disgusted by the display, he felt awed by it instead. His guilt grew ever larger.

The twisted man on horseback sounded slightly disappointed when he said, "You are an odd creature, Bardiya Gorgoros."

"I am the child of my creator."

Clovis grinned sickeningly. "We will see how true that is soon enough," he said; then he pulled on the reins, urging his charger to carry him to the front of the procession.

Bardiya's people looked at him as if he were a ghastly creature they had never seen before. He tried to smile at them, to let them know Ashhur still loved them, but it was for naught. Each of them, even Gordo and his family, looked disappointed. When the order came, they turned away from their spiritual leader and began to march once more. For the rest of the day, none would sing with him, not when he raised his voice as loud as he could, not when he implored them with tales of love, not even when he healed Zulea Doros after she collapsed from sunstroke. They simply marched with their eyes straight ahead, a people defeated.

Heart broken, Bardiya was but a shell of his former self when they crested a final dune to find the Black Spire rising up before them in the valley where the dead of Ker were buried. The obelisk's shadow seemed to swallow all light, all life, all hope, into its shimmering black maw.

CHAPTER 14

The guard's name was Dukat, and Aully knew he was a gentle soul.

"I'm sorry for all your troubles," he said as he led her down the stairs. "Truly, I hope you don't hate me for this."

Aully exhaled deeply. "Then why are you doing it?"

The elf shrugged. "Because I wish for us to be more. As a people, I mean."

"How?"

"I . . . I don't know."

The stairwell veered to the left, and for a moment Aully thought about spinning around, darting up the stairs past her captor, and hurling herself out of Briar Hall's tallest window. *No. That is the coward's way out.*

"You must have *some* idea."

"I suppose. It's just . . . Carskel has said so much of our former glory, of how our people and the Quellan once ruled all these lands. We were free to do as we chose, to go *where* we chose. But now we're either stuck here in this forest or the one farther north. We're surrounded by humans on all sides." He spat then, a thick wad of phlegm striking the floor just as Aully took another step. "Surrounded by vile rats that were handed lands that used to be ours, rats that treat us as outsiders. *We were here first.* That should mean something."

She was taken aback by the anger in his voice. Dukat, once her Uncle Detrick's personal guard, was engaged to Aully's cousin, Mariah. She had never heard him sound so angry.

"So you turn your back on Celestia?"

Dukat laughed. "Celestia abandoned us long ago, Aully. She doesn't care."

That's not true, but she didn't put the thought to words. Playing to his anger, to his perceived role as victim, would only bring his blood to boil. She needed to strike closer to home if she had any chance of escaping.

"But what of me, Dukat? What if Carskel decides to hurt me?"

"He wouldn't do that, Aully. He loves you. You're family."

"Uncle Detrick is family too. That didn't stop Carskel from cutting off his finger."

"That's different."

Aully turned slightly as she descended, saw doubt begin to spread across Dukat's face.

"How is that different? Detrick is his uncle too. If he can hurt him, then he could hurt Mariah. Would you want that?"

Dukat paused on the stairwell, shook his head vehemently. "No. That wouldn't happen."

"Why not?"

"Because Mariah would never talk down to Carskel like Detrick did. Because she's respectful."

"How can you talk of respect and my brother in the same sentence? You know what he did to Brienna. You have to. How can that be forgiven? How can you *trust him*?"

He forcefully grabbed her shoulders, and his face grew firm. "Both Carskel and Ethir told me of your treachery." He spun her around and gave her a shove. "I won't allow you to poison me with lies."

Anger made her heart beast faster. Not that she'd expected anything different from him. He was the same old Dukat she'd known since the cradle: gentle in the heart, dull in the head.

They passed by the entrance to the courtroom where the Lord's Chair resided and continued down. Dukat didn't speak any longer, and Aully let him be. He was dead to her now, a traitor like all the rest, no matter if he was supposed to marry her cousin or how kind he normally was. Betrayal was betrayal, and to Aully that meant a head for a head.

Near the bottom of the winding stairwell was a final door. Dukat roughly stopped her and rapped on the wood. A moment later the door cracked open, and Carskel's grinning face emerged.

"She is here, as you requested, Lord Carskel," said Dukat. Aully gnashed her teeth.

"Ah, so good of you, Dukat," replied Carskel in that much-too-proper voice of his. "Leave her outside, and go back to your duties."

"Yes, my Lord."

Dukat bowed and marched back up the stairs. The door Carskel had been peeping out of closed, and for a moment Aully thought of making a dash for the exit, which was only fifteen feet below her. But then she saw a shadowy figure pass in front of the portal, a spear jabbing into the walkway, and she slumped against the wall.

Chains were unlatched, and the door opened fully.

"Come in, sweet sister," Carskel said, standing aside for her to enter. She brushed past him in a rage.

The room she entered was one she had rarely seen, even though she had lived in Briar Hall for all her life. It was her father's study, and his father's study before him, where the family history and all the great tomes that had been passed down and added to for two thousand years were kept. Unlike the rest of the Hall, it was a dark and dreary place, windowless to protect the books' ancient inks from fading. Aully had never liked being in there then, and she liked it less so now.

She breezed through the stacks of books and into the center of the room, where a great marble desk sat. The few times she'd been there before, this desk had been stacked with teetering tomes, but now it was empty but for a small pile of washcloths and a wooden bowl filled with water. A pair of candles offered sparse, gloomy light. She leaned over the desk, examining the swirls in the marble. Her fingers traced over the corner surface, where two elvish letters had been carved.

Breath was on her neck. "Yes, sweet sister. Father kept his desk a mess, but finally you can see its craftsmanship for how shoddy it truly is. Such a waste of good stone. But what can you expect from the one who built it?"

Aully didn't answer.

Her brother's arm snaked down, and he placed his hand atop hers, tracing the letters with her.

"Those stand for Gradovic Thyne, the first Lord of Stonewood."

Aully jerked her hand out from under his and moved away. She kept her chin up and her eyes on the upper shelves, refusing to acknowledge her brother's presence.

"You were a bad girl, sweet sister, and I hope you've spent the past twelve days considering what you've done." Carskel said, sighing. "Ignore me all you wish; that does not alter that I must punish you."

"Do as you wish," she said finally. She was amazed at how loud her voice sounded in the cramped space. "There's nothing you can do to hurt me."

"Is that so? I would not be so sure of that."

Aully turned to confront him, saw him leaning against one of the shelves, with that wicked smile he was so fond of pasted on his face. Aully hated that expression, but she was thankful for it too, for whenever he gazed at her like that, he looked less and less like her father.

Another rap came on the door, and Carskel clapped his hands together.

"Our company has arrived," he said, eagerly kicking himself off the wall and nearly skipping to the door. Aully took a step back in horror as Ethir Ayers shoved Kindren into the study.

"Thank you for the gift, Ethir. Now please, if you could just stand there and not listen, we three have things to discuss."

"Yes, my Lord."

Ethir took his position against the wall, with his hands behind his back, but Aully didn't linger on his continued presence. Her every thought was on her betrothed as he slowly lifted himself off the ground. His right arm was no longer in a sling, but it hung lower than his left. His face was bruised, his mouth drawn tight with pain, and as he stood, it looked like it was great agony for him to even move. Yet still his lips curled into a smile and his eyes twinkled.

"Hi, Aully," he said.

She rushed him, wrapping her arms around his waist. He grunted in pain but did not shove her away, instead twining his fingers in her hair.

"I've missed you," Aully said into his dirty tunic, the same one he'd been wearing when they were captured. It stunk horribly. She didn't care. She felt close to crying, knowing what Kindren being here meant, and needed to hide her face until it passed. She would not show Carskel any weakness.

"Is that not precious?" said her brother.

Kindren tried to move Aully behind him protectively, but she was having none of it. She gathered herself and twirled around. Her fingers flexed, words of magic forming on her tongue. With Kindren here she felt powerful, and she knew she had nothing to fear. If she could kill Carskel and Ethir quickly, they could sneak down to where her people were being held, gather the rest of her family, and flee back to Ang before anyone was the wiser.

But no electricity sparked at her fingertips, no warmth filled her belly. She couldn't feel the weave anywhere around her.

Carskel shook his head, pointing to the floor and ceiling. Aully followed his finger, saw the markings scattered all over, a series of symbols she had never noticed before.

"Your own home," he said, "and you don't even know the rules. This is the study, child, a library filled with ancient books and ancient knowledge. No magic is allowed in here. The runes demand it. It'd be a terrible tragedy if, for example, a headstrong elven girl summoned a bit of careless fire."

Aully's spirits sank. Even Kindren reaching down and grasping her hand didn't seem to help.

Carskel moved toward the desk and sat down, propping his feet up on it. He motioned to the empty space before him. "Come. Now is when we work out our problems." When neither Aully nor Kindren moved, his frown deepened. "You will come here *now*," he said harshly, "or I will have Ethir force you."

Ethir, from his place against the wall, snickered.

Aully would have refused still, but Kindren released her hand and stepped toward the desk. After a moment's hesitation she joined him. When she looked up at the face of her betrothed, she saw his lower jaw shaking. He was frightened, as he had every right to be. In a way Aully envied him, for she wasn't scared at all; what filled the emptiness inside her was anger.

"There, that's better," Carskel said when they stood side by side before him. He pointed his gaze at Aully, shaking his head disappointedly. "Your stunt at the reception was unacceptable. You know I require your help to bring our people to my cause. It is unfair of you to deny me that. So much time I've wasted mending the discord you sowed."

"I hope you're tortured for eternity in a special underworld all your own," she shot back. Beside her, she sensed Kindren cringe.

"If any underworld exists, sweet sister, I'm sure I will." He let out a short burst of laughter. "Then again, I might enjoy it. I have always rather liked the dark." He brought his attention to Kindren.

"And what of you, Prince of Dezerea? Do you wish to see me burn as well?"

Kindren didn't reply, though it seemed as if he were struggling with some great inner turmoil. Sweat beaded on his brow, turning the dirty hair slathered to his forehead shiny.

"Ah, I see," Carskel said. "Well, I suppose saying nothing is better than saying the wrong thing."

Her brother swung his feet off the desk and shot Ethir a sideways glance. Aully never took her eyes off Carskel and noticed the way his expression changed from one moment to the next. She knew what was to come, and when she looked up at Kindren, she saw that he did too.

"It's okay," he whispered, and she nodded.

"What was that?" asked Carskel from his place behind the desk.

Aully and her betrothed stayed silent.

Carskel let out a disgusted groan.

"You both are being difficult, but I suppose that is understandable. However, we must deal with the very real problem that you have made for me, Aullienna. Our people are restless. They don't trust me. They would have been swayed had you not turned your back on me, which makes me quite upset. War is coming as the eastern god marches through his brother's Paradise, and if we are to survive this, it must be as a united front with our Quellan brothers. That will not happen if I cannot get the people to *trust me*. So I ask you again, Aullienna Meln, my sweet sister . . . will you vouch for me, will you sing my praises to our people? If you do, I will forget all about your betrayal, and we can be like family again."

Aullienna gave him her sweetest smile as he leaned closer for her answer.

"I know how you treat family," she said. "Or should I say, *Brienna* did?"

Before he could react, she spit in his face. He slowly reached for one of the washcloths on the desk and dabbed at the spit dripping down his chin. He then sat back gravely.

"That was unwarranted," he said. "And most unfortunate. Ethir, your sword, please. Kill the young prince."

Aully heard the enforcer step away from the wall, heard the *hiss* of steel drawn from a scabbard, but she didn't panic. Instead, she grasped Kindren's hand, felt him shaking, and glared at her brother.

"You won't kill him," she said. "You *need* him."

"Is that so?"

"You need the Quellan elves. Do you think Lord and Lady Thyne would ever agree to an eventual alliance if their only son is butchered?"

Carskel smiled. "You're wiser than you let on, Aullienna. Though you are right. The prince here is too valuable to kill."

"Then let me go," Kindren said. It was the first time he'd truly spoken since Ethir brought him in, and his voice was shaky. Aully wanted to scream at him to keep his mouth shut.

"It has a voice!" shouted Carskel. "But it will do you no good. While my sweet sister is right that it would be disastrous if you died, she still lacks . . . imagination. After all, the Lord and Lady will accept you back, whether you're whole or not."

Carskel shot up from his chair, his hand flashing through the open space between them, and snatched Kindren by the collar. Aully bit down on her lip so hard that she pierced the flesh as her betrothed was yanked forward. She went to reach for him, but Ethir slapped her hard across the face and sent her reeling. She thudded on the ground, rubbing her swelling cheek, and screaming filled her ears. She looked up to see Ethir holding Kindren's head against the marble desktop while Carskel clamped down on her betrothed's right arm. In his free hand, Carskel held a dagger whose blade gleamed in the low candlelight.

Shaking, Aully got to her feet.

"You leave him be!" she screamed, her fingers balling into fists. "Don't hurt him!"

Carskel looked at her, still smiling. "Do you promise to do as I asked? Will you sing my praises? Will you not betray me this time?"

The part of her that was still young, that still believed in miracles and happy endings, pleaded with her to say *yes.* But when she glanced at Kindren's face, saw the mixture of pain, fear, and defiance in his eyes, she hesitated. She then looked on as he mouthed, *"I love you,"* and the choice was all but made for her.

"No," she said.

Her brother appeared genuinely surprised.

"Very well then," he said. The dagger came down in a flash of silver, striking the desktop with a *clang.* Kindren's eyes bulged in his head and his blood-curdling shriek filled the study. Carskel then lifted the dagger and brought it down again, and Kindren's cries elevated tenfold.

When they were done, Kindren slid off the desk and fell to the floor, right hand clutched to his chest, three fingers missing. Blood spurted from the stumps, spraying his face, painting his youthful features with red streaks.

Aully began to feel faint. She fell to her knees. But she didn't scream.

Ethir grabbed the bowl of water that had been sitting on the desk and knelt before Kindren. He forced the young elf's hand into the bowl, washing it, and then proceeded to wrap the washcloths around it. Aully sat on her knees, paralyzed. Her love would never hold a sword, would never pull back a bowstring. And for what?

"For honor. For dignity. For the love of what is right," a strange voice in her head answered.

"Do you see now?" asked Carskel, and Aully turned her gaze to him. He was sitting again behind the desk, cleaning blood off his dagger. "I seem to have a thing for fingers. First your uncle, now your betrothed." He looked at her, his eyes deadly serious. "Now tell me, sweet sister, have you changed your mind?"

She sat frozen for a moment, staring at Kindren's ghostly white face and blank eyes, before shaking her head.

"I won't," she whispered.

"I have a certain lady in my possession that might think otherwise, sweet sister."

Aully looked at him, wishing she could shoot spears of fire from her eyes and kill him on the spot.

"I know to change your thinking so greatly will take time. I give you a month. A month alone in the cellar with these as keepsakes." He picked up Kindren's fingers and held them out to her. "I want you to spend that time thinking over all I could give you, both as an ally and a husband. And when you come to me with your answer, it best be the right one. For the next time you see me, it will not be the young prince who feels my blade, but our mother. And trust me when I say that there is no one waiting for her return, no one that does not think she is already a breath away from death. Should you deny me, or betray me again, it will not be her fingers I leave with you in your cell. It will be her head."

CHAPTER 15

I should have sliced Catherine's throat when I had the chance, the deceitful bitch.

These thoughts ran through Moira Elren's mind as she urged her horse onward into dusk's waning light. She ripped into a stick of salted beef, swallowing it quickly and then spitting out the salty residue before lifting a skin of hard liquor to her mouth and swigging it down. Her mouth was in horrible shape, her teeth aching and gums bleeding, the unfortunate result of the sickness she'd suffered soon after leaving Port Lancaster.

It had been horrible; her stomach had begun to cramp, her insides revolting against her. She'd spent nearly three weeks holed up in a small hamlet just outside Gronswik, choking down concoctions to heal the illness. It felt like the longest three weeks she'd ever experienced, and the only way she'd made it through was by focusing on her hatred of Catherine and her burning desire to see Rachida again. Failure was not acceptable, and with sheer stubborn will she fought through.

"Should we keep riding or camp for the night?" asked a deep male voice. Moira looked to Rodin, one of the sellswords trotting his horse beside her. His expression was stern yet hopeful while he ran a hand over his shaved pate.

She glanced at the vast fields stretching out to either side of her, half overgrown with weeds. "No. Omnmount is an hour's ride from here at most. We keep on the road. We've had far too many delays as it is."

"Very well, milady," Rodin said, and he pulled back on the reins, retreating to where his cohorts rode behind her.

Moira considered the five of them, and a small part of her started hating Catherine Brennan a tad bit less. The woman couldn't have been all bad; she had allowed her to have her pick of the sellswords under the employ of the house, after all, and the five she'd chosen had been her lifeblood since leaving the city, both literally and figuratively.

The five called themselves "Movers," and Moira knew them each by a single name: Rodin, Gull, Tabar, Willer, and Danco. They were a mostly stoic, headstrong bunch, lifelong friends from some tiny village in the Northern Plains. The Movers believed in the virtue of skill over all else, or so Gull, their quiet leader, was fond of saying. Gull was a man of nearly indistinguishable features—his hair sandy and straight, his nose slightly crooked, his round chin a bit too small for his face—which made him not the most handsome of men. However, his gray-green eyes were intense, and he was the best among them with a sword. He was also prone to lengthy, self-righteous tirades while they sat around the nightly cookfire, tirades his fellow Movers would then debate for hours before finally agreeing with their leader, if they ever really disagreed in the first place. They weren't the brightest bunch, but they held tight to Karak's tenets while damning the god himself, which Moira appreciated. Also, their worship of those of ability was vital to her cause. She had bested each of them in duels over her extended stay in Port Lancaster, and ever since they had treated her with near reverence. It was the reason she'd chosen them in the first place. She would rather surround herself with talented, faux-intellectual dullards who worshipped her than with a man like Bren Torrant, who would betray her for a sack of silver.

She heard one of them pick up the pace behind her, and she swiveled in her saddle, expecting to see Rodin there once more. Instead, it was Willer, the youngest and smallest of the bunch, who had droopy eyes and a head of unkempt chestnut hair. Willer was attached to Tabar like a growth and rarely left the taller man's side unless he had something to prove.

"Lady Moira," Willer said softly. "How long will this meeting with the merchant take?"

Moira shrugged. "Who knows? It's up to Cornwall Lawrence. If he wishes to discuss the contents of Lady Catherine's letter, it might be awhile. If not, it will take only moments, and we can strike out for the docks." She let out a sigh. "And please, don't call me 'Lady' again."

"Many apologies . . . Moira." Willer's eyes grew wide and eager. "The moon is full tonight. If this meeting *doesn't* take long, what do you say to sparring beneath the moonlight and then kissing each other's wounds until we feel them no more?"

Again, Moira sighed. That was another annoyance about the Movers; to them, the carnal pleasures were just as much a game of one-upmanship as swordplay, which meant that Rodin wasn't the only one nipping at her heels. She counted herself lucky that each of them was too noble to have abandoned her while she was on her sickbed.

"I've told you before, Willer, my pearl is reserved for one woman only."

He nodded, dejected. "That's right. The maid. Penetta."

Moira's hand shot out seemingly on its own. She snatched the young sellsword by the collar and yanked "him" toward "her" so violently that he almost fell from his saddle.

"Wrong. And that name will not pass your lips again," she whispered.

He looked confused, but still he said, "All right."

She released him, and he repositioned himself in the saddle, brushing off his boiled leather jerkin as if he could brush away his embarrassment.

"Willer, go back to your mates. I wish to ride alone for a while."

"Yes, Moira," he replied, and did as he was told.

After that they all rode in silence, hooves clomping on packed dirt and the chirping of insects the only sounds. Dusk passed into night, and no one appeared on the road, which was not surprising. It was rare enough to find a carriage or rider about during daylight hours, and the women in the towns they visited said they stayed locked in their homes with their children after dark, for fear of bandits. That was a fear Moira saw as unfounded because not a single man crossed their path during the journey, brigand or otherwise. It was as if the whole male population of Neldar had up and left . . . which, in a way, she supposed they had.

Before very long the road veered to the southwest, and the fields around them gave way to clusters of huts and cabins. All were silent and still; no candles burned in the windows, no telltale puffs of smoke exited the chimneys. These were Omnmount's border settlements, where the transient men and women who toiled in the Lawrence fields put their feet up after a long day's work. Yet they seemed abandoned. She paused for a moment, looking this way and that, searching for signs of life. In some of the windows, she could see human outlines bathed in shadow and the occasional flicker of light off someone's eyes.

"There is no one here," said Gull. "All have fled."

"Stay quiet." Moira put a finger to her lips. "The people are hiding. There must be a reason for that."

"What? Is the great Moira afraid?" laughed Danco, the most roguish of the Movers and a man who thought himself suave. "Moira Elren, a craven? I have seen it all now!"

"I said, *be quiet,*" she shot at him, resting her hand atop one of the swords hanging from her hip. She continued on in an angry whisper: "It isn't cowardice to be cautious. That is how you stay alive, you dolt."

Danco inclined his head, smiling a proud smile. The sick bastard seemed to like being put in his place by her. To Moira, it was bewildering.

They rode onward, passing by more barren fields and a few more clusters of hovels on their way to the central district of Omnmount's township. Hovering at the top of the rise, Moira could see the settlement's single stone building, a tall and rounded structure that looked like a castle rampart and served as a marketplace and place of worship. The tents, burrows, and low holdfasts that surrounded the unnamed building were dwarfed by it, making them look like servants bowing to their godly master.

"Cornwall Lawrence lives in that monstrosity?" asked Rodin from beside her. "I thought you said he was a humble man."

"That's just a building, built for and used by the people," she said. "The Lawrence estate is actually on the other side of the hub, and it is indeed a humble place of residence." She turned to Rodin, frowning. "You've never been to Omnmount before?"

"No." He shrugged. "None of us have."

Not the most worldly bunch. "How in the world could you make it from—"

Something caught her eye, stilling her tongue. She squinted while staring at the sprawling township below, trying to force her eyes to adjust to the mixture of darkness and the moon's bright azure light. Something was amiss down there, something swaying in the slight breeze, but she could not put her finger on what. She wished she had the eyes of an elf.

"What is it?" asked Willer sheepishly, garnering himself a whack upside the head by Tabar.

"Keep quiet," she told them. "All of you, hold your breath for a moment."

They did as instructed, and Moira did the same. She closed her eyes, focusing on the sounds of the land. She heard the soft breath of the wind, distant trees swooshing together, one of the horses snorting, insects chirping, bat wings flapping, and, underneath all of that, a faint yet continuous *creak*.

She turned to the Movers. "We're going down there. Use caution, and only speak if necessary. Understood?"

On cue, each of them nodded.

"Good. Let's go."

Down the gentle slope they went, and the closer they drew to the township, the louder the creaking sound became. Moira kept attentive, with one hand on the reins and one on the sword on her left hip, ready for something to leap out at them from the numerous shadows. Her stomach rumbled, tightening up on her. It was then she noticed there were new additions to the multiple low constructions around the hub: numerous tall wooden poles, like those that would be erected and then strung with decorations and lanterns during the spring festival in Felwood. The creaking noise was continuous.

They soon passed between the closest pair of fifteen-foot-high poles, and all eyes looked up to see a body swaying from each one. Moira lifted her hand, signaling a halt. Her horse fidgeted nervously beneath her. She craned her neck, staring at the dangling forms. They both had feminine shapes, their bodies limp, their necks viciously snapped. One was large, the other much smaller.

"Are they real?" asked Danco. "Up north we hung effigies to ward off crows during the onset of winter, and it is almost winter now."

"They're real," Moira whispered. She didn't reprimand the man for speaking. A gust of wind blew, and the corpses swayed. *Creak, creak, creak.* Without another word she cracked the reins, and her horse trotted onward. Her sellswords followed closely behind.

The town was filled with poles, and each had a resident. Women, both young and old; children; old men—none had been spared. She counted twenty-seven poles by the time her troupe reached the great stone building at the center of it all. A sinking feeling filled her.

"This is horrible."

Willer spun in a circle, his horse baying. "Why would so many people deserve execution? Was it Karak?"

"No," said Tabar as he tugged on a dangling leg, that of an old man with a long gray beard. "These bodies are relatively fresh. Three days dead, at most."

Gull sidled up to her. "Lawrence's work? I haven't met the man."

She shook her head. "Cornwall is rich, but he is *fair*. He would never stoop to such levels."

"When was the last time you saw him?"

She scrunched her face, thinking. "Twenty years ago, at least. After the birth of his youngest."

"Then it *could* be him. Twenty years can change a man."

A loud shriek pierced the night. Moira spun her horse toward the sound but saw nothing except the long wooden structure to her right, one of the temporary barracks. *There are ghosts haunting this place.*

Someone let loose with a shrill whistle, and from within the barracks emerged a myriad of dark shapes. They ran to beat the devil, circling around her and her five companions before crouching into the grass. Moira's jaw dropped as she realized who they were. Children, dozens of them, and in the moonlight she saw that nearly every one held a small, loaded crossbow. Moira drew her sword, as did the Movers.

"Who goes there?" shouted one of them.

"Should we attack?" asked Danco, his head swiveling.

"Keep calm," she said. "They're just children. Do not startle them." Raising her voice, she addressed the one who had asked for their names. "We are travelers from Port Lancaster, down by the sea. We seek court with Cornwall Lawrence, the master of this land."

A flurry of whispers, and then one of them, a boy no older than nine, stood tall.

"You're not from Karak, are you?" he asked.

"No, we aren't," she said. "We are friends."

"Friends?"

"Friends, and we mean you no harm."

"How do we know that?"

Moira glanced at her companions, then sheathed her sword. The other men did likewise.

"There. See?" she said. "No harm intended. All we wish is to have audience with Cornwall, and we will be on our way."

More whispering, and then came the *whoosh* of a tinderstick being struck. The children lit lantern after lantern, until at least six of them stood bathed in faint yellow light.

Moira smiled at the boy in charge.

"We've put away our weapons. Would your friends please do the same?"

"All right," the child said, flapping his arms, and the small crossbows lowered. Moira breathed a sigh of relief. Haven had been filled with children, and she had spent a fair amount of time with them. They weren't the most coordinated creatures in the land, especially when they were this young. Even though the crossbows were undersized and likely not very powerful, she counted her group lucky they hadn't caught an unintentional arrow in the face.

"Now please," she said. "May we go to find Cornwall Lawrence?"

The boy shook his head, an act mimicked by every other child.

"You can't," he said. "Lommy said bring everyone we don't shoot to him."

"Lommy?"

The boy nodded. "Lommy. The Hangman."

Another forced smile.

"Then please, lead the way."

The boy who'd spoken introduced himself as Slug, before waving for Moira and her men to follow him. They crossed through the rest of the township, where even more barracks were situated, tramped across a field that had been flattened and filled with divots, and then climbed the next rise. It was the Lawrence homestead they were headed for, and Moira felt a flutter of hope in her gut.

That flutter died when seven more poles greeted them outside the family's modest home. A bonfire raged outside, and Moira looked up in horror at the face of Loretta Lawrence, Cornwall's wife of nearly fifty years. She had been hanged along with three of her daughters and what must have been the house servants. The crossbow-carrying children stopped on the periphery of the courtyard while Slug led Moira and the Movers to the front entrance, passing right beneath the dangling bodies. The boy whistled the whole time, and Moira realized that he hadn't so much as glanced up at them. *What has this world come to that a child could become used to such a sight?*

As they neared the front stoop, Moira heard the unmistakable sounds of music and laughter coming from inside the dwelling. She gritted her teeth and paused, allowing a bit of distance between herself and the boy that led them. She then put out her arm, slowing Gull and Rodin when they reached her side.

"No move is to be made until I command it," she whispered.

They nodded their approval and passed the message to the others.

Potted plants lined the main foyer of the Lawrence home, a multitude of wilting flowers and browning ferns. The din of laughter rose in volume as they passed first the common area, then a stone kitchen whose hearth still had glowing coals inside it. On their right was a stairwell, and beyond it the hallway narrowed, leading them to the family's dining hall. It'd been so long since she'd been here that Moira had forgotten how misleading the estate was on first glance; it was far larger than it looked from the outside.

"Boy," Moira began.

"Slug," their guide said.

"Slug," she repeated, "where is it we're going?"

"To join the party," he said, as if it were simple.

His small body pushed open the heavy doors to the dining hall, and immediately raucous laughter assaulted them. Moira stepped through after the boy, followed by the Movers. Within the spacious hall the air was hot and muggy, and it stank of sweat and alcohol. Numerous rounded tables had been pushed against the walls, creating a wide-open space in the middle of the room. There were fifteen people in the hall, men all. Fourteen of them wore padded leather, their steel, mail, and plate stacked up on the tables shoved against the walls. There were helms, both great and half alike, resting atop the armor, along with mauls and axes. Moira, transfixed by the sight of the heaped steel, caught sight of a roaring lion sigil poking out from within the pile.

None of the men in the hall looked their way, so intent were they on whatever game they were playing. One of the fourteen sat on the edge of the dais on which Cornwall's seat still resided, and the others had planted themselves in chairs spaced around the room, their swords propped against their seats, forming a haphazard circle and pounding back their cups while simultaneously harassing the fifteenth man. That man was a fool in a lady's bed sheet, his face painted an array of colors. He staggered around inside the circle of torment, accepting a slap from one of them and jab of a stick from another. He moved like an old man, though the paint was so thick on his face that Moira couldn't tell for sure. She could plainly see his eyes were wide with fear. One of the men held a lute, and he played it badly, the song seeming perfectly appropriate to the game they played in Moira's mind. One of the men leapt from his seat, thrusting his hips behind the poor fool, knocking him over. Another reached out and thwacked the fool on the backside with the flat of his sword, sending the man crawling forward. The laughter that followed was as cruel as it was drunken.

Slug seemed hesitant, but he eventually threw back his small shoulders and stepped up to the circle. The lute player noticed him first, gave the boy a confused look, and then his gaze wandered to where Moira stood. His eyes widened, and his fingers struck a final note with a harsh *twang*.

Behind her, the Movers tensed.

With the music ended, the laugher died away as well. All heads turned. The fool collapsed in the middle of the circle, panting and crawling away now that no one paid him any attention. Slug cleared his throat and in his high-pitched voice said, "Mister Lommy, someone here to see you."

One of the men, a thickly built sort with wavy black hair and beady eyes, stood up from his chair.

"L-Lord Commander?" he asked, breaking the sudden silence. He fell to his knees in front of his seat, spilling his cup all over the floor. Four of the others followed his lead.

Moira cocked her head at them, confused.

The one sitting on the dais, swinging his legs, laughed.

"Stand up, you dolts. The Lord Commander's got tits, hips, and an ugly face. This one's got none of the three." The man's gaze turned to Slug. "I thought I told you to put an arrow in anyone who wandered here."

"Sorry," said Slug, shame turning his cheeks pink. "They said they wanted to see Master Lawrence, and they swore they was friends."

The one on the dais sighed and rolled his eyes. "Get out. You disgust me."

"Yes, sir," said Slug, and he turned around so quickly, he almost ran into Moira on his way. The boy struggled with opening the door again, but eventually it slid open a crack, and he slipped out of the hall.

"Children," the man on the dais said to his cohorts, his eyes flicking to Moira once more. He was a wiry man, though his shoulders were thick, and his long hair was greasy. His beard had grown in splotchy, barely covering the pox scars on his cheeks, and he had a hooked nose. There was something familiar about him, but Moira couldn't figure out why. "It seems this conflict has been making orphans left and right," he said. "Found that bunch in a shantytown just south of here, all on their own. Gave them a few coins for their service. They help well enough, but alas, they're still just children." He turned to his cohorts and said, "As for her, she's certainly not the Lord Commander, but definitely a Crestwell. The banished one, I think. Which would make sense, seeing as she has the body of a boy."

"She has a name!" Rodin shouted from behind her.

"I'm sure she does," said the man on the dais.

"Moira," she said, holding an arm out so none of her Movers would make a rash move. "And it is Moira Elren. I haven't gone by Crestwell for a long while."

"Don't see why not," another of them said. "Why confuse folks like that? Just keep the damn name you were given when you were born."

Moira ignored the comment, squinting at the one on the dais. "You would be Lommy?" she asked. "The one they call 'Hangman'?"

The man grinned. "The same."

"So are you responsible for those who were hanged?"

"How else you think I got the name? By what's in my trousers?"

The other men laughed.

Taking a deep breath, Moira took a step toward them.

"What happened here?" she asked. "Where is Cornwall Lawrence?"

"The merchant is dead," Lommy said. "The Wasting took him."

"And those of his family?" she asked. "I saw their bodies. No Wasting took them."

The man's grin widened. "Casualties," he said. "Sometimes when there's a transfer of power, people die. The people of this township seemed . . . hesitant to accept my authority."

Moira narrowed her eyes at him, heard the Movers shuffling behind her. "Transferred to whom? Who are you to claim anything of the Lawrence household?"

Lommy hopped off the dais, strutting up to the fool who was still sliding himself along the floor, and gave him a swift kick in the ribs. The fool let out a yelp and rolled over, hugging his side. Lommy then proceeded to the center of the circle of his men, patting them each on the shoulder in turn.

"I'm the new master of Omnmount," he said. "Lommy Blackbard, first cousin of Trenton of Brent."

That's why he's familiar. He definitely had the Blackbard look to him, all oily and haggard. Their family line was not blessed when it came to appearance, and had built their wealth by owning nearly every brothel in Neldar. *The only way one of them could ever get a woman.* She thought of Loretta Lawrence and her daughters, swaying from poles by broken necks, not to mention the rest of those throughout the township, and her heart began to race. *Anger is my friend.* It took all her effort not to lunge out at the bastard right then and there, but that was something she couldn't afford. She needed to find out more . . .

"What about the armor?" she asked. "That is *soldier's* armor. And how could you confuse me for the Lord Commander?"

"You intruded on my home," Lommy said with a glare. "It should be *me* questioning *you*, bitch."

"Don't you dare speak with Moira Elren in such a way!" shouted Willer.

She silenced him with a look, as appreciative of his defense as she was.

"Humor me," she told Lommy once Willer had calmed.

"Keep your dogs on a leash," the man replied. "As for the armor, isn't it obvious? We were soldiers, taken from our homes in Brent months ago and brought to the delta to serve under your sister."

My sister? Then Avila was Lord Commander now? She wondered at that, at what was happening within Karak's Army . . . and amazingly enough, she felt concern for her brutal sister.

"You left?" she asked, turning her thoughts away from family.

He nodded. "Deserted. Many have. Turned around during a dust storm after we crossed into Paradise."

"And what of him?" Moira asked, gesturing to the fool, who was still curled up on the ground. "Did he desert with you as well?"

Lommy glanced down. "Him? One of Cornwall's protégés. He *was* useful, until he decided to send word to Veldaren." He leaned over the fool. "A lot of good that'll do you!" he shouted, making the man further curl into a ball. "The crown's dead and no one's left to hear your pleas." He looked back up at Moira. "He'll soon join the others in hanging. We wanted to have our fun with him first."

He was testing her reaction, and there was an obvious threat to it as well. If she protested, or desired to stop them, she would just as easily hang like the others. Well, as far as Lommy thought, anyway . . .

"Then let me do as I came to do, so you men may get back to your . . . fun," she said. "I was to deliver a message to Cornwall Lawrence."

"Give it here," the man said, taking a step toward her and reaching out his hand. His ugly face brightened. "If Brennan wishes to make a deal with the master of this house, that would be me."

"Sorry," Moira said. "The letter was for the head of House Lawrence alone." She eyed Lommy and the rest of them carefully, trying to be nonchalant about it. Lommy still had his sword sheathed on his belt and two others held theirs, while the remaining men lingered by their chairs, smiling and seemingly oblivious to the danger they were in. *Good.*

"*I* am the rightful master here!" Lommy shouted. His right hand fell to his sword. "If Matthew wishes to speak, he will speak with me!"

Moira turned around, faced her five sellswords. Rodin and Willer looked ready to explode, while Danco grinned mischievously and Tabar twiddled the frayed edge of his tunic. Gull stood up straight, expressionless. Moira flicked her eyes to the side and nodded to him.

"You are not the master here," Gull told Lommy in that stoic, emotionless way of his. In the past Moira had rolled her eyes at his manner of speech, but now she found it perfectly chilling. "The gods granted us gifts and gave us honor, and you have spoiled both. You turned your back on your responsibilities and murdered women and children to sate your petty desires. Your mothers would weep if they could see you now, and your fathers would wish they'd spilled their seed across their palms instead."

Angry curses sounded from behind Moira. "Who the fuck do you think you are?" she heard Lommy shout.

She spun around, fire in her eyes, eagerness in her smile. "Your executioners."

Gull's speech had done its job, for as they seethed with rage, they'd remained standing instead of making for their tables and armor. Moira drew her twin swords as behind her the Movers readied their own weapons. Lommy's eyes widened, and she saw the hint of fear. They were outnumbered, and she knew a man like Lommy would not think her dangerous, but they would soon discover what true skill meant in the face of cowards and wretches.

Tabar and Rodin acted first, their swords raised, crossing the twenty feet between them and the former soldiers in a heartbeat. Men fumbled for their weapons, a couple clanking on the ground.

The two who'd held their swords leapt in front of Lommy, meeting the dash head-on. Steel clashed with steel.

Moira followed closely behind, both her blades drawn. Men were screaming now, cursing and grunting. She whirled around Rodin and plunged the sword in her right hand into the belly of a pale-faced man. The tip pierced his leather armor with ease, sinking in to the hilt. The man gaped in surprise, a hot stream of stinking breath gushing from his mouth as he reeled away from her. She lost hold of the handle as he did so.

Moira sensed someone behind her and ducked, a sword flashing just over her shoulder. The *clang* of steel followed, and the screaming and curses continued. When she turned back around again, holding her remaining sword with both hands and lashing out, she saw her Movers hacking and slashing their way through the enemy. One of Lommy's men shrieked as Rodin drove a blade into his gut. Another of them scampered away from Danco, tears running down his cheeks, his right arm hanging by a thread. It was chaos all around, clashing swords and animalistic grunts, while Lommy's voice shouted directions to his men. Moira used that to her advantage, slipping her sword around the neck of a man battling with Gull and slitting his throat.

A beefy man turned away from trading blows with Willer, his gaze falling upon her. She ducked beneath another slash from her side and saw the large man charge. He raised his sword above his head, ready to come down on her with full force.

He was five feet away from Moira when she tried to evade the blow, but she was pinned on both sides by fighting men. Instead, she gathered herself and leapt straight up, using the back of the man to her left as a springboard to vault her higher. She did a split in midair, the beefy man's downward lunge missing her crotch by a sliver, and then she kicked off the shoulder of the soldier fighting on the other side of her and leapt over his head. It was a strategy Corton had taught her early on in training; to use her lightness and agility to outmaneuver an attacker rather than meeting them head on, which brings certain defeat.

As she fell, she angled her sword downward. The tip pierced the back of the beefy man's neck, and he arched his spine. Moira fell against the sword's handle, driving it deeper into his flesh. He took the brunt of her weight and fell to the floor in a spasm. Moira rolled off his shaking corpse, leaving the sword embedded in it, just before another blade smacked against the floor.

Blood filled the air along with the screams of the dying. Moira spun around the next man to attack her, colliding with Rodin, who was engaged in his own skirmish. Instead of faltering, Rodin looped his arm around her and spun her low so that she slid between his opened legs. On the other side she picked up a discarded blade and then spun back around Rodin, parrying a killing blow before it took off his face. She then kicked the attacker in the groin and hacked at the back of his neck when he doubled over. The flesh split, spilling blood all over her leather boots.

"Thanks," Rodin said with a grin, and then pressed his opponent into the corner.

Moira was a whirl of motion, flipping this way and that, thankful that her new sword, a short one, was only slightly heavier than her own twin blades. She cut through ankles, stabbed into stomachs, and left everyone who confronted her bloodied. The men they fought were certainly skilled, but she and her Movers were still their betters . . . and they had the advantage of actually having their armor on their backs instead of heaped on tables. Of all the blows she suffered, only one—a slash to the forearm—drew blood.

After jamming her sword through the eye of yet another man, she spun around to see that only three of the conquerors of Omnmount remained standing. One of them was Lommy, who retreated on shaking legs while a bored-looking Gull pressed in on him. Gull lifted his eyes, caught sight of Moira, and then took off

Lommy's sword hand with a downward hew. Blackbard dropped to his knees, his mouth an "O" of shock, staring at the empty void where his hand used to be. The other two men dropped their weapons in surrender.

The floor of the dining hall was a mess of blood and hacked-off limbs as Moira strolled across it, approaching the kneeling Lommy. Gull backed away, inclining his head in respect. She knelt before the would-be lord, who still held tight to his spouting stump, and forcibly grabbed his chin.

"Please . . . ," he whimpered.

"You deserve worse," she said before slitting his throat from ear to ear. A waterfall of red cascaded over his padded tunic. He gargled out a few words before his eyes rolled and he collapsed. Moira watched him until his body stilled.

"What of these two?" she heard Tabar ask.

"Kill them," she said without turning around.

Protests and pleas for life followed, silenced by the sound of steel ripping through flesh.

When it was over, she rose to her feet and looked around. Lommy's thirteen brethren were strewn about the hall, and a near lake of blood rippled on the floor. She felt more alive than ever, her body experiencing no pain, not even her mouth, which had still been sore from the sickness. She took in each of her five sellswords, who were in the process of jamming their swords into the skulls of those on the floor just in case any still breathed. Although they had suffered cuts, and Danco had a nasty gash on his left cheek, they were relatively unharmed. *I made the right choice,* she thought.

Moaning reached her ears, and Moira turned around. The fool was propped up against the dais, his knees drawn to his chest, his eyes filled with horror as he took in the carnage. She dropped her sword and approached, kneeling down beside him. He looked over at her, tears running down his cheeks. He wiped them away, taking clumps of white paint off in the process. Doing so revealed how terribly wrong her initial guess had been; he was likely not any older than fifteen.

"You have a name?" she asked him.

"E-E-Elias. Elias Gandrem."

Moira scrunched her face, knowing that name . . . and then it came to her. "Gandrem? Any relation to Faysia Gandrem from Hailen?"

The youth nodded, his tears still falling. "Faysia is my mother."

She considered him. Faysia was born Faysia Gemcroft, Peytr's sister. Just hearing the name made her think of Rachida, and she felt a longing in her gut. Moira put her bloody hands to Elias's cheeks, rubbing them, trying to calm him.

"Here now, you're safe," she said. "So you sent a bird to Veldaren, even though you were told not to?"

The boy nodded.

"Very brave of you." She rustled his hair. "Very brave indeed."

"Th-Th-Thank you," Elias said.

She helped the boy to his feet and handed him off to Gull, who brought him over to where Danco, Tabar, and Willer were cleaning their wounds. The boy seemed to relax as he went, even laughing uncomfortably when Danco made a crude joke.

"Courageous youngster," Rodin said, sidling up beside her. "But what do we do with him?"

She shrugged. "I have no clue. He is Peytr's nephew, probably sent here by his father to help care for Cornwall's affairs while he was ill. He most likely knows quite a bit about the family business."

"And what about us? Cornwall isn't exactly here to read Lady Catherine's letter."

"Right now we find the rookery, see if there are any birds left, and then send word to the Queen Bitch." She smirked. "And after that, we head to the docks and finish what we came here to do. As deeply as I miss Rachida, I think I've missed swinging a sword just as much."

Rodin grinned.

"Missing a good fight as much as you miss time with a woman?" He laughed cheerfully. "I think all us here know what you mean. Come then. Let's go set some fires."

CHAPTER 16

During the day she had no name, just a corpse walking among the other corpses that populated the city, toiling with them in the fields to the west, supping with them and sharing a cup of dirty water while the sun was still high in the sky. Come late afternoon she became a ghost, slithering through the alleyways of Veldaren's poorest district, unseen even by those who laid their eyes on her, nothing but a filthy rail of a woman with soot in her disheveled hair, grime on her face, and a reeking burlap sack hanging from her shoulders.

But come dusk, life flooded her veins. Come dusk, she was no longer Laurel Lawrence. When she sought out others who lurked in the shadows, binding the weary, the angry, and the frightened into a slowly growing army, she bore a new name, one the tired people gave her out of a mixture of fear and pride. They called her "Specter."

Laurel dashed from one building of drab gray stone to another while destitute mothers and daughters hawked spoiled wares from their carts along the side of the road. She slowed, walking with a pronounced limp, when she spied a Sister of the Cloth, one of many women found guilty of crimes and whose freedom was stripped from them. The wrapped woman glanced her way and squinted, seemingly unconcerned with such a haggard old thing on this cold day. These new daytime guardians of the city always seemed to regard her the same way now—as if she were unworthy of so much as a glance.

The large woman beside her, another nameless female in a veritable sea of them, looked her way and nodded. With the Sister out of sight, she and Laurel picked up their pace, heading west along the Merchants' Road.

"I see her," the large woman, Harmony Steelmason, said. It was still odd to hear her voice after she'd gone so long without speaking a single word.

"Where?"

"Over there." She tilted her head slightly. "The one sitting beside the fish market."

"How can you tell?"

"The note said to follow the scent of fish."

"That could mean anything."

"Yes, but look at the way she is sitting and tapping her feet. This one is anxious, not dejected."

Laurel squinted against the glare of the setting sun, and sure enough she saw the way the girl on the other side of the road shook her legs as if they'd fallen asleep, and her instincts insisted it wasn't from the cold.

"We do this now?" Harmony asked.

"We do."

Together they crossed the road and approached the fish seller's window. Harmony stepped up to the hag behind the counter while Laurel sat down beside the fidgeting girl.

"Tristessa?" she asked, keeping her voice low and slurred.

"Yes?" asked the girl.

Laurel slid closer, keeping her back to the hag at the window.

"Where are they?"

Tristessa hesitated and bit her lip. Harmony continued quibbling with the hag at the window about how much a hunk of catfish was truly worth.

"We have an hour of sunlight left at most," Laurel said in an irritated whisper. "You either show us now, or we leave. We can't be caught outside after dark. You know this."

Again Tristessa bit her lip, and for a moment it seemed she would recant on her promise, but then she rose slowly to her feet and walked down the alley between the fish market and the cobbler to the left. Laurel counted to ten, then followed, doing her best to appear indifferent.

The nervous girl stopped at a door to the rear of the cobbler's. She looked around, the expression on her face one of abject terror, before finally rapping three times on the door. The small portal in the door slid aside, and after a few mumbled words, the door opened with a *creak*. Tristessa slipped inside, and Laurel followed.

The rear area of the stone building was cramped with people. More than half were men, both young and old, starving and gaunt, their faces covered with scars and their arms with sores. The others were women who looked just as frightened as Tristessa had. The men were bandits, forced into hiding by the new lords of Veldaren; the women were former Sisters who had shed their wrappings. Both lived in constant fear of death.

Laurel gazed at each of them, and she was pleased.

An interior door opened, and another woman entered the cramped space. This one carried herself with a dignified air, her nose upturned in disgust at the rancid scents coming off the room's occupants. Her eyes found Laurel, and she shoved her way through the throng, a frown on her face.

"Do I know you?" the woman asked.

"I am a servant of the crown," she said, keeping her voice low and cold, the voice of the Specter. "And I am sure you have heard the stories. Why else would you have left me a note in the fountain?"

In truth, Laurel Lawrence knew the woman quite well. Her name was Ursula, and she was the wife of the cobbler who operated this establishment. They both had shared laughs while waiting for shoes to be repaired, back before Ursula's husband had been conscripted into Karak's Army, before Laurel took on her own new guise. It amazed her that the woman did not recognize her, but then again, why would anyone expect to find a noblewoman such as she cloaked and garbed like a vagabond of the night?

"That was my daughter's doing," Ursula said. "If I had my way, your stink wouldn't be adding to the rest that's already infected my house."

Tristessa stepped forward, clearing her throat. "Mother, don't be rude."

"I'll act any way I wish!" Ursula said, turning on her daughter. "It was not *my* decision to house these miscreants. I'm putting my neck on the chopping block, all for a daughter with more compassion than sense. You are lucky I didn't cast the lot of you out on the street weeks ago!"

Angry murmurs followed, and the pack grew restless. Laurel glanced about and could sense the anger the men and women had toward their caretaker. A fight would follow if the tension were not dealt with, and though the cobbler's walls were stone and this room had no windows, she dared not risk even the slightest commotion being overheard outside.

"We will be leaving soon," Laurel said to all of them. "You will find shelter with us, and food and wine and a safe place to rest your heads. But you must be patient."

"I've been patient enough," Ursula said, hands on hips. "I want them gone *now*."

Laurel pointed an accusatory finger at her. "Don't presume to tell me how this must go," she said. "If we leave now, we will be spotted and risk capture. And if any are captured, they will be tortured, and guess whose name will be on their lips, *Ursula*?"

"But—"

"But nothing. Leave this room. When the sun is almost set, and the Sisters begin their return to their housing, *that* is when we make our move. No sooner, no later. I appreciate all you've done, but the lives of these people are in the hands of the Specter now, not yours."

The woman stared up at her, her head cocked to the side. A question was on her lips, her eyes wide with anger, but she swallowed it down and exited the room. When she was gone, Tristessa approached her, tears rolling down her cheeks.

"Thank you so much, miss," she said. "I know my mother seems bad, but she's just worried about us, that's all."

Laurel placed her hand on Tristessa's head, felt her silky brown hair.

"I know," she lied. "Go to her. Comfort her, and do not worry for the people here. They're under my protection now."

"Thank you," the girl blubbered.

"However, Tristessa, did you have the . . . other items we need?"

"I do," the girl said. She spun around, disappearing through the door her mother had taken, and returned with a pile of moldy fabric heaped in her arms. She dropped the heap in front of Laurel.

"Will that do?"

"It will. Go now, girl, and comfort your mother."

"Yes, milady," Tristessa said with a bow, and she scurried back out of the room.

The bundle the girl had brought was a stack of old cloaks, and Laurel passed them out to the men among them. She counted her new wards: twenty-two of them, thirteen men and nine former Sisters. "Put these on," said Laurel. "It won't be long now." The twenty-two frightened people waiting in the cramped back room of the cobbler's waited some more. Laurel remained by the door until a knock came, two light raps followed by fingertips dancing over wood. She motioned for everyone to step back, grasped the door handle, pressed down, and pulled. When Harmony sauntered in, Laurel slid the door shut, latching it soundlessly. The large woman lifted the stinking chunk of fish she held to her mouth and tore off a hunk. Her thick jaw worked up and down like a cow chewing its cud.

"That"—Laurel pointed at the foul morsel—"is disgusting."

"I'm hungry," Harmony said in return. "A sprinkle of pepper and a pinch of salt can make anything edible."

"If you say so."

From then on the Specter kept vigil by the small portal in the door, watching the sky shift from blue to yellow to pale pink. She heard the rumble of wheels and the grate of shuffling feet.

"It's time," she told the room's occupants.

"What do we do?" asked a frightened voice.

"You follow us," said Harmony. "Walk with your head down, like you are so overwhelmed by life that you have no muscles in your neck any longer."

One of the men stepped forward, frowning. "That's it? *That* is what we needed you for?"

Laurel prodded the man in the shoulder.

"What part of 'We're leading you to a safe place' don't you understand? If you would rather face the Judges' claws on your own, you are free to. The door is not locked. Go and find your own shelter."

She stepped aside, gesturing for him to take the door handle. The man's face flushed red, and he took a step back, murmuring an apology.

"What do we do if the Judges do find us?" one of the others asked.

"You run," Laurel said. A grim smile spread across her face. "And don't you dare pray. Doing that only tells them where you are. Now you men, keep those cloaks tight around you. Let no one see your face."

The twenty-four souls left the cobbler's and turned east, easily mixing with the throng of sullen, departing women. Laurel and Harmony remained in the lead, limping and shuffling their feet. Sunlight shone behind them, casting long shadows that reached like eager fingers. They kept close to the buildings. There were Sisters up ahead, the wrapped women returning to wherever it was they called home for the evening. Laurel glanced behind her, saw the frightened faces of those under her charge, and hoped everyone else was too enraptured by their own misery to notice.

In truth, Laurel was not overly worried. She had made this journey more than fifty times already, and rarely were they threatened with discovery. The new lords of Veldaren were too confident in their hold on the city and in the threat of the Judges' claws to quell any resistance. They were wrong. The only reason Laurel felt uneasy this night was due to how many they transported. Her previous highest had been thirteen, yet now twenty-two followed.

Once the traveling band reached the great fountain of Karak in the center of the city, they turned onto the North Road. The street was crowded, more so than usual, which slowed their progress. Sisters of the Cloth walked toward them, heading for Merchants' Road, dull eyes staring lifelessly from gaps in their wrappings. The sky overhead turned an ominous shade of crimson, the clouds transforming into billowing fire. *This is taking too long,* thought Laurel.

A distant roar shook the air around her.

"No, it's too early!" someone shouted from behind her. She recognized the voice as one from her troupe.

"Oh gods," muttered Harmony.

The crowd was thrown into a frenzy, countless panicked women dashing this way and that, trying to get to the safety of their homes before the Judges emerged from their cages in the belly of the Castle of the Lion. Even a few Sisters of the Cloth seemed hurried. The throng became a stampede, threatening to trample or separate the twenty-four.

"Take hands and into the alleys!" shouted Laurel, and she reached behind her without looking. A meaty hand grabbed hers, and she yanked Harmony into a nearby gap between buildings. She didn't glance behind her to see if her charges had followed orders; if some of them panicked and forgot to grasp the hand of the one in front of or behind them, it could not be helped. They would be on their own, and should they survive the night, they could try again another day.

She pulled them through narrow passages, around bends, and over heaps of festering garbage and human waste. The second roar filled the air, sounding farther away than the first, and Laurel slowed their progress. She could hear those behind her crying and huffing for breath, could almost feel the terrified energy that pulsed all around her. Someone whispered Karak's name, and she stopped short. Harmony almost collided with her backside.

Laurel spun around, anger making her neck grow hot.

"I said no praying," she growled.

Numerous eyes gazed at her. One by one, each of them nodded.

They kept going, the sky growing ever darker above them. Although taking the alleys offered more refuge than keeping to the main throughway, it was also a much longer route. The alleys also had their own dangers; one never knew if some frightened soul might spy them from above and call out to the Judges.

Yet no one caught sight of them, and a few far-off screams told of the Judges dispensing their brutal justice elsewhere. The structures surrounding them began to inch closer together, their walls old wood rather than stone. The scent of feces and rot, prevalent in all of Veldaren, was potent.

They had reached the Black Bend.

The Bend was situated in the northeast corner of the city, a woebegone slum where the poorest citizens resided. The old, the infirm, the orphaned, and the outcast were who lived in this place. Originally, it had been built by the first generation of humans to house the builders who had assisted Karak in shaping his crown city. This section of the city had been forgotten, its land useless for building on due to the natural caves lingering beneath the earth making further construction too risky. Every building was perilously close to caving in on itself, and the mold seeping into the old wood caused horrific illnesses, oftentimes leading to death. Still, the populace here was proud. The downtrodden stuck together, a kinship in torment that embraced the Specter, and she them in return. Only they remembered the tunnels that ran beneath the Bend. It seemed as if everyone had forgotten about the poorer sections of this city save the poor themselves.

Luckily, the king's bodyguard Karl Dogon had been an orphan from the Bend. It was on his advice that the shoddy rebellion had moved there.

They emerged from the darkness and onto a cracked road lined with sewage. Those following behind Laurel gagged, but she and Harmony did not. They both had learned to cope with the incessant reek of the place.

From there they hurried down the street, the pitter-patter of feet echoing dully off sodden, crumbling walls. Shutters were slammed as they passed, candles blown out. It was almost completely dark now. None would grant them entry should Veldaren's rulers fall upon them.

Around the next bend they ran, and Laurel's heart leapt. A single door to a particularly ramshackle structure was propped open, and three men paced in front of it, each holding tight to his sword. The men swiveled at the sound of approaching footsteps, and upon sight of the women, they silently urged speed, waving their arms toward the opened door.

Laurel released Harmony's hand and took her place by the side of the door, ushering her charges inside. She stared over their crouched heads at the man across from her, with his warm hazel eyes and mop of curly black hair. He started to say something, but she put a finger to her lips, silencing him. Another roar broke through the young night, followed by yet another tormented scream. The man took that as his cue, dashing to the back of the line and literally shoving the frightened travelers into the door.

When all were inside, the door shut and barred, Harmony led the throng down a hall whose walls were leaning perilously inward. Into the basement they went, where torches were already lined up for their use. Harmony opened a hatchway in the floor and urged the others to descend into the blackness below. A few hesitated, but all it took was a more violent roar from outside to get them moving.

Only after all the rest were out sight did Laurel follow them into the pit, descending the twenty crude wooden stairs and sneezing at the musty odor of the tunnel. She stood at the bottom of the well and watched the three men shut the hatch, then helped them stack heavy stones in front of the stairwell. Only when they finished did she breathe a sigh of relief.

"Laurel, you worried me," said the man with hazel eyes.

"I worried me too, Pulo," she said with a tired smile.

"You look horrid," said Roddalin, one of the other men.

"She always does when she comes back," said Jonn, the third.

"Enough." She feigned offense, then looked up at Pulo. "Did you make the count on the way in?"

He nodded. "Nineteen. Twelve men and seven women."

"Nineteen," Laurel repeated. "We lost three."

"Most likely the last of the screams we heard."

She frowned. "I hope not."

"They made feasts for the lions," said Jonn, "but their sacrifice probably saved your hide."

"That doesn't make it any better."

Pulo draped an arm around her shoulder, gave her a squeeze. "I know."

"I should clean up," she said, allowing a small, sad smile. "I'll speak with the new recruits come morning. Let Harmony handle it until then."

"Very well. I understand."

Laurel left them, walking down a separate stone passageway. The place was murky and filled with swirling shadows, with a torch burning every thirty feet to light the way. No more were allowed, for the caverns had very little ventilation, and already thirteen people had died from smoke inhalation. At least it was warm down here, which was a welcome respite from the biting chill aboveground. Down here, her knees didn't constantly knock from shivering.

The cavern walls were marked with painted arrows pointing the way to each populated section. The caverns were vast and confusing otherwise, descending deeper into the earth in spots through narrow tunnels. The first time she had visited here, after her rescue from the clutches of the mumbling priest Joben Tustlewhite and the castle dungeons, she had thought it too complex to ever remember. But now the arrows were for the refugees, not her.

The passageway she took was lined with jagged rock, and at a small triangular gash in the earthen wall she ducked down, entering the small fissure that passed for her quarters. Inside were her bedroll, a stinking chamber pot, and little else. What meager clothing she had—most passed on to her by those she had brought here—was resting on natural shelves protruding from the cave walls. Atop a higher shelf was a clay bowl filled with water, a washcloth, and a silver mirror King Eldrich had given her. *All the more to remember who you truly are,* the deposed king had told her at the time, though she had a feeling that he'd given it to her simply so she could make sure she looked her best when in front of him.

Not that she minded. *Let Eldrich have his wants.* In truth, she liked to look beautiful, and always had. But the face that now stared back at her was horrific. Her cheeks were padded with clay and painted with deep rouge to make it look like burst veins crisscrossed her face, then topped with ash and sprinkles of mud. Bits of twig stuck out from the crow's nest atop her head. She smiled, and it looked as if she had only four teeth remaining in her mouth. Sighing, she stepped back from the mirror, stripped out of her hag's garb, and cast it aside with disgust.

Naked, she approached the mirror once again, thankful for the young woman's body she saw, even though she was thinner than ever. After dipping the washcloth into the sweet-smelling water, she began to wash the filthy disguise from her face. The pink of her skin shone through with each stroke, gradually revealing the pretty visage of a naïve young girl who had grown up in Omnmount dreaming of love and marriage and oodles of children. She squeezed the grime from the cloth onto the floor, dipped it back into the bowl, and scrubbed her teeth, removing bit by bit the tar that created her toothless illusion. Unfortunately, the tar was staining, and she couldn't remove it fully, but it was good enough for now. To get the vile taste out of her mouth, she bit and sucked on a lemon wedge.

By the time she was finished combing the snarls, soot, and debris from her hair, using her fingers, she looked nearly herself again; twenty-three and pretty, with womanly curves and a dimpled smile. She debated heading lower into the caverns, to bathe in the place where a natural spring bubbled up into small rocky pools, but shook her head and snatched a simple blouse and breeches from her pile of borrowed clothes. She was tired and needed sleep. The pools would be there when she woke.

The clothes were damp but comfortable, quite unlike the scratchy rags the Specter wore. Laurel squeezed her arms around herself and sat down on her bedroll. It was thin and the cave floor uneven, but she had long grown accustomed to such discomfort. She reclined, laid her head on a rolled-up blanket, and pulled her woolen quilt up over her body. Warmth infused her, and she tried to ignore the aggressive reek of her chamber pot—she'd left in a hurry that morning, forgetting to empty it—and get some sleep. Maybe this time she wouldn't dream of the many she'd lost along the way.

Those nightmares never came, for ten minutes into her slumber she was awoken by a rough shake. Her eyes snapped open, and in the dim candlelight she saw Harmony hovering over her. The large woman who usually accompanied her had cleaned herself as well, and she looked noble with her rigid jaw, piercing blue eyes, and short silver hair. There was a time, back when Quester gave his two personal servants to Laurel and before Harmony cast aside her Sister's wrappings, when Laurel had dubbed her "Giant." She no longer used that name, for it was a title for a woman enslaved, which Harmony Steelmason was no longer. Laurel then thought of Lyana Mori, Harmony's fellow former Sister and granddaughter of the dearly departed Soleh, former Minister of Justice. Lyana was supposed to have been off on her own mission, and Laurel hoped she had returned safely.

"What is it?" Laurel asked, shoving herself backward to sit up against the rough cave wall.

"Your presence is requested," said the large woman. Her voice was deep yet feminine.

"Eldrich?"

Harmony nodded.

"Did he give you a reason?"

"No. He greeted the newcomers and then asked to see you at once."

"That cannot be good."

Harmony shrugged. "Perhaps. Perhaps not."

They exited the cave dwelling, Laurel finding it a bit comical to watch Harmony squeeze her bulky frame through the narrow opening. They crossed through tunnel after tunnel, passing the purple painted arrows marking the walls, until they came to the largest of the caverns, which served as King Eldrich's secretive seat of power. The grotto was the hub of the entire underground dwelling, with thirty-three spines breaking off in every direction. The ceiling was forty feet high, and there were even tunnel entrances lining a rock ledge up above. When Laurel had first seen this place, a part of her wondered whether it was built by the gods long ago with just this purpose in mind. She cringed at the thought. If that was the case, it wouldn't be long until the Judges found them.

The king was there, sitting in his humble chair in front of a rickety table, surrounded by several of his Palace Guards, Pulo, Roddalin, and Jonn. Karl Dogon, the king's bodyguard, lingered at the rear, his square face awash with shadows from the table's six candles. All eyes turned to Laurel and Harmony when they entered. Laurel didn't like the looks on their faces, especially the king's. Although Eldrich had grown even sicklier looking during his extended stay in the caverns, he always seemed to brighten when Laurel entered. *He is quite fond of you,* Pulo had told her, a hint of jealousy in his voice. But now, the thwarted king gazed at her with vacant eyes and downturned lips.

She approached his seat while Harmony hung back.

"Your Grace," she said, curtseying. "You wished to see me?"

"Laurel, sit down," the king told her wearily.

Laurel complied, not liking how the other three men wouldn't look in her direction. Jonn in particular was troublesome in the way he gnawed on his fingernails. She settled into the chair and looked over at Eldrich's pale, deep-set eyes.

"Please, your Grace, what is this about?"

Eldrich sighed. He looked even more faded and despondent than he had that long-ago day when Laurel had told him about the Connington's demands for their assistance in bettering the realm in Karak's absence.

"Karl returned from meeting with his liaison within the castle," Eldrich said. "He learned some . . . disturbing news."

Dogon stepped out from the shadows, and Laurel was aghast at his face, which was covered with cuts and bruises. "Just tell her," he said harshly. "Don't torture the poor girl."

Eldrich didn't reprimand the bodyguard for his harsh tone. Instead, his pale eyes met Laurel's. "Laurel, my dear," he said. "I'm sorry. Your father is dead."

Laurel heard the words, hung her head, and sighed. Cornwall Lawrence had been suffering from the Wasting for years, left to rot in his bed while the disease ate him from the inside out.

"It's a blessing," she said softly. "He is no longer in pain." Even though she spoke the truth, sadness spread within her nonetheless as she thought of how she would never have the chance to tell the great Master of Omnmount how much she loved him, how much he meant to her, how much his guidance had helped shape the woman she had become.

"That isn't all," Karl Dogon said flatly.

Laurel lifted her eyes.

King Eldrich seemed hesitant. His lips, partially stuck together by dried saliva, finally parted, and he said, "There was a message sent by Elias Gandrem, your father's protégé in your absence. The Blackbards . . . they stormed into Omnmount in your father's last days. They demanded your mother hand over the region to them. When she refused, they killed her . . . they killed all . . . all of . . . "

The bodyguard took a hunkering step forward, slamming his fist down on the table and staring intensely at Laurel.

"They butchered your whole family, girl." He looked fierce with fury. "All your sisters, your aunts and elderly uncles, gone. A whole line wiped out. All but you."

Laurel shot back in her seat, her eyes bulging, too shocked for words. "It can't be true," she said. Her voice didn't sound like her own.

"We have no reason to doubt the message," said the king after passing Dogon a glare. "Elias is a good boy of gallant blood. He wouldn't lie about such things, even if tortured."

"How do you know for certain?" she asked. "Someone could have forged the letter!"

Finally, Pulo turned to her. "But why, Laurel? What purpose would it serve?" He reached across the table, his fingers seeking hers, but she pulled away from him.

"Leave me alone!" she screamed.

"Laurel . . . "

She couldn't describe what she was feeling. All the struggle, the misery, the fear—everything paled now. She shoved away from the table as hard as she could, knocking her chair over in the process. Voices called out to her, but she couldn't hear them. The deafening clamor in her head dominated all else.

Into an adjacent tunnel she fled, the shouting growing quiet behind her. She ran blindly, not paying attention to the directional arrows, simply moving wherever her feet chose to carry her. Her mother and father dead, her older sisters . . . it was too much to bear. Their names rolled through her mind: *Lorna, Isla, Rose, Jasmine, Hyacinth.* They'd all had families, and those families were gone now as well, the men forced by their god to fight a war, the children butchered along with their mothers by some damned power-mad merchant. None of her cousins, nieces, or nephews would grow old and have children of their own; none would play again in the shimmering lake behind her parents' home, and her sisters would never again lie in their husbands' arms and whisper sweet nothings. And she was the last. Orphaned. Alone . . . alone . . . alone. Laurel lashed out and punched the wall as she fled, bloodying her knuckles.

She descended through sloping tunnel after sloping tunnel, passing the numerous alcoves where almost eight hundred men and women, nearly half of whom she had helped to save, rested their heads. She ran even when bedraggled people emerged from their nooks, looks of concern painting their faces as they backed away from the whirling demon in their midst. She ran ever downward until she left them all behind, until there was little to no light, and the air around her grew thick with moisture, dripping water the only noise other than her footsteps echoing off wide chamber walls.

She paused, placing her hand on a slick boulder and panting. Tears streamed down her cheeks, and her thoughts waged war between acceptance and disbelief. She cried for her family, for their friends, for the entire township of Omnmount, all those frightened children who were now left rudderless. Alone. All alone. "What's it all been for?" she cried out, hoping a god, any god, would answer her.

None did.

Taking a deep breath, she moved toward a point of light in the near distance. She passed through a low hanging, natural archway, and suddenly there were three shimmering blue pools before her, lit by the flames from the torches embedded in the far wall. A laugh left her throat, the most miserable sound she could ever remember. She had run with abandon, hoping to get lost, hoping to lose her footing and plummet into the depths of some great pit and feel no pain ever again, and yet she'd come here, to the underground bathhouse, a place of cleanliness and rejuvenation. Laurel sank into a corner, hidden by a pair of outcroppings, drew her knees to her chest, and sobbed.

She didn't know how long she cried, but by the time she was finished, she felt numb inside. Her tears had scoured her soul and burned away her emotions, leaving behind a useless shell of meat, blood, and bone. Without her family to protect, what reason did she have to go on? She considered jumping into one of the pools and holding herself underwater until she breathed no more.

That thought was ripped from her with the sound of shuffling footsteps. Laurel remained still, not wanting to be found, and peered through the darkness at the lone, slender figure that approached. It was Lyana Mori, stepping gingerly, wincing each time one of her feet touched the ground.

The girl was eighteen, and her hair had grown out now that she no longer wore the wrappings of the Sisters. The dark curls bounced above her shoulders, light as a feather, and her bright blue eyes shone with the same color as the water in the shimmering pools. The girl shrugged out of her frock and stood naked before the water. Cuts and scrapes covered Lyana's arms and legs, and there was a nasty purple splotch above her small left breast. The girl's feet were also bloodied, and when she sat on the edge of the center pool and dipped her toes in, she winced.

Laurel watched as the girl slipped fully into the water. Though the caverns were muggy, the pools were almost freezing, and Lyana wrapped her arms around herself, shivering. Yet she persevered, forcing her hands to dip into the water, cupping it with her palms and rubbing it over her skin. She looked so young then, so innocent. Laurel was mesmerized at the purity of the vision . . . until Lyana turned away.

Laurel had never seen Lyana Mori's back before. It was covered with a mess of scars, like worms racing across her flesh from one shoulder blade to the other, from her hips to the base of her neck. The skin appeared red and raw, looking even more so in the torchlight. Horror filled Laurel's gut. Not only had this girl been stripped of her freedom and forced to serve the most powerful men in the land, but she had been mercilessly beaten and whipped as well. That horror was soon replaced by hatred, and she remembered the smug look on Quester Billings's face when he passed Lyana and Harmony off to her. *"Take care of my pets,"* he'd said. Only Lyana Mori wasn't someone's pet. She was a living, breathing girl, with dreams of her own and a soul just as worthy as that of any man who might claim her.

But Lyana had believed otherwise. It was only with Laurel's help that she'd cast aside the wrappings, the first of many to abandon the Sisters of the Cloth. With Laurel's help, she'd begun to smile again, to live for herself, to believe her life meant something more than insult and servitude.

Laurel's help . . .

She swallowed down the last of her grief and stood, walking slowly across the rutted, rocky ground. She shrugged out of her clothes as she moved, until she stood just as naked as Lyana. The girl in the pool turned around at the sound of her approach, covering her small breasts with her arms. Lyana saw who she was, and a relieved smile came over her.

"Laurel?" she said. "You frightened me."

Laurel sat down on the stone, slid her legs into the cold water.

"I didn't mean to."

Lyana's head cocked to the side. "Laurel, what's wrong?" she asked, voice like a babe.

Laurel couldn't think where to start, how to reveal the annihilation of her family line. The words died in her throat, and she felt her tears swell anew. She'd thought her soul emptied, but her grief was not yet done. When she opened her mouth, only a soft sob came forth, and then Lyana was there, arms about her, holding her as she broke.

"I'm so sorry," Laurel said, holding her tight.

"You've done nothing wrong."

"Not that," she said, her fingers tracing the scars marring the girl's back. If only she could take them, make them her own. But girls like Lyana, they were legion. And despite their sorrow, their humiliation, they endured. They survived. Laurel drew back, wiped the tears from her eyes, and stared at the girl with her head inclined.

No more tears. Never again. If they endure, so will I. My family may be dead, but I have another, and right now, they are all in chains.

"Laurel?" Lyana asked, clearly worried. "Are you all right?"

"I am now," Laurel said, and despite her sorrow, she smiled.

CHAPTER

17

When the first snowflakes fell, the barrage began. As had happened the past twenty-three nights, boulders pounded Mordeina's walls as arrows sailed over the parapets. Only this time, the thousands lurking inside the settlement were ready. Ashhur had helped erect a massive stone bunker fifty yards from the walls, proclaiming the land between the bunker and the wall a dead zone. None but those assigned as watchmen were allowed to climb the stairs. All the rest were put to work crafting weapons and raising countless domiciles with the last of their timber. It was arduous work, but none complained, not when Ashhur marched among them, an expression of icy determination burning in his glowing yellow stare.

"Karak is baiting us," the deity had said the week before, after allowing his children to cry and shriek praises to the heavens when he exited Manse DuTaureau alive. "He wishes us frightened and helpless. When he thinks us broken, and his strength at its greatest, he will come. When he does, he will not find sheep waiting for him, but wolves."

Patrick should have been happy with this new change in attitude, but he was not. When the nightly bombardments began, he was a man conflicted: Part of him wished to climb the walls, drop down on the other side, and surge against the soldiers as he had when they'd penetrated the outer wall; another part wished to dash into Manse DuTaureau, climb into his mother's bed, and hide.

The fear he now felt as he slogged through the freezing muck on this first dark, wintry evening, carrying a heavy block of ore, was entirely due to the nightmares. They'd begun days ago, assaulting him whenever he shut his eyes to get some much-needed rest. In the dreams he was a man haunted. Nessa came to him, her flesh torn and leaking pus, her hair falling out in clumps, and maggots writhing in the shallow black holes of her eyes. His dead sister hurled insults at him, casting blame his way. *"You are a monster,"* she cried in a voice that was always too far away. *"You never truly loved me. If you loved me, why did you never come looking for me, big brother? Why didn't you search for me? Why didn't you save me?"*

Every time, he woke up screaming.

The worst of it, though, was that of late the nightmares had begun to follow him into the waking hours. Exhausted as he was, he did his best to fulfill his daily duties to Ashhur. But no matter where he looked, he swore he saw Nessa, always just out of sight, mocking him, tormenting him. His head began to grow heavy as exhaustion took its toll. He stopped training his young warriors, for sleep-deprived as he was, he could hardly concentrate. Instead, he performed mindless tasks, moving this and that, gathering water, even spending time in the fields, dragging a plow behind him through the frozen earth, so Ashhur's magic could help bring food up through the soil.

Men and women ducked beneath the stone bunker as arrows *plinked* off the top. They were hard at work, pounding with crude hammers on the blocks of ore Ashhur had lifted from deep within the ground in the northwest corner of the settlement. Some busied themselves stoking the fires that would heat the ore, while still others formed branches into slender rods and passed those rods to others to be fletched with crow feathers. The deity did his part as always, demonstrating to a large group of his children how to work with the ore, before using his godly magic to bend it to his will, stretching it, thickening it, forming it into blades of steel. Patrick watched his god, and when he dropped the heavy block he was carrying, it landed on his toe. In the ever-worsening cold, his thick leather boots did little to soften the blow.

"Fuck!" he shouted, hopping on one foot and squeezing his injured digit. He hated the cold, hated the winter. The only saving grace to the change in seasons was the fact that the corpses stacked on the other side of the stone walkway didn't stink any longer.

Someone snickered behind him, but when he wheeled around to scream at the offender, he saw most everyone was hard at work. Even those whose attention was on him had words of compassion on their lips. Then he caught sight of a demonic, red-haired sprite from the corner of his eye, teeth bared behind rotten lips. When he whipped his head around to look, the vision was gone.

Someone grabbed his shoulder, and he almost reached for Winterbone, which still hung in its scabbard on his back. He breathed deeply, calming his nerves, and turned around to see Judarius standing there, a quizzical look on his face.

"What is wrong with you?" the brawny Warden asked.

Patrick shrugged. "Nothing for you to worry your ugly mug about. What are you doing off the wall anyway?"

If Judarius was insulted by the slight, he didn't show it. Instead, he leaned over and whispered to one of the women fletching the arrows. The woman nodded, handing the Warden a crate made from birch bark and filled with at least a hundred finished arrows. The crate was heavy in her hands, but when Judarius snatched it from her, it looked as small as a breadbox. The Warden tucked it beneath his arm and lifted out one of the arrows, examining the sharpened steel arrowhead, running the pad of his thumb over the tip. Patrick felt confused as he watched him, and wavered on his feet. He suddenly found it so interesting and unbelievable that Ashhur had succeeded in creating nearly a complete armory in little more than three weeks.

"We needed more arrows," Judarius said. "I am not much for archery myself, so I volunteered to retrieve them."

"Oh," Patrick said in a daze.

The Warden cocked his head. "Patrick, something is not right with you. More than usual, at any rate."

"I know. Nightmares. Not feeling well."

"Are you eating?"

"Eating what? There isn't much food to go around, and there are over two hundred thousand people here who would gladly accept my portion. I can go without. I probably wouldn't be able to keep it down anyhow."

"Why? Are you sick?"

Patrick's head grew fuzzy again, his vision doubling. He blinked, trying to get the two Judariuses that stood before him to merge into one image. The one on the left then began to bulge and warp, developing blackened eyes and familiar, slimmer features. The fires burning all around blinded him. His eyes rolled back, and he teetered forward. With his free hand, the Warden snatched Patrick by the arm before he fell.

"Patrick, this is starting to worry me."

"Don't," Patrick said. His thoughts began to wander, his mouth moving as if on its own. "Forget me. Let's talk about something useful. Where have you stationed the other Wardens?"

He didn't know why, but he felt instantly engrossed in hearing the answer. Judarius released his arm and positioned the crate of arrows to be more stable. "There are three hundred assisting with preparations at the south wall. Another hundred patrol the citizens, assisting the people with anything they require. The rest are working the grounds, trying to coax crops from the soil. Why do you ask?"

It was a good question, actually, and strangely enough Patrick didn't have an answer. Something about what Judarius said piqued his interest.

"Is no one guarding the western settlement?" he asked.

"Just the barest of skeleton crews," Judarius said. The way the Warden was looking at him was strange. "There aren't enough people on that side of the settlement, but you already know that."

"And are they all armed?"

"Of course they are."

"Stone or steel?"

"Mostly steel."

Patrick shook his head, cursing silently to himself. His vision righted, and there was just Judarius there now, staring down at him while snowflakes fell in the background. He thought he saw that red-haired devil again, but he refused to believe it. *It's all in your head. Just stop it already.*

"Doesn't hurt to double-check these things," he said, trying to convince himself as much as Judarius.

"Patrick, you don't look well, and I think I know why," the Warden said in a flat tone. "You need a good, violent fuck. And you could rip the bitch's throat out afterward."

Patrick stumbled back a step. "What?"

The Warden inclined his head. "I asked why such interest in the Wardens?"

"Wait. You didn't . . . " Patrick shook his head. "I'm sorry, Judarius. Might be best if you head back to the archers. I'm not even making sense to myself."

"Are you sure you do not wish—"

A low *thud* sounded, followed by another, and Judarius's mouth snapped shut. The Warden stepped out from beneath the bunker and gazed at the wall. Patrick followed his stare. The rain of arrows had ceased, at least for the moment. Snow fell on his forehead, and the cold drove a spike of pain between his eyes.

Judarius turned around and faced north just as another muted thump rumbled the air. Patrick stood confused. The noise sounded like far-off thunder, which was rare during a snowstorm as light as this one. Even stranger was the pattering of rain he heard next.

Only it wasn't rain, for a few moments later eight horses raced around the hill on which Manse DuTaureau sat. Each rider carried a torch, and the faces those torches illuminated were filled with fear.

"They are bombarding from the north!" one of the riders screamed. "Come, hurry!"

"Damn," Judarius growled. He gazed down at Patrick, obviously angry with himself. "You were right. We should have had more men guarding all along the wall, not just here. Rosler told me he thought he counted fewer catapults than yesterday, but there was liquor on his breath, and I did not listen. Damn, damn, damn." He slammed the crate of arrows into Patrick's chest, almost knocking him over. "Take these to the archers. I will head up the new defenses." Then he turned about face and began running along the ranks of confused people who stood outside the bunker. "Come, Marius! Grendel, Bosipherus, Ariel—to me! Karak is attacking to the north!"

At least twenty Wardens and another fifty humans joined Judarius in his mad sprint as he chased after the now-retreating eight horsemen. Soon they disappeared into the darkness, and a hush fell over all of those standing around watching. It seemed the only sounds to be heard were the crackling torches and the howl of the wind, until a *ping* rang out, and something whistled past Patrick's ear. He started, stumbling in place, almost knocked over by the weight of his own sword.

"The arrows are falling!" called out a booming voice, and Patrick pivoted to see Ashhur marching along the long bunker, shoving people beneath it. "Take shelter now. Get yourselves—"

The god's words were drowned out by a giant crash. Patrick whirled around and saw a boulder sailing over the wall, carrying with it bits of parapet. Nessa's face was imprinted on the boulder, staring down at him with a wicked grin. He was frozen in place, too confounded to move, too frightened to do anything but watch as the huge chunk of rock began its descent. People screamed, trying to scamper out of the way of the flying boulder before it crushed them like the others had so many nights before. The scene was pure bedlam.

Something large flashed by him, knocking him over. He landed face first in the snow as arrows fell like rain on the white-sheathed ground. With great effort he lifted his head and looked on as Ashhur collided with the boulder. Patrick's ears ached from the ensuing *crack*. Shards of rock rained down, and people shouted Ashhur's name. Yet as the dust settled, Ashhur remained standing, hatred shining in his glowing eyes, making the area in front of him appear as bright as day.

Ashhur ordered his children to retrieve whatever weapons they could in the lull that followed. Patrick stood up, watching as myriad forms scurried to and fro in the space between the bunker and the wall. He shook himself out of his stupor and looked at the ground around him, seeing the birch bark crate smashed and arrows strewn about in the snow. Cursing, he snatched a large square of burlap from inside the bunker and laid it out on the ground, then proceeded to toss as many arrows as he could find atop it. He rolled the blanket and picked it up. It was heavy, but he didn't care. He climbed atop the bunker and hopped down on the other side, heading for the wall.

It was difficult with his mismatched legs to maneuver through the slippery muck. All the people frantically trying to collect the enemy's arrows made it even more difficult. Finally, he slipped, colliding with someone and sending them both to the ground. Rage burned inside him, and when he shook the snow from his eyes, he saw Nessa getting to her feet opposite him, inhumanly tall, her gray tongue dangling out, her lipless mouth smiling. Maggots tumbled from her eye sockets, only to turn into smoke when they touched the air.

Patrick forgot all about the arrows, about the archers atop the wall. All that mattered was the demon ghost. It hefted a large ax and stared at him.

"You aren't Nessa!" Patrick shouted. "Stop fucking haunting me!"

He reached behind his back and grabbed Winterbone by the handle. In a single yank it was in his hands and he charged. His hatred gave him strength as he rumbled forward, sword held by his ear. The demon Nessa's face contorted as she raised the ax in defense. Patrick screamed at the top of his lungs and leapt into the air, ready to split the beast in half with one mighty hew.

A large body collided with him from the side, sending him tumbling. He lost grip of Winterbone, the sword disappearing into the snow. He heard a crunch and shrieked. Needles of pain assaulted him from his neck down to his groin, and he curled into a ball and writhed.

"What is *wrong* with you?" asked a roaring voice.

Patrick looked up. Ahaesarus stood above him, shoulders rising and falling as he huffed. Patrick shifted, looking around the Master Warden to the crouching figure beyond. It was another Warden, Judah, holding his ax tight to his chest.

"I asked you a question," demanded Ahaesarus.

Patrick rolled over, slumped onto his rear, and rubbed the sides of his head. His whole body was sore, his anger gone. For the first time in a while, his thoughts seemed clear despite his fatigue.

"I'm sorry," he said as he glanced about for the bundle of arrows he'd dropped. "I didn't know that was Judah . . . "

"Who else could it be?" Judah asked while he stood and shook himself off.

"I don't know . . . it's just that . . . Judarius asked me to bring arrows to the archers while he rushed off to the northern side of the wall . . . and . . . and I've been seeing things . . . I'm sorry again . . . "

Patrick puffed out his cheeks and exhaled, closing his eyes.

"He called me 'Nessa,'" he heard Judah say.

A moment later soft fingers touched Patrick's misshapen cheek. He opened his eyes to see Ahaesarus squatting before him. The Master Warden looked at him with concern, almost pity, instead of anger. To Patrick, that was worse.

"Patrick, what is happening?" he asked.

"I . . . don't . . . know . . . "

"Are you thinking clearly?"

He shook his head. "I seem to be now."

"Did you call Judah your sister's name?"

"I think I did. He had her face, rotten and disfigured."

"Have you seen her often?"

Patrick hesitated and considered lying, but it would do no good. The Master Warden would smell the untruth as soon as it left his mouth. "Yes. I've been seeing her all the time. In both my dreams and my waking hours."

"That is not normal," Ahaesarus said, clutching his knee and leaning forward. "Let me see if I cannot find someone else lurking around in there." He gazed deep into Patrick's eyes as if searching for something. A few seconds later the Warden shook his head and leaned back. "I see nothing. No curse, no magic—only you. How do you feel?"

"Well, better," said Patrick. Strangely enough, he did.

"Stress can be a demon for all of us, Patrick," said Ahaesarus. "You have been working yourself to the bone and not sleeping. It is not healthy, and we *need* you healthy and alert. Go back to your friends. Lie down. Drink yourself into a stupor if you must. Just *get some rest.* I will bring the archers what they need."

With that, the Master Warden gave him a pat on the leg, found his bundle of arrows in the snow, knocked the white stuff off it, and headed for the wall stairs. Patrick watched him through the falling snowflakes until he disappeared into the gathered blackness at the base of the wall. He then stretched, cracked his back, and stood up, slapping his forehead. *Perhaps I should do as he says,* he thought, though he also realized that, oddly enough, he really did feel better than he had in quite some time. Drained maybe, and more than a little tender in his joints, but his mind was clear. And when he glanced this way and that, taking in all that went on around him, there was no sight of his red-haired haunt.

He took a step back toward the bunker, but when he felt the lack of weight on his humped back he turned around. He had to find his sword, his precious Winterbone. Dropping to his hands and knees, he searched through the snow where he fell, and then he spotted a sword-shaped indent in a drift ten yards away. A smile stretched across his face as he crawled toward it, digging into the snow and muck with his numb fingers until they wrapped around the handle. He then rose once more, bringing Winterbone up along with him, and wiped the handle with the inside of his heavily padded jerkin before stuffing the blade back in its sheath. After that he began walking once more, the dream of drunkenness and passing out taking priority in his mind.

A few seconds later arrows again began to fall, and he had to run as fast as he could to get out of their range lest he catch one in the back. As he hopped up on the bunker and then dropped down on the other side, he spotted a wraithlike figure lurking in the shadows just out of sight.

"No," he whispered, trying his best to ignore the apparition as he walked. "Please go away. Please, just leave me alone."

His hope for sleep abruptly left him.

CHAPTER

18

The walls are thick, but they are weakening, thought Velixar with a smile as he held the dragonglass mirror. *It will end soon.*

He and his god stood five hundred feet from the wall in a giant crescent—two hundred shield men to the front, protecting the three hundred archers who stood behind them, with seventy of the Ekreissar arrayed fifty feet behind the human archers, launching arrows with their stronger bows and superior aim. The rules of engagement were simple, the same as every other day: Pound the walls with the catapults, fire arrows over the ramparts, and keep Ashhur's frightened children awake and afraid. The only new wrinkle was Lord Commander Gregorian's surprise bombardment to the north, an attack meant to make Ashhur's people panic. Panic meant casualties and yet another strike to their morale. The soldiers uninvolved in the attacks, more than twelve thousand of them, slept in the camp a quarter-mile away. Their bodies needed to be rested if they were going to continue the hunt for the food needed to feed an army, as well as the labor required to finish building the engines necessary to end the siege.

Karak glanced at the mirror as Velixar put it away.

"Have you learned anything new?" the god asked.

"I have," he said. "I had a breakthrough tonight. I could actually see through his waking mind. Your brother, he is making weapons, swords, and axes along with replenishing their stores of arrows. They have built a bunker, a six-hundred-foot trench running along the left of the main gate, shielded by a stone partition that faces the wall."

"What else?"

"They have only five hundred Wardens left, who act as nursemaids, as usual. Also, the only section of the wall where they have mounted permanent defenses is right here in front of us. The rest, mile after mile of it, has been ignored." Velixar grimaced, picturing the Lord Commander ordering boulders thrown against—and over—the wall to the north. "It might have been useful to know that earlier. But perhaps it is not all bad. They will now thin out their resources to keep the entirety of the wall guarded. When we choose to make our final push, they will be hopelessly outnumbered and unable to resist."

"What of my brother's children? Are they capable warriors? Is there a secondary gate into the settlement that our scouts have not yet found?"

Velixar frowned. "I do not know. I am still finding it difficult to pierce Patrick's mind; he resists me far more than I expected and I must rely on trickery and exhaustion until he breaks. I thought him a buffoon, but he seems cannier and wiser than he lets on. In addition, I must be careful. When I was finally let in tonight, Patrick suffered a violent outburst. He almost cut down a Warden because of the visions I sent him. Should any take a closer look at him, or even worse, his sword, whatever advantage we might have would be lost."

"Then use caution," Karak said. "It will be some time still before we are ready to commence the final assault. Any information we can gather before then would be most welcome." The deity grinned, looking up at the blackened, snow-dappled sky. "Once the walls fall and we are inside, there will be no limits to what we can do."

No limits, thought Velixar, and frustration overcame him.

"My Lord," he said, "the sun will rise in three hours. Do you have any further need of me this evening?"

Karak gazed down at him, his glowing eyes quizzical. "Do you wish to rest?"

"Not exactly, my Lord."

"Ah," said the deity, nodding deliberately. "I assume my High Prophet must broaden his horizons?"

"Something of the sort."

"Very well then. Off to your pavilion. May you find the order you seek in your studies."

"I am sure I will, my Lord. I am sure I will."

Velixar bowed low and pivoted on his heels, marching back toward the waiting camp. The phalanx behind him parted, creating a human passageway for him to walk through. His cloak snapped in the wind and pride welled inside him. Ever since the night Karak had visited him in his pavilion, when the deity admitted his failings, their relationship had flourished. No more did Karak affront him, no more did he cast doubt on his actions. When they spoke, it was with respect, and Karak always listened intently to any counsel Velixar had to offer. Velixar had found himself in the one place he always longed to be—on equal footing with his god.

Yet that was not completely true, and he knew it. He still had his limitations, and there were aspects of the demon's knowledge inside him that he could not quite grasp. For nearly a hundred years he had studied the legends of the beasts, had nearly every event of Darakken, Velixar, and Sluggoth's hundred-year war with the elves imprinted on his memory. Unfortunately, the creature had not come with instructions, and his efforts to control its power were sluggish at best. He needed to find out more, and his only other recourse was to go to the source and rip that knowledge from the demon itself—or at least from the consciousness Jacob Eveningstar had cast aside.

It took him a half hour to trudge through the muck and snow to his pavilion, his heart beating out of control. He stepped inside, not bothering to remove his boots or cloak. He ignored his desk and bedroll and strode directly toward the chest on which he had placed the head of Donnell Frost. The onset of freezing temperatures, and the fact that Velixar felt no need to heat his pavilion, had done wonders for preserving the head. Though the one good eye had shrunken like a tiny white raisin and the flesh had taken on a brownish hue—as much due to the wax coating as to rot—no more maggots squirmed beneath the skin.

He hung the dragonglass mirror on the support strut behind the chest and knelt down before the head. His heart continued to race. The snow coating his cloak had frozen, and when he bent his elbow, it cracked and flaked away. Velixar brought his hands up, placing them on Donnell Frost's cold, waxen cheeks. Almost immediately the fires within him were stoked. This was the time. He knew it. Years of planning, of practice, had led to this moment. It took every ounce of restraint within him to keep calm.

"Life is a hindrance," he said, slowing his breathing. "The secrets of the universe do not dwell in the realm of the living, but of the dead. While the body corrodes, the soul endures. Only in decay can there be true knowledge. Bring that knowledge to me."

He closed his eyes, focusing on the words now streaming into his consciousness. When they came to him, he said them aloud, his voice sounding strange to his ears, as if he were speaking through a pool of molasses. Donnell's head seemed to melt beneath his fingertips, growing hot as magma bubbling up from a crack in the earth. His body felt suddenly weightless, and a strange feeling overtook him. His excitement grew. *It will work this time.* After so many weeks of trying, he was near success. The demon Velixar had commanded an army of undead elves during the great Demon War; it should have been simple for the new Velixar to commune with a single dead soldier.

Everything around him fell away. When he opened his eyes, he floated through a watery darkness. The skeletons of entities long dead floated past him, things that should not have been there but were, men and women and children and gods and demons, all wandering aimlessly through Afram in search of a place of peace. *Only in this emptiness can there be true knowledge.* In the distance, a small glow appeared, near and far at once, the conscience of the demon he'd swallowed calling out to him, though he could not move toward it. He had expected this to happen. A smile stretched across his ethereal lips.

"I seek Donnell Frost!" he called out into the nothingness. "I seek my guide through the land of the dead!"

The remnants of beings long passed parted, and a lone ball of light drifted forward through the murk. It had no shape, no characteristics at all, and the sight of its frenzied non-form nearly drove Velixar mad. *The human mind was never meant to take in such things. This is the true kingdom of the gods, and gods create form from nothingness.* He concentrated, and the twisting ball of light took shape, becoming the likeness of the man Donnell had been.

The apparition stared at him with hollow eyes, features flickering in and out of existence. "Donnell Frost, faithful servant of Karak," Velixar said, "I call you to serve once more."

It seemed to want to speak, but it could form no words. Velixar sensed a wave of hate emanating from it, however, as if Donnell was not happy to be torn from the afterlife he had been given.

Use that to your advantage, he told himself. *It is a spirit, an after-image. It wishes for only one thing . . .*

"Departed soul, in death you have been granted the inherent wisdom of the void. I seek the resting place of the demons of old, the discarded creations of the ancient Kaurthulos. Show me, and I will release you to the peace you knew."

Donnell's image seemed to nod. It did not reach out for him; it did not move in any discernable way. Yet Velixar felt invisible fingers prying through the miasma of his ethereal form as Donnell's spirit tugged him through the black.

He had expected to be taken on a long journey and be privy to wondrous sights, but time seemed to have no meaning here. Instead, it felt as if he went nowhere at all. One moment the glowing phantom shimmered before him; the next a giant, iridescent wall passed *through* him, and the ghost he had called to his aid disappeared. Instead of a black void, he was now surrounded by great swashes of swirling color, indigo and purple and crimson and ochre; the shades of creation, of un-creation, of eternity itself.

Velixar did not hesitate. "I call on the Beast of a Thousand Faces!" He screamed into the swirls, his human voice like the squeak of a mouse beneath a crashing ocean wave. When nothing happened, he called out again, and this time the colors before him shifted, pulling apart and then drawing together in millions of patterns. Through the chaos an image came forth, that of a face with eyes that glowed as red as Velixar's, concealed within an unearthly façade that shifted from one moment to the next. They were a multitude of faces, both elven and things different, darker, harder to comprehend, the molds never once repeating. The mouth didn't move when the thing spoke a single accusatory word that stretched throughout perpetuity, its tenor shaking the fabric of the universe.

You.

Velixar gazed in wonder at the creature, and for the first time since he had cast aside its consciousness in the throne room of the Tower Keep, he felt a moment of doubt. The beast was so immense, so powerful; it was no wonder a mortal as tiny and human as Jacob Eveningstar would find it difficult to master all the wisdom of this demon.

Leave this place. You are not wanted here.

"I will not!" shouted Velixar. "I have come to commune with you, Beast of a Thousand Faces, the creature I admired for all of my short yet eternal life. I will not leave until you tell me what I wish to know."

We have a name. You will speak our name.

The beast's image wavered like colored waters mixing together, and Velixar realized it was frightened of him. He might have only been a man, but he had defeated the creature already. It was now dead, just as its brother Sluggoth the Slithering Famine was. It was a spirit, but not powerless; it was a creature of the void, whereas Velixar was but a visitor, and it still had its knowledge. A show of strength was necessary.

"You have no name," he told the demon. "I cast you out. I shredded the cords binding you together. You are legion no longer. You. Are. Powerless." He lifted an invisible, ethereal hand, ancient words of magic leaking from his visage and making the demon shrink from him. The thing shrieked, the sound like comets colliding. It was the most beautiful thing Velixar had ever heard.

Stop. We relent.

Velixar smiled, and he wondered if his true body, still kneeling with hands pressed against Donnell Frost's cheeks, was smiling as well.

"I do not come to you out of malice," he said. "I only come seeking knowledge."

Then ask.

"Tell me the secrets of the dead. Once you controlled legions of them, yet I have failed in all my attempts. What spell was used? How did you control them?"

The demon seemed to mull this over, its shifting face swirling along with the myriad colors. *You ask the wrong question of us. The dead are useless shells, merely vessels for the power that fills us. It is that power you must seek.*

Velixar was confused. "Why must I seek that power? I consumed all that you were, consumed your very soul. I should have *your* power."

You are powerful, yet a fool. The Beast of a Thousand Faces laughed. *You consumed memories and echoes, nothing more. And souls themselves are not power, but merely vessels for power, which stems from the gods. We have always known this; we are surprised you do not.*

"But what of a world where the gods do not exist?" he asked the beast. "Where does power stem from then?"

The gods exist everywhere, human. In every rock, in every ocean, in the very air of any habitable world. Everywhere there is life, there are the gods, for all life was created by them. Their power lingers, shadows imbued into the fabric of everything, lurking in wait for one who knows how to wield it. Draw from it if you desire, or draw from the deities themselves; it is no difference.

Velixar felt his frustration growing. "I have channeled the essence of my god, demanded power of him, and felt it flow through me . . . yet it is not enough. There must be another way."

You know nothing, said the demon, just as Karak had told him so many times before. *The well you draw from is as infinite as the universe itself, yet you mewl it is not enough. The gods' power is greater than even the gods themselves. We channeled our creator, the grand Kaurthulos, and became so potent, we almost slew the goddess. You can do the same, Velixar. We can show you how.*

It seemed a promise too good to be true, and he instinctively distrusted it.

"Wielding such power would break me," he said. "My mortal form would not endure."

The beast laughed, and the endless space seemed to ripple along with it.

The soul is limitless. With our help, you will become as mighty as the gods themselves.

Velixar found his consciousness assaulted by tiny pinpricks of light that gradually built up within his ethereal form, expanding it, filling him with knowledge. The pain was exquisite, and when he screamed, his voice seemed to rip through the heavens, pulverizing stars, exploding galaxies, causing time to fold in on itself.

"Why!" he screamed amid it. "Why would you help me?"

Laughter was his only answer, and then he opened his eyes. He was back in his pavilion, the head of Donnell Frost a heap of liquefied flesh and bone stuck to his fingers. He fell back, his rump splashing in the puddle of melted snow behind him. Rising to his feet, heart pounding, mind racing, he pulled the pendant from beneath his tunic and watched the bas-relief of the lion atop the mountain pulse and throb with a dark purple glow.

The soul is limitless. Velixar gritted his teeth and squeezed the pendant, feeling its warmth thump in his hand like a heartbeat.

"As mighty as the gods themselves," he whispered.

CHAPTER

19

"Not much farther now," said Nole, one of the soldiers leading Rachida Gemcroft and her band of six hundred sellswords through the frozen white north. Nole and his six mates were thin to the point of malnourishment, their flesh pale and covered with ugly purple splotches and raised veins. Despite being young—Nole in particular looked to be barely out of his teens—they moved with the awkward gait of much older men. Each time their feet touched the ground, breaking through the thin sheen of ice and into the powdery snow beneath, it looked as if they might fall over.

Rachida shivered against the cold as she sat atop her horse, pulling her cloak tight around her. For fifteen days she and her legion had marched through cliffs and valleys, circling the bases of mountains, the last half of the journey spent trudging through snow, ice, and freezing rain while hungry wolves haunted their nights. At last they had arrived on the outskirts of Drake. Only instead of the people of Paradise, they'd happened upon this small band of Karak's soldiers. The soldiers' eyes had widened with what looked like relief when they'd emerged from the frozen wilderness, greeting her and her men as saviors. Rachida had introduced herself as Commander

Mori, breathing a sigh of relief that her hired army still bore the standard of the lion on their chests.

Quester sidled up to her, pulling at his blond beard and appearing amused. "So what do we do now, milady?" he asked. "Draw swords?"

"Not yet," Rachida whispered back. "Our enemy thinks us their ally still. Best we see the state of our opponent before we act."

"Yes, milady," Quester said with a grin before falling back into line with the others.

The snowy path they traveled veered into the forest, revealing the soldiers' camp. There were numerous tents scattered about, and though a great many cookfires burned, the scent of food was noticeably lacking. It was the middle of the day, yet there was a gloom in the air. The tree branches above were weighed down by a thick coat of ice, glimmering in the murk like crystalline, skeletal fingers.

Men emerged from their tents as they rode through the center of the camp. There were so many of them. Countless eyes, deep-set and bloodshot, gazed hungrily in Rachida's direction. She felt a chill and shivered once more, pulling her cloak even tighter around herself. Many of the men were hunched over as if their spines weren't strong enough to hold up their bodies any longer. Others simply stood with their mouths hanging open, revealing rotting teeth and blackened gums. Still others sucked on handfuls of snow like sweet combs of honey.

It was one of the more frightening sights she'd ever seen.

At the head of the camp, set against a backdrop of trees with thick, imposing trunks, was a large pavilion. "Dismount here," said Nole as they approached it. The young soldier then disappeared into the pavilion. Rachida patted her horse and swung out of the saddle, then looked back the way they had come. The sellswords formed a line through the trees, the rear of the procession concealed by fog. Her men eyed the soldiers warily, fingers dancing on the hilts of the swords on their belts. They dismounted and gathered around the wagons they'd brought with them, those containing what was left of the provisions harvested in Conch. Karak's soldiers ogled the wagons, wantonness showing in their eyes.

Quester appeared beside her. His air was serious, much different from the flippancy he usually displayed.

"Get the captains," she whispered out of the corner of her mouth.

"All of them?"

"Yes. And be prepared for the worst."

The Crimson Sword nodded.

The captains of the other five sellsword companies gathered, nary a word spoken between them. A moment later Nole stepped out of the pavilion.

"Captain Blackwolfe will see you now," he said, gesturing to the tent flap. Rachida took a deep breath, then stepped into the pavilion, Quester and the other captains on her heels.

The men awaiting them inside looked like death warmed over. Their flesh was pale, eyes rimmed with purple, hair snarled into oily tendrils. The plate and mail armor they wore was rusting at the joints, and the roaring lion sigil on their chests appeared somber, not threatening. They looked like men who'd been lost in the wilderness for an age.

Despite their downtrodden appearance, the one in the center, a tall, lanky sort with a matted beard and intense eyes, smiled. "You came," he said. "You actually came."

"We did," Rachida said, though she had no clue what he was talking about.

The man stood boldly upright, as if he'd just remembered protocol, and bowed to her.

"Captain Talon Blackwolfe at your service," he said. "It is an honor to receive you, Commander Mori."

"It is an honor to be received," Rachida answered. Behind her, the sellsword captains fidgeted.

"Please know we appreciate your arrival," the man told her. "It wasn't expected. To say we're relieved would be an understatement."

The others in the pavilion hastily nodded their agreement.

A cold wind blew, billowing the sides of the tent around them. Talon Blackwolfe shivered and looked at the soldiers standing on either side of him, as if seeking guidance from them. It was such a strange thing. To Rachida, these men appeared much too green to be officers, and Talon was in no way captain material. He was too young, too gruff; a foot soldier, not a leader.

"Captain," she said, "what has been going on here?"

Blackwolfe gave her a queer look, glancing at his eight officers. "Were you not told already?"

"Would you prefer to waste my time with assumptions, or would you answer the question I asked?"

The man sighed, his shoulders slumping. "There were five thousand of us here, making life miserable for those spellcasting bastards in Drake. Casualties were low, supplies good. But then our first commander, Wallace Ball, was taken from his pavilion in the middle of the night. We looked, found some footprints leading to the river, but that was the last trace of him we've seen since. Not long after, Captain Joseph Marten took command and ordered us on the offensive.

"We were just meant to harass, you know. Those were Karak's orders—just harass, not assault. So long as the people of Drake stayed up here instead of going south to help Ashhur, we were doing our job. But our new captain wanted blood, though truth be told I think he was just spooked and thought he'd vanish like Wallace did. So we crossed the river, like good little soldiers."

Rachida had heard stories of the spellcasters of Drake, but had yet to witness their power. A part of her ached to have been here during the assault.

"How did you fare?" she asked.

To that, Talon laughed.

"We died, Commander Mori. That's how we fared. Arrows, lightning, fire, shards of ice . . . if it exists, and can kill you, they threw it at us. But we took the tower, just like Joseph said we would. Course, the only reason we took it was because the people fled back to their homes. After that they created a . . . barricade of stone around the township, and we've kept it besieged ever since."

There was defeat in his voice, and Rachida felt a morsel of pity for him.

"We brought our supplies with us from the Tinderlands camp when we crossed the Gihon," he continued. "But it wasn't enough for how long we've been here. There were less than a thousand citizens in that damned township, and after they sealed off their homes, they should have starved. But if they have, they're hiding it damn well. Us, though? Captain Marten died in our last attempt on the township, as well as his left hand, Remmy, which meant a duty I wasn't prepared for fell to my sword. Winter has driven the deer and elk into the mountains. We've lost more than half our original numbers, be it from sickness, arrow, or spellcaster magics, and Omar over there even caught a couple of the men roasting one of their dead brethren over a fire out of desperation." One of the younger soldiers, obviously Omar, nodded grimly. Talon said, "We dealt with those men accordingly, but the seed had already been planted. No one expects to find victory here, yet if we abandon the siege and travel south, we will die by Karak's hands for our cowardice."

Rachida knew she should be pleased with how poorly things had fared for Karak's men, but hearing the exhaustion and frustration in Talon's voice as he told his tale kept such easy emotions away. Lion on their chest or not, they still suffered and endured terrible hardships, and for what? Fear of Karak's retribution? When first entering the tent, she'd thought to kill them all, but now . . .

"You say we weren't expected," said Rachida. "Why is that?"

Talon appeared unsure how to respond. "Well, shortly after Captain Marten died, I sent word to our god of our troubles, pleading for reinforcements and supplies. We received word back from Karak's prophet three weeks ago."

"What did this prophet say?"

The disgust on the man's face was plain as the snow on the ground outside.

"That we are on our own now. That we disobeyed orders, and our current predicament is of our own making. The letter said we would receive no reinforcements, no supplies, though our mission hasn't changed. We are to keep the spellcasters here in Drake, and abandoning that duty will be considered treason against our god."

Rachida could plainly see the anger in the man's eyes, anger that was echoed by the other eight advisors in the pavilion. That was good.

"So you have two options," she said. "Remain here and perish, or flee and perish."

"Exactly."

"I can see now why you're so relieved we are here." She glanced over at Quester and the other sellsword captains. "Captain," she said to Talon, "I wish to speak with you . . . alone."

The man raised an eyebrow. "Very well."

Talon gestured for his young advisors to exit the pavilion, which they did without question. The sellsword captains, however, hesitated.

Quester leaned into her. "What are you up to, Rachida?"

"Trust me," she told him. "Now get out."

When they were finally alone, Rachida unlaced her cloak and removed it, exposing the Twins on her hips. She felt Talon's eyes on her as she made her way across the pavilion, tossing the cloak on the captain's desk. The man was visibly wary. She could use that.

"Tell me, Captain Blackwolfe," she said, "what do you wish to come of your predicament?"

"I wish to fulfill the will of my god," he told her, though his fidgeting and tone said otherwise.

"Do not lie to me, Captain," she said, removing her belt and placing her swords on top of her cloak. She then moved back to the center of the space. "Tell me how you truly feel about this, how your *men* feel. We are here now to help you. You will receive no punishment for the truth."

Talon leaned back in the chair, rubbing his temples. "You wish to know the truth?"

Rachida nodded.

"The men want . . . they want this conflict over," Talon said, nearly whispering the words. "Though a few of us have discovered the thrill of conflict, were born for it even, most of the men are cut from softer cloth. They had lives once . . . farmers, merchants, pages, blacksmiths, potters, bakers, miners. They lived and died and loved and lost as free men. Yet they are free no longer. We are all starving and near death. We've suffered in a wasteland for so long, and for what? To be told by our god that we are to be abandoned, that our lives are worth nothing because we followed our leader's instructions? How is that fair?"

"It isn't," said Rachida.

Talon seemed taken aback by the statement. "Thank you, Commander. So now you know of the men's wishes. What would you have us do?"

"I said earlier that you had two options, both ending in death. What if I offered you a third?"

"I would kiss you on the mouth, if that option did not also end in death."

Despite his obvious exhaustion, he smiled, and Rachida decided she liked him.

"I offer you an opportunity to live your lives as free men once more," she said. "The chance for this siege to end and for you all to walk away, fully supplied for the task ahead. Your men could cross into the Tinderlands and return home, or flee to some remote corner of Paradise. Those who have developed a taste for conflict can join me and my men and wage war against the very god that abandoned you."

At that, Talon started. In a single sharp motion he took a step back and grasped the handle of his sword, though he hesitated to pull it. His eyes flicked toward the table on which Rachida's blades rested, then back to her. Rachida made no move to claim them.

"Who are you really?" Talon asked, his voice shaking.

"Just who I said I am. Rachida Mori, a child of Karak's First Families."

"You speak of treason."

"I do."

Talon's indecision seemed to grow.

"Karak swore he would punish us for the betrayal."

Rachida forced a smile.

"Did he? Do you think he'll hunt down each and every one of you? Scour the lands, and for what? Petty revenge? Our beloved creator cares not for such things, and he cares not for *us*, his children. His war against Ashhur is all he loves. You have a choice, Captain Blackwolfe. Remain here in the cold and die, or take your life in your own hands."

"It's madness," Talon said, though his eyes began to show a spark of hope. "How would we even do such a thing? How would the men be fully supplied? Are your wagons fully stocked?"

"They aren't."

"Then how?" he asked, frowning.

To that, Rachida smiled. "The spellcasters, Captain. You said they aren't starving, so I say we find out why that is the case."

Talon shook his head. "It won't work. I told you, they'll kill you the moment you try to attack."

"Who said anything about attacking? I mean to walk up to their gates and ask."

"You're going to *talk* to them?"

"If you want this siege ended, if you want your freedom, that is the only way."

"And you're confident it will work? You think they'll listen?"

Rachida shrugged. "Look at me, Captain. Do I look like a woman men turn away from?"

Timidly, the young captain smiled. "I suppose not."

"It is settled, then. Tomorrow the deed will be done."

"And what will you need from me?" Talon asked.

Rachida grinned. "All I need from you is for you to keep your men in line. And dedicate yourself to me when this is all over with."

Talon shook his head as if he couldn't believe the conversation was actually taking place. "That I can do, Commander Mori. That I can do."

"You best. And please, Talon, do not call me Commander. Rachida is fine."

The captain was true to his word. When the sun rose the next morning, she found the soldiers gathered just outside camp, nervously fidgeting yet appearing expectant. Talon stood tall by a ring of stunted trees, gazing out at the white world that stretched out before them while stroking his mangy beard. Rachida approached him.

"What bothers you?" she asked.

Talon grimaced. "I mean no offense, nor doubt on your part, but those spellcasters can't be trusted."

"Your doubt does offend me, Captain. This Escheton will hear me out, and after he listens to what I have to say, he will open his doors and let me in."

"What will you tell him?"

She winked. "You have your secrets, Captain, and I have mine."

The man chuckled nervously and kicked at the snow, lifting a small cloud of it. "That's fair, I suppose," he said. His tone then dropped. "As long as you're true to your word. Should you turn against us, or return a failure, I can't be held responsible for my men's actions. Men are at their cruelest when they've had hope kindled, only to have it snuffed right back out."

Rachida stepped in closer, grabbing him by the shoulder.

"If you want to see cruelty," she said, "make such a threat again. I assure you, it won't be my blood painting the snow red."

An hour later, Rachida, Quester, Pox Jon, and Jon's second in command, a polite young sellsword named Decker, made their way across the snowy field outside camp, heading for the Drake Township. The mountains squeezed in on them from either side. The land they rode on was wide and flat but strangely bereft of wildlife. It was odd, especially when Rachida remembered the stories her parents used to tell her about the massive grayhorns that lurked in the upper northwest corner of Paradise. On her journey she'd seen squirrels, deer, a giant brown bear that assaulted one of their food wagons one night, and the ever-present wolves, but no grayhorns.

Finally, after an hour of trotting through the snow, they spotted a white mass rising up before them, like a wall made of pure ice that blocked out the horizon. The mountains to their left leveled out, revealing the wide and roaring Gihon River, its surface marked with rushing whitecaps. Pox Jon whistled while keeping a gloved hand over his face to keep warm.

"Is that Drake?" asked Decker.

"I would assume so," said Rachida.

"I thought Blackwolfe was exaggerating about the barricade," Quester said.

"Looks like he wasn't," said Pox Jon.

"Enough," said Rachida, her attention on the top of the white wall. She swore she could see movement up there, and movement meant defenders. The last thing she needed was an arrow or fireball to come flying at them while they were bantering like oblivious teens. "Eyes forward. Stay ready, just in case. And Jon, prepare the flag."

They paused a few hundred yards away from the structure and waited while Pox Jon unfastened the long pole from his saddle and Decker tied a dirty white bed sheet to the top of it. Rachida took it from Jon and set her horse to trotting once more, holding the pole up high so that the bed sheet snapped and fluttered in the wind. Quester kept his own horse close to hers, free hand firmly planted on the hilt of his sword. Rachida laughed inwardly at his futile effort; the Crimson Sword's blade would prove useless when faced with a twenty-foot-high wall.

When they reached the base of the fortification, all signs of movement ceased. They sat there for what felt like forever, staring at the white wall while their four horses whinnied and paced impatiently. Rachida's arms began to grow numb from the effort of holding the seven-foot pole, and a groan accidentally leaked from her throat.

"Let me take that from you," said Quester.

"Forget it," she snapped. "I do not need your help."

The handsome sellsword rolled his eyes. "Fine then. Be the martyr."

He hopped down off his steed and approached the snowy wall, stroking his blond beard as he did so. Rachida watched him, hoping he didn't try anything stupid. A low crunching sound could be heard when Quester broke the outer layer of ice with his fingers, and then his hand disappeared into the powdery stuff underneath.

"It's solid rock below," he said, removing his hand and shaking the snow from it before putting his glove back on. He glanced up at the wall and shook his head. "Looks to me like whoever's inside doesn't care we're out here. What do you say we ride around it, see if there's a way in?"

"There's no way in unless we *make* one," said a voice from above.

Rachida started, lifting her head to see at least thirty bearded faces staring over the wall at them. The one who had spoken, the one in the center, had a bright orange hat of some kind atop a head covered with wavy red hair. His lips played into a roguish smile as he took in each of the visitors in turn. "You'd think you Karak puppies would learn," the man said. "A flag? Surrender? Is that your new ploy?" The man's eyes lifted, scanning the trees on either side of the long clearing. "Where are the others? Preparing for a mad dash the moment we open a door?"

Rachida guided her horse forward. "This is no ploy. And we are not from Karak."

"Your men are wearing his armor," another of the men said.

"True," said Rachida with a nod. "*That* is the ploy. To get behind enemy lines, one must look and act the part. However, the one we seek resides behind your walls. Turock Escheton is his name. Are you he?"

The odd redhead frowned. "Depends. Who is asking?"

"Rachida Gemcroft, daughter of House Mori." Rachida bowed in her saddle. The pole she held wavered in her grip. "I am joined by sellswords from the east, an army of six hundred. It seems that you and I have things to speak about."

Those peering over the wall disappeared for a moment. They heard bickering through the thick wall of ice, coupled with long pauses of silence.

A few minutes later, the redhead in the funny hat reappeared at the top of the wall. "Seems our magic can't find anyone lurking about," he said. "So to answer your question: Yes, I'm Turock. Now disrobe down to your smallclothes, and I mean all of you, not just Rachida. Pile your armor and weapons in front of the wall. Come on now, mush, mush."

Pox Jon grumbled and made a fist. "Are you hoping to freeze us to death, or have you forgotten about the damn snow everywhere?"

Turock laughed. "Do you think I asked just because I want to see you in your skivvies? You're coming into our home, and we're going to make sure you do it without any hidden blades, scrolls, trinkets, or ancient rings capable of blowing us all to the fucking sky. So if you want inside . . . smallclothes. Now."

"Pleasant fellow," Rachida muttered, tossing aside the pole. She hopped off her horse, her cloak billowing, and began unlacing. She glared at her cohorts, who still appeared both offended and ready to challenge the strange man's authority. "Do as he says."

Grumbling, the three of them obeyed.

Swords and armor piled in front of the white wall, the four of them stood in nothing but the parchment-thin smallclothes they had worn since departing the Isles of Gold. The wind chose that moment to pick up, making Rachida shiver, but she refused to cross her arms over her chest for warmth. All eyes were on her, and as she'd learned in Conch, men of the west were the same as those from Neldar when it came to a beautiful woman standing before them. If she had to use her feminine assets, there were worse sacrifices she could make. Sure enough, someone up above whistled, and another man cleared his throat uncomfortably.

"Well, I suppose a bargain is a bargain," Turock said. "Back away from the wall a few more feet, would you? I'd hate for one of you to lose a hand or something."

They did, taking ten paces backward, bare feet crunching in the snow. The men peering over the wall disappeared, and Rachida heard chanting from the other side. A speck of light appeared before her, just in front of the wall. It was small at first but then grew until it became a swirling blue disc at least seven feet tall. Rachida gasped at the sight, her eyes bulging, a reaction echoed by the others. Five burly men then stepped out of the light, attempting to keep their eyes averted from her near nakedness and failing miserably. They tied the horses to a nearby tree, gathered up Rachida and her cohorts' armor and weapons, and then disappeared back into the blue void. Rachida simply stood there, confused.

"Come now," she heard the red-haired man shout from somewhere within the swirl of light. "I can't hold this thing open all day. Step through already!"

Quester glanced in her direction, shrugged, and jumped into the light, disappearing just as the others did. His laughter as he vanished seemed to echo all around her. Swallowing her fear, she followed him, wincing when the light hit her skin. For a moment she feared that she would be seared alive . . . until she landed on her two feet on a street bereft of snow, completely unharmed. Quester grabbed her arm, and she stood up to see they were surrounded by the men from atop the wall. The red-haired leader stood with two others in the forefront, their hands glowing, their fingers making strange gestures. A thud sounded, and Pox Jon and Decker emerged from the portal behind her. Both looked as bewildered as she felt.

Finally, the lead spellcaster dropped his hands to his sides and took a deep breath. The swirling blue portal behind them blinked out of existence with a barely audible *pop*. A young man with a beard nowhere near as impressive as the others' came forward with boots and heavy cloaks for each of them, and when Rachida slipped hers overhead, she swore she heard all in attendance moan. Turock, whose heavy robe was the same garish orange color as his hat, stepped toward them. He opened his mouth to speak, but Rachida cut him off.

"That was a fine spectacle you put on."

"The portal?" The man laughed. "Nothing, really. Simply rearranging some elements and cutting a hole through space and time. Easy as baking a baneberry pie. So! You had things to discuss?"

"Not here." She patted his shoulder and breezed past him. Those gathered behind parted for her, looking baffled and whispering among themselves. When she had passed them, she stopped and took in her surroundings. She could see the barricade was an earthen wall seemingly raised from the ground itself, just as Talon had said, circling the entirety of the village. The ice and snow that covered the outside of the wall were absent on the inside, revealing the drab brown of rocks and packed dirt. The village itself was large and bustling. Men, women, and children filled the streets, bundled up against the cold and acting as if there was nothing strange going on. She took them all in, noticed that none seemed to be starving. In fact, quite a few of them looked downright robust.

Perhaps even stranger, however, were the buildings lining the cobbled road. They were grand structures possessing a sort of unnatural architecture she had never seen before. Outhouses, shops, domiciles, gathering places; it didn't matter what they were, they were all constructed of interlocking granite blocks and topped with a thick layer of snow that only added to their impressiveness. Even in Veldaren and Port Lancaster, the most advanced cities in all of Neldar, there were no structures as striking as these. And lining the road were numerous poles, each topped with an odd reflective square that seemed to glow on its own.

"Is there a place where we can speak that isn't so cold?" Rachida asked as Turock hurried to join her side.

"Of course there is," he said. "Just because we made you strip doesn't mean we're bad hosts here in Drake. Follow me."

The odd man walked ahead of her, his hat flopping on his head, his robe fluttering. Rachida and her men followed, Turock's men taking up the rear. They formed a sizeable caravan marching down the road, and finally the people of Drake seemed to notice them.

Turock led them to a two-story building fronted with something that Rachida had rarely seen—four giant panes of frosted glass, at least eight feet long and five feet high. She marveled at the windows as Turock led her through the wide double doors and into the building. Glass was rare, a luxury for the wealthy in the kingdom her god had created, difficult to make and even harder to maintain. To have glass in Paradise, which by all accounts was a simple land where advancement wasn't necessary, went against her expectations. Then again, all of Drake exceeded her expectations.

The inside of the building was crammed with people. At least two hundred men and women filled the vast area, sitting at tables, drinking cups of wine, stuffing their faces with food. The scents of spices and roasted meats assaulted Rachida's nostrils, made her mouth begin to water. Turock noticed and chuckled.

"Impressive?" he asked.

Rachida glanced behind her as her men and Turock's filed into the building. The look on Pox Jon's face told her he was just as astounded. Even Quester looked overcome.

"It is," she said, whistling. "Where did you come across such a bounty?"

"Follow me, my beautiful Rachida, and I'll show you." He looked to his right and gestured to an ornate door cut into the wall. As he led her toward it, he called out over his shoulder, "Bartholomew, please get our other guests situated. Food for all, and have Margot prepare a bath if they want."

"Okay," said young Bartholomew. "Remember, Abby is expecting you."

"My wife can wait," Turock grunted as he grasped the door handle. "Have her come to me if she's impatient."

The door opened into a large study, the whole outer wall of which was one huge window. The space was filled with gemstones, each type stacked in its own pile. There had to be millions of them. Rachida whistled at the sight, and Turock leaned against the wall and folded his arms over his chest.

"What is going on here?" she asked him finally. "Where did these come from?"

"Your husband, Peytr, supplied us with half of it. He's frequented the islands off the coast of Conch for two decades now. My wife loves the ocean, and we visited Conch often, backward little village that it is. He often talked of your splendor, though it was in a bored sort of way, so I figured he was exaggerating."

Two decades? He'd been hiding his true wealth from her for twenty years! Add that to Peytr's attempt to have her killed, and it was yet another nail in his casket. "He does that. Exaggerate."

Turock grinned. "Not in this case."

She sighed. "So Peytr gave you half. The rest?"

"The rest we mined ourselves from the very mountains surrounding us."

"And the food? How large your stores must be!"

"Ha! We have no stores. All we have," he gestured to the piles of gemstones, "are these, in more abundance than you could ever know."

She looked at him, confused.

"Here, I'll show you," Turock said. He bent over and picked up a stone from one of the piles. He held the tiny, glittering green pebble between his thumb and forefinger. "So, Rachida, what is your favorite food?"

She gawked at him and squinted.

"Humor me."

After thinking for a moment, she said, "Roast quail."

Turock flipped the gem into his palm, made circles over it with his other hand, and whispered a few incomprehensible words. The miniscule gem glowed brightly, and then its form shifted. Before she could blink, a single steaming leg of quail rested on the spell-caster's palm. He reached out, offering it to her. She hesitated.

"Go ahead, eat it," he said. "It won't kill you."

She took the small leg from him and bit down. Juices filled her mouth, dripped over her chin. Even though the taste was somewhat dull, she almost moaned.

"I don't understand," she said after she'd swallowed.

The man's smile grew broader. "Magic requires give and take, and different minerals hold different properties. For example, the stone I just held was topaz, which is used in the conjuring of foodstuffs. It was one of the earliest tricks my teacher showed me, and the first that I taught to my own students. We've been mining the mountains for nearly as long as your husband has been mining the Isles of Gold, Miss Gemcroft. We have enough topaz within these walls to feed all of us for years."

"Oh" was all Rachida could muster.

"Now," Turock said, serious once more, "you obviously didn't come here to talk about food. What brings you to Drake?"

She swallowed, still tasting the quail on her tongue. "I need you, Turock Escheton. The gods are at war, and my sellswords wish to join it. However, we came here not to fight *with* Karak, but *against* him."

"And why would you do something like that?" asked Turock, looking curious.

"Because Karak does not have our best interests in mind. He has turned his back on his own principles and has lost the love of his children as a result."

"That's all well and good, but why seek *me* out?"

"Because Karak fears you and your students. Why else would he send a quarter of his army up the Gihon to do nothing but keep you busy?"

"That may be true," he said, shifting from foot to foot. "But the same faction you just spoke of still lurks beyond the empty grazing fields, as they have been for months. As I told the Master Warden before he left with half my students, *I will not discard all I've built.* This is my home, my life's work. I won't see it destroyed because Ashhur and Karak can't get along; the rest of Paradise be damned."

The statement was absurdly selfish, but Rachida did her best not to react. "You won't have to abandon it, Turock. Those soldiers out there are destitute and miserable. They've been abandoned by their god. If you were to open your arms to them, if you were to give them the means to travel back to their homes, this siege would end. You would be left alone."

"Is that so?" he asked with a chuckle.

"It is. I can broker a meeting between you and their leaders. You say you have enough gems to feed yourselves for years? Prove it. Prove your generosity. There is no love for Karak out there in the cold, Turock. Of that you have my word."

The spellcaster picked up another gemstone from the heap and bounced it in his palm. He seemed to be thinking long and hard, his lips puckered. Finally, he snatched the hat off his head and twisted it in his hands.

"Absolutely not," he said.

Rachida stepped back, her neck flushing. "No?"

"No. Why should I? Those people have tormented me and mine for *two years*. They're freezing? They're dying? Good. Let them. I'll use their corpses for kindling later."

A knock came at the door, and Rachida jumped. Turock let out a deep breath.

"Come in, Abby," he said, sounding irritated.

The door opened, and a short woman with curly hair colored a deep crimson breezed into the study. There was something eerily familiar about her. She was an attractive woman, in a cutesy sort of way, with dainty features and eyes the color of seaglass. She had an air of poise about her that made the simple blue dress she wore, rimmed with fur on the hem and neckline, look like a queen's gown.

"Turock, why must you make me come find you?" the woman asked. "Who are those men in the dining hall? You know I hate surprises, especially on a day when I had a special—"

The woman's voice stilled as her eyes found Rachida. She tilted her head to the side and frowned. "What is this?" she asked, almost growling. "Who is *she*?"

"That's Rachida Gemcroft, darling," said Turock.

"The merchant's wife?" the woman said, eyes wide.

"The same," answered Turock. "And Rachida, this is my wife, Abigail, daughter of House DuTaureau." The man smiled, but Rachida could see a hint of contempt behind his eyes. "It seems you two have something in common, being daughters of First Families and all."

That explained why she looked familiar. Rachida had spent many months with the woman's brother and sister when Patrick brought Nessa to Haven. For a moment, she pined over the son DuTaureau had given her.

Abigail turned her narrowed eyes to her husband. "What are you doing in your study, all alone?"

At that, Turock laughed. "The lovely lady wishes for me to offer food and supplies to the soldiers who've been plaguing us."

"Is that so?"

Rachida inclined her head. "It is, Lady Escheton," she said.

"For what purpose?"

"To end the siege."

"Is that possible?"

"It is."

Abigail again turned to her husband. "And you said yes, correct?"

"Um . . . no," the odd man replied. "I told her to piss off."

The crimson-haired sprite shook her head. She then shrugged her shoulders back, lifted her chin, and walked confidently up to Rachida, placing both hands on her shoulders and looking her right in the eye.

"He'll do as you ask," Abigail said.

"I will *not*." He very nearly whined.

His wife turned to him. "You will, and you'll do it soon. You'd turn aside an opportunity for a normal life all to hoard a few gems and satisfy petty revenge? How selfish are you?"

Quite, Rachida thought, but remained silent.

"It's not a normal life she wants," Turock said, face darkening. "She wants us to go to war."

Abigail's mouth drew into a thin line.

"My family is in Mordeina," she said. "Byron, Jarak, Pendet—our *children*—are there. You swore to me the only reason we did not aid them was because of the siege. We had to protect our people, you said. But if the siege breaks . . . "

Her voice trailed off, the silence full of questions and threats. Turock dropped his arms to his sides, head drooping.

"If the siege breaks, to Mordeina we go," he said.

"I thought so," said Abigail before looking back at Rachida. "I'm sorry if he was being difficult. Men can be stubborn and stupid. You're a wife. I'm sure you understand."

Rachida grinned but did not reply.

The next day, after the first solid night's sleep since she'd left Port Lancaster a lifetime ago, Rachida brokered peace between Drake and the soldiers of Karak. For a full day they held a massive feast outside the township's earthen walls as the weary soldiers ate and drank and even cried. *Harsh times make for strange bedfellows,* thought Rachida. Her words to Turock were proven true the day after, when the majority of the two thousand men departed across the roaring Gihon, filled to the brim with supplies the Drake spellcasters conjured for them. They had the look of hope on their faces, even though they were a long way from home, and she was certain many wouldn't survive such a harrowing journey in the dead of winter.

Talon also stayed true to his word, as the captain and two hundred others vowed themselves to Rachida's cause. Three days after that, when all the supply wagons were packed once more, this time including a hefty pile of topaz for the spellcasters to use to create food, they began the march south. Her six hundred soldiers had swelled to nearly eight hundred with the defectors added, and a glum Turock joined her along with twenty-two of his remaining spellcasters. He had pledged a promise to Abigail that he would return with their children. His wife, the rest of the townspeople, and most of the civilians, stayed behind in Drake, protected by their earthen walls and with enough men of magic to feed and protect them.

"To Mordeina?" Quester asked, trotting alongside her on his horse.

"To Mordeina," she answered.

"I'll be honest with you. I'm more than a little eager. Haven't had a good scuffle in weeks. My sword arm is itching."

The sun overhead was bright, and the air was warm for the first time in quite a while. For a moment she was reminded of Haven and the home she and Moira had built, but that thought led to another about Peytr and his deception.

"Mine too," she said, and kept on riding.

CHAPTER 20

The storm was on them. A freezing rain blew sideways, the wind howling directly into their faces as they peered over the rise. To Moira, this was ideal. The wind blowing toward them meant they were upwind from their targets, so they needn't worry about making too much noise. Any stray step or clank of steel would be covered up by the pounding rain and incessant wind.

"What are we facing down there?" asked Tabar. He had to raise his voice a bit to be heard over the clamor.

"There is a clipper, four barges, and many rafts," Moira answered. "Seventeen soldiers are working around the rafts. Looks like they're preparing to load them. And another twelve in red cloaks wandering about. Who are they?"

"Acolytes," said Gull.

"Acolytes," Rodin agreed.

Moira stretched, propping herself up on her elbows to get a better view. She and her Movers were spying on the docks built by Karak's Army for transporting their goods across the river, then to be carried by horse and wagon to the standing army half a world away. The docks were forty miles from Omnmount, and Elias Gandrem had said that the acolytes left Omnmount with the last of the autumn harvest weeks ago. Moira had been disheartened by the news at the time, fearing the sixteen tons of food taken from Omnmount would be long gone. But luck was with her, and when she arrived, she found the three storehouses packed full with dried fruits, salted meats, and crate after crate of pickled vegetables, eggs, and mushrooms. She still had the chance to deny her god his much-needed supplies.

One of the soldiers turned toward their position at the top of the ridge over the river's edge, and she ducked down out of sight behind a mound of dirt. For the briefest of moments she'd seen his face; the man looked tired, moved sluggishly, and Moira realized that these soldiers had likely traveled all the way from Paradise to bring the food back to their god's army, because Catherine had killed the few hundred soldiers who'd remained in Neldar. Danco sidled up to her, his long, dark hair sticking to his face.

"Why haven't they sent it all west already?" he asked.

"They haven't been able to." She grinned. "For once, fortune smiles on us."

"So what is the plan?" asked Willer.

Moira smirked at him. "We go down there, kill them all, and to the victors belong the spoils."

"That's a lot of spoils for just six men," said Gull. "What would we do with it all?"

Moira turned about, gazing into the forest behind them, sensing eyes on her. "Don't worry about that. Let's do what we came here to do; I'll figure the rest out later."

"Now *that* is a plan I can support," said Rodin cheerily.

A few minutes later, Moira was running along the edge of the ridge, keeping herself out of sight. The strategy was simple: She and the Movers would fan out, sneaking around while hidden by the many storehouses and boathouses, taking out as many sentries and acolytes as they could. Should anyone encounter trouble, they were to sprint for the open space closest to the river, screaming to alert the others. Then the rest would come running, and together they would fend off their attackers.

Moira knew it wouldn't come to that.

She reached a pair of wooden structures and ducked between them, using the slickness of the sodden earth to her advantage. She was able to move quickly, sliding from one post to the next while barely lifting her feet off the ground. She slithered on her belly once she reached the end of the structures, approaching the hill that led down to the docks. Freezing, muddy water splashed into her mouth, sending a sharp pain through her teeth, which were still sore from her recent sickness. A moment later she heard what sounded like a faraway grunt and an even fainter splash. Those down below would think it nothing, but Moira knew the Movers had claimed their first life of the evening.

There were two forms lingering by the bottom of the hill: a soldier and an acolyte. The soldier stood tall and rigid while the young acolyte squirmed, constantly squeezing rainwater from his soaked red cloak. The soldier was saying something, but she couldn't hear what. Moira remained on her belly, keeping close to the unkempt grasses as she inched along. When the soldier suddenly turned, she froze, thinking herself foolish for assuming it'd be so easy. He seemed to stare right at her, his face bathed in darkness as the rain beat against him, but a moment later he turned back around, his shoulders visibly slumping.

She was mere inches from them when she gradually rose to a crouch. The rain picked up, growing louder and masking the sound of her drawing her swords. When the acolyte looked in the other direction, she jabbed upward with her left hand, the tip of her sword dipping beneath the soldier's helm and piercing the base of his skull. Moira shoved hard, driving the blade into his brain, before quickly yanking her sword free. The soldier teetered forward and then fell. Finally the acolyte seemed to notice something was wrong. He took an inquisitive step forward, standing over the fallen man. "Pate?" he asked, sounding confused. Moira slipped behind him and crossed both swords in front of his neck, pulling backward. The blades sliced open his jugular, and the young man collapsed on the muck-covered ground, clawing at his throat as he gargled the last of his breath away.

Three down, at least.

Moira remained in her crouch, turning this way and that, searching for her next target. With the rain falling as hard as it was, she could see only vague outlines. In front of a storehouse she thought she saw three men hustling along. As she rose to her feet, she heard a screech in the distance, followed by steel meeting steel. Heart racing, knowing someone had been discovered, she leapt into action.

Of the three, she took two out quickly and easily, piercing one through the back and into heart, and the other with a wicked tear across his throat. In her haste she missed the killing blow on the third, her light sword whacking harmlessly off his gorget instead of piercing his throat. The surviving soldier wheeled around, and she caught his terrified expression in a flash of lightning. The man hacked wildly with his sword, but Moira was a blur. She parried his chop with one sword while ducking down and lashing out with her second. The blade carved a chunk out of the soldier's knee, where his boot met his chainmail, and he began stumbling. His sword fell from his hand as he begged for his life.

She was about to kill him when something collided with her from behind, sending her crashing into the pleading soldier. They both tumbled to the sopping earth in a wild tangle of arms and legs, and she lost hold of one of her swords as she fell.

Muddy water was in her eyes, blinding her, but she felt a tingling sensation in her gut and rolled to the side, away from the gasping soldier. The flat end of a pole whacked against the soldier's face, snapping his nose with a *crack* that could be heard even over the wind and driving rain. The soldier shrieked. Moira ducked into a summersault, avoiding yet another attempt to strike her.

When she got out of her roll she frantically wiped at her eyes with her sleeve. There were three short, young men in red robes pressing in on her, each holding a long rod out before them. Their movements were tentative and uncoordinated, and what she could see of their faces showed them to be just boys, the oldest thirteen, perhaps fourteen at best. *It doesn't matter. They're acolytes of Karak, and acolytes become priests.* Still, it was difficult to look at the frightened youths' eyes and not feel sorry for them. She backed away, holding her remaining sword out in front of her, hoping they would turn and flee, so she wouldn't have to kill them.

In the end, Gull did the deed for her. The stoic man appeared from out of the rain, his longsword swiping in measured arcs, cutting down each of the acolytes before he had a chance to turn. The deed done, Gull drove his blade into a fallen soldier's throat and then whipped it out before him, flicking the blood from the steel before sheathing it on his back.

"It's over," he said. He bowed to her and turned away. Moira sheathed one sword, retrieved the other, and joined the rest of her Movers at the storehouse.

All seventeen soldiers were dead, as were ten of the twelve acolytes, the other two having scampered off into the night.

"Should we give chase?" Rodin asked.

"Leave them," Moira said, kneeling beside Willer, the only man injured of their group. "The wolves or coyotes will find them before they cross the miles to the nearest village."

"What if they return?" asked Danco.

"Won't matter," Moira said, still staring at Willer. "They're two boys. Not a threat."

"I . . . I'm sorry," Willer blubbered. He lay in Tabar's arms, hands clutching his gut, which bore a deep, bloody stab wound. "I thought I had him . . . "

Moira met Tabar's eyes, and she mouthed her question. In answer, the seemingly unsympathetic man slowly shook his head.

"Hush now," said Tabar calmly. Willer obeyed, sniveling in silence as rain pelted his body. Tabar placed his palm over Willer's eyes, slid his dagger from his belt, and drove the blade into the young man's heart. Blood poured over Tabar's fist as Willer's body offered a few last spasms and then fell still. The deed done, Tabar slid the young Mover off his lap and stood up. The other Movers gathered around their fallen companion, heads bowed in respect.

"He died fighting," said Gull. "A worthy death for an unworthy man, for on this day, he was not good enough."

"Here, here," the rest of them answered, and then they went back about their business.

It was a shockingly chilling goodbye, Moira thought.

They hauled Willer's corpse, along with those of the dead sentries and acolytes, onto the clipper. After dumping a barrel of lamp oil onto the deck of the clipper and the four barges, Gull set them aflame. When the lines tying them to the dock were cut, the five flaming ships moved slowly south with the Rigon's current, like sluggish, indifferent hell beasts. Moira and her Movers proceeded to shatter the rafts with axes from the boathouse before setting fire to the boathouse itself, the barracks and the docks along with it.

Before long the rain stopped, and with the fires raging it was as bright and hot as a summer day in the delta. Only the stable and the four shacks housing the food stores remained untouched. Moira gazed at them, then the stables, and finally at the six rickety wagons sitting idle at the top of the rise. She thought of what Rachida, always the altruistic one in their relationship, would have done. *She would help as many as she could.*

"What do we do now?" asked Rodin, throwing his arm around her. "You've completed the task Lady Catherine set you to." Moira thought to wiggle out of his grasp but decided against it. Her emotions were still on edge after the deaths of Willer and the young acolytes. She would take comfort from whoever offered it, even if that someone was a cold-hearted bastard like all her Movers were.

She rested her head on his shoulder, pretending he was Rachida. The mirage almost worked.

"There are nine horses in the stables," she said wearily. "They're old, but they'll do to pull those wagons up there. I'll load them up with food and then strike out north. I'm sure there are many folks starving right now. I can feed them on my way to Veldaren."

"What's in Veldaren?"

She shrugged. "The king of Neldar, and hopefully Cornwall Lawrence's last surviving heir."

Rodin gazed down at her, giving her a knowing half smile.

"Don't look at me like that," she said, playfully punching him. "I promised Elias I would bring Laurel safely back to Omnmount to take her rightful seat. I'm not one to turn my back on promises."

She thought of her promise to Rachida, and her bed play with Penetta, one of Catherine Brennan's maids, and guilt snapped her mouth shut.

Thankfully, Rodin changed the subject as they climbed back up the rise together. "What of the rest of the food? It will go to rot eventually, if it doesn't attract predators first. Seems like such a waste."

"Oh, it won't be wasted."

"No?"

"Absolutely not."

"And why would that be?"

She smiled up at him, and once they reached the top of the hill, where the muddy access road stretched off to the northeast, she shoved away from the man and cupped her hands around her mouth. "Hey, all of you!" she shouted. "I know you're out there. Come show yourselves."

Rodin passed her a queer look, but she simply nodded to him and tapped her foot. For a long while there was nothing but the rustling of the leafless trees in the wind, but then a few shadowy forms emerged. There were only a couple at first, but more and more exited the forest on either side of the road. They were old men, women both young and old, and children; at least two hundred staggering beings, all wandering up to them with wary yet hopeful eyes. The children led the procession, a familiar disheveled boy at the front.

The rest of the Movers had joined them at the top of the hill by then.

"What is this?" asked Danco. His hand fell reflexively to his sword.

"Don't," Moira said. "They mean no harm."

"Who are they?" asked Tabar.

"The children from Omnmount, along with those who were hidden in the cottages when we arrived."

"What are they doing here now?" asked Gull.

She looked up at the stoic man and shook her head. "Surviving." She took a step then toward the approaching mass of humanity. They stopped in their tracks, staring at her. Moira nodded at the boy Slug, who grinned in return.

"There is food in the storehouses," she told them, raising her voice to all. "I will be taking some of what is in that one,"—she pointed toward the third rickety building—"but the food in the other two is yours to do with as you please."

A hundred disbelieving smiles stared back at her.

"Can we get it now?" asked Slug.

"You can," she replied. "All of you can."

The wary, the bedraggled, and the starving tottered past her and her Movers. Moira watched them with a smile on her face, each thankful gesture warming her heart. When they had finally reached the first of the shacks, she finally let out a breath and confronted her Movers.

"So what are you all going to do?" she asked. "Return to Port Lancaster? Find your way in a new town, with new masters? I hear there are many about in need of quality swords."

Rodin and Danco laughed at that, and Tabar chortled, but Gull simply stared at her with that deadly serious expression of his.

"We will do neither," Gull said. "Our place is with you, Moira. You have proven yourself to be greater than any of us." He withdrew his bloody longsword and crossed it over his chest. "Until you are bested, our loyalty lies with you."

"With you," said Tabar.

"With you," said Danco.

"With you . . . always," said Rodin.

It was an answer Moira had somewhat expected, but she was grateful for it nonetheless.

"Here's to making a new life for ourselves up north," she said. "But first, if you truly are dedicated to me, you need to find me a trained bird somewhere. We can kill all the bastards we want to later, but right now I need to send the last letter to Catherine before she makes my life completely fucking miserable."

CHAPTER 21

Hope and faith were two things Bardiya Gorgoros had always possessed in abundance, but even those were beginning to fade. He was exhausted, disenchanted, and in a state of constant, spine-rending pain, a creature made to stoop day and night while chained to three wagons, alone though surrounded by people, the shadow of the Black Spire falling over him as the sun crawled across the late afternoon sky.

They are toying with you, nothing more, he thought, yet he found it difficult to believe that was true. And songs of joy no longer sprung from his lips. He couldn't save his people, no matter what he sang to them. *I have failed.*

His brothers and sisters in faith milled about in front of him, serving watered-down wine and salt pork to soldier and elf alike. He looked on as Tulani Hempsman and a large group of Kerrian women, their gazes empty, slaved away over large steel pots, stirring and shifting a horsemeat stew. Behind them, just in front of the Black Spire, the men of his group worked under the watchful eyes of the elves, constructing a dais from disassembled wagons. *Tonight there will be a feast,* Clovis Crestwell had told him. *The largest feast Dezrel has seen in a thousand years.*

Of all his emotions, and there were many, confusion reigned supreme. They had camped in front of the Spire for nine long days, and each morning his people suffered a different form of torture. Some days it was constant insults and beatings, whereas on others the captured were wined and dined and treated as equals, even respected. One afternoon twenty married women were gathered up and taken by soldiers in the sand while their husbands, bound and gagged, were forced to watch. The very next day those same twenty fraught women were given fine elven silks to wear while they and their husbands were waited on hand and foot by the same soldiers who had abused them the previous day. After the sun set, none knew what would happen when it climbed the opposite horizon come morning. Some begged for death; other begged to be made servants, if only to know what would come from day to day.

And for all this, it seemed Bardiya was the catalyst. On the bad days Clovis would stand before him in the morning, proclaiming him evil, disparaging Ashhur's teachings, telling the people that what was about to befall him was his fault. On the good days he was proclaimed a king among kings, men placing a crown of woven wicker about his head. He became an object, a giant human tool and nothing more, useful only when needed. When the soldiers were kind, he was ignored; when they were not, his people lined up before him to receive his healing touch . . . a touch that seemed to be failing. With every man, woman, and child he mended, he found himself growing weaker, so much so that just yesterday he had failed to restore Jacco Bendoros's broken leg. He now watched Jacco limp across the assembly, his leg in a splint. A soldier, the one with the small scar on his cheek, helped him along.

"Do you not see what this is?" shouted a voice, and Bardiya turned, the harness around his neck creaking. The voice belonged to the elven prisoner they called Ceredon, a hundred feet away, strapped to a plank above one of the supply carts, with his arms splayed wide. The elf had been kept up there day and night, yet unlike Bardiya, it seemed nothing his captors did could stifle his rebellious spirit. He continuously railed against everyone, screaming accusations and insults until his throat ran dry and he could scream no more. But then the meals would come, another elf climbing atop the cart to feed him hard biscuits and water, and he would be right back at it again. Strangely, he was ignored.

"You are all cravens!" Ceredon proclaimed, and then he laughed aloud. "Can you not see? This is your last meal! The beast will devour you, and then the scavengers on the dunes will pick through your remains!"

Bardiya turned even further at those words, gazing toward the near rise where once he had saved Kindren Thyne, the Dezren prince, from certain death. He could see nothing but shifting white sand along the ridge, though he swore that every so often he could see a glimpse of something moving up there. He thought of the distant pursuers he had noticed on the horizon as they marched, and then of Patrick DuTaureau, the longtime friend he had turned away when he'd come to plead with Bardiya for help. At night, when Bardiya lay awake, he swore he could hear the jangling of metal and shifting sand in the distance, drawing ever closer, and though he passed it off as a trick of the frigid desert winds, a part of him still hoped it was Patrick, come to help, come to save him from himself.

No! There is no one man who can save me. There is Ashhur and there is love, or there is nothing.

If only he could truly believe that. His back began to ache once more.

"Open your eyes!" the bound elf screamed to deaf ears. "The goddess will judge you, and she will judge harshly!"

"Do not listen to him," said a gravelly, inhuman voice. Bardiya swiveled his head slowly, every muscle screaming in agony, until he saw a hooded Clovis Crestwell squatting beside him. The first child of Karak was wearing a white shawl instead of his armor. The loose fabric hung off him, and Bardiya could see just how sickly he truly was. More skeleton than man, Clovis's every bone was noticeable beneath his parchment-thin flesh. When he moved, his joints seemed to creak, like a wet twig being twisted. His eyes were sunken deep, and his lips had retracted, exposing his blackened gums and oversized teeth. He was death incarnate.

Bardiya turned away and closed his eyes.

"Come now, giant," said the horrific man. "Look at me. Look at how weak I am."

"No."

Bony fingers dug into his cheeks, forcing his head to turn. Bardiya was too exhausted to offer any resistance.

"You will," Clovis said. "You will look, and you will see."

"I see nothing," he said, his anger welling inside him. "I see a godless thing that will soon die, only to suffer for eternity in its own special pit in the darkness."

Clovis offered him a horrendous grin. "I thought you preached love and forgiveness? What happened to that? What happened to the *singing*? And giant, if I am to die, how will it happen? Will you destroy me?"

Bardiya almost lunged at him, but instead let out a deep sigh. "Your depravity will destroy you. The gods will not allow it. Why else would you be fading away before my eyes?"

"You assume much, giant. I am not the only one fading away." There was a bag at the man's feet, and Clovis reached inside it, removing a flattened piece of reflective glass. He then held the glass in front of Bardiya, chuckling. The red glow of his eyes intensified.

The face in the mirror was indeed that of Bardiya Gorgoros, but it was sunken now, the skin stretched, much like Clovis's. Numerous deep crevasses sprouted from the corners of his eyes. His cheeks drooped, forming jowls, and atop his head was a thick thatch of white curls.

Bardiya sat back, aghast at his own reflection. He was so in shock he knew not what to say; though he had never stopped growing, by appearance he had remained unchanged for more than seventy years. He slumped down, letting the harness carry him to his side. Realization came over him: The pains now running through his body were not his constant growing pains, but the ache of time, of life, of *age*.

Clovis laughed at him as he stuffed the mirror back into his bag. "Your god has abandoned you, giant, but I have not." The man leaned in close, and Bardiya could smell decay on his breath. "I once promised that you would bring *true* beauty back to this world. It is time you fulfilled your duties. The feast begins now."

With that, the man stood. His emaciated form hobbled away, heading for the now-finished dais in front of the Black Spire.

"Do not listen to him!" shouted Ceredon. "The beast lies!"

Bardiya was too busy wallowing in his despair to listen. *Ashhur, why have you discarded me? Have I not lived as you desired?*

A horn blew, echoing across the desert and drawing the attention of all to the dais. The people of Ang were herded to the front of the assembly while soldiers approached Bardiya and forced him with prods and whips to stand. He leaned against the roof of the wagon to his left, heavy chains clinking about his wrists and feet.

Clovis climbed the dais and stood in the center. The Black Spire loomed behind him like a portal to the underworld. All in attendance, prisoner, soldier, and elf alike, began muttering among one another. Clovis rubbed his hands together, and his eyes burned a deeper red than ever before, eliciting shocked gasps from his audience.

"This is a glorious day!" Clovis declared, his lips peeling back further. His voice was harsh, as if flames were ejecting from his gullet along with his words. He looked down at the three hundred people of Ang who huddled before him. "Tonight, we celebrate the end of our time together. Tonight, all sins are forgotten with a purging feast. When that feast is done, you will be freed." The soldiers grumbled; the elves, both Quellan and Dezren, passed suspicious glances back and forth.

"It's a trick!" Bardiya heard one of his people shout.

"No, no trick," Clovis said, his grin growing ever wider. "I am a . . . man of my word. When the feast is over, consider yourselves free souls in Karak's eyes." He folded one arm over his withered chest and propped the other atop it, fingering his chin as he scanned the crowd. "In fact, I feel a demonstration of trust is necessary. Your singing has brightened many of my evenings since we have been together, and it has saddened me that all but the giant has stopped. I wish to hear a song once more."

More grumbling followed, but no one stepped forward.

"Come now, can we not have some beauty during these dark times? I wish to hear a song, an innocent song, a *pure* song, the one about mothers and lions and mountains. You know the one."

A woman suddenly began singing, only to be hushed by a wave of Clovis's hand.

"No," he said. "I wish for *innocent* voices. Are there any children among you who will sing for me? Will you come join me, allow your voices to fill me with warmth? Should you do so, you will be freed . . . "

The man gestured to a group of soldiers off to the right, and three of them shuffled through the sand in front of the prisoners, looking each child up and down. Finally one child stepped forward, then two, then more, until there were seven. The soldiers climbed the dais steps, urging the young ones to follow them. Bardiya noticed one of the soldiers was the one he had healed. Clovis knelt down, kissing each of the children's hands before directing them to form a line on the front of the platform.

Bardiya's heart was overwhelmed as he stared at those seven angelic faces. He knew them all, of course: Keisha, Sasha, Minora, Robbet, Yassar, Boren, and Stev. They were all eight years old or younger, and their eyes were filled with worry as they gazed down at the audience of nearly one thousand. Keisha Hempsman raised her head, her eyes finding Bardiya, and she nodded to him. *This is for you,* her look seemed to say.

"Now sing," Clovis demanded.

Keisha and Sasha were the first to open their mouths, but soon the other five followed. The sound of their seven voices melded into sweetness and honey.

"On a crisp and chilly morn
the mother came to me,
whispering the secrets
of the wind and the trees.
She spoke of times past
And times yet to be,
Everything in balance
Everything forever free."

Bardiya closed his eyes, allowed the singing to wash over him. His energy seemed to return, the pain in his body subsiding. He even began to sway, humming along with their song.

"On a warm and vibrant day
a lion came to me,
whispering the rules
of how not to be.
He said go forth with joy,
he said you now are free
so long as you remember
in whom you believe."

He remembered the first time his mother had sung this song to him, when he was still a very young child suffering night terrors beneath the blankets in their hut. He thought of his father, the mighty Bessus, and how he had chastised his wife for filling young

Bardiya's head with foolishness. His heart ached, especially when the next verse began. His father had been right all along. It was beyond foolishness; it was a complete lie.

"On a dark and lonely eve
the mountain said to me,
you're all my precious children,
stretching from river to sea.
I made you full of joy.
I made you to be free.
So love each other, live with grace,
and no harm shall come to thee."

"Enough," Clovis said, his voice loud and shrill. Bardiya opened his eyes and saw the man standing behind the row of smiling children, his eyes bulging with excitement to the point of popping from his skull. Clovis whispered something to the soldier beside him, whose face paled, whose hands shook.

"No," Bardiya said, dread overcoming him.

Clovis shoved the soldier and grabbed the sword hanging from his belt with quickness that someone in his state should not have possessed. He ripped the blade free with a glare, and the two other soldiers, including the one Bardiya had healed, needed no more invitation. They too drew their blades and approached the children from behind. The crowd in front of the dais pitched forward in a frenzy, and those standing guard struggled against their mass.

"NO!" Bardiya cried.

Clovis lifted his eyes, and it was like they were on fire, they glowed so brightly. He stared right at Bardiya.

"I will set their souls free," he said. "Now let us bring some beauty to the world! The feast begins!"

The man reared back and brought the longsword across in a wide arc. Bardiya surged ahead, pulling against his chains, the ox harness, the wagons themselves. Tears streamed down his cheeks as he watched the blades, Clovis's and the soldiers', find purchase in innocent flesh. Keisha was the first to die, her head sheared clean from her neck. In a matter of seconds, there were seven corpses atop the dais.

Women shrieked, and the anger and dread of Bardiya's people spread like a disease. Gordo shoved past a soldier and climbed onto the dais. Bardiya saw the parents of the other slain children emerge from the sea of humanity, and his massive heart thrummed so hard that it might have shaken the earth itself. He thrust his arms with such force that the four-inch-thick iron chains binding them shattered. His mind went blank, and he threw his head forward, splintering the ox harness about his neck. His vision went red as he watched Gordo cradle his daughter's headless body, and when a pair of elves rushed Bardiya, he lashed out without thinking. He grabbed them each by the top of the head, even after one slashed at his wrist with his khandar, and slammed their heads together. Their skulls exploded into a bloody pulp that coated his hands even after he tossed their corpses aside.

"NO!" he screamed, shaking his bloody fists before him. It seemed the very heavens echoed his call.

More soldiers charged, but Bardiya focused on Clovis. The skeletal man was hopping up and down in what appeared to be excitement, his gaze aimed somewhere to the side. Bardiya looked that way, his blood racing, and saw men sprinting down the tall dune. They were dark skinned and brandished weapons of steel, and they bellowed their battle cry as they ran. He recognized every one of them.

Bardiya only looked away when a soldier stabbed him in the side. He reached down, grabbed the soldier by the leg, and then threw him as hard as he could against one of the wagons. The soldier's body crumpled like a dried leaf, his head spinning around on his torso until it hung there by a single, gummy thread. Bardiya yanked the sword out of his side, such a tiny thing in his massive fingers, and flicked it away. Four more soldiers and two elves came at him next from all directions. He swung his arm, and the thick iron chains still locked around his wrists pulverized two men's skulls. The rest he smashed with his fists until they were formless piles of flesh, bone, blood, and steel.

All around him was chaos now, his people fighting with their captors while the elves met the stampeding newcomers. Steel met steel with a *clang*, and the sounds of screams and the smell of blood filled the air. Bardiya jerked his foot, snapping the last chain binding him to the wagon, and hurled his body headlong into the fray.

In his rage his mind was on fire, his body young. There were none that could touch him, and though he was struck and prodded and stabbed from all sides, nothing could hurt him. Each time he saw one of his people put to the sword, his fury burst anew. He snatched up a Quellan, ripped his body in two, and used those two halves to beat the elf's brethren to death before continuing toward his destination: the dais, and the emaciated man who still jumped and laughed atop it.

Blood was in his eyes, the salt making his vision blurry. He elbowed his way through the bedlam, tossing bodies into the air, stomping them underfoot. When he finally reached the dais, he stepped onto it as easily as one would walk up a stair. He towered over the deplorable, twisted human, who rubbed his hands together as he cackled.

"This feast has begun!" Clovis cried.

Bardiya said nothing. Instead, he reared back and brought his fist down on the man. Clovis never tried to defend himself, never even attempted to dodge. Instead, he took the brunt of the blow, the side of his head caving in, his teeth shattering. His body crumpled like a pile of dry bones, the red glow from his one remaining eye slowly going out.

In a fit of rage, Bardiya kicked the mangled, shrunken body off the rear edge of the dais. He threw his head back and roared, then turned about. The battle still waged below him, and as he looked over the combatants, he saw a cluster toward the center of the countless struggling forms gradually moving his way. The faces in the cluster were those from his past, faces he had not seen in months. There was Loom Umbridge swinging a two-handed sword; Gale Lumber coming down on an elf with a maul; Antar Fidoros using a large ax to lop the scalp off a helm-less soldier, and countless others wielding weapons of their own . . . including Ki-Nan Renald. Bardiya narrowed his eyes, watching his old friend fend off attackers with a long, curved blade.

They had returned to him, all of them, at the time when he needed them most.

Bardiya got down on one knee, staring at the seven mutilated children on either side of him while swatting aside elf and soldier alike with his bare hands. He could feel Ceredon's eyes on him, gaping at the carnage from his plank above the wagon. Men and elves died all around. Ki-Nan and his pack emerged from the swarm, panting and bleeding. The others formed a protective wall, allowing Ki-Nan and two others to approach the raised platform unharmed, holding above their heads a long crate. If not for the current of hatred flowing in Bardiya's veins, he might have cried.

When they reached the dais, two of Ki-Nan's men hefted the long wooden box they were carrying, sliding it onto the platform right in front of Bardiya. Ki-Nan leaned forward, his dark hand touching the giant's massive foot. Behind him, the battle continued to rage. Ki-Nan said not a word. He didn't need to. The determined look in his old friend's eyes told Bardiya all he needed to know.

Slowly the giant reached down and unlatched the long, heavy box. He lifted the lid, and within he saw the gleaming steel of a seven-foot-long sword. It was the same blade that Aullienna Meln and the rest of the Stonewood Dezren had shown to him that day on the stony beachhead.

Ki-Nan stepped back. Bardiya grasped the sword's handle and lifted the heavy blade from the box. The steel felt cold to the touch, but there was an underlying burn that seemed to leach into his skin and set his nerves afire. It was the first time he had so much as touched a weapon of this sort, and somewhere beneath his anger he was both amazed and saddened by how natural it felt in his grip. He took a swipe with it while still on his knees, getting a feel for it.

"No time, Bardiya!" shouted Ki-Nan, pulling him from his private trance. "We are breaking!"

The giant's head shot up. To his right he saw small bands of his people scurrying away from the fighting, huddled together like a flock of kobo fleeing a diseased land. Wounded human soldiers were fleeing right behind them, casting aside their weapons as they ran. Bardiya watched as, to the left, the protective barrier formed by Ki-Nan's men slowly crumbled beneath the attack of the combined elven forces. Men screamed and blood misted in the air.

Bardiya gritted his teeth and launched himself off the dais. He soared, sword held out to the side, and landed with a *thud* in the midst of the carnage. The elves and the few soldiers who remained in the fight turned his way, and in that brief opening, those left of his people made a dash for safety. The Dezren and humans looked fearful, ready to take flight as the Quellan sounded their battle cry. Bardiya let loose a cry of his own, one that sounded like the universe collapsing in on itself.

He swung his new sword with a single hand, as if it were the scythe he had used to cut wheat in the days when he was much younger and much smaller. The strength he possessed was enormous, and he hacked through five bodies at once before looping the blade up and over, ready to attack again. His second swipe killed eight more, his third another five. The bodies mounted around him, their blood pouring from severed arms, necks, and torsos, soaking into the sand.

All the while the Black Spire loomed above them like the God of Death himself.

Those who remained of Ki-Nan's original large force followed behind Bardiya, picking off any who escaped the giant's devastating slashes. At one point the soldier whose life Bardiya had saved, the one who, along with Clovis, had then butchered the children on the dais, crossed his path. The young soldier threw down his arms, pleading. Bardiya sliced him in half from head to groin, thinking nothing of it. His mind was focused on a single objective: Kill, kill, kill.

It was visceral. It was liberating. It was *pure.*

As the sun began to sink below the horizon, the battle ended. In the aftermath Bardiya hovered over the heaped remains of his enemies. He shuddered and dropped his sword, marveling at the destruction. There had to be five hundred corpses strewn about the camp, and another two hundred injured, pulling themselves through the sand as they whimpered and gasped their dying breaths. The vast majority of the dead were elves, their perfect flesh hacked and shredded. Bardiya looked down at one of them, a Quellan who was still writhing, and stomped on his head, crushing it.

Dear Ashhur, has this always been my purpose? Is this *what you made me for?*

He flexed his hand, his elbow, his knee. Despite the sting of the many stab wounds and slashes that pierced his skin, he felt better than he had in ages. It made no sense, not when he had lived his life in constant agony from his forever growing body. Instead of making him feel vital, it only caused his newfound anger to rise.

"Bardiya," said a tired voice. "Brother, I am sorry."

The giant slowly turned, and there was Ki-Nan, kneeling with those who had arrived with him. Tuan was kneeling as well, and

Yorn, and so many of the others who had remained in Ang. Bardiya looked down at his old friend, breathing heavily.

"Brother, we had to wait," Ki-Nan said. "We have been wai—"

"It does . . . not . . . matter," Bardiya growled.

He glanced up at the remains of the camp, at Ceredon, who still remained, motionless, atop his wagon, at men and women dressing the wounds of the injured, at fathers and mothers crying; tears of agony for their slain children, tears of joy for those who survived. There was sound all around him, but it was wailing and moans and the final breaths of the dying that he heard. There was no singing. Somewhere inside him, he knew the songs of joy and love and life had died, possibly forever.

"If I am but your tool, your Grace, I do not belong here," he whispered.

"What was that?" asked Ki-Nan.

"Gather up all who can still fight," Bardiya said. There was ice in his veins. "Scan the dying for Karak's soldiers, find out what they know about the whereabouts of the eastern army."

"I will, but why?"

Bardiya cast his eyes to the north.

"Because I'm going to kill a god."

CHAPTER

22

The sun set over the desert, revealing a wide, cloudless sky filled with millions of twinkling stars. The Black Spire shimmered in the faint light, though its glow seemed strange, unnatural, as if the great and mysterious obelisk were somehow lit from within.

Ashhur's dark-skinned children were making preparations for their journeys ahead. The women, the old, and the infirm were given carts and horses to assist them on the trip back to their home by the sea, while the healthiest of the men—both those who had been marched as prisoners and the horde that had arrived later, bearing weapons of steel—mounted their own borrowed steeds to begin their march north.

Ceredon watched it all, still strapped onto the plank above the wagon. Everyone ignored him, even when the very cart his plank was affixed to was pilfered of useful goods. The Quellan prince's befuddlement grew. Unable to free himself, he struggled in his bonds as Darakken butchered the children, the demon instigating the spiritual leader of the Kerrians until the giant lost his mind and revolted. He'd been helpless when even more western men descended on the standing army, taking them by surprise, their ferocity and force of will helping to counteract the elves' and soldiers' far superior skill with sword and maul. He'd had no choice but to look on while the demon's decrepit human shell jumped and cheered atop his dais, seemingly overjoyed by the massacre going on below him until the giant confronted him and smashed the demon's skull.

It loosed a monster upon the land, he thought as he stared at Bardiya. *A creature powerful enough to decimate two hundred men on his own. Why would the demon do that?*

While all items of use were being packed away, Ceredon kept his eye on Bardiya as the giant worked his way through those who suffered with grave injuries, offering each one a healing touch before moving on to the next. The glow of his hands seemed faint, the healing not as potent as it had been when Ceredon watched him stitch back together the soldier he had gutted the day they'd arrived at the site of the Spire. Those who received his touch would struggle to their feet, still in obvious pain, and limp along until they joined their brethren. It was a gloomy spectacle, the cold yet determined expression on the giant's face. Just as in Dezerea, Ceredon felt guilty for how harshly he had judged these tortured people, and even guiltier for the harsh words he had shouted from his slab.

Why must there be such suffering?

"Such is the way of life, the way of the universe," came the reply. He wasn't sure if it was the goddess or his conscience answering.

In the end he received his penance. When the carts were filled and the horses bridled, the two separate groups complete, the Kerrians began their separate journeys. One of Bardiya's men pointed Ceredon's way, the giant having to bend down to hear the whispered question. He then stood up straight, gazing at the bound elf.

"Let him free," the giant said in a rasping voice that echoed throughout the sandy dell. "It was his voice we should have listened to long ago."

One of the soldiers came and scaled the side of the wagon, stood on the rickety roof, and cut his bonds. Ceredon slumped to his knees, throat parched, back and arms aching from his imprisonment.

"Water?" he asked the man who'd freed him.

"Bardiya said to let you free. Didn't hear nothin' about water."

At that the man joined his brethren, leaving Ceredon alone among the carnage. A silent command given, the humans departed the area, leaving Ceredon alone among the shattered wagons, innumerous corpses, and thirteen bound and dying soldiers of Karak who had failed to flee. Glittering above them all was the Black Spire. With the din of civilization now departed, he could hear the throaty purring of the sandcats as they stalked the area, drawn by the scent of blood and the promise of an easy meal. A cold wind blew, and a violent shiver rocked his bones.

A metallic *clank* reached his ears, and his adept eyes caught movement along the ruins of the collapsed dais. Instead of the sandcat Ceredon expected, a human form emerged from the wreckage. The man stood tall, cracked his back, and then brushed himself off. When he turned his way, Ceredon saw the man's face; the long, dark hair; the diamond-shaped scar on his left cheek.

"My prince, are you alive?" Boris Marchant asked.

It took Ceredon a moment to remember that human eyes could see nowhere near as well as his own. "I am. And I believe I told you not to call me prince."

Boris chuckled.

"Aye, that you did. I hope, given today's circumstances, you'll forgive me for the blunder."

Ceredon slowly climbed down off the wagon, standing uneasily on tired legs as Boris joined his side.

"You took your time freeing me," he said. "In fact, I dare say you never did."

"Apparently not. Again I apologize. I told you, I needed to wait until the moment was right, until it was safe."

"So you waited until the demon set off the giant and got his entire regiment slaughtered?"

The human laughed. "Well, let's just say that I didn't know *when* it would be safe. I had hoped it would be before my friends from the west launched their assault, but I had no way of knowing Darakken would be so . . . careless."

"You knew of the humans trailing us?"

"I did," Boris said with a nod. "The one who led them I've known for quite some time. He is a pupil of my uncle and a very capable man. He and his people have been following the convoy since we departed Ang, waiting for their opportunity."

Ceredon shook his head, trying to push through the cobwebs in his mind. Something wasn't adding up.

"They can't have followed us for so long without my brothers spotting them."

"They *were* spotted," Boris said, shrugging. "Darakken didn't seem to care. He laughed and told the elves to ignore them."

Ceredon turned his attention to the thirteen men of Karak still bound and gagged. Boris's eyes followed, and the scarred man frowned deeply.

"Give me a moment," he said, drawing a dagger. "I'll take care of them."

"No," Ceredon said, grabbing the man's arm. "The crows and sandcats will be here soon. Let vermin die by vermin."

Boris raised an eyebrow, hesitated a moment as if in disbelief, and then sheathed his dagger.

"Damn," he said. "I thought I was cold. So what now?"

"I was hoping you would tell me. So far you have been the one with the plan."

"That I am." Boris clapped the elf on the shoulder. Ceredon knew he should be insulted by such familiarity between a human and himself, but at the moment, he decided he didn't care. "Well, you're free to go, Ceredon. Return to your home and tell your people of the need for cooperation with the humans who share your land. My Connington uncles will be more than receptive to any talk of compromise between our peoples."

"We've lost so many," Ceredon said, casting his eyes to the dead. "Perhaps it is finally time we sought peace instead of bloodshed."

"I'm thinking that time was months ago," Boris said, winking. "But as they say, better late than . . . "

Boris's voice was cut off by a loud cackle that shook the sand beneath their feet. A blinding purple light followed, shining from the Black Spire and causing both Ceredon and the human to cover their eyes and turn away. The cackling eventually died down, the light dimming, but not completely flickering out.

"What was *that*?" asked Boris, his voice frantic.

Ceredon spun around and gazed in horror at the Black Spire. It was black no more, its surface a swirling cavalcade of dark colors that covered the surface like water over a stone. The stone rippled, and then a slender human figure emerged, dressed in a blood-splattered white robe. He walked unevenly at first, but slowly gained his balance as he climbed to the top of the wrecked dais. Ceredon and Boris were still standing beside the wagon Ceredon had been tied to, toward the rear of scene of battle, but even though he was a hundred yards away from the dais, Ceredon knew who the being was. Darakken laughed once more and threw back his hood, and Ceredon could hear no trace of humanity in the demon's tone. He watched as Darakken hefted a large bag from the wreckage, reached inside, and lifted out a giant tome, the same book that the beast had shown him the night he'd murdered Ceredon's father, the very same book that Boris had given to Darakken.

"Oh, shit," said Boris.

Ceredon picked up a discarded khandar and began to stalk toward the beast, slowly, cautiously. Behind him, Boris stood frozen.

The demon in its faltering human shell knelt on the pile of debris, the swirling light from the Spire making it seem like a wraith made flesh. The side of its face the giant had pulverized knitted back together, the jaw snapped back into place. It flexed its mouth, eyes burning with such brightness that it seemed to blot out the glow coming from the hunk of black stone behind him. Those eyes bore into Ceredon, a wicked smile coming over the demon's maw.

"The feast has begun," Darakken said.

Ceredon took another step forward, his insides burning with both anger and terror. Finally he'd had enough; he bellowed and began to sprint, khandar held above his head. The demon glanced up at him and raised its hand, and Ceredon was hurled backward as if struck by a boulder. He hit the ground hard and rolled, his momentum stopped by a mound of dead elves. His side ached, and Ceredon got up on his elbows, staring once more toward the remains of the dais. His thoughts were a muddle of confusion, and his vision shook.

"There is no interrupting the feast," Darakken said, scowling. The demon then placed the book down and whispered incoherent words of magic. The tome flopped open, its pages rifling all on their own until they fell still. The demon's gaze remained fixed on Ceredon, its rotten-toothed grin growing all the wider. It then lowered its glowing gaze to the book.

"'*In order to create worlds of their own, the gods require self-sacrifice,*'" the creature read, its voice like a bear trying to mimic speech. "'*Celestia placed a piece of her essence into the heavens, forming the heart of Dezrel. The world spun around that piece of the goddess, taking shape, growing outward, giving birth to the land, the mountains, the oceans, the rivers, the trees. Yet when the eon passed, that piece remained. Small, slender, it is most sacred.*'" Darakken lifted his glowing eyes to Ceredon and Boris. "So wrote the elves of ancient times; so wrote the man who penned this very tome."

Ceredon struggled to his feet, his fingers finding the dropped khandar and lifting it once more. He looked to the side, searching for Boris, but the human was nowhere to be found.

"Coward," Ceredon whispered. "What have you done?"

"He has given me a chance at new life!" the beast laughed. "The Black Spire is a piece of Celestia herself. Within that crystal lie the secrets of the universe, a gateway to realms long forgotten, a portal into the very heart of creation." The demon pounded a withered fist against its human chest. "Within lies the power to recreate the truest beauty that ever roamed this land, a beauty created by the great Kaurthulos himself!"

Ceredon took a deep breath and gritted his teeth. He then took off at a run once more, careening toward the kneeling creature.

Darakken watched him approach, eager. The thing looked like a child given a present, barely able to contain himself before opening it. The distance shrinking, it began reading from the book once more.

"*'Antidrok lakkath!'* With the blood of the children of the goddess that banished me, I shall be reborn!"

The beast continued to chant, its words becoming more and more desperate. Ceredon reached the edge of the smashed dais, let out a guttural cry, and leapt over the debris. He jammed the khandar into Darakken's chest. The beast threw its head back, its mouth opening wide, and a spiraling tube of shadow erupted from its maw with such force that Ceredon was thrown backward. He landed hard atop the corpse of an elf, knocking the wind from his lungs.

He rolled off the corpse and onto his hands and knees, looking on as the body of Clovis Crestwell deflated and then collapsed as if there were nothing left within it to keep its form. The living shadow that had been trapped within it writhed and billowed in the night sky, forming a giant cloud above the thrumming Black Spire.

So huge, Ceredon thought. *How did that frail body ever contain it?*

A primal scream seemed to emanate from the very air. The light from the Spire was bright, so bright it hurt to look; yet despite the pain, Ceredon watched as the living cloud stabbed into the pulsating rock. The Spire began to shake, fissures forming along its surface like cracks in thin ice. The corpse of the elf beside Ceredon quivered, as if something inside were trying to escape. Ceredon backed away from it on his hands and knees, watching in horror as the corpse's eyes exploded. Thick, coagulated blood seeped from its every orifice, flowing along the sand in thin streams.

Ceredon struggled to his feet, panic making it difficult to think. All around him the lifeless bodies of Dezren and Quellan elves performed the same perverted dance as the first, their blood spewing from their bodies until the combined streams became a great river flowing in the direction of the Black Spire. The thirteen human soldiers left bound by Bardiya's men writhed against their chains, screaming in agony as their blood burst from their eyes, mouths, and nostrils. Only instead of it joining the flowing river, it flew backward, as if the Black Spire deemed it unworthy.

The wreckage of the dais collapsed further as the river of elven blood surged over it. The dark fluid pooled around the base of the Spire, and the tall, pulsing formation of dark crystal began to drink it in. Its glow became darker and yet more forceful. The book Darakken had read from lifted into the air, rotating on an invisible axis, itself bathed in a strange light. A deep rumbling shook the ground.

Ceredon started running as the corpses themselves rolled toward the pulsating obelisk. He dared not turn around, not when he heard the sickening *crack* of bones being pulverized, nor the rip of flesh and muscle torn asunder. He kept his eyes on his goal, the tall dune that led west toward the very edge of Ker. Boris Marchant's words to him the first night he visited him repeated over and over in his head.

"Because after Darakken destroys Ker, he'll turn his back on his promise to your people. He will fulfill the purpose he was created for: devouring elves. Stonewood will come next, then Dezerea, then Quellassar."

Ceredon ran until the whole of him burned as he crossed the treacherous, shifting sand underfoot. When he reached the top of the dune, he collapsed, panting, and looked up to see a whitened cliff face before him, radiant in the moonlight. He caught the flash of feline eyes hidden within the softly blowing grasses at the base of the cliff. Sandcats. He clenched his teeth, ready for them to chase a helpless meal, but they did not. They remained where they were, partially concealed by the grass.

Hiding from the most dangerous of all predators.

A low, hornlike bellow sounded. Dread gripping him, Ceredon stood and faced the Black Spire. With distance it looked almost appealing: a fountain of swirling colors pulsed out of it like those in the sky over Mount Hailen during the winter northern lights. That appeal died the moment he spied the monstrous blob of writhing gray flesh, made from the remains of his people, in front of the Spire. Hoofed feet sprouted from the rear of the heap, and clawed, pawlike appendages from the front. A spiked tail grew like a snake wiggling from its leathery egg. The gray flesh took on a bumpy texture, and though Ceredon was too far away to know for sure, it seemed like scales slowly covered its hide. A backbone formed, rippling as it writhed, and pointed spines grew from each bulging vertebra. Last came the bulbous head, the snout growing outward, stretching to each side as a horrific face took form: wide-set black eyes, huge slotted nostrils, a hinged jaw. The still-forming thing threw its head back, opening its maw to silently scream. Teeth poked through the pink flesh inside its mouth, and a monstrous pair of tusks popped out from either side of its maw, creaking as they grew ever outward, not stopping until they extended far beyond its triangular, fleshy nose.

The shifting of its body wound down as it fell to all fours. Ceredon imagined bones growing, muscle tissue knitting together, organs sprouting from the combined remnants of nearly six hundred dead elves. Despite his horror, he marveled at the size of the thing. It had to be thirty feet long, perhaps forty given its spiked tail, and it looked like a ghastly combination of a bull and one of the giant water lizards that once roamed the Rigon Delta, but with the tusks of a grayhorn. The book was nowhere to be seen.

Silence fell over the desert. Even the wind seemed to die, as if Celestia herself were holding her breath.

The Black Spire throbbed a few final times, and then a high-pitched scream discharged from within. All light combined into a blinding white, leaping from the obelisk and swallowing the newly made creature. Ceredon threw his arm over his eyes, unable to bear its brilliance. And then, with a deafening boom, the Black Spire exploded. In millions of bits, it flew into the air, soaring for miles and then falling like an ashen rain. As Ceredon looked on, tears in his eyes, the last of the light faded, and only a blackened hole in the sand remained of what had once been a part of his goddess.

Through the dimness Ceredon watched the creature suck in a long, labored breath. Its eyes, formerly filled with shadow, began to glow, bringing forth that same red resonance Darakken had possessed when it dwelled inside Clovis Crestwell. The beast shook its head, snot flying from its bull's nose, and rose to its full height. Maw lifted to the heavens, it let out a booming roar that seemed to go on and on.

Ceredon fled west, one foot in front of the other, pushing his aching body to its limits. He didn't know what he'd do, what he *could* do. But he had to gather himself, figure out a way to keep Aully and Kindren safe. He had to protect his people. As the terrifying roar continued, he realized it was not just a primal howl, but a single word, stretched out and mutated, full of terror, full of exaltation.

"REBORN!"

CHAPTER

23

The snow had stopped, and Mordeina was quiet for the first time in gods knew how long. No shouts from the army outside their walls, no barrage of heavy stones, no screams and shrieks of the frightened and dying.

Ahaesarus didn't like it, not one bit.

The Master Warden pulled his heavy woolen cloak over his shoulders as he exited Manse DuTaureau. He gazed out at the calm night, taking in the eerie white world around him. From atop Manse's high hill, he saw Ashhur standing at the crest of the wall. The god's back was to him, white robe fluttering as he stared at the army that gathered across the valley. Ahaesarus lowered his eyes, reflecting on how the settlement he now called home looked so different. What had once been a rambling green land filled with rolling hills and small pockets of trees now closely resembled the village he had lived in his whole life, back on Algrahar, the same village that was decimated when the winged demons descended from the sky to lay waste to everything.

Ahaesarus shuddered.

He turned left and walked along the footpath circling the manse, his keen eyes observing. To the south there was the heavy gate cut into the inner wall, with seven-foot-tall stone barricades lining the road leading into the settlement. *Murder row,* Ashhur had called it. Much like the causeway between the two walls, should the enemy succeed in pushing through the portcullis, the tall barricades would hem them in on either side, and they would be helpless as Ashhur's defenders hacked away at them from above.

Fifty yards behind the gate was the bunker his god had raised, a six-hundred-foot long crescent that ran from the far side of murder row to well past Celestia's tree. The trench was shielded by solid rock on the side facing the walls; it opened on the other, allowing the defenders to hunker down inside and work on molding steel into weapons, or await their next shift atop the wall. Right now he saw the glow of a few fires inside the bunker as those still awake burned the midnight oil.

Farther east, in a slight vale, sat the remains of the storehouses where the winter provisions had once been held, along with the old well that had been Geris Felhorn's prison. The rickety storehouses were long dismantled, the wood used to construct the many huts that had risen up all throughout Mordeina. There were over thirty of those twenty-foot-by-twenty-foot huts down there now, each crammed with three or more families. Even on the footpath high above, he could still be hear the soft cries of children.

Ahaesarus walked north around the manse. Mordeina's frozen fields came into view, partly covered with snow and ice and partly muddy and dark, the result of Wardens painstakingly tilling the land with Ashhur's assistance, the god using his magic to raise crops to feed his children. Those crops were stunted, pathetic, barely enough to feed two hundred men, never mind two hundred thousand. The earth was used up, its nutrients sapped over the long year, and too much of Ashhur's energy was in use keeping the magical barrier around the walled settlement intact. It seemed even a god could not make something out of nothing.

Beyond the fields were the grazing grounds, where barely two hundred cattle, swine, goats, and sheep milled about, watched over by a small cluster of Wardens. Butted up against the grounds were the stables, where most of the fifteen score horses had settled in for the night. Ahaesarus sighed. When they'd first raised the walls around the settlement, there had been almost two thousand animals here, most owned by House DuTaureau, but also many others brought into the settlement by those seeking the protection of Mordeina's walls. With the stores all but used up, and crops a near impossibility, it had come to only the meat the animals provided to sustain the masses. Nearly four hundred of them had been slaughtered over the last month alone, even newly born calves and kids. Not even heavy rationing would slow it down. People had to eat, after all, and Wardens too. At this rate, they would exhaust their food supplies in less than two weeks. As for the horses, some of them had begun to die off as well, no matter the healing touches the Wardens gave them. Horses belonged in the plains, running and breeding and free. To be locked within a confined space was against their nature. The only saving grace was that whenever a horse died, one cow was saved from slaughter for another day.

The Master Warden groaned, seeing the distant Birch Forest nestled into the northwest corner of the settlement and the camp that had sprung up around it. A sense of longing filled him, for these were the last trees in all of Mordeina; the maples, elms, chestnuts, oaks, and willows, whose wood was much sturdier than birch, had been cut down to help build shelters and weapons. Wood was so scarce now, such a valuable commodity, that it was prohibited from being used for fires. The people needed to use hay and dried blocks of dung instead, which created an ever-present pungent smell.

A few people moved within the camp, which now included four large, white-topped shacks that housed the majority of the two thousand who lived there. Ahaesarus sighed. Patrick was down there somewhere, probably twisting and writhing in his bed. Ever since the brave and disfigured DuTaureau had seemingly lost his mind, his presence had become scarce in the southern portion of the settlement, where Mordeina's defense was being prepared. The Turncloaks kept a watchful eye on him, and they'd told Ahaesarus that the poor man was in a horrific state of mind after the death of his sister. Ahaesarus found that strange, as Patrick had learned of Nessa's death months ago. *Everyone processes grief in their own way. This is Patrick's. He needs time to heal.* Though truth be told, he wished the man would get on with that healing already. In his absence, Ahaesarus had taken on many of his duties, including his shift atop the wall at dusk. The combined efforts were rapidly eating away at him. He hadn't slept more than two hours on any given night in over a week.

If I go on like this much longer, I will drop dead from exhaustion.

Beside the forest was the enormous camp of those who had accompanied Ashhur on his long journey from the Rigon River to Mordeina. The white landscape was dotted with many heavy tents and rude hovels, positioned in square grid patterns following Warden Leviticus's design. This part of the settlement stretched out lengthwise for nearly a full two miles, butting up against the wall and reaching all the way to a hundred feet below Manse DuTaureau's high hill. By rough count, there were over a hundred and fifty thousand people residing in this quarter of the settlement, as Ahaesarus was always painfully aware due to the rancid odor of human waste constantly wafting from it.

Finally, Ahaesarus's eyes fell on the settlement's darkest segment, one that no one wished to acknowledge. Positioned thirty yards west of the inner gate and a hundred yards from the end of the populated area, this section was relatively small, cordoned off by a short stone wall that Preston Ender had ordered built. Within that cordoned space lay the corpses of all those who had died within Mordeina's walls. By last count there were almost six thousand bodies in there, from the soldiers of Karak—those whose lives Patrick and the Drake spellcasters had ended in the causeway—to citizens of Paradise who had perished due to battle, disease, or boulders falling from the sky. Ahaesarus had demanded they be burned to prevent their stench and sickness from spreading, but Ashhur denied him.

"The dead will serve their purpose," Ashhur had said, refusing to elaborate further.

Ahaesarus finished his revolution around the manse and found Howard Baedan standing in front of the building's front stoop, with King Benjamin by his side, both bundled in furs. The youth appeared frazzled, gazing with trepidation out into the quiet night. The steward's hand was firmly on the boy's shoulder, and whenever the young king shivered, Howard squeezed and shot him a disapproving look.

"Stand tall," the steward said. "Stand *strong*."

"But it's *cold*."

"It'll be colder when you're dead," Howard said. "You need to display strength, not whine like a child."

"But there's no one here to see me but you."

"Does my opinion mean nothing to you?"

"Should it mean something to me, *servant*?"

Ahaesarus couldn't believe the haughtiness in Benjamin's voice, couldn't believe the nerve of the child to speak to the Master Steward that way. Those were words that would have come from Isabel DuTaureau's mouth, not from a plump youth prone to bouts of whimpering. Even though the matriarch of House DuTaureau had been confined to her quarters within the manse, her sway over the boy king remained.

"You would be wise to listen to him, boy," Ahaesarus said, unable to keep his mouth shut. "You've experienced nothing of life, yet dismiss those with wisdom who seek to help you. Ashhur would not be pleased."

The boy's head snapped around, his eyes widening as he lifted them to Ahaesarus's approaching form. Howard Baedan, on the other hand, seemed unsurprised. He chuckled under his breath and offered the Master Warden an appreciative nod.

"Has it begun?" Ahaesarus asked.

"It has," said Howard, gesturing to the huts that rested where the storehouses once were.

Down below, people were exiting their crude shelters and trembling against the night's cold. Three men worked their way around each chalet, alerting those inside that their grim duties were about to begin. He also spotted a group of Wardens, including Judarius, marching across the frozen land, heading for the darkened area of festering death. Confusion abounded among them; what Ashhur had ordered them to do this night was unusual to say the least.

"Did you get what you needed inside?" Howard asked.

"I did." Reaching beneath his cloak, Ahaesarus removed a clay jar filled with a salve Azariah had made for him. "Smear it on your hands. It should protect you from any sickness you touch. A little bit beneath your nose will also help with the odor."

Howard cocked his head. "You wish me to join you?"

"Of course. We all must do our part," Ahaesarus said, and he pointedly stared at King Benjamin when he spoke.

Howard turned to Benjamin. "Go to bed, boy." And Benjamin did, casting a nervous glance in Ahaesarus's direction on his way out. Once he was gone, Howard relaxed.

"I'm tired of playing nursemaid to such a brat," he said. "Thank you for the invite. Getting my hands dirty will alleviate my frustrations."

"I thought you enjoyed being his mentor now that Isabel is no longer . . . a viable option."

To that, Howard let out a humorless laugh. "Isabel had her claws in him for over a year. Making the boy unlearn what she taught him will take time and energy, and I doubt I will have enough of either before entering my grave."

Hearing Howard speak so surprised Ahaesarus to no end. The man had been the house steward for more than twenty years. He assumed if any would be on her side, it would be Howard.

"Sir Howard, what of Isabel?" he asked, hoping to draw more out of the man. "I have not seen her since Ashhur banished her to her room."

He shrugged. "Who cares? The bitch and her husband can rot in their bed, for all I care." His gaze shifted up, staring into Ahaesarus's eyes. "And please, never call me 'Sir.' I loathe that title."

Ahaesarus was taken aback. "I thought it was what you *wished* to be called?"

Again Howard laughed. "Absolutely not. That was Isabel's doing. She was the one obsessed with the Wardens' stories of knights and honor and centuries of glory. I asked her once if we should perhaps take up jousting, for entertainment. In my youth, my friends and I would pretend to be the knights from those stories." His lips bent into a frown. "When she heard that, she laughed. 'Does Howard think he's a knight?' she asked. I'm a steward, as my father was before me. A servant in her eyes, and obviously those of our brat king as well. Servants aren't warriors. She made sure to remind me of that daily."

Ahaesarus placed his hand on the man's arm. "I am sorry, Howard. I never knew."

"You never asked," Howard said, shrugging off the hand.

The Master Warden and Howard descended the high hill, falling in behind the ninety-six men who had been awakened. By the time they arrived at the corpse pit, Judarius and his fellow Wardens had removed the long boards that formed a ramp leading up to the top. Within, bodies were stacked atop bodies, some fully intact, some missing an arm, a leg, even a head. The men lined up as Ahaesarus placed a glob of Azariah's salve in each of their hands. Their collective misting breath formed a cloud above them.

"Why are we doing this?" asked one of the men.

"Because Ashhur requested it of us," Ahaesarus replied.

"But *why*?"

"Do not question, just *do*," the Master Warden said. He turned to Judarius, nodded. "Break open the wall."

Judarius lifted a great maul he'd had custom built over the past month, solid wood with an enormous steel head. Walking over to a wall of the pit, he braced himself, swung, and smashed it in, exposing the piles of the dead. Another swing and the hole grew, granting them a wider entrance. The men slowly surged forward, clearing out the smaller pieces of rock, unblocking their path, and then they began the work Ashhur requested.

In teams of two, they wrestled bodies from the pile and carted them to the wide empty area in front of the bunker. The corpses were stiff, the bloat all but gone, and their flesh felt slick. Ahaesarus was beyond thankful for the cold, for it had kept the bodies from reaching a far more grotesque state of decay. Removing them from the carts, the men placed them on their backs, shoulder to shoulder in the snow. Ahaesarus worked with Howard, and was impressed by the man's resolve. He would always look at the face of the man or woman they carried, offering a softly worded prayer before lifting the legs while Ahaesarus took the arms. Never once did he grow green from disgust, nor did he panic or dump the contents of his stomach on the ground, as many of the others did. He remained stalwart and tough, a pillar of strength among much weaker men. Though there was silence between them as they worked, the Master Warden's opinion of Howard grew.

For five hours they toiled, hauling corpse after corpse out of the pen and placing them in three rows in front of the protective bunker. During the last hour Ashhur descended the wall, joining in with his children, lugging eight cadavers at a time. The god remained quiet, a downtrodden look on his face, which greatly concerned Ahaesarus.

They finished as the sun was climbing the eastern horizon, sending shoots of yellow and crimson above the walls. Howard's shoulders were slumped, though his eyes were still alive with determination. Judarius led the Wardens to the low wall surrounding the area where the corpses had previously resided, while the rest of the workers began trudging back to their families, with heads hanging. It was only at Ahaesarus's prodding that Howard joined them.

"Get some rest."

Howard sighed. "I will. And Master Warden . . . you have my thanks."

"And you mine."

Before he could leave, Ahaesarus reached out and grabbed him by the shoulder, holding him still.

"Howard . . . do not lose hope, and do not diminish your own worth. With you at the king's side, there is still a chance he could grow to be as fine a man as you are. Our kingdom would be blessed by such a fate."

The Master Steward hesitated, and then he smiled.

"Blessed indeed," he said, and then began the tiresome climb up the icy hill to Manse DuTaureau. Ahaesarus felt as tired as Howard looked, but he knew he should join his fellow Wardens in dismantling the rest of the low wall.

"Howard is a good man," said a powerful voice from behind him. "Only I fear he wrestles a darkness within him."

Ahaesarus turned around. Ashhur stood there, his long golden hair fluttering in the cold breeze. Brown blood and sticky yellow fluid tarnished his white robes, staining the image of the mountain on his chest.

"Then he is no different from all others who walk this land," Ahaesarus said. He pointed at the corpses. "Even you, your Grace."

His words sounded harsher than he meant, but before he could apologize, Ashhur sadly shook his head.

"I fear you are right, my friend. My children think our enemies evil men, but the works of evil men are cracked and small and easily seen. It is when a good man succumbs that the earth truly trembles."

Ahaesarus frowned.

"My lord . . . what is wrong? Has something happened?"

Ashhur ran a hand through his golden hair. "Bardiya has been broken. His soul cries out to me in anguish, in hatred, in self-loathing."

"What happened?"

"I know only that he has taken life."

Ahaesarus shook his head, confused. "But what does that matter? We have all taken lives here, even you, your Grace. Why should the son of Gorgoros be any different?"

"Because he *was* different," the god said. "Of all men in this world, he stood the tallest, and now he has fallen. I can sense his fury, his confusion. It may lead him to greatness, or it may consume him completely, leaving me nothing of the beloved child whose father I once lifted from the dust. Tragedy or triumph; is that not what all great risks leave us with in the end?"

His god fell silent, an aura of melancholy hovering over him. Ahaesarus looked to the rows and rows of corpses, knew he could stand the uncertainty no longer.

"Why are they here?" he finally asked. "This is wrong, all of it wrong, I sense it in my bones. What is it you plan?"

Ashhur met his eye, and in the depths of the god's stare, Ahaesarus realized there was an ocean of knowledge of which he knew nothing, and a debate fearful in its ferocity.

"My path is set," Ashhur said, his face darkening. "Do you ask for your own information or in hopes of dissuading me should the path be one that frightens you?"

The Warden felt so small, so humiliated. He lowered his gaze, wondering what had happened to the being of justice and grace that had saved him and his people.

"Forgive me. What are your orders?"

Ashhur turned to face Manse DuTaureau, and Ahaesarus saw Azariah was hurrying down the hill toward them.

"Prepare our soldiers," Ashhur said. "I sense my brother's fury. It should not be long now."

Not an hour after that, the final onslaught on Mordeina began.

CHAPTER 24

"*Where is it?*" Nessa hissed. Her red hair danced around her head like snakes. "*Tell me where it is.*"

"I don't know!" Patrick shouted back at her. "You're not real! Leave me alone!"

The wraith pressed forward, pus dripping from her eyes, her rotting teeth gnashing together. Patrick turned, but there was nowhere to go. He was surrounded on three sides by black cliffs that rose high into the heavens above him, cliffs whose surface seemed soft and malleable, expanding and contracting as if the very stone were alive. He backed up against one of the walls, and a stream of stinking fluid poured over his shoulder.

"Get away from me!" he screamed.

"*You would forsake me?*" Nessa asked. "*You never loved me. Look at what you have created, you with your malformed body and black heart.*"

Patrick lashed out, his fingernails digging into her flesh. The skin tore away with ease, exposing the white of her skull. Maggots crawled over his fingers. With a primal howl, the wraith shoved him backward. Patrick's feet tangled in the muck, and he toppled over. Nessa landed atop him, pinning him, vomiting putrid slime all over his face.

"Stop! Please stop!"

"The second gate," the vile image of his sister asked. *"No walls have but one door. There must be another. Tell me where it is, dear brother, and I'll leave you be. Tell me where . . . "*

Something heavy struck him in the cheek.

"DuTaureau, snap out of it, dammit!"

Patrick blinked, and it wasn't the wraith he was seeing, but Preston Ender. He glanced around. He sat on his bedroll in the long shack that had recently been built in their camp next to the Birch Forest. Sweat beaded up on his brow, and the whole of him was shaking. Preston knelt before him, hands on his shoulders. Behind the older man, the rest of the Turncloaks looked on with tired yet concerned eyes.

"Patrick, how do I look to you?" Preston asked him. "Am I myself or someone else?"

"You're you," Patrick said, shaking. "Ugly as sin, but you."

"Good."

"Was I asleep this time?"

The man ground his teeth together and grimaced. "Not exactly. Tell me . . . what do you remember before your delusion?"

Patrick breathed deeply, trying to gather his thoughts, but nothing would come to him. All he saw was Nessa's decaying flesh; all he heard was her voice, her pointed questions . . .

"Nothing," he said. "Last I remember, you were helping me into the shack after I collapsed."

"That was two days ago," said Preston. "You've been in here ever since."

"I have?"

Preston nodded. "You were rife with fever. Ryann and Joff took turns wetting you down."

"I thought you said I wasn't sleeping."

"You weren't. You awoke after we returned from supping with the others. You seemed in good spirits. You told us about the time you took your sister to the delta and ran across the bandits attacking Crian Crestwell's wagon, the day he handed you your sword."

"I don't remember any of that," Patrick said in disgust. "What happened after?"

"You just . . . drifted away. Began mumbling, but your eyes were open. An hour ago you started thrashing, and I tried to restrain you, but you shoved me off. Then you started asking me nonsense about hidden gates. What is it that *you* remember?"

Patrick frowned, straining his memory. To have been out for so long, surely he'd dreamed many dreams, but it had gone by so *quickly*.

"I was being chased," he said. "By Nessa's spirit again. She asked me about a hidden gate." He looked at Preston gravely. "This isn't random, Preston. This isn't my subconscious or guilt haunting me."

"No?"

He shook his head vehemently, rapping his forehead with his knuckles. "Something is . . . *in* here, damn it. Something, someone, I don't know who or how, but Ahaesarus was wrong, he had to have been wrong . . . "

Little Flick stepped forward. "Mister Patrick? Are you gonna be all right?"

"Shut it, you halfwit," snapped his brother Big Flick. He yanked the large youth backward. "Leave the man be!"

"Enough, both of you!" Preston roared before turning back to Patrick. "These delusions have gone on for weeks. You need to speak with Ashhur. I'll go to him if you won't."

"Um," said Tristan with a frown, "I think that might not be possible. The god organized some big deal for tonight. Something about the bodies in the nook. He'll be busy."

"Then we interrupt him," snapped Preston. "This is more important than corpses, I'd say."

Patrick watched the conversation, his mind wavering once more. "We might not have to. I know of . . . of someone . . . who might . . . be of . . . Az . . . Az will . . . *go away*!"

Nessa stepped out from behind Preston, grinning her skeletal grin. Preston grinned along with her. Patrick's vision began to swim. *Not real, not real! Get out of my head!* But his brain reacted on its instinctual fear. His fist lashed out, catching Preston square in the face. The man fell backward, clutching at his nose as blood seeped between his fingers. Patrick rolled to the side, avoiding his sister's ghost when she lunged for him. His fingers found Winterbone's handle, the sword resting beside his bedroll. He yanked the blade from its sheath, shrieking as if a demon infested his soul. *Stop it, stop it!* his mind screamed, but he couldn't control his actions. It felt like he was being compressed, driven into himself by some potent outer force. His vision slowly darkened.

At last! an ethereal voice proclaimed inside his skull.

He felt his body turn, and he sensed words on his lips. *It's all right,* his mouth was about to say, words his brain didn't believe, but the Turncloaks were on him before he could make a sound. They shoved him to the ground while he thrashed, Patrick cuffing Preston's son Ragnar on the side of the head and kicking Joff Goldenrod in the groin. In payment for that, Big Flick clouted his misshapen jaw.

Stars filled his vision, and Patrick felt his eyes roll into the back of his head.

There was murmuring above him, but he could see nothing but blackness. Inside that blackness lurked Nessa. He clutched Winterbone tightly to his chest, like a lifeline. Why was he holding it so tightly? He bit down hard on his tongue, trying to force himself back to reality. It worked, at least a little. He chanced opening his eyelids just a tad and saw Preston kneeling opposite him, blood trickling over his lips and drenching his gray beard. Patrick rose up on his elbows. Every inch of him felt tight yet dulled, as if he were a guest in his own body. *I know you're in there, you bastard,* he told the invader in his head. No one answered, but he felt the presence nonetheless. It was wary now.

Patrick sat up with a grunt, his world wavering. It took a great effort to stand. His knees felt stiff, unresponsive. It took an even greater effort to lurch toward the wall and snatch Winterbone's sheath. He shoved the sword inside, shaking all the while, and held the scabbard out to Little Flick. The large young soldier hesitated for a moment, then took it from him before handing the blade to Preston.

The whole time, the other Turncloaks watched him in silence.

"What do we do?" Joffrey finally asked.

"Take me to Azariah," Patrick said, meeting Preston's worried gaze. "Fucking carry me if you have to."

Everything was a daze as Patrick's friends guided him through the cold night. It was everything he could do to stay upright on his horse, Big and Little Flick riding on either side of him in case he fell over.

There was pressure behind his eyes, and he squeezed them shut. *You won't see,* he told the invader in his head. *I won't let you.* Eventually the pressure relented, and he allowed himself to look at his surroundings once more. Even the darkness seemed much too dark, and he caught a flash of red in the distance, dashing through the black.

Not this time. Not . . . this . . . time.

Preston led the group up Manse DuTaureau's high hill, and the Flicks helped Patrick out of the saddle once they reached the top. The two large boys supported him on either side, nearly carrying him through the front doors after Preston opened them. The rest of the Turncloaks followed behind them in silence. Patrick could almost feel their concern.

"Azariah!" Preston bellowed as they walked through the manse. The old soldier had Winterbone balanced across his arms, and Patrick eyed the sword greedily. "Azariah, come quickly! You're needed!"

Patrick heard a few people yelp from somewhere deep in the manse, obviously surprised by the sudden intrusion at such a late hour. Patrick hoped his other sisters had the good sense to stay in their rooms. In no way did he want them to see him in such a state.

Finally, the short Warden appeared as they approached the makeshift throne room at the far end of the manse. Azariah stood watching them, a look of bemusement on his face, the white robes that he now always wore draped around him. Patrick eyed him weakly, feeling drunk, his head bobbing from side to side.

"What happened?" Azariah asked.

"I . . . we're not sure," said Preston. "Patrick wants you to look him over."

Azariah leaned over Patrick, hesitated a moment, and then stepped back, eyes widening. "Quickly, bring him inside."

The Flicks lugged him through the doors and set him down on the slab upon which Ashhur had once been laid. The Turncloaks stepped back as Azariah went to work, checking Patrick's pulse, feeling his neck. The Warden's lips twisted into a grimace. Patrick felt a wave of hatred rising up in him, followed by a desperate desire to kill Azariah where he stood.

"Flicks," he murmured. "You might want to hold me down . . . "

The next time Azariah went to touch him, Patrick's fist flung for his face. Thankfully for the Warden's sake, the two big boys were faster.

"He's feverish," Azariah said, seemingly nonplussed by the outburst. "How long has he been like this?"

"Weeks," said Preston. "Maybe as long as two months. He's not certain."

"Sickness?"

Patrick vehemently shook his head, which made Azariah's mouth tighten.

"He's been seeing his dead sister," Preston said. "Visions, nightmares—things like that. It's strange because . . . he said he thinks someone's in there with him. Is that possible? Ahaesarus looked him over a couple weeks ago but saw nothing."

Azariah gazed down at Patrick. "And you thought I could see what he could not?"

Patrick nodded fervidly. The Warden allowed himself a smile.

"I suppose I should feel proud of your confidence," he said touching him. This time when the revulsion came, Patrick fought it down without need of the Flicks. "And something is awry, I'm certain of it. It's subtle, though. I'm not surprised Ahaesarus failed to notice it, especially if you weren't as bad then."

"What is it?" Ryann asked. "What do you see?"

Azariah's eyes were closed as he spoke.

"It's like smoke coming from his eyes," the Warden said. "Little tendrils of it, so faint . . . but not connected to anyone afar. No curse, no ancient wards, just tendrils . . . connected to . . . "

Suddenly every single warning instinct in Patrick flared. He surged to his feet, flooded with strength he never knew he had. Both Flicks hurled themselves against him, each holding an arm, and even then it was not enough to keep Patrick from ramming his head into Azariah's chest. As the Warden stumbled back, more men grabbed hold of Patrick, slamming him down onto the slab. His every muscle tensed, Patrick struggled, screaming out mindlessly.

Azariah whirled around, still clutching his chest. *"Give me his sword!"* he screamed. Without another word he leapt at Preston. The old soldier almost threw Patrick's massive blade at the Warden. Azariah snatched up the scabbard and hastily threw it down on the slab beside Patrick.

"A hammer!" the short Warden shouted. "Anything! Something hard and heavy! Now!"

Ryann Matheson released Patrick's arm to hand him the undersized maul the young soldier kept hitched to his belt. Azariah quickly grabbed it and lifted it above Winterbone's handle. Patrick watched it all happen, and in his heart he knew—he *knew* what would happen.

"Don't!" he shrieked. "It'll kill me, you bastard! *It'll kill me!*"

Azariah brought down the maul. The dragonglass crystal adorning Winterbone's handle shattered.

A puff of smoke rose from the splintered crystal, and Patrick snapped back into himself. His hand recoiled, the strain in his muscles gone just like that. The fog in his mind lifted, and the dullness of his muscles faded away. For the first time in a very long while, he felt like himself. He glanced nervously to the side, searching for Nessa's ghastly image, but she was nowhere to be found.

"It's gone," he said, turning to the short Warden. "Praise Ashhur, it's gone!"

Azariah remained leaning over Patrick's sword and the broken crystal, his expression one of pure dread. "Dragonglass is a powerful mineral. Within it is a bit of the fire that created it, and within that fire is the very power that made the dragons. Two large pieces of it could create a gateway of sorts, and it can be useful in communicating over long distances. Also, if a piece is close by, it can be used to manipulate the mind of another." Azariah let out a disgusted grumble. "I allowed an old friend of mine to experiment with it on me once."

"Let me guess," said Patrick, sliding off the slab. "Would that friend be our beloved Jacob Eveningstar?"

Azariah nodded. Patrick grunted, squeezing fingers into fists until his nails bit into his palms. His anger made his neck grow hot.

"If Jacob or Velixar—or whoever—has been inside your head for some time, he has seen everything you have," said Azariah. "He knows our weaknesses and our strengths. And if he knows, so does Karak."

"They don't know everything," said Patrick. "He kept asking about a hidden gate of some sort, but I never knew if one existed. Does it?"

The short Warden leaned over and looked into his eyes once more, as if making sure Patrick was alone in his head. "There is a hidden postern gate," he said. "The entrance is just outside the birch forest, veiled beneath a false floor covered with discarded branches. It was Ashhur's last resort, a tunnel wide and tall enough to accommodate a whole fleet of carriages, if worst came to worst."

"Where does this tunnel end?" asked Preston.

"It empties out into a rocky precipice three miles from here, by the river."

Patrick leaned forward, grinning. If felt good to do so again. "Perfect."

Azariah looked at him quizzically. "Perfect?"

"Yes, perfect. Azariah, listen to me. I need you to go tell Ahaesarus what just transpired. Tell him that Karak likely knows everything about our defenses. And do it quickly. I have a feeling Karak won't wait long to kill us once and for all."

"And what will you do?" asked the Warden.

Patrick's grin grew wider. "For the first time in months I feel like myself again—and not just that, Azariah; I feel *pissed.* I'm taking whoever will come with me through that secret tunnel. We're going to loop around and attack the bastards from behind."

Preston grinned, and it was obvious to Patrick whom his first volunteer would be.

"This is reckless," Azariah insisted. "Such desperation is suicide."

"Might very well be," Patrick replied, rage churning within him. "But I'm tired of waiting here to die, and I want my shot at revenge. Your old friend has been tormenting me for weeks now, using my own sister against me. It's about time I give him a taste of his own medicine. He wants to know everything I know, see everything I see? So fucking be it. I'll cut off his damn head and carry it around wherever I go, no dragonglass required."

When the dragonglass shattered, severing the link, Velixar leapt back into himself, panting. He shook his head to clear the mist, then threw his chin toward the sky and screamed. The canvas walls of his pavilion billowed with the force of his rage. The red glow of his eyes dwindled.

So close! He'd broken the misshapen man, had finally been able to step inside his mind and take control, just as the Beast of a Thousand Faces had done to so many elves a thousand years before. Patrick's erratic behavior would have been at an end, granting Velixar an assassin on the inside. Patrick was far stronger, resisting far longer than the mutated wretch had any right to, and in the end it failed. Dragged before Azariah, it was only a matter of time before the Warden discovered the dragonglass crystal and destroyed it. Velixar felt the waste of too much precious time, spending all these weeks torturing Patrick, manipulating him, gaining only a few modest scraps of information for his efforts.

If there was one thing Velixar loathed, it was wasting his time.

He stood with a huff and stormed out of his pavilion into the cold night air. Pulling his robe about himself, he shivered once before forcing his body to be still. There were soldiers standing nearby, guarding against deserters, and he was High Prophet of Karak, the swallower of demons. The cold should hold no sway over one with such power. He could not show weakness before them.

Velixar gazed at Karak's pavilion looming over the camping army three hundred feet away. A rare fire burned within, making its walls glow softly. He heard Karak let out a groan. Velixar started toward his chosen god's dwelling, hastening his steps. Something felt wrong. Something felt *very* wrong. By the time he'd crossed half the distance, he'd broken out into a run.

He burst through the pavilion flap to find Karak sitting in front of the raging fire, his knees drawn up. The deity held his head in his hands. The groaning Velixar had heard was actually a growl that sounded eerily similar to that of the Final Judges when offering a sinner their special form of justice.

"My Lord?" he asked as he knelt on the other side of the fire.

Karak's eyes rose to meet his, bearing sorrow, frustration, and the exhaustion of eternity. As they stared, Karak's troubles infused his every fiber. Such a reaction. Few things could spark it, and in his gut, Velixar had a suspicion . . .

"The demon," Velixar said. "What has he done?"

Karak's jaw tightened.

"Darakken has regained its old form, in the flesh."

Just as he'd thought, then. Troublesome, especially if Karak placed the blame on his head. Had he not promised to control the beast? Was it not his journal that contained the required spell to bring back the demon's mortal form?

Speaking of which . . .

"Is my journal with him still?" he asked. There were many other secrets within, secrets he disliked the idea of the ancient demon reading.

Karak shook his head. "The Darakken will carry your book always, High Prophet. That book now lies within the heart of the creature it helped bring about. Just like the Black Spire, it cannot be seen again."

"What happened to the Spire?" asked Velixar.

"In the aftermath of Darakken's creation, the Black Spire was exhausted of its magic and shattered."

Velixar looked down. His journal was gone, and the Spire as well.

"That is . . . unfortunate."

"All is not lost," Karak said. "You have the knowledge of ages within you, High Prophet. You can pen your journal anew, if that is what you wish to do. As for the Black Spire, its loss is fortuitous. It was the Spire that created the desert at the heart of Ker, its power draining all life from the earth surrounding it. With it gone, the rains will soon come, as will grass and trees. Vibrancy will emerge where once there was desolation. Those lands will be truly hospitable once more."

"Lands that will soon be yours," Velixar said, realizing why Karak considered it a boon. Still, the loss stung. Velixar had hoped to prod the secrets from the crystal one day.

"Now that Darakken is whole once more," Velixar asked, each word tentative, "will it be joining us?"

"No," said Karak. He slid his legs beneath him and sat up straight, the reds and yellows from the fire casting flickering shadows across his face. "As if from a dream, I remember when we were whole and gave life to that . . . thing. It is nothing but hunger and desire, my prophet. It will not come to us. Without Clovis to help guide it, the thought will never even enter its head. It was formed for one purpose, and that purpose will take it to the Stonewood Forest."

"To slaughter the elves."

Karak nodded.

"Forgive me, my Lord," said Velixar, crossing his arms over his chest and bowing his head in supplication. "In my pride I thought to control it, to use it as a tool. Whatever consequences such failure deserves, I accept them humbly."

"You were a fool to think your power sufficient," Karak said, and his words burned into Velixar's chest. "But at least you now understand your foolishness. As for the ancient demon . . . for now it will spread chaos, and for once, I feel that chaos is exactly what we need."

That sounded like blasphemy to Velixar, but how could words of blasphemy come from the lips of a god?

"I don't understand," he said, figuring that a safe enough response.

"Despite all the horrors Celestia has allowed to fall upon her children, she still loves them. They are her creations, her greatest achievement." Karak's gaze turned distant, and he smiled. "Her focus will be drawn to the elves and their struggles. If she is prompted to intervene again, it will be to defend them, not Ashhur."

"Or it will cause her to loathe this war all the more," Velixar dared suggest.

Karak slowly shook his head.

"If she seeks to end it, then let her end it. I will not let fear of her guide my actions. All around us, this entire world is filled with chaos, but within the chaos I am learning to see threads of order. We can cling to this still, find opportunity even in the worst of hardships. This is one such opportunity, my friend, and one we must take advantage of immediately."

Velixar stood, his entire body shaking with anticipation. "What do we do now?"

"Everything has aligned, the threads coming together, with Darakken's creation the final knot. We have an army that will soon go hungry, yet despite our lack of resources, they have worked diligently. Though the magical barrier my brother raised still stands, I now have thirty-six towers and twenty-nine catapults, along with as many ladders and rams as we could possibly utilize. The time to attack is *now*, my prophet. Once inside Mordeina's walls, that barrier will be useless. Once inside those walls, the might of the demon you swallowed will at last be put to the test."

Velixar grinned. "I look forward to that, my Lord."

"Our strike will be quick and deadly. Before the sun rises, I want all divisions mobilized. Inform the Lord Commander of everything you have learned from the mutant's mind, of all defensive positions and resources my brother has at his disposal."

There it was, the mention of the malformed DuTaureau. Velixar opened his mouth to admit yet another failure to his chosen god, but Karak continued.

"This will be our day in the sun," said the deity. "This is the day that will usher forth a united Dezrel. Do not dwell on your failures or what you feel was lost. When Ashhur falls, when his people bear witness to my might and bend their knees, all shall be forgotten. Now go forth and ready the soldiers for what lies ahead."

"Yes, my Lord."

The sky above him was dark as Velixar withdrew from the tent, the type of deepened black that comes just before sunrise. He walked a straight line through the snow, the walled settlement of Mordeina a faint outline in the distance. No longer did those walls seem unassailable. Karak's approval had steeled him, had let him see that the outcome of the coming battle had already been written. They would storm those walls, and they would conquer the people within. For Karak was the god with vision—the deity willing to risk everything to bring about that vision—whereas Ashhur was a sentimental fool. It was that timidity, that naïve trust in feeble, foolish humankind that had led Velixar to choose the god of the east. Karak was the stronger. Strength led to destruction and chaos, and from destruction and chaos would emerge creation and true order. Might was visceral, *real*; compassion was a belief and nothing more.

Heart soaring, Velixar marched through the sprawling camp, seeking out the Lord Commander. The day of reckoning was at hand.

CHAPTER

25

The attack began as the sun crept above the horizon.

It started with boulders smashing against Mordeina's walls from all sides, pounding and pulverizing the thick stone. Ahaesarus raced along the western wall, shouting out orders, the warning Azariah had given him coming too late, the assault beginning too quickly for him to get all of his charges to safety. Though the walls remained standing, cracks soon formed. Just like the many times before, many of the heavy boulders soared over the walls as well, only this time, just as Azariah had said, they were not flung blindly. Each falling chunk of rock landed much too close to the defensive formations Ahaesarus had formed. The defenders scattered, Warden and human alike. The huts where weapons were hammered out and stored were pulverized. Boulders fell onto the fields in the north of the settlement, crushing the weak crops; smashed into their horse stables; dropped onto their dwindling livestock. Animals fled the destruction of their habitats, horses, cattle, pigs, and goats tramping through the settlement to avoid the death raining from above. Snow and mist filled the air. The people were thrown into a panic. All was chaos.

With one final *boom*, an eerie calm descended on the settlement. It had been by far the most extensive attack yet, with what seemed like five hundred boulders. When it ceased, Ahaesarus rushed up the stairs to the top of the wall, sprinting along the ramparts with Judarius by his side as they examined the damage. A great many cracks lined the interior of the outer wall, a few of them large enough to fit a man or even three through, but those would be easily defended. *Karak, you have misjudged your brother once more,* Ahaesarus thought with a smile. He then crossed the plank to the outer wall itself, gazing out at the forest that lay a mere quarter mile away, and his heart froze in his chest.

Skeletal branches snapped as giant wooden towers emerged from the frozen, dead forest. Soldiers of Karak, bundled in furs and grouped in clusters of fifty, shouted as they shoved their wheeled towers through the packed snow toward the wall. The five regiments he saw were evenly spaced, with at least three thousand feet between them. The archers among the soldiers raised their bows, pulled back the strings, and loosed their arrows. Ahaesarus ducked behind a merlon, eyes wide. The bombardment had been a brutal distraction, forcing those inside to cower while the soldiers moved their towers into position and approached the walls. Karak had spread out his force, presumably coming at them from all sides. So far as Ahaesarus could guess, the tall towers would be close enough to mount an assault in a half hour at most. Given the size of the settlement, he had no opportunity to fully organize their defenders, most of whom were positioned by the southern portcullis. By the time he gathered the archers and climbed back to the top of the wall, the soldiers would already be here, and given how much space was between them, the pitiful two hundred archers would be less than useless.

"Damn it," he muttered.

"Ahaesarus!" shouted Judarius. "We need orders!"

The Master Warden gazed over at his compatriot and saw anger boiling over in his green-gold eyes. Judarius was breathing heavily, his elegant hand held firm over the giant maul fastened to his belt.

For a moment he thought Judarius would leap over the wall, the sixty-foot fall be damned, and charge the approaching clusters himself, but instead his expression stiffened. Arrows continued to fly over their heads. Down below, the people of Mordeina, their wards, were screaming and running for cover.

"What is your command, Master Warden?" asked Judarius, and strangely enough, he seemed suddenly calm. "Do I fetch the archers?"

Ahaesarus tapped his fingers on the parapet's compacted stone. "How many towers did Leviticus report at last count?" he asked.

"Over thirty."

Ahaesarus chanced another look around the merlon and saw the wobbling tower growing ever closer.

"There is no time for archers," Ahaesarus said. "No time for anything but melee weapons and pikes. Judarius, go down to the people. Find the bravest men and make them lead. Have them gather as many as they can and bring whatever they have at their disposal—old tent posts, rocks, buckets of grease, anything—up here. Tell them they must delay the soldiers as best they can."

"They will die," Judarius said, his tone devoid of emotion. "These people are not properly trained."

"Does it matter? Delay Karak's men, Judarius; that is all I ask."

Judarius nodded. "Stay safe, my friend."

The black-haired Warden sprinted back across the plank connecting the two walls, ducking to the left and right to avoid the flying arrows, until he disappeared over the stairs. Ahaesarus took a deep breath, counted to ten, and then began to run south along the wall walk. He stayed as low as he could, but it was difficult to stay below the merlons and move at a decent speed. A sharpened arrowhead grazed his back, slicing through his thick leather surcoat and opening a small wound across his spine. He barely felt it. His booted feet crunched on the snow packed on the wall walk. Sweat poured down his face despite the cold.

The wall was long, the distance far, and Ahaesarus forced his legs to churn. He gave up on his hunched run and stood up straight, allowing his long, loping strides to carry him farther and faster. Ashhur's booming voice filled his head, the god magnifying his voice to relay commands to his children spread throughout the settlement. Ahead and behind he saw people climbing to the top of the wall, men with tall wooden shields protecting the spellcasters from Drake in their drooping furs. Strangely, he didn't see an archer among them. Arrows *thunked* into the shields, causing those bearing them to waver. Ahaesarus then looked on as the hands of the spellcasters began to glow. One by one, the stone planks connecting the inner and outer walls exploded in a rain of pebble and dust.

Ahaesarus ran faster.

An arrow passed in front of his eyes, startling him and causing him to lose his footing. He slid forward on his hands and knees, the sword on his hip dragging through the snow behind him. His mind racing, he scampered back to his feet and kept on going. Celestia's tree, rising above the wall like a broken guardian with half its branches snapped off by hurled boulders, was a half mile ahead of him. If he simply kept his feet moving and was lucky, he would be there in minutes.

Minutes are all we have. He chanced a look out at the valley outside Mordeina. He had passed by the dead forest, and now the sprawling white world to the south opened up before him. Thousands of soldiers, like black ants on a white backdrop, rushed the walls. Their camp stretched from one corner of the land to the other on the horizon. Over the rush of blood in his ears, he heard the soldiers chanting their warbling battle cries. He was once more reminded of the winged demons descending on Algrahar, the memory filling him with crushing hopelessness. Death from above or death from below—it didn't matter. Both ended in the same way: with the destruction of everything he knew and loved.

No! he told himself, catching a glimpse of Ashhur pacing in front of the lengthy bunker, instructing his children to defend. This time they could fight back. *This time, there is a god on our side.*

Past a chunked and crumbling section of the wall he flew, Celestia's tree growing larger and larger in his sight. The inner rampart was now crowded with people, his wards and fellow Wardens alike, working feverishly at lugging heavy pots of bubbling grease along the slippery walk or hammering away at the stone planks the spellcasters had yet to destroy.

The arrows had ceased flying once he finally reached Celestia's tree. He nearly separated his shoulder when he collided with its steel-hard trunk. He immediately climbed to the top of the nearest merlon, grabbing a thick branch for support. He had been correct: From this vantage point, he could see eight towers approaching, each pushed by regiments of fifty. A massive phalanx of what looked to be five thousand soldiers marched behind the towers. He heard a heavy *thud* from below and leaned over the wall. His breath caught in his throat. There was a veritable hive of soldiers pressing against the base of the outer wall, some hammering away with large mallets at the weakened sections while others nailed differing lengths of ladder together. His gaze shifted, and just below him he saw at least a hundred elves on horseback. Their leader, the largest elf he had ever seen, with scaly black armor and a pair of wicked swords crisscrossed on his back, shouted orders. Thirty of the elves dismounted, snatching ropes from their saddlebags. One by one, they tossed the ropes over the lowest branches of Celestia's tree, pulling them taut.

And then they began to climb.

"Warden!" he heard a man's voice shout over the din of crashing hammers and jangling armor. Ahaesarus lifted his gaze. Right in front of him, fifty feet away and slowly closing in, was a wobbling tower. The cloaked man standing atop it had glowing red eyes and black hair that seemed to whip about like writhing snakes.

Ahaesarus recognized the man's slender jaw, his easy posture, the intensity of his stare.

"Jacob." Ahaesarus's voice was a wisp.

The First Man smiled and lifted his hands. Shadow oozed from his fingers, forming a swirling ball before him, growing larger and larger by the moment. Jacob then thrust his hands forward, and the ball shot through the air, straight for Ahaesarus's head.

The ball of shadow was thick, its surface shiny and rippling like oil. Ahaesarus saw faces in the sphere, those of his long-dead wife and children, and their screaming visages held him fast. A loud hum shook him as the sphere collided with the invisible barrier Ashhur had raised. A sound like the shrieking of a thousand murdered souls filled the air as the ball of shadow exploded outward, creating a web of writhing black smears that hovered in mid-air before gradually fading into nothingness. Ahaesarus took a step backward, his heart pounding, his thoughts awash with revulsion.

Atop the approaching tower, Jacob Eveningstar laughed.

"Master Warden!" someone called out from behind him, and Ahaesarus whirled around. A crowd had gathered on the inner wall walk, their expressions just as horrified as he felt. A spellcaster was standing there among them—Potrel Longshanks, one of the original four from Drake. The man inclined his head at Ahaesarus, tugging on his thick, bushy beard.

"Master Warden," he said again, pointing at the stone plank he stood before.

Ahaesarus needed no further instruction. He dashed across the plank; it was not even a second after his feet left it that Potrel decimated the stone catwalk with a flash of blinding blue light. Ahaesarus shook his head, trying to dismiss the stars in his vision as he weaved in and out of the frightened cluster of defenders who busied themselves on the wall walk. Then the first of the towers collided with the outer wall, and soldiers began climbing over the ramparts, steel drawn. All around him, people screamed. Ahaesarus grabbed the handle of his sword, and torn, he struggled with what he should do. He heard Wardens shouting orders, Mennon and Florio among them. Ashhur then called out his name from somewhere down below, and Ahaesarus spun around.

Down the steps he flew, his feet slipping on the ice-slathered stone. When he reached the bottom, he hastened across the long section where the thousands of dead bodies had been laid out in a macabre display. His stomach cramped, doubling him over, but still he kept his eye on his destination: the long bunker, and the god who stood with hands on hips, his golden eyes aglow, behind it.

Ahaesarus leapt over the stone barricade, landing on both feet on the other side, glancing to the right and the left. Hundreds of people were hustling about, bundles of freshly fletched arrows in their arms and steel slung over their shoulders. Nearly to a man, their eyes were wide with fright. Ahaesarus turned to the side and saw Ashhur a hundred feet away, staring at him. The god nodded. The Master Warden righted himself, standing tall and throwing his shoulders back while he stared at the masses huddled in the trench.

"Stand your ground!" Ahaesarus bellowed. "No matter what occurs, remember what we are here for! We must defend the innocents with our very lives!"

"We can't stand against all that!" someone cried.

Ahaesarus gestured to the side, where Ashhur stood, larger than life. "Your god is here to protect you," he said, spittle flying from his lips as he paced the line. "Accept his strength, and know that nothing is impossible when we stand with him. Karak may come at us from all directions. His soldiers may wield the sharper steel. *But we have righteousness on our side!* We have glory! We have *Ashhur*! For the sake of him, we will stand tall, and should death come to us, we will be well met in the Golden Forever, drinking our fill for eternity!"

A few muffled cheers came from the huddled masses. It wasn't much, but it was enough. Men climbed out of the trench, and a few women as well, their new steel clutched tightly in their pale fingers. They faced the southern wall, and it seemed for a few moments that all sound ceased. Ahaesarus glanced behind him to Manse DuTaureau atop its hill and saw a pair of figures, one tall and one small, standing outside the structure, surrounded by a mass of women and children who crowded together in the snow. The standing figures worked their way through the crowd, seeming to offer solace to the masses. King Benjamin and Howard Baedan. It seemed the Master Steward had continued his tutelage of the boy after all. For a brief moment, Ahaesarus allowed himself the very hope he preached.

A great horn sounded, and the dying began. Ahaesarus stood his ground, surrounded by his wards, watching intently for any sign of what might be going on atop the wall. He could see nothing but slight shadows and the occasional pike raised high in the air, but the noises of battle were unmistakable—the *thump* of blunt objects colliding with shields, the *clang* of steel against steel, the *thud* of men falling seventy feet to the frozen ground, the *crack* and fizzle of the spellcasters' magics. *I should be up there on the wall. I should be defending my wards with my life, not waiting down here for the enemy to come to me.*

However, he followed Ashhur's command, and the defenders seemed to be holding.

From his right, where seventy-five yards away the barred gate on the inner wall stood, he heard more shouts, these on ground level, only they were not wails of the dying. It seemed there were living souls down there. "They are in the causeway!" he proclaimed. He snapped his head around, looking to where his fellow Wardens were gathered. "Judah and Olympus, take twenty of our brothers to the gate. Bring pikes and spears. Do *not* allow the soldiers to batter it down."

The Wardens rushed off. Ahaesarus turned his attention back to the top of the wall. The form of a man appeared, hobbling into the gap between merlons where the stairs to the ground descended.

The man teetered as he walked, holding his stomach. His head flopped back, his arms falling to his sides, and blood and a mess of red entrails pitched from his abdomen. The man took another blind step forward, his foot missing the edge of the stairway, and he plummeted. His body folded over itself when he struck the frozen ground. His intestines, trailing behind him, landed wetly on his twisted form. Behind the Master Warden, someone vomited.

"Stay strong!" he called.

It was then that bedlam erupted. A bright purple light flashed above, painting the sky a lingering crimson, and the battle atop the wall spilled over the ramparts. Countless flailing bodies dropped from above, waving as if their arms could turn to wings and help them soar. Potrel Longshanks was among them, as was Warden Mennon, his tall, graceful form falling sharply. Their bodies struck the ground like a living rain, landing amid the rows of corpses, bones breaking, flesh torn asunder, their screams cut off as their heads were crushed. Ahaesarus winced and drew his sword. With measured breath, he glanced to the side, watching a virtuous glow envelop Ashhur as his flowing robes transformed into the god's immaculate plate armor. The deity raised his hand, and his divine sword sprung forth, casting a brilliant blue light over a land painted white, gray, and red. Ashhur climbed atop the bunker before him and threw his head back.

"KARAK, FACE ME!" he bellowed, and the ground shook beneath Ahaesarus's feet.

As if to answer him, Karak's soldiers began descending the stairwell as ropes were thrown over the side of the wall. *They must have used planks of their own to cross the gap,* Ahaesarus thought. The defenders were too green, too inexperienced, to properly defend the walls. Ahaesarus grunted just as Ashhur hopped off the bunker, taking menacing steps toward the center of the field of corpses. Elves swung over the top of Celestia's tree, flipping from branch to branch with ease as they descended. They were like an army of invading locusts, moving ever onward. Ahaesarus looked to the left and right, and saw that the very same scene was taking place all around him. His wards tensed, and his fellow Wardens began shuffling this way and that.

"When, Master Warden?" someone shouted.

"Soon," said Ahaesarus. "Those with swords and spears, out of the bunker now. Form up behind me."

The men did as they were told, passing the order down the line and gradually exiting the bunker to form a row of five hundred behind Ahaesarus. The Master Warden again looked to the field of corpses, this time seeing Ashhur stopped midway through, holding his divine sword out before him while he was peppered with arrows from both the enemy atop the wall and the elves near Celestia's giant tree. The soldiers continued to descend the wall, forming ranks once their feet touched the snowy ground, waiting for the rest of their brothers to join them. Their numbers swelled. There looked to be more than a thousand there, awaiting the order to charge.

Any hope Ahaesarus had felt earlier threatened to leave him. The sight of all those pale faces, of those armored shoulders rising and falling, of their steel glinting in the morning light, told him this was the end. Just then something hard thwacked his shoulder, and when he turned, he saw Judarius there, leaning with one hand against the lip of the bunker, his massive bloody maul held tight in his hand. His face was spattered with red.

"Soldiers approach from behind," Judarius said, breathing heavily. "There was little we could do to stop them."

Ahaesarus nodded. "What of the others?"

"The teams of Wardens guarding the northern wall are broken. Many are dead, and the rest are fleeing this way. I do not know about the rest of the settlement, but I assume it's the same."

Ahaesarus nodded again. "I know. It does not matter. They are here now, and we must fight."

Judarius lifted his head above the bunker, staring at both Ashhur, as he held his ground against the assault of arrows, and the massive throng of soldiers gathering at the base of the wall. The Warden shook his head, smoothed his long black hair with a bloody hand, and snarled.

"We charge now."

"No," Ahaesarus shot back. "You will do no such thing. You are to gather up all of Ashhur's children that you can, all those who cannot defend themselves, and bring them to the hidden postern gate. Lead them to safety. Protect them."

"No," Judarius said.

"You will do as I say."

"I will do nothing of the sort. You wish for a nanny, then find my brother. It's what he's suited for." Judarius stood up straight, slapping his maul against his free hand. "I was built for better things than that."

"I am your Master Warden!" Ahaesarus shouted, coating Judarius's face with spittle. He cared not that an audience was gathering. "You will do as I say, and you will do it now, or else—"

He never had the chance to finish that statement, for one of the soldiers lifted a horn to his lips and blew. When that bellowing trumpeting ceased, the army of Karak charged.

Ashhur stepped forward to greet the soldiers, looping his massive glowing blade, cleaving through flesh and steel with ease. Yet he did not kill many, for the soldiers gave him a wide berth, passing right by him and rushing headlong for the bunker. It was the elves who kept Ashhur distracted, continuing to pelt him with their arrows while others rushed him from behind and the side, slashing and jabbing and leaping out of the way of his blows.

"Now or never!" Judarius screamed, and oddly enough he was grinning. "Any who aren't cravens, come with me!"

"No!" Ahaesarus shouted back.

"We must fight, or are you a craven as well?" sneered Judarius.

Ahaesarus grabbed his fellow Warden by his collar, pulling him close. Judarius's eyes widened in surprise. "The time to fight will come," Ahaesarus said, seething. "For now, follow my orders."

Ahaesarus released him. Judarius stepped back, gripping his maul with both hands.

"Archers up," Ahaesarus ordered. His breath hitched as the soldiers drew closer. There was no time for second thoughts. He looked down the line and saw all of his archers were in place, arrows nocked. "Loose them." No one did anything. "I said *LOOSE THEM*!"

Ashhur's children heard Ahaesarus that time, launching volley after volley at the onrushing soldiers. Many were struck, some fell, and others used the bodies of their comrades as shields as they continued their stampede. Even the remaining spellcasters could do little to stop them with their fireballs and bolts of electricity. Ashhur turned his attention away from the elves and rushed the soldiers from behind, slaying many, filling the morning air with a bloody mist, but still they came.

The archers continued to fire, but they were hurrying their aim. Many of their arrows missed their marks, even though the soldiers were only twenty feet away and closing fast. The hands holding the bows shook, and tears streamed down the archers' faces. Finally, Ahaesarus had had enough.

"All of you, get back!" he ordered. In an instant the archers hustled from their positions, running behind the wall of men holding swords, spears, and axes. Judarius stood by Ahaesarus's side, huffing, his gaze intense.

The first wave of soldiers hit the curved barricade guarding the bunker. They were so close now that Ahaesarus could see every crease in their foreheads, every speck of mud on their cheeks, every starburst of color in their eyes. He offered no orders to his defenders this time. As the soldiers scaled the barricade, he simply screamed and pointed his sword at them. The men holding spears rushed forward. The soldiers who jumped first were impaled on the sharp points. Judarius and others bearing blunt weapons bashed in skulls. Blood spilled. The shrieks that filled the air were deafening.

Ahaesarus heard more screaming from behind him, and when he pivoted around, he saw the countryside awash with violence for as far as he could see. Soldiers of Karak and the children of Ashhur clashed, and blood soaked the snow red. Steel against steel, man against man, the trained against the untrained. For every one soldier the brave citizens of Mordeina felled, they lost five of their own. There was slaughter on all sides of him. Finally, he swung back around, narrowly avoided being impaled by a pike, and saw Ashhur still tramping through the soldiers, his movements sluggish as men hung off him. They were rushing the god now, trying to overwhelm him with sheer numbers.

And it was working.

Ashhur collapsed to one knee, tearing soldiers off him, crushing them in his fists and hurling them away, their bodies soaring through the air like so many shattered birds. Ahaesarus's mind went blank. If his god couldn't help them, no one could. The soldiers closed in on Ahaesarus and his men.

No. No, no, no!

"Attack!" he shouted as he hacked away with his sword, swinging with all his might, trying to press closer to the bunker and his distressed god. But there were just too many of them. Judarius fought at his side, swinging his maul with abandon, sending soldiers careening. Blood flew into Ahaesarus's face. Together, he and Judarius cut a path through the throng until they reached the bunker. They both leapt atop it, fighting like old, experienced warriors, killing and maiming. Ahaesarus hopped down on the other side of the bunker, only to catch a sword in his left arm. He fell back against the barricade, screaming in pain. Judarius bolted out ahead of him, shoving through the mass of steel and flesh. His every move was determined, his every swing willed by rage. The black-haired Warden shattered a soldier's jaw, caved in another's helm, splintered yet another's arm.

Ahaesarus swallowed his pain and drove in after him, slicing throats and severing limbs. *We will make it! Ashhur, we are coming!*

Only they never did. Just as Ahaesarus drove his sword through a soldier's mouth, he caught sight of Judarius whirling around, his maul flailing, keeping dozens of men at bay, but even his power was not enough. A soldier leapt atop him from behind, jamming a dagger into Judarius's shoulder. The Warden screamed, grabbed the man, and hurled him into his own comrades. Another swing of his maul, but it was slower now, weaker. Blades cut into his sides, a horde of attackers, and as Ahaesarus watched in horror, a glimmering length of steel pierced through one side of his throat and out the other.

"Judarius!" Ahaesarus shouted. He tried to cut his way through, but he found himself surrounded. A blade chopped at his lower leg, almost severing it at the knee, and he collapsed while above him the soldiers continued the onslaught. He was kicked and stepped on, his wards and brothers dying left and right, and though he took out as many feet as he could by blindly swinging his sword, it was no use.

He was stomped on, bombarded, until a pair of strong hands gripped the back of his damp, cold tunic and hauled him backward. At the bunker, his unseen rescuers lifted him up above the crowd, trying to get him over. It was then that a loud *boom* rocked the morning. Many of those standing around fell to their knees, blown back by a rush of hot wind. Ahaesarus was released, sliding down the bunker wall as black smoke billowed from Mordeina's main gate. Thick iron rods fell from the sky. The bodies of his fellow Wardens hung limp atop the barricades that formed the murder row, bits of stone and steel jutting from their lifeless forms. Of those he had sent, he saw only one standing—Judah, who limped away, clutching his dangling right arm.

More soldiers emerged from the smoke, charging and howling seemingly without care, their swords and axes held high. Then the captains stepped forward, the horns on their great helms painted red, and they shouted as well. Those who had descended the wall stampeded across the snowy, corpse-strewn ground. Men on horseback galloped through the chasm, veering to the side and riding perpendicular to the long bunker. Ahaesarus watched them disappear into the distance before he slid fully to the ground, but he had no time to question what they were doing, not with death staring him right in the face.

The battle had changed. Lying prone amid the chaos, Ahaesarus saw flares of magic lashing the air above, constant, violent, and powerful. He couldn't see what was happening from flat on his back, but he didn't need to. They had lost the day. Mordeina would fall, and all of Paradise would belong to the east.

CHAPTER 26

Just as Azariah had said, the tunnel leading out of Mordeina was three miles long and dumped out into a rocky, ice-covered gulch fronted by a bubbling stream. Beyond was the thick forest. By the time Patrick and his band of twenty-two brave souls re-entered bright sunlight and snuffed out their torches, the morning was growing long. Preston gestured for the Turncloaks to ride two by two, and Denton Noonan, young Barclay's father, tried to do the same with his group of fourteen common men. Patrick looked back at the cave mouth they had just exited and shook his head. The trip had taken longer than expected.

Preston trotted up to him on his horse as they circled the lip of the gulch. "So that was . . . impressive. Where are we now?"

Patrick pointed to the west, where another thick grouping of trees stood. "The sea is forty miles that way. Fifty miles north will be the Whitetail River." He grinned. "And if we loop around this wood here, it's another couple miles until we reach the Gods' Road."

"You know this place?" asked Tristan.

"I do," he nodded. "That cave has been there for as long as I've been alive . . . though it didn't always run as long as it does now. I spent a lot of time in there as a child, exploring all the odd things that lived in the darkness. Good times."

"You loved spending time in caves?" Joff asked.

"Of course," Patrick told him. "When one looks like me, the darkness can be liberating."

Big Flick scrunched up his face. "What's that mean?"

"It means I was teased a lot as a child. Children can be cruel, as I'm sure you know."

"But you were a child of a First Family," said Ragnar. "Doesn't that mean something?"

"Only if your mother wishes for it to have that influence." Patrick grunted. "Alas, the great Isabel wished for me to learn to deal with the japes on my own."

They rode for an hour, the sun slowly inching higher into the sky. An eerie feeling crept up Patrick's spine. Despite the relative quietness of the day, he could hear odd sounds below the howling of the wind. It sounded like the far-off caw of an eagle combined with the rumble of a grayhorn stampede. He knew what it meant. Guilt at his decision to go on this vengeful quest formed a lump in the back of his throat. He had left his people behind. His armor suddenly felt too constricting, the furs on top too heavy.

"You hear that, don't you?" asked Preston.

Patrick nodded.

"Hear what?" asked Edward, a bit too loudly.

"Shut *up*," Patrick snapped before Denton could clout the young soldier. He turned to Preston, who stared in annoyance at his son. "The attack began. Sounds like it's for real this time. We should have stayed."

Preston chuckled to himself and shook his head. "We are twenty-three men, Patrick. If Karak has begun a full assault, what difference would we make against fifteen thousand trained soldiers?" A grin stretched across his wrinkled mouth, pulling up the sides of his beard. "But out *here*, away from Mordeina, we might do some good. I would wager Karak will attack with all he has, all at once, without the slightest possibility of defeat entering his head. If he does that, then only a sparse force will remain behind to guard his supply wagons."

"So this might not be a suicide mission after all," Patrick said. His guilt subsided slightly, replaced by the nervous excitement that he had felt in Haven when Karak's Army first attacked.

"We'll have surprise on our side." Preston peered over his shoulder. "So long as no idiot gives away our approach."

Edward hung his head. Ragnar, his brother, trotted up to him and placed a comforting hand on his back. *They are seasoned men in battle, yet sensitive boys when not thus engaged.* Patrick almost burst out laughing at the absurdity of it all. His humor, however, lasted only until Ryann spoke up.

"If Karak takes Mordeina, what's the point of torching a few wagons?" Ryann asked. "Won't the war be over?"

Patrick swallowed down a massive lump in his throat.

"You can't think like that," he said. "We do what we can, to the best of our ability. Let the gods deal with the rest."

He led his troupe into the wood, following a winding path he still remembered, even though it had been more than fifty years since he'd stepped foot on it. Snow crunched under their horses' hooves; ice fell from the leafless branches overhead; and the clamor of war grew ever louder. The farther into the forest they went, however, the more stumps of felled trees they found. It looked like the center of the woods had been clear-cut—no doubt the result of hundreds of campfires and the numerous siege weapons Karak's Army had built. Patrick's heart began to race, and he reached behind his head, pulling Winterbone from its sheath. Having a weapon at hand seemed to help, at least a little.

The trees again rose up, the closer to Mordeina they drew, these ones brittle, their trunks hollowed out and devoid of life from when Ashhur had drained them of their essence to create the grayhornmen. Patrick halted his mare, and those following did the same. He climbed out of the saddle, as did Preston, and together they trudged through the dead wood. They were at the edge now, and with no foliage to conceal them, he felt naked. If anyone looked their way, they would be spotted immediately.

"Looks like I was right," Preston said.

Patrick squinted, rising up on his toes and straightening out as much as he could with his humped back. He saw countless tents populating the valley's ridge, and behind them were a seemingly never-ending row of covered wagons. "I don't see any soldiers," he whispered.

Preston chortled lightly. "The soldiers are there," he said, pointing. Patrick followed his finger and saw a line of perhaps sixty of them, small as figurines as they stood in a line farther out in the snowy valley, facing Mordeina's walls.

"But what about other people?" Patrick asked. "Those who, you know, service the camp. Wouldn't they be needed?"

"Not here, not in Karak's Army," said Preston. "When Karak started this war, he pulled from their lives nearly all the men old enough to fight. Need a blacksmith? There are a hundred soldiers who have been blacksmiths all their lives. The same with chefs, tailors, and horsemasters—any profession that would be of use to a traveling army is here. If something needs doing, there is a man to do it, one who can still pick up his sword and run into battle when the time comes."

"But all men?"

Preston nodded. "You will find few women here, perhaps none at all. Our regiment in the Delta had only seven, not counting the Lord Commander, and all of those seven were sent away early on."

"Why? Would they not be useful in battle as well? After all, Moira and Rachida were two of the best fighters I've ever seen. By gods, a quarter of our warriors in Haven were women. Many of the archers in Mordeina are too."

"Neldar holds a . . . different view of the fairer sex," said Preston with a nod. "I assume Karak feels that having women on the battlefield will be nothing but a distraction. It is simply the way life is in Karak's Army, and also yet another reason why Ashhur must win.

Should Karak come out the victor . . . and to the victor goes the spoils . . . with all those men who have not lain with a woman for more than a year . . . ”

“I get it,” Patrick grumbled. “No need to spell it out.”

“Very well.”

They turned around and headed back to their awaiting compatriots, who had remained deeper in the dead wood. “What do we do?” asked Little Flick when they both climbed back atop their horses.

Tristan shifted eagerly in his saddle, his hands flexing. “Yeah, what’s the plan?”

“We charge,” said Preston. “The soldiers are all lined in a row, though there may be more inside the tents. Their attention is on the siege, so be quick, be brutal, and ride fast. No yelling, no talking. Let the horse’s hooves be the only warning. The tents are arranged into rows, like we had in the delta. Ride between them, so your horses don’t trip. For those of you new to this, each of you follows behind one of my boys. They’ll show you the way.”

Denton and the fourteen others went white as fallen snow, but they nodded nonetheless.

With that, Patrick led them out of the forest a little farther back on the Gods’ Road. When they emerged they spread out five wide, with each of the young Turncloaks leading one or two of the new warriors brought by Denton Noonan. They sat in place for a few moments, Patrick allowing the nerves of all present to harden before offering a brisk nod and bringing his horse to gallop. Preston fell in beside him, with Ragnar, Edward, Tristan, and Joff forming the first line. The repetitive sound of hooves beating the frozen earth was like the endless rumble of thunder.

They swerved around a bend in the road, and the camp of Karak’s Army opened up before them. The soldiers’ attentions were still fixed on the battle waging in the far-off city, and for a second Patrick doubted their plan. Their rush was so loud, it was sure to attract their attention, and should that happen, they would have at least two minutes to prepare themselves for what was to come. If there was one thing Patrick had learned about battle over the last three years, it was that two minutes could be a lifetime.

Yet the soldiers never turned, instead keeping their eyes on the distant walled settlement as if transfixed. Patrick allowed himself to glance up, and he saw bright flashes light up the sky above Mordeina. *That can't be good,* he thought. He tore his eyes away and had to shove aside worry for his sisters, nieces, and nephews, all locked away inside Manse DuTaureau. Should any harm come to them . . .

Stop it. Focus. He lifted Winterbone and held it out before him like a lance.

He veered his horse through the rows between the tents, keeping his vision fixed on the soldiers. He saw one of the tents billow, but he wasn't sure if that was due to the bitter wind or someone moving about inside. Not that it mattered. Any who emerged would receive their due when the most present threat was taken care of. On and on thumped the hoof beats, but the battle from afar was so loud and full of chaos, it appeared to be an unexpected blessing.

They were only twenty feet away from the soldiers when finally the one at the end of the line turned. He was an older man, and a smile was on his lips. That smile faltered when he saw Patrick on his horse, and it disappeared completely when Patrick hacked down with Winterbone, cleaving his face from his skull. The man collapsed, clutching at the bloody ruin where his face had once been. He disappeared as Patrick's horse shot past the soldiers, galloping out into the field a good fifty feet before he yanked the reins and turned around.

The rest of the soldiers whirled in a confused panic just as Patrick's mates descended on them. Seventeen fell during that first pass, the twenty-two other riders fanning out and hacking away. The unharmed soldiers fumbled for their weapons, but they were too shaken, too surprised. By the time the first few had pulled out their swords, each of their attackers was charging once more.

Another fourteen died on the second pass.

This time when Patrick and his regiment tried to turn around, they had to maneuver through the tents to do so, allowing the thirty remaining soldiers to ready themselves. Panicked orders rang out among Karak's men, and they spread out, dashing this way and that in an attempt to separate their assailants. Patrick's militia didn't fall for it. Denton and two of the other men from Paradise, David and Michael, sheathed their swords and pulled out their homemade bows. They fired shot after shot at the soldiers while the rest continued the assault. Patrick spied the three of them over his shoulder for just a second, in awe that these men who had only seen a true battle once could adapt so well when the moment called for it.

Patrick chased after three soldiers who scooted between the rows of tents, heading for the supply carts. As he rode, this time he did see two other men emerge from the canvas enclosures, looking bewildered and frightened. These two never had a chance to draw their weapons, for Preston and Ragnar were on them a moment later, running them both through.

The three soldiers veered once more, and instead of swerving along with them, Patrick went against Preston's advice and charged straight through the tents. His mare trampled them, scattering iron cookware, piles of smallclothes, and stones across the snow. Once the horse's rear hoof became tangled with the corner of one of the tents, but after a momentary stumble the beast righted itself and kept on galloping.

He came upon one of the soldiers an instant later, driving Winterbone down and piercing the man through the back of the neck. The soldier lifted off the ground, impaled on the sword's blade, his legs still kicking. Patrick's forearms screamed at him with the extra weight, and he jerked upward. The razor-sharp blade ripped through the soldier's scull, shearing it in half and freeing the sword. Blood sprayed everywhere as the soldier fell. Patrick winced, switched the massive sword from one hand to the other, and shook the pain out of his arm.

Big and Little Flick had cornered another of the fleeing men, viciously hacking at him. Patrick pulled back on the reins, bringing his mare up on its hind legs for a moment. When the beast returned to all fours, he spun in a circle. He saw no more standing soldiers, only his twenty-two brothers-in-arms, all hovering over the last of their kills.

Patrick whirled back around, searching for the final fleeing soldier. Grunting, his blood racing through his veins, he sheathed Winterbone, hopped off his horse, and began to walk down the line of supply wagons. Each cart was surrounded by a mound of snow that rose to the top of the wheels, and he noticed that one of those mounds had a deep impression in the center. When he reached it, he ducked down and saw a pair of feet pushing against the snow, desperately trying to get away.

"Got you," Patrick said.

He grasped the booted feet with both hands and yanked, and the soldier slid out from beneath the wagon with ease. When he was fully exposed, Patrick roughly kicked him onto his back, grabbed him by the neck of his breastplate, and lifted him to standing. The soldier screeched and tried to get away.

"Please!" the soldier said. "Don't hurt me!"

Patrick released him and took a step backward. The soldier before him was young, no older than Joffrey, the youngest Turncloak. He had a head of silver hair, a slender jaw, and light-blue eyes like seaglass. He looked like he could have been Moira Elren's brother in another life.

Tears streamed down the young soldier's cheeks. "Please," he groveled, clutching his hands to his chest like a small child. "Please, I-I don't want to hurt anyone. I just want to go home."

"You want to go home?" Patrick asked.

The boy nodded. Patrick almost pulled the dagger out of his belt and shoved it into the boy's throat right there, but something stopped him.

My son will be that age one day, he thought. He dropped his hands to his sides.

"Go," Patrick said.

"What?" asked the soldier.

"I'm not going to tell you twice. Go. *Now.* Before I change my mind."

"Thank you, thank you, thank you," the young soldier repeated as he crept along the side of the wagon. When he reached the edge, he turned and began running through the snow, heading south toward the Gods' Road. Patrick watched him go, his inner thoughts in turmoil. Then he saw a shadow pass over his head, and a moment later the fleeing boy fell. His body shuddered for a moment and then stilled, an arrow protruding from the back of his head.

"You got him, Denton!" he heard one of the other men shout.

Patrick turned, his fists clenched, and spotted Denton Noonan sitting atop his horse, three of his compatriots patting him on the back. Patrick was about to charge him, but strong hands grasped his wrist, spinning him back around.

"Don't," Preston told him.

"I let the boy go," Patrick growled.

"Denton didn't know that."

"He should have."

Patrick shrugged out of Preston's grasp and stormed through the snow, approaching the body of another of the soldiers he'd felled. He kicked the corpse, and it spun over. He gazed down at the face of a boy not much older than the one he had decided to set free. This one had wavy chestnut hair and eyes of a deep green that were already beginning to grow milky with death.

"Children," he muttered.

"Karak left behind those he thought either too old or too young to fight," Preston said.

"How many?"

"Seventy."

Seventy men, killed in less than ten minutes. It was a horrific thought, and one that threatened to make him pitch the wine still sitting in his stomach all over the ground.

"Karak turned children into monsters," Patrick whispered. "We're no different. Joff is fourteen."

"As the books say, war makes monsters of all of us," said Preston. "We do what we must do to survive, and that is all. It's something we all must accept at some point."

"This used to be Paradise," Patrick said, his mind in a daze. "It used to be beautiful. Now it's just like me."

"Patrick, don't say such things. You don't know—"

"Shut it, old man," Patrick snapped. "You don't get to tell me how to feel."

Preston put his hands up and backed away. In the background, the battle raging within Mordeina's walls rose in volume. Patrick's anger began to churn once more. He peered over his hump at the grayed soldier.

"Go get the tindersticks," he said, his voice low and grave. "Set fire to every wagon."

"Hurry," Preston shouted to the others. "If we're quick, we can be back to the cave in no time."

"No," Patrick said, grabbing him by the shoulder and spinning him around to face him. "We're not running. There's a battle raging, and we'll go galloping in head first."

Preston's hard, pale eyes stared into his.

"And if Karak has won before we reach the melee?" he asked.

Patrick felt his blood run cold, but this was something he would not budge on, was something he knew was right.

"We charge, even then. Even unto death. If we're going to die, we'll die as good men protecting the innocent. Not as monsters. *Never* monsters, not ever again."

CHAPTER

27

"KARAK, FACE ME!" Ashhur had said.

Velixar let the memory of the western god's challenge wash over him. There had been so much anger in those words, and he swore there was a hint of fear as well. He glanced up and saw Karak smiling as he stood before the gate cut into Mordeina's inner wall, his glowing eyes lighting the dim, cramped space. Behind him was the pile of rubble from Velixar's previous failed attempt to overrun the settlement, and behind that was the ironlike trunk of Celestia's tree. All around were the broken bodies of the dead and dying, those who had plummeted from the top of the wall during the invasion. Half were men from Paradise; the rest, soldiers of Karak.

So many reminders of my failures on the day of our greatest victory.

From within the settlement came the *clang* of steel, the shouts of the aggressors, and the shrieks of the dying. Velixar glanced behind him, where Lord Commander Gregorian stood by the hole the soldiers had battered into the weakened stone of the outer wall, and then stared up at his god. He took a knee before him.

"My Lord, we are beyond your brother's protection. Allow me the privilege of opening the final gate."

Karak put a hand on his shoulder.

"Do it," he said.

Velixar stood and approached the gate, strangely aware of the many eyes watching him from just outside the fissure behind him. Beyond the gate, the slaughter had commenced. His fingers touched the pendant around his neck, feeling its warmth, then found the iron bars, eight inches thick and unbendable. Velixar smiled. *That which cannot bend will easily be broken.*

He swiveled his head slightly and looked at the Lord Commander. Malcolm had his arms crossed over his chest, his milky left eye seemingly glowing through the slit in his great helm.

"Best keep your men back," Velixar said. The faithful man nodded to him and held his arms out. The eager soldiers gathered behind retreated from the opening.

"Hold nothing back, High Prophet," said Karak from behind him. "This is the hour of our victory."

Velixar squeezed his eyes shut and took a deep breath. He thought back on the words of the demon whose power he now possessed. In the darkness behind his eyelids, he created a temporal rift within him, expanding his soul outward and inward at the same time. His essence became a shimmering sphere filled with magma swirling at its center. He imagined all of the cosmos, everything connected, and his pendant became a funnel, stretching out into the stars, seeking the heart of the sun that burned above him.

That sun was Karak. Those flames were his might.

For you, my Lord. All for you.

Velixar siphoned the power into himself.

He felt the energy flow. His nerves tingled, and his hairs stood on end. There was a tightening sensation as his flesh began to stretch with the hugeness of the power he had absorbed, threatening to burst his entire being. *The soul is limitless. It is the mind that restricts us.* He pictured his body as water, flowing free and formless, and allowed the essence of his god to infuse every particle of his being.

Soon, in the world behind his eyelids, he had grown nearly as large as the world itself and just as mighty. He felt close to bursting.

Do not push it too far. Not yet. Keep yourself restrained.

He opened his eyes.

The world seemed to warp in his vision, pulsating with vivid colors. With his body tingling, he raised his hands and fanned his fingers, looking on in awe as shadows flowed around them. He opened his mouth, and words of magic sprung forth, raucous and potent.

Dark lightning leapt from his hands. A deafening explosion followed as the gate—and a good five feet of the wall bordering it—blasted inward. Smoke billowed and purplish fires blazed that no water could quell. Screams sounded from the other side, filled with terror and pain. Velixar looked behind him at Karak.

The god seemed pleased. Velixar's heart soared.

"Go forth," Karak said. "Prepare Paradise for my coming."

"Lord Commander!" Velixar bellowed when the thick smoke dissipated. "Send in your men!"

He stepped to the side as Malcolm led the soldiers through the gaps in both walls. The constant drumming of their feet and clank of their armor was music to Velixar's ears. It seemed to take an age for all four thousand to pass through. Only when the horsemen entered, their chargers huffing and snorting in the lingering smoke, did he enter as well, leaving Karak alone in the chasm.

"All this will be yours," Karak told him, his thundering voice confident. "All you must do . . . is seize it."

Excitement simmered through Velixar's core, and he hastened his steps. Lionsbane, impotent next to the power at his disposal, swung on his hip. The place he entered was awash with blood, death, and confusion. The twin barricades that had once turned the causeway that stretched out from the gate into a thin culvert—*murder row*, as Patrick DuTaureau's mind had dubbed it—were obliterated, lying in smoking piles of debris on either side of him.

Corpses, both human and Warden, covered the ground, their bodies twisted and ruined. More than one had the remains of the gate's iron bars protruding from him. Velixar stepped off the causeway, and all around him were small pockets of fighting. The heat from his energy and the blast had melted the snow, leaving muddy earth beneath his feet.

No matter where he looked, he saw bloodshed. Karak's soldiers pressed onward, the Lord Commander forming his massive regiment into a brutal column that sawed through the settlement's defenders. Off to the side, Aerland Shen, the Ekreissar Chief, was storming through ranks of opponents, cutting them down with his dual black swords. Screams filled the air. Though they now had steel weapons at their disposal, the people of Paradise had little training and were poorly armored. Men and women fell like blades of grass beneath a swinging scythe. Velixar lifted his eyes and saw the squat, bulky form of Manse DuTaureau sitting on its hill, surrounded by a massive throng of people, tiny as ants in the distance. *So many of them. They will be stomped just as easily.*

A bright flash came from his right, and Velixar turned toward it. He saw a cluster of soldiers collapse as small fireballs and waves of electricity washed over them. Beyond those fallen soldiers he spotted six men in heavy cloaks surrounded by a phalanx of Wardens. The spellcasters worked diligently, their hands and mouths in constant motion despite their obvious exhaustion.

Velixar grinned and twisted his fingers into runes. So powerful was the energy running through him that he didn't need to utter a single word before two of the Wardens collapsed into shapeless, fleshy heaps, every bone in their bodies crushed. He imagined organs rupturing, and blood erupted from another Warden's mouth with such force that it rose twenty feet into the air. Shadows leapt from his fingertips, swirling around three more Wardens, spinning them, twisting their bodies until their limbs were ripped from their torsos. Eyeballs boiled in their sockets, hearts burst, faces caved in. The six spellcasters were the last to fall, four of their stomachs splitting open and their entrails vomiting out of them. Those entrails in turn became writhing snakes, choking the life out of the remaining two.

To Velixar, his work was brutal, effortless, *exhilarating*.

He sensed danger approaching and pivoted on the balls of his feet to find an arrow careening toward his head. He had no time to cast a spell to bat the bolt aside, not even time enough to duck, but his confidence didn't waver. He simply smiled as the arrow caught fire, burning to a cinder as it passed through the swell of energy surrounding him. By the time it struck his billowing cloak, the arrow was nothing but ash. He looked in the direction from which it came, and there was Ashhur, knee deep in soldiers, fighting them off with all his might. Ropes looped around his neck, and as the deity lumbered forward, hacking away with his ethereal sword, he dragged soldiers behind him.

Velixar hooked his fingers, and a shadowy conduit shot forth, five feet wide and screaming with dark energy. The conduit roared along the ground, obliterating bodies both living and not, kicking up a bloody mist as it sought out its target. It struck Ashhur in the side, enveloping the deity in pulsating tendrils. The god screamed, as did the soldiers attacking him, and then the whole of the area was overcome by a ring of darkness. Purple flames licked along the surface of the swirl like a potent cosmic storm. Velixar laughed and brought his hands together, wringing the dark energy, compressing it, crushing all that was inside. He imagined Ashhur, his heavenly form squeezed thin as a reed, the magma of his life flowing out his mouth, eyes, and ears.

"I have you."

Only he didn't. Just as his palms met, and the swirling shadow constricted with an audible *thwump*, Ashhur leapt from within the black. He soared twenty feet into the air, arms and legs splayed, golden hair trailing behind. His silver armor was dented, the plating seared black, but his flesh was still immaculate. When the deity landed on the other side of the stone barrier that rimmed the southern edge of the settlement, one knee and one foot driving into the earth along with his fist, he lifted his glowing yellow eyes to Velixar and seethed.

Not even in Haven had he seen Ashhur so full of rage. The god appeared angry enough to crush the entire world in the palm of his hand. With a wrathful deity's attention fully on him, Velixar felt dread for the first time. Ashhur's presence also seemed to steel both the Wardens and his children, for they fought with renewed vigor, even those mortally wounded.

Velixar lifted his hands, and the heads of forty of the corpses surrounding him tore free from their necks. With a whoosh the heads were alight with purple fire, searing away hair and flesh. The skulls left behind still burned, and when he thrust his arms forward they took flight, trailed by licking flames. They flashed through the air, heading for the throng on the other side of the bunker. It was a maneuver to frighten as much as injure, one he had seen utilized in the memory of the Beast of a Thousand Faces, when Kaurthulos's demons laid siege to Kal'droth's last elven stronghold.

It might have worked then, but not now. Ashhur didn't cower; instead, the deity reached up a single hand, stopping the skulls midflight. He made a fist, and the fires extinguished, bits of smoking bone raining down on the blood-drenched snow. The western god then took a menacing step forward, pointing an accusatory finger Velixar's way.

Ashhur's voice echoed in his head, though the god's mouth never moved. *Betrayer.* The force of the accusation was nearly enough to drive him to his knees.

"BROTHER!"

The sound rocked the countryside, feeling like the moment Celestia split the land to form the Rigon River.

"YOUR KINGDOM IS MINE."

Karak's voice was swelled with contempt. Ashhur's eyes shifted to the smoking hole in the wall where the gate had once been, and Velixar looked that way as well. Karak came sauntering out of the hollow, his armor a black so deep it seemed to swallow all light, making the very air around him dim. He held his own ethereal sword in his hand, its blade alight with flames and swirling with shadow. The Divinity of the East took five steps and then stopped, leveling his gaze at his brother.

Ashhur stared at him, standing as still as the mountain embellishing his scorched breastplate. It seemed as if everything ceased, nearly all combatants stopping mid-swing to gawk at the stare down between the brother gods. The only sounds were the wind, the moans of the dying, and the sobs of those attempting to comfort them.

It was Ashhur who moved first. He lifted his chin, stared at the bright afternoon sky for a half an instant, and then glared back at his brother. The western deity was statuesque, the embodiment of beauty and dignity with his flowing golden hair and firm posture. Velixar hated him all the more for how much he admired him in that moment.

"Leave," Ashhur said, his voice low and menacing. The blue glow of the sword in his hand brightened.

"No," Karak said.

"Then I will make you."

"As always, you lack wisdom," said Karak. "You will not lift a hand against me."

As Ashhur tilted his head and narrowed his eyes, seeming puzzled, a low rumbling sound reached Velixar's ears. Karak gestured down the road behind his brother. Ashhur turned his head, and Velixar could see him visibly deflate, the god's shoulders hunching.

The rumbling was the sound of innumerable marching feet. A multitude approached from the northwest, urged onward by soldiers on both foot and horseback. Babes cried, mothers sniffled, old men pleaded for their lives. It was one of the most pathetic scenes Velixar had ever seen.

The soldiers who'd scaled the walls at distant parts of the settlement had been given firm orders: Be brutal when confronting pockets of resistance, but do not harm the innocents or those unwilling to fight. Instead, they were to gather as many as they could, as quickly as possible, and march them to the southern gate. The five hundred soldiers pushed and prodded the people through the center of the road, where the remains of countless humans and Wardens surrounded them. Bodies were shoved aside to allow room for the bedraggled populace to stagger forward. Velixar was shocked by the numbers he saw: There had to be more than five thousand.

The captain leading the charge stopped the procession three hundred feet from where Ashhur stood, surrounded by a ragged collection of bleeding defenders. The crowd was close enough now that Velixar could see their faces, see the fear and dismay that showed in their tear-filled eyes.

"Citizens of Paradise," said Karak, his voice elevated so that it could be heard from seemingly miles away. He proffered his hand to the still-smoking gate behind him. "These walls were built not to protect, but to *enslave*. Your creator would deny you your liberation! He has kept you as infants when you should have become strong. *My* faithful embody the strength you lack; *my* faithful have been given the means to flourish. Ashhur gave you all you desired, even the very weapons your defenders now hold, but I . . . I allowed my people to grow on their own. The towers outside were crafted by their sweat and labor, the steel they wear and hold molded by their brothers. Accept these gifts. Accept the knowledge I offer. The time for remaining children has passed. I do not wish to destroy you. I wish for you to be *FREE*!"

Velixar watched with interest as the multitudes shuffled and mumbled among themselves. A woman stepped forward. She was old, with white hair and wrinkled flesh, but her posture was straight as an arrow. She glanced once at her deity, then threw her head back and stared at the god who opposed them.

"And if we refuse your liberation?" she asked.

Behind her, the massive crowd murmured. They were growing unruly.

Karak crossed his sword over his chest. "A land divided is a land of chaos, and I will have order in my kingdom."

"This is not your kingdom," Ashhur proclaimed. The Wardens and humans surrounding him began to spread out, lifting their weapons.

"The peoples' lives are in my hands, not yours," Karak said, eyes narrowing. "Tell me truly, whose kingdom does that make it then?"

The western deity frowned.

Karak shook his head and turned back to the throng. "Come to me, people of Paradise. Turn your back on this feeble god." He pointed toward Velixar. "Do as the first of your kind did long ago. Come into my arms. Allow me to make you as powerful as he."

Velixar's heart filled with pride, swelling the power that already existed within him. He took a step forward and looked toward the unkempt citizens, holding his arms out wide, feeling the heat on his cheeks as the glow of his eyes intensified. *I will be an example for them. I will be a beacon of Karak's glory.*

Amazingly, the old woman who had stepped forward lowered herself to her knees. The thousands behind her were hesitant at first, but eventually they followed her lead. The sound of the knees of the assembly hitting the ground, one after the other, was like a stampede of horses through a sodden field. Velixar smiled warmly, his pride growing. His eyes kept returning to Ashhur, trying to gauge the deity's reaction to his people turning their faith to Karak, but his face was like stone.

Karak stepped through the maze of corpses with long, purposeful strides. It was then that Velixar noticed something odd, something he had not noticed during the rush of battle. More than half of the bodies on the ground were long dead, their skin gray going on blue, their joints stiff to the point of immovability. Those bodies had not been there two days ago, when last he had seen the outside world through the eyes of Patrick DuTaureau. He could think of no reason for them to be there now.

Karak spoke, yanking that contemplation from his mind. "My new children. I welcome you into my arms. You may not be forever safe and warm in them, but you will . . . "

His words trailed away as the old woman who first knelt began to sing. It was a sweet song, one filled with hope and love. *"And let Ashhur always hold us in his arms,"* she crooned. Soon a few of the others behind her joined in, the song rising in volume, voice added to voice until at least half of the immense congregation was lifting their song to the heavens. To Velixar's ears, the sound was like the scraping of steel on stone. His mouth dropped open. These people . . . these *children* . . . would they prefer death to the freedom of creating one's own life? Would they rather cower in the arms of Ashhur than stand strong before Karak's dignified order? It made no sense. They were frightened, confused, and they knew with each word they sang, they sank deeper into their own graves. Yet still they sang.

Still they sang.

Velixar looked to Ashhur. The god's face was still as stone, but tears flowed from his eyes.

"You leave me no choice," Karak said, his voice thundering over the chaos of the five thousand. "Above all else, I will have order."

"You never will," Ashhur said, and though it was spoken as a whisper, Velixar heard it with ease. "Not this year, not this century, not this millennium will you ever have the order you crave. You are chasing illusions, and I will not let you destroy my people in your wake. I promised to protect them, no matter the cost, and so I will."

His head dipped as Karak bellowed for his soldiers to ready their blades.

"No matter the cost," said Ashhur.

A brilliant light flared from the god's eyes, so bright that Velixar could not look lest he be blinded. As he covered his face with his hands, a single, deafening word rocked the landscape.

"RISE!"

Mordeina grew larger and larger in his vision as Patrick slapped the reins again and again. Steam rose from his mare's bobbing head, and hoofed feet pounded into the icy, snowy ground. His half helm bounced against Patrick's head while Winterbone, its scabbard fastened to the side of the saddle, thudded against the horse's flank.

His body ached from being tossed around, but he gnashed his teeth and ignored the pain. He could hear the conflict inside the walls escalate, even over the constant *thud, thud, thud* of charging hooves. Karak's voice came clear, and Ashhur's as well, so loud that they might as well have been five feet away from him instead of five thousand. The sky above the walls lit up with flashes of light. A series of low, resounding *booms* followed.

"Faster!" he shouted. Only one thing was important now—getting through the walls and defending his place of birth.

The walls were close, so large in his vision that all he could see was a backdrop of mottled gray and black stone. He counted nine wooden towers butting up against the walls, empty and forgotten. Two of them were on fire. In the wide space between two of the towers was a gaping chasm in the wall's thick stone. He leaned over, urging his mare to quicken her pace. With the afternoon sunlight shining down, brightened five times over by the snowy landscape, he realized that it wasn't a single fissure he was seeing, but two, one through each wall, each wide enough for ten men to stroll through abreast, leading directly into the settlement. He swore he could see a flurry of activity on the other side.

They were now two thousand feet away and closing fast.

Shadows appeared on either side of him, and Patrick glanced in both directions. Preston had ridden up on his right, the old warrior's face a hard mask of calculation, while Denton Noonan kept pace with him on the left, his eyes ablaze with anger and focus. The hoots and hollers of the younger Turncloaks echoed behind him.

When they were a thousand feet from the gap, the blood-curdling screams of those inside were almost deafening. Patrick bore down, chancing to take one hand off the reins and grab Winterbone's handle. He saw clearly into the heart of Mordeina, where countless tiny forms were locked in combat. He tensed his neck and shoulders to keep his upper body steady while his lower bounded with his mare's strides. Numerous bustling shadows then appeared within the jagged hole in the wall, moving hastily. A second later, soldiers poured out of the opening. They ran haphazardly, shrieking as they stormed through the slick snow. Patrick slowed his mare ever so slightly

"Ready!" he shouted as he tore Winterbone from its sheath.

CHAPTER 28

The thousands of dead littering the ground took to their feet. To Velixar's ears, the sound was like a million twigs being snapped all at once. Screams followed, from followers of Karak and Ashhur alike.

"Kill them!" ordered Karak. "Kill them all!"

Velixar's feet were seemingly frozen to the ground. An immensely tall figure rose from within the melee; the Warden Judarius, his fellow member of the Lordship back when Velixar had been Jacob Eveningstar. Only Judarius's face was wrong. His flesh had gone gray, his eyes milky, and the left side of his neck was a mess of flayed skin. The Warden moved his head slowly to the side, his lifeless stare lingering on the soldier standing in front of him. The soldier appeared bewildered, his dazzled blue eyes shining in the intense light Ashhur created. He never looked up, not even when the Warden lifted a bloodied maul and brought it down on the back of his head. The sound of steel and bone shattering echoed over Karak's furious screams.

Bedlam ensued as the walking corpses lashed out at the soldiers with whatever weapons they still held; those that had nothing bit with their teeth and scratched with pale bleeding fingers. Men fell, their bodies torn asunder, while Ashhur's children fled in all directions, looks of abject terror painting their faces.

Velixar couldn't believe what was happening. He'd seen images like this in the memory of the demon he'd swallowed—the Beast of a Thousand Faces had raised an army of undead elves to march against Kal'droth during the great war—but he had never expected Ashhur to take such an extreme measure himself. But no . . . that wasn't right. He'd seen this before. His thoughts retreated to the moment when the western deity had animated the corpse of Brienna Meln, the elf Jacob Eveningstar had loved. Terror filled his soul.

A cold hand grabbed him around the neck, ripping him from the painful memory. In desperation he whirled around, flailing violently, and the hand fell away. When he pushed back his hood, he saw a staggering dead man with a slit throat before him, the symbol of the roaring lion embossed on his breastplate. The walking corpse righted itself and stared at him with eyes that shone with soft yellow light. The dead thing reached out for him again, fingers curled into claws, and Velixar stepped back. His horror and disbelief made him weak; the link funneling the power from Karak into him vanished. Still, he was strong enough to take out a single undead monster. Words of magic spat from his lips and the thing crumpled into a mound of useless flesh and bone.

When he turned, everywhere he looked there were undead. Thousands of them, men, women, and children from Paradise, along with a great many dead soldiers of Karak. They fought with mindless intensity, even those who appeared to be long deceased, their movements forceful but erratic. The living soldiers were thrown into panic, unsure of whom they should defend themselves against. Whenever one of their brethren fell, a moment later he stood again, eyes shimmering with that sick yellow light.

The whole time, Ashhur conducted the chaos, glancing this way and that, steering his undead horde.

Velixar desperately searched for Karak as the battle raged around him, found his god flinging the walking corpses left and right as he shouted for his army to remain strong. None were listening. Soldiers fled for the hole in the wall, first a few, then many. Even Aerland Shen and his Ekreissar, though they handled the undead with relative ease, retreated toward the opening. Velixar wanted to scream at them, to pulverize their bodies with a word, but a group of seven corpses lurched toward him, their jaws chattering wordlessly. He impaled one with a lance of living shadow, crushed another's skull, set a third aflame, but that didn't stop their advance. They knew no fear, no pain. Even the one he'd impaled with shadow continued on despite a gaping hole in its chest and the entrails spilling out around its knees.

Four more continued on, so close now. Velixar fled, the shame of it burning in his chest. Toward Karak he ran, veering side to side, nearly having his head lopped off by a cluster of living, terrified soldiers. He ducked beneath the attempt and kept on going, his gaze focused on his beloved deity.

Karak seethed as he stared at his brother, looking like he was ready to leap into the air and pounce on him had it not been for the undead that clawed at his godly form. "Face me!" he shouted, his words aimed at Ashhur, who still played puppet master behind the stone bunker. "Come face me yourself!"

The undead pressed even harder as Ashhur watched from across a sea of writhing corpses.

The *hiss* and *clink* of his fellow warriors drawing their weapons was music to Patrick's ears. He raised Winterbone, holding it steady despite its great weight, and prepared to strike. He was on the first soldier in moments and drew back, ready to slash with all his might. But when he caught sight of the soldier's expression, his eyes bulging with fear, Patrick faltered. Instead of lopping off the man's head, his blade glanced off his helm, raising a flurry of sparks, and the soldier rushed right past him. Patrick pulled up on the reins, forcing his mare to rear and nearly pitch him from the saddle. When he spun the horse around, he saw that the soldier had simply kept on running, his feet trudging desperately through the snow.

He heard the ring of steel meeting steel, and he whirled in a circle. The Turncloaks and Denton's brave civilians had followed his lead and halted their horses as well, randomly hacking at the charging soldiers, yet meeting no resistance. None of the running men wearing Karak's sigil tried to assail them. *They aren't charging. They're fleeing.*

"STOP!"

Hesitantly, his mates ceased lashing out at the soldiers, Big Flick punctuating the stillness when he brought the hilt of his longsword down on a soldier's head with a *clang*. All twenty-three sat slack-jawed and bewildered, their horses fidgeting nervously as hundreds of terrified men hurried past. They were like stones in the middle of a surge of water.

"What's happening?" yelled Tristan over the din.

Patrick grinned, his heart rate quickened.

"He's winning! Ashhur is winning!" he proclaimed. "Come on, follow me!"

Patrick urged his horse forward, working his way through the fleeing soldiers. Their numbers parted like the knees of a wanton maid after too much wine, allowing them uninhibited passage through the holes in the walls. He could smell blood and smoke in the air, as well as the sickly sweet stench of burning flesh. He crossed through the break in the outer wall, followed closely by his compatriots. He was past the ten-foot chasm between the two walls in the blink of an eye.

When he charged through the second fissure and into Mordeina, he found himself surrounded by absolute madness.

There were people fighting everywhere, tight-knit clusters swinging swords, mauls, axes, rods, and even hands and fists. It was so crowded that the hordes pushed up against both sides of his mare, sealing off any possible escape. A helmeted head collided with his knee, and something heavy shoved at him from the other side. A spray of blood caught him in the face, momentarily blinding him. Invasive fingers grabbed at Winterbone, trying to pry it from his grasp. For a moment he thought he heard someone shout his name, but it was impossible to tell. There was so much conflict, so many voices, that it was as if nothing existed save screams and clashing steel. He glanced about him in a panic, but couldn't make out anything except the flurry of bodies locked in struggle. He couldn't see Preston, Big Flick, Edward, Denton—anyone. It was all confusion.

It was like the night he had led the Turncloaks against Karak's soldiers in the chasm, only a hundred times worse.

Another stream of blood splashed against his cheek, and his mare shrieked in pain. The beast reared back, this time far enough that Patrick tumbled out of the saddle. He threw his arms up as he plummeted, keeping Winterbone high in the air. His back collided with a seemingly solid wall of humanity, but the force of his fall carried him, and those he crashed into, to the ground. Someone gasped—the first distinguishable sound he'd heard since entering the settlement—and he rolled over, his elbow splashing in gore-soaked muck. The man who had broken his fall writhed, face down, arms and legs pounding the sodden ground, weighed down by his heavy plated armor.

Even though a swarm of bodies crushed in on him from above, seeing the struggling soldier caused Patrick's head to clear. He glanced at his right hand, saw that he still held his sword, his fingers clenched so tightly they had turned white. Quickly, he scampered to his feet, seeking higher ground. As he had learned that night in the chasm, Winterbone was nearly useless in close quarters.

He shoved his way through the throng, stabbing at those in armor to try and keep them at a safe distance. He took a nasty slash to the bare flesh of his left wrist between his vambrace and his mailed glove, but he couldn't turn enough to see who delivered it. Instead, he put his head down and churned his uneven legs, bulling his way through.

Finally, he reached a gap in the fighting, nearly falling when suddenly there were no obstacles blocking him. Ahead of him was the bunker, but in front of that were two soldiers locked in battle with a Warden with long auburn hair. Patrick recognized him as Ludwig, and he was badly hurt. The soldiers hacked away mercilessly at him, and though Ludwig was much larger than they were, he was not nearly as good with a sword. It was all he could do to bat aside every third blow. Two of the fingers on his left hand were gone, a massive gash yawned on his chest, and innumerable other tiny cuts covered him.

Patrick charged, relishing the freedom of not being crushed by countless bodies, and came down hard with Winterbone. In the clamor, the soldiers never heard him coming. His blade sliced through steel, flesh, and bone alike, severing the arm of one of the men. It flopped uselessly on the ground. He then drove the tip of his sword through the slit in the soldier's helm, and the man fell backward. The second had turned when he realized his partner no longer fought with him, giving Warden Ludwig a chance to stab him through the neck from behind.

With both soldiers down, yet more approaching, Patrick rushed to the Warden and drove his shoulder into him, forcing the injured being against the outside of the bunker. "Climb, dammit!" he shouted, and Ludwig complied, albeit weakly. Patrick pushed and prodded until the Warden had reached the top of the five-foot curved wall. Only when he disappeared over the other side did Patrick's fingers find a crevice in the stone. With bodies beginning to flail toward him once more, he pulled himself up.

For a moment he stood atop the bunker and gawked at the carnage, but a second later he began running along the curved surface, slashing at the soldiers standing below. He noticed a Warden with a wide back and thick black hair, carving his way through a group of Karak's men. Patrick hacked off a soldier's sword-wielding hand as he tried to climb the bunker, then looked back up at Judarius and smiled. The Warden was a beast with his maul, an animal of single-minded fury. He crushed three skulls before turning around, and when Patrick saw his face, he stopped in his tracks. The Warden was horrific, his jaw dangling, his loose-fitting tan leathers saturated with red. Yet it was his eyes that riveted Patrick. Judarius's eyes had been green, but now they were pale and glowing slightly. His expression was blank.

That's when Patrick noticed that he himself was being mostly ignored. He looked this way and that, his eyes growing wider as he took in the battle scene around him. Soldiers were fighting soldiers. Soldiers were fighting men and women whose flesh was every shade from gray to blue. Soldiers were fighting attackers missing one or both of their limbs.

"What the fuck . . .?"

Velixar swung Lionsbane, taking half the head off a naked dead woman, and slid to the snow-and-gore-covered ground when five more reached for him. Fingers snagged his cloak, and he lifted his arms, allowing it to be torn from his body. He almost lost Lionsbane in the process, but his grip on the sword's handle was true. He scampered to his feet, his pendant bouncing against his chest as the undead descended upon the cloak as if he were still in it. Without protection from the elements, the cold hit his sweat-soaked body like an icy wave. He shivered but kept running.

He was almost to Karak when the deity raised his hand and a gush of purple flame and shadow, eight feet wide and spiraling, leapt from his palm. The spinning shaft decimated all in its path, living and dead alike, as it careened toward Ashhur. The God of Justice locked both arms in front of his face and lowered his head, and Karak's magic hit an invisible wall a few feet in front of him, sending tendrils of destructive energy flying in all direction, killing even more soldiers.

Those soldiers, their bodies smoking but still intact, rose a second later.

"COWARD!" Karak roared.

Velixar reached his chosen god's side, shoving Lionsbane through the chin of yet another grasping undead. The blade exited the top of its skull with a *pop*. He yanked it free and turned to Karak. The god sent another magical attack Ashhur's way, only to see his brother deflect it once more. The anger in the deity's eyes was so great, Velixar thought his god would set the whole world on fire if it led to Ashhur's defeat, consequences be damned.

"My Lord!" he screamed.

Karak's glowing eyes turned to him, and for a moment it seemed the deity might burn him to a cinder. Velixar kept his gaze intent on the god's, using his elbow to smash away another dead attacker.

"It is lost, my Lord," he said, his voice ragged and gasping to his own ears.

"It cannot be! I will not let it!" snarled Karak, turning back to Ashhur and sending another blast of energy his way.

"It is, but not forever," Velixar said. "My Lord, we must fall back. When next we come for him, we will be ready!"

Another undead slammed into Velixar. He kicked the thing to the ground and removed its head with two frustrated hacks.

Karak looked at him once more, his gaze softening. Velixar swore he saw not only rage behind those divine eyes, but embarrassment as well. The deity nodded to him, then leapt forward, gathering twelve grasping, snapping beasts in his arms. He hurled them straight ahead, toppling the hundred now approaching like so many saplings.

"Soldiers of Karak, my brave warriors," his god called out. "We must retreat. We have failed this day, but we must live to fight again!"

His voice carried throughout the settlement, and the remaining Eastern soldiers turned tail and sprinted for the hole in the wall. Karak placed his hand on Velixar's shoulder, and the strength that had previously left him returned tenfold. The pendant on his chest pulsed as he slid Lionsbane back into its sheath. Together, the god and the First Man raised a wall of fire, shielding the retreating soldiers from the advancing undead. Grunting, he poured all his anger into the spell, heightening the flames. Finally, the last brave stragglers limped through the gate, and the god and his prophet followed suit, Karak having to duck beneath the jagged opening.

Once outside, Velixar saw thousands of soldiers tramping across the snow-covered valley toward their distant camp, where black smoke billowed. *No.* The last of their supplies were burning. He shot one last glance behind him, saw the undead pouring out of the gap in the wall, but noticed they didn't pursue. They stopped the moment they emerged, forming a wall of decaying flesh, their dimly shining eyes staring straight ahead. Not wanting to see any more, Velixar turned away, quickening his pace to keep up with Karak's much longer strides. Where once there was confidence, frustration now simmered.

"All this time . . . for nothing," Velixar said. "How did this happen? Victory was there, we held it in our hands . . . "

Karak gazed down at him, and the pendant on his chest throbbed.

"I made a mistake, High Prophet," the god said. "And now all of Dezrel shall suffer for it. I offered mercy, yet only death will suffice for my brother and his people. So be it. If he will turn his own dead into soldiers, then let us make soldiers of his entire kingdom as we burn it to the ground."

A bright flash came from Patrick's left, followed by a gust of hot wind that knocked him off the wall. He lost hold of Winterbone and landed on the ground on the other side with a *thud*, then rolled down into the bunker. His head rattled and he shook it. Lying just in front of him was Warden Ludwig. The Warden's eyes were open and unblinking, already gone milky in death. Patrick watched in horror as a faint light began to shine deep within those unblinking eyes. The body shuddered once, and Ludwig lifted his head. He looked right at Patrick, though there was no recognition in his gaze. The Warden slowly hauled his body off the cold ground and walked, hunched over, out of the bunker. The flap of flesh on his chest sagged like a panting tongue.

Patrick scampered after him, picking Winterbone up along the way, and watched as Ludwig hopped over the bunker and re-entered the fray. Another bright flash came, momentarily bringing stars to his vision, and he blinked and turned around. There he saw Ashhur, standing not two hundred feet away from him and surrounded by a crowd of bleeding humans and Wardens. Ashhur looked imposing, a scowl on his face and his hair fluttering behind him like golden smoke. The light coming from his eyes was so intense that Patrick couldn't gaze at it directly. He turned his head slightly and squinted, watching as the deity raised his hand. Another *whoosh* ensued, and a massive spiral of dark matter detonated not ten feet in front of the god, sending streamers of dissipating energy in all directions. Patrick had to duck before one of those streamers struck him in the side of the head.

"We have failed this day, but we must live to fight again!"

He recognized that voice. How could he not? It had been seared into his brain in the aftermath of the attack on Haven. In a daze, he took a step backward and peered over the low wall. Sure enough, there in the distance he saw Karak, the deity just as imposing as Ashhur in his black armor and with his flaming ethereal sword. The god was backing away through the horde of vicious dead things, fending off dozens of them at a time. And beside him, his eyes alight with crimson, was Jacob Eveningstar. God and man both then lifted their hands, and a massive sheet of flame rose into the air. The flames raced across the ground, becoming a wall all their own, blotting out Patrick's vision. A good number of the walking dead were set alight, but that didn't stop their forward momentum. They continued to pursue even though their skin charred and smoked.

Then, not ten minutes later, it was over. The wall of flame fizzled away. A few hundred living soldiers remained within the walls, dashing this way and that, trying to escape any way they could. He even saw a score of them along the far wall to his right, tiny from such a great distance, attempting to climb the staircase. A cluster of men and women wearing burlap chased after them, fists pumping as they shouted. He couldn't hear what they were saying, for the sound of weeping and moaning drowned out all else.

There were wide patches of muddy earth all around him, littered with discarded bits of armor and even a few wriggling limbs. There were also the corpses of at least two hundred horses out there, somewhere among them his own mare. Yet though the dead horses stayed on the ground, the human corpses persisted in walking. There were thousands of them streaming out the gap in the wall, but they didn't pursue Karak and his soldiers across the snowy field. Instead, they spread out once they exited the outer wall, lining up in a formation of living death. Patrick felt disgusted just to look at them . . . and his horror peaked when he saw Denton hobbling among them, his right arm dangling by a thread, his gait lurching. Patrick closed his eyes. Barclay would be overcome with grief, if the boy still lived.

Finally, he allowed himself to consider the battlefield again. Dazed people were moving about all around him, appearing almost as mindless as the living dead. The wounded were tended to, and he even saw a young man wandering among the numbers of the walking corpses, eyes brimmed with tears as he scanned every face. Patrick turned away from the sight, but in doing so he was forced to look at his childhood home as it sat atop its hill. There was a crowd packed around Manse DuTaureau, more people than he had seen in a single place in all his life. For a moment he wondered if they were cheering or sobbing over what had just transpired, or if they were like Patrick and felt nothing but revulsion.

War makes monsters of us all.

"Fuck that," Patrick muttered.

He jammed Winterbone into the earth, turned on his heels, and marched toward Ashhur, farther along the bunker. His sorrow bloomed, even though he caught sight of Preston and Edward assisting with the injured. He also saw Tristan, and the youth raised a weary hand to him in greeting. Patrick ignored him and picked up his pace. Just as the soldiers had done when he rode through the walls, the multitude of weary people gave him a wide berth as he walked. When he reached Ashhur, he found the god on one knee, hovering over Master Warden Ahaesarus. Ashhur touched the Master Warden's chest, his hands lighting up a brilliant white, and Ahaesarus cried out. A chorus of *snaps* and *pops* followed, and Patrick watched the Warden's nearly severed leg gradually stitch back together. There had been many times in the past when Patrick had felt awed by such a spectacle. Now was not one of those times.

When the deed was done, three Wardens helped Ahaesarus to his feet and supported him as he limped away. Other men and women began approaching the god, but immediately retracted when they spotted Patrick coming up from the rear. Ashhur turned around and looked at him. The deity wasn't smiling. In fact, he looked more exhausted than he had back in Haven.

"My son," Ashhur said.

"Your Grace," Patrick said softly. He spoke his next words without thought. "Does that name even fit any longer?"

"How dare you?" shouted an injured Warden flanking Ashhur. Patrick recognized Judah, one of Ahaesarus's closest confidants.

"Leave, Judah," the deity said.

"I cannot, your Grace. He has—"

"Leave."

Judah, his eyes showing hurt, gradually bowed and backed away. Ashhur turned his attention back to Patrick.

"What in the ever-living fuck did you do?" Patrick asked coldly.

"I did what was necessary," answered Ashhur, even more coldly. "There are no more rules now, my son. I must protect my children."

"This . . . " Patrick waved his hand at the undead streaming out of the wall. "This is an abomination."

"Is it any greater an abomination than the thousands of my dead children Karak has laid at my feet?"

Patrick felt his righteous fury beginning to falter.

"But at what price?" he asked. "What of allowing your children to mourn their dead? There is supposed to be *peace* after death. That's what you always told us. Not . . . not *this*!"

"Their souls are safe in the afterlife," said Ashhur. "I have raised their earthly bodies and nothing more. What you witness are empty shells."

"But what about your children? What of their grief? How do you think they feel watching the corpses of their loved ones strolling about? Did you think of *that*?"

The deity looked disappointed. "One cannot grieve if one is dead."

Patrick went to retort but held his tongue. *Good point.* Finally, after a long pause, he said, "But what happens when Karak returns? You know he will. Will your army of corpses help us then?"

"Karak will not have a chance to return. *We* will pursue *him*, even if we must chase him all the way to his own pathetic kingdom."

For a moment, it seemed like smoke curled out of Ashhur's eyes, a sight that made Patrick shiver. "His army is in shambles, his lines broken."

"But how can we, with all we've lost?" asked Patrick. He glanced over his shoulder at the decimation of Mordeina to prove his point.

Finally, Ashhur's expression softened, and his massive fingers wrapped around Patrick's shoulder.

"It is true we have lost much," he told him wearily. "But should we allow my brother to gather himself and come back at us, we will lose *everything*. Karak began this war, and I will end it, even if I must empty every grave in all of Dezrel."

CHAPTER 29

It was risky to linger outside the Castle of the Lion, even during daylight hours. Sisters of the Cloth were constantly about, keeping close watch on the weary female populace as they shuffled through their daily routines. The Sisters seemed on edge now, presumably because over a hundred of their numbers had disappeared in previous months. They eyed everyone with suspicion. Civilians who appeared the slightest bit dubious were grabbed and dragged pleading into the castle for interrogation.

Over the seven days she had spent spying on the castle, Laurel Lawrence hadn't seen a single one of them reemerge.

She was there again, sitting in a rickety chair by the side of the cobbled road, a seller's cart filled with inexpensive baubles in front of her. The cart had been pieced together out of discarded lumber from crumbling houses; the trinkets had been collected from the belongings of those hiding out in the caverns beneath the Black Bend. Laurel was dressed in her Specter's garb, a decrepit old woman with tangled hair and filthy skin. She made certain to look each passerby in the eye and call out in her false old crone voice. "Half a copper for a top! A quarter copper for a set of rings! One gold for the elixir of love!"

She had no such elixir, only a capped porcelain vial filled with cheap brandy, but she felt compelled to shout it anyway. With most of the street merchants offering at least one expensive, unbelievable item, it would have been suspicious if she didn't. She also thought it a small rebellion to sell a love elixir in a city where there were so few men.

The weary citizens passed her by as always, bundled against the cold. Only one woman stopped, a child hanging off each arm. There were heavy purple bags beneath her eyes and her skin was pale. One of the children was sleeping, his rosebud lips pressed against the woman's neck; the other, a small girl no more than three, sat in the crook of her mother's right arm, draped in an outrageously large fur blanket. Neither looked in Laurel's direction.

"Ooh," the little girl said, pointing at something on the table. Her fingers were sickly and white.

"Yes, Soleh," said the mother, her voice sleepy. "Which one are you looking at?"

The little girl pointed more exuberantly. "The dolly. It's pretty."

"It is, Soleh. Very pretty."

Laurel was taken aback by the sound of the girl's name. While it was a relatively common practice for those in and around Veldaren to name their children after the First Families—she had even met a handful of people named Thessaly, the most forgettable of Clovis Crestwell's children—she had not heard anyone utter the name of the former minister in quite some time. She took a step backward, gazing intently at the mother, but the woman showed no interest in meeting her gaze.

"I want, Mommy," little Soleh said.

The mother finally lifted her eyes, and Laurel could see a hint of recognition on her face.

"How much for the doll?" she asked.

"Um . . . it's . . . ," began Laurel, but she quickly snapped her mouth shut. She'd forgotten her old crone voice. She cleared her throat and said, "two coppers" in a hoarse croak.

The woman squinted at her, cocked her head slightly, and then looked at her daughter. "I'm sorry, Soleh. We only have a half copper left."

Stupid, stupid, stupid, Laurel chastised herself inwardly.

Little Soleh's bottom lip jutted out, and her eyes grew watery. "But I *want it.*"

"We can't, dear." Her eyes began darting left and right, her words in a rush. "Please, darling, don't make a scene."

"I want the dolly!"

The child's display had caught the attention of the Sisters lingering nearby. The mother glanced up at them, fear washing over her face. "We can't, Soleh. I'm sorry."

The mother started to walk away. The child continued crying.

Laurel snatched up the doll and circled around the cart, this time making sure to limp the way the Specter always did. "Wait," she called out, and the mother turned. The Sisters were approaching them now, and the mother's eyes flicked in their direction.

"Here," said Laurel, placing the doll into little Soleh's reaching, needy hands. "No payment necessary—seeing the smile on your daughter's face is enough." She rustled Soleh's hair while the girl gathered the doll to her chest and hugged it.

"Th-thank you," said the mother.

One of the Sisters had reached them, a short girl with arresting blue eyes. Laurel backed away. The Sister placed her hand on the mother's shoulder and stared intently at her.

"I'm . . . I'm sorry for the disturbance," the mother said. "I was just out for some bread."

The Sister nodded to her, then turned to face her approaching brethren. She held up her hand. The other Sisters inclined their heads and turned away, heading back to their posts. The mother breathed out a shaky sigh. The short Sister reached up and playfully flicked little Soleh under the chin before gesturing for the mother to be on her way.

"Thank you, thank you," the mother repeated as she hustled down the road.

The Sister swiveled around and looked at Laurel. Those soulful blue eyes flicked to her cart, and Laurel immediately turned around and limped back toward it. The Sister fell in beside her.

"Thanks," Laurel whispered out of the side of her mouth.

Lyana, her face obscured by her wrappings, said nothing.

When they arrived at the cart, Lyana performed the ruse of examining all of the baubles resting on the cart's flat surface. She cast a quick look behind her before asking about what had happened in her hushed, childlike voice. She held up a small tome that was for sale, its leather cover layered with stains and dust.

Laurel leaned forward as if looking at the tome along with her. "Just a scared woman."

"Why did she panic?"

"Because I forgot to disguise my voice. If she were caught and brought before the judges, we both know what would happen."

The girl nodded, and Laurel could not suppress her shudder. It was eerie to see Lyana back in her wrappings. Sometimes she found herself wondering if her young companion would fall back into the thrall of her former order.

"How did you forget to alter your voice?" Lyana asked. "You're always so careful."

Laurel thought about telling her, but decided to lie. "I'm just tired. I'll concentrate harder next time. We still have a few hours before it's time."

"Good."

Lyana's eyes glazed over, and she pivoted on the balls of her feet, carelessly tossing the tome back onto the cart before walking away. Again, Laurel felt unease. She knew it was an act, but still . . . when Lyana donned her wrappings, she became a different woman altogether.

The hours dragged by. Few customers approached her cart, their meager coin needed to pay the fish, meat, bread, vegetable, and medicinal sellers instead. That left Laurel with ample time to lose herself in thought. It hadn't been an easy decision to start coming here, lingering just outside the castle's portcullis in full view of the frozen corpses that still swayed on the wall. Laurel often felt like a sheep wandering into the lion's den, causing her to wonder if this was worth the risk of exposure.

Of course it's worth it. What else can we do?

The situation for those who railed against Veldaren's new leadership had grown worse by the day. The fountain was now watched, and many who had helped those fleeing Karak's law, including Ursula and Tristessa, the mother and daughter from the cobbler's, had been executed before that very fountain, their heads lopped from their bodies while a broken populace looked on. No more communications reached the rebellion, no more stray Sisters, bandits, or other frightened souls entered their midst. The Sisters of the Cloth pressed closer and closer to the Black Bend, putting fear in the hearts of the masses. They began pulling the poor and downtrodden from their homes, hauling them away for judgment. The Judges also spread out their area of search during their nighttime hunts. They were simply getting much too close. Ten days ago the male lion had devoured one of the families living in a ramshackle building on the outskirts of the Bend itself. Those who resided aboveground in the Bend were frightened beyond belief, and though most topsiders didn't know there was a settlement growing daily beneath their feet, Laurel knew it was only a matter of time before the caverns were discovered.

It had been Karl Dogon, King Eldrich's bodyguard, who demanded action.

"The Judges may be the swords that stalk the night, and the Sisters the ax that rules the day," Karl had said, "but the arm that wields them both is a single man. Joben Tustlewhite is the true ruler of this city. Were the mumbling priest out of the picture, it would be left to the acolytes to carry on in his wake, and they are but boys.

The cowardly councilmen who remain in the priest's employ would turn on them in a heartbeat and lock the Judges away for good. We need to kill him. How difficult can it be to take the life of a single man?"

As it turned out, *very*.

The mumbling priest spent his evenings in Karak's Temple in the undeveloped far eastern corner of the city. Every morning just after sunrise, a carriage containing twelve Sisters would ride up to the temple to retrieve him. They accompanied him all the way to the castle. The priest would them remain in the castle all day, never once showing his face outside until an hour before sunset. Then he would reappear, again accompanied by twelve Sisters—it was impossible to tell whether they were the same twelve or not—and the wagon would carry him back to the temple, where the acolytes waited for him to arrive. The man was never alone.

For the last seven days, Laurel and her cohorts had charted the man's movements, hoping that his routine would change. Yet, he always kept the same schedule, the time only shifting because the days were growing longer. At first they thought they could secretly place one of the former Sisters among them, perhaps Harmony or even Lyana, and slip a poison into the cup of cider and brandy they brought him each morning. Pulo insisted that was too risky, as a man of Tustlewhite's importance would most likely choose his guardians carefully, perhaps even make them stand before the Judges to prove their loyalty. They couldn't chance attempting the kill close to the castle, for with all the Sisters around, whoever did the deed would be subject to death or, even worse, capture. Also out was attacking the carriage once it reached the Road of Worship. Twenty men wouldn't be enough to overpower the Sisters before Tustlewhite called the Judges, as Dogon claimed he could. Two hundred men could easily run through the Sisters, but the same problem remained: Should the priest summon the lions before he was killed, whatever size force they brought would be decimated.

And so they watched, and they waited, hoping to find an opening they could use. But it seemed the only thing going their way was the warming of the weather. It hadn't snowed for almost three weeks now, and though there was still ice on the ground, the snow within the city was almost gone.

Laurel watched as the sun finally drooped near the horizon. The other sellers began packing up their carts, so she did the same. The exhausted women then shoved their wares along the road, flanked by the Sisters. One of them joined Laurel as well, and she needed to check twice to make sure it was Lyana. She breathed a sigh of relief and steered her cart around the corner, allowing the other street merchants and their tails to pull ahead of her. As usual, none seemed to even notice she had fallen behind. Someone always had to be the last in line, after all, and she appeared to be an old woman. By the time she rounded the corner onto South Road, the others were far ahead.

Once out of view of the castle, she and Lyana glanced around to make sure no one was looking and then hastily shoved the cart into a slender alley, cutting between an abandoned apothecary and a smithy. They slid open the side door to the smithy and pushed the cart inside, careful to not make much noise. Then Laurel stripped out of her heavy, beaten shift and fur jacket. The cold made her teeth chatter as she reached below the cart and slipped her arms into a padded jerkin.

"That's better," she whispered.

"Ready?" asked Lyana. Laurel turned to her, saw the girl's expression shift beneath her wrappings. It looked like she was grimacing.

"Ready," she said.

They shut the door and climbed to the top of the smithy, which allowed them a clear view of the castle and its walls. The roof was the safest place to be at this time of day, as the Sisters were now making their way home and no longer watching the city from above. The Castle of the Lion was just south of the great fountain at the hub of the city, and the area around it had at one time been densely populated. The buildings lining South Road were set close together, their roofs often separated by mere inches. Because of that, when Laurel peered over the edge, it was like gazing at a landscape of pointed clay dunes and flat drab platforms.

"He's coming," Lyana whispered.

Laurel narrowed her eyes at the distant castle and saw the wagon exit the portcullis, five Sisters hanging off either side of it. The driver, another Sister, cracked the reins, and the two horses pulling the wagon began to trot. They turned west out of the castle, heading their way.

"Let's go," said Laurel.

The two of them hopped from rooftop to rooftop, taking care to keep themselves out of sight, as the Sisters were still present on the streets. At one point Laurel slipped on a slanted roof, sending a clay shingle sliding over the side, where it smashed on the ground below. "Shit," she muttered, her fingers tightly gripping the roof while she panted. No Sister came to investigate the noise. After a look from Lyana, they kept on moving.

The wagon was a half mile behind them, slowly lumbering along the road. Whenever it came upon another conveyance, the Sisters would stare menacingly at the driver until they gave room to pass. The sun dipped lower. In less than an hour, it would sink below the horizon, and the roars would begin.

Laurel and Lyana didn't follow the road directly to the fountain; instead, they veered off to the right, heading for the residential sections that sat in the elbow between South Road and the Road of Worship. The buildings were spaced farther apart here, forcing them to descend and walk on the road, but it was actually safer there than it had been on the rooftops. With nearly three-quarters of Veldaren's residents now gone, either to Karak's Army, beneath the Bend, or to the grave, the place was nearly deserted. It was also the area where some of the Sisters resided during the night, which meant they would be free to move as they pleased until just before sunset.

Soon the houses ended, and the foundations of unfinished buildings and stacks of rotting timber peppered the landscape. Laurel and Lyanna kept far out of sight, dashing through the field a good half mile away from the Road of Worship. Here the snow was still present, and they ran through the tall grasses, recently uncovered by the thaw, to hide their approach. On the distant road they could see the wagon lumbering along behind them, the Sisters peering out, hands cupped over their eyes to block out the low-hanging sun.

Finally, after running for nearly forty minutes, they arrived at Karak's Temple. It was an unseemly rectangular structure, five stories high and black as midnight. The onyx lions outside its front entrance were captured in mid-leap, their mouths hanging open in an eternal roar. Lyana grabbed Laurel's hand, pulling her across the field and toward the building. The wagon was close, almost close enough for the Sisters to see them. Once they reached the small thatch of evergreens that stood on their side of the road, Lyana helped Laurel climb one of the trees before bounding up effortlessly after her.

Finally at a vantage point where they felt it safe to watch without risk of exposure, they sat still and waited.

The wagon pulled up in front of the temple as acolytes stepped outside. The mumbling priest got out of the wagon, what remained of his white hair flapping in the breeze. He pulled his cloak up over his head and approached the boys in red robes. The acolytes escorted him inside. The door closed. The Sisters piled back into the wagon, the driver turned it around, and they plodded away.

The same as every other day.

The sun dipped even lower, half of it now obscured by the mountains to the west. Laurel glanced up at the red lines streaking across the sky. A riotous roar shook the air, vibrating the branches of the tree they were in, knocking bits of ice to the ground. Still she held on, staring out at the blackening structure. She had to remind herself to breathe.

"Laurel, we must go."

"Not yet," she replied.

Darkness slowly descended over the land, the last rays of light making the windowless temple look like it was constructed out of living fire. Nothing was happening. Nothing at all. The lion roared again, and Laurel heard it echo all around her.

"Laurel, please. Roddalin will be here come morning. Our time is over."

Laurel's head snapped around, and she stared at the girl. *"Not yet."*

"We must. The Judges will work their way toward the Bend. If we are not there before then . . . "

Laurel reached out and grabbed the girl by her wrappings with both hands. "Listen to me, Lyana. We *must do this*. There has to be something we haven't seen. Something, anything . . . "

"Even if there *is* something, how would we know? The temple has no windows, Laurel!"

In her panic her voice rose, and Laurel placed a hand over her breast to calm her.

"I don't know, Lyana. But I need to watch, I need to *try*. Please allow me that. None have stayed this late already, which means we are seeing things others haven't."

"Even if that is nothing?"

"Even so."

Lyana huffed and sat back against the branch. She unwound the wrappings from her head, gradually revealing the pretty young girl beneath, the girl that looked so much like her grandmother, the dearly departed Soleh Mori. Laurel found herself staring. She'd grown fond of the young sprite. After all, they had so much in common. Neither had a family any longer. All they had was each other.

She was so focused on Lyana that at first she thought the sound that reached her ears was a trick of her imagination. But then she saw Lyana's eyes widen, and she turned around, inching forward on the branch until she could see the whole of the temple clearly.

The top of the structure rose above their spot in the tree, and it was from there that the sound originated. It was the singing of a plethora of innocent voices. She saw outlines on the roof of the temple in the dying light, and many flashes of red.

It was the acolytes, marching in a circle as they sang Karak's glory.

She squinted, confused, and then strangely, in the center of the temple above the massive door, a single shutter opened. There stood the mumbling priest, Joben Tustlewhite, breathing in the cold night air. Laurel could see everything inside the room—the bed, the cupboard, the candles, and a writing desk against the far wall. She looked on as the priest turned away from the window, went to the desk, and sat down.

Still, the acolytes sang on the roof.

Lyana was suddenly beside her, head poking out of the branches. "What's going on?"

Laurel threw a hand over her mouth and shoved her to the side, almost losing her balance and falling out of the tree in the process. She held her breath as Joben stood up, came to the window, and peered out into the oncoming blackness. When he saw nothing, he returned to sit at his desk.

Putting a finger to her lips, Laurel pointed to the ground. Lyana got her message and silently descended the tree, making sure to help Laurel along the way. It was times like these that the last surviving member of House Lawrence ridiculed her own childhood love of girly things. Had she shadowed the boys for even half her youth, she would be much better prepared for the deeds before her.

Their feet touched ground, and they waited a few moments as the acolytes continued to sing. As one song ended, another started.

When it became apparent that they wouldn't be stopping soon, Laurel and Lyana crept back along the tree line and then began running, praying that the boys were too intent on their praise of that bastard Karak to look down and notice them.

None did. They passed by Karak's Temple and continued to head east, then north into the forest bordering Veldaren, their footfalls crunching much too loudly in the thin layer of icy snow. The sky was completely dark now, the stars shimmering overhead. It was only when the temple was the size of a child's block behind them that they chanced stopping. Lyana whirled in place, searching for signs of the Judges, and Laurel doubled over and coughed.

"What was that?" asked Lyana.

Laurel spit a wad of phlegm and wiped a stray strand off her chin, which in turn removed some of the caked-on mud that assisted her Specter disguise.

"That, Lyana, was our opportunity," Laurel said with a tired smile. "Now let's get going before the lions find us. We need to talk to Pulo and King Eldrich. We have a priest to kill."

CHAPTER 30

After a while, it was hard for Ahaesarus to tell the difference between the walking dead and their living counterparts—other than those missing limbs, that is. They all had the same blank expressions on their faces, moved with the same hunched, uneven gaits, and were covered with equal amounts of filth. If not for the tears shed by the living and the gaping wounds marking the flesh of the shuffling corpses, they might as well have been one and the same.

Over the last four days, Ahaesarus had taken a rough count of the reanimated dead that stood guard outside Mordeina's walls. Their numbers included four thousand soldiers of Karak's and sixteen thousand of Ashhur's children. The remaining three hundred and twenty-nine were Ahaesarus's brothers in servitude. They towered above the rest, majestic even in death, their skin pale and their clothes tattered. Of the original thousand that had been saved by Celestia and Ashhur when the winged demons descended on Algrahar, only one hundred and eighty-three remained living. Ahaesarus thought of the destruction he had witnessed during those fateful days, of the screams of his family and the ripping of steel through flesh, and it came to him that everything had come full circle. His second life had become just as anguished as his first. In his dark moments before sleep, he wondered if it all had been worth the trouble for him and his brothers.

Of course it was. We helped create Paradise. We helped forge peace.

Yet now that peace was gone. Now Paradise was in shambles, Karak setting fire to the countryside as he fled back to his kingdom across the river. The eastern sky glowed red day and night. All of it, ruined. And for what? What remained now that all safety and prosperity was gone? He looked down at his right leg. Beneath the thick fabric of his breeches, there would be a white scar there, encircling his calf entirely, a reminder of a wound that would have been mortal had Ashhur not been there to mend him—though the god had been too weak, too overly strained, to heal him completely. He flexed the leg, and felt the dull ache of pain in his bones. It was a sensation he knew would follow him to his death, whenever that happened to be, and loathing churned in his gut.

There is justice. There is retribution.

He heard a familiar pleading voice above the murmur of beseeching sobs and looked up. The living citizens of Paradise were weaving their way through the wall of undead, seeking out their loved ones as they had been for days now. He scanned their numbers, searching for the voice he'd heard, and found Judarius standing above the other undead, his dark hair matted and clumped in greasy tendrils, his face a mask of ruin. Azariah was standing before him, grasping his dead brother's hand. The shortest Warden muttered words of a long-forgotten prayer, an entreaty to Rana, the god of their long-dead world. It was a prayer Ahaesarus knew well: "Treaty of the Fallen," an appeal to the god of Algrahar to watch over the souls of the deceased. Ahaesarus had spoken those words many times in his former life, when he had been a priest in the Temple of Forever Light. He gulped down the bile that gathered in the back of his throat and began walking.

By the time he reached Azariah, the Warden had released his brother's cold, dead hands. Azariah's eyes were downcast, his arms crossed over his chest. The long white robe he wore was splotched with mud and dried blood. Azariah had spent much of the last four days among Mordeina's wounded, mending bodies and souls alike, and Ahaesarus wondered if this was his first trip outside the walls. He placed a hand on the shorter Warden's shoulder. He wanted to say something comforting to his colleague but couldn't think of the proper words.

"He often surprised me," Azariah said without looking up.

"How so?"

Azariah shook his head, a sad smile on his lips. "Back home, Judarius was a ruffian. Callous, belligerent, full of anger, and always drunk. All he ever wished to do was fight, and it was only when Father had had enough of his antics and sent him to the Citadel that he harnessed his anger. Judarius took to the teachings of Rana's paladins, and he calmed. He was only forty-three when he was christened a knight of the Order of the Two Suns, the youngest ever given the title."

Ahaesarus looked down at his friend, stunned. "He was accepted into the knighthood? He told me he was simply in the honor guard of Rana's Shrine."

"That is because his past shamed him," said Azariah, gazing back up at the ruined face of his undead brother. "The knighthood was his penance for his past sins. If not for his misdeeds, he would never have been sent to the Citadel, and the paladins would never have taken him under their wing. To him, the title he bore was a constant reminder of all those he had hurt."

"That *is* surprising. I never knew Judarius to be sentimental."

"He was. To a point."

The short Warden fell silent, staring down at the ground and shuffling his feet. Finally he lifted his head and looked over at Ahaesarus once more.

"Do you know why he never created a knighthood here in Paradise?" Azariah said. "I asked him once. *'The concept of a knight might be noble, but by definition it teaches a life of violence. I would never form a knighthood here, for I see no use in it. I do not see the need for this young race to ever learn about violence at all.'* Those were his exact words."

Ahaesarus thought of the battle, of the violence consuming their new world.

"Do you think he felt that way at the end?" he asked softly. "He fought valiantly; he fought viciously. He seemed to think he was made for it."

Azariah shrugged and gestured toward his brother. "He was, and he did, but you would have to ask him. And I think you might find it difficult to pry the answer from his lips."

Azariah then turned away from Ahaesarus and began walking through the crowd of people, both living and dead. "We will be leaving on the morrow," Ahaesarus called out after him. "Will you be joining us?"

"No." Azariah stopped and turned, facing him again. "My place is here, among my students. As I have told you before, this world needs healers as much as it needs warriors, perhaps even more so. Our roles have shifted, Ahaesarus. My brother is dead. You are now the warrior, as he was. I . . . I am now the priest, like you once were."

With that, he turned and approached a throng of fifty youngsters huddling before the wall of the dead, focusing on two in particular: a tall boy and girl with sandy hair and flesh a shade darker than the others around them. If Ahaesarus remembered correctly, their names were Barclay and Sharin Noonan, siblings who had traveled with Ashhur when the god trekked from one corner of Paradise to the other, collecting his children and bringing them here to Mordeina. Both the youths' cheeks glistened with tears as they stared at one of the standing dead men, most likely their father. Ahaesarus looked on as Azariah touched the dead man's forehead, whispered a few words to the grieving youths, and then wrapped his wide arms around them. He guided them away from the swarm, heading for the holes in Mordeina's walls.

Ahaesarus shook his head. "You were right, he *is* the sensitive one," he spoke, looking at Judarius's corpse. "And perhaps he is also the smartest of us all." He looked up at Celestia's tree, its branches pressing upward into the late winter sky, and followed Azariah and his students into the settlement, walking with a slight limp.

Unlike the exterior, inside the walls there was no time for sadness and disbelief. The last four days had been spent repairing what had been lost. With Karak having fled, Ashhur dismantled the bunker he had raised, using the stones to rebuild and expand on the murder row lining the road leading into the settlement. The usable lumber from shattered edifices was repurposed into new constructions. The numerous dead horses were hauled away, to be butchered and salted for the nearly starving populace.

Those four days also featured preparations for the march east, which was set to begin on this day at noon. The remaining horses were saddled, supply wagons built, weapons gathered. Discarded armor from Karak's Army had been collected, the black painted over before being distributed among those who would depart. All supplies were amassed at the base of Manse DuTaureau's hill, and the crowd was thick. Wives and mothers offered their husbands and sons teary goodbyes. Young King Benjamin was out as well, Ahaesarus was happy to see, with Howard Baedan steering him through the people, along with Isabel DuTaureau's children and grandchildren. And halfway up the hill, Ashhur knelt in the sparse snow, holding court with a gaggle of youths. Ahaesarus felt his heart plummet at the sight. Ashhur was always at his benign best when speaking with children, his godly face beaming, the glow of his eyes bringing vibrancy to the landscape that didn't exist even on the brightest of days. Yet none of that was in evidence at the moment. The deity appeared sidetracked, exhausted, even glum, as if he wanted to be somewhere else, and from the looks on the children's faces, they noticed it.

Ahaesarus glanced up at the manse and thought he saw the outline of a redheaded waif in one of the windows. Isabel seemed to look right at him despite the distance. He shook his head and turned away.

The decision to pursue Karak had been met with bewilderment at first. In the aftermath of the bloodiest day in the history of Paradise, and with the shock of seeing the dead rise, not many knew how to react. Ashhur had preached, trying to convince his creations that what he wished for was righteous, but the response he received from his people were hesitant at best. It wasn't until Patrick DuTaureau, his Turncloaks, and a collection of two hundred men and women who resided in the northwest corner of Mordeina voiced their enthusiastic support for the plan that the others joined in. Whereas Ashhur pleaded with their sense of justice and the need to survive, Patrick drew on a much more base desire—vengeance. The morning of that second day, he had stormed through the assembly, screaming at the top of his lungs, fire in his countenance. Many then joined the cause.

In the end, more than thirty thousand volunteered, men and women, the young, old, and infirm. So many offered their services that most had to be turned away. There simply weren't enough armor and weapons to go around, and Ashhur was adamant that he wouldn't send his children into battle unprepared.

A little too late for that, Ahaesarus thought at the time, then felt guilty immediately after.

Now he scanned the crowd, looking for Patrick, but could see only the elder leader of the Turncloaks guiding his young cohorts in saddling the last of the horses. Finally, he spotted the malformed redheaded man, riding from the front gate, that giant sword of his resting on his lap. The look on his face was intense, his posture strangely rigid. A young girl ran up to the side of his horse and pulled on the leg of his mailed breeches, but he shoved her hand away. Ahaesarus frowned at the sight. He had always known Patrick to be a carefree sort, crass yet loving, and even insightful at times. To see him act this way made him feel the same as when he saw Ashhur teaching the children—distraught.

The misshapen man rode up to him. "Master Warden," Patrick said, no humor in his tone.

"Patrick."

"It's time."

Ahaesarus nodded. Neither said another word.

Ashhur rose to his feet and lifted a giant horn to his lips. His golden hair flowed around him like a mane of silk. When he blew into the instrument, the trumpeting rang throughout the walled settlement with the force of an erupting volcano. All work ceased, all eyes turned to their god.

"Citizens of Paradise, my precious children, the time to forge your own destiny is now."

The fighting men and women formed haphazard ranks. Horses were tethered to the wagons and whips cracked. Ashhur gave the word, and mismatched armor clanked and spears thudded against the ground as the new army of eight thousand surged forward. They were a flood of flesh and steel, flowing toward the newly reconstructed front gate, too disorganized to form the lines necessary to pass through without creating a logjam. One hundred seventy-five of the remaining one hundred eighty-three Wardens marched at their lead, trying to get them under control.

Ahaesarus lingered by Ashhur's side in front of the inner wall, watching the force approach. Patrick and the Turncloaks were there as well, and the Master Warden studied them. The soldiers who had turned against Karak didn't seem as somber or frightened as the rest, and they gazed up at Ashhur with utmost respect. Even Patrick seemed to join in, his sullen mood interrupted when one of the youngest of the Turncloaks leaned over and whispered in his ear. Patrick threw his head back and laughed. "A tit?" he said through his guffaws. "He thought it was a *tit*? Ha!"

Then came the rumbling, and all laughter ceased. The ground shook, causing the advancing army to stop and hold their arms out to keep their balance. Ashhur took a step forward, his image wavering in Ahaesarus's vision. The god gazed skyward, and the quaking of the earth ceased. The people of Mordeina shuffled about nervously, murmuring to each other. Something odd was happening, they could feel it in the air. Ahaesarus hurried to the front of the army, to where Ashhur marched, seemingly oblivious to the now fearful brightness of the sun.

"My Lord," the Warden said, putting a hand on Ashhur's forearm. Before his god could respond, Ahaesarus heard the voice. It was soft, feminine, and seemed to float on the wind.

My love . . . my love, you must stop this folly.

Ahaesarus immediately understood who spoke. It seemed all the land stood still, and when he looked about, it was truer than he thought possible. The horses were frozen, the people unmoving. Though the Warden felt wind blowing from all directions, not a strand of hair blew, nor a single thread of clothing. Even the sparse clouds in the sky remained in place. Only he and Ashhur seemed unaffected, and standing there in the sudden stillness chilled Ahaesarus to the bone.

Ashhur inclined his head and closed his hands into fists. "I cannot, my love."

Celestia's voice came again. *Allow your brother to return to his home. Do not pursue.*

"We must," said Ashhur, lifting his gaze to the heavens. "I have no choice."

There is always a choice. My world weeps, and I weep with it. Seek peace, not more death.

When Ashhur spoke next, it was with rage that matched his fury at the sight of his brother storming through the walls of Mordeina.

"You come to *me* with a plea for peace? I, who never wished for this war? I, who beseeched my brother until the final moment to turn back? I have done nothing but defend the lives of my creations! If you wish for this to end, my love, go to *him*! Demand Karak leave this land and never return. Do it, and see how he answers!"

When the god's mouth snapped shut, the eerie silence stretched on and on. Ahaesarus was afraid, too afraid to voice his fear, and could only stand by his god and wait for the goddess to reply.

Is that your wish? Walk with care, my love. I spared you once, but not again. My world will not crumble as yours did. You, and the people you have created, are on your own.

"We have always been on our own," said Ashhur. "You left us to starve and die, and for what reason? Balance? Come to me! Come look me in the eye and tell me I am no different from my brother. Tell me we need one another, and the world must have us for your precious balance. My heart yearns to hear just how many lies your lips can spill before your own world turns against you."

Ahaesarus was stunned by the god's anger. He'd always thought these two so close, so dear to one another, integral in forging Dezrel into the land it now was. But this . . . this was frightening. When next Ahaesarus heard the goddess speak, there was a fire in her voice.

I offered you solace. I offered you a chance for redemption, to atone for your mistakes. You spoke of a new world, and tempted me with the spectacle of creation. I have witnessed many wondrous things, but the terrors have started to overwhelm the glory. These lands you squabble over are mine, not yours, yet they run with blood.

"Lands given to us," challenged Ashhur. "And it is *our* blood that spills."

And more still will be shed. My eyes are upon you. Do not forget it.

The ground shook, and with a sudden rush of air Ahaesarus realized they were once more within the normal grip of time. People looked about; shrieks filled the air, and to Ahaesarus it sounded eerily similar to five days before, when Karak overtook Mordeina's walls. An enormously loud series of *cracks* came next, followed by what sounded like a massive landslide. Ahaesarus rushed forward, trying to calm the panicked horde of people, but he lost his footing when the land beneath him shifted. It felt like the whole world was crumbling. He imagined giant fissures opening up and swallowing Ashhur and all he'd created.

"The tree!" someone shouted, and soon a veritable chorus joined in. Fingers pointed toward the wall. "The tree is falling, the tree!"

Ahaesarus winced as he stood, his bad leg throbbing, and looked toward Celestia's tree. The giant branches swayed and broke loose, sending people screaming for cover. Its trunk developed a sickly gray color and caved in on itself. Great puffs of ash rose each time another portion fell. The sound of the chunks plummeting to the ground was like the heavens ripping open.

The tree continued to collapse, until it finally caught fire and broke apart. The branches bounced against the wall as they descended, leaving deep gouges in the stone and exploding into billowing clouds of ash. The fire in its center gave forth one final bright flash and then darkened. In a matter of moments, all that remained of the colossal tree was a lingering haze of dust and smoke.

Although most backed away, Ahaesarus approached the gap in the wall that the tree had blocked. He could see the undead out there, clear as day, unmoving as they stared east.

"Damn," he heard Patrick say. "Well, at least it'll be easier to march all these people out now."

Glancing over, Ahaesarus saw that Patrick wasn't smiling. He then turned to his god, who shook his head while he stared at the gap. He looked tired and annoyed, and the golden glow of his eyes was faded.

"What do we do now?" the Master Warden asked.

"I must fix the breach," the god replied. "I will not leave those who remain behind unprotected."

"Are you strong enough?" Patrick asked.

"I have to be."

"Yes, but what then?" asked Ahaesarus. "After the wall is fixed? Karak has enough of a head start as it is."

"This changes nothing," said Ashhur. The god gazed through the fissure, staring at the red glow that lit the horizon. "We must simply ride faster."

CHAPTER

31

An army of people waited outside Port Lancaster's walls, milling about as if they had nothing better to do. Behind was a line of wagons that stretched for nearly a half mile, with smaller groups of people congregating around each wagon. The vast majority were women. Catherine Brennan shook her head as she stared down at them from atop the wall tower that loomed over the city's main portcullis. The door to the elegant carriage at the front of the procession opened, and out stepped a white-haired woman and two bald men dressed in draping crimson frocks, their powdered noggins dull in the twilight gloom. Catherine groaned. The brothers had written her requesting a meeting to discuss a thin stretch of land that resided between Riverrun and Thettletown, which Matthew had laid claim to for years. The two families had often battled over that parcel of land, where there was a convenient fjord in the Queln River and an impressive number of massive trees. Catherine now knew for certain, with the amount of people in the Connington's party, that the meeting was a ruse. She'd expected as much.

One of the brothers—it was difficult to tell which one—lifted his head to her and waved. Catherine let out a disgusted grunt and waved back.

"You want me to get rid of them, boss?" asked Bren Torrant.

"No," Catherine said. "Allow those three in."

"Just the brothers and the woman?"

"For now."

"What about the rest?"

"They can wait outside. Now let's go down there and welcome our guests."

After descending the wall tower, Bren spoke through the bars to the Conningtons before organizing those under his command, lining up his sellswords on either side of the entrance. Their eyes were locked on the gate as it slowly lifted. "Swords and spears resting on shoulders," Bren told his charges, pacing up and down the line. "Let them be wary."

Catherine smiled as Bren took his place by her side. She fluffed out the long, frilly skirt she wore, trying to further hide the swell of the baby growing inside her. *Some things they mustn't know about,* she thought.

When the gate was all the way up, Romeo and Cleo Connington strolled inside, portly as ever, joined by the white-haired woman. It was the woman on whom Catherine focused. She was quite tall and had a stately manner, and despite her age, she walked upright as if a rod had been shoved up her ass. Catherine recognized her immediately; even if she had not met her a few times before, the resemblance to her sons, with her circular and hefty nose, low cheekbones, and squinting eyes, was obvious.

Catherine furrowed her brow. Lady Meredith Connington almost never left Riverrun: She was the village steward during her sons' frequent periods traipsing throughout Neldar on business ventures. Her presence validated Catherine's fears.

The Conningtons wanted Port Lancaster.

"Ah, my dear Catherine," said Cleo Connington in his high-pitched voice. "So good to see you." The fat man approached her with his hands clenched over his heart and his head tilted to the side. He then bowed before her and took her hand in his, kissing the back of it. His fingers felt soft as a baby's bottom; his lips, like a pair of worms after a rainstorm.

Cleo stepped aside, and Romeo, the elder and gruffer of the two brothers, took his place.

"It is kind of you to allow us entrance into your city," he said, though his frown and tone belied the sincerity of his words. Regardless, he echoed his brother's actions, bowing, grabbing her hand, and kissing it. Thankfully, Romeo's hands felt rough, like a man's should be. His lips, however, were just as moist and disgusting.

Lady Connington didn't approach her; instead, she curtseyed from a distance. Catherine nodded to her before turning back to the brothers.

"Your letter said nothing of bringing such a large entourage."

"My, my, Catherine, how blunt you've become," said Cleo with a snigger.

"One must be blunt when a rival arrives at your doorstep and expects you to feed a thousand new mouths."

"One thousand two hundred and thirty-eight to be exact," Romeo said. "And who said anything about *you* feeding them?"

Catherine chuckled. "I'm the regent of this city in the absence of my husband, and if I allow them to enter, they will be guests within my walls. Who else would it fall on to feed them if not me, you halfwit?" She almost said more, but doing so would betray her suspicions. So she kept quiet.

Romeo scowled and sucked on his upper lip.

"Now, now, Brother," Cleo sang out, prancing between them. He was light on his feet for a fat man. "There is no need to be unpleasant. You are speaking with a widow." He then turned to Catherine, bowing once more. "You have our condolences, milady Brennan. Matthew was a splendid man, and shrewd. You must tell us how he perished. And also you must please forgive us for our presumption. Rest assured, you will not need to feed those we brought with us. There is enough grain and vegetables and salted meats in our wagons to feed three times that many for a month."

"I don't need your pity, Cleo. And I assume this bounty of food you've brought is also a bribe to let your people through our gate?"

Cleo clapped his hands together. "Such splendid frankness! Do you see this, Brother? Whatever happened to the demure Catherine we've always known?"

"She became the leader of a city, with real problems to worry over," Catherine replied. Though Meredith Connington had yet to speak, she glanced at her anyway. The left corner of the older woman's lip twitched for a moment, then fell still. Catherine knew that was the closest thing to a smile she could hope to get from the woman.

"Ah, yes," said Romeo with a nod. "The housewife is now the grand ruler of Port Lancaster. How lovely."

"I think it splendid!" squealed Cleo.

Bren fidgeted beside her, and all it took was a quick glimpse to see that the sellsword was wringing his fist around the hilt of his sheathed sword. Catherine knew he wanted to hack the fat brothers to bits. She couldn't blame him.

"Enough of this foolishness," said Lady Connington. Her voice was cold, her words like tiny shards of ice. "You have business to attend to, and I have many people to get situated."

Romeo glowered while Cleo grinned. Neither acknowledged that their mother had spoken. The older woman frowned, the lines in her face deepening. A long pause followed, until finally Romeo said, "We came here to meet, so we should meet. There is much we have to discuss."

"Yes, yes, that we should do," said Cleo.

"Will you accept the people of Riverrun into your city?" asked Romeo. The question clearly pained him when it left his lips, and he seemed to realize this, adding, "You certainly have the room to spare," in his offhand, insulting way.

"We do, and we will," Catherine told him. She turned to her sellsword captain. "Bren, have your men escort the train to Rat Harbor. And make sure the contents of the carriages are counted and marked. I wish to know the extent our new bounty by the morrow."

"Okay, boss," said Bren.

"Rat Harbor?" said Romeo, aghast. "You're settling our people in the slum?"

"It's the best I can offer right now," Catherine purred. "You said you would only be here for a short while to discuss your rights to Matthew's land holdings. Rat Harbor has been abandoned; it is the easiest place to set up temporary residences for your lot."

Romeo opened his mouth, but it was Cleo who spoke. "It is understood, milady. Truly it is." Cleo gently touched both Catherine's arm and his brother's shoulder. Romeo glared at her while he straightened out the wrinkled top of his frock. He then spun around and faced his mother.

"Mother, don't just stand there like a simpleton! Go back to the commoners. Our wives and children require counseling."

The white-haired lady pivoted on her heel and gracefully loped away. Catherine gestured for a group of ten sellswords to follow her, which they did. She then stared rays of hatred into the back of Romeo Connington's head.

This one hates women so much that even his own mother doesn't rate.

With preparations underway to accept their people into the city, the brothers Connington considered Catherine once again. "My sweet Lady Brennan," said Cleo, "shall we conduct our business here, or will you escort us to more . . . comfortable accommodations?"

Offering her best charming smile, Catherine extended her hand to the carriage that awaited them a few hundred feet down the road, a pair of sellswords lingering outside it. "We will speak at the estate.

Now please, do your host the honor of waiting for me in the cart. I will join you shortly."

The brothers bobbed their heads and began to waddle toward the waiting carriage. She could hear Cleo's excitable tone in his remark about some benign nonsense as they walked, though Romeo remained deathly quiet. *This will certainly be interesting.*

Bren sidled up beside her. "Boss, you sure about this?"

"I'm not one prone to fits of doubt," she said. "Were the girls given their tools?"

"They were."

"Excellent. And whom did you assign to protect me? I cannot see from here."

"Tod and Rumey. The quiet and sinister ones."

"Good." She tugged on Bren's sleeve. "Then we have nothing to worry about, do we?"

"If you say so, boss."

"Oh, and Bren? One more thing."

"What, boss?"

"Remember that you're in a city that loves me. Remember what the women of Port Lancaster are capable of when confronted with those who would turn against those they love."

Bren nodded and walked off to help the rest of his sellswords escort a hundred carriages and over a thousand people through the gates. Catherine made her way to the covered wagon. It didn't escape her that Port Lancaster had barely sixty horses within its walls, and now that number would be more than tripled. In no time at all, the streets would reek with horse dung.

The carriage was covered and ample, yet with five people inside, including the portly brothers, seating was still cramped. Cleo and Romeo sat on one bench while Catherine took her place between the two blank-faced sellswords opposite them. She struck the carriage ceiling with an open palm and heard the female driver say "Hyah!" The carriage began lumbering forward to the sound of clomping hooves, clinking chains, and crunching gravel.

Catherine stared at the brothers, and they at her. No one said a word for a long while. They were like gamblers playing a game of switchback, waiting for the first player to give away his hand. Catherine remained stoic and unmoved. She would not be the one to flinch.

Romeo blinked, his eyes darting to the two sellswords sitting on either side of Catherine. He raised a plump hand and pointed at both of them. "Why do you still have your mercenaries?"

Catherine shrugged. "I keep them paid and fed."

Tod and Rumey nodded but kept quiet.

"I think what my dear brother is trying to ask," said Cleo, "is *how* they are still with you. I don't know if Matthew ever showed you the note we sent him, but all our hired swords and Sisters were conscripted by the acolytes and Karak's soldiers."

Of course she knew about the note. She'd been the one to intercept it before Matthew could read it.

"I know. I read it. I'm sorry for your loss."

"Then you know we even lost the captain of our guard, our Crimson Sword. Yet Bren is still here, and a hundred hired men."

"Eighty-one to be exact," she said, adopting Romeo's offensive tone from earlier.

Romeo grunted. "So, how are they still here? I assumed the acolytes would demand all you had to give."

"They tried. We killed them before they could take any."

The brothers Connington took a long moment to overcome their dumbfounded shock.

"You what?" asked Cleo.

"We killed them, my dear visitors. All of them. Acolytes and soldiers. Every man who stepped foot into our city demanding we give them our resources for nothing."

"But how . . . ?" began Romeo.

"Matthew's sellswords are resourceful," said Catherine with a wink. On either side of her, Tod and Rumey grinned.

Cleo lurched forward and clamped his hand on Romeo's knee, making the older brother yelp.

"Brilliant! I never thought Matthew capable of such treachery! Perhaps we were wrong about him. Why did we not think of doing so, Brother? We had twice the mercenaries our dear Matthew had, not to mention over a hundred Sisters trained with sword and dagger. Think of the possibilities!"

Romeo shot him a look, and Cleo retracted his hand, nodding knowingly. Catherine made note of that quiet exchange, though she did not now what to make of it. Then Cleo's face brightened, and he leaned forward once more.

"But Matthew's treachery was certainly not without cost," he said, almost singing the words. "We'd heard your husband died, but how was always a bit of a mystery. Am I correct to assume now that it happened during the battle?"

She put on her best sorrowful face and nodded.

"And what of Moira?" he asked. "It's surprising she is not guarding you."

"Moira left. I sent her away."

The fat man clapped his hands and kicked his feet. "Oh, how wonderfully incongruous! Dear brother, this trip gets better and better!"

In response, Romeo chuckled without mirth.

The carriage stopped ten minutes later, and the driver opened the door. Catherine stretched her legs, which were cramped from keeping them pulled up tight to her bench to avoid rubbing Cleo Connington's knees, and then exited the carriage. Her two sellsword protectors and the brothers Connington followed her up the steps to her estate.

She led them through the foyer, down the hall, and up the staircase, heading for the solarium on the estate's fourth floor. She heard soft murmurs when she passed the third story, and imagined her children sitting with their nursemaid Brita while the old woman taught them their lessons. She pictured little Ryan, staring out intently from beneath the tangled curls atop his head, absorbing Brita's every word in silence. He was much like his father—his *true* father—in that way. Always listening, always learning, silent until he needn't be any longer. *I will be with you soon, my son. After my work here is done.*

By the time they reached the door to the solarium, Cleo and Romeo were bent over at the waist, panting and clutching their crimson frocks. Catherine hid a smirk and opened the door for them. They entered in a wobbling fashion. The sellswords Tod and Rumey went to enter as well, but Catherine stopped them.

"Please wait outside," she told them. "I'll handle things from here."

The two men nodded and took their places on either side of the doorway. Bren was right to assign these two to her. They were indeed quiet and sinister, but more important, they didn't question orders, which was exactly what Catherine needed at present.

She shut the door and turned around. The Brennan estate's solarium was a huge room that spanned the full fifty-foot width and forty-foot length of the structure below. Its walls were lined with display cases and ornate stands holding some of the more exotic sea life Matthew's father and grandfather had discovered on their early ventures out on the open ocean. The merchant's desk—*my desk now*—stood to the right, fronted by a heavy round rug colored teal and yellow. The rug was a new edition, for the bloodstains left by Matthew's executed whores wouldn't come out of the old one. As for those who'd been tasked with scrubbing those stains, they were present now: her maids Ursula, Lori, and Penetta were in the room, tending to the brothers' needs, while two other young women in simple, white household garb sat in the chairs in Matthew's old lounge area, playing lutes. The soft tinkle of music filled the air.

The Conningtons stood in front of the two musicians, warming their hands at the fireplace that took up one-third of the solarium. Each held a cup of spiced brandy provided by Penetta. They whispered back and forth to one another, and Cleo in particular kept glancing up at the bare stretch of wall just above the hearth. They were clearly stalling. Catherine walked up to them and cleared her throat.

"Would you rather talk business or stare at a blank wall?"

"Oh, my sour and candid Catherine, we will talk trade soon enough," said Cleo. "My brother and I were simply remembering the monstrosity that once hung there."

"The sword Lancaster Brennan had forged as gift for Karak," Catherine stated.

"Yes, that," Romeo said. "So impressive, despite its impracticality."

"The sword reached the giant," Cleo said in his singsong way. "Our . . . associate . . . is right now following Gorgoros and his people as they march through the desert. The deed will be done soon."

They are uninformed. If what Ki-Nan wrote is true, the battle is already over, and he is with the giant heading north. You best stay safe, my love. You best return to me.

"That is good," said Catherine. "Now, this business about the land up north—"

"Can wait," Romeo said. "Right now, we are famished. The brandy is only sparking my appetite. Will you offer your guests some sustenance?"

"Of course," Catherine said with a curtsey.

Her maids left the solarium, returning a few minutes later with plates of peppered goat, cornmeal biscuits, and bowls of venison and barley stew. The brothers sat down in front of the fireplace, throwing casual conversation Catherine's way as they picked at their food. She watched them with interest, politely answering each of their meaningless questions. The conversation was benign, and

Catherine was growing impatient. It was hard to keep her frustration in check.

Finally, after the brothers had scarfed down the pork pastries Penetta offered them, Catherine stood from her chair. "You came here for business. Now that you've eaten, are you ready to talk?"

"Yes, we're ready," said Romeo. Cleo sniggered.

They made their way to the other side of the room. Catherine circled around the desk and sat down while Lori and Ursula brought over two chairs for the brothers. The Conningtons sat down without giving thanks. Romeo acted as if her maids weren't there, treating them much like he had his mother. Cleo leered at them, something in the sparkle behind his eyes making Catherine grip the edge of the desk tightly, feeling the handle of the dagger strapped beneath it.

"Now about the lands and the fjord," she said. "Matthew's father purchased both from your grandfather years ago. It has been in his family ever since. The trees are valuable, the river crossing and docks even more so. If you wish to take possession of them, the price will be steep."

"Still so frank!" exclaimed Cleo. He then frowned playfully. "However, that bit of business can wait for later. We have much more important things to discuss."

Catherine's lips twisted into a grimace.

"Such as?"

Romeo smiled at her show of discomfort.

"Such as the state of your holdings here in Port Lancaster," he said. "We have come to relinquish that burden from your shoulders."

Catherine sat back in her chair and stared at the brothers, silent.

"We wish to help you, dear Catherine," said Cleo. "We will take the reins of Matthew's shipping empire and allow you to fulfill your womanly duties to your children. It must be difficult, worrying your pretty little head over all Matthew once controlled."

"It can be," she said, inwardly seething.

Romeo nodded. "We assumed so. We have an offer for you. We will take control of House Brennan's holdings. We will operate the shipping and go about building new ships to replace those that have been lost."

"We would take a fee, of course, for doing this," added Cleo, "but the majority of Matthew's coin would remain yours to do with as you choose. We know how difficult it must be for a housewife to manage these . . . intricate details. You will be free to love and raise your children."

Catherine frowned. "Which means you'll be staying here indefinitely."

"That is correct," answered Romeo. "Until your son reaches age, and we relinquish control to him."

"The perfect outcome for everyone!" Cleo sang.

Shaking her head, Catherine leveled her gaze at both of them. "No."

The brothers Connington gaped at her.

"Do you think me a fool? Do you think I was born yesterday? You've tried to ruin Matthew for years, and now you wish to help his widow? I think not. Ryan would never live to see his fifteenth birthday. Then, according to Neldar law, Matthew's possessions will go to the first man to claim them. Which, since you'll already have control, would be you."

"How could you . . . " Cleo said, eyes wide and disbelieving.

"You had your own daughter killed, Cleo. Why would my son be different? Arrogant fool. You think you can come into *my* city, without guards of your own, and wrest power from me?"

To that, Romeo slammed his meaty fist on the table. "You think you're *not* a fool? You think you have the upper hand in this? Ha!" He glanced toward the window, and a wicked grin stretched across his face. "By now, our mother has offered your sellswords everything they could ever desire to turn on you. Without them to protect you, what do you have?" He laughed aloud. "You *will* accept our offer, Catherine, or else another member of your family will suffer a mysterious death such as Matthew did!"

"Is that so?" she asked.

"It is," scowled Romeo.

"So be it."

Catherine stood and gestured to her maids. Romeo glowered, then tipped forward, readying to lift his fat body off his chair. He never made it to a stand. A gasp left his mouth as his eyes flitted to the side, staring at Penetta as the young maid held the sharp edge of a knife against his throat. Blood dribbled down his neck and stained the front of his frock an even deeper crimson.

"Oh," Cleo said weakly, and Catherine turned to see Lori behind him, the maid holding a knife to his throat similarly. The two young lute players appeared on either side, each leveling a small crossbow. The Conningtons' eyes darted to and fro, taking in their plight. Romeo collapsed back into his chair.

Catherine's smile widened, and she made a show of sitting back down in her seat, billowing her skirt in a playful manner, still careful to hide her pregnant bulge. "Such fools. You have no idea whom you're dealing with."

"Obviously not," said Cleo, a hint of humor still in his voice.

Romeo grunted, blood trickling from his neck. "If you wish to kill us, just do it."

"Unlike certain others," she said, "I don't wish to kill those who might be my greatest allies." She jutted her chin at her maids, and they withdrew their knives, backing away toward the fireplace. Romeo and Cleo visibly exhaled, the former bringing his hand up to staunch the flow from the small cut on his throat.

"Who *are* you?" asked Cleo, the mirth finally leaving his voice, breathless shock taking its place.

"I am the simple wife of a merchant. One who always kept her eyes and ears open. I watched Matthew's dealings. I studied his actions, both the good and bad. I stowed away half the gold he earned without his knowledge, hiding the sums in ledgers that the priests and tax collectors from Veldaren were too lazy to scrutinize. And when Matthew's vices finally outweighed his uses, I killed him."

At that, both the brothers' jaws dropped open.

She leaned forward, propping her elbow on the desk. "You think yourselves scheming?" Venom leaked from her every word. "You think you have conspired? You're nothing compared to me. I know *everything* that has gone on in this kingdom. I know of your plots against Matthew, as pathetic as they were. I know of your murders, of your love of torture. And I know of your moles in Karak's Army. There is no move you've made that I'm not privy to."

"But how?" asked Cleo.

"I'm no damsel waiting for my fat heroes to come save me," she said. "I have spies of my own roaming the world, and given my status as a lowly woman, none think of me as a threat when I seek information. I played my part so well that even my own husband, the man who *shared my bed*, didn't know my plans. How could you have any idea, you who live so many miles away? How could you know that the women of my city are now armed and skilled? The sellswords were not the ones who butchered Karak's soldiers; it was the women who've toiled as I have, who've been subservient to the males of our species for nearly a hundred years. We are no weak settlement to be trampled by whichever man wishes to conquer it. These women will protect each other. They will protect *me*. With their lives, if need be."

The right side of Cleo's lip twitched while Romeo gripped the armrests of his chair so tightly his fingers turned white. Neither said a word, and she saw the lump in Romeo's throat rise and fall with each gasp of air he took in. They were afraid. Of a *woman*. Catherine chuckled softly at the thought.

"Don't look so pathetic," she said, folding her arms. "Even though you wished to overthrow me, I bear you no ill will. I know who and what you are, and you needed to learn that I am just like you, if not your better." She smiled. "If anything, you should be *thanking* me. All those plans you dreamed up will come to pass."

"How so?" asked Cleo, sweat beading on his bald pate.

She smiled wide. "I'm a widow now, and I will soon remarry after the grieving period is done. When that time comes, I will marry Ki-Nan Renald, your own protégé, and take his name."

Once more, both brothers gaped.

"We have been lovers for a long while now," she said, answering the question before it could be asked. *They mustn't learn about Ryan and the pregnancy,* she reminded herself before continuing. "All while Matthew toiled and stumbled, nearly losing all of the wealth his family had built over the last ninety-odd years." She leaned back, regaining her womanly posture as she placed her clasped hands in her lap.

"And you will marry him?" asked Cleo.

"Yes," she replied. Though Romeo was still scowling, she could see the hint of a smile play on Cleo's face. That was good, even if maddening. She hated revealing so much to these men, but she had no choice. If she didn't prove herself worthy of their respect, or even their fear, all her plotting would be for naught.

"The dark-skinned bastard," muttered Romeo. "That's what happens when you take a savage from Paradise and show him the world."

"He simply learned well from us," said Cleo. "*Too* well, perhaps." He turned back to Catherine. "And what will happen if our dear Ki-Nan doesn't return from the war?"

Though the question killed her on the inside, she couldn't let it show. She shrugged and spoke the most painful lie of the many she'd told in her life. "Life will go on. Perhaps that would even be best. I will still be regent, and without a husband who holds loyalty to you."

"Why, then?" asked Romeo, dumbfounded. "Why treat with us at all?"

"Because you're the strongest merchant house," she replied simply. "Your holdings are double mine, even considering how much Karak has stripped from you. I would be a fool to turn my back on that sort of power. Not if we are to endure the coming chaos."

"And if Karak returns?" asked Cleo.

"Then we're fucked, and all the plotting in the world won't matter."

At that, Cleo clapped, his jollity returning. "Such language! What do you propose we do, sweet Catherine, should Karak fail to return?"

She leaned her head against the back of her chair. "I see it thusly: When the god who created us disappears, this land will endure unrest never before seen. Every family, no matter how small, will seek to conquer another. But those who are ready—those who bond together in unity and mutual self-interest—those could reap wealth beyond imagining. Therefore we must decide who is trustworthy, who is worthwhile, and who is expendable. You know that Trenton Blackbard, the slimy bastard that he is, will move against us all if given the opportunity. Tod Garland is noble, but pious and beholden to Karak's law. Tomas Mudraker is ambitious but a dullard. Peytr Gemcroft is wily and bold, but he is also unpredictable."

"What of Cornwall Lawrence?" asked Romeo in his sullen tone.

"That house has been all but wiped off the map," she told him. "I received word that a renegade cousin of Trenton Blackbard butchered the entire family. Of them, only the youngest daughter is still alive, and she is trapped in Veldaren, unable to lay stake to her claim."

Romeo's eyebrows lifted. "That is no good," he said. "If Blackbard has control of Omnmount . . . "

"He doesn't," Catherine said, cutting him off. "The cousin—and his men—were brought to an end."

"By whom, pray tell?" asked Cleo.

"Moira, and five other sellswords I sent north."

Cleo sat back and clapped once more. "I should have known! How splendid! You said you sent the lost Crestwell away, but never why or where. You truly *are* a devious one, sweet Catherine!"

For a woman, she thought dismissively, but let it go unsaid.

"As of now, young Elias Gandrem is keeping hold of the settlement," she continued. "His father has sent a party to assist him at my request. However, this doesn't matter. All that matters is that this tragedy is something we can use to our advantage. None but Elias and Moira know that the Blackbard cousin acted on his own, and that story can be . . . twisted to suit our needs. The way I see it, Trenton is our greatest threat. And with the Gandrem house beholden to Peytr Gemcroft and now myself, it is another coin in our pockets. We can use this against Blackbard and convince the others to do the same."

Both brothers leaned forward, assuming similar poses with their elbows dangling between the draping fabric of their frocks. "House Gemcroft will be in turmoil soon," said Cleo. "We have seen to that . . . " He trailed off there, eyes flicking over his shoulder. Catherine glanced over their heads, at her maids and the two crossbow-wielding lute players, and nodded. The five girls bowed and exited the room, leaving her alone with the brothers Connington.

"What is it you propose?" asked Romeo. The man sounded truly intrigued, even awed, which filled Catherine with pride.

"First, we must decide whom to deal with, and whom to cast aside," she said. "When the gods no longer walk the land, it is up to us, the people, to guide our own fates. Those who feed our citizens, keep them safe, will be loved the most." She smiled wide. "And those who gain the most love? Why they will be us, and we will have the power not only to sway kings, but to *choose* them."

"The truth in those words is inspiring," said Cleo, inclining his head in respect. "However, I regret to tell you that there is no guarantee Karak will lose this war. Even with all our preparations, toppling a god is no easy task. How can you be so confident?"

"Because I'm a mother," she said with a casual wave of the hand. "Everyone seems to forget that Dezrel is a world of three deities, not two. And the strongest one is the one who created it. The goddess is the mother of her children no less than I am to mine, and mothers are protective of what they've birthed. When this conflict between the brother gods threatens all she has created, she'll end both of them forever."

"Are you certain of this?"

Catherine grinned. "Would you like to ask my dear beloved Matthew that question?"

CHAPTER

32

Darkness was Aullienna's only companion, and it was a poor one at that. It whispered evil into her ears whenever she felt a glimmer of hope, suffocating her though she lay in open space. Her cell was kept dark at all times, even when food was brought to her. Those who brought it were formless in the black, invisible demons offering her disgusting slop. Every noise she heard was haunting, from the skittering of rats to the sound of footsteps tramping the soil above her head. With not even the faintest light to meet her keen elven eyes, her mind created the scenes for her, and each one was horrific. Monsters with tentacles whipping around them, hounds with fangs dripping blood and saliva, shadowy phantasms whose presence would make her shiver in her skin; each nightmare was worse than the last. It became nearly impossible to tell when she was dreaming or awake.

Yet the thoughts of her loved ones were far worse than the monsters in her mind. They came to her in waves: her nursemaid, Noni, with a knife popping out of her skull; Aaromar with an arrow through his eye; her mother's face, bleeding and covered in bruises; Kindren, her love and betrothed, whose fingers had been sliced off by Aully's wicked brother. *Kindren's fingers.* She felt around the dirt floor of the cellar that was now her prison until they fell on a swathed clump of rolled fabric. She held the fabric close to her, beneath her chin, and felt the knucklebones of the fingers inside. The thing reeked of decay and was slimy to the touch, but she dealt with the stench and discomfort until her stomach inevitably cramped. *Please, Celestia, help me stay strong,* she pleaded with the darkness. *Give me the strength to fight.*

This time, just as most others, she received no answer.

The stench of the rotting fingers became too much, and Aully gently placed them down beside her. Not that the smell improved much. She'd been forced to both relieve her bladder and defecate right there on the floor. The whole place smelled wretched, of sweat and shit and piss and death itself. She didn't think she could ever get used to the reek.

A wave of dizziness hit her, and Aully curled into a ball. She felt bile in the back of her throat and gagged on it. Sensations such as these had been happening more and more often of late. She assumed it had something to do with whatever it was Carskel was feeding her. But in a way, she didn't mind the discomfort. When she vomited, at least it was clear to her that she was awake.

A sound reached her ears—a *real* sound, the creak of a door being opened, footsteps moving slowly down the darkened hall. She lifted her head from her arms, and her stomach cramped once more. She reached blindly into the black, desperate for sustenance. It didn't matter if what she was being fed was killing her. She needed to eat.

The footsteps ceased a few feet in front of her, and for a few languishing moments there was no sound at all. "Aullienna?" a voice asked. It spoke in a muddled whisper, and she couldn't tell if it was male or female.

She croaked out a reply, her constricted throat not giving enough breath for words.

"There you are," the whispering voice said.

A flame struck, filling her world with wonderful light. At first Aully recoiled from it, but then she lurched forward, reaching for the source of the illumination like an elf lusting for water after a week in the desert. But her hands never found the light. Instead, they rapped hard against the wooden planks that held her prisoner.

She sat back and drew her knees to her chest, gazing at the flickering light through the gap in the boards. The light revealed her accommodations—a twelve-foot-by-twelve-foot room surrounded by earthen walls on three sides. The cellar had once been used to store wine and tobacco, but now it stored only her. The dirt floor was covered with her bodily waste instead of skins and broad leaves. It was disgusting, but given that she could see for the first time in a long, long while, there was a part of her that found it beautiful nonetheless.

"Oh Aully, look at you. I'm so sorry."

She squinted and inched along the slatted wall. Grabbing one of the boards, she pulled herself up and gazed through one of the lower gaps. The light was so bright out there in the passage that it seemed almost as bright as the stars in the heavens. The source of the light was high up, held in the hands of an immensely tall, shadowy being.

"Celestia?" she whispered. Tears formed in her eyes.

The form squatted down, and a hand touched hers. Three fingers and a thumb squeezed her palm. Aully squinted, trying to make her eyes adjust. Eventually her vision cleared and she saw the face of her Uncle Detrick staring back at her.

"Not Celestia," she grumbled. Her hand slipped out of his, and she slid down the boards until she lay flat on the soiled ground once more.

"Aully, please," her uncle said, pleading. His voice rose. "Sit up. Talk to me."

Aully groused, inaudible to her own ears.

"What was that? Aully, I couldn't hear you."

She lifted her head. “Go away, Uncle.” Her voice was rasping and weak.

Shuffling came from the other side of the boards, and soon the light assaulted her face once more. Detrick was kneeling now, looking at her through the bottom slat. She simply stared back at him, her mind blank. Her uncle opened his mouth to say something, then snapped it shut. He reached beneath the boards, feeling the opposite side with the fingers of the hand Carskel had mangled, his mouth curving into a grimace of concentration. The thick boards were positioned in even intervals, with a seven-inch gap between each one. Detrick worked his way up, touching each board, steadily moving the light away from her as he rose.

“Bring it back,” she whispered.

“Bring what back?”

“The light. Please.”

Once more Detrick knelt down, and the wonderful light bathed her again. Aully tried to smile, but she wasn’t sure if she knew how to anymore.

“Carvings on the boards,” her uncle said. “Magical wards.”

“I know,” Aully said. She’d realized that the first time she’d tried to cast a spell. Her wicked brother had placed the same sort of protective net around the cellar that existed inside her father’s old study.

“How long has it been?” she asked. Despite the coldness she felt toward her uncle, he was still alive, and carried both voice and light. She had to keep him there, keep him talking.

Detrick sighed. “Twenty-eight days,” he said, the disgust plain in his voice.

Twenty-eight days.

“Where is Kindren?” she asked meekly.

Her uncle went on as if he hadn’t heard her. “He is a bastard, Aully, a sick bastard who will do anything to get his way. I should have known from the start with that one. I almost told your father when first I laid eyes on him as a screaming babe that he should toss the hideous thing into the Corinth and be done with." He looked away. "I never did," he said, "but I wish I had."

"Kindren," she whispered again. "Where is Kindren?"

Detrick blinked at her and reached through the gap. She shuffled away from his grasp. Her uncle sighed and leaned back.

"Kindren is safe," he said. "He is in my chambers within Briar Hall. Your brother left him in my care."

"His hand," Aully sobbed, more to herself than to her uncle.

"I know," said Detrick. "He was feverish for days after Carskel dumped him on me. I burned and bled the stumps of his fingers, but infection took root. For quite a while I thought I might lose him, so high was his fever. But your betrothed is a strong one, Aully. He pulled through." Her uncle lifted his own mangled hand, gazing at the stub where his discarded finger had once been, and a solemn smile crossed his face. "We have bonded through our mutual disfigurement."

How wonderful for you. You bond, while I lay here and rot, slowly poisoned with each passing day.

Suddenly annoyed, she inched closer to the slats and cleared her throat. "Why are you here?"

"To make sure you are well."

Aully laughed, and with her coarse voice she sounded much older than her fourteen years. Her uncle tilted his head at her, moving closer to the gap, a frown on his lips.

"So tell me," she rasped. "Do I look *well*?"

Detrick leaned closer to the boards, angling the candle he held through the gap and straining his eyes to look into the area beyond. Seeing the precious light up close, Aully mindlessly moved toward it, reaching out like it was a holy relic promising immeasurable power. Her uncle's gaze found her.

"My goddess," he gasped. "Aully, you are all skin and bones!"

She grabbed an empty clay bowl off the ground—she kept it close to the wall of boards, for if her jailers couldn't find it when they came to bring her more slop, she would be left unfed until they returned the next day—and jettisoned it through the space between the boards. The bowl missed her uncle by inches, shattering when it struck the wall behind him. He fell back, almost losing hold of the candle when he withdrew his hand from the gap.

"I'm being poisoned, uncle," she said. "Each day I grow sicker. My brother is trying to kill me."

Detrick sighed and rubbed at his temple. "He is not trying to kill you, Aully. That would defeat his purpose for placing you in here."

"If that is so, why am I sick?"

He waved his hand at her. "You have been living in your own filth, breathing it in. It is painful, yes, but not fatal . . . so long as you are allowed out of here soon."

A gasp froze Aully's throat. Just the thought of freedom made her feel dizzy.

"Uncle, please," she said, pleading. "Please, release me. Break those boards and let me out. Let me gather up Kindren and my mother and flee this place. You can come with us! You've long told me how much you despise Carskel . . . and after what he did to your hand, after how he betrayed your brother . . . please, please, Uncle, help me! We can run away and find a safe place where we never have to look at his face again!"

Detrick looked away. His eyes watered.

"I am sorry, Aullienna. I cannot."

Aully deflated, her moment of hope dashed. She crumpled again on the soiled ground and rolled into a ball, squeezing her eyes shut. "Go away," she whispered, but it was so quiet she didn't think her uncle could hear.

"My sweet niece," Detrick said. His hand was on her then, his fingers running through her muck-soaked hair. "It would do no good to flee. The gods clash not two hundred miles from us. The lands to the east are burning. There is bedlam all around us. The only safety we have is here, in our forest." She opened her eyes and saw him shaking his head through the gap. He smiled, and it was forced. "As much as I hate your brother, as much as I wish him dead, he is right. The only way to guarantee our safety is to change, to conform. It may not be so bad. Carskel was young and brash when he hurt our dear Brienna. With you, he may be gentle. With you, he may be noble."

"Go away," she breathed.

"What was that?" her uncle asked.

"I said *go away*!"

Detrick flinched and pulled back his mangled hand. "I am sorry, Aullienna, but I know no other way."

"Of course you don't," she muttered, remembering her father's words when she'd asked him why he had been made Lord of Stonewood when Detrick was the older of the two. *"My brother is docile,"* Cleotis Meln had said. *"Detrick is no leader. He is a follower through and through. It is simply what he does best."*

"You can't save me," she said.

"That's right," her uncle answered. "I cannot."

"Then what am I to do?"

He leaned back into the boards, and they creaked. "Your brother will visit you in three days. When he comes, he will ask you questions, and he will expect you to answer correctly. He wishes for you to love him, Aullienna, for you to dedicate your life to him. You must do this. It is our only hope. Should you do this, and should he find your answer true, you will be free. Your mother will be safe. I will be allowed to marry her, to assume the Lord's Chair at her side."

"You?" she asked, her voice still drained. "What of Carskel?"

"He is nervous. He's had trouble bringing the whole of our people to his cause, and he has not heard from his contacts in Dezerea for quite some time. So after you are wed, you and your new husband will leave Stonewood and head for Dezerea with the Dezren prince. After that . . . to be honest, my sweet niece, I have no idea.

I have heard from Ethir Ayers that Carskel has been promised a position on the Quellan council for his part in their schemes, but I don't know for certain."

She heard what he offered, and this time Aully couldn't keep from crying.

Detrick's hand found her yet again, gently caressing her filthy bare shoulder. "Hush, child. It is difficult, I know. But please, I beg of you . . . accept what your brother offers. Swear your love to him, pledge him your hand. I tire of seeing you suffer so. I tire of *all* our suffering." His tone changed, becoming deeper, almost accusatory. "If you are given a chance to end that suffering, and you refuse, it would be most selfish of you."

Those words stilled her sobs. She glanced up at him, seeing only the frame of his eyes and upper brow through the gap. Her lower lip quivered and she sucked on it, tasting the grime caked there.

"Selfish?" she asked.

"Yes, my sweet niece. Selfish."

She bowed her head, hatred flowing from deep within her. She had to keep from lashing out at her uncle, from reaching through the boards and scratching out his eyes with her chipped fingernails. And yet his words also told her exactly what she needed to do.

"I'll do it," she said.

"Do what?" Detrick asked.

She sat down and looked up at him, doing her best to act the little girl he surely thought she was. "I'll promise to love him as best I know how."

"Do you promise, Aullienna?"

She nodded. "Yes, Uncle, I promise."

"Very good," Detrick said, and he gave her a genuine smile. "I know how much of a sacrifice this is. I know how hard it will be for you. Simply stay strong, and remember your loved ones—"

"Uncle, please stop," she said, cutting him off. "I wish to be alone now."

"Alone? Why?"

"Because I have three days to learn how to love my brother. Let me be alone with my thoughts."

"Ah, yes. I see." Her uncle then drew back from the slatted boards and bent over. When he reappeared, he slid a bowl containing three apples and a halved and salted beet. He also slid in a flask of wine. "Think well, my sweet niece. I pray you will be successful in your efforts."

With that, her uncle walked away, taking the precious light with him. Aully was cast back into darkness, but this time she didn't care. She smiled instead, thinking on what she'd told him. *I will promise to love him as best I know how.* Those words weren't a lie, for the best way Aully knew how to love Carskel was to set his whole body aflame.

Celestia forgive me, she prayed, and pushing aside the thoughts of what would happen to her loved ones once her brother died, she took a bite from the apple instead. She had never tasted anything so sweet.

CHAPTER 33

Veldaren was bordered to the north by a thick wood that stretched all the way from the river in the west to where it ended when it curled around the Road of Worship. It was through that wood that Laurel, Pulo, Roddalin, and Jonn marched, silence among them as the gray day slowly darkened. Hunting had become a rare occupation of late, what with it being winter and there being few experienced hunters remaining in the city. Even the women who'd learned the art of trapping stayed away. It was tough enough to catch a squirrel or rabbit during the warmer months; in the snow and cold, it was a useless endeavor, a waste of good traps and precious time. So for two hours they walked in silence, seeing nothing, hearing no one, until the wood ended and Karak's Temple loomed before them.

"There's still time to turn back," Pulo said.

Laurel shook her head. King Eldrich had pleaded that it needn't be her to do this, and now Pulo was doubtful as well.

"Someone needs to drive a knife into Joben's chest," she said, "and tonight that privilege is mine."

They hid there in the wood, huddled at the bases of four separate trees. For a fleeting moment Laurel feared Joben Tustlewhite had become suspicious and altered his schedule, which would have wasted four days of planning. Just the night before, Karl Dogon and Ennis Coldmine had been attacked by the Judges on their way back from this very temple, with Ennis dying and Dogon almost perishing as well. What a waste of a good man it would be should the priest not arrive. But finally she heard wooden wheels rolling over the packed dirt road. Laurel inched along the hard, snowy ground on her elbows and then peered over the bank she'd built. She watched the priest exit the wagon, climb the steps of the temple, and disappear inside. The acolytes closed the door behind him. The wagon carrying the Sisters turned about and headed back the way it came.

Still they waited. The minutes ticked by, and the sky darkened even further. Again Laurel worried something had changed, but sure enough the acolytes began to sing. Peering over her mound of dirt and snow, she saw the window to the priest's study swing open. The four conspirators then exited their cover and gradually approached the western side, where Karl had told them the wall along the roof was highest.

The land was barren around them, and a chill worked its way up each of their spines. It seemed they all shivered at once as they stepped onto the road and approached the temple stairs. It was eerie to feel so alone, even with the singing coming from the roof. It was as if the world had gone and died on them. The feeling worsened when they scaled the steps and passed between the two onyx lions. The statues' black eyes seemed to stare at them accusingly. She glanced up at the open window of the study, and for a moment she thought for sure that Joben Tustlewhite's pale face would emerge, staring down at them. Again a quake ran through Laurel's body.

They reached the entrance, and Laurel took a deep breath. Behind her, the other three men tensed, hands on their swords. Laurel grasped the handle of the massive door. She had with her tools to pick a lock, yet when she twisted the handle to the side, it opened.

"Well, at least we have some measure of good luck," whispered Roddalin.

The interior of Karak's Temple was as vast and desolate as the land surrounding it. The antechamber was empty save a stack of cloaks off to the right and a rod resting against the far wall. As Jonn gently closed the door, Laurel glanced about. The ceiling was high, at least fifteen feet, and just ahead of them was another set of huge double doors. She assumed those were the ones Harmony had said led to the monastery. To the right of the doors was a passage lit by torches resting in elegantly carved vases. At the end of that hall was a stairwell leading up. They went that way, walking lightly and trying not to make any noise, though a glance back showed they were leaving behind wet footprints. Hopefully, no one would be seeing those until the priest was dead and they were long gone.

The stairs were steep. They passed the second floor and then stepped off on the third, hastening their steps. Though the acolytes still sang on the roof, their song seemingly coming from the polished stone walls of the temple itself, Laurel and the men had no way of knowing when the musical rejoicing would end. The last thing they needed was for the faithful boys to stumble in on them while they were doing the deed.

The third level was carpeted, thick fibers that concealed their movements even more than before. Laurel quietly exhaled. The corridor was lined with doors, fifteen of them on either side. Most of the doors were open, and she poked her head in to see a small bedchamber containing a single dresser, four skinny cots, and a shrine on which a sculpture of a lion rested. The acolytes' rooms, obviously. She backed away from the chamber and moved on, signaling for her colleagues to follow.

The door to the priest's study was obvious; nailed to it was a plaque on which the Laws of Karak had been carved. Laurel stopped before it. Pulo pressed his back to the wall on one side of the door and drew his shortsword; Roddalin and Jonn did the same on the other. Laurel took a moment to fluff up her wavy hair. She undid the clasp on her cloak, shrugged it off her shoulders, revealing a sheer, barely there ensemble with thigh-high boots and a firming leather bustier. She had borrowed the clothes from a girl named Famke, a whore from one of the brothels along Merchants' Road, who sought protection in the caverns. Laurel placed her hands beneath her breasts and shoved the bustier up, making her bosom swell in an obscene way. She glanced at Pulo, who retained his air of dignity, though his cheeks were red. She didn't want to see how Roddalin and Jonn were reacting.

Now or never. She reached out and rapped her knuckles on the door.

Nothing happened.

Laurel bit her lip and frowned. She knocked again, but still nothing. She pressed her ear to the door and listened, but not a sound could be heard on the other side. Taking a step back, she looked over at Pulo. He was scowling.

"He'll call for the lions the moment he sees you," Pulo whispered. "Even with you wearing . . . that."

"I only need a moment," Laurel whispered back, glad the singing easily drowned out her whispers so that there was no way Joben could hear from the other side of his door. "Just one moment of confusion and lust."

She grabbed the handle, pressed down the latch, and swung open the door.

There was no priest. Instead, what she saw were lions, one male and one female, each of them six feet tall while standing on all fours. Their golden fur shone in the torchlight, and their eyes glowed with intelligence. The heads of both lions swung her way, and an expression that she didn't think possible for a feline came over their snouts: they smiled. The male then took a menacing step toward her and opened a mouth filled with giant, sharp teeth.

"Laurel," said Kayne.

"Lawrence," answered Lilah.

"Betrayer," they both said at once.

Laurel shrank back in horror, her heart hammering at the inside of her ribcage.

The Final Judges slowly sauntered toward her as she backed away from them. Their heads lowered to the ground, their nostrils flared. Yet they didn't charge. Laurel tripped as she backed out of the room, and she almost fell. Jonn was there to catch her from beside the door. His arm wrapped around her waist and seemed to suffocate her.

"Laurel, what is—"

He glanced up, and his words became nothing but a wet whistle. Jonn released Laurel, letting her fall to the floor. She landed on her elbow with a thud. Finally her throat unlocked and she yelped. Jonn quickly sidestepped in front of her, his shortsword held before him, pointing at the lions as he blocked the exit. His sword arm trembled.

"Um, Pulo . . . Rod," he said, his voice cracking and shaky. "Some help would be nice."

The two other men joined him, forming a human shield before Laurel, though she could see their knees knocking. Laurel rose to her feet, cringing at the pain in her sore elbow. The Judges had stopped advancing and now sat on their haunches, looking like living statues as they stared at the four intruders.

"You have defiled the Divinity's temple," came a voice deep in the room. From beyond sight of the door stepped the priest, joining the lions. Joben Tustlewhite was gaunt and pale as a ghost. His robe hung open, revealing a skeletal chest scored over with four gigantic scars.

Roddalin's lips parted as if he was about to say something, likely a bit of ill-timed wit, but only a feeble whimpering left his mouth.

The priest began to pace, the Judges' eyes following him, though their bodies never moved.

"The flesh is a funny thing," Joben said, staring at the floor. "On its own it is innocuous, simply a shield for what lies beneath, but that also makes it the most important substance in the universe. Flesh feeds the beasts of the wild; flesh holds our insides within our bodies; flesh both quells the desires of men and leads them to betrayal."

"Betrayal," said both lions at once.

"Flesh is also a great teller of truths," the priest continued as if the lions hadn't spoken. "It reveals all our past iniquities, like living memory. Should you be cut by a blade, a scar will remain. Should a woman be unfaithful to her husband, her inner flesh will be marked by another male's entry. We forget sins with ease, but the flesh remembers; the flesh bears its marks, an undeniable truth. Yet if you strip it away, the pain will bring forth the forgotten memories, the lying tongue made to speak without lies." The priest stopped pacing and finally looked up at them. A broad smile stretched his lips. "And the flesh of the guilty is the easiest to strip away, as my masters will surely show you."

"Guilty," said Lilah.

"Flesh," said Kayne.

Roddalin took a deep breath and somehow found the nerve to speak. "How?"

"It matters not."

"Why are you yammering and not getting busy with the killing?" asked Jonn. Though his words were confident, his body shill shook.

"Because Karak is just, and Karak is fair," the priest answered. "Just like all betrayers of the faith, you will be given the chance to repent before the Final Judges. They will seek out the faithfulness in you . . . and tear the impure flesh from your bones."

Roddalin and Jonn exchanged a look, then glanced at Pulo. The man who had once been the captain of the Palace Guard frowned at them, but still he nodded. His free hand snaked behind him, grabbing Laurel's.

"Pulo, what—"

Before she could finish her statement, Roddalin and Jonn bellowed at the top of their lungs and charged into the room, swords raised. The priest never moved to defend himself. As Pulo whirled around and shoved Laurel down the hall, she couldn't help but watch as a pair of blades arced downward for Tustlewhite's bald pate. They never reached their mark, for the Judges were upon them, leaping over the priest's head and knocking both men over with powerful swipes of their oversized paws.

Laurel saw no more, for she was running, Pulo dragging her along. But she heard, yes she did. Heard bones breaking. Heard flesh tearing. Heard her friends screaming.

Heard lions roaring.

Down the stairs they flew, seeking the door and desperate for the safety beyond. Fear clawed at her throat, and she thought there was no way she would reach it in time, but then the door to the temple was before her. Pulo grasped for the handle, but there was nothing but an empty hole where it had once been. His eyes widened in horror and he shoved her aside, hands searching all over the enormous surface, seeking a way to get it open.

"No, no, *no*!" he said. His fingers dug into the crack where the door met the frame, but nothing he could do would make the door budge. Finally, he started flinging his body against it, hoping to break it open with his weight. Laurel swallowed her fear and joined Pulo in trying to get the door open, hoping two bodies were better than one.

Still it refused to budge.

"This temple offers no escape for you," Laurel heard Joben say, and she turned to see him emerge from around the corner. "Just as the caverns beneath the Black Bend hold no safety for your fellow blasphemers."

The female lion rushed past him, her golden skin soaked with blood. Laurel screamed, and Pulo turned just in time to see Lilah leaping toward him. He fell to his back, jabbing his sword at the beast, trying to keep its snapping jaws at bay. Its claws raked down his chest, shredding his leather armor and opening gouges in his flesh. Joben Tustlewhite shook his head in disappointment as Kayne joined his side from the staircase, Jonn's severed arm hanging limp in his mouth.

Seeing the look on Joben's face, and hearing Pulo's continuing cries of terror, urged Laurel to act. She scampered to her feet, only to be knocked back down again when the temple door suddenly swung outward, and a long, heavy object was thrust inside. The wide lance, the object she'd run into, thwacked against the female Judge, causing Lilah to leap off Pulo, hissing at the now opened door.

The lance retracted, and two Sisters of the Cloth entered the temple, one large and one small, covered head to toe in wrappings and each carrying a pair of curved daggers. The large one reared back and tossed her dagger at Lilah just as she was readying to leap, the spinning blade striking her dead on in the nose and sinking in deep. The lion squealed and roared and swiped at the hilt sticking out of her face. The cry of distress angered Kayne, whose glowing eyes expanded in fury when he saw his injured mate.

"False faithful," he roared from his blood-soaked snout. Jonn's arm flopped to the carpet.

Hands fell on Laurel's shoulders, tugging her across the floor. She looked up to see Lyana's familiar deep blue eyes peering out at her from the gap in the wrappings. The priest was shouting. Laurel struggled to her feet, feeling lightheaded, and heard a woman scream. She looked on in horror as the large Sister, Harmony Steelmason, met the charge of the lion head on. She slashed with her dagger, scoring tiny cuts that seemed to do no damage as she leapt around, pushing her large frame to move in a way that didn't seem possible.

"No!" Laurel shrieked, and almost ran toward her, but a firm hand gripped her by the back of her bustier, choking her of breath and will and ripping the skimpy garment in the process. She was hauled outside, slipping and sliding on the icy staircase. She fell to the side and had to grab onto the rear leg of one of the onyx lion statues to keep from tumbling down the stairs.

The door slammed shut a second later, and that sound was followed by Harmony's screeches. Laurel stared straight ahead in shock, her mind racing.

"Laurel, we must go!"

She turned her head and there was Lyana, a badly injured Pulo leaning on her. The girl's wrappings had come undone around her head, and bits of dark hair sprouted out like so many dead saplings. Much to Laurel's shock, thirty other men and women stood at the bottom of the stairs behind them. Most of them were those Laurel had brought to the caverns beneath the Black Bend.

Inside the temple, Harmony had ceased her screaming, joining Roddalin and Jonn in death. The lions roared, the sound shaking the door of the temple. Laurel didn't need to be told what to do next. She slipped around Pulo's other side, threw his opposite arm over her shoulder, and together she and Lyana hauled the wounded man through the snow and toward the wood. The others who had come with the two former Sisters hacked away at the statues of the two lions with mauls, rocks, and anything else they could get their hands on, until the onyx bases broke. They grunted as they heaped the two statues in front of the closed temple door. After that, half of them stayed behind, fear in their eyes while they held their weapons at the ready, while the rest rushed toward Laurel and Lyana to help with Pulo's wounded form. From atop Karak's Temple came a series of gasps as the acolytes, their song long finished, stared down at them as they fled.

For the first time since the brothers Connington had opened her eyes to the sins of her god, Laurel began to pray. Only this time, it wasn't to Karak.

The caverns were mostly quiet when Laurel, Lyana, Pulo, and the rest who had helped them flee the temple descended the stone staircase. They had fled through the wood, seemingly blind, the fear of being mauled from behind by the Judges making every shadow in Laurel's vision become threatening. But luck was with them, and they returned to the Black Bend without further incident. Only time would tell if those who had stayed behind would arrive as well.

Laurel shook her head. They were dead already, and she knew it.

She glanced at Pulo as they entered the caverns, his normally tanned flesh appearing pale and clammy in the sparse torchlight. His body was raked with slashes and gouges from Lilah's claws, and he had lost copious amounts of blood. Both Lyana's wrappings and Laurel's tattered whore's garb were covered with it as well. Together, the two women guided the injured man and those who carried him toward the cave that Harmony had once called home. The large former Sister had kept a bevy of salves and healing herbs among her belongings, and now, being dead, she would have no need for them any longer.

Laurel's spirits sank even lower at the thought. Her staunchest supporter, the mighty Giant, was gone. A part of her wanted to lash out at Lyana for disobeying her order and following them, but she knew that was folly. She and Pulo would be dead if they hadn't. *I will remember you always, Harmony,* she told the dank cavern air, and then pushed those thoughts from her mind to focus on their next step.

After leaving Pulo in the care of Lyana and those who knew better than she how to deal with the injured man, Laurel snatched up one of her young companion's daggers, straightened herself, and began marching through the snaking caverns. For a brief moment she considered going to her own private grotto and changing her clothes, but decided against it. She was an open wound now and would be seen as such. She clutched the dagger tightly, turning it over and over in her hand, feeling its weight.

She remembered Joben's words: " . . . *the caverns beneath the Black Bend hold no safety for your fellow blasphemers . . .* "

The constant bruises, the flayed strips of skin, the mysterious contact within the castle. It was all too obvious to her who had betrayed them.

She entered the large central hub, and sure enough, there was King Eldrich Vaelor, sitting at the long table and nursing a cup of some sort of alcoholic beverage. The gaunt king never slept when she was out of the caverns, his concern for her growing by the day. Karl Dogon was with him, the bodyguard looking worse for the wear, with his arm in a sling and his face mottled with bruises. His sword rested on the table before him, still in its sheath. Vaelor's gaze lifted to Laurel at the sound of her entrance, and his eyes bulged in their sockets. She didn't know whether he was reacting to her scant clothing or the sight of blood drenching her, but it didn't matter. She stepped up to the table and slammed her fist down on it, making the gaunt king flinch. She tapped the tip of the dagger against the table. Dogon's eyes found hers, looking tired yet surprised. It was on the bodyguard that she focused her attention.

"Why did you do it, Karl?"

Vaelor tilted his head at her and squinted, but said not a word. Neither did Dogon.

"You told them everything. From the beginning. Why?"

King Vaelor seemed puzzled, his eyes flitting from Laurel to Karl and back again. "What's the meaning of this?"

Laurel peered at the king. "They knew we were coming, my Liege. The Judges were waiting for us. They know about the caverns.

I'm sure they even know we've been gathering people here." She pointed an accusatory finger at the bodyguard. "All because of *him*."

Eldrich pushed himself away from the table, the legs of his chair scraping against the stone. "This cannot be right." The king gawked at his longtime guardian. "Tell her this isn't true."

Karl Dogon chuckled. It was deep and throaty, and in a way he almost sounded relieved.

"With all due respect, my Liege," he said, "you're an idiot."

The man stood up sharply, kicking his chair so that it tumbled and crashed behind him. He pressed the knuckles of his left hand into the table and leaned forward, squinting at Laurel. She took a single step back, holding the dagger out before her. *I am the daughter of Cornwall Lawrence. I will show no fear.* Yet she still couldn't stop from glancing at the sword on the table, inches from the large man's knuckles. She should have thought to bring Lyana with her.

"You were supposed to protect the king," she said, summoning her strength, "not betray him."

"You understand nothing," said Karl. His gaze lingered on hers. "I've *always* protected my king, and always shall."

"Then why give our secrets away?"

The man laughed, winced, and shook his head. "Secrets? We have no secrets, girl. The priest knew about the caverns from the start. Joben grew up a child of the Bend. He knew it was the most logical place for us to go when we fled."

"When were you planning to turn on your king?" asked Laurel, waving the dagger before her.

"Never," Karl declared.

"Bullshit."

Karl scowled at her. "Eldrich was never in danger. I love my king, no matter how foolish he may be. The pact was long ago sealed, back before Karak marched his army into Paradise. How else do you think we could have escaped the throne room when the

Judges and Sisters attacked? Do you really think that Joben would fail to leave the only other exit out of Tower Honor unguarded? The only reason we lived was because Joben *allowed it.*"

King Vaelor gaped at him.

"It was all for you, Eldrich," the man said, turning to the king and dropping to a knee before him, his face twisting in pain as he moved. "We were raised as brothers after your father brought me out of the gutters. Never once would I allow harm to come to you. That is why I have done what I have done."

"I still don't know *what* it is you've done," the king said.

"He's signed our death warrants," declared Laurel.

"Yours, perhaps." Karl glared at her. "But not yours, my Liege. You were to be protected, no matter the outcome. You may not have been allowed your station, but you were to be allowed to *live.*"

"And the others?" Eldrich asked.

"Fuck the blasphemers," spat Karl. "They're the useless fodder of gods and lions. It is to you I've pledged my life, not them."

"That's it," said Laurel, and both the king and Dogon glanced over at her. "That is why they haven't assailed us even though they knew where we are. They were waiting for us to collect all of those who turned against Karak's law." She looked at the king, saw the horror in his eyes. "We haven't been building a rebellion, my Liege. We've been packing a slaughterhouse."

Dogon opened his mouth as if to retort, shut it again, and then moved for his sword. Even wounded and with his sword arm in a sling, he was still as quick as could be when he snatched the hilt with his left hand and flicked the scabbard aside. Laurel backed up a step and hunkered down, the dagger shaking in her hand. She was half Karl's size. Even as hurt as he was, if he decided she needed killing, she was a dead woman.

Yet Karl didn't move from behind the table. Instead, he gawped at her, his eyes watering and his lips trembling. A thin trickle of red liquid dribbled out the corner of his mouth. Laurel glanced to the left and saw the wrapped leather handle of King Eldrich's knife sticking out the side of Dogon's neck. In a violent motion, Eldrich swung his arm outward, showering the table with blood as Karl's throat tore open. The man fell backward, clutching at the gushing wound, kicking so hard that he almost upended the table. King Vaelor took a step away from him, bloody knife still in his hand, a look of dejection on his gaunt mug.

"My Liege . . . " Laurel said.

"Laurel, what's done is done," said the king. His voice trembled with disappointment and agitation all at once.

"What do we do now?" she asked.

He looked up at her, his gray eyes distant and fierce.

"Now, we wake everyone in these caverns. They're no longer safe."

"But what then?" Laurel asked. "Where is there left for us to flee?"

A sad smile crossed King Eldrich's lips. "Flee? No, dear Laurel. It's time we stopped being the sacrificial lambs of the gods. It's time we showed Karak's faithful just how lethal the free citizens of Veldaren can be."

CHAPTER 34

Bardiya's people restlessly slumbered beneath crude tarps while a light drizzle fell from the sky. Their horses, taken from the dead elves and soldiers, whinnied. The horses' coats were wet and glimmered in the darkness. The air was cold, but at least the winds had died down. Luckily, they were on the crags of eastern Paradise now, and though the rocky terrain was slippery, it was solid. This was preferable to the desert, where the once shifting sands underfoot had become like clay, packed and solid at times and dangerously solvent at others due to the unheard-of rain. On more than one occasion, the people had needed to throw ropes to those trapped in the quagmire as the greedy, drenched sand sucked them into the earth. So far two men and one horse had been lost, disappearing under waves of undulating bog, never to be seen again.

Yet still they soldiered on, traversing the land, now camping a few short miles south of Ashhur's Bridge.

The rains had come the morning after he ushered his herd, which included those accompanying Ki-Nan, away from the Black Spire and the valley of slaughter beside the ancient relic. It was the first precipitation Bardiya had ever remembered seeing in the desert. He'd assumed it an oddity that would quickly pass, but he'd been wrong. The rains had not let up since, raging for six days strong.

What he first took to be an anomaly became a harbinger of doom, a physical manifestation of the god's disappointment in him. *You faltered. You turned your back on what is right.*

Three days before, when the people had made camp, Bardiya had sat naked in the rain and gazed across the sopping northern expanse, his legs folded beneath him, his hands clasped in his lap. He'd been trying to find the center he had lost, and that's when he'd felt *him*. Karak was there, on the Gods' Road far on the other side of the soaked terrain, heading for the bridge leading into the Rigon Delta. The fires the deity left behind made the northern expanse glow red. Bardiya had lifted his eyes to the heavens, and he mouthed a *thank you* to the hidden stars. His rage, which had been his only comfort since he had lost control, began to ebb. *Do not leave me,* he had demanded, and his conscience obliged. All he need do was picture the seven innocent children standing on the dais as their bodies were hacked to pieces.

Bardiya stood on the edge of a quay, the path leading down uneven and precarious. The flooded vale was behind them, leaving a damp but passable area filled with rolling hills between them and the road. He gazed northeast. Though he couldn't see it, he knew Ashhur's Bridge was only another day's ride away. He turned and looked north at the glowing horizon. They had moved ahead of Karak slightly, picking up speed at Bardiya's command. Come morning, they would strike out north at a rapid pace and hopefully take the god by surprise. Again his doubt churned. He was running blind into whatever lay ahead. He didn't know how many soldiers Karak had with him currently, and Bardiya had barely four hundred. The only thing that gave him hope was the fact that the deity was heading away from Mordeina, but whether Karak had been victorious or Ashhur had defeated him, he did not know.

Bardiya would learn which soon enough, once Ki-Nan returned.

A soft, sloshing sound emerged, making him tense; his grip on the great sword tightened. From out of the dark night came three men on horseback, Ki-Nan in their lead. All three were tired yet smiling, holding their shoulders back with pride as they bounced in their saddles. Bardiya nodded to them, and Ki-Nan halted his horse, whispering something to his cohorts. He dismounted, handing the reins to the other two, who would tend to the horses before heading to their sleeping rolls.

Ki-Nan approached the giant, his smile slowly fading the closer he drew. The two old friends shared an uncomfortable silence for a moment. Then Bardiya turned and loped down the quay, seeking asylum in the small basin of stone below. Whatever the news, he wanted it told out of earshot of his people. Ki-Nan followed him.

"What happened?" Bardiya asked once they reached the floor of the basin. Even though it was only drizzling, water cascaded down the rocks, pooling at his feet. "Did you find the encampment?"

"We did," answered Ki-Nan. "Karak's Army sleeps in the forest beyond the Gods' Road. It was difficult to stay out of sight, what with the fires raging behind them and the elves in their midst, but I think we managed."

"What shape is the army in?"

"The soldiers back at the Spire said that Karak traveled with fifteen thousand soldiers, but so far as we could tell, there weren't nearly that many. I would say a third that at most. And many of the men we spotted were in dreadful shape. Injured, hungry, and exhausted."

Bardiya nodded. "This is good."

"It is, brother. It is. If the weather improves tomorrow evening, we can sneak up on them while they sleep. Darkness will be our ally."

"No," said the giant, shaking his head. "They will have reached Ashhur's Bridge by the time the sun sets. Whatever we do, we do on the morrow, come daybreak. When I face Karak, it must be in Paradise, not in the delta or Karak's own kingdom. He cannot be allowed to cross the bridge."

"But . . . are you certain this is your path, brother?" asked Ki-Nan, breathless. "You have little experience with that sword, and fighting a deity is much different from fighting soldiers half your size."

"Ki-Nan, my decision is made."

Silence again passed between them, with Ki-Nan averting his gaze as Bardiya stared at him. These silences, and the arguments that preceded them, had become all too common in the weeks before Ki-Nan had left Ang months ago, and were the same way now. Only with the others did Ki-Nan ever seem at ease, never around Bardiya.

The giant sat down cross-legged on the drenched stone. When sitting, he was as tall as Ki-Nan was standing.

"My friend," he finally said, "what happened to you?"

Ki-Nan's eyes lifted to meet his. "What do you mean?"

"We were close once," Bardiya said. "We once could speak of anything. You would regale me with stories of your adventures at sea when you returned from your trips. Only Onna, bless his soul, entertained me nearly as much. Now, you will not so much as smile at me."

"Times change, brother. The world darkened."

"Yet not so much that you cannot share a laugh with the others."

"You don't understand. Being with you is . . . difficult."

"Why?"

Ki-Nan shifted on his feet, his eyes downcast. "Because of our past. Because of the disagreements between us. You let our people be executed. I pleaded with you to fight; yet you refused. I knew you would never understand until you experienced the pain for yourself. I have always loved Ashhur, brother—how could I not love the god who created me? But I was not willing to suffer needlessly for him."

They were words Bardiya had heard many times over, but the *look* of his friend when he spoke them was different. It was as if the atmosphere around him wavered, becoming darker for a barely perceptible moment. Bardiya shook his head, and his vision cleared. Sighing, he said, "And now I have seen, and I have turned against everything I once held dear. I hope you take comfort knowing you were right."

"You know I don't." His friend took a step forward, placing a hand on the giant's massive shoulder. "How many times have you told us that doing the right thing is rarely easy? I fear that's where your anger takes us now. The hard path is overcoming our grief and learning how to kill. The hard way is questioning everything we ever knew and believed. Death, though? Death is easy, especially when clothed in honor and vengeance."

Again the air around Ki-Nan flickered, and Bardiya felt a strange yet undeniable tightening in his gut. Ki-Nan was . . . lying. About what, he wasn't sure, but his friend's words echoed in his head.

"Learning how to kill . . . "

Bardiya shoved Ki-Nan away. The much smaller man stumbled and almost fell to his knees on the water-drenched stone.

"You lie," Bardiya said, his deep voice rumbling.

Ki-Nan's expression turned into a worried frown. "Lie? About what, brother?"

"I watched you on the battlefield. You wielded your blades with precision, cutting down trained soldiers with ease. How could you, and all those who fled from Ang with you, be so adept in the art of warfare?"

"We trained, day and night, for what was ahead," his friend replied.

This time, Bardiya saw no wavering, but his gut was still knotted. He sucked air into his lungs. *Stay in control.* So Ki-Nan and his people did train . . . but there was more to it. More, hiding in the words.

"*How* did you know to train?" Bardiya asked. "You lived your whole life in Paradise and never touched a sword until that day on the beach when the elves showed us the cache of steel."

"We . . . we did as best we could," Ki-Nan insisted. "Our race was . . . our race is flawed, brother, built for war. You saw when you held that sword in your own hands! The soldiers you destroyed, the men whose lives you ended . . . it came as naturally to you as breathing!"

Again that certainty, cinching and snarling in his gut. "You hide yourself from me," Bardiya whispered. Sadness swelled within him. "I sense it each time you open your mouth. Have I been blind until now? Have I ever truly known you?"

"Brother," said Ki-Nan, scrambling to his feet. He held his arms out to Bardiya. "You're tired, confused. Please, come back to the camp. We can discuss this when we—"

"NO."

In a single motion, Bardiya snatched his friend by the front of his tunic and slammed him to the ground. Ki-Nan gasped, spittle flying from his lips, the air knocked from his lungs. Bardiya loomed over him, a gigantic fist pressed against Ki-Nan's chest. His anger was beginning to take hold. *It would be so easy. A simple push of my shoulder is all it would take . . .*

"All lies," he said instead. "I give you this one last chance, Ki-Nan. If you tell the truth, I will let you live long enough to answer another question. If you lie, you will receive the same fate as those who perished before the Spire. Do you understand?"

Ki-Nan nodded, breathing heavily, his eyes bulging from his skull.

"Good. Now tell me who trained you to wield a sword."

He removed his fist from Ki-Nan's chest, and the man began coughing, rolling over onto his side. When his gaze rose to meet Bardiya's, he was quaking with fear.

"I met them nine years ago," he said, "during the summer of my twenty-second year."

"Met whom?"

"Traders from the east, stranded in an ill-built ship by the bluffs surrounding the southern islands. They'd pierced their hull, and I helped save their crew as the ship sank."

The tightening in his gut released, and his vision was clear, so Bardiya knew this was the truth. He nodded for Ki-Nan to continue.

"The masters of the boat were two fat brothers, Romeo and Cleo Connington. In the aftermath, the two fat men lauded me for my help, but they couldn't stop staring at me. I don't think they had ever seen anyone like our people, brother. I *intrigued* them, they said. We talked for hours on end, and they regaled me with stories of Neldar, and I shared of Paradise. They asked if I wished to experience life outside our humble existence of fishing and hunting and praying."

"And you said yes."

"I did." Ki-Nan was shaking now, rubbing his chest where Bardiya had pressed against him. "I have long been restless, brother. What harm can there be in learning of the world beyond our borders? So they taught me the ways of the east, of money and trade and self-defense. They made me a part of their *family*, for Ashhur's sake! They said I was to hold an important place in their house. The men I came to know in the Connington household grew to mean more to me than my eleven brothers and sisters." Soundless lightning flashed overhead, brightening the night and washing out Ki-Nan's features. He looked like a living ghost. "To those of the east, I became a man of importance," he said, "while here at home, I was simply a fisherman."

Bardiya ran a hand through his sopping hair and looked at Ki-Nan sadly. "Do you really require more than what you have been given by Ashhur?"

"Not all of us were granted leadership and respect at birth, brother."

"Do *not* call me 'brother' again," Bardiya snapped. "You are my brother no longer. Now tell me: Your leaving me, our disputes—were those sincere, or were they guided by these Conningtons you speak of?"

"Those . . . those were real, broth— . . . Bardiya."

A lie. Bardiya lurched, swinging wide to strike Ki-Nan down. The man shrieked and lifted his hands, a feeble attempt to protect himself.

"I did what I was told!" he shouted.

Bardiya backed down.

"I was supposed to convince you to fight," Ki-Nan rambled desperately. "But you were so stubborn, so damn stubborn. I delivered those weapons to the coast with the intention of feigning discovery later, but then the elf princess found them first. And still you refused. So I did as I was told and left you alone . . . until the time was right."

Fear seemed to have finally scattered the last of the lies off Ki-Nan's tongue. A dark thought crossed Bardiya's mind. "The demon in the Clovis Crestwell guise . . . did you know of that? Did you know what the creature had planned?"

At that, Ki-Nan shook his head. "I didn't. I swear on that which I love more than anything else that I didn't."

Again, no lie. The words, however, gave him pause. "What you love more than anything else . . . it isn't Ashhur anymore, is it?"

Ki-Nan hesitated, then shook his head. "No. I . . . I fell in love early on, during a trip to Port Lancaster, a city on the southeast coast of Neldar. She was the most exciting woman I'd ever met. Elegant. Exotic. And strong, so strong. I fathered a child by her, though I've never seen his face, and she is with my child once again. It is them I wish to return to, whom I wish to build a life with."

"I see." Bardiya hung his head and rubbed his eyes. "A woman. Children. Glory and praise. And for these selfish desires, you would betray the god who created you?"

Ki-Nan opened his mouth, then closed it and remained silent.

"I should kill you," Bardiya said. "You have no place in Paradise any longer. What you have done to me, done to all of us . . . is unforgivable." His hand clenched into a monstrous fist around the hilt of his sword.

"Please, brother, no!" His old friend clambered to his knees before him. "You preached of forgiveness your whole life. Please find a way to give me that. You asked once if my intentions were pure, and they are! Is there anything more pure than love? Than dedicating yourself to a wife, to your children?"

Bardiya lifted his sword. "You speak to the wrong man, Ki-Nan. Ashhur has abandoned me as you have abandoned him. I am his weapon now, nothing more, and what you have done is unforgivable."

"Ashhur hasn't abandoned you," Ki-Nan insisted, eyes widening at the rising sword. "You—you're strong as ever!"

Bardiya shook his head. "Ashhur robbed me of my youth. I am but an old thing now, my outside rotting as quickly as my faith."

At that, Ki-Nan cocked his head. "Old?" he asked, his voice still shaking. "How so?"

"Look at me. Look at the wrinkles in my face. Look at the whiteness of my hair. My body aches as it decays. The only act that stifles it now . . . is violence."

"You aren't making sense," said Ki-Nan. "You look the same now as you ever have."

Bardiya started to argue, then realized he saw no lie in the words. He bent over, peering at the darkly shimmering puddle of water that had gathered between his feet. A moment later came another flash of lightning, and for the briefest moment he saw his face. It was old, wrinkled, and ugly.

But in his gut, he felt that knot of certainty.

The image was a lie.

Come the next flash of light, he held his eyes wide open, and there he saw himself, flesh dark and smooth, his hair curly and black as it had ever been. There were no creases around his eyes, no deep grooves in his brow.

The demon . . . it showed me what it wanted me to see.

Bardiya looked on the cowering Ki-Nan, and his own words echoed in his mind. *Unforgivable* . . . How many times had he insisted to his people no action went beyond forgiveness? No action could prevent them grace? But here he was, sword high, denying those very words. And still Ashhur was with him. Ashhur was there . . . as was the certainty in his gut. The revelation of the lies. Wardens had that power, given to them by Ashhur. Did he now have it as well? But the weight of the blood he'd spilled hung about his neck. The vision he'd seen, the image of himself old and breaking, he'd felt every bit of it. Taking the lives of so many, it wasn't Ki-Nan he'd seen as unforgivable. It was himself. He'd seethed and raged and declared himself abandoned . . . all while Ashhur remained.

He dropped to his knees, releasing the sword in the process and allowing it to clatter away from him. Ki-Nan backed toward the edge of the chasm, the water trickling over the side dripping on his head. Bardiya thought of how hard he'd struggled to be perfect, to stand tall above his people. First Family of his god, wiser than his parents, wiser than Ashhur himself . . . he'd thought himself crushed by his own fall from grace, but he was a fool. He was only human. Even with his great height, he'd barely had any distance at all to fall.

Another bolt of lightning struck, and his bones and joints ceased to ache.

"Ki-Nan, my friend, will you forgive me?" he asked.

The frightened man's eyes narrowed as if he didn't believe him. "Why?"

"Because our ability to forgive, to see the faults in our brothers and sisters and still love them, is all that separates us from the animals that roam the wilds. *That* was the lesson Ashhur meant to teach, because he knew we would eventually experience the strife we now face. *That* is the reason he created Paradise—to nurture those aspects of ourselves, to give them a chance to grow before we must rely on them."

"Even if that's true," Ki-Nan said, "you've done nothing for me to forgive."

Bardiya shook his head.

"I declared you my brother no longer, as if my love for you has limits. As if I were a cowardly, bitter, selfish man. Some things cannot be undone, but at least with this, let me try."

Ki-Nan looked speechless. He took a step forward, and he swallowed down a lump in his throat.

"Even after the lies?" he asked.

To that, Bardiya laughed.

"I have spent the past years lying to myself," he said. "I certainly won't condemn you for yours."

The man paused a moment; then he smiled and wrapped his arms around Bardiya's neck.

"You're still a bloody fool," he said. "But damn it, I'm tired of all the lies and secrecy, and even with all their fat combined, the Conningtons are half the man you are."

Bardiya rose to his feet, and he felt lighter than air. To think he'd put the weight of Ashhur's teachings on his shoulders, to think he'd believed himself the only one capable of giving wisdom to his people. But when presented with the need to forgive, forgive others, forgive himself, he'd failed so thoroughly that for the first time in ages he felt he had so much more to learn. Years ago, such a revelation would have horrified him. Not anymore.

"So what should I do?" Ki-Nan asked, stirring Bardiya from his thoughts.

Bardiya put his hand on his friend's shoulder.

"This woman you love, these children of yours, you should go to them," he said. "But only after you do whatever you can to ensure their safety. I think you owe them, and Ashhur, at least that much."

Ki-Nan hesitated a moment.

"And if I die before seeing them again?"

"Every breath may be our last, be it in war or in the most peaceful of days. Make each breath matter. Give each one meaning. Who are you, Ki-Nan? Who is the man beneath it all? Are you one who would flee to his family and pray from afar you'll be safe? Or are you a man who will fight to make it come to be?"

There was no question, not when put that way. Ki-Nan struck his chest with a fist, a gleam entering his eye.

"I'm a man who will fight."

By the time they exited the basin, the drizzle had stopped, and dawn began to stretch its crimson fingers across the cloud-filled sky. The warriors of Ker were already awake, shuffling about their temporary camp, stretching their sore backs and moaning. Small cookfires were flaring, and the smoke from the damp wood filled the air. Bardiya gathered them all together, nearly four hundred warriors who had never known conflict until less than a week ago.

"Brothers!" the giant proclaimed, and his voice carried over the rocky cliffs. He pointed north. "Beyond those hills lies a scourge that wishes to rip from us the very love that each of us has felt for all our lives. We must not allow that to happen! Karak is out there, brothers, and he is running. Ashhur has already proven to be his better. It is now for us to finish the task our creator started."

The crowd before him began to murmur.

"Will we face them alone?" someone asked. It sounded like Tuan Littlefoot.

"Alone?" Bardiya shouted. "We will stand between the eastern god and passage into his kingdom, but not alone. We will face his forces to preserve our way of life, but not alone. We will ensure *none* of our loved ones will ever suffer such blight again, and when we do, we will not be alone. We may die. Every last one of us. But we will not die alone. We have truth on our side. We have *love*! And should our pure hearts cease beating, we will find splendor in the Golden Forever. This is what Ashhur has promised you. This is what he has guaranteed!"

The murmuring grew in volume, but the people seemed hesitant. Ki-Nan then stepped to the foreground and faced his brethren.

"Come now, my brothers!" he bellowed. "You have tasted battle before, and you *won*! Onward we march! For glory! For freedom! For *Ashhur*!"

"For Ashhur!" the throng shouted in reply, and though it was slightly less than enthusiastic, Bardiya knew that was the most he could hope for given the certain death they faced. They'd march needing a miracle, but it seemed they walked in an age of miracles, and for once Bardiya felt free from the doubts that had dug their claws into his heart so deeply.

CHAPTER 35

The morning was warm and filled with lingering smoke as Velixar watched the soldiers dismantle their tents and don their armor. These brave souls, who had fought so valiantly not seven days before, were beaten and weary, nearly to a man. Their movements were laborious, their expressions dour, and their lips sagged with disgust as they tore into their meager tack—all that was left of their provisions after the supply wagons had been set to the torch. Wolves had taken the rest. The tall trees surrounding them made them appear small, like squirrels desperately foraging for nuts before winter's wrath fell upon them. All the while, the animals of the forest chattered and scurried all around. Flocks of birds soared overhead, heading back north.

Winter is all but over. We should be taking stock of our bounty, not licking our wounds.

Velixar felt for each of them. This was supposed to have been their moment of glory. The two years of preparation, the long march into Paradise, and the siege of Mordeina should have ended with Ashhur beaten and his children liberated. Instead, Karak's Army had fled back to their kingdom across the river, their once mighty force decimated by death and desertion. Velixar's heart thrummed in his chest, seemingly loud enough to act as the drum cadence for the march ahead. He had never dealt well with failure—not when he was Jacob Eveningstar, and certainly not now, as the swallower of demons. The reality of their situation irritated him, and his anger boiled over. The smoldering landscape a few hundred yards behind them, charred and blackened by Karak as the god set fire to Paradise while they tramped through this once pristine land, did nothing to lift his spirits.

Ashhur's raising of the dead had caught them off guard. Even days after, the images still fresh in his mind, it didn't seem real. The *scale* of what Ashhur had accomplished was astonishing. So many thousands of undead, so many tons of rotting flesh, all turned against them. It was no wonder the soldiers who remained were so dismayed.

I should have known. He fingered the pendant dangling beneath his new cloak. *I should have seen Ashhur's plot the moment we stepped within Mordeina's walls. The Beast of a Thousand Faces would have understood.*

That, more than anything, formed the crux of his anger. He could point blame at Ashhur, at the Master Warden, even at the mutant Patrick DuTaureau, but this didn't stave off the fact that he, Velixar, had been caught unaware. The best of humanity had been tricked by a naïve, peace-loving deity. *"Your ego will be your downfall,"* Karak had once told him. And so it had come to pass. He knew he had failed his chosen god, even if Karak did not castigate him.

A dark shadow appeared beside him, and Velixar glanced over to see the Lord Commander standing there, his fingers clenching and unclenching. His black breastplate was dented and scratched; the chainmail covering his right arm, bent and split. His good eye stared straight ahead, intent on his charges, while the milky left one seemed to glow within the nest of scars that marred his face. Malcolm's mouth hung open, and he breathed deeply. Velixar knew the man well enough to understand that he wished to say something, but he remained silent. Malcolm Gregorian knew his place in the world. He would only speak with the High Prophet of Karak after Velixar acknowledged his presence.

"What is it, Lord Commander?" he asked.

Malcolm cleared his throat. "High Prophet, the men are hungry. We have been on the Gods' Road for six days now. Should we not have come across our resupply wagons by now? They were due to arrive a month ago, yet still there is no sign."

"I don't know," Velixar answered. This was a problem he had been pondering since long before the assault on Mordeina. No birds had arrived from Omnmount, and though supplies were supposed to have arrived every ten days, they had received no aid for nearly two full months. A part of him wondered if some blight had taken place in the staging grounds, or some of the treachery Karak had said he saw in his visions, but he quickly quashed that contemplation. There was no room in his mind for any more thoughts of failure.

"Wagons or no, we progress as we have," he said. "We will be home soon enough either way. The snows have passed, and the days are warming. Have the men forage for nuts if it comes to that, and those strong enough should go hunting when we make camp. They will have to make do."

"Yes, High Prophet."

"Is that all?"

Malcolm shifted his feet. "No, High Prophet. The Quellan are restless. Chief Shen is adamant that his Ekreissar take no part in our struggles any longer."

"He told you this?"

"Yes," Malcolm said with a nod.

"When?"

"This morning, as I was making my rounds in the minutes before the sun rose."

Velixar frowned. *Of course they wish to depart us. The Quellan are proud. They deal with failure as horribly as I do.* That they had chosen each night to make their camp far away from the human soldiers was proof enough of how they felt about the situation. That knowledge doubled his irritation over the fact that the elves had been among the first to flee Mordeina when the dead stood up and began fighting. *Karak will punish them for this. If they turn against the pact they agreed to, when we storm back into Paradise and bring Ashhur to his knees, they will receive nothing in return. Their people should count themselves lucky if Karak simply lets them live.*

"High Prophet," said Malcolm, "what will we do about this?"

Velixar's brow furrowed, and he tapped a finger against his pendant. "Where is our god now?"

Malcolm held his chin high. "I spotted mighty Karak lingering on the edge of the forest, gazing toward the Gods' Road."

"Very well. Go back to Shen. Tell the thickheaded oaf that the Divinity of the East demands to speak with him. If he and the Ekreissar wish to turn their backs on us, let them tell the deity himself."

"Yes, High Prophet."

Malcolm bowed, the massive sword Darkfall clanking in its sheath on his back, and then the man marched away. Velixar watched him until he disappeared behind a thick copse of evergreens, and a sense of longing filled him. Malcolm was a good man, a *faithful* man. He was one of the few who had showed no fear when the dead rose. If they'd only had a thousand Malcolms at their disposal, Mordeina would have fallen.

He grunted, adjusted his cloak, and began to walk through the bustling cluster of soldiers. Eyes rose to meet his, but they quickly turned away, wary of his presence. It was a reaction that had grown all the more prevalent since his massive displays of power. A sense of disconnection began to wash over him. *I am no longer of their ilk. I am closer to the gods than to humankind. They realize this.*

Karak was standing alone at the head of a long stretch of grassland when Velixar found him. The Gods' Road lingered five hundred feet below them. The deity's eyes were fixed on the west, gazing down the expanse of packed dirt that snaked into the horizon. Both sides of the road were blackened wasteland, where small fires still burned in the hearts of the husks of trees, the end result of Karak's godly influence. Each sunset, while the soldiers set up camp, Karak raised his hands and instantly set the landscape ablaze. That hellish ruin stretched for as far as the eye could see behind them, culminating at the Wooden Bridge over the Corinth River, which the god had destroyed after his army crossed.

Velixar sidled up to his chosen god. Karak glanced down slightly, a frown on his lips. The deity then looked south for a moment before bringing his attention back to the smoldering western expanse.

"My Lord, we must speak," said Velixar.

"They are coming," Karak said, as if he hadn't heard.

The High Prophet gazed up at his god. "Who is coming, my Lord?"

"My brother and his children. I sense him as strongly as if he were standing beside me. The dead are with him."

Velixar was taken aback. He had expected Ashhur to remain in Mordeina and pick up the pieces after the invasion, to coddle his children as always. He'd never thought the weak-minded god would pursue them.

"Why did you not sense him before, my Lord?" he asked.

Karak's lips twisted into a grimace. "He was not this close before. We are going too slowly. A journey that has taken us seven days he has completed in three."

"But how?"

"Soldiers require rest, High Prophet," said Karak, his frown deepening. "Wardens require much less, and they can heal their wards and horses when exhaustion threatens to topple them. As for the dead . . . they require no rest at all."

"Oh." Velixar pursed his mouth and peered at the span of the Gods' Road running east. "How far behind are they?"

"A day. A single day."

Velixar slapped at his leg. "Then it matters not, my Lord. We will arrive at Ashhur's Bridge before this day leaves us. Once we have crossed into the delta, we will set up a defense within the swamp."

"No," said the deity, anger churning in his voice. "That we cannot do."

"Why not?"

Karak raised a hand and pointed to the lands on the other side of the road, above which thick black storm clouds were just beginning to disperse. "Another force approaches from the south," he said. "I have felt them as strongly as I feel my brother. Though I cannot discern their numbers, the presence I feel is monstrous. There seem to be thousands of them."

"A force from the south?" Velixar chewed on the statement for a moment, and then his heart sank. "Your brother's dark-skinned children have come into the fray."

Gravely, Karak nodded. "Led by the giant Gorgoros. Do you see that trace of black on the horizon, beneath the storm clouds? That is the remains of their cookfires. They are only three miles away and advancing quickly. They will reach the Gods' Road in less than two hours."

Damn you, Darakken, Velixar thought. Then he puffed out his chest, trying to force his old confidence back to the forefront. "It matters not, my Lord. No matter their numbers, our soldiers have more training than the Kerrians. We must meet them head on. We must *crush* them."

Karak shook his head. "As magnificent as that sounds, High Prophet, it is a course we cannot take. To meet the Kerrians in battle will allow Ashhur to gain ground on us. I do not wish for my children to face a two-front battle when they have already lost so much."

"What of your power?" Velixar asked. "You struck low the walls of Mordeina with a single spell. Could you not do the same to those from Ker?"

"And leave myself weakened for when my brother arrives?" Karak asked. "No. I have something better planned, something that will buy us needed time."

"Then what do you have planned, my Lord?" asked Velixar.

At that moment, a rustling sound came from behind them. Velixar swiveled around to see Aerland Shen, dressed in his black scaly armor, exit the forest and approach them. His two black swords were crisscrossed over his back. The thickly built elf was nearly upon them by the time Karak turned.

"What is the meaning of this?" Shen asked in his garbled version of the common tongue. "Why was my presence demanded?"

Velixar opened his mouth to reply, but it was Karak who spoke.

"I have heard of your decision to leave my ranks," the god said, his voice booming. Velixar's eyes widened in surprise that the deity had already known, but he shouldn't have been caught off guard. Karak was a god, after all. The deity reached out and snatched the Ekreissar chief by the front of his armor "That will not do."

Shen shrank away from the god, his pointed ears twitching. It was the first time Velixar had seen the elf afraid.

"We . . . have lost . . . " Shen began. Then, "It is useless . . . to go on with this charade . . . "

Karak shoved the elf backward. Shen fell to the ground and slid on his rump. The deity gestured to the swords strapped to his back.

"Tell me, Aerland Shen, son of Moerlind and Lorientas, what are the names of those weapons you wield?"

Shen twisted his head to the side as if thinking of the correct words. "Salvation and Condemnation."

"Ah, powerful names for powerful blades. And tell me, Chief Shen, how many have you slain with those swords? How many were given the gift of the swords' names?"

"I don't know. One hundred? Two hundred? Too many to count."

"Is that so? And how many of those countless numbers did you slay before this conflict between Ashhur and I began?"

In answer to that, Shen snapped his lips shut and looked away.

"I thought not," said Karak. "You never killed a soul until our pact was sealed. The Quellan like to proclaim themselves a proud and powerful race, regaling the tales of their conquests, and yet none of your kind has seen war for over a thousand years. I offered what your goddess did not: the opportunity for your people to reclaim lands that had once belonged to you, and now you wish to abandon your promise to me?" Karak stood up tall and swung his arm out wide as if presenting the scorched terrain to the elf as a gift. "Look at the devastation. Do you truly think I would allow you to turn against our pact and suffer no consequences? Should you leave, you will have doomed Quellasar to the same fate as Paradise, and when I am through with you, none of your kind shall remain."

Shen narrowed his eyes. "You speak of victory, yet it is we who flee east. Why should we believe your brother will not hold your head in time?"

Karak's eyes narrowed, and his fury seemed to make him taller.

"My brother has raised the dead, and in doing so, he has changed the rules of the game. I will give him a gift just as deadly. Look upon it, and then decide if my doom is still so certain as you imply."

Karak held his arms out to his sides and threw his head back. The brightness of his eyes increased tenfold. A gleaming layer of darkened light swirled around him. Aerland Shen struggled to his feet and spun in place as the forest behind them became a flurry of snapping branches and animalistic grunts. Velixar's movements echoed the chief's. The surprised and frightened shouts of the soldiers back at camp reached his ears. It was as if the forest were collapsing in on itself.

"What are you doing, my Lord?" he asked. He had to shout to be heard over the din.

"I told you that Ashhur offered me a half measure when he created the wolf-men. Now he has dispensed with pretense, and I shall retaliate in kind."

All creatures great and small burst from the forest in a stampede of fur, teeth, and legs. Elk, deer, wild goats, wolves, even squirrels emerged from the trees. A pair of black bears, early risers braving the end of winter, made themselves known. Migrating birds swiveled in the air and changed course, descending to join the fray. The caws and growls and snarls and chattering of the wildlife was so loud that it was like standing beneath the crest of a crashing wave.

The sloped clearing they stood in was large—perhaps a mile squared—yet not ten minutes after Karak had bellowed his silent call, there was nary a patch of bare earth to be seen. Velixar drew closer to his god as a litany of eyes stared at him, both black and docile, glinting and predatory. And still creatures emerged from the wood, clambering over one another, jaws snapping, antlers jabbing, drawing ever nearer to the three beings that stood at their center, becoming a nearly solid wall of undulating fur and teeth.

"What is happening?" Aerland Shen shouted, his normally hard voice wavering.

"You wish to see true power, child of Celestia?" Karak said without looking at the elf. His words bellowed across the countryside with enough potency to cause pebbles to bounce at their feet. "When a god is in need of soldiers, he *creates* them."

In a violent motion, Karak threw his arms out wide and his head pitched back. He screamed; it was a sound so horrible that it might as well have been the shriek of a dying star. But Velixar was not afraid. He felt the magic flow out of the deity, could see the threads exiting Karak's body, bore witness to the well as it filled with strength, pulsating. *This is creation,* he thought, awed. In his mind's eye he could see cells split and combine, looked on as the primordial sludge of unreality became the template for life itself.

Light poured from Karak's mouth, creating a second, earth-bound sun. The countless animals that had gathered—possibly close to one hundred thousand, both in the ring and hidden behind the trees—cowered from the god's radiance. The energy that exited Karak's body hung in the air, a brilliant golden cloud, and then slammed back down to the earth, coating the landscape with living fire. Velixar flinched and Aerland Shen screamed, but neither was touched by the descending light.

It was the animals that were engulfed. They screeched as one, the clamor so great that Shen dropped to his knees and covered his ears. Velixar looked on in wonder as creatures great and small began to writhe, their bodies warping and contracting, the bones beneath their flesh snapping and elongating. Fingers tipped with claws formed at the ends of furry appendages, snouts shortened, knee joints cracked as creatures that once walked on four legs rose up on two.

All the while, the transforming creatures bawled in pain. Every last one of them.

The blinding light that had engulfed the entire vicinity then disappeared with an audible *pop*. Karak's mouth snapped shut, his arms fell to his sides, and he collapsed to one knee, panting.

"It . . . is . . . done . . . " the god gasped.

No longer did the beasts cry out in anguish. In fact, the only sounds to be heard were the rasping breaths of untold thousands. Chief Shen had both his swords drawn and stood hunkered down as if he expected a battle. Velixar touched the large elf on the shoulder. When Shen turned to him, Velixar saw his eyes were wide and shimmering.

For the second time that day, the chief of the Ekreissar was afraid.

"Put your swords away," Velixar told him. "You have nothing to fear."

He stepped in front of the elf without another word, gazing out at what his god had created. Animals that had once been creatures of the forest now stood with the posture of hunched men. Each beast's body had nearly doubled in size: the elks were eight feet tall and slender; the wolves as large and broad as any soldier; the squirrels like malevolent, two-foot-tall imps; the birds varying from three feet to six in height, with talons sprouting from the ends of their wings. All of their eyes glowed yellow, much like those of Karak's lions, the Final Judges Kayne and Lilah. Those eyes stared back at him, brimming with recognition. Then, in an act that surprised Velixar to no end, the beasts dropped to their knees, one after the other.

As one, their snouts opened, revealing fanged and stumped teeth alike, and their tongues undulated in their mouths as they tried to speak.

"Ka-rak," they said in the voices of primitive children.

Velixar stepped up to what had been a goat a moment before. He placed his hand beneath its maw, lifting the creature's head. Its eyes met his, and he could see fear, confusion, and anger in its stare. The thing growled. Velixar released it and stepped away, looking over the sea of fur and teeth. It was then he noticed the grass beneath his feet. Its color was a dull yellow, no different from before. He spun around and looked to the forest, where an audience of befuddled soldiers had gathered on its edge. Velixar saw that although the trees had no leaves, they still appeared hearty and healthy; their bark was still crisp, their sap still flowing from broken branches. He thought back to when they'd first arrived at Mordeina, to the dead valley they had entered, where the trees of the bordering forest were crumbling, brittle things.

"How?" he asked, gazing across at his god.

Karak raised his head. The deity's flesh had lost its luster; his stately brown hair was matted; the glow of his eyes, dim; and his lips, like gray slugs in the middle of his face. Yet still he smiled.

"A piece of me lies within each of the creatures that stand before you now," Karak said, his voice weak and rasping. "The same essence that created you, Velixar, the same essence that forged humankind on this land, now pulses in their veins. With the beasts Ashhur made, he gave not of himself, but took from the land. Mine, due to my essence, will be wiser. Stronger. Better."

Velixar looked away, examining one of the wolf-men up close. Saliva dripped from its fangs, and it snorted when he drew near. *So many of them. I cannot begin to imagine how much power this required.* Velixar faced his god once more. Karak wavered on his knee and had to place one of his giant hands on the ground to keep from falling. There was also something odd about the expression on his face, a slight upturn to one side of his lips and his right eye twitching. It made Velixar recall Cotter Mildwood, the old man who had been driven mad when he read the scribblings in Velixar's old journal. That was how Karak appeared now—a whisper away from madness.

"But at what cost, my Lord?" he asked.

"A necessary one," Karak answered, a feverish grin crossing his features. "A willing sacrifice in the name of maintaining order. Now come to me, High Prophet, swallower of demons, and the greatest of all humanity. I lent you my power when you required it; it is time for you to return the favor."

The pendant resting on Velixar's chest leapt and pulsed. He felt his lips stretch into a grin. With determined strides, he stepped past a gawking Aerland Shen and marched up to the deity, holding out his hand. Karak's fist engulfed his. Velixar closed his eyes, picturing the land in all its magical glory, siphoning the godly energy from the very air itself, filling the cosmic well. Power infused him, raced up his legs and into his heart, then down his arms and into Karak, filling the deity with renewed vigor.

The creak of steel sounded, as well as a low grunt. Velixar opened his eyes and craned his neck to see Karak standing at his full twelve feet, wavering slightly but radiating strength. The deity released his hand and stepped away from him. The thousands on thousands of beast-men dropped lower to the ground. Karak slowly turned in a circle.

"Beasts of Dezrel!" he shouted, and though he wasn't nearly as thunderous as he'd been in the past, his voice was still imposing and incredibly loud. "You are my children now! I have given you strength beyond measure. I have given you knowledge. I have given you a second life! Who is it that you worship? Who is it that you adore?"

"Karak," the beasts growled.

"Now heed my words, my children. A pair of enemies approach, enemies that wish harm to your creator. You will defend me with your claws and teeth. You will defend me with your very lives if need be!"

"KARAK," came the vociferous howl of the beasts once more.

"Ia mapa ammen," muttered Chief Shen.

"Now go, children of the forest! Bring pain to any that do not worship my name!"

Once more, it was a stampede. Thousands of newly altered creatures began to run, adeptly veering around the three in the center. Never once were they touched. The entire procession took nearly a half-hour to complete, until the last stragglers passed them by, barreling down the steep hill toward the Gods' Road. On reaching the road, two-thirds of the beast-men veered to the west while the remaining third ran directly south. Velixar tore his eyes away from them, noticing the awed expressions on the audience of soldiers watching from the tree line. He then looked on as Shen stumbled up the hill, heading for the throng of elves that awaited him on the edge of the forest. *They will not abandon us now. They would not dare.* A chuckle escaped his throat, and he looked back at Karak.

"Will they be able to bring Ashhur to his knees?" he asked.

"If my brother is weak," said Karak, eyes distant. "It is the delay that matters, and the indecision that their mere existence will cause my brother to feel. But they are strong, and my essence is with them. Even if they do not find victory, thousands of our enemy will die. Let us see just how committed to the chase Ashhur's people are after the animals of the wild descend upon them."

CHAPTER 36

The Kerrians made good time as they crossed the border of Safeway and trudged north toward the Gods' Road. The sun had burned away the storm clouds, and the air had a slightly crisp feel to it. The horses maintained a steady canter while those on foot jogged alongside. Bardiya remained at the head of the procession, his heart overflowing with his newfound faith as his inhumanly long legs carried him forward easily. The only discomfort was his giant sword, which had been tied with hempen rope and draped over his left shoulder. The steel *thwacked* against his back with every loping stride.

"Onward to the drylands, to snatch the maiden fair," he called out over his shoulder, a rhyme Warden Ozyel had taught him before his dearly departed father asked the elegant beings to leave their land. When he'd grown older, he'd realized how obscene the rhyme was, but in his youth he had repeated it nonstop while with his friends.

"The maiden's legs are lengthy, I'll stretch them once I'm there!" his people shouted back to him. Bardiya glanced to the side and saw Ki-Nan bouncing in his saddle, a smile on his face. It seemed like a scene from a time long passed—a collection of young men heading out for the hunt, excited for the thrill ahead.

Except this hunt would most likely lead to their deaths.

They descended a slick embankment where small patches of snow and ice still remained. Bardiya looked around in wonder. The cold hardly ever invaded the lands he called home, with only the rare flurry during the most brutal of winters, such as the one from the year before. Even then it was rare for him to see such sights. It had been so long since he'd ventured away from Ang, Safeway, and the desert of Ker. Once more he felt young again, and he wished to see a pure white landscape for the first time in forty years.

The simple desires ended when the embankment flattened, and they progressed across a broad, barren plain. There had once been grassland here, and tiny villages as well, but all was gone now, razed by Karak as the rancorous god's army worked its way toward Mordeina. Bare earth squished and clumped beneath Bardiya's bare feet, sending a chill up his ankle and through his calf until it took root in his spine. He shivered, a spasm so intense it felt as if his whole core had become unstable. *A portent.* He gazed across the ruined steppe.

Something wasn't right.

No matter how decimated the land was, Bardiya still knew precisely where they were. The plains they currently cut through, nestled beneath the red cliffs to the west and the hills bordering the Rigon River to the east, stretched out for another two miles until ending at the Gods' Road. Yet as he peered ahead, trying to see the horizon, all he saw was a black fog of some sort. It almost seemed as if there were another storm raging, this one hovering only a few feet off the ground.

He planted his foot and came to a halt, the rhyme dying on his lips. Behind him, the rest of his party followed suit.

Tuan Littlefoot sidled up to him. "What is it?"

Bardiya frowned at him and faced north. He heard a sound like that of a waterfall, faint at first yet growing progressively louder. He squinted, noticed that the black cloud ahead stretched nearly as wide as the valley itself. A feeling came over him, a smothering sensation he had experienced only once, years before, when he'd run across the flock of dying kobo. It was as if nature itself was crying in despair, railing against some ill-fated blight.

His eyes snapped open, and he ran forward a few steps, the questions his people tossed his way nothing but a dull murmur to his ears. It was then that he realized the cloud he saw was dust and ash being kicked into the air by countless stampeding feet.

It was a living wall of animalistic fury, undulating as it approached, jaws filled with sharp, snapping teeth. Bardiya had never seen anything like it in all his life. The creatures of Dezrel had been warped into something vicious. He knew right away this abomination was Karak's doing.

"Ashhur save us," he whispered.

The others must have noticed as well, as behind him Ki-Nan and Yorn Loros were riding in a frantic circle, forming their four hundred mates into a packed cluster fronted with swords and spears. Yorn rode up to him.

"Fight or flee?" the man asked, sweat beading on his brown skin even though the day was quite cool.

Bardiya looked back at the charging, mutated beasts. "No fleeing," he said, and offered Ki-Nan, who lingered nearby, a knowing nod. "We must do the opposite of the antelope when confronted with a stalking sandcat; our best defense lies in keeping them before us. Just like the antelope, if we run, there's a better chance we die."

Ki-Nan's face flushed and he turned away.

Yorn wheeled his horse around. "We need arrows!" he shouted.

A group of fifty men dashed forward, fanning out beside Bardiya, raising bows they'd liberated from elven corpses. The bows were larger than the ones the people of Ker normally used, and many of the men had difficulty drawing back the string. The task was made no easier by the fact that they were all terrified, their arms shaking uncontrollably.

The wall of fur, teeth, and claws drew nearer.

"Do not aim!" the giant shouted over the din of hoots and growls as he yanked the giant sword off his back. "This is no hunt. Just loose as many as you can!"

Bowstrings were released and arrows sailed into the afternoon sky. The elven bows were more powerful than those bearing them had expected, and the first volley sailed over the heads of the charging beasts, disappearing in the mass. Nevertheless, the arrows found purchase. Pained yelps and screeching sounded. Standing as tall as he did, Bardiya could see the charging horde was just as deep as it was wide. There were thousands of them, too many to count, too many for his meager four hundred men to hold at bay.

And so it ends here.

The archers adjusted their aim, and this time when the arrows sailed they carried in nearly a straight line across the hundreds of yards separating them. A few of the beasts in front collapsed and were trampled by those rushing up from behind. The archers nocked anew and fired. Still another handful fell, but they kept on coming. They were close enough now that Bardiya could see the beasts approaching them were of vaguely human form and nearly twice as big as they should have been. He saw the echoes of wolves, big cats, flightless birds, deer, otters, even sheep, their faces mockeries of humanity with distended brows, jutting snouts, oversized teeth and beaks, and glimmering yellow eyes.

For every one the archers felled with their shaky volleys, another ten took their place. In a matter of seconds the horde had halved the distance between them, so close now that Bardiya could almost smell the stench of old meat on their breath. "Get back to the others!" he told the archers. "Fight together! Fight with purpose! The Golden Forever awaits us all!"

The archers turned tail and fled back to the others, and he glanced down to see another group of men had joined his side. Allay and Yorn were among them, as was Ki-Nan. Half of them were on horseback.

"Should we die, we die together, brother!" Ki-Nan proclaimed.

Bardiya nodded, then held his massive sword above his head with one hand and pointed at the rushing beasts with the other. A primal scream exploded from his throat, and Bardiya and his fellow warriors charged, ignoring the arrows that now whooshed past them on either side. Hooves and feet pounded the wet, burnt land.

Just before they arrived, the creatures let out a simultaneous cry. Its pitch varied, high and low, an uneven wave of sound, but the word was all the same, and the sound of it chilled Bardiya to the bone.

"KARAK!"

The giant crashed into the line first, slicing three beasts in two at the waist with a single sideways hew. Then the mass of the stampede slammed fully into him, knocking the breath from his large and powerful lungs. His fellow warriors followed his lead. Their horses reared back and shrieked as claws tore into their flanks, spilling guts and riders alike. Men began screaming, and Bardiya swore he could hear Ki-Nan's voice rise above the others as he shouted curses at the beasts.

A pair of upright-walking wolves crashed into his chest while a cat-man came at him from the side. Teeth raked against his flesh, claws dragged down his back. His shoulder was impaled by an antler that he snapped off with a single flick of the wrist. Bardiya grunted as he grabbed the beasts in turn with his powerful left hand, tossing them back over their swelling numbers as if they weighed nothing. He thrust forward with his sword, impaling six beasts through the chest like they were on a spit. A smaller creature tried scaling his leg—a squirrel-man, by the looks of him—heading for Bardiya's most sensitive area with its teeth bared. The giant snatched the two-foot-tall thing off him and made a fist. The writhing squirrel popped like a rotten fruit, bathing his hand with entrails.

Still the beast-men swarmed, relentless. These were not mindless things, Bardiya realized. They were attacking in clusters, the larger beasts such as deer and elk in front, the lesser predators behind, while the smallest of the forest creatures dashed through the legs of their larger brethren, using the bodies of the larger creatures to mask their movements. Bardiya hacked the head off a giant elk-man in a single swing, narrowly missing being skewered by its antlers, and then turned to see one of his fellow defenders whipping around and gargling blood, a human-shaped gopher attached to his throat. A pair of wolves fell upon the poor soul, ripping into his chest and sending intestines flying. The body was flung to the side, and Bardiya could see it was Tuan Littlefoot, one eye gone and leaking blood while the other one stared at him, lifeless.

The same was happening all around him. Every horse that had charged was now gone, swallowed by the ungodly numbers of beast-men, and he could see only a handful of the men still clashing with their savage opponents. He wondered if Ki-Nan was one of them, before his thoughts were interrupted by the flash of feathers in his face. Bardiya plucked the bird-man off him, a crane with stumpy claws at the end of its wings and serrated teeth inside its beak, and snapped it over his knee.

Three more beasts rushed him, only to be cut down swiftly. Bardiya pivoted on his heels and saw the cluster of four hundred men being overrun. The larger beast-men raked and snapped at those on the outside of the circle, while the smaller of their species leapt off shoulders, careening through the air and descending into the center of the desperate defenders. Blood began to fly into the air, Bardiya's people being decimated from both outside the circle and within.

He went to storm forward, but an impossibly heavy weight collided with him from behind, knocking him face first to the sodden ground. He lost hold of the sword when he landed with a splash, and he rolled just as powerful jaws closed around his left forearm. Wickedly sharp teeth pierced his flesh and scraped against bone.

Bardiya cried out in pain, beating at the gigantic, fur-covered head with his free hand. The thing's grip was insanely strong, as if it were made from solid rock.

A beast with a pair of black eyes, faintly glowing yellow at the center, rolled in his direction. Bardiya recalled the day he'd been attacked by timber wolves while hunting with his father in his youth, and did the same now as he had then. He plunged three fingers of his free hand into the beast's eye socket. The eye itself was large, the size of a mango, and it slipped and sloshed against the tips of his fingers as they snaked around the backside of the orb. The beast's gyrations became all the more violent. Bardiya then tore his hand away from the socket, ripping out the eye with a sickening *plop*. The beast finally released him, rearing back and lifting its snout to the sky as it roared. Bardiya kicked away from the thing, searching for his sword, while smaller beast-men scurried past him, heading for his doomed brothers in faith.

Bardiya hastened to his feet, his left arm aching and leaking blood. The beast that had attacked him ceased its bellowing and faced him, and Bardiya could now see that this monstrosity had once been a black bear. It was taller than Bardiya by at least two feet, and with its bulk it must have weighed as much as four of him. The thing stared, its empty eye socket oozing while the intact left eye radiated hatred. The bear-man growled, and Bardiya was buffeted by its hot, stinking breath from ten feet away. *"Hurts,"* he heard the beast growl. It then ran at him, its claws like ten long daggers aiming to pierce his heart. Bardiya braced for impact, knowing this would be the end of him.

He caught the claws when the bear-man collided with him and shoved him backward. His heels dug into the damp earth. The beast was strong, so damn *strong*. It leaned forward, bending Bardiya's arms nearly to the point of breaking. Its maw pounced, snapping with six-inch incisors. One of those massive teeth scraped against Bardiya's cheek, opening up a new, gushing wound.

He fell to one knee, the bear-man crushing its full weight down on him. *I love you, Ashhur,* he prayed. *I am sorry to have failed you.* He screamed as loudly as he could, trying to shove back against the bear-man's crushing weight.

Amazingly, he succeeded.

The bear let out a sharp cry as it stumbled. When it righted itself, the beast suddenly flailed, its good eye bulging as it whimpered and grunted. Then there was a flash of silver between its legs. The bear pitched forward, clawed hands grasping at the gaping vertical mouth that appeared where its nether parts should have been. Innards as thick as a human arm poured out of the wound, slopping onto the earth. The beast gawked at Bardiya as if insulted, taking a single step forward before its colossal bulk toppled over.

Another form was dragging itself toward him. Bardiya regained his wits quickly enough to bat a bird-man off his shoulder and draw back his fist, ready to strike. The head of the beast lifted, and beneath a wolf's nose there was the lower half of a grimacing brown face.

It was Ki-Nan. His old friend was entirely covered with blood, and the wolf's nose was actually a head, severed at the jaw line. Ki-Nan rose to his feet, revealing a giant gash running along his side, and tottered before Bardiya until his eyes rolled to the back of his head and he fell. The giant caught him, gently lowering him to the ground. All around him, the beasts continued their attack. A few even nipped at the back of Bardiya's neck. He batted them away, and they left him alone, rushing instead toward the easy meal a couple hundred feet away.

"Finish . . . this . . . ," he heard Ki-Nan say beneath the racket. "Finish it."

"I don't know how," he told his friend sadly. The circle of his fellow Kerrians was nearly broken, the beasts tearing into men left and right. It was a slaughter.

"You said . . . you said we couldn't lose," Ki-Nan said. "Not when Ashhur was with us. Now *prove it*."

His hand dropped to the side, falling atop Bardiya's sword. Bardiya looked at it, a thing he'd long viewed as evil, and knew it had to be something more if they were to survive. Reaching down, he lifted the sword, and felt comfortable, at ease. Rising, he took a slow step, then another, steadily gaining speed as he left Ki-Nan behind. With his size and strength, the beast-men gave him a wide berth, thrusting themselves into the greater melee of his people. *Cowards,* thought Bardiya. *Cowardly animals, evil things.*

Are you with me? Bardiya prayed as it seemed the very ground shook beneath his feet while he ran. *Because I need you now. Let me show them. Let every last vile thing sense your presence, and let them be* afraid*!*

The sword weighed nothing in his hands. He'd thought it evil, thought it a curse he never hoped to endure. But before him was true evil, hate with claws and teeth, created solely to murder and kill. And with his sword, he would end them. Clutching the weapon tightly, he let out a bellow, all the pain in his body gone. Into the ranks of the beasts he slammed, and he swung his sword with all his might—but not at any animal. An overpowering instinct guided his hands as he drove the weapon with a massive overhead swing straight into the ground.

The earth rumbled and broke.

The shock wave rolled over the battlefield, knocking aside man and beast alike. The creatures yipped and howled, twisting back to their feet as Bardiya ripped the sword from the ground and held it high above him. The blade shimmered with light, and the things snarled defensively, shielding their eyes with their misshapen mockeries of human hands.

"Say his name!" Bardiya cried. "Say the name of your god!"

"Karak," hundreds of them whimpered and growled, the word seemingly pulled unwillingly from their throats.

Again he slammed his sword into the broken earth. The ground roiled, and air blasted in all directions with the force of the mightiest storm. The beast-men let out cries of fear and confusion as behind them the people of Ker backed away, the soil firm beneath their feet.

"Say his name!" Bardiya roared, the challenge so loud it hurt his own ears. He could hardly believe himself capable of such volume. "Say the name of he who gives you strength!"

"Karak," they answered, quieter. Even fewer were willing to meet his gaze, yet none dared turn away. Their attention was his. Simple beings, he knew. They were driven by fear, only fear. Fear of Karak, the god who made them. It filled their hearts and minds. But fear was weak, lacking loyalty or faith. Fear he could conquer. Fear he could break.

"Karak's strength?" Bardiya asked. "Show it to me, you unclean things. Show me his strength!"

They did not move, only tensed their muscles. Despite the blood dripping from his body, despite the exhaustion he felt tickling in the back of his mind, Bardiya grinned.

"Fine," he said. "Then let me show you mine."

He rushed them, sword pulled back to swing. The sword's light flared brilliantly, and the creatures howled. When Bardiya swung in a wide arc, it was as if there was no end to his weapon's length. Ten times his height it slashed out, cutting the beasts down, severing their bodies with shining white. Pulling the blade back, this time he flipped it around and drove the blade downward, and as it pierced the rocky ground, a wave of chromatic brightness rolled in all directions. The beasts it touched let out cries as their hair burned away, and their skin turned black and rotten. The sound was deafening, and with it came the stampede. All of them, thousands, from the greatest to the smallest, fled north. Bardiya stood there, watching them, chest heaving as he breathed in and out, the glow on his sword slowly fading away.

When the last of them were gone, Bardiya collapsed to his knees, and he had to clutch the hilt of his sword to remain upright. The steel of the pommel was cold against his warm cheek, and he closed his eyes and held it to him as if it were a long lost friend.

"Thank you," he whispered.

Slowly Bardiya rose to his feet and turned to face his countrymen. Where once there had been four hundred, now there was barely half that number. All of them were bloodied and injured, a few near death themselves. Of those he had known best, only Allay Loros remained standing. They stared at him with wide eyes, a mixture of fear and awe that Bardiya would never forget.

"Ki-Nan?" Bardiya called. He turned and staggered through the corpses until he found his friend. Ki-Nan's left side was mangled, and a gash in his neck was soaked with blood. His lips moved, but Bardiya couldn't hear the words. The giant lowered himself to his knees and leaned closer to Ki-Nan's mouth.

"I knew it," the dying man said in barely a whisper. "I knew . . . you could."

Bardiya didn't hesitate. He placed his hands on Ki-Nan's chest and allowed the healing energy to flow through him. This time, he felt no pain as Ki-Nan's wounds mended. When it was finished, the man rolled over and coughed.

"Stand," he told his old friend. "You have a woman and family to find, remember?"

Bardiya helped Ki-Nan to his feet, and together they made their way to their maimed brethren. The giant flexed his arm as he went. The wracking pain of the injury he'd sustained from the bear-man's jaws was now a dull throb, but he knew the pain would return in time. Still, there was more he had to do before he looked to himself.

Bardiya turned to his friend as he walked. "What is the name of the woman you love?"

"Catherine," said Ki-Nan.

"After I heal our brothers, leave this place and do not return. I wish never to see your face unless this Catherine is at your side."

"But what of Karak?" asked Ki-Nan. "If you think I'm going to abandon you while the rest of our people—"

"Enough," Bardiya said. "Let me work."

For the next two hours, as the sun reached its highest point and began to descend, Bardiya spent his energy healing the remaining one hundred and eighty-two of his people. By the time it was over, he was exhausted, and his arm pulsed despite the bandage he'd tied about it. He slumped down on his rump, feeling much smaller than the giant he was, and gazed at the sea of corpses, both beast and man, that surrounded him. He then looked back at those he had just healed, who hovered a few feet away. They were torn, overwhelmed by grief yet given hope by his display of strength. But Bardiya knew their purpose was done. After today, they would follow him to the ends of Dezrel. Yet, after today, he would never ask them to.

"Go home," he told them.

Once more that day, all eyes turned to him.

"What?" asked Allay Loros, tearing his sorrowful gaze from his brother's corpse.

"I said go home. There is nothing left for you here but death, and that is never what I wanted for you all."

"But what of Karak?" asked Midoro, a middle-aged man whose white sideburns nearly glowed against his black flesh.

"Karak is a god," Bardiya said. "There is nothing you can do to him."

"But I thought we—"

"It matters not what we thought," said the giant gravely. "Your *lives* are all that matter. So take off that borrowed armor, toss it to the ground, and go back to Ang. Be with your wives; play with your children; bring joy and laughter into the world once more. You have witnessed enough ugliness for five lifetimes, never mind one."

"And what will *you* do?"

The question came from Ki-Nan, and Bardiya could see the pain in his old friend's face. Ki-Nan might have betrayed him by desiring to be someplace other than the land where he was raised, but in that single look Bardiya understood just how much Ki-Nan still loved him.

"I will continue on," he said. "This is my burden. Whatever trust you have, put it in me now. Let me carry it alone."

Ki-Nan gazed at him solemnly.

"I know I'll never understand what we just saw," he said, "but even that will never be enough. You will lose, brother."

Bardiya nodded, his massive body casting an imposing shadow over his remaining mates.

"I know, my friend," he told him. "I know."

CHAPTER 37

Patrick sighed. If it wasn't one thing sapping Ashhur's strength, it was another.

The first had been the task of sealing the huge gap in Mordeina's wall after the collapse of Celestia's tree. That effort had taken the deity almost six hours to complete and was accomplished only with the help of the nine spellcasters who hadn't been killed during the raid on the settlement. Next the god raised a temporary passage to replace the Wooden Bridge, which lay in ruin—Karak had apparently splintered the structure after his army crossed. After that came Ashhur's efforts to quell the fires that raged on either side of the road as they marched. The deity had also taken it upon himself to pass along his healing touch to any who might need it—human, Warden, or even horse—as they proceeded at breakneck pace toward the east.

And now this.

"There's so many," Tristan whispered, the young soldier's eyes wide and disbelieving as he stared at the impossible things surrounding them.

Patrick glanced at the boy. He looked as frightened as Patrick felt. "No shit," he said, trying to break the tension.

No one laughed.

They had come out of the smoke that billowed from the shattered lands bordering the Gods' Road—beasts of every species imaginable, wolf and elk and hawk and boar to name a few, standing upright as they broadened around the massive convoy. Luckily Ashhur had sensed the beasts' presence before they'd appeared. The god stopped the march, ordering his eight thousand brave warriors to bunch up while the undead he commanded surrounded their ranks, forming a wall of dead flesh. If he hadn't, the exhausted new army of Paradise would have run smack into Karak's new pets.

As it was, while the beast-men snarled and howled and snapped their jaws when they first emerged from the smoke, they hadn't yet attacked. They simply leapt about, their numbers far too many to count, encircling the undead in the same way as the undead encircled the living, rarely coming within ten feet of Ashhur's deceased sentinels. Occasionally, one of the more wild-looking beasts would venture close to the walking corpses as if testing its strength, but not once had any truly attempted to cross the barrier.

Those trapped in the middle of the undead were in a state of unease just as great, if not greater, than the pacing beasts. The air was filled with the sickly sweet scent of their fear. Patrick felt it as well, a churning deep in the pit of his stomach that made his throat run dry and his shoulders quake. *I have it better than most,* he thought, and that was the right of it. At least he knew the gods were capable of such feats of alteration, having watched as Ashhur created fiends like these on two separate occasions. For the others, seeing wild beasts that walked like humans must be like living a nightmare.

"Form up!" came a firm voice from Patrick's right. There he saw the Master Warden Ahaesarus walking among the men, four other Wardens behind him. His face was stern, and he ambled with ease, hands clasped behind his back. *At least someone isn't frightened.* Though, perhaps it was only an act to help calm the nerves of his wards.

If it is, it's a good one.

"What do you think they're waiting for?" asked Preston Ender.

Patrick looked up at the old soldier. Preston sat atop his horse, eyes narrowed and brow furrowed, hand cupping his thick gray beard as if deep in thought. He didn't seem afraid in the slightest. *That makes two.* Patrick thought.

"I don't know," he said aloud.

"How many do you think there are?"

Patrick shrugged. "You tell me. I can't really see from down here." He had lent his new stallion to a man named Duncan earlier that day, saying that he wanted to jog for a short while to get his blood pumping. A funny suggestion, considering running was extremely painful for Patrick given his uneven legs. It was something he only did when absolutely necessary. But Duncan was a proud man, and he would have taken offense if he'd known that Patrick had only made the offer because Duncan looked like he was ready to pass out from exhaustion. *Stupid fucking git,* Patrick chided himself, wishing he had that horse now.

Preston leaned forward in his saddle. "Impossible to tell for certain. They keep moving around. But there are certainly lots."

"That's helpful," Ragnar muttered from beside his father.

Preston cuffed his son on the back of the head, and Ragnar rubbed the spot, looking upset. Little Flick laughed at him, which made his brother, Big, laugh as well. Edward chuckled. Soon, the whole of the Turncloaks were guffawing like a pack of hyenas in the midst of frightened lambs. Patrick smiled truly for the first time in quite a long while, feeling the tension break. The other men in close vicinity seemed put off by the display. Warden Barnabus even shushed them, but the Turncloaks didn't listen.

"You know," Patrick said after the laughter died down, "your boy has a point. You don't even have a guess for us?"

"Fine," said Preston, shaking his head. "Let us say . . . a hundred thousand."

"A hundred thousand?" said a panicked voice from among the others.

"Only a guess!" the old soldier shouted, and he glowered at Patrick. "You see? *That* is why it's not a good idea to make assumptions, especially out loud."

"Got it," Patrick replied.

Preston gestured for Patrick to come hither, so Patrick placed a hand on the man's horse and got up on his toes.

"Though there *do* seem to be twice, maybe three times as many beasts as there are undead," he whispered, serious as a lightning strike.

Patrick rolled back flat on his feet, any joviality he felt fleeing him. Ashhur had more than twenty thousand walking corpses at his disposal. The math was demoralizing.

"Shit."

He spun around, elbowed a man wearing a comically large helm to get him out of the way, and began walking between two columns of frightened people. "Where are you going?" he heard Preston ask.

"I think a god might have a better grasp on numbers than you," he shouted over his shoulder.

Ashhur lingered just inside the ring of undead, standing beside one of the wagons holding their paltry food stores and fronted by a company of thirty Wardens. The frightened men and women of the convoy kept edging closer to the deity, seeking out his protection, but the Wardens shielded the god while Ashhur remained inexplicably standoffish. Patrick approached the line of Wardens, preparing a tirade for when they would try to stop him from advancing, but oddly their numbers parted as he clanked toward them, allowing him passage. He cocked his head, uncertain. Warden Judah nodded to him on his way by.

He sidled up to the deity, who was standing mere feet behind the wall of undead, gazing out at the legion of beast-men in the same way Tristan had. His flesh was still chalky; his hair seemed to have lost its golden luster; and his normally pristine silver armor now looked a dull gray, but that somehow only made him seem more statuesque and imposing. Patrick cleared his throat, and Ashhur's softly glowing eyes lowered to him.

"Patrick," the god said.

"Your Grace," Patrick replied.

"I have been waiting for you to come to me."

"You have?"

Ashhur nodded. "Please, climb atop the wagon."

"Um, all right."

Patrick did as he was asked, using his powerful arms to haul his bulky frame onto the wagon's roof, where his sightline was almost even with Ashhur's. Boards creaked beneath his feet. For a moment he simply stood there, in awe. The multitude of beast-men had seemed daunting when he'd been down below, but up here, able to fully witness the sea of writhing fur that seemed to stretch out for a mile in every direction, the view was entirely different. It wasn't a daunting task that faced them, but an impossible one.

"Your brother's been busy," he said, trying to keep from careening into despair.

"Indeed he has."

Patrick thought back to the morning Ashhur created the grayhorn-men, pictured the landscape darkening and turning brittle as the life-giving energy was siphoned out of it. "But your Grace," he said, "to make so many . . . he must have gutted half of Paradise to pull it off . . . "

Ashhur frowned. "He did no such thing. These beasts are different. Remember when I formed the wolf-men, so long ago? You asked me why I did not make them more intelligent, and I told you it would greatly weaken me. Karak has taken no such precaution. Just as we did when we created humanity, he gave these creatures a piece of himself, each and every one of them. Though they are still close to the beasts they were, in time their intellect will grow, as will their drive. And they will be loyal, entirely, to Karak."

Patrick gave the deity a queer look. "That makes no sense, your Grace," he said. "Why go through the trouble of making these beasts smart, if they're not smart enough to realize when we're sitting ducks?"

"If they were mere beasts, they would have already attacked," said Ashhur. "It is that intelligence at work here. Karak wanted them to surround us. They were created to make me choose."

"Choose? Choose what?"

"That which is more important to me: my need to pursue my brother or the need to keep my children safe."

Patrick frowned.

"I don't get it."

The deity turned to face him. His expression was exhausted and filled with a mixture of anticipation and doubt. It was not a look befitting a god, and it made Patrick nervous.

"I can scatter them if I wish," Ashhur said, lowering his booming voice and directing it so only Patrick could hear. "They are still base creatures, and whatever intelligence they have, I can still overwhelm with fear. But these . . . things will move deeper into my lands, and when they do, they will hunt my children, without warning, without mercy. Yet if we fight the beasts, our forces will suffer casualties, and it will give Karak ample time to distance himself from our troops."

"So what will you do?" Patrick asked. His voice sounded small and insignificant in his ears.

The deity inclined his head. "We stay the course," he said, "and hope my children are intelligent enough to hide within the walls I've raised for them when the beasts arrive."

"What of those who aren't in Mordeina? There must be thousands of them."

"Those, we simply pray for."

"And who does a god pray to?"

Ashhur sighed once more, his glowing eyes aimed at the gray-blotted sky. "Anyone that will listen." Patrick didn't think he'd ever heard anything more depressing in all his life.

Ashhur turned away from him. Patrick was left to stand atop the wagon alone, surrounded by frightened humans and Wardens on one side, and countless undead and beast-men on the other. The beasts' grunts and growls rose in volume, their eyes following the god as he progressed along the line. Patrick could see hatred in their glares, but awe and dread as well. In that way, the creatures were very much like himself.

The deity strode ahead, the line of undead bulging outward as he neared their numbers. The beast-men outside the protective circle howled and snarled, backing away as the walking corpses pressed closer to them and snapping their jaws at Ashhur. The god held out his hand, and his ethereal sword appeared from the mist, massive and glowing.

The sea of decaying flesh parted, and Ashhur walked past them, each step measured, determined. The beast-men snarled, a guttural chorus that caused the very air to quiver. Patrick looked on uneasily as twenty or more of the braver beasts, former wolves and elk, charged the deity, claws outstretched. Ashhur swung his sword with such speed that the blade became a glowing half-circle as it cut through the attacking beast-men. Bodies were carved in two, the beasts' blood washing over Ashhur. In a matter of moments, all of those that had attacked were dead.

The other beasts close to the deity nervously backed away. For a moment Ashhur simply stood there, staring at them, while blood fizzled and popped on his glowing blade. Eerily calm, he knelt down and placed his fingers on the already scorched ground. Flames immediately sparked to life, racing away from the god in either direction like twin waves and rising twenty feet into the air. The wall of fire raced along in front of the swaying undead as it circled around them. The inferno blocked Patrick's view of the beasts, but their shrieks and howls of pain could be heard over the violent crackle of the flames. He had to shield his eyes from the brightness as the atmosphere became superheated. Sweat rolled over his brow.

Ashhur shuddered for the briefest of moments, and the flames died away, retreating back toward the being who had created them, revealing a ring of smoking, humanlike corpses. There had to have been more than a thousand of them. Patrick squinted, looking on as his god forced himself to his feet. When he took his first step, his right knee buckled, and he almost fell. His face was more drained than ever before.

And then it was over, the beasts' howls echoing across the land as they fled into the distance. Ashhur strode back toward his children, the deity's armor caked with blood, his expression tired. Men rushed Ashhur, falling to their knees before him, begging the god to say he would keep them safe. Patrick thought he saw Ashhur's dimly glowing eyes well with tears as he knelt down among his flock, allowing them to gather around him and offering reassuring words. This seemed to lift the mood of the men, a sentiment that passed through their great numbers like a wave. Soon many of them wore smiles, even if most were wary. The din of the fleeing beast-men drifted into the background, seemingly forgotten. Patrick couldn't help but think of Mordeina and the many villages outside Paradise's capital settlement. It seemed they would need Ashhur's protection far more than those here at his side.

Patrick glanced behind him as the last of the beast-men disappeared into the lingering smoke. A cluster of brawny wolf-men was the last to leave, casting hateful stares at the god of the west before they themselves disappeared. For a moment Patrick took in the reality of all that surrounded him, and had to fight back despair; where there had once been forests and grass, there was now a country of glowing, smoldering coals. It hardly looked like a land worth fighting for.

Yet fight we will. His resolve grew as he watched his god calmly nurture his children. Patrick climbed down from the wagon and sought out the company of his Turncloaks, his brothers-in-arms. *If Ashhur is willing to sacrifice so much of himself, how can we do any less?*

The Wardens reorganized the people into their formations, and soon the march began anew. Ahaesarus took the lead, his extremely long legs churning as he jogged, sword raised, ushering his wards onward while Ashhur loped behind him. Patrick found Duncan and retook his stallion, his knees throbbing as he climbed into the saddle. He exchanged a few casual remarks with Preston, Edward, and Tristan as they cantered, but his gaze kept finding its way back to his god. Ashhur looked like he might fade away right then and there. Patrick wished there were a steed large enough to carry him.

The caravan moved onward, the undead dragging their carcasses along, somehow keeping pace despite their stiffness. The sun crept low behind them, casting long shadows over the Gods' Road. A few of the horses faltered, two of them snapping legs, forcing a shaking Ashhur to heal them. It seemed not even broken mounts could stop the march. They were near to Ashhur's Bridge now, much too close to consider stopping.

The smoldering ruins of Paradise abruptly ended, replaced by fields of grass, dull green from the winter's snow, and trees that were hearty despite their empty branches. The smoke that constantly seemed to envelop them all but disappeared. Patrick looked all around him, taking in his surroundings. After the desolation they had passed through over the last three days, he thought he'd never seen anything more beautiful.

Then the convoy came to a halt once more; only this time a tired grin stretched across Ashhur's sallow face as he gazed upon the obstruction in the road. The wall of swaying undead parted, and the god stepped through them, trailed by his Wardens. Patrick shot Preston a look, and the two men followed.

The obstruction in the road was a group of what looked to be at least two hundred dark-skinned people. They were camped right in the center of the Gods' Road, sitting around cookfires, wearing only their bloodstained smallclothes. Piles of mismatched armor, once worn by Karak's soldiers, were stacked outside their small clusters. Their horses—only a handful of them—grazed lazily on the field of flattened grasses to the south of the road. The men of Ker all rose when they spotted the eastern-marching convoy, appearing pleased as they gazed up at Ashhur. Oddly enough, though they looked at the numerous undead with startled expressions, they didn't withdraw in fear. It was almost as if seeing such horrors had become commonplace for them, which struck Patrick as particularly discouraging.

He scanned the assembly for a sign of his giant old friend, but Bardiya was nowhere to be seen.

Three of the Kerrians talked with the rest of their group and then approached Ashhur, meeting the deity halfway. All three dropped to their knees before him.

"Your Grace," said the one in the middle, a tall youngster Patrick didn't recognize. In fact, as he scanned the Kerrians' faces in the dying sunlight, he realized he couldn't identify any of them. Had it been so long since he'd traveled farther than the Black Spire? It didn't seem like it.

Then again, the passage of time is fleeting when you don't age.

He rode his stallion up to Ashhur's side, and the three men of Ker turned their eyes to him. All three looked at him with suspicion, and two seemed repulsed by his appearance. Patrick frowned. It had been a long while since he'd experienced such a reaction; he'd almost forgotten how insulting it was. He wondered if they would have reacted the same way if Bardiya had been with them.

"Allay, Midoro, and Nusses—my children," said Ashhur, thankfully drawing their attention away from Patrick. "Why are you blocking the road? We wish to pass."

The one in the middle bowed low, his black skin gleaming in the waning light. "We were waiting for you, your Grace."

"If you desire to join our ranks, I ask that you pack up your belongings, mount your steeds, and find a place among the column. The bridge bearing my name is but a few hours away, and we will ride through the night if need be to reach it."

"Are you pursuing Karak, your Grace?" asked the one named Allay.

"Of course."

"Then the bridge to the delta isn't where you need to go."

"Is that so?"

The one named Midoro, a bulky young man with a wide jaw and piercing hazel eyes, nodded. "It is, your Grace." He pointed north, toward a lengthy backdrop of rolling hills that ended at a thick wood. "The god of the east went that way."

Ashhur faced the direction in which Midoro pointed. His pale lips twisted into a grimace, and he shook his head.

"Of course," the god said.

"Bardiya already ran off after him," said Nusses. "He ordered the rest of us to go back home, but those you see here couldn't bring ourselves to abandon him."

"Wait," said Patrick. "Bardiya is going after Karak on his own?"

Allay, Midoro, and Nusses nodded.

Ashhur seemed to mull over the men's words for a moment before turning about and facing his legion of Wardens. "We will make camp here, with my children from Ker," he said. "But only for an hour or two. Pass the message along to the others. There are no safe passages across the Rigon, north of the bridges, and the terrain is rocky and perilous. We will be greatly slowed."

As the others dispersed, including the Turncloaks, Patrick trotted up to his deity. "I wish to go on ahead."

"Do not worry for Bardiya," said Ashhur. "My child knows what he is doing."

"Are you sure of that, your Grace? What if he's not in his right mind?"

Ashhur tilted his head forward. "I have felt him in my thoughts, my son. He has recaptured the grace he thought he lost. He is as complete now as he has ever been." A sad smile came across the deity's face. "However, if you wish to forge ahead, you may. The undead will find the footing treacherous in the forest. Form a party with the Master Warden, and search out my brother's army. But you will only look—not engage. Not until the full of my force is with you."

Patrick almost opened his mouth to protest, but decided against it. "Very well, your Grace." He dropped to a knee, bowing low.

Ashhur placed a hand on his head and then turned away, heading back toward the swaying undead and the short-lived camp that was now being raised between them. He lingered there for a long while, staring up at the northern wood. He knew his desire to rush to Bardiya's aid was rash. It was selfish. *He's my friend. I don't want to lose him too.*

Gods knew he had lost enough already.

Chapter 38

Moira Elren was in a boiling rage as she raced toward Veldaren. The horrific images she'd seen the day before refused to leave her, a nightmare that haunted even her waking hours. She leaned forward in the saddle, gritted her teeth, and dug her heels into her horse's flank, urging the animal to gallop faster. The pounding of hooves filled her ears as the Movers struggled to keep up with her frantic pace.

They exited the forest and entered the city from the south, passing by the Watchtower, the setting sun reflecting off its spire. Moira could see none of the City Watch roaming around the entrance to the tower, but that wasn't surprising. In every village and shantytown they'd delivered food to during the long journey north, men of fighting age were a scarcity at best. She and her Movers had only seen a handful of roving bandits, and those disheveled men kept their distance when they caught sight of her four large companions and their steel. It seemed that in all of Neldar, only Catherine Brennan had rebelled against Karak's demands and kept afloat what her husband's family had built. The farther Moira traveled, the more her once seething hatred of the woman transformed into genuine respect.

Perhaps if Erznia had someone like Catherine leading them, I would not have found what I did.

She bore down, the drab gray buildings lining the South Road flashing by on either side. Tears of fury formed in her eyes as the memory crowded in.

The decision to visit Erznia had been an impulsive one. She hadn't stepped foot in the settlement since she and Rachida had fled to Haven more than fifteen years ago, and the closer she drew to the hidden community within the trees, the more her excitement built. Even though the Moris had been subjected to great losses over the last couple years, those who remained had been like a surrogate family to her. To see Yenge, Alexander, Caleigh, Ebbe, Dimona, and Julian again would fill her heart with joy. To sit and share a drink with Oris, the scarred beast of a man with a heart of gold, would bring a smile to her face. She wanted nothing more than to relax, to recharge. Laurel Lawrence could wait a few days while she filled her belly with Yenge's signature spiced lamb kabobs served over a bed of leeks and turnips . . . so long as the fall harvest had been plentiful.

Yet what awaited her there was not relief, but horror. The gate was smashed, and half the elegant cottages inside Erznia's fifteen-foot-tall wall of pine and steel had been put to the torch. The causeway through the center of the hidden township was torn up, marred with the impressions of boot heels. The lavish gardens that had been a staple of each family's land were wilted and dead, crushed by the now melted winter snows.

But worst of all were the bodies. They were everywhere, some lining the side of the road, most strung up upside down from trees and the roof overhangs of the homes that weren't reduced to ashes. The corpses were stiff, their flesh parchment thin. Many of their stomachs had been opened, and the animals of the wild, let in through the smashed front gate, had picked through the remains. The upper torsos of those dangling were reduced to bone and sinew; many of their heads and arms had been chewed off altogether. It was a dreadful sight, and for a long moment Moira just sat there atop her horse while her Movers set out to investigate the scene, staring in disbelief at the carnage.

It wasn't until Rodin persuaded her to ride toward the northwest corner of the settlement, where the estate of House Mori resided, that she broke from her stupor. Whereas other parts of the village featured a sort of macabre order, here was disarray. It looked like the cadavers remained as they were when they died, numerous arrow shafts jutting from their long-dead hides. Moira dismounted and examined the one closest to the estate's entrance. It was female, with a faded yellow dress and a head of dark, curly hair gone pale from exposure to the elements. Her flesh was ravaged, half her face gnawed away by both time and beast, but it was clear who the woman had been. It was Yenge, Vulfram Mori's widow, now joined with her husband in Afram, if such a place existed at all. Moira leaned closer, examining the arrows protruding from the dead woman's hide: one in the neck, two in the flank, three jutting from the lower abdomen, one in the eye. The rest of the deceased had been pelted in much the same way, with just as great an abundance of arrows. Karak's Army had come here, and for whatever reason had killed *everyone*.

Women and children, young and old—none were spared, not even the village's Magister. It was a thousand times worse than the scene she had run across in Omnmount. Moira had thrown her head back to the heavens and screamed.

Suddenly, the need to find the last surviving Lawrence became all the more vital.

And now here she was, back in Veldaren, the city where she had spent much of her youth, looking for a single woman in a city of presumably thousands of females. She rode and rode, hoping to run across one of Karak's representatives, no matter who he or she might be, she wanted to watch blood cascade from the wounds of one of the god's faithful.

"Whoa, Moira, slow down!" shouted Danco from behind her. "We must gather ourselves!"

Reluctantly she pulled back on the reins and swiveled her steed around. The Movers had stopped riding and were now sitting atop their horses and gazing with apparent wonder at their surroundings. Although Port Lancaster was a sprawling city in and of itself, most of the buildings erected were humble wooden constructions that had ample space between them. Not so in Veldaren, a city designed by a god. It was the most densely populated location in all of Neldar, housing twice the residents Port Lancaster did, necessitating tightly packed buildings of gray stone that loomed over the road like ancient guardians in formation. And more had been added since Moira had last seen the place, which made simply riding down the road a study in claustrophobia.

Moira trotted up to her men, examining their expressions. Rodin was awestruck, looking around as if he felt small and didn't like that feeling one bit. Tabar scowled, fingers restlessly tapping the hilt of his sword, and Danco laughed nervously. Gull, as usual, was expressionless. Even the fading sunlight reflecting in his gray-brown eyes did nothing to enliven him.

Rodin shook his head as Moira approached. "This is strange."

"What is?" asked Moira.

"This city. So large and intimidating . . . so empty."

"Empty, indeed," said Tabar. "Where are the people?"

Moira turned about and glanced down the length of the South Road. There wasn't even a hint of movement. She looked to the buildings abutting her—a mason's shop on one side, a silversmith on the other—and saw that their shutters were open, the windows dark. It was only in the apartments above the shops that she caught sight of what might have been a pair of eyes, staring out from the blackness within. But those eyes quickly disappeared. Then she noticed that no smoke came from the many chimneys, even though it was cold. Again she thought of Omnmount, of the people hiding within the cabins in the border settlements.

"It's the same as before," she said. "They're locked away. Afraid."

"Of what?" asked Danco, his voice rising slightly.

Moira thought of the scene in Erznia.

"Of Karak's faithful, I'd wager." She cocked her head and grinned. "Have any of you seen the castle before?"

"No," said Gull flatly.

Of course not. Stupid question. She pointed up the road, where the major artery split, one continuing farther north, the other veering to the right. "Well, the Castle of the Lion is right down there. You can see the towers over the buildings. What do you say we pay the honorable King Eldrich a visit? Perhaps he can tell us what we don't know."

"Perhaps," Rodin said. "However, I hope this goes better than the last time we went to meet with a man of great importance."

Moira sighed. "Me too."

"I also think proceeding with caution instead of riding flat out would be best," added Tabar.

They all agreed, clomping down the road in formation, with Moira and Rodin in front, Tabar and Danco in the rear, and Gull between them. Tabar expressed regret that Willer had died, but only because the energetic young Mover had always acted as their forward scout. Moira couldn't help but shiver at how detached they were when it came to the loss of their friend.

The curve in the road neared, and Moira's heart began to race. She didn't know what to expect once they reached the castle, and that lack of knowing played evil games with her mind. She tensed, feeling the weight of her twin swords as they bounced against her hips. Her hands flexed inadvertently around her horse's reins. She could barely feel the cold wind that blew against her face. A bird cawed overhead.

"Halt," said Gull. They were mere feet from the bend in the road.

"What is it?" asked Rodin.

"We're close," Moira said. "Let's just get to the castle and out of the open. It's making me nervous."

Gull put up a finger, his head cocked to the side. "Do you hear that?"

At first Moira heard nothing, but then she noticed a faint undercurrent beneath the wind and creaking stone—a barely noticeable *tink, tink, tink,* followed by another bird's caw.

"Conflict," Danco said. He didn't seem so uneasy any longer, and he actually smiled.

"But where?" asked Rodin, looking about.

Gull stretched out his arm in an exaggerated manner and pointed. "To the north. Come, we must ride."

"We should go to the castle," said Moira firmly.

"We will," Gull replied. "However, if you are correct and the people are hiding within their homes, it means oppression is occurring here just as it did in Omnmount. If that's the case, it's possible the skirmish we hear is an act of rebellion. Would you, Moira, the woman who gave heaps of Karak's liberated food to the starving, turn away from those in need?"

Moira nodded sharply. "Of course not. You're right."

"Then we must move, albeit cautiously."

Again Moira nodded, and she took the lead as she guided her Movers along the South Road.

The road to the castle passed by to the right, dark and ominous in the twilight. The structures around her became taller, more densely situated as she approached the center of the city. Now she could see actual people watching her from above, mostly women, peering out their windows. Moira didn't focus on them, didn't acknowledge their presence. She simply urged her mount to pick up speed.

They veered around Veldaren's massive central fountain and continued onto the North Road. There the sounds of conflict heightened, and Moira could plainly hear actual human voices screaming. Her heart began to pound in her chest, and this time she allowed one hand to slip from the reins and grab hold of a sword.

She would clearly need it soon.

She caught movement out of the corner of her eye and veered sharply to the right, bolting down an alley between a pair of boxy stone buildings. Moira didn't think; she simply kept her eyes straight ahead until she exited the alley. Then she pulled up, forcing the Movers to do the same, their horses skidding to a halt on the slate walk. Danco nearly fell from his saddle. The screams surrounding them were all encompassing.

Moira's eyes bulged in her head as she gaped at what lay before her. The alley emptied out into a wide square lined with smaller, more humble domiciles. She knew this place. The locals called it Haremdale, which many of those who had come from northern Neldar called home; it was a sort of city within the city, where those of like occupation and heritage could gather together and speak of how much more difficult it was living here than it had been in Felwood, Hailen, Winterhall, Stonybrook, and the like. It was where nearly every resident had hair the same color silver as Moira's, with eyes just as pale blue. They would toil on the streets, sell furs and junk from the north, and laugh and drink their odd green wormwood concoctions in six small taverns. In truth, being here had always made her uncomfortable, for given the populace's similar appearance to Moira's own family, it was like being surrounded by an endless sea of Crestwells.

Now, instead of drunken songs, she heard shrieks and the clang of steel, and all that she saw was pandemonium. Also, there were *men*. Lots and lots of men. At least a hundred flooded the square, some exiting the buildings, dragging helpless women behind them, some clashing with other women. There were women fighting women as well. It was a flurry of swords and daggers that was dizzying to watch.

Gull urged his horse a few steps forward, gazing at the bedlam with cold, calculating eyes. They were off to the side of the conflict and had yet to be noticed. Moira followed the stoic man's line of sight, and looked on as a grimy man ran a sword through a woman with short blond hair. She fell to the cobbles, clutching the gaping wound that opened her from neck to belly and crying out. The grimy man quickly jammed the tip of his sword through her ear, silencing her.

Rage built up in Moira, and it only doubled when she saw that Gull made no move to protect these poor women. The other three sellswords were just as passive, remaining behind their leader, awaiting orders. They were obviously itching for action, with their legs shaking and fingers clenching and unclenching, but they did nothing.

"What are you waiting for?" yelled Moira.

Gull shook his head and held up a single finger, his gaze returning to the battle in the square. Rodin shrugged in her direction, but he didn't move otherwise. Another woman fell, and then another and another. Blood coated the cobbles.

"Caution is best," said Gull.

It was the first time her sellswords hadn't jumped at one of her commands, and her blood began to race. "Fuck off then!" Moira shouted. She kicked her horse's flank, startling the beast and dashing forward, drawing both her swords as she did so. Gull shouted for her to stop, but she ignored him. Her screaming had caught the attention of the combatants. A group of nine men turned toward her, appearing confused. They were distracted enough by her rapid approach that two of them had their throats slit from behind by dagger-wielding women. The other seven were then jumped by women with fists flying, teeth biting, weapons slashing. Moira grinned and leapt from her horse, landing on an open patch of road, with both swords held out wide.

Hysterical sobbing reached her ears, and she turned quickly toward the sound. A gruff older man with a shaved pate was dragging a young girl by her hair out of one of the boxy brick homes. Tears streamed down the girl's face as she kicked her feet and clawed at the strong hands that held her. The man pulled her up by the throat, growling something into her ear. The girl's eyes bulged, and she started shrieking all the louder as the man continued to tow her along, heading for another of the side alleys.

Moira burst into action, ducking around individual skirmishes until she had a clear line on the man and his helpless quarry. The man never looked up at her, so intent was he on his destination. Moira kicked herself into a leap, spinning the swords in her grip so they pointed downward, and stabbed as she descended, hoping to skewer the man just below the base of the neck, as she'd done during the fight in Cornwall Lawrence's estate. This time, however, she missed her mark. The girl stopped her screaming when she saw Moira, which in turn captured the man's attention. He swiveled at the last moment, a shocked expression on his face, and then released the girl's hair and fell backward. Instead of piercing the back of his neck, Moira only succeeded in slicing through the front of his filthy tunic.

She landed straddling the girl, who was now inching away from her would-be captor. The man reacted almost the same as she did, pushing himself backward on his rump while staring wide-eyed at the wound on his chest. Moira took a menacing step forward, preparing to lunge again as the man fumbled with the sword on his hip.

"Who *are* you?" he shouted, glancing all around him, as if hoping help would come. "Don't you underst—"

Moira crossed her swords in front of her and then flung her arms outward, cleaving through the man's throat. He clutched at the gushing wound and fell backward, blood spurting between his fingers. If any of the other combatants noticed, none came to avenge him. Moira pirouetted and rushed toward the girl, who was now on her hands and knees, hurrying away.

She grabbed the girl by the back of her thin shift and lifted her. The girl struggled against her just as she had with the man. A fingernail dug into Moira's cheek, and she yelped and released the girl, who backed herself against the stone wall of the dwelling she'd been ripped from, panting.

"Hey!" shouted Moira, touching her cheek and coming away with blood. "I was trying to *help* you!"

The girl said nothing. Her eyes flitted from side to side, as if taking in the action going on around her, before she rushed back into the home. Moira sheathed one of her swords and gave chase.

"Come back here!" she yelled.

The door to the dwelling slammed in her face.

Something hard collided with her, knocking her to the side. Moira stumbled but kept on her feet, spinning and holding up her blade defensively. Her confusion was overwhelming. It was a woman standing there, one with a rigid jaw, short black hair, a scar on her forehead, and holding a curved dagger. The woman looked down at Moira and scowled, then rapped the dagger against the door that had just closed. She wore a bloodstained cloak, and when the door opened and she stepped inside, that cloak flapped, revealing legs wrapped in off-white cloth. Moira stared after her as she disappeared, remembering the letter the Conningtons had sent to Port Lancaster, in which they'd revealed that their many Sisters of the Cloth had been taken from them by Karak's acolytes. Moira turned back around, gazing over the turmoil of battle toward the alley where she and her compatriots had emerged.

Her Movers were gone.

From the corner of her eye, she saw a cluster of movement. In a flash she had her second sword drawn and twirled around, raising both swords just in time to parry two blows from onrushing attackers. Steel clanged off steel, numbing her arms, and she tucked her head between her knees, rolling between two more pairs of cloth-wrapped legs. She quickly shot to her feet, hunched over, and watched as her two assailants whirled to face her. She could only see the Sisters' eyes; the rest of their faces were hidden beneath their wrappings. One held a curved saber and the other, a dirk.

Stupid, stupid, stupid, she thought. *You knew the priests had demanded the Sisters be confiscated from the merchants. What else would they be used for?* She also realized that although there were many men engaged in the fight, a good number of them were women *dressed* as men, wearing heavy leather armor and chipped and rusted helms. Her confusion rose so greatly that she almost didn't react in time when the two Sisters charged her, graceful and deadly at the same time. Moira lashed out, batting away their blows as she backed up. She was more adept with her right hand than her left, which meant the Sister attacking on her left side was able to press much too close. The Sister slashed upward with her saber, aiming for Moira's midsection. Moira couldn't drop her left sword quickly enough; the only thing that saved her was another pair of combatants, who tumbled in front of her just as the blade was about to pierce her side. A man howled in pain. Given a momentary reprieve, Moira hacked mercilessly at the lone Sister now before her, beating her back. The wrapped woman's eyes widened with each violent hew, and Moira finally landed a solid blow to the Sister's wrist. The sword dropped to the cobbles, knocked aside by blindly shuffling feet, and the Sister grasped her leaking wrist. Moira thrust with both blades, but the woman spun away as quickly as Moira had before, disappearing into the throng. Moira's sword cut through the empty air.

She heard hooves, but was not quick enough to react. Hands were on her then, snatching her from behind and yanking her from her feet. She was thrown aside, just as a press of at least a dozen Sisters—some fully wrapped, some not—charged. She landed on her hip, startled, and lost grip on one of her swords. She looked up to see her four Movers, still on horseback, battle the Sisters back. Gull led the way, brutal and efficient with each looping arc of his longsword. In a matter of moments, the twelve Sisters were either dead or had fled, but more moved in to take their place. Moira scrambled to her feet, snatched up her second sword, and charged into the fray.

Suddenly, a roar split the night, and though a few individual scuffles continued, most of the discord ceased. A second roar thundered through the square, from the opposite direction as the first, gravelly and high pitched at the same time. Moira glanced up at her sellswords, then at the mob. Everyone appeared nervous, even the Sisters. A few of the wrapped women disappeared inside one of the many buildings.

"We will not back down!" shouted a feminine voice. "You Sisters still enslaved to the priest and his Judges . . . there is still time for you to see the light. We are the people of the city, and we will not back down! Karak has abandoned us, and he has abandoned you. Join us! Throw aside your wrappings and be free!"

Heads turned, gazing up at a point above Moira's head. As if in a trance, Moira backed up toward the center of the square, following their gazes. There was a young woman standing on the rooftop of the two-story building behind her, her form silhouetted by the sliver of sun that now poked over the horizon. She was striking, this woman, with a head of flowing auburn hair and stately features. She wore a masculine getup, with slacks and a heavy jerkin, but the power of her youth and confidence made it seem as if such clothes were the most natural things for a woman to wear. Her shoulders were thrown back, and the group of men standing around her, purple sashes fluttering in the breeze, seemed to regard her with reverence.

"Now go!" the woman proclaimed to the formerly embattled crowd. "Seek shelter before they arrive! We must live to fight another day!"

With that, she offered a knowing smirk and disappeared over the other side of the building. Once more the square descended into madness. The Sisters, both clothed in wrappings and not, tore through the throng, heading for the squat brick homes lining the square. The men and disguised women scurried left and right, darting down the various alleys. It was then that Moira noticed a handful of men sporting the same purple sashes as those on the roof, and others who wore helms painted with gold stripes—symbols of the Palace Guard and City Watch, respectively.

Another roar resounded off the stone buildings.

The square was still emptying out when men and women screamed from the darkness of the alleys. Moira's heart leapt and she took a few jogging steps forward, leaving behind the safety of her sellswords. A wave of people flew back out of the alley as Moira approached, re-entering the square, their faces frozen in terror as they dashed along the wall of homes and shops, searching for another way out. Moira inched even closer, her mind awash with turmoil. She looked on in wonder as a body came soaring out of the darkness, arms and legs flailing as it spun, until it landed with a *splat* on the cobbles not ten feet in front of her. The corpse's flesh was shredded, its face a mess of pulpy gore. Entrails formed a red path behind it, disappearing back into the alley. Moira thought of Erznia, of the horror that had happened there, and hunkered down, holding out her swords.

Just as the sun disappeared over the western horizon, bathing the city with a reddish hue, a lion stepped out of the darkness of the alley. It was a female, six feet tall, her eyes shining with a golden light. Moira's arms dropped ever so slightly, the tips of her swords dipping, as she stared at the beast.

"Lilah?" she asked, her voice filled with wonder and childlike fear.

She hadn't seen Soleh Mori's pets in ages, and as far as she knew they had been kept locked beneath the Castle of the Lion for more than forty years. She recalled her younger days, when Vulfram would wrestle with Kayne while Oris and Ulric cheered him on, and the girls of the house would groom the lioness. The lions had been huge even then, but nothing compared to what she now saw. This was no childhood pet or even a beast of the wild.

What stood before her was the personification of Karak's rage.

Lilah swiped at those trying to flee, scoring the back of one man and knocking a woman into the air, splitting her ill-fitting helm. A ragged collection of men and women in armor then began inching along the walls, approaching the beast. The lioness's glowing eyes glanced toward them and then locked on Moira. The lioness froze. Lilah sniffed the air, a guttural rumble vibrating her throat. Her tongue, nearly the size of Moira's arm, licked the blood off her maw.

"Moira," the lioness spoke. *"Blasphemer."*

Moira stood slack-jawed, knowing she should run but convinced that the moment she did, the lioness would leap.

"You know what to do," Gull shouted from behind her.

Lilah dipped her head and charged. The sight of those gleaming claws in the burgeoning darkness broke the spell upon her. She spun to the side just as the lioness leapt. A single claw dug into her leathers, gouging her forearm as the beast sailed past. Moira ground her teeth against the pain and rolled.

Despite her massive size, Lilah touched back down with barely a sound and whipped her body around. Moira was back on her feet, frantically considering her next action. Although Corton had taught her how to fight men much larger than her, she doubted such maneuvers worked well against a thousand-pound lion. As if to mock her, she heard another roar, and more screams, erupt from behind her. She chanced a look over her shoulder, spotting Kayne, the male lion, as he bounded into the square from the opposing alley. The beast had a man dangling from his jaws, and when he jerked his massive neck, the body ripped loose from the neck. The corpse splattered against the side of one of the buildings while the lion bit down on the head in his mouth. The crunch that followed nearly turned Moira's stomach.

"We're dead," she whispered.

"I would not be so sure about that."

Moira spun her head back around and saw her four Movers standing before her, three facing the lioness while Rodin stood by her side, his eyes locked on the male. "Form together!" Gull shouted, and they all backed up until their shoulders were almost touching, forming a five-person circle in the center of the square.

The lions began to circle around them, eyes squinted and glaring as they examined their prey, angling nearer with each revolution. By that time the center of the square was empty but for the hundred or so corpses that littered the cobbles, though the armored men and women lingered in front of the alleys as if waiting for something. Kayne dipped his head into the gaping chest of one of the corpses while passing it by, slurping down a mouthful of entrails.

"They speak," said Gull out the side of his mouth.

"Seems that way," Moira replied.

"How intelligent are they?"

She shrugged, tracing the lions' movements. "I don't know."

"Let us see then, shall we?"

Gull stepped away from their defensive circle, holding his long-sword out before him. He had a self-assured manner about him as he began to mirror Kayne's movements. He flicked the tip of his sword to the side and fully faced the beast, his legs spread out wide. His empty hand lifted, and he made a mocking, beckoning motion to the lion.

"I challenge you," Gull stated, his voice still strangely flat despite the danger facing him. "Let us see if a beast can indeed be anything but a beast."

Kayne scowled at him, his massive head dropping. The lion moved slightly to the side.

"Are you afraid, animal? Do you fear a mere human with a sword?"

"What are they waiting for?" Danco whispered in Moira's ear. He jutted his chin at the gathered, armored people who lingered beyond the lions' claws.

She didn't need to answer, for a half second later the separate groups of people bellowed at the tops of their lungs and charged toward the lions. Danco and Tabar followed suit, taking off at a run in opposite directions, their swords held up high, their feet pounding the gore-soaked cobbles. The lions ceased their pacing and looked ahead and behind before rushing Moira's sworn men. Moira kept her eyes on the male, watching in horror as the beast shook his head, his sodden mane like a ring of snakes, and then hunkered down on his haunches. Tabar flew past Gull and lashed out at the lion. A paw came up, absorbing the blow, and when Tabar streaked past, Kayne pounced. The lion's powerful jaws clamped down on the man's left arm, halting his momentum, snapping his head to the side. Tabar howled in pain. Kayne drove forward, forcing Tabar to his knees. There was a pop as his shoulder dislodged from its socket.

Without making a sound, Gull strode forward, moving quickly and easily across the square, and brought his longsword down on one of the lion's legs. Kayne released Tabar's arm, which was now dangling as it bled, and roared. When Gull's sword looped back around, there was only a smattering of blood on the blade. The other charging men and women then reached his side, hacking and slashing in vain at the lion.

"Moira, we must go!"

A strong hand clasped around Moira's injured forearm, and she was nearly yanked off her feet. She spun, batting the hand away, and caught a glimpse of Danco as he danced around the lioness, joined now by another thirteen combatants. It was difficult to see in the spreading darkness, but she swore Danco was limping. He had placed himself between the buildings and the open space of the center square, severely restricting his opportunities to flee. People pressed in around him. Lilah bore down, ready to strike.

Again Rodin grabbed at her. "We must leave while we have the chance! No harm can come to you!"

"No!" Moira yelled at him. Her teeth gritted and she glowered. "I am Moira Elren. I fought Karak's Army in Haven. I do . . . not . . . run."

She drove her elbow into Rodin's chest, knocking him aside, and then charged toward the faltering Danco. Danco now favored his left side, his free arm pressed against his own waist as blood turned his breeches red. Moira leapt at Lilah, plunging both her swords into the lioness's flank. The lioness whirled around with a quickness that should have been impossible for so large a creature. Moira landed and flattened herself on the ground, barely avoiding the giant claws that soared over her head. She then rolled beneath the lioness's torso and jammed one of her swords into Lilah's gut. The beast howled and rose up on her hind legs as a gush of blood left the wound. But Moira watched in horror as the cut closed, fur overlapping the gash until it disappeared.

Danco grabbed her ankle, dragging her across the ground and nudging aside the swarm of people that surrounded them, before the lioness dropped back down on all fours. She heard Tabar swear somewhere behind her. Moira kicked Danco away, scampered back to her feet, and went to charge the lioness again, knocking a man in a rusty helm in the back of his head with the butt of her sword in the process. This time Rodin snatched her around the waist, pulling her tight to his own body while Danco fought Lilah off.

"Do you want to die?" Rodin growled into her ear.

She kicked him in the shin, eliciting a yelp, and then flung her head back as hard as she could, striking him square in the nose. The hands around her released, and she charged back toward the fighting lioness, flinging herself into the air to stab down with her twin blades, soaring over six new corpses.

She never had the chance.

The lioness turned at the last moment, lashing out with a heavy paw. Moira managed to slip one of her blades into the thick webbing between the beast's toes, but that wasn't enough to stop the large, sharp claws from piercing her padded leathers, shearing her armor and flesh at once. Her breasts were scored over, ripping nearly to her ribs. She lost hold of her blades and tumbled back to earth, her forehead smacking against the cobbles. For a moment she blacked out, and then the world and all its pain came rushing back at once. Moira screamed as blood flowed from her wounds.

"Everyone, back!" she heard someone order. "Now, to the alleys!"

Gull shouted to her, and then the *whoosh* of countless arrows sounded. The ground shook as the lioness tramped past her. Moira opened her eyes, but there was blood in them. An explosion rocked the square, much too close to her, and the sudden light drove into her brain like hurled spears. She shrieked and covered her face with her arms. Something heavy approached her, and she knew she was done for. She reached out with desperate fingers for her swords, but then she heard steel slide across stone nearby and knew someone else had picked them up. She cursed to the heavens as loudly as she could.

"Calm yourself, Lady Moira."

Hands slid beneath her back, lifting her from the ground. Her life became a cavalcade of pain as whoever carried her ran across the square.

"Now, do it now!" she heard a man's agony-filled voice shout.

The cascade of arrows continued, the *twang* of bowstrings nearly constant, as was the *thud* and *clomp* of many retreating feet. The lions began to roar and screech behind her. She could actually hear the arrowheads embedding themselves in the creatures' thick hides. Though she was in agony, a smile stretched her lips.

More voices, hushed and urgent, directed those who carried her. Hands shifted beneath her a few moments later, and her body was lowered. Moira heard a door slam, and everything went hazy. She felt like she was close to vomiting.

Another door slammed, more hands lifted her, and this time she did heave, pitching the contents of her stomach all over herself.

She heard a man and woman grunt in disapproval, but her forward progress didn't halt.

"Put her there," a woman said. It was the same voice as the woman from the roof.

"And you four, over there. You, over there, find someone to tend their wounds."

"And what of her?" asked Rodin.

"She's in good hands."

Again, Moira felt herself being lowered. This time when her back touched the ground, a warm, wet cloth pressed against her forehead, wiping the blood from her brow. She opened her eyes. Sure enough, the young woman who'd been standing on the rooftop was above her, lips drawn downward in a frown. Gull was beside her, the side of his neck bleeding, but otherwise not the worse for wear.

"That was very foolish," Gull said, though there was no disappointment in his tone.

The young woman nodded. "We found your men watching the battle from the mouth of an alley. They offered to help guide the lions to the center of the square so that our archers could buy our people enough time to flee." She chuckled, shaking her head. "They seemed certain they would make it out alive, even though we lose five or six good soldiers every time we attempt the same trick. Looks like they were right."

"The fire," gasped Moira. "What started . . . the fire?"

"A special powder King Eldrich's advisors came up with. Fire seems to be the only thing the Judges are afraid of."

"Did it . . . kill them?" she wheezed.

The woman's face twisted into a frown. "Unfortunately, no."

She then put comforting hands on Moira's shoulders, dabbing her cheeks with the cloth. The wound in Moira's chest flared, and she gritted her teeth. The young woman grimaced, then reached behind her, producing a bowl.

"Here, drink this," she said, lowering the bowl to Moira's lips. The liquid was thick and bitter, and it stung going down her throat. She threw her head to the side and coughed, causing the pain to flare up once more.

"Bryan, get over here; she needs help quickly," the woman said. She then looked back at Moira. "I know the poppy is disgusting, but in a few moments you'll sleep. Don't worry. You have the king's own physician here to assist you. You'll be fine. Scarred, but fine."

Moira's vision started to go hazy, her defenses dropping. The woman above her was beautiful. "Who . . . are . . . you?" she asked.

"Laurel," said the woman. "Laurel Lawrence."

Moira burst into a fit of laughter that didn't cease until the tincture did its job and she lost consciousness.

CHAPTER

39

In the north, the Rigon wasn't the gentle and majestic river it became farther south. No, up toward the border of the Tinderlands it was a raging rapid seven hundred feet wide. This massive swell of water was created by the Gihon River that flowed from the mountains in the northwest corner of Dezrel, dumping its contents into the larger Rigon. The constant churn of liquid wore away at the banks, creating treacherous sandstone cliffs fifty feet high that regularly crumbled under the weight of time and erosion. Ice still clung to the crags, forming deadly downward-facing spires nearly three feet in length. Up here, even with the sun high in the sky, it was bitterly cold. There was still ample snow on the ground.

It was in this location that Karak wanted to build a bridge for what remained of his army to cross the massive waters. The terrain was rocky with shale and granite on the other side of the river; yet the trees were plentiful and hearty with wildlife. With spring nearly upon them, they could march through the Northern Plains and feed the soldiers with deer or hedgebeasts, massive, elklike creatures three-quarters the size of a grayhorn, with deadly antlers that could grow up to twenty feet wide. With sustenance, the men would be able to pick up their pace. With a greater speed, they could reach Veldaren in a week and a half.

Velixar stood on the edge of the river, Malcolm Gregorian beside him, kicking at pebbles and watching them drop fifty feet to the rapids below. He remembered a time when he had done the same thing along the banks of the southern portion of this very river, back when he was pretending to be Ashhur's most trusted, when Martin Harrow was newly deceased and Geris Felhorn still had his sanity. So much had changed since then, himself more than anything. He was powerful now, nearly as powerful as a god. But he doubted he was strong enough to do what Karak desired.

The remnants of Karak's Army spread out behind him, fidgeting and moaning. They had lost forty-three horses during their trek through the dense forests and steep hills of northern Paradise. Most had to be put down, snapping limbs on the uneven terrain, but a few had simply disappeared, along with their riders and precious supplies. If he had been an optimistic man, Velixar might have guessed the culprits to be wolves. But more likely they had taken their horses and deserted into the night.

It was becoming a common occurrence.

"It is time," Karak said.

Velixar turned and examined the deity. Somehow, Karak looked smaller than usual. Black veins traced across his too-pale flesh, climbing up his neck and spreading like webs across his cheeks. He had a mad gleam in his golden eyes as well. It was that gleam that made Velixar nervous.

"Are you certain, my Lord?" he asked.

"Are you questioning our god, High Prophet?" snapped Lord Commander Malcolm Gregorian.

Velixar ignored him. "My Lord, it is rather high here, very wide. Should we not travel farther north, closer to the fork where the cliffs are lower and the river narrower?"

"No. It is here that the deed must be done."

Velixar started to argue more, but stilled his tongue. If Karak said this was the place, this was the place. Karak was confident in his abilities, and so Velixar should be as well. Velixar ought to trust him; Karak was the deity, after all.

"Very well, my Lord," he said, bowing.

Karak stepped toward the edge of the cliff and held out his hand. Malcolm backed away, joining the remaining seventy-seven Ekreissar, who hovered near the front of the mass of soldiers. Aerland Shen looked on with a distrustful eye. The Ekreissar Chief seemed to have recaptured his bearings over the last four and a half days. Even though the square-faced elf had witnessed Karak's power when the army of beast-men was created, he was still doubtful. But then again, it wasn't the god's power they were relying on now, and Chief Shen knew it.

Velixar scowled at the elf before turning back to the river. *He will see. They all will.* Karak held out his hand and Velixar took it. His cloak billowed in the stiff wind; the pendant on his chest grew so hot, it nearly seared his flesh.

"Are you ready, High Prophet?" Karak asked.

Velixar nodded.

He closed his eyes and concentrated, allowing the energy to wash over him. Still, he couldn't erase his doubt. This was nothing like the trick that god and prophet had performed before, when the army crossed from Neldar and into Paradise; the Rigon was slimmer at that point, its banks more traversable. And all they had done in that instance was build stone columns within the river, allowing the soldiers to lay down heavy planks to form the bridge. Those planks had washed down the river after the god demolished the bridge; which meant they now had to use the barest of elements to create the passage, all while Karak was very weak. Velixar's uncertainty caused his strength to waver.

"You are able, my son," said Karak. The god's eyes were closed, and he looked almost contemplative.

"I will try."

"You will not fail me, Velixar."

"Yes, my Lord."

Karak began chanting, and Velixar joined him. He felt heat on his cheeks as the glow of his eyes intensified. Rocks shimmied on the edge of the cliff, and a few of the weak saplings that sprouted between the cracks twisted and writhed. A fissure then formed on the lip of the cliff, snaking along the ground and running between him and Karak. The earth on either side of the fissure folded upward and over. The soldiers behind them gasped.

Yet for all the men's wonder at the display, it was just that—a display. With Karak in his current condition, it was up to Velixar to create the foundation of what was to come . . . and he had no idea how.

"The soul is limitless. With our help, you will become as mighty as the gods themselves."

This best be true, he thought.

Slipping his free hand beneath his cloak, he grasped his pendant, felt it throb in his fingers. With one hand in Karak's and one clutching Karak's gift, he closed his eyes, feeling the warmth radiate off his flesh. The connection between himself and Karak's internal well was made stronger. All sound, but for the thrum of his heart in his ears, washed away. Once more he ventured through the empty, ethereal plain of creation, becoming a pinprick of light barely perceptible among the stars. The pendant funneled him toward the blazing sun that was Karak; only this time that sun was wreathed in shadow. Portions of its surface appeared frozen and cracked, the darkness slowly spreading toward the center, the very core of the deity himself.

Yet when he made contact with the sun, it instantly brightened, the chinks sealing shut, the inferno reignited. With the link made stronger by his physical contact with Karak, energy pulsed into him in greater quantities than it had before. He felt himself growing larger, more powerful, until he became a small star himself.

I am infinite! I am one with everything!

And still he should not stop, for Karak's power would not be enough. The words of the demon from the void came back to him, and he focused his energy deeper within Karak's soul, seeking connection after connection. *The universe created the gods; the gods are the universe.* He soared down hundreds of individual threads, from Karak to the supreme god that spawned him, Kaurthulos, the one made many, and then to the multitudes that came before. He bathed in the gases of the cosmos, waded through the glowing particles of a dying sun. His essence swelled and swelled, until it seemed he would absorb it all, Dezrel and beyond.

Then pain struck him behind the eyes, making him scream. He fell to his knees, releasing Karak's hand in the process. His whole body quaked, and smoke rose from his chest. He opened his eyes, and his vision was boiling in a red haze. When he lifted his hands and stared at them, he saw his flesh split, tiny fractures that wound along his palms, releasing puffs of shadow and licks of purple flame. The ground on which he knelt sizzled, the rocks melting and becoming magma that flowed around his knees. He felt close to bursting.

The mind restricts you, for the soul is limitless, he tried to tell himself, but the scope of what he experienced overwhelmed him. He was a god and a man, all at once, and the contradiction threatened to tear him to pieces.

"Do it now," he heard Karak say from somewhere behind him, and he swore he heard awe in the deity's voice.

Velixar finally understood. He rose to his feet and stepped closer to the cliff's edge. There were no more words of magic, no more chanting. All he needed was the power of creation that boiled within his swelling body. He held out his hands, focusing on the red, rocky soil. In his mind he pictured the land extending across the deep chasm. The light from his eyes outshone even the sun above, and the whole cliff began to rumble. Boulders a thousand years old shuddered and split, the dense core of them extending outward in snaking tendrils. Reddish sediment from the river that raged below climbed up the side of the cliff, attaching to the narrow protrusions, combining them, giving them solidity and form. Velixar felt the power flow out of him in red-hot waves, making the air in front of him hazy. The stone melted and cooled, melted and cooled, thickening as it grew. He then gazed across the river, to the other side of the cliff, and amazingly it seemed he could see two places at once. He watched the ledge before him expand on itself, and at the same time observed the process beginning anew on the other side.

Soon there were two spires pointed outward from either cliff, racing toward each other. Velixar twirled his hands, and a spiral of shadow appeared between the two rapidly growing sections, pulling them, stretching them. The particles in the air itself were condensed, adding to the thickness of the stone and sediment augmenting its sides, its surface, flattening it. The two pointed spires then touched, became liquid, and melded like one snake swallowing another. The whole of the new structure bulged, widened, and then bulged again. Velixar clapped his hands together, releasing one final wave of heat. He felt his core lessening, all the power he had gathered poured into the completed bridge. The funnel of shadow dissipated into the air.

When it was done, Velixar collapsed, panting. His mind swam and his vision wavered. And the pain, *the pain*! He sat back on his calves and took a few deep breaths to steady himself. Though it was indeed frightening to wield that much godlike power, now that it was gone, he missed it terribly. When he felt mostly normal again, he looked upon his creation. A sturdy earthen bridge now spanned the gap between the cliffs, seven hundred feet long, twenty feet wide, and at least fifteen feet thick at its thinnest section. Stray granules of dirt skimmed across the top and dropped over the side, raining on the furious river below. He glanced at his hands. There were no cracks there any longer. His skin was smooth and flawless.

"I did it," he said, in awe of himself.

"Indeed you did, High Prophet," said Karak.

The deity was beside him once again, holding out his hand. Velixar took it, allowing Karak to assist him in standing. He turned around, gazing with a painful sort of pride at the soldiers gathered behind him. Eyes were opened wide, jaws hung agape, hands were pressed to chests. Even Chief Shen seemed overcome. Velixar wanted to laugh at them, to strut before them and proclaim them in the presence of two gods, not one, but he stayed his tongue. *That path leads to blasphemy.*

The army crossed. The earthen bridge groaned and creaked beneath the feet of four thousand soldiers and a hundred horses, but it remained stable. They gathered on the grass-covered granite of the opposite bank, a collection of men too exhausted to continue on, yet too overcome by the powerful forces that guided them to do anything but continue.

It was only when the feet of the last soldier left the bridge that Velixar and Karak crossed. Deity and prophet walked side by side, and Velixar's delight in his accomplishments began to leave him. Karak still looked like a shell of himself, and there was a sort of frustration in his stare that was disturbing to see.

"You are not a god," Karak said, breaking the silence between them.

"I know, my Lord," said Velixar, and he felt a chill at the reminder of how in tune his god was to his own private thoughts.

"You best remember. The demon you swallowed is but a parasite, siphoning the power of others more deserving. You will never be as strong as a true child of the heavens."

"I will do my best, my Lord. Though the draw of such power is . . . tempting."

Karak nodded. "I imagine it would be. But simply remember this—when my soul recaptures its former glory, when I become the deity I was before my brother and I arrived on this world, you will witness feats that will drop you to your knees. You must keep your head, High Prophet, for when that happens I want you by my side. Although you will never truly be a god, what you accomplished this day proves you are worthy of something much greater than what simple humanity can offer you. Is this something you desire?"

"Yes, my Lord. Very much so."

"Good."

When they finally reached the other side of the bridge, Karak ordered Lord Commander Gregorian to march the troops east. Malcolm did as he was told, like the faithful man he was, barking out commands. Nine thousand booted feet stomped the granite-infused soil, the army forming into three columns as they marched into the trees, heading for the Northern Plains. The Ekreissar were in the lead, with the horsemen taking up the rear.

Soon they were gone, leaving Velixar alone with his god. Karak looked down at him, his eyes narrowing. The god's shoulders were still hunched, his flesh still cracked. He seemed sorrowful somehow as well, and when he spoke, his tone swelled with compassion.

"High Prophet, I apologize that I require your strength so much as I do," the deity said.

"There is no need for an apology, my Lord."

"There is," the god said with a sad nod. "I have not been feeling myself."

"It is fine, my Lord. You will soon heal; you will recharge, and you will be as you were once more."

To that, Karak nodded. "Until that time comes, however, you must be my sword. You must—"

The god's eyes widened, his jaw clamped shut, and he whirled his head around, staring down the bridge. His fingers clenched and unclenched rapidly.

"What is it, my Lord?"

"It cannot be," said Karak.

Velixar followed the deity's glowing eyes, gazing at the bridge and the thick wood on the other side. He could see nothing out of the ordinary. "What is it?"

"He is here," said the god gravely. "My brother could not arrive so quickly. It is not possible."

"Ashhur is here?" Velixar looked around desperately but still could see nothing. His heart began to race. "What do we do?"

"The bridge must be destroyed."

Karak took a stride toward the bridge and raised his hands. The bridge began to shimmy, its surface developing deep cracks. Velixar joined his god's side, mimicking his every motion, and soon chunks of the bridge broke off, plummeting to the river below.

Velixar held his breath, awaiting the moment Ashhur would come bursting out of the wood. *Not now! Karak is too weak.* I *am too weak!*

Finally a form exploded from the trees, advancing at blinding speed toward the bridge, and Velixar stared at the approaching monstrosity, baffled beyond belief.

Karak had been wrong. It wasn't Ashhur at all.

CHAPTER

40

Though fishing, farming, and praying were a part of daily life for those in Ker, to reside in the desert and southern plains of Paradise was to live the life of a hunter. Tracking was a skill nearly all children learned early on, trailing game through the prairies and thick forests, that night's meal dependent on finding and dispatching their quarry. It was a skill Bardiya excelled at, even though he hadn't put it to much use over the last fifty years.

Not that he needed to be a talented tracker to find the trail Karak and his soldiers had left for him. Just north of the Gods' Road he saw flattened grassland littered with the dung of thousands upon thousands of animals. From there, the hollow prints of booted feet led directly into the forest. All he had to do was follow the trampled earth and scored trees, which were in abundance.

Days came and went, and much to Bardiya's surprise, he was never hungry. His stomach never grumbled, his muscles never twitched, his throat never ran dry. He was being guided by a force larger than himself, a duty he had blinded himself to for a long time. It was his faith that now sustained him, as filling as the heartiest meal, as intoxicating as the strongest wine.

The soldiers and elves marched into the distance, leaving Karak and Jacob alone on the opposite cliff face. It wasn't a perfect situation, but Bardiya knew it was the best he would get. He bowed his head and brought his fist to his mouth, kissing his knuckles. "Ashhur, protect me," he whispered, and felt lightness infuse his being. It was the first time since he'd ordered his brethren home that he'd prayed. Before that moment, he hadn't dared.

Bardiya clutched his giant sword tightly and began to run. His heart rate remained even as his legs churned, carrying him with ease through the dense foliage. Branches slapped at his face, chest, and legs as he ran, but their impact brought no pain. His shoulder collided with a thick tree trunk, and he heard a *crack* as its roots were ripped from the ground. His feet created deep divots in the packed soil. Still his breath came as easily as if he were taking a stroll along the edge of the ocean.

A series of snapping sounds reached his ears, and when he exited the dense forest, felling two small trees as he did so, he saw that Karak and Jacob were standing on the other side of the river, hands up, eyes shimmering. The bridge was slowly collapsing, large chunks of it dislodging and tumbling to the furious waters below. Bardiya felt his first moment of panic, experienced the first twinge in his muscles. His heart rate quickened, as did his breathing. The sword grew heavy in his hand. A primal scream left his mouth, renewing his courage, and he bounded onto the bridge without care for his safety, racing across the seven hundred foot span with inhumanly long strides. All around him, it continued to break apart.

He saw the First Man's eyes widen in surprise. Amazingly, Karak's did as well. God and man continued their chanting, the glow of their eyes brightening as their visages grew larger in Bardiya's vision. He focused on Karak, who seemed as large as the continent itself, and felt a twinge of fear. The bridge shuddered beneath Bardiya's feet. He was only two hundred feet away from the end, at most.

I will make it! Ashhur help me, I will make it!

A large, earthen section of the bridge dislodged from the structure, making the bridge dip to the side. Another long stride carried Bardiya to within fifty feet of the end, and when his foot planted he leapt into the air, aiming for the chanting pair. He soared, arms outstretched and legs splayed, easily traversing those last fifty feet. Karak took hurried steps backward, but Jacob stood his ground. The First Man raised his hands, whispering words of magic. Bardiya felt a tightening in his chest and a trickle of blood drip from his nose, but the discomfort was slight. Jacob then swore and turned, trying to get away, but he wasn't fast enough. Bardiya hit the granite ledge hard, one knee striking the ground while the other rammed Jacob's back, sending the man reeling, his cloak like a cloud of smoke as it billowed. The ground shook beneath Bardiya, the violence of his impact creating a small crater.

Jacob Eveningstar stopped rolling and fell still. Karak looked over at the unmoving man before bringing his glowing eyes back to Bardiya. He tilted his head and smiled. The look caused a chill to run up the giant's spine.

"The child of Gorgoros," Karak said.

Bardiya nodded before shoving off the ground with his fist, standing upright. Being this close to the deity, separated by barely twenty feet, Karak seemed not so huge. The giant took a step up and out of the crater he had made. His sword swung lightly in his grip, ever pointed toward the god. Karak himself held no weapon, and he didn't appear in a rush to defend himself. He simply stood there in his glinting black armor, arms dangling loosely by his side, and grinned.

"Your sins have brought this down upon you," Bardiya said as he approached. "Even a child of the heavens must be held accountable when so many innocents perish in his name."

"Is that so, Gorgoros?" asked Karak, laughing. For a moment, Bardiya felt threads of fear at his tone. "Are you here to kill a god?"

"Yes."

Bardiya reared back, grabbing the sword with both hands, and then swung with all the force he could muster. Time seemed to slow down. While the tip of the giant blade cut through the air, the space around Karak's right hand shimmered with mist. A sword grew from that mist, a radiant, ethereal blade sprouting purple flames and ringed with swirling shadow. Time sped back up, Karak becoming a blur as he turned his sword upward. The blades of giant and god met with a deafening *clang*. Sparks flashed like lightning. Spikes of torment assaulted Bardiya's hands and arms. He screamed. The deity shoved forward, forcing Bardiya's feet to skid across the rocky ground, pushing the blades ever closer to his face. The flames from the deity's sword leapt outward, singe-ing Bardiya's eyebrows.

"You are a fool," the god said.

Karak gave Bardiya a powerful kick to the stomach, sending the giant flying. He struck the ground and bounced once before slid-ing fifteen feet. The jagged earth beneath him sliced into his back, opening wounds that bled onto the rocks. His ribs were a swirl of agony, possibly broken. Though Bardiya had lived his whole life in pain, nothing he had ever experienced compared to this.

His slide ended at the lip of the cliff. Groaning, Bardiya rolled onto his side. He hadn't released the sword when Karak kicked him, but when he stared at the weapon in his hand, his spirits plummeted. It was red and smoking where the god's sword had connected with it, and he could see the steel warping even as he watched. He waited for it to glow as it had when he'd frightened off the beast-men, but no matter how much he prayed to Ashhur, it remained nothing but steel.

"Did you truly think a blade forged by man could challenge one forged in the heavens?" Karak stormed toward him.

Bardiya scampered to his feet, keeping his knees bent, his back hunched. He perspired, though it was cold, and a drop of sweat dripped onto his reddened sword, releasing a *hiss* and a small puff of steam. Dread threatened to overwhelm him. *I cannot win. All is lost.* His lips began to quiver. *I am sorry I have failed you, Ashhur.*

A queer sort of warmth then spread unexpectedly through him. It began in his heart, slowing the organ's violent thrumming, and worked its way out from his ribcage, stilling his shoulders, his hips, his arms and legs. Ashhur's voice was within him, the most soothing words he'd ever heard, reverberating throughout his body. *All is never lost, my son. No matter your failures, your love, your virtue, has always been true. You are the greatest of my children, heartfelt and wise and willing to sacrifice everything for your brothers. One day, all of humanity will look on you with awe. Reject your doubts. In my embrace, there will be no more pain, no more fear.*

"I am your servant!" Bardiya cried. "Ashhur, my life for you!"

His sudden outburst caused Karak to hesitate ever so slightly, allowing Bardiya to straighten himself out and hold the twisted steel before him. The deity then glowered and closed the ten feet between them in a heartbeat, bringing his ethereal sword around in a mighty cleave. Their swords met once more, and Bardiya held strong, gritting his teeth as he tried to keep from being shoved over the edge and into the river. Karak's sword burned through his. Glowing molten steel flowed down the shaft, causing the blade to bend backward. The deity laughed at him, madness in his radiant eyes. It was a stare that would have reduced any other mere mortal to quivering, but Bardiya simply would not back down. Though the god's sword had nearly worked its way through his own, he gathered his strength and shoved back. Amazingly, Karak's grin wavered as his face lit up with cobalt radiance.

The god's eyes widened, and when Bardiya shifted his gaze to their locked swords, he saw that his was no longer made of folded steel. What he held in his fists was a column of pure energy, blazing white and blue and white again. *For you, Ashhur!* The light from his blade and the dark flames around Karak's seemed to forge a battle all their own; eddying and lapping, one force of nature trying to overtake another.

Strength poured into Bardiya's soul. As with Karak's man-beasts, he couldn't explain the glowing sword, his newfound vigor, or the way his instincts directed him—but it felt *right.* He chanced to release one hand from his weapon's handle, swinging a meaty fist around and connecting with Karak's cheek. The deity's head snapped to the side, a grunt escaping his lips. He stumbled and had to hold an arm out to keep his balance, and his ethereal sword dipped. Bardiya used the opening to attack, hewing low, so the tip of his blade passed beneath the god's. The lighted shaft met Karak's leg, burning through his black armor and slicing the godly flesh beneath. The deity shrieked and staggered away from the giant, his free hand groping for a wound that leaked liquid shadow.

Karak glanced at the gash and scowled.

Bardiya gave him no reprieve. He charged the god, hacking away like a crazed woodsman. Karak parried blow after blow, inching backward each time, constantly on the defensive. There was no skill in Bardiya's attack, no style to his fighting; he operated on predatory aggression alone. Embers leapt into the air each time their swords met, falling all around the combatants as if they fought within a ring of fireflies. And still Bardiya pressed on. His muscles felt no wear; his bones didn't ache. He was simply a tool of his god, acting on intuition, defending that which he knew to be righteous. He might be violent on the outside, but on the inside he sang.

When they drew close to the trees, Karak pivoted, heading instead back toward the center of the granite cliff. The wound in his knee had stopped seeping, but still he limped. Gone was the look of madness, replaced by something Bardiya would never have expected to see on the face of a deity—concern. Bardiya hacked left, brought his sword around, and then chopped to the right, throwing the god off balance. Karak attempted a desperate lunge, which Bardiya easily sidestepped. The maneuver left the god open to attack, and Bardiya thrust his luminous blade at Karak's shoulder. The tip found a slight gap between breastplate and pauldron, slipping into the god's flesh as easily as a stick into a muddy pool. The deity threw his head back and screamed. The glow of his eyes dimmed, and the purplish flames surrounding his sword sizzled as if doused with water. Spools of thick shadow leapt from the new wound, crackling when they came in contact with Bardiya's shining blade.

The giant kicked Karak square in the chest, knocking the deity flat on his back. His sword withdrew from the god's shoulder with a sound like a murmur on the wind, the shadow fizzling on its surface. Karak's sword hand opened when his head struck the ground, sending the blade tumbling away. It turned to mist mid-spin and disappeared.

Bardiya loomed over the prone deity. Karak panted, his face now wreathed in the shadow that poured from his shoulder. The god's throat rumbled as he tried to lift himself off the ground, but Bardiya stomped on him, forcing him back down. The god's armor was hot against the soles of his bare feet. He shifted his grip on his sword, aiming the tip downward while he raised it high above his head. Its brightness intensified, becoming nearly as intense as the sun above.

"Your depravity shows in your weakness," Bardiya proclaimed just as he began to bring his blade down, intending it to strike Karak's head.

"Not nearly so weak as you assume," came a voice from behind him.

Bardiya never had time to turn. Inky blackness enveloped his vision, blinding him. Something powerful wrapped itself around his forearms, stilling his downward thrust. He was then towed backward. The invasive force was strong; it felt like his bones were being crushed. Vigorous laughter filled the air.

Dragged to his knees, Bardiya hurriedly lifted his blade, slicing through the wall of suffocating black that ensnared him. His head snapped around toward the source of the laughter, and there was Eveningstar, kneeling where he had fallen, hands raised. His cloak billowed around him; his eyes blazed red. Tendrils of shadow leapt from his fingertips, undulating as they raced through the air. Bardiya lifted his glowing sword, cutting through them. He gritted his teeth as he fought to stand.

A furious pain then hit him, tracing him from shoulder to ribcage. His heart skipped one beat, then two, then began to hammer in his chest as if it were trying to escape. Glancing down, Bardiya saw Karak's sword, simmering with dark flames, protruding from his bare chest. The flames had cauterized the wound, which was a smoking, pulpy line that began at his collarbone—the same one scarred by Ethir Ayers in the mangold grove so long ago. His bones had held then, but not this time. Not when the force of a deity fell upon him.

In his hand, his own glowing sword faded until it became warped steel once more. His thoughts dulled, his vision became cloudy. Karak's sword pulled out of him, leaving behind a dark, shadowy afterimage that slowly dispersed into nothingness. Bardiya teetered on his knees like a reed in the wind, and the pain that filled him washed away. He felt his heart stop beating—he actually *felt* it—and his eyes rolled until they stared at the bright afternoon sky. Then his eyes closed, his body pitched forward, and he struck the ground face first with a crunch.

"Ashhur," he breathed, the word inaudible to his own ears, "remember me."

Always and forever, my child.

Bardiya rolled onto his back, body flopping as if in resistance to his every order. Karak and Jacob towered over him, staring down. No words on their lips. Just cold anger. It seemed strange to him, that anger. As he felt the life fading from him, felt the world collapsing inward, their anger inspired only pity in his motionless heart.

Bardiya?

The sky was opening. He saw golden light, felt his body separating, his presence expanding. Even the sound of Ashhur's mighty, crestfallen bellow from miles away could do nothing to stifle his wonder.

Do not grieve for me, my god. I understand now. It is so, so beau—

Chapter 41

For a fleeting moment, the war almost ended.

From his hiding spot within the trees on the other side of the river, Ahaesarus watched the giant Gorgoros battle Karak. Patrick DuTaureau, Preston the Turncloak, Warden Judah, Allay Loros, and the twelve others who had formed their advance scouting party gawked at the clash with eyes wide. It seemed none of them, Ahaesarus included, dared to so much as breathe.

They saw the giant hit his knees, Karak stalk toward him, and Bardiya's sword begin to glow. They looked on as the spiritual leader of Ker attacked with a vengeance, somehow beating the deity back with blow after vicious blow. They gaped as Karak fell to the ground and the giant lifted his radiant sword, preparing to strike it through the god's skull, only to be yanked away by oily tendrils of shadow. Then they watched in horror as Karak sliced the giant through from shoulder to chest.

Bardiya's sword dimmed and he fell, his life extinguished.

Not a moment later, Ashhur's distant, mournful cry added to the miasma of despair.

"No!" shouted Patrick. The deformed man flexed his massive arms, his sloped forehead crunching downward and wrinkling as tears streamed from his eyes. He reached for the sword strapped to his back and took a menacing step forward, ready to burst from their secluded spot and charge across the crumbling bridge. Ahaesarus grabbed his forearm and squeezed. Patrick's head whipped around, spraying tears like mist from a waterfall.

"Do not," said Ahaesarus, trying to keep his tone even.

Patrick slapped his hand away. "Don't tell me what to do!" he shouted, his shoulders rising and falling with each rasping breath.

"He's . . . he's gone," whispered Allay. He ground his teeth together.

"Listen to me," Ahaesarus told them, stepping back so he could address them all. "There is nothing out there for you but death. You witnessed the giant's fate. Don't let that be yours as well."

"His name was *Bardiya*," snapped Patrick. The malformed man then turned to the others. "We go now!" he shouted. "Let Karak try to defeat all of us at once!"

Before Ahaesarus could say anything more, the other men lifted their swords to the sky and bellowed. Patrick tore away from the Master Warden, slamming through the brush like a raging bull. The others followed him, all but Warden Judah, who remained at Ahaesarus's side. Judah glanced at him, uncertainty showing in his smooth features.

"They cannot cross," Ahaesarus told him before scowling and chasing after the men. It took mere moments to leave the cover of the forest, and the broad stretch of the cliff face stretched out before him. With his long strides, he easily caught up with the one at the back of the pack, the Turncloak Preston, snatching him by the armor and using his superior strength to toss the older man to the ground. Then another man went down, then another and another, rolling on the gravelly earth, their anger abated by surprise. Behind him, Judah further kicked the now prone men, keeping them down.

Patrick was the first to step foot on the bridge. It was a wide structure that looked to be made of solid granite and sandstone, but it was no longer stable. Half of its northern face had crumbled, raining dust and debris. At the middle section, large chunks of the earthen bridge had already fallen, leaving behind a dangerously sloped surface that threatened to drop the charging men directly into the rapids below. The pursuers ran with their swords, axes, and spears held high, wounded animal cries roaring from their throats, oblivious to the threat.

Ahaesarus came to a skidding stop at the edge of the bridge. Only five had rushed the crumbling structure; everyone else had been successfully thwarted. Of the five who had made it, only one now dashed without care—Midoro, one of the Kerrians. The others seemed to have lost confidence in their spur-of-the-moment attack. Patrick, in particular, was teetering back and forth, his sword resheathed, his uneven legs spread wide as the bridge shuddered beneath him.

From the other side of the river came the sound of laughter.

The Master Warden lifted his gaze. Karak and his prophet stood in front of the giant Gorgoros's corpse, and it was the god who laughed. Karak's eyes blazed gold, Velixar's red. Though the deity stood twice as tall as the First Man of Dezrel, to Ahaesarus, in that moment, the human was much more frightening.

They outstretched their arms and began chanting. The uneven bridge began to tremble.

"All of you, to me!" Ahaesarus shouted, dread filling him. "Quickly now, come! There isn't time!"

Patrick's panic-filled eyes found his, and the hunchback pivoted on the balls of his feet, his uneven gait carrying him back across the failing structure. A great *creak* sounded, followed by a horrific splintering. Huge sections of the bridge broke off, plummeting seventy feet and crashing into the river, shattering as they struck the rapid's jagged rocks. Allay Loros was the first to reach safety, followed by another of the Turncloaks, a boy named Tristan, and then a slender, brown-haired youth named Tosh. Patrick, with his uneven stride, was still twenty feet away; Midoro had passed him and was now halfway across, not slowing down, slip-sliding along the pitched section of bridge while still wailing his battle cry.

With a final, violent crack, the bridge fully collapsed. In the distance, Midoro tumbled along with heavy sections of granite, his ax spinning in the air while he toppled, head over heels, like a leaf in autumn.

Closer to Ahaesarus, not ten feet away, Patrick scuttled along the rapidly dropping slope, eyes wide with terror, his misshapen face scrunched. The only sound was the terrible shattering of the bridge. Patrick leapt forward, powerful arms outstretched, thick hands grasping at air. Without thinking, Ahaesarus reached for the falling man. Their palms met, Patrick's fingers wrapping around Ahaesarus's with such strength that it felt like the Master Warden's bones would be crushed.

The bridge completely fragmented, coming fully detached from the side of the cliff. Patrick fell along with it. Ahaesarus held on for dear life, Patrick's weight wrenching and unbearable. The Master Warden dropped to his knees, then flat on his chest, his shoulders stretched to their limit. Patrick's momentum caused him to swing inward and slam against the rock face, sending a jolt down Ahaesarus's spine. He cried out in anguish as DuTaureau dangled in his grasp. Patrick's eyes were downcast, as were Ahaesarus's, watching the remnants of the bridge crash into the violently flowing Rigon.

Hands were on him then, many of them, tugging on Ahaesarus's clothes, pulling him backward. Sharp stones and debris cut into his stomach as he was dragged across the ground, but his grip on Patrick's hand remained true. Finally, the others succeeded in yanking Ahaesarus back far enough that the hunchback could clutch the many raised stones, pulling himself up and onto the ledge. When he finally reached safety, Patrick collapsed on his side and panted. Ahaesarus shook his head and closed his eyes, exhausted.

"Ahaesarus," came Judah's voice. "We need to leave."

Ahaesarus glanced up at his fellow Warden and saw him gazing with a locked jaw over the chasm's now empty span. The Master Warden rolled over to look, his every joint smarting. Karak had stepped back, and the First Man now stood at the edge of the opposite ledge, his cloak fluttering in the cold breeze. It was difficult to tell from seven hundred feet away, but he suspected Velixar was smiling.

"Ahaesarus, the great teacher of man," Velixar hollered, his voice echoing across the chasm. "Did you truly believe you and Ashhur's pet freak could dare Karak's might?" There was laughter in his tone as he pointed at Bardiya's massive corpse. "You witnessed the fate of the last challenger."

"I'll fucking kill him," Patrick uttered, still on his stomach and panting. There was no strength behind his words.

"Not now," Ahaesarus said as Karak's prophet raised his hands. "Run," he told the rest of his allies. "All of you, *run*!"

Ahaesarus scampered to his feet, heaving Patrick up and along with him as he trailed after those dashing back into the forest. He didn't turn around—not when he heard the First Man chanting, not when he felt a scorching heat on his back. He focused on putting one foot in front of the other, hoping beyond hope that Patrick's stumpy legs could keep pace with his much longer ones.

They dove into the surrounding trees just as the entirety of the cliff face went up in a blaze of purple and black flame. Those flames licked above Ahaesarus's head as he dropped to the ground and tumbled down a slight decline. Whipping tendrils of living shadow snapped all around him even as he rolled, their texture solid and oily when they lapped against his bare flesh.

The ground dropped out from beneath him, and Ahaesarus fell. He collided with the root-covered ground hard, an *oomph* leaving his lips as the wind was knocked from his lungs. Patrick landed right beside him, his flailing right arm striking him directly on the chest. The force of the blow was made all the more painful by the coldness of the day. Ahaesarus lay there, clutching his chest and moaning, until the ache diminished.

When he lifted his head and glanced about, he saw they had landed in a ravine. The odd purple flames still licked at the air fifteen feet above their heads. All members of the scouting party save Midoro were present, tending their various injuries. The only one that seemed not to be hurt was Preston. The old Turncloak sat with his back against a tree, stroking his thick gray beard as if deep in thought. Ahaesarus thought of the charge toward the bridge, how Preston had been the last in line and had gone down rather easily when Ahaesarus grabbed him. It was as if he'd been stalling on purpose. *That one knows better than to challenge a god. Seems he should dispense some of that knowledge to his friends.*

DuTaureau shook his head while he gently dabbed at a deep gash in his elbow. "I'm sorry, Ahaesarus," he said without looking up. He looked so miserable, with his tear-soaked cheeks and gnashing teeth, that Ahaesarus couldn't stay upset.

"I understand," Ahaesarus said.

Patrick's eyes flitted upward, staring at the Master Warden from under his distended brow. "You do?"

"I do. However, do not be so foolish again. We cannot afford to lose you."

At that, Patrick laughed grimly. "So say you."

"Yes, so say I. You are the greatest of Ashhur's defenders. Our god cannot afford to lose his ultimate warrior because of a need for vengeance."

"You watched him die too, Ahaesarus," said Patrick, looking away. "He was my friend."

"He was. And his loss is painful to all, especially Ashhur. However, he played his part well. If not for the First Man, he might have killed a god. So go ahead, weep for Bardiya Gorgoros as you wish. Even Ashhur has shown his sorrow on this day. However, know that the giant now awaits us all in the Golden Forever. In some ways, he is lucky. His pain is over. Ours, I fear, is just beginning."

"What a wonderful thought," said Patrick, a hint of a wry smile playing on his lips.

Judah, who had been leaning against the earthen wall of the ravine, glanced up at the sputtering flames above them and then looked to Ahaesarus. "What do we do now?"

Ahaesarus leaned back on his hands and thought. At Patrick's insistence, Ashhur had sent the party ahead of the bulk of his force, for their progress was indeed slowed, the undead and horses having a difficult time negotiating northeastern Paradise's harsh forest terrain.

"Now, we return to Ashhur," he said. "We will follow the river and look for a better spot to cross as we walk.

"What then?" asked Tosh. The other youngster, Tristan, rolled his eyes as if the answer were obvious.

"Then we go after them," Patrick said, anger returning to his tenor. "Ashhur will face his brother and make him pay for what he's done. There's no stopping what has begun. There will be justice, or there will be death. Perhaps even the heavens will fall."

Ahaesarus shivered, though he couldn't have said it better himself.

CHAPTER 42

That coldhearted cunt," Turock grumbled. The older spellcaster bounced with each of his horse's strides, his mane of wavy red-blond hair bobbing on his shoulders. He clutched his pointed green hat in his lap, twisting it as if trying to squeeze the last drop of juice from a lemon. "She has *my children in there*! How dare she keep them away from me? Icy little bitch. It probably snows when she pisses. I'm glad my wife doesn't take after her."

Rachida Gemcroft rolled her eyes and shook her head, irritated. She had heard this same rant, over and over again, during the five days since they'd been denied entrance into Mordeina.

Turock continued his tirade while Quester Billings trotted up on the other side of her, grinning. "You want me to silence him?"

"Heard that," said Turock, glaring over at the handsome young sellsword. "I'd like to see you try. You don't want to know what happened to the last man who trifled with me."

"Testy, aren't we?" declared Pox Jon, who rode to Quester's right.

Turock glowered.

"Enough, all of you," Rachida said. "It's like riding with children."

She snapped the reins, forcing her steed up to a canter. Her frustration boiled over, and she let out a long groan. Even imagining shoving a shank into Peytr's groin did nothing to lift her mood.

They had taken a circuitous route to Mordeina from Drake, sticking close to the mountain chain bordering the Gihon and heading inland only when the forest of Dezerea came within view. In all, the trip had taken thirteen days, and though the spellcasters' gemstones had kept them well fed and the weather grew warmer, they still needed to sleep out in the elements, and the anticipation of what lay ahead of them had everyone on edge.

Yet that angst had not been justified, for when they arrived at the settlement itself, they found Mordeina surrounded by a gigantic double wall that put the one around Port Lancaster to shame. Even Turock was awestruck, staring up at the sixty-foot-tall wall of gray stone, and he was speechless for the first time since the journey started. Instead of Karak's Army, they found an empty valley whose grass and trees, now bare due to the early thaw, were brown and dead. Instead of warfare, they found silence. Instead of being greeted as saviors, the people behind the wall turned them away.

No matter what Rachida told the black-haired man and the rather short Warden who had confronted her on the other side of the portcullis, they would not let her group inside. Even when Turock came forward, confident he would be able to sway the man he called *Howard* to open the gates, they were greeted with indifference.

"The men you travel with are emblazoned with Karak's sigil," Howard had told them, and the short Warden nodded in agreement. "After what our people have gone through, the sight would not be a welcomed one."

No promise to strip the men of their armor would change their minds. The insults and threats Turock had lashed them with certainly hadn't helped either. And so they had ridden away from the settlement, frustration steadily progressing through their ranks. Only Talon Blackwolfe and the other two hundred of Karak's soldiers that had joined their cause up north kept a level head throughout the ordeal.

Arguments abounded. Turock and the spellcasters wanted to head back north to their people; the sellswords wished to return to Neldar and their masters' employ; and the two hundred turncoats called for pursuing Karak to the east. It was Talon's men who won that argument, as they were the ones who sided with Rachida. She had stood proudly before her eight hundred men and told them—*told*, not asked—that they would be staying the course. She reminded the sellswords that they would be burned as blasphemers should they return to Neldar as known betrayers; Turock and his spellcasters she persuaded by promising them their pick of the treasures deep within the Isles of Gold. Peytr might not be happy with the deal, but then again, after she dealt with her plotting husband, he would never object to anything again.

And so they continued on the course Karak and Ashhur had taken, riding through a razed landscape, only to be thwarted at the Wooden Bridge. The bridge was in tatters, its ropes snapped, half its planks dangling. There was no way to get eight hundred men and three hundred horses across. Going back north was out of the question, for the way was too rough and slow, which left them with only two options: Circle around Lake Cor, which would bring them into the Dezren Forest, a place Talon Blackwolfe had informed them was under the control of Karak's Army; or march south toward Stonewood, where the elves were supposedly more docile. Again they fell into arguments, and once more Rachida was forced to put her foot down.

They would head south toward Stonewood Forest and attempt to make passage where the Corinth River was shallow enough for the horses to cross without drowning.

Now here they were, on the cusp of Stonewood itself, and the only saving grace was the warm southern air. Turock continued his outburst, throwing out curses that made even Quester blush. Rachida rode ahead to get away from him, bringing her horse to a gallop as she neared the huge trees bordering the forest. She sensed eyes on her and felt ill at ease. The only path curved inland, away from the river, and though Turock assured her that the path bent back to the east once they entered the trees, she felt naked without those flowing waters to dive into should trouble arise. The only thing to her right here was a bank of tall trees that sat at the edge of a field, two hundred yards away.

When she was far enough ahead, she turned her horse around just in time to see Turock angrily flick his wrist while yelling, "Cunt!" A tiny fireball zipped from his fingertips and singed the grass bordering the beaten path they treaded. Young Decker, Pox Jon's second in command, quickly snuffed out the fire. Rachida looked on as Talon and eight of his men began to sneak up on the spellcaster from behind. Behind them, Turock's students noticed this happening and themselves began to approach, scowling. It would be all-out war between them if she didn't do something.

She drew one of her Twins and urged her horse to gallop toward them.

"All of you, enough!" she shouted, holding the sword out wide. Turock looked her way, glaring. Talon obediently halted his movements. The other spellcasters, all twenty-two of them, pulled up before they collided with the soldiers' rears. At the sight of such a display, many in the sellsword divisions laughed.

Rachida rode sidelong up to the angry and flamboyant man. Turock puffed out his chest as if to challenge her, which Rachida answered by swiping at him with her sword at such speed that he didn't have time to react. The blade flashed against his cheek, creating a thin red line. The man flinched, his hand coming up to touch the wound as a dollop of blood dripped onto his bright green robe.

"You bitch," he said, eyes wide.

Rachida leaned forward in her saddle, resting the flat edge of her blade against Turock's neck. "Call me bitch one more time, and I slice your throat. Trust me, as of now nothing would bring me greater pleasure."

Turock's expression suddenly brightened, and he forced a smile. "Why, dear Rachida, I wouldn't *dream* of it."

"You best not."

"And don't think to cast some sort of spell, either," said Quester with a wink. "My man Pox Jon over there is deadly with throwing knives. He can bury four in you before you get the words out of your throat. Isn't that right, Jon?"

Pox Jon nodded, reached into his belt, and pulled out three stumpy blades. "Got a few right here, matter of fact."

Turock visibly swallowed, looking all around him. His fingers started twitching, and sweat pooled on his collar, even though the temperature during this early afternoon was mild. To Rachida he seemed ridiculous; this was a man of Paradise, surrounded by soldiers from the kingdom that was now, technically, the enemy, and yet it was as if he had just then realized that fact. For an obviously brilliant man, he was rather stupid.

"I . . . I'm sorry," he told Rachida in a low voice.

"Say it louder," demanded Talon.

Rachida held up a hand. "No, that is fine." She sheathed her Twin and sidled closer to Turock, leaning in. Even though her sword was secure, he still seemed wary. "Listen: I don't wish to hurt you. But we are about to enter Dezren territory. I don't know how relations are between elf and human in Paradise, but it is chilly at best in the east. So please, let us not attract undue attention to ourselves while we tread through their land. Once we cross the Corinth, you can go on all you like. Do we have a deal?"

She stuck out her hand. Turock hesitantly took it, his head cocked oddly to the side.

"Deal," he said, though it sounded like his thoughts were far away.

"Good. Now let's go."

The spellcaster cleared his throat. "Uh, one more thing, Rachida my dear."

"What?"

"What's happening over there?"

His eyes glassed over as he pointed across the field at the thickly packed forest that bordered the Corinth River. Rachida followed his gaze, seeing movement within the trees, the branches swaying, and the underbrush rustling. It was probably just a wolf or an elk or—

It wasn't a wolf, or an elk, or any other animal for that matter. Instead, a tall elf, with deeply bronzed flesh and long, satiny hair, burst from the foliage. He was a Quellan and therefore very far from home. The elf ran with abandon, his arms and legs pumping vigorously as he crossed the field of swaying reeds. Rachida's hand fell to her sword, preparing to draw it should the elf attack, but she noticed that he brandished no weapons. He was running strangely, as well, leaping into the air every few moments and waving his arms at them.

Sensing her men tense behind her, Rachida raised her hand and signaled with a fist.

"Hold!" she ordered.

The elf was on them in an instant, and as he passed them by, dashing through the ranks of soldiers and sellswords, Rachida heard screaming, endless streams of syllables that were alien to her ears. The sound of his shouts elapsed as fast as he did, like the screech of a falcon as it soared through the sky and disappeared over the horizon. The men parted for him, allowing the elf to sprint across the opposite field and disappear into the massive trees of the Stonewood Forest. When he was gone, Rachida gawked at her sellswords, confused.

"What in the name of the gods was *that*?" asked a bewildered Pox Jon.

"An elf," Quester told him.

"No shit."

"He was saying something," said Rachida. "What was it? I couldn't make it out."

"Sounded like nonsense to me," Talon said, trotting over toward the spot where the elf disappeared. "Just gibberish."

"It wasn't gibberish," said Turock. Rachida turned toward the absolutely terrified-looking spellcaster. It made her uneasy to see him so. What's more, she now heard a steady thrum, one that vibrated her saddle.

"What did he say?" she asked.

"Noro, nuru e taryet," the spellcaster said. "It's Elvish for 'Run, death has arrived.'"

As if on cue, a horribly loud trumpeting rang out, causing most of the eight hundred men gathered on the road to cover their ears. Countless birds squawked and flew from the treetops in bunches. Quester clammed up and actually appeared frightened for the first time since Rachida had met him. Rachida's head whipped back around, and she looked on as the tall trees to the east began to sway, their budding branches snapping like so much kindling. Her horse whinnied nervously and then bucked.

Then, in a flash of dust and an explosion of dirt, the tree line exploded outward. What rumbled out of the forest was huge. Menacing. Evil. Impossible.

And it was coming their way.

"Flee!" shouted Rachida. Her mind blank with fear, she spun her panicked steed around and hastened into the forest in the other direction, followed by the soldiers and sellswords, while death closed in from behind.

CHAPTER

43

And so history repeated itself.

Aullienna Meln, the princess of the Stonewood Dezren, walked along the twisting skywalks that formed the causeways of the city within the trees. Only this time, Carskel didn't walk behind her, prodding her along. Instead, he was by her side, his hand in hers, a triumphant smile plastered across his face. He looked down, his eyes unabashedly taking in every inch of her.

"You look beautiful," he said.

She did her best to force her cheeks to flush, thinking about the first time she and Kindren kissed. "Thank you, my love," she said, speaking with her best innocent quiver while squeezing her brother's hand. "It means a lot that you should think so."

Carskel beamed and turned away, gazing down the jewel-lined skywalk and the group of elves that had gathered toward the center of Stonewood. "Desdima did her best work. I am glad I spared her life."

Desdima had been Lady Audrianna's personal tailor, one of the original thirty-two that had escaped from Dezerea and the Quellan oppression. The *work* Carskel referred to was the garb Aully now wore; a gown of spun satin, white as the northern snowcaps, embellished with shimmering crystals. The gown was long and flowing, the train trailing five feet behind her. The sleeves were form-fitted, the material billowing out at her wrists like a flower, and the collar clung tight to her neck all the way to the base of her jaw. The back was bare, though her naked flesh was hidden by her long, golden hair, teased and curled and pinned with roses, cornflowers, and pink silkwood blossoms. The dress was formfitting yet comfortable, a work of art that conveyed the conservative nature of the Stonewood culture while still suggesting the sensual nature of a coupling. It had been made originally for her wedding to Kindren.

Now, she detested it.

Aully groaned at his words, a sound that Carskel misinterpreted. He began to rub his thumb along Aully's palm, causing her to shudder. Again he misinterpreted, and bent over to kiss her on the cheek as they strolled. It was all Aully could do not to turn away in disgust.

"This . . . this is wonderful, sweet sister." Carskel rose back up, a jolly hitch in his step. "Today, we announce our engagement to our people. Tonight, we feast. Tomorrow, they love me. And the day after that, we depart for Dezerea for our nuptials. It truly is an exciting time, is it not?"

"It is, my love," she replied demurely.

He glanced down at her once more, this time appearing more somber. His eyes even began to tear up.

"You do not know how concerned I was, sweet sister. When I entered your chamber to ask of your decision, I was prepared to lash out at you. And then I saw you there, kneeling, hands clasped before you, radiant despite so much filth . . . you were a sight to behold, Aullienna. And when you told me yes, when you whispered those words of love into my ear, I knew you spoke the truth. You must understand that I never wished for you to suffer so. You simply had to *learn*. Can you find it in your heart to forgive me?"

Only when your entrails are hanging from the skywalks like garlands. "Of course, my love," she said. "My own foolishness dictated my punishment, nothing more."

"I am glad to hear that." Her brother released her hand and squeezed her shoulder, pulling her close in the process. She allowed him to do so, just as she had allowed him to embrace her after thirty days spent rotting away in her cellar prison. She performed perfectly, nurturing her malevolent brother's pathetic need for acceptance, and then spent the following two weeks cultivating her hatred. Every bite of exquisite food she ate, all the primping and preening of oblivious handmaidens, only ripened her rage. She plotted and planned, dreaming up wicked schemes, all the while praying to Celestia for validation. The goddess's silence was all the answer she required. Her mind was made up; her will, resolute. She would become Jimel Horlyne, the elf who Kindren said had killed one of the ancient demons all by himself. Aully had pictured herself as the statue of that great elf, reaching down from the ceiling, her face warped by both torment and triumph. By the time Carskel had come to her this morning, after Desdima had finished sewing her into the ornate gown, she'd felt primed to burn an entire nation to the ground.

The sound of clapping filled her ears the farther along the skywalk they tread. Just as before, her people hung from the other walkways, nearly three thousand Dezren gathered en masse. The cheers rose in volume as she rounded the bend, circling onto one of the lower skywalks. Rose and tulip petals were tossed into the air, fluttering down like dead butterflies. Every face she saw was filled with a reserved sort of joy. Aully began to hate every one of them. *How can you not see what's right in front of you?* Most have them had lived for far longer than her fifteen years. Surely, they weren't so blind.

They will see. When today is over, they will understand.

Carskel steered her toward the forest city's central causeway. Ethir Ayers and Mardrik Melannin guarded the entrance to the walk, the rough elves like stone guardians staring straight ahead. Both bowed when she and Carskel passed them by, and Ethir's mouth twitched ever so slightly when his eyes met hers. *He doesn't trust me,* thought Aully.

He was right not to.

Aully's uncle Detrick once again waited on the causeway's central platform, dressed in a long, flowing brown robe with deep green stripes running up the sides. He held a book in his mangled right hand, appearing eager as he watched his niece and nephew approach. Aully had to refrain from scowling at her uncle. She'd come to despise him over her time in seclusion, perhaps as much as she hated her brother. Carskel was an evil, plotting bastard, but at least she knew where she stood with him. Detrick was a craven weakling with the face of a friend.

Detrick dropped to one knee when they reached the center platform, planting a kiss first on the back of Carskel's hand, then on Aully's. Then he stood and faced the crowd that surrounded them. He raised his hands, and the mob quieted. Aully glanced about her. She saw Desdima standing on one of the middle skywalks, along with the others that had escaped Dezerea with her, but Kindren and Lady Audrianna were nowhere to be found. She shuddered.

"Nervous?" Carskel whispered.

"Yes," she responded. This time, she didn't lie.

Detrick drew their attention. "We come here today," he said, patting the book in his hand, "to celebrate a return to the values of old. It was written by Ignacious Thyne, the first of our race whom benevolent Celestia blessed with life, that the royal house was to stay united, the family line kept pure. For five hundred years we held true to those teachings, until our people strayed, thinning the royal blood. That thinning has left us weak, and we refuse to be weak any longer! Today I announce, in the spirit of Ignacious himself, the betrothal of Carskel and Aullienna Meln, whose marriage will lead our people to a great and bright future!"

The massive gathering of elves broke into soft applause. Aully could plainly see at least half of those packed onto the skywalks looked confused, a couple even disgusted. "Brother and sister?" she heard someone proclaim. "Unnatural!" It was all Aully could do not to grin.

"However," said Detrick, ignoring the objectors, "there is a slight problem that must be overcome first. Our texts say that when a Dezren is betrothed, there are only two instances in which the promise can be broken: by death or a renouncement. Princess Aullienna has already agreed to forego her engagement to the Prince of Dezerea." He turned to her, and she nodded, though her stomach was clenched with dread. "However, it takes two to enter a pact and two to break it. Now bring forth Kindren Thyne!"

Aullienna looked away from him to see the dullard Dukat and one of Ethir's sentries escorting Kindren and Lady Audrianna along the adjacent skywalk. Her mother was in front, Aully's betrothed three steps behind, and both walked with their heads held high, needing no prodding. A collective hush came over the throng of elves as Aully's jaw clenched. *Come on. You expected this. It changes nothing.*

Detrick gestured for the pair to be shepherded onto the causeway. "And what betrothal is complete without a blessing?" he bellowed to the crowd. "Audrianna Meln, the former Lady of Stonewood, is here to provide it!"

That statement drew even more hesitant grumbles from the throng. Even those who had been cheering so vociferously before stopped. Aully realized that almost no one was looking at her anymore, but at her mother. A great many gawked with what could only be described as reverence.

Kindren and the Lady of Stonewood made their way down the gently swaying causeway, holding tight to the rope handrail. Kindren stared intently at Aully, as if no one else existed. He blinked three times in rapid succession. At first Aully couldn't decide whether he was nervous or trying to send her a message, but then he nodded to her while grimacing, and she understood, right then and there, that he knew what she was about to do and approved. As if to prove his point, he held up his spoiled hand, of which only his thumb and little finger remained. Aully grimaced at the sight, then gathered herself and blinked, telling him silently that she understood.

Her mother, however, was a different story. Audrianna waved to her people, her lips parted in a kind smile. It was her mother's public face, similar to the one she would wear when the Lord and Lady of Stonewood held court during each Spring Festival. When she had that familiar face on, it was nearly impossible to tell how she truly felt. Cleotis had often joked that if his wife were to put on that expression for him, she would be just as likely to bludgeon him as kiss him.

Thoughts of her father caused a wrenching in Aully's heart. She closed her eyes and breathed deeply.

When she opened them again, Kindren and Audrianna were standing before her, with Detrick off to the left. Her uncle sang a short refrain from his book, some nonsense about the glory of the Dezren, eternal life, and smiting enemies. He then tucked the book beneath his arm and stepped between Kindren and Audrianna.

Her uncle took Kindren's good hand in his own. "Do you, Kindren Thyne of Dezerea, denounce your betrothal to Aullienna Meln of Stonewood? Do you release her from the ties that bind?"

Kindren lowered his head. He hesitated, but eventually his lips moved, though with the murmuring crowd, it was difficult to hear what he said. Beside Aully, Carskel tensed.

"I am sorry, but we could not hear you," said Detrick.

"I will," Kindren stated, loudly this time.

Detrick released his hand and proceeded to do the same to his sister-in-law. "And now, Lady Audrianna Meln of Stonewood, do you bless this coming union, with all your heart and with Celestia's sanction?"

Carskel visibly cringed at the sound of the goddess's name.

"Of course," Audrianna said, turning her head from side to side. She kept her voice raised so all could hear. "Of course I do."

Detrick smiled warmly and stepped back, which brought Aully's anger back to the surface. Kindren continued to stare at his feet while the Lady of Stonewood waved to her admirers. Then the elegant and beautiful elf, in the briefest of moments, peered at her daughter and mouthed, *Do it.*

Aully's breath came so quickly that she almost didn't realize that Carskel had leaned back down, his chin resting on her shoulder. "Now is the time," her brother said. "Address your people. Half of them are mine already. Once we reach Dezerea, you will be the Lady of this city. Tell them how much you love me. Tell the disbelievers that the stories they have heard aren't true. Tell them we will bring them glory that Stonewood has never seen."

Aully nodded and took three steps away from him. She placed both her hands on the platform's hempen railing, gazing out at the swarm of elves. She scanned their numbers, seeing face after familiar face. She spotted Hadrik, Mella, and Lolly as well as her cousin Mariah, lingering on one of the upper skywalks. They were among those who appeared downcast, defeated. Aully closed her eyes and remembered the last time she'd stood here. She recalled how she had fought inwardly about whether she should do as Carskel told her. How she had taken a half measure by shouting out his sins instead of ending all the pain, all the torment, right then and there.

That would not happen again.

"They are waiting," she heard Carskel say, impatience in his tone.

Aully faked a smile and raised her left hand to wave at the crowd. A smattering of cheers answered her. Her right hand she kept by her side, holding her middle three fingers out straight while bringing her thumb and little finger across her palm until they touched. The words of a spell entered the forefront of her mind, and she could feel the web pulse as the land's magic infused her.

"For you, Celestia," she whispered, softly as she could, and stared at the circle of bright sky amid the canopy.

"Invaders!" shrieked a loud, panicked voice. "Lord Carskel, they're coming!"

The spell died on Aully's lips. She whirled around and glanced up to see Davishon Hinsbrew, the Surveyor of Stonewood, slinging down from the top of one of the nearby trees. His face was a mask of panic, eyes wide and teeth grinding together.

The elf landed on the causeway, pitching the hanging walk into an exaggerated sway. Carskel stormed toward the elf, his clenched right fist inching ever closer to the khandar on his hip.

"What is the meaning of this?" he roared. His normally pale cheeks were flushed.

Davishon scampered along the causeway, pointing east. "They are *coming*, Lord Carskel!" he screamed. "Karak's soldiers! They are *here*!"

The Surveyor's voice was so loud that those standing on nearby skywalks heard him, and panic ensued. Elves dashed this way and that, scrambling to climb the ladders to their homes. Ethir and Mardrik barked orders to the other sentries, who snatched their bows from their backs and dashed along the walks. The din was so loud that Aully could barely hear herself think. Hands were on her then, gathering her close. She looked up. It was Kindren who held her, while Lady Audrianna began shoving them toward the other end of the hanging causeway.

"Move!" Audrianna shouted. "Come now, one foot in front of the other. Quickly!"

They shuffled along the causeway, and that's when the first of the humans appeared. They burst from the forest, their horses kicking up clumps of damp earth as they galloped. The soldiers wore armor painted black, with bits of silver, and Aully could see the red sigil of Karak's roaring lion on their breastplates. They passed beneath the hanging platform, which hung only a few short feet from the tops of their helmed heads, but didn't stop. They simply kept on going, leaning over in their saddles, disappearing into the trees on the other side of the clearing.

"Kill them!" Aully heard Carskel cry out. "Kill them all!"

Arrows rained down from above, and Aully shrieked. Kindren stopped lugging her along and instead tossed her onto the causeway's wooden planks, then fell on top of her, shielding her with his body. He used his left hand to snatch Lady Audrianna by the hem of her dress and tug her down as well. There they huddled, swaying, as soldiers passed below them. The soldiers screamed. Arrows flew.

One of the soldiers yanked back on the reins, spinning his horse around. He flipped up his helm, revealing a youthful face with crystal blue eyes and strands of hair that were so silver they were almost white. Aully remembered seeing a man like that once, the one who had dueled with Ceredon Sinistel during her and Kindren's betrothal, though in her panic she couldn't remember the man's name.

"We aren't your enemy!" the man bellowed in the human's common tongue. He pointed a mailed first toward the direction from which he'd come. "There is death coming, huge with horns and hooves! You must—"

Arrows zipped past him. One struck his horse in the flank and one *clinked* off his armored shoulder. "Fuck this," the soldier swore, veering his horse back around and galloping into the forest.

"What are you *doing*? Get off my betrothed!"

It was Carskel's voice. Aully shoved aside Kindren's arm to see her brother stalking down the causeway toward them, khandar in hand. "No!" Aully shouted as he reached down and grabbed Kindren by the back of his tunic. Kindren's eyes widened in surprise, locking with Aully's before he was forcibly lifted off her. Kindren was then cast aside, tumbling to his rear on the slatted walk. Though Kindren was the same height as Carskel, her brother had a great advantage in both age and strength.

Carskel raised his khandar, appearing ready to hack Kindren to bits. Aully scampered to her knees and lifted both her hands. The magic within her rekindled, and she uttered the words in short, sharp bursts. A small ball of flame formed inches in front of her palms, and she sent it flying. The spinning fireball struck Carskel in the back, setting his white frock aflame. He yelped and lurched away, beating at the flames with his free hand.

Aully glanced to the side, where Lady Audrianna was kneeling. "Mother," she said, somehow calm despite the chaos. "Help Kindren. Get him off the causeway."

"You are coming with me!" Audrianna pleaded.

Aully shook her head. "No, Mother," she said. "I can handle this myself."

A hard, determined look came over her mother's face, and Lady Audrianna sharply nodded. She ran, hunched over, across the walk, until she collided with Kindren, who was halfway to standing. Her mother and betrothed both toppled over the side of the causeway, falling down among the charging soldiers below. Aully felt a sharp needle of panic plunge into her gut, but she did her best to ignore it. She had to trust that her mother knew what she was doing.

Aully reached down within herself, said more words of magic, and traced a line across her gown with a scorching hot finger. When she was finished she stood up, the billowing part of the dress falling away along with the train, smoking where it'd been singed. Then she stepped confidently toward her bastard brother, arms outstretched. Electricity sparked between her fingers, even as the arrows came down. Carskel finished batting down the flames, which had burned away a large portion of his frock. It dangled in two pieces from his back.

She stopped ten feet away from him. "Brother!" she shouted.

Carskel spun around, still hunkered down, khandar held at the ready. His eyes widened when he saw her. Aully thrust her hands forward and shouted the words, and lightning shot from her fingertips, arcing across the span between them and striking Carskel square in the chest. The elf fell flat on his back, the khandar bouncing away from him as his body shuddered violently. The electricity continued to course through him. Aully took one step toward him, then two, not letting up. Smoke rose from Carskel's chest, and she could smell burning flesh. When she saw his eyes roll into the back of his head, she drew her hands back to her sides. The lightning ceased to crackle. Carskel fell still.

She snatched up the fallen khandar and knelt beside her brother, the would-be ruler of the Stonewood Dezren. He appeared dead, though his chest rose and fell. Aully crept along his side until she reached his shoulders. She placed the cutting edge of the khandar against his neck.

Carskel's eyes snapped open, and amazingly, he grinned. Aully started in surprise, her moment of hesitation giving her brother the opportunity to shove the blade away from his neck. Stars then exploded in Aully's vision as his fist connected with her cheek. She dropped the weapon and fell away from him, grasping at the side of her face. It was on fire. Her eyes watered, blurring her vision.

Still the arrows rained down, and the soldiers galloped.

"You have injured me," Carskel said, almost playfully. "That will not do."

The elf stepped toward her, bending over and picking up the khandar just as she'd done a moment before. His hand reached out and grabbed a handful of hair. Pain spiked in Aully's scalp as he dragged her along the causeway. "You won't do that again, sweet sister. Consider your precious Kindren's life forfeited, as well as—"

Carskel doubled over, a wad of phlegm ejecting from his mouth. His grip on Aully's hair loosened, and she pulled free from him, scurrying away on her hands and knees before turning back around. What she saw, she couldn't quite understand. A shadowy elf was now on the causeway, his fists pummeling her bastard brother, knocking him from one hempen rail to the other. Carskel's head snapped back; he doubled over when struck in the gut; he fell to the side when battered on the ear. Finally, the shadowy elf grabbed Carskel by the back of his breeches and tipped him over the rail. Aully's brother disappeared from sight. The shadowy elf then turned to her, and for the first time she saw his face. Aully's jaw dropped open.

"Ceredon," she said.

Ceredon grabbed her hand and held it tight.

"Run."

Above them, the forest city of Stonewood exploded in a shower of wooden shards.

"Run," said Ceredon. His knuckles were bleeding from striking the elf that had been attacking Aully, and his entire body was sore from untold days trying to lead the demon Darakken away from Stonewood, a plan that he realized was doomed to fail from the start.

Aully just stood there, gaping at him. *No time for this.* The massive beast that was Darakken burst forth, demolishing trees and homes, forcing his hand. He snatched up Aully by the waist and lifted her, leaping over the side of the rope bridge just as it collapsed.

Behind him, Dezren elves screamed and wood shattered. Rising above it all was the demon's trumpeting howl.

He landed on the hard-packed earth and held Aully tightly to his chest, shielding her from harm as they rolled. When they stopped, he hastily got back on his feet and glanced up at the huge, raging beast. The thing was clawing at Stonewood's tall trees with its lizardlike claws, deeply scoring the bark and using its horns to pry into the still intact domiciles. Its spiked tail lashed from side to side, impaling an unfortunate soldier through the chest; the horse he rode galloped off riderless. The demon then plunged its snout into a treetop home, its horns collapsing the side of the structure. Its jaws snapped shut, and when its head withdrew, it had a female elf trapped in its maw. Blood poured from the poor elf's mouth even as she beat at the beast's scaly hide, pulverizing her own fists on its scales. Darakken tensed, its jaw trembling, and with a loud *crack* the elf split in two. Her upper torso and legs plummeted to the earth while the demon gulped down her midsection. From inside the ruined domicile, children shrieked. Ceredon's stomach churned.

He turned away from the morbid display, only to see that Aully was still staring. "Do not look," he coaxed, gently touching her cheek to avert her head.

"Lolly," she said with a whimper, her eyes bulging. "Hadrik, Mella . . . "

"Do not think of them. Just run."

Aully nodded, but she still appeared too frightened to move. It was chaos all around them, with both elves and human soldiers storming across the clearing, trying to get away from the giant, ravenous beast. Not all of them fled mindlessly, however. A few of the soldiers paused to allow stranded elves to climb onto their horse with them. One of those was a woman dressed all in black, a beautiful creature, for a human, whom Ceredon recognized. He'd seen her when he raced past the human caravan on his way into the forest. The woman looked determined, but not overly frightened, impressive given what she faced. She rode off, followed closely by an odd-looking man wearing a bright green cloak. Then he too was gone.

It was time Ceredon followed suit.

He grabbed Aully's hand and began to run, but the young Dezren princess fought against him. "No!" she shouted.

"We have to *go*, Aullienna!" he yelled back at her. The demon continued to feast on elves in the treetops.

"No, we have to find Mother, we have to find *Kindren*!" Aully exclaimed. "I won't leave without him!"

Ceredon nodded, fighting off the urge to throw her over his shoulder and scamper off. She seemed to have shaken off her paralysis, and though her flesh was still pale as the sky on a cold winter's day, there was a determination in her eyes that he couldn't deny. He hadn't come all this way to protect just her; he knew he couldn't turn his back on the others.

He took her hand, and together they ran toward the center of the clearing, where the remnants of the hanging bridge now lay ruined. Human soldiers still charged through the clearing, looks of pure terror on those faces not covered with helms. They flashed by on either side of Ceredon and Aully, so close that wind whipped through Ceredon's hair. There were bodies littering the ground, and horses trampled them. In their terror, a couple of the soldiers blindly ran down the fleeing Dezren, crushing them beneath heavy hooves. Bones snapped. Blood flew into the air and seeped into the soil. It was pandemonium.

"There!" Aully shouted.

Ceredon followed her gaze, and finally he spotted Kindren and Lady Audrianna, holding one another while they limped across the frenzied clearing. A man on horseback veered too close to them, clipping Lady Audrianna in the process. The Lady of Stonewood was tossed aside, falling on top of Kindren. They lay there shouting while another soldier passed by, missing them by mere inches.

"Come!" Ceredon shouted. He grasped Aully and took off.

He swerved through the turmoil, his feet moving with a survival instinct all their own. The gap between him and the huddling pair was crossed in seconds, and Ceredon and Aully both reached down, helping them to their feet, then shuffling them toward the tree line. Aully bathed Kindren in kisses, and the young prince reciprocated her affections, oblivious to the horror going on around them. Tears cascaded down both their cheeks.

Another riderless horse came hurtling toward them. Ceredon shoved the three frightened elves away and dashed for it, reaching at the reins. He snared them, though just barely. With the reins firm in his grip, he dug his heels into the ground. The horse's momentum yanked him off his feet, but it had obviously been well trained.

At the pulling of the reins, the beast slowed and then stopped, shuffling nervously in place.

Ceredon stood up, his knees shredded from being dragged across the stony earth. "Aully, Kindren, *now*!" he shouted, bringing the two young elves running. Ceredon helped them into the saddle, Kindren in front and Aully behind. "Now go. Follow the soldiers."

"But Mother!" yelled Aully.

"I will care for your mother. Now *go*!"

He whacked the horse on its flank as hard as he could, and the beast took off, disappearing with its precious cargo into the surrounding forest. Ceredon quickly made his way back to Audrianna.

"Come now, Lady Meln," Ceredon said to her. "Take my hand." The dazed woman's fingers wrapped around his palm and he lifted her. She clung to him as if her life depended on it. He began to trudge forward as fast as he could, Audrianna quivering in his arms. When he glanced behind him, he saw that Darakken had finished its treetop feast. The demon crashed down to earth, shaking the ground beneath Ceredon's feet. Its blazing red eyes stared hungrily at the fleeing elves. Its trumpeting howl sounded once more, and the beast lurched forward.

Lady Audrianna screamed in Ceredon's arms, her body quivering like jelly. He lugged her into the shelter of the forest, the demon closing in from behind. It batted aside trees with its tusks, its hoofed rear legs tearing through the underbrush. He could almost feel the evil creature's rank breath on his back. All around him dashed Dezren elves and human soldiers, forming a bulging line as they fled from the beast.

I did not come this far for nothing! In the seemingly endless days since Darakken had resurrected itself, he had spied on the beast as it learned to be alive once more, constantly trying to lure it away from Stonewood until finally, the day before, it had turned around and started headlong for the forest. *If I had simply come here as I'd planned, we could be far away by now.*

Too late for regrets now, he knew. So he just kept putting one foot in front of the other and prayed Lady Audrianna wouldn't stumble and fall. If that were to happen, they would end up food for the demon.

Somehow the Lady of Stonewood kept her footing as they tramped over vines and roots. Even when they slipped on a thatch of slick leaves, all it cost them was a momentary stumble. The demon continued to track them somewhere off to the right, the sound of its feet striking the forest floor like a constant, raucous drumbeat. Trees broke and splintered. Ceredon's arms grew weary and his legs, numb. Breath was hard to come by. Lady Audrianna suffered the same way; she'd stopped her screaming and now simply wheezed.

He glanced to the side and saw Darakken's slick, scaly hide flash between the foliage, much too close. The thing then lurched to the left, colliding with a thick elm. The roots tore free from the ground and the tree toppled over. Ceredon squeezed Lady Audrianna and forced his feet to move faster, running diagonally, knocking over a fleeing soldier in the process. The tree landed behind them with a *whoosh*, crushing the soldier and a group of unfortunate elves. His mind was awash with both fear and confusion. Darakken was acting oddly, running alongside them like a shepherd's dog, threatening, but not attacking, as if penning them in.

When he finally exited the thick wood, running at full speed, Ceredon discovered that's exactly what the evil thing was doing.

Darakken had forced the fleeing masses to the southwest, where Stonewood Forest pressed up against the Corinth River. A two hundred yard stretch of flat, rocky grassland spread out before him, leading to a sheer cliff that dropped to the mouth of the river below. To the south was a line of thick trees that abutted the cliff; to the north, a slender patch of land with an upward slope. Those who fled had been hemmed in, trapped between the forest and the river. A large contingent of panicked elves attempted fleeing along the slender northern corridor, but Darakken burst through the trees, snapping a few of them up in its jaws. Other elves fell off the cliff screaming.

Then the demon disappeared back into the forest.

Ceredon took a deep breath, squeezed Lady Audrianna, and set his feet in motion once more. He hurried to the edge of the cliff, where at least two thousand elves and soldiers lurked, looking around as if they didn't know what to do next. Those on horses galloped back and forth across the center of the clearing as if their options might change each time they swiveled around.

"Aully, Kindren!" he shouted as he swerved around the horsemen.

"Here!" Aully's voice hollered back. The sprite emerged from the throng, dragging Kindren behind her. Kindren held the leads of the horse they'd ridden, struggling to make the beast match his strides. Ceredon rushed up to them and released Lady Audrianna.

"Let the horse go, Kindren. Then all of you get back," he said. "And don't fall."

He didn't wait for a reply, instead hastening along the mass of panicked elves and humans. He spotted the familiar, beautiful woman he'd seen earlier, still sitting astride her horse, her wavy dark hair like onyx threads. She appeared supernaturally calm, her shoulders thrown back while she squinted toward the forest, tracing the demon's movements behind the trees.

"You!" Ceredon shouted when he drew near.

The woman glanced down at him and stared. On one side of her was a young soldier with a forked blond beard, and the odd, redheaded man in the bright green robe was on the other.

Ceredon stopped running and bent over, hands on his knees, as he panted. "Do you lead the soldiers?" he asked in the human tongue.

"I do," she replied.

"We haven't much time. Gather your men. Horsemen on the flanks, foot soldiers in the middle. Anyone else of use, have them line up in front of the cliff. We'll assault the demon with all we have."

The woman nodded. No argument, no questions. A human with a solid head on her shoulders. Ceredon opened his mouth to say more, but he was silenced by the shattering of trees on the far edge of the forest. The demon emerged howling.

Whatever meager plans they had made would have to do.

The Darakken had come to feast.

CHAPTER 44

Laurel hid beneath a mound of stinking hay that was heaped in the back of a wooden cart. Lyana was beside her, dressed in civilian rags this time, dagger held firmly in her hand. They waited for the soft sound of marching feet to pass them by before pushing aside a few moldy strands of hay to peek out into the city beyond. They could see nothing.

"All clear," whispered a man's voice. "It's safe to come out now."

With a sigh, Laurel pushed herself out of the heap and dropped to the cobbled road. Lyana did the same. They stood there for a few moments, brushing hay fibers from their clothes while keeping a vigilant eye on the empty streets. The sky was growing dark, and there was no sign of anyone else approaching. That meant the two women were either the last to arrive or the only ones who would.

The owner of the cart, an old farmer named Jinkin Heelswool, tipped his cap to them from atop the wagon. "Where you be day after next? Here?"

"I don't know," said Laurel.

"Okay," the old man said, nodding. "If needs be, you know how to contact me."

"We will. Thank you again, Jinkin."

"It's my pleasure, milady. You take care of yourselves now."

"We'll try," said Lyana. "You too."

Jinkin ushered the two wretched mares that pulled his cart onward. Laurel watched him go as she and Lyana crept toward the shadows cast by the building to her left. She hoped he made it back to his meager fields without incident. Jinkin had been a boon for them; his family had a longstanding relationship with House Vaelor, Jinkin's own son serving as master chef at the Castle of the Lion before the war had come and yanked all men of fighting age away. When the Forgotten King's Renegades, as those who fought loyally with Laurel had come to call themselves, had been forced to flee the caverns beneath the Black Bend, the king himself had called upon the old man, asking his assistance in moving around unnoticed. Jinkin had been the only planter who kept proper stores when winter hit, and when he presented that bounty to Veldaren's new ruling class—namely the zealot priest Joben Tustlewhite—he was given uninhibited access to the city. His wagons came to deliver foodstuffs to the castle and beyond daily, guided by him and his eight daughters. Now, however, they carried with them other cargo as well—the rebellion itself. When Laurel had asked him why he would agree to so dangerous a task, his answer was inspiring. "What future is there for us if we ain't free?" he'd said. "In the world as it is now, we're nothin' but slaves. I think we deserve better. By the abyss, Karak *promised* us better."

She couldn't have agreed more.

"Come, Lyana," she said. "Let's see if the others made it."

Laurel hurried down an alley until she reached the rear entrance of a massive storehouse. It was one of three similar buildings that sat side by side on Merchants' Road. The storehouses had become home to the destitute, those who had lived in the streets and feared the lions' claws, in the time since Tustlewhite and the Judges took power. At least that's what Laurel had heard.

The storehouse door entered into a space forty feet long, sixty feet wide, and twenty feet high. Nearly every inch of space was occupied by people, jammed together shoulder to shoulder. Most turned to her and Lyana as they gently closed and barred the door. It was quite dark, as the building had no windows, and there were very few candles lit. Despite that and the anxious look in their eyes, Laurel smiled at them. Though there were many she didn't recognize, she did notice quite a few familiar faces, some that she herself had saved from the streets.

People nodded to them as Laurel and Lyana snaked their way through the human maze, but none spoke. Silence was tenet now. The Judges were leaving the castle earlier and earlier, and on this day their first roars had come more than two hours before sunset. That being the case, and with the rebellion switching locations every two days, they were forced to move about during daylight hours. If not for the old man's aid, they would've been snuffed out long ago.

The storehouse had a loft area ten feet up the wall, and she could see people lingering about up there as well. She started to walk toward the hanging ladder, only to notice that the massive gathering of people kept clear of a section of floor to her right. She went there instead, Lyana stalking silently behind her. Those gathered in the circle backed up even more. One of them, a former bandit Lyana had brought to the caverns, stepped forward. He bent over, grabbed a metal ring embedded in the floor, and pulled. A solid set of boards lifted, exposing a portal into the darkness below. Laurel silently thanked the man, then knelt down and found the ladder.

She descended into darkness, and when she reached the bottom, there were three men there to greet her, the one in the middle holding a candle. They were former members of the Palace Guard, still wearing their purple sashes with pride. They helped her off the ladder's final rung, which hung two feet off the ground. "Jericho, Luddard, Crillson," she said with a nod. The men smiled. Minister Mori had once told her that it meant a great deal to the guards for those they protected to call them by their true names, simply because so few did. It was a lesson Laurel had found true.

The three guards then stood back as Lyana effortlessly dropped from the ladder. Their smiles melted away when they nodded to the girl. Their expressions grew hard, understanding. To the guards, Lyana wasn't a ward to be protected; rather, she was a warrior, even if she was the granddaughter of the woman they loved best. Though Laurel was revered by them, Lyana was treated like a sister, perhaps even an equal.

"Where is the king?" Laurel asked.

Luddard turned to her, his pale brown eyes flicking farther into the darkness. "Down that way," he said. Crillson then handed her a candle and lit it with a tinderstick. Laurel mouthed, *Thank you*, grabbed Lyana's hand, and guided the girl away.

She walked slowly. The floor was earthen and damp, and the wide chamber stunk like old compost. "What *is* that?" Lyana asked, coughing out her words and covering her nose and mouth with the crook of her elbow.

"Just what it smells like," answered Laurel. "Rotting plants. These large fruit cellars get like this if left unattended for too long. Most of our storehouses in Omnmount had one dug into the earth beneath them."

"Oh."

Murmuring voices broke through the silence of the cellar, and Laurel followed the sound. Eventually she reached a wooden barricade—most likely the part of the cellar that once stored wine and other liquors. The voices were coming from the other side, where light shone between the slats. There was a crude door, hanging cockeyed on crumbling iron shingles. Laurel wrapped her fingers around the wood and pulled.

The room was lit by eight flickering candles scented with lavender to mask the stink of the cellar. Conversation ceased. King Eldrich, sitting on a stool above the rest, smiled warmly at her. Pulo

Jenatt was there as well, and his smile was just as wide. Also present were the four hard, odd men who called themselves the Movers, along with the woman who led them—Moira, the lost Crestwell. Everyone in the small, sealed-off room, save the king, still bore injuries from the Judges' claws, though they hid their pain well.

"Darling Laurel," King Eldrich said. "You made it."

"I did. Thankfully."

She walked in and sat down on the ground beside Pulo. Lyana took her place beside Laurel. Moira, who was on the king's other side, offered her a kind, almost blissful grin. Laurel had never met the woman until their attack six nights ago, but she had seen her sister, Avila, in the castle on a few occasions. It was amazing how similar and yet different the two women were. Their facial structures were nearly identical, all the way down to their quaint, pointed noses, and both had straight, silver hair. However, where Avila's blue eyes radiated coldness, there was warmth in Moira's gaze, especially when she looked at Laurel. She sometimes tilted her head coyly when they talked. It was odd, but the woman's soft, almost innocent laugh more than made up for her personality quirks.

Laurel looked away from Moira's intent gaze. "How many did we lose today?" she asked the king.

Eldrich shook his head. "Three."

"Three? That's not so bad."

"It's still too many," said King Eldrich. "If we are to succeed, we must have all possible manpower."

The one who called himself Gull cut in. "I was just telling the king, we should draw from those who already called the storehouse home. They are mostly women, yes, and many are hungry and weak, but what better fodder to protect us during the assault? Force them out in front. When the Sisters respond to our threat, they will have to cut through them first. When you speak of attacking a well-guarded castle, time is of the greatest essence. They will buy us that time."

Moira cuffed the man on the shoulder, wincing and grabbing her chest afterward. "I already told you no, Gull. We don't sacrifice innocent life."

King Eldrich glanced at her. "It is I who will make that decision," he said, though not unkindly. He then looked at Gull. "But no, we will not use these poor souls as fodder. If I am to die tomorrow, then I will die with a clean conscience."

"Men with clean consciences do not win wars," Gull said flatly, then let the matter drop.

"Laurel," the king said, turning to her, "you have remained silent on this issue for days. I would like your input."

Laurel shrugged. "I'm no warrior, my Liege."

"Could've fooled me," said Lyana, playfully nudging her leg. "You're as brave as anyone."

"Brave, perhaps," Laurel acknowledged, "but weak and useless with a sword. I can give a good speech, I can make people like me, but I'd be a hindrance on the battlefield."

Moira looked at her appraisingly. "I think you may underestimate your usefulness."

Eldrich waved her off. "I'm not asking you to fight, Laurel. I'm asking your *advice.* Say all you wish about your lack of skill, but the fact remains that the strike against the remaining councilmen and the Sisters that protected them was *your* idea, and it worked beautifully. You have a skill for planning, my dear. That is all I wish from you."

But Marius Trufont and Lenroy Mott still live, Laurel thought with a sigh. "Alright," she said. What the king said was true; but they had lost upwards of eighty men and women in the attack. Laurel felt her responsibility keenly. Nevertheless, if her king wanted her input, she was obliged to give it.

"I don't like the plan," she said.

"Why not?" asked the Mover named Rodin. "It's straightforward and simple."

"That's just it," said Laurel, inching forward on the dirt floor until she was directly in front of the seated king. She drew a circle in the dirt with her finger. "You're talking about a full-on assault on an armed fortress. We have—what? Eight hundred people at our disposal? We will lose half of them just squeezing through the portcullis."

King Eldrich frowned. "We must send a message. We must be swift and brutal."

"Yes, but you can be both and not stupid at the same time." Laurel cringed at her own boldness, but Eldrich's expression never changed. He appeared rather intrigued, and she continued. "Instead of striking an hour after first light, as we discussed, we move on the castle at midday. And rather than a suicide run, we use the resources we have."

"Such as?" asked Gull.

"Well, more than a third of those who now fight in the king's name are former Sisters," she said. "The wrappings of the order aren't difficult to come by; many still carry them in their sacks. At midday, the Sisters are spread throughout the city. The largest force walks among the merchants who line the streets. All eyes are *away* from the castle, looking for threats from outside. If we were to dress our women warriors in Sister's garb and send them through the portcullis in small groups, we could gather them at the rear stables. By Karak, we could even put some of our more slender men in the garb as well." She offered Pulo a sly smirk, but the subsequent moans she heard told her that others were unsettled by her speaking the name of Veldaren's god. Pulo ran a hand through his dark, curly hair.

"That gets us people inside," he said, "but what then?"

"Then they take the courtyard from the inside. The rest, the Palace Guard, Watchmen, and former brigands, will be lurking in the abandoned shops nearby. When a signal is sent, they can rush the streets and enter the portcullis untouched. The priest, and the surviving members of the Council, will be ours to do with as we wish. When the castle is ours—and hopefully we can lock the Judges in their cages before they know what's happening and join the fight—we have a defensible position. We'll have a gods-damned *castle*."

The ones named Tabar and Danco, who had remained silent thus far, perked up. "That could work," Tabar said, rubbing at his shoulder.

"It's brilliant," said Moira. She pitched forward, silver hair dangling in her face as she grinned. "I like this one. A lot."

Rodin leaned into the lost Crestwell and spoke softly. "Remember the letters, Moira. Remember what happened last—"

"Shut it," Moira snapped, elbowing the man in the chest. "It's not like that."

Gull fingered his sword. "It is a logical strategy."

"So what say you, my Liege?" asked Pulo as he threw his arm around Laurel. Laurel in turn rested her head on his shoulder, enjoying the smell of sweat on the man's clothes.

King Eldrich gave them a disapproving look. "It could indeed work. But I worry about how long it would take to organize such an assault. Say what you will about our peoples' ability with swords and spears, and their willingness to die for our cause, but none of us have truly fought a war, only skirmishes. Will they listen? Will they follow instructions? Will they even *understand* them?"

Laurel shrugged. "Who knows?" she said. "You wanted my advice, and I gave—"

The ground shook, cutting her off. Dust and dirt rained down from the ceiling. The candles flickered, growing dimmer before dancing upward once more.

"What in a maiden's twat is that?" shouted Danco.

Again the ground trembled, and this time half the candles went out. Screams split the silence and feet began to pound the floor above their heads as the people in the storehouse proper began to panic. The entire structure seemed to be creaking.

"Will it collapse?" asked Pulo.

Rodin glanced up. "Let's not stay here and find out."

Everyone in the small room leapt to their feet. They threw open the door and dashed down the hall, keeping King Eldrich between them. The other guards in the cellar waited by the ladder, hurriedly gesturing for them to climb.

One after another, they entered the storehouse's main room. Laurel was the second one out, and she helped the others, still in pain from their injuries, get to their feet. She then gawked at the scene before her. The people were indeed panicking, shouting and clustering even more tightly together in the center of the wide space. A few fights broke out as others sought safety within the wall of flesh. Then a trumpeting sounded, like the loudest horn in all of Dezrel. Laurel's heart nearly pounded out of her chest.

That's when Laurel noticed Moira's eyes were wide with terror. The silver-haired woman slowly turned to her and then walked right past her, heading for the barred door. The Movers were right on her heels, and Laurel and Lyana followed suit, King Eldrich and Pulo behind them. Danco and Rodin lifted the heavy bar and dropped it to the ground. The horn blew again. They all walked outside.

It was dark now, the night moonless. Laurel stared east, toward the heart of the city, in wonder. For the longest time, Veldaren had been quite dark during nighttime hours, but now there was a brilliant yellow glow that lit up the black. It was like the days before war, when taverns and inns saw business throughout the evening. Despite that deafening horn and the way the ground shook, Laurel felt a sliver of hope.

Then came a booming voice that shook her teeth, and that sliver disappeared.

"MY CHILDREN, COME TO ME!"

Those who had called the storehouses home before the arrival of the rebellion began to stream out of the buildings, wandering hesitantly toward the glowing center of the city.

"Karak has returned," said King Vaelor, looking dead already.

"Oh shit," said Pulo.

"We have never fought a god," said Gull. "It might be interesting."

Moira stared over at Laurel, her eyes rimmed with purple. "So much for your plan." There was no humor at all in the statement.

All Laurel could say was, "I know."

CHAPTER 45

To Velixar's eyes, Veldaren was a shadow of the city it had once been. It was dark and silent, save for the faint whimpering sounds that drifted along the wind like a cricket's song. The streets were empty. The larger buildings were scored with giant claw marks; the thatched roofs of outlying homes were burned, leaving behind hollow stone shells. From darkened windows peered the weak and craven, unwilling to show their faces as their god's army returned. Karak had told Velixar, before the fateful final attack on Mordeina, that the Final Judges now ruled the city, but he couldn't have imagined what that meant.

If only Karak were with him now.

Velixar led the remaining four thousand of Karak's Army onto the cobbled North Road. The barrenness of the city caused the soldiers' moods, which had been high when they first caught sight of the Castle of the Lion's three spires, to plummet. The only thing that brought them any sort of relief was the fact that they were now on solid ground. The journey through the Northern Plains had been harrowing; the untamed ground coated with thick mud from the thaw, sucking at booted feet and the horses' hooves and making the nightly camp a dirty, uncomfortable affair. After such a long time away from home, fighting their Divinity's war, the soldiers likely wished for nothing more than the warmth of a hearth and a soft bed to rest their bones. Velixar couldn't blame them, though he doubted their comfort would last long. Ashhur would be here soon. And when that happened . . .

My Lord, where are you?

Karak had left them in Felwood, the deity walking away from Velixar and Lord Commander Gregorian in a huff one night and riding the shadows away. That had come after Velixar found the god overlooking what had once been the most populated village in the Plains. Felwood was now virtually abandoned, many of its homes crumbling from winter's heavy winds and snows. Only a few stragglers remained, mostly starving women and their malnourished children. Just as the citizens of Veldaren now hid, so had they. The soldiers were left to plunder whatever stores were still available, which were paltry. It seemed as if most of the village had taken all they had and simply left.

"There is no faith in me here," Karak had told him that night. His tone was odd, a mixture of anger and sadness.

"There are few people here, my Lord," Velixar had replied.

The god shook his head and clenched his fists. "I am not speaking of this village, Prophet, but my *kingdom*. My ability to draw from my essence grows less and less potent each time one of my creations turns his back on me."

"You are simply weakened, my Lord," Velixar had replied. "You require time to heal."

"No. I require *faith*." The god had gazed down at him, golden eyes ablaze. "All deities draw strength from their faithful. It is what gives us purpose, what gives our existence meaning. Without devotion, we would fade away to nothingness, re-entering the heavens a speck of what we were, eventually forgotten."

"Yet you still have power, my Lord. You are still mighty."

"That is only because of you, my son. Your faith is great; it builds upon my own. As does the Lord Commander's, and that of others like him." The deity sighed. "Alas, that is not enough. I will require more, and swiftly, if my vision is to come true."

"What will you do, my Lord? How will you make the downtrodden love you once more?"

At that, the deity had laughed. "I do not require love, High Prophet. I require *faith*. And there is more than one way to bring that about."

And then he was gone.

Velixar grunted at the memory, guiding his horse onto the North Road and the city proper. To his left rose the spire of the Tower Keep. Simply laying eyes on the keep had once filled him with pride, but he felt none of that now. It was an empty structure, devoid of meaning—a partially completed dream, just like this war had become. He thought then of Mordeina, of the walls surrounding Ashhur's prized settlement, and again felt disgusted with himself. The seventeen years he had spent forming the groundwork for this war could have been put to better use. He should have waited, worked to build up Veldaren instead, raising a wall around the city like the one surrounding Port Lancaster in the south. He should have assisted the First Families instead of undermining them, helping to build Karak's children into something fearsome, something powerful. He glanced behind him, at the rows of soldiers that marched and rode solemnly through the street. It was entirely possible that these four thousand were the last men in all of Neldar. What future was there if that were the case?

"Something troubles you?" asked the Lord Commander.

Velixar glanced to the right. Malcolm now rode beside him, looking proud in his scratched black armor. He wore his horned helm, its visor down, his milky left eye glimmering in the starlight. That eye was dead, Velixar knew, but it still seemed vibrant more times than not. It was as if all his love for Karak shone out of that single, pale orb.

"I am simply thinking," Velixar said.

"Fear not, High Prophet," said Malcolm. "Karak will not abandon us."

"I know this," he said with a sigh. "I fear for him."

"Fear for him?" Malcolm said, frowning. "Why would you fear for a god?"

"Because he is greatly weakened, Lord Commander."

The one-eyed man scoffed. "Weakened? Karak is never weakened. He is the purest image of vitality and wisdom."

Velixar hesitated. He wanted to inform the man of Karak nearly losing his head to the giant Gorgoros's glowing sword. He wanted to tell him how if he himself had not dragged the monster of a man off their god, giving Karak the opportunity he needed to end the fight, everything they had fought for would have been lost. But he said none of that. He remained silent.

Malcolm reached over and squeezed his shoulder while the horses beneath them continued to trot along the North Road. "You are doubtful of that," he said. "Your expression reveals as much. I know, for I have felt the same. But no longer. I have seen the glory of Karak's supremacy, as I have seen yours. With the strength of the righteous behind us, we cannot lose."

"Your faith is admirable, Lord Commander."

Malcolm released his shoulder. "As is yours."

After that they fell silent as they led the soldiers farther into the city. They passed by the road leading into the slums of the Black Bend, entering a densely built district lined with gray stone abodes with slanted clay roofs. This was the region of the city that Karak had built, with his own hands, before the creation of man, a span that stretched a mile from the central fountain in every direction. Although drab, the structures on either side of the road were formed into an exacting, gridlike pattern—the purest illustration of architectural order that anyone in Dezrel had ever seen. Finally, confronted with an example of Karak's true vision, Velixar sensed his spirits begin to rise.

They rose further when a glow appeared in the distance, rising like a dome from Veldaren's central fountain. A lion's roar split the night. A charge seemed to fill the air, and columns of soldiers marching behind gasped. Even Aerland Shen and the Ekreissar rangers seemed awed. The glow on the horizon became brighter, the dome growing ever larger.

"I told you, High Prophet," said Malcolm with a hearty laugh. "Karak has not abandoned us!"

And so he hadn't. Karak waited at the city hub, kneeling in front of the massive fountain guarded by his life-sized likeness. The dome of light that had been cast seemed to come from the fountain itself; the water inside glowed and sparkled. The Final Judges were with the deity, Kayne to Karak's right and Lilah to his left. They purred as the god ran his fingers through their golden fur. Velixar felt taken aback by the sight of them. The Judges had always been large, bigger than any wild cat he had ever seen, but the closer he drew, the more he saw how truly *massive* they were. When Karak noticed their approach and stood, so did the lions. Even on four legs, they rose higher than the deity's waist. It was awe inspiring.

Whimpers could be heard beneath the lions' droning. That was when Velixar noticed there were gallows erected just behind the fountain. Nine people were strung from the wooden scaffolding, one old man and eight younger women, their wrists bound and hanging from the upper plank, their feet roped to the lower. They all writhed in their bonds, their flesh bruised and gashed, tears flowing down their cheeks.

Behind Velixar, the soldiers began praising their god's name.

Karak gestured for the soldiers to fan out to either side as they approached. Velixar led them to the left, Malcolm to the right, and the four thousand men fell in line. The Judges watched them with intelligent, scrutinizing eyes the whole while. The soldiers gathered in six even rows beside the gallows, curving around the sides of the fountain. Though the hub was large, it was still cramped with so many gathered on only one side of the fountain. The air was filled with those praising Karak. Velixar and Malcolm led the way.

"Glory be to Karak! Glory be to Karak!"

The god turned to face them and lifted his hand, and the chanting ceased. Karak reached to the side, his palm open, and a large, thick staff at least twenty feet high formed from the mist. He slammed the staff into the ground once, twice, three times. Each time it struck, the earth shook. A giant horn, its likeness never seen before by human eyes, materialized in his other hand. Karak lifted it to his lips and blew. The sound it made was deep and ominous, echoing throughout the city and beyond, loud enough to form cracks in the fountain. The soldiers covered their ears and fell to their knees. The horses reared back, nearly tossing their riders.

When he was done, the horn disappeared into mist. Karak, staff held firmly in his right hand, lifted his chin to the sky.

"MY CHILDREN, COME TO ME!" he cried, almost as loudly as the horn. After that a deep silence fell over the throng. Anticipation made Velixar's heart beat out of control.

They came from all around; Sisters of the Cloth first, then young women with frightened children, and then the bedraggled, old, and infirm. For almost an hour the soldiers and elves stood there at attention while the citizens of this once-great city gathered. The Final Judges grumbled and snarled, but Karak stilled them with a glance. The people fell to their knees before the fountain, thousands of them, squeezing in like the fish in a lucky fisherman's bucket after an ample catch. All the while, those strung up on the gallows wriggled and begged.

As the last trickle of humanity fell to their knees, Karak gestured for Velixar to join his side. Velixar climbed down off his horse and walked, head down, around the fountain. He neared Kayne, and the lion's nose sniffed the air. Velixar felt no fear. A throaty gurgle sounded, and amazingly, just like the beast-men Karak had created, the lion spoke.

"Prophet," he said in his rumbling, inhuman baritone.

"Faithful," Lilah answered.

The gathered mob gasped, a sound like a million fissures spouting steam around a volcano.

Velixar rubbed the flesh beneath Kayne's bloodstained maw, and the gigantic cat purred. He nodded to the beast and took his place at Karak's side. Only then did Karak speak.

"My children, my creations, the moment of judgment is upon us!" cried the deity. It seemed like the wind picked up in that moment, blowing back the hair of the kneeling women present. "I have been gone too long, and the war I have righteously waged against my sinful brother has not gone as planned. Whose fault is that, I ask you now? Is it the fault of your creator, he who put breath in your lungs and vibrancy in your limbs? Or is it the fault of you, his wayward children, who do not love their Divinity as they should?"

A collective, frightened murmur raced through the thousands of kneeling onlookers.

"It is you, the faithless, who have thwarted me!" the deity bellowed. Feminine voices shrieked. "You have turned your back on your creator. You have turned against *order itself*! I come to this city now, and all I see is chaos. What kind of children would repay their father for his kindness by betraying his very ideals? I look upon you now, a mass of swarming cowardice that only show love for their next meal, and not for the god who provided it for them!"

Velixar felt a shiver run through him, the burgeoning fear of thousands being chastised by a rage-filled deity lingering in the air like fog. The pendant grew hot against his chest, his nerve endings tingling. His eyes widened as he gazed up at the deity.

I require faith. There is more than one way to bring that about.

Karak's voice lowered in volume, becoming nearly sympathetic in tone.

"All is not lost, my children," he said. "Even now my brother marches on this city, along with a legion of walking dead, bent on bringing an end to all I have created. We can defend that which is mine. We can stop Ashhur, demonstrate for him the true meaning of virtue. It is up to you now, my children. You must show faith in me. You must give to me the very souls I gave you. Betrayal will no longer be tolerated." The god shifted to the side, extending his hand toward the nine dangling people. "Those you see are the faithless. This man, Jinkin Heelswool, and his daughters have turned their backs on my glory, as many of you have. You know them as the ones who offered sustenance to this great city when it was most needed, but the gift they offered was tainted. In their hearts there is blackness; there is chaos. They have consorted with those who wish to bring down their own architect. The Final Judges have deemed them guilty, and so have I. They must be punished."

"Fuck you!" shouted the old man as he thrashed. "You are no true god! You are a *liar*!" The other eight, his daughters, simply cried and pleaded for their lives.

Karak ignored them. "In the quest for order, there is no mercy. Those who blaspheme against my name shall be punished with fire."

The deity snapped his fingers, and the nine hanging from the gallows burst into flame. It raced over their flesh, making it bubble. Still they writhed, flaming bits of them falling off their bodies and scorching the wooden planks below. Their screams pierced the night, the air smelled of burning flesh. A few of the soldiers standing close by the gallows vomited. The massive crowd wailed and moaned. The smell of fear wafting off the thousands, once pungent, became overwhelming.

The golden glow of Karak's eyes brightened.

It took the blasphemers nearly ten minutes to die. When they finally fell silent, their charred remains smoked and crackled. Karak stared at the corpses, smiling, and turned back to his children.

"Ashhur is near," he bellowed. "My brother will arrive with the rising sun. He will be vicious, and so shall we. Now go, my children, all of you. Use whatever you can to bring Ashhur's irreverent faithful to their knees. When the undead march into this city, when those who wish to enslave you in the name of justice batter down your doors, you will cry out my name, and you will fight."

"Karak," came a wavering voice from the mob.

"Karak," said another.

Soon the night was filled with human voices shouting the deity's name. It began somberly at first, but then grew louder and more certain. Male voices joined in with the female throng. The soldiers banged the swords and spears against their shields, creating a cadence. Even the Ekreissar joined in, Aerland Shen slamming his swords together as he guided his rangers in calling out the God of Order's name. *"KARAK, KARAK, KARAK!"* went the refrain. *"KARAK, KARAK, KARAK!"*

The crowd began to disperse, still chanting, still pumping their fists. It was then that Karak went down on a knee before Velixar, staring him right in the eyes.

"What you did," said the prophet, "was . . . inspiring."

The deity nodded. "Now is your time, Velixar. It is you I am counting on."

Velixar's eyes opened wide as he bowed. "I am your humble servant, my Lord."

"You are more than that. You are the swallower of demons. You are power incarnate. It is through you that this battle will finally end. When I left your side, I went back to the mountains for a short while and thought of my clash with the giant. He might have sent me back to the heavens—*would* have—had you not intervened. Although my brother and I are too evenly matched to kill one another, a righteous follower can." The god's smile widened. "You have the power within you, High Prophet. You have the strength to overwhelm a god. I can see it as plainly as I can see the order in chaos. You are the salvation of Neldar, my son. You are the most perfect of all the gods' creations."

Velixar felt short of breath as he listened to his chosen god's words. Even so, a grain of doubt tickled his thoughts. He clenched his hands before him and dropped to his knees.

"I will remain strong, my Lord. I will pour my entire soul into destroying Ashhur. However, I must ask . . . what if I fail? What if my strength proves not great enough?"

Karak reached out and touched Velixar's forehead with his massive index finger. "Just as with faith, there is more than one way to obtain order. I will show you."

Images assaulted Velixar's mind. Fire filled his vision, horrifying and purifying, wondrous and terrible, all at once. Velixar fell back, holding his hand before him, watching everything around him burn in his mind's eye.

"So . . . beautiful . . . "

CHAPTER 46

Veldaren opened up around them as Patrick rode along the road in the city's southern district. Even the vividness of the early spring sun could do nothing to brighten what looked to be a depressing wasteland of drab gray. To the right appeared a stone tower with a hollowed nook at the top. Though tall and indeed threatening, it too appeared dreary. "I'm not impressed," Patrick muttered, bouncing on his stallion. He'd seen the amazing architecture his brother-in-law Turock had erected in Drake, the precise buildings designed by Warden Boral in Lerder, and the elegant Gemcroft estate in Haven, all of which made the boxy sameness of Veldaren less than inspiring.

"Your eyes tell a different story," said Preston.

Patrick offered him a scowl. "Shut it."

But there was no denying the truth to the man's words. The sheer size of the place most certainly stilled Patrick's heart. Even Drake, with all its advancements, was a place where many people resided in shanties and tents scattered just outside the central square. Veldaren had none of that. There was no grass to be seen. The street was cobbled, the walks lining it gray slate. The plain structures were numerous, built close together, most rising at least two levels up. And that didn't include the three massive spires that cut into the sky ahead and to the right. Those were the most imposing of all.

"I've never seen a city before," Patrick said. "A *true* city, like those in the Wardens' stories."

"Of course you haven't," laughed Edward.

There was edginess in the youth's laughter. He'd been like that during most of their journey to this city across the river. Most everyone was tense, from the Turncloaks to the Wardens, to Ashhur's children. Even Ashhur seemed anxious. The only ones who showed no fear were the thousands of undead that marched around them, their numbers so great that those on the perimeter of the ring were constantly colliding with the many buildings lining the road.

As for those inside the circle, so crammed were their conditions that they rode in three slender columns. When Patrick peered over his shoulder, he couldn't see the tail end of the convoy. They were still exiting the forest to the south.

"I don't like that," said Patrick. "It doesn't look good."

"It isn't," Preston replied. "Being stretched this thin, we're easy targets."

"But what about the undead?" asked Tristan. Though he was nervous, the young soldier had a warm smile on his face as he gazed all around him at the dingy scenery. *He's from here,* Patrick recalled. *This is a homecoming for him.*

"The undead can protect us only so much," said Preston. The older man jabbed his thumb behind him. "And their presence will mean nothing if the god controlling them falls."

Tristan turned around, as did Patrick. Ashhur wavered as he walked, his gaze intent on some distant point, his arms hanging limp by his sides. He had been this way for days, ever since he had raised a provisional bridge over the Rigon once they'd reached the scorched remains of Lerder. It looked as if it took his every effort simply to stand upright. It had gotten so bad that at night, when their tents were put up and the men of Paradise gathered around their cookfires, they would express their doubts about whether Ashhur was right in bringing them east at all. Not that Patrick could blame them. He was starting to have those thoughts as well.

"Too late to turn back now," he whispered.

"What was that?" asked Preston's other son, Ragnar.

Patrick waved him away. "Nothing. Talking to myself."

The force progressed down the road, the constant clomp of hooves on cobbles ringing in Patrick's ears. Their advance was indeed noisy, but it struck him as strange that despite how much of a ruckus they made, they attracted no attention. The opened windows of every building they passed, large and small, were empty. There wasn't even a hint of movement inside, which was strange in a place that looked like it had once housed thousands upon thousands of people.

"You think the people left?" he asked Preston.

The older man shrugged.

"Perhaps we won't find Karak here after all," said Patrick. He reached over his shoulder and tapped Winterbone's now naked handle for luck.

"I wouldn't be so sure about that," Preston said with a frown.

The old soldier's words proved prophetic, for a few minutes later a commotion broke out at the front of the column, half a hundred yards from where Patrick rode. The wall of undead collapsed inward a bit farther up, and Patrick heard Ahaesarus sound his warning horn. The men from Ker, who had been interspersed throughout the column, lifted their elven bows and nocked them with arrows. The horn sounded again. Words of caution were passed from the front of the column to the back.

"On the roofs! Look to the roofs!"

Patrick shouted the same warning to those behind him, then raised his eyes to the tops of the surrounding buildings. Hundreds of people appeared, their hair long and grimy, their clothes tattered. To Patrick it looked as if they had ridden into a den of feral women. The women held various objects in their hands, from rocks to sharpened lengths of wood to the type of iron cookware—pots and ladles and fire pokers—that Patrick had seen used in Haven. There were some wielding bows and arrows as well. Seemingly at once, the women raised their makeshift weapons above their heads.

"Shields up!" Patrick shouted, unhitching from his saddle his borrowed shield—which still bore Karak's sigil—just as the women released their wares.

Those that had shields lifted them; those that didn't tried to get close to those who did. Heavy objects rained down on them, pounding against the solid wood and metal of the shields. Men shouted down below while women sounded a primal war cry from above. Patrick braced himself, a heavy chunk of iron striking his shield, cracking it, and bathing his eyes with splinters. A spike of pain jolted through his forearm on impact. An arrow struck his mailed thigh, but not hard enough to pierce it. He glanced down as yet another heavy object thudded against his shield and saw that the arrow was crudely made, simply a sharpened stick with feathers attached to the shaft with twine. He plucked it from the ring it was stuck in and tossed it aside.

The Kerrians fired arrows back at those attacking from the rooftops, their aim truer, their bolts more deadly. Many of the women fell back, disappearing over the other side of the slanted roofs; others caught arrows in the chest and tumbled twenty feet to the ground, only to stand up a moment later and join the undead horde.

A horse galloped along the edge of the convoy. It was Master Warden Ahaesarus, inhumanly tall in his saddle. He shouted at the Kerrians as he passed them by. "Get to the center! Do not waste arrows on the citizens! Save them for the real soldiers!"

A few stubborn Kerrians still loosed arrows, but most men followed orders, pressing their horses into the column to find someone with a large enough shield to hide beneath. Still the rain of debris continued. Patrick lifted his shield slightly and peered at Ashhur.

The god had remained silent, even as he was pelted with heavy objects. Each time one struck him, he would wince, but he kept on walking, determined.

At last, the god spoke. "To the right!" he bellowed loudly enough for those still a half-mile away to hear. "We head for the castle."

Up ahead, the procession turned. Patrick remained beneath his shield, though his stallion was taking a beating. It whinnied every time it was struck, and once a large chunk of stone hit the stallion in the flank, almost breaking its leg. "Easy," Patrick said, doing his best to soothe the beast. "You have it. You can do it." The stallion remained true. Others weren't so lucky. Edward's horse was taken down by a crude spear; Big Flick lost his when a large iron tub crushed the poor thing's skull. The numbers of those who carried on by foot grew by the second. The dead men rose to join the undead army while the horses formed obstructions the rest of the convoy had to maneuver their way around. If Patrick thought the road had been a cluttered mess before, it was nothing compared to now.

There were urgent shouts coming from up ahead. As Patrick took the turn onto the adjoining road, guided by the crush of bodies around him, he could see why. Human forms charged from the structures lining both sides of the road and crashed into the wall of undead, hacking and slashing with daggers, spears, small swords, and hatchets. There were hundreds of them, all feminine in shape, yet they were covered head to toe in what looked to be off-white bandages. Patrick watched them battle the undead, slowly cutting through their thick mass. He then peeked around his shield, still held above his head, and saw that the barrage from the rooftops had ceased.

"Small victories," he muttered.

Then he glanced forward, saw the three giant spires they had been marching toward, rising above a thirty-foot wall, and realized just how small that victory truly was.

The convoy was more packed together now, a writhing mass of bodies rather than three distinct columns. Those on the outside moved hastily toward their undead protectors, hands shaking as they held their weapons at the ready. Not a good sign. The strange, wrapped women seemed to fight without fear, as if driven by some otherworldly force. The barely trained defenders of Paradise, though more numerous, would be cut through in moments. Patrick exchanged a glance with Preston. The old soldier gritted his teeth and leaned forward in his saddle.

"Turncloaks, ride!" he shouted.

Patrick ripped Winterbone off his back and led the way, inching his stallion through the press of struggling bodies until he reached the edge of the undead wall. One of the wrapped women sliced the head off a deceased Warden and shoved her way past the reaching, now-headless corpse. Patrick was there to greet her, hacking down from atop his stallion, clipping the woman on the side of the head. She fell back shrieking, blood spurting from where the wrappings had been sliced on her cheek, until the undead horde swallowed her whole. Patrick felt his stomach clench as he watched the walking corpses tear her apart.

Then Ashhur screamed, and everything went to shit.

Patrick veered around, looking on as his god grabbed the sides of his head and fell to his knees. The undead he commanded stopped in their tracks, swaying in place, looking like indecisive simpletons who couldn't decide which way to go.

"Uh, Patrick?" he heard Preston say.

"Yeah, this isn't good," Patrick replied.

They retreated back toward the center as the wrapped women barreled over the suddenly motionless undead. They made no sound as they charged, but it didn't matter, for whatever noise they might have made would've been swallowed by the war cry of Karak's soldiers. They stampeded down the road in front of Ashhur's brave warriors, a massive wave of flesh, armor, and sharpened steel, while another division simultaneously assailed the rear of the convoy, which was still wrapped around the corner on the main road. The clash of steel and the screams of dying men overtook all else. Patrick, his heart beating a mile a minute, snapped his head around, staring at the wall and towers of Veldaren's castle. Only two hundred yards at most separated them, but it could not have seemed farther away.

All the while, Ashhur remained on his knees and hunched over, screaming in pain.

Patrick glanced at Preston. "Forward!" he shouted, holding Winterbone out before him. "Never stop moving! Head for the castle!"

The Turncloaks, as well as a small group of Ashhur's children and Wardens, heeded his call. Twelve horses and thirty men on foot fell in behind Patrick as he urged his stallion through the road's cramped confines. All around him was commotion as the wrapped women leapt and stabbed and hewed, sending geysers of blood into the air. Fortunately for those from Paradise, given how tightly they were bunched and the borrowed armor they wore, more attackers fell than defenders.

That close proximity and armor would mean nothing once Karak's soldiers met their ranks, however. And they were approaching fast, the whole screaming lot of them. Patrick finally reached the front of the line to find Ahaesarus, no longer on horseback, trying to organize the terrified men who formed the front line. Half of them had no shields. There were undead here too, standing still, wavering, and useless for anything but a simple obstruction.

Patrick tossed his shield to one of the men without one. "All of you, do the same!" he shouted to his ever-growing squad. One by one they handed over their shields to the men forming the barricade. "And any of you who wish for a good death this day, follow us!" A few chose to line up behind him, but most simply knelt there, shivering behind their shields. A couple of them even tried to scurry back away from the front. Patrick turned away quickly before he snapped at them. The Master Warden could handle the cravens. He had better work to do.

"Onward!" he shouted, kicking at his stallion. He took off at a gallop, knocking aside bunches of stagnant undead and charging straight for the onrushing soldiers. The Turncloaks fanned out to either side of him. Pikes and shields were raised, but that didn't slow either party's advance.

Patrick crashed into the first row of soldiers, barely turning his body to the side fast enough to miss a lunging pike. His stallion hollered in pain as the animal was battered by a soldier's hardened steel, but it pressed onward, urged on by his commands. From atop the beast Patrick brought Winterbone down again and again, cleaving through armor, batting aside enemy blades, slamming those who tried to yank him from the saddle with his elbows. And still he kept yelling, *"Hyah!"* to keep his stallion pushing forward.

The unified cry of a thousand souls broke above the din of battle, and Patrick kicked a man in the face and turned around. It seemed Ahaesarus had decided a new strategy was necessary. Instead of waiting to be run through by the enemy, the massive throng of Paradise's defenders had followed Patrick's lead, hurtling past the dormant undead and into Karak's soldiers. Bodies collided, steel crashed. It was absolute pandemonium.

Whirling back around, Patrick continued onward, determined to reach the castle walls. He fought the urge to check on the location of his mates; that would only slow him down. He kept bringing his sword down again and again, the muscles in his powerful arm singing with strength. Men died by the score, their flesh torn asunder, their armor no match for Winterbone's gleaming edge. He sat high above it all, dishing out death in the name of Ashhur.

"DuTaureau!" he heard Preston's voice call out from somewhere amid the chaos. "Horsemen!"

Patrick lifted his head and saw at least two hundred men on horseback appear from a pair of alleys on the right side of the road.

They galloped toward him just as arrows began to fly from above, descending into the mass of humanity far behind him. He glanced up at the rooftops, only instead of disheveled women, he saw tall, elegant beings up there, launching arrow after arrow with quickness he had never seen before. *Elves,* he thought. *Great.* Patrick turned away from the sight of them, slashed through the helm of a soldier wielding a giant hammer, and charged toward the horsemen.

He never reached them.

A solid blow took his stallion out from under him, and the animal screeched as it toppled sideways, crushing two soldiers. Patrick fell from the saddle, landing solidly on a group of men, armor clanking. He rolled, avoiding stomping boots and plunging blades, before swiftly getting to his feet and pitching backward. A soldier's face was crunched by his armored hump, and he snarled as two more soldiers turned to face him. He went to lift his sword, but it was snagged behind him somehow. One of them got in a good swing, his sword catching Patrick on the vambrace and sending a shudder through him that rocked his shoulder, but the other one didn't attack. Instead, his eyes bugged out of his skull as the pointy end of a spear ejected from his neck. His blood splattered against Patrick, who freed his sword and ran it through the first man. He felt someone closing in from behind and whirled around, Winterbone leading. His blade met Preston's with a resounding *clang.*

The old Turncloak grinned. "Not today, my friend."

Patrick nodded. The two of them swiveled at once, their swords unlocking, and began scything their way through the soldiers. Sharp edges found gaps in his armor, opening what felt to be a hundred tiny cuts all over him, but he didn't care. He noticed many others wearing the white-painted armor of Ashhur's legion behind him, including most of the Turncloaks, and grinned. His people were with him. He could ignore his pain so long as that was the case.

When the horsemen entered the fray, crashing through their own brethren as if they didn't care about their lives, Patrick went back to work. He sliced at the horses' legs and sides, severing tendons and spilling intestines. His men followed his lead. Many of the horses toppled over, tipping their riders into the melee. After felling yet another horse, nearly severing the beast's head with one massive hew, Patrick spun around and was almost run down. He fell straight backward, slashing out to the side with Winterbone at the same time. The blade cut through the horse's front leg, snapping the bone and separating it just above the ankle. The horse crashed head over heels. Bones crunched, and more men screamed.

Someone helped him back to his feet, and then he felt himself being shoved from behind, carried along by his men's rush. He bounced off soldiers, punching and stabbing at them, until finally he fell forward into open space. He tumbled, smacking his cheek on bloody cobbles, jarring his neck in the process. But there was no time to wallow in his pain. He shot to his feet, ready to face his next challenge, only to see that he now stood a mere twenty feet in front of the castle walls. There was nothing but the slate walk between it and him—no soldiers, no horses, no wrapped women, nothing.

He'd made it.

Before he could turn around and defend against the dangers behind him, he glanced up the full height of the wall. The top of the wall shimmered in the sunlight, drawing his eye to its horrors. He wanted to look away but couldn't. Tristan had told him about the corpses that hung here, and though he knew the boy hadn't been lying, a part of him still hadn't wanted to believe him.

Yet there they were, bodies dangling from the wall, at least fifty of them. Some were fresher than others; those to his far left looked like they had been recently hung. Patrick stared at their faces, rotted and drooping, holding very little resemblance to the humans they had once been. The slate walk beneath them was stained black and a wretched shade of green. Patrick couldn't help but gape at each and every one of them, men and women alike, not stopping until he found the one he was searching for.

Patrick's heart shattered. He fell to his knees.

There she was, a decomposed husk of the vibrant girl she'd once been, now not much more than a skeleton covered with a thin sheen of gray, peeling flesh. The mane of curly hair, its bright red faded to a dull auburn, coiled around the eyeless skull and fell over the shoulders. Patrick leaned back, staring up at Nessa's corpse. Her death hadn't been real before; it had been a message from another—more rumor than fact, even if he'd believed it completely. But now, to see the proof directly in front of him . . . something within him snapped. He threw his head back and howled at the sky, then scampered to his feet, breathing heavily as tears streamed down his cheeks. The din of conflict going on all around him seemed far away.

"Where are you!" he bellowed. "I know you're here!"

When he turned, he saw that the entire square in front of the castle had become one giant battleground. Soldiers of Karak and Ashhur clashed with a frenzy, while elves, those strange wrapped women, and the Wardens were intermixed as well, killing and dying just as easily as everyone else. Ashhur, his beloved deity, was nowhere to be seen, swallowed by the horde, his undead swaying uselessly between pockets of combat.

That only served to further enrage Patrick, and he focused on that rage. When one of Karak's soldiers ran at him, he drove his sword through the man's face, kicked the corpse off the blade, and continued to rumble along the castle wall like a bull seeking a target to spear with his horns. There was one man that mattered, the one that had haunted his dreams with visions of his dead sister, the one he now blamed for everything that had gone wrong.

And then he found him: Jacob Eveningstar, the First Man who had betrayed Ashhur and cast all of Dezrel into war. He stood in front of the castle portcullis, flanked on either side by onyx lion statues, his eyes glowing bright crimson. A ring of soldiers in black armor protected him. His cloak billowed as if he was caught in a harsh wind, and his body was surrounded by swirling shadow. The man chanted, his hands in constant motion, fingers twisting into odd shapes, a look of pain on his face. Patrick never thought twice. His instinct was to let out a scream, one that contained all the rage and heartbreak he had ever felt, but he snapped his lips shut and simply charged.

One of the soldiers in front noticed his approach and turned. He wore a massive helm topped with a pair of horns, and stepped toward him. The soldier held before him a sword as hefty as Winterbone, with a curled black handle. Patrick snarled, kept his feet moving, lifted his own sword above his head, and chopped down as hard as he could when he was within reach.

The soldier easily parried the clumsy strike, kicking Patrick away in the process. Patrick hit the ground and rolled, falling directly on Winterbone. The sharp blade sliced through his armored left shoulder and cut deep into the flesh beneath. Patrick let out a cry of fury and pain and rolled back over, clutching at his gushing wound. The same soldier then yelled something Patrick couldn't hear.

As Patrick got to his feet, an ear-splitting roar sounded. From above the castle wall leapt two lions, a male and a female, far too huge to be normal. They soared over his head and landed amid the chaos, their jaws snapping and claws swiping. Men were shredded from both sides. One of the Wardens, Sabael, lost his head in an instant.

"You have lost, blasphemer!" someone called out. Patrick turned back around to see that the soldier who had thwarted his attack had lifted the visor of his great helm. Scars ran down half his face, and one of his eyes was milky white. The scarred man took a step forward, pointing a mailed finger in Patrick's direction.

"You will fall next," he said.

Patrick took a defensive posture, ignoring the pain in his shoulder, waiting for the man to attack. Behind him, swords clashed, and he heard a youthful voice—either Tristan or Joffrey—screaming his name. He ignored it.

But the helmed soldier didn't rush him. Jacob Eveningstar didn't hurl a ball of shadow in his direction. Instead, from out of the portcullis swarmed fifteen elves, moving effortlessly around Jacob and the guarding soldiers, forming a secondary layer of protection for the First Man. Their copper skin glistened in the sunlight, and their pointed ears twitched. The elf in the center stepped forward. He was a massive beast of a thing, square headed and thick shouldered. His armor was black and rutted, like scales. From behind his back he drew a pair of gleaming swords just as black as his armor. The elf leaned forward and scowled at Patrick, clanging his swords together in front of him, causing sparks to shower to the cobbles.

Patrick heard rapid footfalls approaching from behind and threw an elbow, cracking the jaw of a rushing soldier, then stood sideways and faced the giant elf.

Perhaps this is the one to prove me mortal?

"Who cares?" he growled. The ageless Patrick DuTaureau charged.

CHAPTER 47

Eldrich Vaelor, the puppet king of Veldaren, stood atop the roof of the tallest public dwelling in the city, gray eyes staring across the narrow alleyways toward the Castle of the Lion. Moira followed his gaze. It was bedlam down there, thousands of combatants, nearly all of Veldaren and Ashhur's entire armies, mashed into a tiny space. Even as far away as they were, it sounded as if the war were raging right below them.

Moira moved to the edge of the roof, squinting. Her blood was pumping in anticipation, and despite her injuries, which were not yet fully healed, she wanted to dive in down there, where she was most needed. And she knew she would get that opportunity. Though the king had claimed his rebellion was only traversing the city to observe the clash between the brother gods, she knew that the people's need to make a difference would override his hesitation. Eldrich might not be the same man she had known as a child, a spoiled braggart afraid of his own shadow, but he wasn't the strength behind the rebellion.

No, that strength was drawn from the one Moira had come here to save. Laurel Lawrence, that brilliant, beautiful, and fearless young thing, was the *true* power behind the forgotten throne.

As if on cue, the woman stepped toward the ledge beside Moira. Laurel was dressed in a pair of loose-fitting breeches covered by a mannish frock, but there was no denying her beauty or the potency of her will. Moira was intensely attracted to her, and even awed by her. From what Moira had learned, this woman had ventured out each day into a city that wanted her dead, determined not to stop until she had saved all the people she could. This was not a woman who would allow her king to stand idly by.

Laurel turned her haunting hazel eyes to King Eldrich. "We must fight."

Behind them, those from the rebellion who had gathered on the roof cheered.

Eldrich furrowed his brow. "We will lose."

"We may," said Gull, running a whetstone along his saber.

"Either way, it will be exciting," added Tabar.

The king frowned at these two men he barely knew, before turning around and facing the fifty or so gathered on the rooftop. The rest of the rebellion congregated on the empty streets below.

"Do you all wish to join the fight?" he asked, voice raised.

A raucous shout of approval answered him.

"Even if you fight for yet another god?" the puppet king asked. "Karak or Ashhur, it matters not. Whichever wins, we will still be in chains, only of a different kind."

"We don't fight for any gods," said Laurel proudly. "We'll fight for *ourselves*."

"Besides," scowled Danco, "Ashhur was swallowed by a wave of soldiers. For all we know, he's gone for good."

That statement drew another riotous cheer, even louder than the first. Moira lifted her sword above her head and joined them, grinning.

Eldrich appeared glum but seemed to gather himself as he shushed the crowd. "And so the choice has been made," he said. "Any who wish to join the battle can do so of their own free will, but we will force none. It will be the people's choice whether they sprint to their deaths." Moira was surprised by the strength behind his voice, but that still didn't stop her from scoffing at the man giving everyone *permission* to do as they chose. The man was a puppet king. He held no real power.

Another cheer began.

Laurel hushed them. "Listen, all of you. We're behind the castle, so let's keep it that way. When those who want this fight are collected, we'll circle around the wall to the west, since our view of what is happening on the other side is blocked. Karak hasn't made himself known yet, but he still might be nearby. Try to stay out of sight until you're within fighting range. We don't want anyone becoming lion meat." She gave King Eldrich a smirk. "Then, my Liege, you will have the straight-on assault you wanted."

Moira laughed, this time not bothering to hide her amusement.

"Now go, everyone," said Laurel, "and if I never see you again, know that you were well met."

Those on the roof began hopping down the stairwell, heading for street level. Laurel gave Pulo Jenatt, the curly-haired former captain of the Guard, a hug before he limped after the others. Moira noted the look of jealousy on King Eldrich's face, before going to join her Movers.

"Moira, wait," said Laurel, stilling her.

Moira turned to see Laurel arguing with the young girl with the dark, wavy hair and deep blue eyes, who was constantly at Laurel's side. Moira walked up to them, listening to the songs of battle the people heading down the stairs sang and longing to be with them.

"What?" she asked.

Laurel's stare was intense. "Moira, how hurt are you?"

"A bit." She rolled her shoulders. "Still smarting, but once the blood starts flowing, it should fade away."

"Good." Laurel gestured to her young companion. "Lyana is adamant that she be allowed to fight. She is a girl of age now, eighteen and her own woman. However, I must ask . . . can you protect her?"

“I can do my best, I suppose.”

“That’s all I can ask.” Laurel then looked deep into Lyana’s eyes. “You stay safe. Stick by Moira’s side like sap. I *will* see you again, do you understand? You are important, one of only two members of the First Families remaining in this horrid city. Your survival will serve as an example to the rest.”

“I’ll try, Laurel.”

“You best.”

Moira watched the conversation, the sounds of battle melting away as she gaped. She nearly slapped herself upside the head. That was why the girl looked familiar. Lyana. Lyana *Mori*. Rachida’s niece and last surviving family member. Though Moira hadn’t seen the girl since she was in the cradle, the resemblance to the house matriarch couldn’t be denied.

“No,” Moira said, too harshly. “She isn’t coming.”

Laurel and Lyana snapped their heads toward her.

“Why not?” asked Lyana.

“Because of who you are. Because of what you mean. If your Aunt Rachida finds out you died out there, she’d never forgive me for allowing it. I’m sorry, but absolutely not.”

With that, Moira dashed toward the stairwell, ignoring Lyana’s angry shouts. She descended the stairs three at a time, hoping that the girl was obedient enough to heed her warning and stay far, far away.

For though it was true she’d probably die in the next few minutes, she had to hedge her bets just in case. Lyana would make a splendid present for Rachida should they ever be reunited.

Her Movers awaited her just outside the tall building, and upon her arrival, they began sprinting without a word. From what Moira could tell, more than half of the eight hundred men and women fit to fight had decided to join them on the dash to their deaths. The Palace Guard and Watchmen wore their uniforms, but the commoners were dressed mostly in lighter armor, if they had any armor at all. Those that didn't had strapped scraps of wood to their arms and wedged heavily stuffed pillows beneath their smallclothes for protection.

As a group they sprinted down the alleyways, crossing the span between them and the raging battle in mere minutes. The roar of it grew more and more deafening with every step Moira took. Then came the fear and excitement, and—just as she'd told Laurel—the pain from her wounds melted away behind a wall of electric anticipation.

They reached the rear wall of the castle, the three towers rising high above them, and ran at a measured pace along it. The fighting had spilled over to the side, as soldiers in sloppily painted white armor fought those in silver and black. Ashhur even had a few Wardens on his side, the tall beings more than holding their own against the armored hordes. The Judges were also in the mix, working their way through the melee, ripping men apart. Moira paused, looking toward the neighboring rooftops. There were elves up there; she could see them now, taking aim and launching arrows into the hordes.

"Movers, to me," she said.

Gull, Rodin, Tabar, and Danco sidled up to her, waiting intently for their instructions. She also called over twenty others.

"Forget the fight on the ground," she said. "See those buildings over there? Get on the roofs and kill those elves. They are likely the ones who are best with a sword, so I want *our* best with a sword to face them. I'm sure there are more on the other side of the square, but the less death coming down on us from above, the better. We have enough to deal with when there are Judges and soldiers and Sisters about."

Her Movers nodded sharply, pride in their eyes, and took off without a word, leading the twenty others. "I hope to see you again," she whispered. Moira then took a deep breath and faced forward. Pulo Jenatt was peeking around the wall. He held up three fingers and counted down. When his fist closed, mayhem sparked.

Moira ran screaming into the fray, holding both her swords out to her sides. She used one of her own men as a launching point, kicking off his back and rising into the air. As she descended she spun, hacking at a pair of soldiers' throats. One she killed, severing his windpipe easily; the second she sliced through the cheek instead, causing his flesh to dangle, exposing his teeth. The soldier fell to the ground, clawing at his face.

She landed amid the turmoil, sprinting into motion once more. She stabbed and slashed, bounding off shoulders and helms, using her lithe frame and agility to keep from dying. Arrows flew all around her, making her spin to the side or arch her back to keep from being struck. Always she eyed the two lions, which were at least two hundred feet away, sending bodies flying into the air. It was then, as she stabbed another soldier in the back of the neck and once more leapt into the air, that she noticed something strange. There were a great many people who weren't engaging in the battle. They simply stood there in the middle of everything, swaying, eyes blank. Some looked to have taken grave injuries, many missing limbs or with gaping wounds on their bodies that somehow did not leak blood. The momentary confusion caused Moira to falter. She missed her mark, roughly colliding with a soldier's back and then landing in the midst of countless tramping feet.

At least the arrows won't reach me here.

She stayed crouched, inching along the ground and hamstringing as many men as she could. A queer sort of panic filled her when one of the men whose ankle she severed fell to the ground, only to have his face stomped by oblivious feet. Though the man's armor was that of Karak's Army, there were splotches of white paint covering the breastplate. Moira scooted to the side, avoiding another soldier's blade, and noticed that almost all of Ashhur's followers were simply wearing the standard of the lion, only painted over. With the crude paint chipping away during the battle, it would be nearly impossible to tell one side from the other.

The concern fled her when she heard a cry rise above the clamor. It was the scream of a tortured soul, of pain beyond physical, and she recognized the voice. She stood, grabbed a soldier from behind, hoped it was one of Karak's, and slit his throat. Using his body as a shield, she spun around, looking for her opening. When she found it, a three-foot space of empty, bloody cobbles, she tossed the man's corpse at the skirmishing men and ran in the opposite direction, putting as much force as she could behind her next jump, arrows be damned.

Batting away blows on either side, Moira hustled toward the sound. Luckily, the arrows were no longer flying on this side of the square, which meant her Movers had done their job. She had to keep one eye ahead and one eye on the castle wall, but then she saw him—Patrick DuTaureau, the father of Moira and Rachida's child, sprinting along the wall. His expression was one of pure agony, pure *hatred*; in that moment, he actually looked like the monster many had assumed him to be. She had fought by his side in Haven, and he'd never looked like that. She wondered what had transformed him so.

Then her eyes traced upward, and she wondered no more.

"Fuck no," she muttered.

Hanging on the wall amid a long row of corpses was one that stuck out from the rest—a small, withered thing with red, curly hair. And beside her, his chestnut locks like reeds blowing in the wind, was Crian. Her brother, the only one in her whole family who had never judged her for her dismissal of the family code, hadn't made it to Paradise after all.

"No!" she screamed.

A woman possessed, she hacked and slashed blindly, not caring in the slightest which side she killed. The frenzied nature of her assault created a wide gap in the packed group of combatants. When finally she dove out of the fray, she twirled around, whirling both swords in her hands, and split the faces of two soldiers who were brave enough to challenge her. When they fell, she followed the sound of Patrick's ranting. She found him battling with a giant elf who wielded a pair of black swords. Patrick shouted obscenities each time he dove into a hysterical attack, only to be beaten back by a tumult of parries and jabs. The elf had split the chainmail on Patrick's thigh and damaged his right vambrace so much it dangled off the hunchbacked man's massive arm. His skill was too great; and Patrick, too angry. He was swinging wildly, carelessly. Before long he would open himself up and receive a sword in the face for his troubles.

Moira sprinted toward the clash, ducking out of the way of charging soldiers, leaping over a couple others. She reached Patrick's backside just as the large elf launched into a flurry of cleaves and slashes. Leaping upward, she used Patrick as a steppingstone, kicking off him to continue her forward assault. Flying frontward, she twisted to give her slashes even greater power as she came crashing down. The elf edged away in time so that only the tips of her blades caught his flesh, scoring both his cheeks at once. Moira landed on both feet in a low crouch, her shortswords held one over the other in a defensive stance. Behind her, Patrick staggered ahead, almost falling on his face.

"What the *FUCK*!" he screamed.

"Sorry," Moira called out, chancing to glance over her shoulder.

Patrick's eyes widened as he huffed. "Moira?"

"It's me," she said. "Look out!"

Patrick tilted to the side, and a soldier's blade passed through the air where he'd been. The hunchback planted a meaty fist in the soldier's face, breaking his nose before gutting him with that massive sword of his. When he shoved the dying man away, he looked back at Moira. His face whitened.

Moira whirled back around and saw that another five elves had joined the one in black, who looked wild with rage, the dual scars, like red teardrops, tracing down his cheeks. Moira shifted position, standing sideways with her front leg bent and the rear leg straightened, one of her shortswords angled above her head while the other one was held out straight. A moment later Patrick was by her side, holding his blade by his waist with both hands.

"Just like old times?" he asked out the corner of his mouth.

"Just like old times," Moira echoed. "Only channel your anger. Don't be stupid."

"Yes, mistress," the deformed redhead said.

The elves rushed them, and Patrick sprang forward, this time swinging with measured strikes. Moira used his back as a pole, spinning from one side of him to the other, parrying jabs, and knocking aside slashes. One of the elves fell, then another, devastated by Patrick's sword. During one of Moira's revolutions, the elf in black was there to greet her, planting a boot squarely in her chest. The wounds the Judges had given her flared to life. She shrieked and twisted back to the other side, but there was no relief there. Another of the elves lashed out with his khandar, a blow Moira had no choice but to block. Had she tried to duck beneath it, the blade would have dug into Patrick's neck. A spike of pain coursed through her upper body when their swords met.

A hand wrapped around her, and Patrick scooped her up while ramming his shoulder into the elf in black. Patrick screamed, that shoulder obviously wounded and soaked in blood, but he pumped his legs nonetheless. He used his strong arm to toss Moira into the air. She did a pirouette, driving her foot into the square-faced elf's nose. He barked and stumbled away, blood gushing from his nostrils.

Patrick faced the massive elf while Moira landed and scampered back around him. They stood back to back, staring at the enemies that surrounded them.

"Sorry our reunion ended so quickly," said a winded Patrick.

"It's not over yet," answered Moira.

"No? Too bad. I'm getting tired of this."

"You can rest when you're dead."

"Ashhur help me, that's sort of the point."

The elves charged from all sides, holding their khandars like spears. Moira tensed for impact, but then the elves were thrown off balance by a mighty gust of wind. A round of explosions came next, as if people themselves were suddenly bursting all at once. Blood and viscera flew into the air in geysers all around, so thick that it fell like rain, coating everything.

"What the *fuck* was that?" shouted Moira.

"The undead," said Patrick hesitantly, obviously confused. "They . . . exploded."

A single word then rumbled over the battlefield, as potent as a million thunder strikes happening all at once.

"ENOUGH!"

It seemed for a moment as if the battle had ceased. In the middle of the chaos rose Ashhur, his silver armor layered with blood. He took a massive step, scattering the soldiers, Sisters, and Wardens before him. Never before had Moira seen a god look so angry, not even Karak. One of his hands was gathered into a fist, and the other held the limp form of one of the massive Judges—Lilah, the female. With a mighty swing of his arm, the deity tossed the giant lioness through the air, where she crashed down into another group of combatants. Moira heard a feline whimper. The thing wasn't dead.

Neither was the male. Kayne bounded through the throng, roaring, trampling soldiers beneath his claws. Ashhur slammed his palms together just as the lion hurdled toward him. The god's fingers knotted together, and he clobbered the male upside the head, snapping Kayne's head to the side and sending him soaring as well.

"KARAK, SHOW YOURSELF!" the deity roared.

"You will only face the true god of the land if you prove yourself worthy!" said another voice, softer but no less threatening, from behind her. She turned just as the soldiers guarding the portcullis parted, revealing a man she recognized standing there, his eyes glowing red, his cloak fluttering even though there was no breeze.

"Jacob, stand aside," Ashhur said coldly. "You do not frighten me."

Jacob Eveningstar? thought Moira. *Here in Veldaren?*

Beside her, Patrick growled.

"I am Velixar," the cloaked man said, laughter playing on his lips. "And honestly, my Lord, I *should* frighten you. Even the gods trembled before the beast."

The man who had once been Jacob slammed his hands together. A massive arc of black light shot forth, swallowing all in its path. Moira was caught in the wave and sent careening through the air along with at least two hundred others, Patrick included. They all landed in a heap fifty feet away, clearing a path between the god and the man who challenged him.

Moira groaned and shoved at the men piled atop her, trying to get loose. Nearby she heard Patrick cursing. Armor creaked, dying men moaned out their last breaths. But the one sound Moira *didn't* hear was the clash of steel on steel.

She finally wedged herself free from the tangled mass of humanity. Patrick was nearby, his powerful arms quivering as he tried to pick himself up off the ground. She ran to him, urged him to stand. The fighting around her began anew as Moira and Patrick fled to the shelter of the half-demolished stables nearby. While the others waged war, their attention was fixed on Ashhur and the First Man.

Ashhur held out his hand, and a radiant sword of pure light appeared in his grip.

"This ends now," the god said.

Moira couldn't turn away.

CHAPTER 48

Castle gates didn't exist. All that mattered was Ashhur. He would assail the deity while Karak remained inside the castle, waiting for the moment Ashhur was near defeat before emerging to finish him off.

He reached into Karak's deep well, siphoning the god's power as he had done many times before. Drawing upon the fount of knowledge of the demon inside him, he reached across time and space, deciphering ancient spells and incantations, building up his inner reserves, imprinting them onto his brain. He cast out a wide web, drawing energy from not only the God of Order but the God of Justice as well. *I am the child of two gods. I am the child of ALL gods!*

Velixar's body thrummed with energy, the very air around him growing unstable with charged particles, as if his tiny pocket of creation existed wholly separate from the world on which he stood. Electricity caused the pendant around his neck to vibrate. Thunderclouds billowed before his eyes, lightning crashed. Never before had he swallowed this much power. His nerve endings were on fire, pushing well past the threshold of pain. He ignored a speck of cowardice, which cried, *It is too much—too much!* For Velixar knew it was *never* too much. The demon whose name he had taken had told him so.

He closed his eyes, and the labyrinth of magic opened up. Millions upon millions of intersecting lines, like dust motes flittering through multiple shafts of light, became clear. For the first time Velixar understood, truly *understood*, the nature of the universe, the connection between all things, the web Celestia had woven, built up and over those that had come before, stretching all the way back to the beginning of time itself.

And in the middle of it all stood Karak and Ashhur, faulty vessels of once-powerful cosmic entities, entitled to the power of the universe but restrained, limited and made solid, by singular ideals.

It was Ashhur he focused on, illuminating the filaments of living energy that connected the deity to his multitude of marching corpses, bringing them to the forefront of the web. With the secret revealed, he leapt forth, snagging each of the threads in his own ever-growing web, pumping his influence into them.

The Beast of a Thousand Faces had once commanded an army of the undead, now so would he, even if he had to rip control from a god to do so.

He felt Ashhur's pain as his energy traveled along the ethereal filaments and surged into the god, contaminating his essence. The thread doubled in width as Velixar and the deity fought over control, but he couldn't sever Ashhur's connection. The undead stopped moving, the contradictory orders passed along the invisible threads locking them in place.

They struggled, god and man-turned-god, the tide shifting one way then the other, then rolling back again. Ashhur suffered, the toll of his weakened state made all the more horrific by the constant push and pull. Velixar felt none of that; he was beyond pain. Though he knew his soul was expanding far beyond what should have been possible, he felt nothing but the exhilaration of conflict, of power, the thrill of driving a god to his knees.

Potency continued to pulse into him. The cosmic dust of the universe seeped out of his pores. Velixar expelled more and more of himself, a conduit draining energy from one source and shoving it into another. Ashhur was falling, failing, growing weaker by the moment, but the deity wouldn't surrender. Velixar grinned, his hair lashing about his face, and poured as much as he possibly could into the spell. The threads binding the undead swelled, became volatile. It was then that Ashhur did relinquish control, and Velixar withdrew in horror. The energy he had hurled in an attempt to thwart the deity instead surged into the undead in a single, violent current. The corpses expanded as the force infused them, their every particle alive with more power than their frail forms could hold. The bodies exploded, filling the afternoon sky with torrents of blood and bits of bone.

The energy snapped back into Velixar, causing him to recoil from its force. His knees buckled, but he didn't fall. The pain returned. His view of the web crumbled, revealing the battle that still raged, the combatants bathed in the falling blood of the undead. But still he felt vital, he felt *strong*. And then Ashhur stood from the swarm of battle, himself bathed in blood. The deity beat back the Judges, who attacked him on sight, and then bellowed to the heavens.

"KARAK, SHOW YOURSELF!"

"You will only face the true god of the land if you prove yourself worthy!" Velixar called out. The soldiers who had been guarding him, including the Lord Commander, scattered.

The deity leveled his gaze at him. "Jacob, stand aside. You do not frighten me."

"I am Velixar now," he shot back, laughing. "And honestly, my Lord, I *should* frighten you. Even the gods trembled before the beast."

There were thousands of people between he and Ashhur, and Velixar again drew on the endless pit of strength, creating a violent wave of dark energy that threw everyone, both friend and foe alike, into the air as if they were scraps of parchment caught by a gale-force wind. When it was done, an expanse of bloodstained cobbles stretched out before him, he standing on one end and Ashhur at the other. Those tossed aside, the ones who were capable enough stood up and began fighting once more.

Ashhur held out his hand, and his ethereal sword grew from nothingness. The god then ran forward, streamers of blood trailing behind him, the glowing blade held above his head, ready to cleave him in two.

Velixar laughed as he reached back inside, tapping into Karak's might. His power doubled, further pushing against the boundary of his physical form. Ashhur thought him unarmed; the deity didn't realize that to Velixar, every corpse, every puddle of blood, every bit of bone, was a weapon.

The pools of crimson lining the open space shimmered. Dark, oily vines shot out of them, wrapping around Ashhur's legs, his waist, his arms, his head. The god was a mere twenty feet away when his momentum stopped, the bloodvines growing more elastic and potent with each word Velixar spat from his mouth. Ashhur grunted, trying to snap the tendrils, but every broken one was replaced by another, and then another, until practically the whole of the deity's form was wrapped in their pulsating, meaty limbs. Ashhur dropped to his knees. Soldiers skirmishing close by, sensing an opportunity, rushed the struggling god, stabbing at him with swords not strong enough to even scratch Ashhur's armor. Some jumped on his back, trying to gouge the deity's neck, but their blades scraped off his shimmering flesh.

Velixar's fingers worked quickly, twisting into rune after rune. The soldiers attacking Ashhur, all twenty of them, screamed at once, their bodies bulging within their armor as they were lifted into the air. The High Prophet of Karak then flipped his hand over, and the men's insides came pouring out their mouths. Their bones crunched and pulverized, creating tiny shards that ejected along with the spray of blood and minced organs. When it was done, their armor clanked down to the cobbles, filled with empty husks of flesh. The mess of blood, viscera, and bone began to swirl around the fraught deity, growing faster with each passing second. Velixar laughed and laughed, shoving as much power as he could into the smallest fragments of matter. The rotating cone closed around Ashhur, squeezing him. Smoke rose from the top of the funnel as charged blood particles singed his godly flesh; the hardened bits of bone pricked him like a million tiny needles. Velixar brought his hands together slowly, attempting to crush the deity, but the resistance was great. Ashhur bellowed, his sword slicing upward through the wall of blood and bone that crushed in on him. The spell broke. Once more the power snapped back into Velixar, knocking him back a step.

Ashhur tore the remaining bloodvines off him, scowling as he slowly rose to his feet. Velixar gritted his teeth and cursed, eyes flitting across the arena of war until he caught sight of what he was looking for: a pair of giant bodies covered with bloodstained fur, struggling to stand amid the chaos after being walloped by a god.

"Kayne, Lilah, to me!" Velixar shouted, just as Ashhur let out a cry and brought his sword down with all his might. Velixar raised a globe of shadow and purple fire around himself. When Ashhur's sword struck the outer edge of the sphere, the blade dug in, sending out geysers of flame that singed the god's armor. Yet still Ashhur pressed against the sphere, buckling it, cracking it.

Velixar battled against the force of the deity as best he could, driven to his knees beneath that brutal strength. He then saw the two Judges limp out of the mayhem. Velixar squeezed his eyes shut, confident that his shield would hold for a time, and transferred energy from himself to the lions. They shuddered, dropped to their bellies, and then stood up once more. When they took their next steps, neither was limping. Kayne roared and Lilah followed suit.

Ashhur glanced behind him, then back at Velixar, his face a mask of rage that appeared and disappeared between wisps of shadow and jets of flame.

"They aren't enough," the god said, his words grinding into Velixar's skull.

"I know," Velixar retorted through clenched teeth.

The strength he held, while great, was inadequate. He had to dive deeper into the well, find a new source of power. Placing one hand on the ground, he closed his eyes and concentrated, felt the burning heart of Dezrel buried deep beneath the soil, the fragment of Celestia herself. *Who needs the Black Spire when you have the power of a god?* A cackle escaped his lips as he focused on that energy, on that massive blazing mass, drawing its power up through the bedrock and into him. His eyes bulged from his head, and his skin felt on fire, so quickly did the transfer come. Outstretching both arms toward the approaching lions, he poured it into them.

The lions fell back on their haunches, bellowing. Warriors from both sides scurried away from their writhing forms. Ashhur ceased attempting to break through the shield and spun around.

Velixar looked on in wonder, feeling the inferno of Dezrel's everlasting heart as he consumed it. That same inferno now raged in the Judges, burning them, altering them, *improving* them. The lions' fur began to smoke, smoldering away in a flash of white light. The seams in their flesh split, leaking magma that melted the cobbles beneath them. The flesh itself became like stone, black and scorched like the onyx statues guarding the portcullis behind him. Men screamed. The lions' teeth and claws became like black diamonds as they writhed.

When it was over, the smoking forms of the Judges rolled over and stood, shaking their heads like dogs shedding water. Kayne took a thunderous step forward, the blood on the cobbles boiling where his paw landed. His mane was a ring of fire. Lilah opened her maw and roared. Both lions then swiveled their heads toward Ashhur, flames raging in their eyes, their nostrils, their mouths.

"The impure god," Kayne said, his voice like a boulder tumbling down a mountainside.

"The bringer of chaos," added Lilah.

The fiery Judges leapt at Ashhur. The god slashed with his sword, batting the male aside, sending chunks of volcanic rock from the lion's body where his blade struck. Lilah bounded at the deity from the other side, her jaws closing around Ashhur's forearm. The lioness's teeth pierced the god's vambrace, cracking the unearthly metal. Ashhur screamed and battered the lioness with his opposite fist, sending more chunks of blackened rock flying but doing little damage to her.

Kayne pounced as Ashhur tried to free himself. The lion's flaming maw wrapped around the god's neck, its teeth digging in deeply. Ashhur threw his head back and screamed. Magma poured from the god's wounds, further stoking the Judges' fire. The deity's glowing eyes dimmed ever so slightly. The blazing female jerked backward, shattering Ashhur's vambrace and flinging it aside, smoking. She then bore down and lunged, her maw opened wide.

Ashhur's fist shot out, plunging deep into the lioness's flame-filled throat. Lilah's burning eyes bulged, even as her jaws snapped shut, further crunching and melting the god's armor. Ashhur's face scrunched, and he let out a roar as he whipped his upper body around, sending the female Judge careening across the battlefield, crushing and burning those unfortunate enough to be standing in the way. The deity then raised his hand, coated in red-hot rock, and snatched Kayne by his fiery mane. He forced the lion's head back, the teeth withdrawing from his neck. With a mighty heave, he lifted the gigantic lion up above his head and slammed it back down. The ground cracked on impact.

Velixar's eyes widened. The energy from the heart of the world continued to flow into him uncontrollably, and he poured all he could into the Judges. The lions were on their feet a moment later, assaulting Ashhur with all they had, but the god was more than their equal. He batted away jaws, slammed his fist into their faces when they snapped at him, driving them backward. He was like a raging comet, his force not to be withstood. Velixar couldn't understand where he found the strength. He looked about him, where the battle had once raged. It raged no more. Combatants from both sides simply stood there, gawking at the clash of god and ungodly beasts. The Wardens who still lived, as well as half of the human soldiers, were kneeling, looking up at Ashhur with pleading reverence in their eyes. Everyone was coated with blood, making it impossible to tell whose side they'd fought on.

"No!" shouted Velixar, turning just in time to see Kayne leap at Ashhur. The deity ducked out of the way and slashed upward with his sword. Kayne's momentum carried him directly into the blade, slicing him from nose to rear. The two halves of the flaming lion soared through the air, and when they landed, both halves exploded into chunks of smoking, molten rock.

The lion's mate let out a rumbling howl of despair and charged as well. Ashhur plunged his fist into the lioness's snout, driving her maw into the ground. Then he sidestepped and brought his glowing blade down on her neck, splitting through the solid stone and roiling molten rock. The gaps in Lilah's stony flesh ceased to glow, smoke rising instead. Ashhur grabbed the beast's severed head by the ear and lifted it. He turned to Velixar, showing the head to him before tossing it aside.

From all around the god came a chorus of gasps, cheers, and prayers.

With the Judges gone, the power that forged them had nowhere to go but back to its originator. It slammed into Velixar, the combined energies churning, boiling over. He fell to his knees as Ashhur stormed toward him. His shadowy, protective sphere dissolved. Smoke billowed from Velixar's throat when he tried to speak. He tried to form runes with his fingers, but his flesh bulged and rippled. He screamed in pain as the pendant on his chest burned through his ribcage.

"It . . . cannot . . . be," he gasped.

"Indeed it can."

Ashhur snatched him up by the front of his cloak, lifting him into the air. Velixar felt no fear of the god; he was too fearful of what was happing inside him to worry about much else. He felt his flesh expand, his blood boil, his bones begin to shatter under the massive weight of all that he'd swallowed.

The deity lugged him off the slate walk while awestruck onlookers gaped. Velixar couldn't blink, couldn't move, couldn't defend himself; it was like he was filled with a raging star that pressed against his limits, ready to explode. He felt impossibly stiff. Almost gently, Ashhur set Velixar's two feet on the ground and stood before him, glowing sword in hand, shaking his head. Velixar glanced above the deity. He was now facing the Castle of the Lion, its three towers rising above the wall and into the afternoon sky like stone fingers.

"This . . . should never . . . have happened," he murmured, looking up at Ashhur. "The soul . . . is limitless . . . so said . . . the demon . . . "

Ashhur shook his head. "The mortal body is not." He almost sounded compassionate. "Never listen to a demon. They lie."

The god stepped backward and swung his radiant sword. The blade cut through the man's shoulder, sliced down through his ribcage, and stopped upon hitting his spine. A rush of white-hot pain surged through him. All of the energy Velixar had absorbed came rushing out of him in a giant shaft of translucent fire. People screamed and fled. Ribbons of heat curled around the entirety of Velixar's being. The beam of energy slammed into the wall around the castle, instantly disintegrating the bodies that hung there. The wall then detonated, crumbing, the heavy stones toppling one after another. The beam continued on its way, growing ever larger as it punched through the bottom of the three towers. The sound of crunching rock filled the air as the towers wavered, falling against one another, losing form as they collapsed, stone by stone, brick by brick, with a sound like an avalanche. The beam continued on, pulverizing the opposite side of the wall.

And then it was over. Velixar fell, his innards spilling over the cobbles, adding to the gore. The castle and its wall kept crumbling while Ashhur stood over him, a look of triumph on his godly face.

I am sorry, my Lord, Velixar thought, reeling with the pain of a mortal wound. *I have failed you once more . . .*

CHAPTER 49

Nothing had ever filled Aully with as much dread. Not being thrown in the dungeon, not watching the butchering of Noni and Aaromar, not those long days she sat fearing for her mother's life, not even being forced to sit there helpless as Kindren had his fingers sliced off, one by one. No, the thing that lunged out of the forest before them, toppling trees as it roared, was terror incarnate.

Aully grasped hold of her mother and Kindren and wailed. Her entire body was quivering. She thought of her old friends, now gone after the massive creature tore through the city in the trees, devouring all it came across. Aully had escaped that fate, but now she and those who fled were trapped between the rampaging demon in front of them and the sheer cliff that plummeted into an ocean inlet behind. The choice between becoming a monster's snack and plunging to her death was not a choice at all. Not even having with them Ceredon, the Quellan prince who had sacrificed so much to save them back in Dezerea, gave her a glimmer of hope.

"Keep steady!" Ceredon shouted, running along the line of survivors. The horde was huge, over two thousand as far as Aully could guess. Most of them were her fellow Stonewood Dezren, but interspersed among them were a number of the eastern deity's human soldiers, their armor polished black. Although the humans seemed anxious, as if looking for a fight, the elves stared ahead with wide eyes, gawking at the beast rumbling toward them as their feet shuffled backward, edging closer and closer to the rim of the cliff. Few of them were warriors, and those that were had long before pledged their allegiance to Carskel. Aully spotted her bastard brother among their numbers, standing alongside Ethir Ayers, both of their expressions blank with shock, and for a waning moment hatred bubbled up within her, overtaking her fear. She scowled and shoved away from her mother and Kindren's embrace, heat growing on her fingertips as she mouthed the words to a spell.

A hand grabbed hers. It was Ceredon. "Save it," the handsome prince told her. "We will need it."

The spell dispersed.

Ceredon kissed her on the cheek and dashed away, heading back toward the small cluster of human soldiers. When they spoke this time, it was hurried, hands waving, voices raised and frantic. Finally a woman, the most beautiful human Aully had ever seen, grabbed a man with a forked yellow beard by the collar, growled at him, and shoved him away. She handed Ceredon one of the shortswords that hung from her belt. A funny-looking man with a thick red beard and wearing a bright green, bloodstained robe, laughed. The odd man smacked Ceredon on the shoulder and hurriedly called out to the throng of humans in the common tongue.

The demon lurched into action, barreling across the stony ground like a charging bull. The thing was huge and bulbous, at least forty feet long, with a lashing spiked tail. Its rear legs ended in hooves that tore up the ground with each lumbering stride, sending bits of gravel and dirt into the air. The front legs each ended in five long, wickedly sharp claws. Its head was like that of a reptilian horse, with a triangular, slotted nose above a wide mouth filled with huge teeth that dripped with the blood of her people. A pair of giant tusks curled around from the hinge in its jaw, each coming to a point on either side of that slotted nose, and as it ran, it dipped its head, those tusks gouging into the earth. Its eyes were like a raging red inferno. Its forked serpent's tongue licked the air. It was a nightmare made flesh.

Every remaining human soldier who had a horse mounted up. The beautiful woman swung up onto her charger, drew her sword, and sounded the charge. Hooves pounded the gravel-strewn ground as the humans fanned out. Those who had no horses ran behind, clustered together. There had to be four hundred of them.

"Do not just sit there!" screamed Ceredon. The prince stormed toward Davishon Hinsbrew, who stood gawking just outside of Carskel and his party, and slapped him across the cheek. Davishon staggered back, eyeing the Quellan with fright. "You have a bow—use it," Ceredon growled at him before dashing away.

Davishon glanced back at Carskel for a moment before he seemed to gather his wits. The elf ran along the line of terrified elves, picking out those few who held bows, and pleading with them to follow him. He snatched his bow as he ran, nocking it just before he reached the front of the line. Only twenty other elves joined him. Their arrows sailed high into the air before descending toward the charging beast.

"Aully, Kindren—with me!" Ceredon yelled. Aully looked away from the archers and saw her protector dashing through the crowd. She was too numb to argue, so she simply followed his command, grabbing Kindren's hand and putting one foot in front of the other as if in a dream. Lady Audrianna shouted at them to stay put, but her voice was carried away by the ruckus.

Ceredon reached them, grabbed them both by the hand, and then yanked them through the crowd, where another contingent of humans awaited. Unlike the other humans, these wore simple furs and knitted breeches instead of armor. The oddly dressed man in the pointed hat was among them.

Aully felt herself flying forward as Ceredon shoved her and Kindren in the odd man's direction. "That's all you have?" the man asked.

"For now, yes. All that I know of. Now go!"

With that, Ceredon sped off, chasing after the stampeding humans on foot. Aully could do nothing but gape as she watched him run headlong for the towering beast.

"You two, get in line!" the odd redhead shouted. "If you have magic, use it!"

"Turock, they might be elves, but they're children," one of the other spellcasters added.

"I know."

Aully's head slowly turned, and she saw Turock, the redhead, frowning at her. He shook his head and faced forward, along with the other sixteen men who made up his troupe. "All you have!" he exclaimed. "Do it now!" Their arms raised, words of magic poured form their mouths.

Hands wrapped around Aully's waist, pulling her away just before she was struck by the jagged stream of lightning that leapt from the hands of the man closest to her. Kindren wheeled her around, staring at her intensely. His cheeks were flushed, and he blinked rapidly as if he'd just awoken from a horrible dream.

"Aully," he said. "Aully, we can help. I know it's frightening, but together we can be strong."

"Together we can be strong," she repeated. She glanced down at her hands. There was a tingling in her chest, a sensation she hadn't felt in far too long. "Together, we can be strong."

"We can."

They turned about and faced the rampaging beast. Arrows bounced off its thick scales, the spellcasters' fireballs, bolts of energy, and electric strikes dissipated against its hide, seemingly to no effect. And yet the monster's progress was slowed as the soldiers on horseback raced past it, lashing at its legs with their swords and axes, gouging it with pikes. The beast reared up, its lashing tail thumping a trio of riders, impaling one and knocking the others off their steeds. With its underbelly exposed, the soldiers on foot hurled spears, if they had them. A couple found gaps between the large scales and dangled there like ornaments. Most of them simply bounced off.

"Damn it all, if you're going to help, *help*!" shouted the man in the funny hat.

Aully and Kindren nodded to each other before raising their arms. Aully quickly turned her eyes away from Kindren's mangled hand, not wanting to see his thumb and small finger sticking out on either side of his fist like lost lovers separated by an ocean of scars. She focused on his voice instead, on the confidence with which he spoke. Suddenly, despite the hopelessness of what they faced, Aully felt at ease. She remembered what she'd lost, what she still had. She remembered traipsing with Kindren through the desert, eating foreign foods and laughing with the locals. She thought of the times they'd met in the crypts beneath Dezerea, of Kindren's broad smile as he spoke to her of legends and days long passed.

But most of all, she remembered what it was like to love and be loved, to live each day knowing that no matter what might happen, she would remain strong, that the strength she held inside her was not hers alone, but a gift to be shared with *everyone* she loved.

Aully chanted, and a raging stream of fire leapt from her hands. It was thicker than those created by the other spellcasters, even the man in green. The stream arced through the air, blazing through the monster's horns and lashing against its face like a crashing wave. The beast dropped down on all fours and turned its head to the side, seemingly wounded. Aully heard Turock utter, "That was unexpected."

To her left, Kindren's winding electrical charge zapped across empty space and struck the creature in the shoulder. The massive thing shrugged it off and took a hurtling step toward the soldiers clustered in the middle of the open ground. The men shrieked and tried to retreat, tripping over one another. The monster threw back its head and opened its hinged mouth. The horns that extended in front of its maw swung out wide like an insect's mandibles.

"It's going to eat them!" Aully cried.

Instinctively, she reached out and grabbed Kindren's hand, in that hurried moment not caring it was his mangled one. She slid her fingers around the stumps of his. She squeezed her eyes shut, quickly mouthing the words of a spell she had never used. She felt Kindren's inner strength, his connection to the weave, and then her eyes snapped open. Still chanting, she watched the ground in front of the soldiers rise and fold over, the solid bedrock beneath the cliff's surface forming a stone shield that curled atop the fumbling men. The beast's head came down, maw cracking against the earthen shield with a solid *crunch*. The mandible-like horns snapped shut, wrapping around the shield and skewering two men, but the deed had been done. With the monster dazed, if only for a second, the soldiers were given their opportunity to flee. They scattered across the rocky field in all directions.

"More!" Turock shouted. "No relenting!"

The spellcasters, along with Aully and Kindren, continued their assault. Other Dezren stepped forward, joining with the others, their magics weak. But at least they were trying. The creature dislodged itself from the earthen barricade, shook its head, and was thrown into a rage. It lashed out at the soldiers on horseback that circled it even as its hide was pummeled with magical attacks. Two men died, then four, then another six, their armor shredding as easily as their flesh beneath the monster's claws. The blood of men filled the air.

"The spells—they aren't strong enough!" hollered Kindren, launching a weak salvo of energy at the beast.

"I know!" Aully said.

The creature rumbled to the right, using its tusks to knock men off their horses. No more arrows fell toward it—the elves had likely exhausted their supply—and the magical attacks were pathetic. The spellcasters were growing tired. Aully herself was drained almost to the point of collapsing. Finally, when she uttered the words and flicked her fingers, nothing happened. Her magic was gone.

Now unimpeded, the demon turned about and hurtled toward them. The throng of elves behind Aully shuffled backward. Screams filled the air as a few of them backed up too far, plummeting off the edge of the cliff, their bodies crunching when they hit the rocks below. The soldiers on horses, who had been attacking the beast, turned tail and fled. The demon's eyes were like liquid fire, growing larger by the second, radiating both hatred and hunger. Aully grabbed Kindren and turned, running toward the lip of the cliff, searching for her mother. Lady Audrianna gathered the two youths in her embrace, and all three knelt down on the uneven, rocky soil.

"Goddess above," said Aully's mother, "we give our lives to you, to protect and hold once we reach your side."

"I love you all," Aully said.

Kindren squeezed her tight. "Always and forever."

The demon howled, sounding much too close, and though Aully didn't want to look, she did anyway. The beast veered to the side, a rope around its neck. Aully's eyes followed the length of the rope, which ended in the hand of brave Ceredon, standing atop a galloping horse. The elf then jumped, dangling by the rope, holding on for dear life as the demon swung its head and him along with it. The beast skidded to a halt, the hail of rock and other earthen fragments bombarding the cowering elves as its claws dug into the ground. The demon swiped at Ceredon, knocking him around like a pendulum, until the rope broke and the elf fell to the ground. Defiant, he scampered back to his feet, ripped the shortsword the human woman had given him from his belt, and hurled it at the beast. The sword ricocheted harmlessly off the creature's snout.

"Darakken!" the elf shouted, shaking an angry fist at the beast. "You want a meal, you devour *me*!"

The demon reared back, its tusks retracting once more, and then a mouth filled with giant teeth lurched toward the lone, defiant elf.

Aully tore away from Kindren and ran, knowing she would never get there in time, knowing there was nothing she could do even if she did. Kindren tackled her from behind.

"Ceredon, *no*!" she screamed.

Ceredon dropped to his knees, his head back as the demon's maw rapidly descended on him. He couldn't help but smile. It hadn't mattered what anyone had done, how brave any of the soldiers had been in defending their lives. It didn't matter how much magic they threw at the beast, how many arrows plinked against its hide. In the end, it was Boris Marchant's version of the story of how the evil thing was defeated before that told him all he needed to know. Because of that, he finally understood the true meaning behind the words Celestia had whispered to him in Dezerea. *Become the mountain.*

A mountain is resilient. A mountain stands unmoving and accepts whatever abuse nature brings upon it without complaint. A mountain offers up its surface as a sacrifice for all the creatures that call it home.

The descent of Darakken ceased.

The ground rumbled beneath Ceredon's knees, shaking him to the core, but he didn't move. He kept his gaze up, staring at the ancient demon as its fiery red eyes widened. It huffed, casting down a gust of breath that reeked of smoke and rotten meat. The thing then reared up on its hind legs, pawing at its chest.

Ceredon looked on in astonishment as the ground rose up around the beast, swallowing its hooves, its reverse-jointed knees.

The earth rumbled once more, and Ceredon finally scurried backward as lances of stone burst from the ground, pointed tips driving into the demon's hide, shattering its scales, making it bleed. *Demon's blood,* Ceredon thought as he put more distance between himself and the demon. *Elf's blood.*

Spires continued to break out of the soil. One lanced Darakken's shoulder. One broke through its clawed hand and exited the other side before embedding in its neck. One punctured its back, extending outward until it punched through the creature's neck as well. The demon struggled, gurgling in pain, but only succeeded in thrusting the earthen spears deeper into its body.

Soon, at least a hundred of those granite lances locked the demon in place, bent upright. The blood continued to gush from each and every wound, but the flow slowed, the blood seeming to harden as it rolled over its scales, as if it were turning to mud, then clay, then solid granite. Its struggles diminished as well, and there was an audible *creak* each time a limb bent. The area beneath the demon's scales, where its heart should have been, began to glow, and Ceredon swore he saw the darkened outline of a book in the center of the light. That light was soon covered over by a thick glob of soil-like blood that oozed from the demon's throat.

Darakken's scales slowly changed color, transforming from green-black and shimmering to a deep red and then to a pale shade of brown. Ceredon looked on in awe as those same scales seemed to calcify, nodules rising on them, covering them over, filling in the gaps between them. The thing was turning to stone before his eyes.

Become the mountain, indeed.

The earth swallowed the demon from the bottom up, snaking over the stone spires, congealing, becoming solid. The last thing Ceredon saw of the beast was its eye, the red now faded, as it rolled and stared down at him in both fear and hatred. Finally, that too was covered over by the upward cascade of dirt, clay, and stone.

Darakken was no more.

"That . . . how did you do that?" Ceredon heard the spellcaster named Turock ask.

Ceredon stood in front of what was now a stony hillock. The thing took up much of the clearing, closing his view of the forest behind. The soldiers who had survived the demon's assault rounded the massive obstruction, some on horseback, most on foot, limping. Rachida, a woman Ceredon had met once long ago when Karak's First Families visited Quellasar, rode elegantly into view. He nodded to her, and she nodded back before going about taking measure of her losses. Ceredon lifted his gaze to the sky, tears welling up. He faced north, toward Celestia's hidden star, and whispered, "Thank you."

The deed is not yet done. Her voice was an enraged whisper on the wind. Ceredon whirled around and faced the mob of Stonewood Dezren that lingered by the cliff's edge. All their eyes were on the heavens, their expressions of relief washing away, replaced by confusion. Even Aully, Kindren, and Lady Audrianna, who had been striding toward him, stopped and stared. Had they heard the voice as well? Was that possible?

My children have disappointed me, the goddess said, and sure enough the Dezren *did* hear, for many of them fell to their knees, breathing in panicked breaths. *You were blessed with lives longer than any other mortal beings, and yet those lives were squandered by hatred and war. Beauty was handed to you, and yet it was not enough. All you had was bartered to a childish god, for greed, for fleeting power and shallow pride. Such immaturity, such ugliness. I have stood aside and allowed you to err, but no longer. Your sins shall not be tolerated.*

The elves surged forward, their pleading voices rising to the heavens, while the humans stood around and gawked at the scene, confused. Ceredon lowered his eyes and saw one elf standing out among the rest. For a moment, Ceredon was taken aback—the elf looked like a thinner, younger version of Cleotis Meln. The elf raised his hands to the sky.

"You owe us!" he shouted. "It was *you* who turned your back on *us*!"

Out of the corner of his eye, Ceredon saw Aully glaring at the elf, her hands curled into fists.

The wind blew silently for a moment before Celestia spoke once more.

You were to be the wardens of humanity. Her voice came from all around, on the wind and in the stillness between, and it was laced with fury. *And when your leaders refused, I accepted your choice. I let you be, with two simple doctrines: Protect the beauty of this world, and remain impartial in the affairs of man. Both have been broken, and those who have broken them, in all the lands you call home, shall be punished. No longer will you know beauty. No longer will your lives be long. You will only know an undying hunger, an empty pit in your souls where my love once resided. You will always remember all that you once had, and the knowledge that it is no longer yours will drive you mad.*

Some of the gathered elves began weeping. Others shouted angry decrees at the heavens. Ceredon pivoted on his feet and walked toward Aullienna, gathering the young princess in his arms, holding her head to his chest. Kindren was soon there as well, followed by Aully's mother. The four of them stood there amid the lament and anger, holding each other silently.

Vile children of mine, I revoke my love. Take my curse instead.

The land filled with the screams of a thousand voices. Ceredon, Aully, Kindren, and Lady Audrianna separated, looking all around them. One out of every two elves had dropped to the ground, where all of them writhed in pain. Among them was the elf who looked so much like Cleotis Meln. Their bodies contorted, their teeth bared. It looked as if there was another entity beneath their flesh, fighting to get out. Ceredon backed away from them, toward the hillock that had once been a demon, dragging the three frightened Dezren with him.

"Celestia, what is this?" he whispered.

He looked to the sky and saw a dark cloud approaching. It moved faster than any cloud he had ever seen before, churning and bulging, growing bigger and bigger on the horizon. He dragged Aully and the others a few steps onto the hill, keeping his eyes up, and as it drew nearer, he realized that what he saw was hundreds of winged horses, flying in formation, descending as they approached.

You faithful few, accept my sanctuary.

"Aully!" he shouted. "Kindren, Lady Audrianna, all of you who haven't fallen, come!"

Ceredon raced up the rocky side of the steep hillock, the others on his heels. The winged horses were so close now that he could see the mist from their noses when they exhaled. He continued to climb, stumbling over loose stones, holding tight to Aully's hand just in case she fell. The first of the horses broke away from the rest, sailing over his head, soaring toward the other side of the knoll, and pivoting in midair. It was a she, and she landed on the broad, flat surface at the top of the hillock, whinnying and snorting and kicking her hooves. Another of the winged horses landed just behind her.

Ceredon raced for the mare, dragging Aully behind him. The horse bent her front legs, lowering herself so they could climb on her back.

"Two on each horse!" he shouted to the throng of elves as they crested the hillock's short peak. More and more winged horses landed while the rest circled up above, waiting for space atop the narrow crest. Ceredon helped Aully onto the horse's back and then climbed on in front of her. "Hold on to me tight," he told her. He glanced over at Kindren, who was helping Lady Audrianna climb atop another of the majestic, winged beasts. The boy prince looked at him, and he dipped his head. "She will be safe," Ceredon told him.

Their horse rose to her feet and galloped along the ridge. Then, she took to the air, her massive wings flapping. Wind blew through

Ceredon's hair; Aully's arms squeezed his waist. The horse banked low and to the side, turning toward the east, and when she did so, Ceredon gaped in both horror and wonder at the scene down below. Elf by elf, winged horse by winged horse, the Dezren took to the sky behind him. The human soldiers had tried to scamper up the side of the hillock, but it was too steep, and they were slow, weighed down by their armor. The cursed elves had risen. Their skin was gray, their faces hideous, and they attacked the humans with a sort of bloodlust that made Ceredon's skin crawl. Men screamed, swords clashed, blood spilled. Once more violence had come to Dezrel.

The winged horse pitched back to level out, and thankfully Ceredon could no longer see what was happening below. Soon, even the sound of the clash faded away as they soared higher and higher, rising above Stonewood Forest and the demolished city within the trees. He took in all he saw, and though the wind was freezing this high up, he barely felt it, for what filled his vision was beautiful.

"Where's Kindren?" Aully shouted, still pressed against his back.

"Right behind us," Ceredon called out over his shoulder. "With your mother."

"And where are we going?"

"Home." He couldn't say where they'd find it, but he knew that's where they were going.

CHAPTER

50

Velixar lay on his side, his blood leaking away as Ashhur towered above. Scarlet drops caught fire on the god's shimmering blade. He couldn't begin to interpret Ashhur's stare. Was it anger? Regret? Or detachment, the curiosity of one who'd stepped on a strange insect?

All around them, those who had been fighting for Dezrel's soul gawked.

"You," Velixar gasped, and despite his grievous wound he tried crawling toward his former god. If only his power had been stronger. If only he hadn't pushed his limits, if only his human body weren't so pathetically weak. "You won't . . . "

The ruins of the castle shifted, followed by the *boom* of heavy footsteps that shook the ground. Ashhur looked away and lifted his sword. Velixar heard Ashhur sigh, and he knew Karak had finally emerged from the wreckage.

"You should not have come," said Karak.

Ashhur's mouth twitched, the faintest hint of a smile on his face.

"You knew I would," Ashhur said. "This conflict must end."

It was pandemonium as those who had been battling in the gods' names fled.

Karak was just beyond Velixar's sight, and he turned his head to look. His god wore his brilliant armor; his short, dark hair was blown back by a breeze, and he held his fiery blade in both hands. His armor was stained with soot and clay, and a grim smile played across his face, eagerness in his eyes that burned greater than his sword. This battle, Velixar realized, both had been yearning to revisit since their fight in Haven ended in a draw. Damn the followers and armies and supplies and movements. There would be no retreat this time. Their blades were drawn, their power naked. Here they would fight until one of them would forever die.

Velixar's fingers pressed against the blood-soaked cobbles, and he begged for strength. Only the magic of the ancient beast within him kept him alive, kept his rent body together, kept the blood pumping through severed veins. The pendant that had singed his chest pulsed with energy. It was agony, and took great concentration, but he would not die. Not yet. Before he passed, he would see a victor. The damn world owed him that much.

"What happened to the paradise we were to create?" Karak asked as he braced his back leg for a lunge. "What happened to the perfection we swore would blossom? We watched worlds burn. Ours was to be different. Ours was to be better. How did our creations fail us so?"

Ashhur settled low, readying his blade, preparing for the charge. "They never failed us," he said. "Not as much as we failed them, as *you* failed them."

Karak's smile spread full, and it was a look Velixar hardly recognized. His god seemed . . . crazed. Feverish. "You are right," his deity said. "We gave them their free will. Knowing their imperfections. Knowing their sin. Every murder, every blasphemy, it is on our heads. It is our failure, our greatest failure, and once your body breaks before me, I will sweep across this land correcting it."

Ashhur looked horrified.

"You would strip them of their will? Their choices? Their *very souls*? This conflict was your doing, not theirs."

The fire on Karak's blade burned all the greater.

"You still don't understand?" he asked. "Life is chaos. Creation is stubborn and wild. There is only one way to obtain true order. Only one way to obtain true justice, yet you are too blind to see it. Emptiness, my brother. Pure, quiet, blissful emptiness. We were doomed the moment we stepped foot on this land and sought to create anything other than monuments to ourselves. Proud gods are we, but we must be prouder still. We must cast off these inferior beings, cast off our need for their love, our yearning for them to live and grow and understand things they will never truly comprehend. They will only know suffering, misery, and confusion before they succumb to their graves. You cannot cast dirt to the stars and expect it to understand the vastness, and that is all these humans are, the dust beneath our feet. Let me help you before it is too late. Before these wretched things, by their very existence, result in the death of a god."

Velixar was in too much agony to understand it, his god's words flowing over him like a frozen wind, their meaning horrifying yet so simple, so frighteningly believable, just like the vision of a burning, peaceful world Karak had shown him. Looking to Ashhur, he thought there was no way another perfect being could hear and not agree. What counter could Karak's brother offer? What wisdom could he refute it with? The god stood still as a statue before the ruins of the castle as Karak waited for an answer. And when it came, it came with tears in Ashhur's eyes.

"No," he said, his deep voice but a whisper.

"Why?" Karak asked, not hiding his frustration and disappointment.

"Because I love them. And I will die to save them."

Ashhur leapt forward. Velixar craned his neck to watch, his dying breaths stolen away. Ashhur's sword swung, Karak blocked, and at their connection the very ground shook from the shock wave, further toppling the castle's ruins. The massive throng of terrified onlookers shrieked. A mindless roar rumbled from Karak's throat as he pushed back, muscles bulging, the world beneath him breaking from the strain. At last Ashhur relented, only to swing again. Sword striking, sword blocking, each became a blur, light and fire twirling, mixing. A chunk of the wall still standing was crushed beneath the might of their struggle. Suddenly it was a display Velixar no longer felt worthy to witness, and casting his eyes to the bloodstained cobbles beneath him he crawled, dragging his lower half behind him. He cried out in pain as he lurched over the remnants of one of the onyx lions that had guarded the castle portcullis. He had to be closer. What power he had left, he wished to give to his god. No matter what, Ashhur could not win. Not after all he, Velixar, had given . . . all he'd lost.

As Velixar crawled, his ears ringing from the awesome noise, he felt magic begin to grow around him. It was low at first, a tingle, but soon it seemed the very air was saturated by some ethereal presence. Velixar didn't know what it was, but it made him afraid, and he crawled faster. His intestines threatened to burst out of him entirely with each movement, but he used the power within him to keep his flesh together, to hold on just a little bit longer. The gods were so close now, and a glance showed them deadlocked, their movements mirrored. No attack went unforeseen; no feint succeeded; every thrust was parried away.

"Karak," Velixar groaned—another inch crawled. He was nearly deaf now from the riotous clash of the gods' ethereal blades. Even the screaming host of humanity fell away. It seemed impossible that two weapons could make such a cacophony, but each connection between them was like the collision of worlds.

They had to see it, didn't they? See how the air was turning a shade of green, how dark clouds swirled above them like the heart of a tornado? His terror grew. So thick with magic now, multicolored sparks shimmering in and out of existence everywhere he looked. Something, or someone, was coming.

Crawl! He flung himself forward onto the remnants of the castle courtyard, strewn with rubble, without fear of the conflict, but only the deep innate sense he felt that somehow time was running out. The battling gods were close now, mere feet away. The dust vibrated before him; he saw a foot, and then he reached out. Just as he touched Karak's heel, he heard a sound that shook through his body. It was like a crack of thunder, only greater, so much greater, and it carried the power of a goddess.

Time halted. His heartbeat froze. No blood dripped from his body. The ground vanished, and though he felt a smooth surface beneath him, there was nothing there but a blanket of stars that seemed to stretch out to infinity. Karak took a step, breaking Velixar's touch, and suddenly he could not move, could not speak. He could only watch. Both gods turned to face the intruder, and to Velixar's eyes she was a stunningly impossible vision. He felt an ache in the back of his mind as he tried to give form to the light shining before him. There was a face, a feminine form, hair like light, eyes like stars, and in seeing her, Velixar realized how *whole* she was. This was not the same goddess he had watched descend from the heavens to find comfort in Ashhur's bed. This was *true* divinity. The brother gods, compared to her, were incomplete. They were broken, lacking her power, her authority. Right then, Velixar had no doubt that in her realm, the brother gods were mere interlopers.

"This ends," Celestia said, hovering before them. Her voice was beautiful and terrifying. "No more destruction. No more wasted life. Only the two of you, as it always should have been. Find a victor."

Karak and Ashhur lifted swords gleaming with energy, light, and fire. If they were upset with the goddess's intervention, they did not show it. Instead, Ashhur's brow furrowed, and his gaze narrowed with concentration as Karak grinned wide.

"There is only one possible victor," said Karak. "We both know who is stronger. Your heart is soft, brother, and it will lead to your downfall."

Ashhur braced for an attack.

"Too many of my children have died by your hand," he said. "Come see how little mercy for you is left in my heart."

Karak lunged, his sword lashing out, and when Ashhur blocked, it seemed all of eternity shook from the impact. The blades pressed harder and harder against each other, until it seemed they intertwined completely, fire and light swirling together. When they pulled back, neither god appeared fazed in the slightest. Up and around went Karak's sword, swiping wide for Ashhur's side. He blocked again, and the shock wave was just as strong, the impact fusing the weapons together once more. Mouth hanging open, Velixar watched as they repeated the dance again and again, sometimes Ashhur taking the offensive, most times not.

This wasn't like Haven. That wasn't even close to the battle he'd just witnessed. For once, Velixar saw the gods not bound by flesh, but by something different, something more. The strength of their blades was no longer dependent on the strength of their muscles. Both their eyes shone white with power, and as their intensity increased, so too did their visages grow otherworldly. They were men standing on stars, swinging blades amid the heavens, beings of strength and power that made the very cosmos shudder. Force of will drove them on. Time, already an elusive thing, became meaningless, and Velixar was nothing but a spectator, his own heart not beating, his lungs never once drawing in a breath of air.

Strike. Parry. Swing. Block. On and on, a dance unending, neither able to surprise the other, neither able to bring down his brother with either power or strength. If it tired them or gave them pause, neither showed it. A thousand times their blades struck, then a thousand times more. Through it all watched the goddess, her luminous form saying nothing, only silently waiting for the end.

And then, just when it seemed they would endure forever, their battle stretching on as infinite as the field of stars they warred within, Velixar saw Karak's blade slow. It wasn't much, just the faintest spark of white across the tip. It was the goddess, Velixar knew. It had to be. His god would not fail. He felt seething rage in his breast as Ashhur's sword slipped over the block, through Karak's armor, and into his chest. It plunged in deep, and instead of shadow, shimmering crimson blood poured forth. A symbol of how weak they were when confronted with true power. Karak stood there for an endless moment, mouth open, his fiery blade vanishing into the ether.

And then he fell.

Velixar wanted to scream, to cry out, but he was helpless. There would be no denying the goddess, not then and there, her collected might gathered and furious. Whatever terror he'd known, it only magnified. Karak had lost. Ashhur was victorious.

"I've won," Ashhur said as Karak knelt before him, clutching his bleeding chest. Karak glared at him but said nothing, would not admit defeat even then. Velixar waited for the horrible moment when the final blow would come, wishing he could shut his eyes, but unable to do even that.

"You have," Celestia said, and it seemed she grew closer, more human. "But what does your victory mean?"

Ashhur seemed perplexed by the question. He looked down at his sword, stained with the blood of his brother, the blood of a god. His fist tightened. The glow of the blade brightened.

"I end it," he said.

"There is another way," Celestia said, and she hovered between them, a ghostly presence. "Let him suffer exile to the world you came from. I allowed your entrance, and I can deny it just the same."

Still Karak said nothing. Velixar wished his god would object, would cry out at the injustice. Celestia had interfered—did they not all see? The whore had broken the dance, tipped it to her lover. Ashhur was not the stronger. He was not!

"Another way," Ashhur said, gaze boring into Karak, who shuddered and held tight to the oozing wound in his chest.

"Or you can take his life," Celestia whispered, and it seemed her voice echoed from a thousand directions. "Take his power into your own. All of Dezrel will be yours, if you desire it. Make your choice."

Up came the sword. Velixar couldn't imagine the debate raging within Ashhur, but he could see a glimpse of it. He could see the pain, the exhaustion, the indecision, the doubt and fondness. But then he saw it all replaced by a glimmer, a hint of something he'd seen in Darakken, and in himself. A longing for power. When did a god ever resist power?

Down came the sword.

"STOP!"

Ashhur's sword shattered. Eternity quivered. The goddess stood between them as a flaring nova, and there was no denying the fury that overwhelmed her every word.

"You still seek blood?" she asked as both gods lifted up, helpless in her grip. "You, Ashhur, my lover . . . you would seek power over mercy? You, Karak, you would have death and emptiness if it granted you order? You entered my world through my grace, my desire to save you, and you have ruined it with fire, flooded it with beasts, and spilled the blood of your own children. I will not have it, even if I must be the one to pay the cost."

The heavens ruptured. High above, Velixar glimpsed a world beyond his own understanding. The only thing he could perceive was its vastness. Something—a wall, a light—divided it, and with a sound akin to shattering stone, Celestia cast the gods into either side. They faded, growing farther away. Yet still the goddess spoke.

"The souls that awaited you . . . take them. They are yours."

A chasm then appeared, rising from below him from the black. Next came the murmur of thousands of voices, and then Velixar watched the people ascend from the chasm, which now stretched out into the heavens as if it had no end. They passed through stars as if the distance was but a step, and they sang and cried and danced. *The souls of Afram,* Velixar realized. Velixar looked to the dividing line, and the sight of it made him wish to weep. The faces were different, the bodies strange, but Velixar saw some he recognized, people Jacob Eveningstar had known; Roland Norsman, Nessa DuTaureau, Crian Crestwell, Vulfram and Soleh Mori, Harlan Howey, Oscar Wellington. Ranks of Wardens streamed past him, Judarius and Ezekai, Loen and Grendel, Bareatus and Jaquiel, and countless others. The spirits of the humans went to the gods who'd created them, and the Wardens to Ashhur, until the stars sealed, and only the twirling void met Velixar's eyes.

He was alone with the goddess.

"Karak," Velixar wept. "Karak, please, fight her . . . fight free!"

Celestia turned to him, and he felt paralyzed with terror. Her eyes bore into him, and it seemed she saw him for the very first time. Pointing a finger toward him, she spoke.

"You were banished. You are again."

The power of Velixar, the Beast of a Thousand Faces, ripped out of his very essence. No pain ever felt by the man once known as Jacob could compare. He screamed, he writhed, as the ancient power fled him like red curls of smoke, disappearing into the void. It was like losing a hand, only worse—like forgetting how to breathe even as his lungs burned. Yet he could do nothing, only weep, while the stars vanished.

In his chest, he felt his heart beat, just once, before his body spilled apart.

As he lay dying, the clouds above him rumbling, the world returning to his sight, he heard the goddess's words echo across the land.

I banish you, never to walk my land again. If you would war forever, then let it rage among your creations. Let it be your curse, one they will bear until the breaking of days.

His body convulsed, his vision gone dim, and with ears gone deaf, he heard only silence. Death was coming, death for the ageless First Man. For the briefest moment, he thought perhaps it would be a welcome relief. At least he would war no more. At least he would bear no more burdens for either of the gods. As he felt himself slip away, his only regret was that, in the end, he and his chosen god had lost.

Not yet.

It was a voice he could never forget. Karak's invisible hands were on him, his power flooding into Jacob's every particle of being. Skin knit shut where he'd been cut in twain. The strength he'd lost from the demon was replaced by something purer, holier. His body convulsed, but he felt no pain as his sight and hearing returned. Against his chest he felt the emblem of his god burning into his flesh. The pendant glowed like a dying star. Letting out a great cry, he staggered to his feet. Karak's voice overwhelmed him.

This is the last I have to give, my faithful prophet. The war is not yet done. Be my voice in a world that will soon know only silence. Be my Lion.

Velixar looked down to his hands as he realized what it was he'd become. His heart no longer beat. His lungs drew in no air. When he spoke, his voice was a projection of his will, deep and rumbling.

"Death," he whispered.

Prophet, said his god.

Velixar looked about, saw the countless men and women who moments ago had been trying to kill each other, now confused and lost, blinking away their blindness from the sudden deluge of light. They didn't know what to do, how to act. Who would rule them? Who were they to worship? And what of the war, the gods?

They'd need him, Velixar saw, now more than ever. But it could not be here, not as he was, a wretched, scarred body coated with his own blood. He had to recover. He had to grieve. To his left he ran, toward the shadows lingering between two wrecked sections of the wall that had once protected the Castle of the Lion. He leapt into those shadows. Karak's power flooded him, and he knew the words without thinking. A doorway opened for him; he fled through, and then he was gone.

CHAPTER 51

I banish you, never to walk my land again. If you would war forever, then let it rage among your creations. Let it be your curse, one they will bear until the breaking of days.

Patrick blinked, his vision finally coming back after that sudden flash of brilliant light. The billowing clouds overhead parted, allowing sunlight to once more shine down on the blood-covered square. The ruins of the castle were now devoid of conflict. All it had taken was a single lightning strike, and Ashhur and Karak were gone. Jacob Eveningstar seemed to have vanished as well. In their place were the words of the goddess, echoing through Patrick's mind as he stood gawking at the scene.

Patrick wiped blood from his forehead. The rush of conflict had all but left him, quivering in his nerve endings like a forgotten memory. He looked to Moira, who appeared just as horrified as he, and snaked his hand into hers. He slid Winterbone into its scabbard. Together they exited the confines of the wrecked stable, wandering out amid the ruin.

"Did you hear it?" Patrick asked. "Celestia's voice?"

Moira looked over at him and nodded. "I did." She then gestured to the packed, bloody square. "They *all* did."

The people of both Paradise and Neldar shuffled about, their expressions blank. There was sobbing to be heard, and moans, and a few voices whispering urgently, but other than that there was silence. He sought out familiar faces, but it was difficult to distinguish one man from another when their faces were all painted red with blood. The whole time, Moira prattled on about finding Rachida, her voice strained, seemingly on the verge of tears. Patrick's heart went out to her. Then, someone shouted his name, and he halted in his tracks. Moira stopped as well, turning toward the sound with him.

From out of the stilled swarm marched a dignified soldier Patrick instantly recognized, flanked by four others. The tears that flowed from Preston's eyes washed the blood from his cheeks. There was an unmoving form draped across his arms, its limbs and neck flaccid. Big and Little Flick, marching behind him, each held a body as well, with Ryann and Joffrey beside them.

Patrick held his ground as they approached. The remaining Turncloaks laid the bodies of their dead onto the bloodied cobbles before him. Patrick stared into the older man's steely gray eyes as they twitched. There was such deep sorrow there, it broke Patrick's heart.

He looked down at the three bodies, each caked with blood. Young men all, brave men all. Two were Preston's sons, Edward and Ragnar. The third was Tristan Valeson. Tristan's neck was a gory mess of pulverized meat. His eyes were open, growing cloudy in death, staring unblinking at the sky. Patrick knelt down, clutched the young soldier's fingers with one hand, and closed his eyelids with the other. His heart, already broken from Celestia's harrowing words, shattered some more.

"I'm sorry, Patrick," he heard Moira say.

"You will be missed," he whispered. He leaned over, gave Tristan a kiss on the forehead, and then did the same with Edward and Ragnar.

"They died good deaths," said Preston. His voice cracked when he said it.

"Was there ever such a thing?" Patrick answered softly.

There were people shuffling around now. Patrick turned away from the corpses of his friends and looked toward the empty ruins of the castle. Kneeling in front of it was a man in heavy plate armor. His head was thrown back toward the heavens. "Release him at once, you bitch!" the man shouted in his anguished voice. "Karak, Karak, fight her! You cannot lose!"

Another soldier walked up to the kneeling man and tried to pull him away. The man turned suddenly, snatching the soldier by the front of his breastplate, and Patrick saw his face. It was the one who guarded Jacob Eveningstar, the soldier with the great horned helm, the marred face, and the dead, milky eye. The man shoved the soldier away, spouting obscenities. His shoulders hitched, and the sound of his sobs mixed with the others. Patrick rolled his neck and rose painfully to his feet. He looked to Moira, who wasn't paying attention to him. Her eyes were focused on some point in the distance, widened in what could either have been shock or delight.

"I can't believe it," she said. The lithe woman took a few steps forward, as if in a dream, before bursting into an all-out sprint. She careened through the maze of corpses and dazed people until she ran headlong into four men who limped through the crowd. "Rodin!" Patrick heard her say as she threw her arms around a bald and strapping, blood-soaked man.

Something else caught Patrick's eye right then. There were elves winding through the massacre, their neutral-toned clothes torn and spotted with gore. There were quite a few of them, coming from every direction. Someone shouted in the elves' native tongue, breaking the eerie almost silence. Patrick whirled around, only to see the square-faced elf he and Moira had battled, standing with both his black swords in hand.

The elf was calling his brethren to him.

Patrick sidestepped around the three bodies at his feet, sidling up to Preston. The old soldier had gathered his wits; the only signs of his sorrow were the clean trails that snaked down his bloodied cheeks.

"Be wary," Patrick said out of the corner of his mouth, tilting his head in the elf's direction.

Preston understood. His hand fell to the handle of his sheathed sword. The other Turncloaks followed his lead.

The elves continued to gather a few feet from where the anguished soldier of Karak wailed. Patrick did a quick count, coming up with forty-three. The colossal elf in black gathered the others around, shouting in their queer tongue. When that was finished, the elves sheathed their swords and slung their bows over their backs. They began to cross the blood-splattered square, only to stop a moment later. It appeared as if each of their heads looked up to the sky at once.

A whisper on the wind reached Patrick's ears, nearly undecipherable. Though he couldn't make out the words, it was obviously the goddess speaking once more, her voice soft and snipped and threatening.

The elves fell to their knees. Their eyes bulged, and their heads were thrown back. Their mouths opened as if to scream, but no sound came out. Patrick inched forward, Preston and the surviving Turncloaks following. Patrick couldn't believe what he was seeing. The elves' flesh bubbled and warped, the color darkening to a slate gray. Their eyes retreated into their sockets, and their brows distended. Each of them lurched forward, gagging on an unseen blockage, their lips pulling back, their incisors growing slightly larger. They looked dangerous, feral. Then they all collapsed and writhed there for a moment, until they all fell still.

"What in the name of the unholy?" whispered Preston.

The scene had drawn a crowd around Patrick, blocking his vision and making him wary of the wall of human flesh that closed him in.

He might not have been stunted, but with his hunched back and warped spine, he was shorter than most, and he had to hop up to see what was happening. He heard the crowd gasp before it started to back away. Frustrated, he and his remaining Turncloaks elbowed their way through the mass of bodies, seeking the front.

When they reached open air, they saw each of the elves standing and staring at their hands. They no longer looked like elves. Instead of looking noble, they seemed savage, their skin covered with pocks and scars. The large one with the black armor saw Patrick and jolted his head forward, snapping at him. Patrick jumped backward and yelped, his hand instinctively reaching for Winterbone.

The twisted elf's eyes lost their focus. His head lifted, seemingly glaring at each and every face that stared back at him. Behind him, his brethren did the same. They grunted and hissed. A few of them tried to form words, but their tongues tangled in their mouths.

Then, suddenly, the large one's head swung around. He gawked stupidly toward the demolished castle, until those deep-set eyes narrowed. A primordial scream left his mouth, and the former elf took off running, drawing those two black swords from his back. His brethren gaped at each other stupidly before they started to run as well.

They were heading for the wailing man, the one with the dead, milky eye.

Patrick didn't know why he felt inclined to do what he did next. "No!" he shouted, and then took off, grabbing hold of Preston's sleeve on the way by, tugging the old soldier along. Patrick ran as fast as his uneven legs could carry him, heading diagonally toward the kneeling man. Somehow he kept pace with the sprinting feral elf. He reached back and tugged Winterbone loose, his breath coming in short, painful rasps.

The kneeling man's head whirled around just as the feral elf drew close to him. The man fell back on his hands, groping on the ground beside him for something, but he wasn't quick enough. A pair of black, glinting blades cut through the air.

Patrick dove forward and lunged with Winterbone. The feral elf's swords crashed into his with a hollow *clang*. The elf's strength was immense, but somehow, even though pain spiked into his back, Patrick's powerful arms didn't yield an inch. Their blades remained locked, just a whisper away from the kneeling man's face.

The man's good eye looked from Patrick to the elf and then back again. Patrick took a deep breath and brought his arms up with as much force as he could. The large elf was knocked backward, giving Jacob Eveningstar's protector a chance to roll out of harm's way. The other deformed elves closed in from behind, brandishing their own weapons and squealing like rabid animals. Patrick stepped back and hunkered down, preparing to be rammed, preparing to die.

Then the shouting began. Preston barked orders, inspiring those who'd been gawking to snap into action. A large crowd of humans collided with the feral elves, battering them with swords and axes, shoving them over the ruins of the castle wall. Patrick saw two of the odd wrapped women among the fray, their wrappings soaked with blood, slashing at the new enemy in their midst as if they could erase all the knowledge that their god was gone by simply destroying these primitive beasts. It was a vicious spectacle, and his watching of it almost ended him.

So focused was he on the brutality of his fellow humans that he almost didn't see the large elf come at him from the side. At the last moment he bent backward, and two black swords sliced across the space he'd once occupied. The perverse elf roared at him and threw a fist, catching him full in the face. His nose snapped to the side, blood pouring from his nostrils. Patrick staggered, having to jab Winterbone against the cobbles to keep from falling.

The beastly thing was on him again a second later, hacking and slashing with wild abandon. It fought with no skill, only pure rage, beating Patrick back. Another three of its mates, apparently having escaped death at the hands of the riotous mob, joined the large elf's side. All four of them bore down on Patrick. With his eyes watering from his broken nose and his limbs gone weary, it was all Patrick could do to hold Winterbone up. Blades scraped his armor and pierced his flesh.

One of the feral elves to his left then howled as the tip of a colossal sword exited his chest. The thing's eyes bulged from his sockets and he looked down at the protruding blade as if in disbelief. In a single, brutal motion, the sword then flashed up, tearing the dark elf up through the bottom of his neck. The dead elf was knocked to the side. In its place stood the man who'd been kneeling, his horned helm back atop his head, his ample sword held firmly in both hands. The man's good eye sparkled through his visor, and he nodded curtly before hurtling himself toward two of the elves, his sword strikes measured and deadly.

The larger of the feral elves, the one in the black armor, remained fixated on Patrick. Sparks were flying in all directions as his two swords met Winterbone again and again. The elf was much larger than him, and despite his feat of strength earlier, he knew he couldn't keep up this fight for long. The elf finally threw him off balance, thrusting with one sword, a move that Patrick lifted Winterbone to counter. The other sword then slipped beneath his raised hands. The blade clanged off the bottom of Patrick's breastplate and plunged easily into his belly. Patrick lurched forward as pain overwhelmed him. The feral elf slammed his forehead into Patrick's. His head snapped back and he collapsed. The blade slid out of him as he fell. Patrick felt blood gush from the wound, drenching his crotch and thighs.

The feral thing hovered over him, cackling in an odd, callous way. The sun glimmered over his black scale armor as he held both swords out to his sides, the blades dripping with Patrick's blood. The elf's muscles tensed as he prepared to strike. Patrick showed the beast his neck, hoping it would be quick. The twisted elf then paused for some reason, his head tilting to the side. It didn't stop tilting until the head came loose from the neck and tumbled over his shoulder. The body fell, collapsing next to Patrick on the gore-stained cobbles with a sickening *splat*. The elf's swords clattered away.

Patrick looked up at the gigantic image of a god looming above him, a halo of light shimmering around its body. The figure then leaned on a sword and crouched down beside Patrick, his silky golden hair just as soaked with blood as everything else in this godsforsaken place. Patrick looked into those intense blue eyes and laughed, causing a coughing fit to overtake him. That was no god.

"Ahaesarus," he said between painful chuckles. "You made it."

"Barely," the Master Warden said.

"Couldn't you see he was going to kill me? I would think you'd have at least given me that before you cut off his head."

Ahaesarus patted him on the shoulder. "Sorry. Today was not your day to die, Patrick. After what just happened, you are needed."

"Too bad I'm gutted."

The Warden laid down his sword and rubbed his hands together. "Let us see what we can do about that."

Another form then appeared above him, blocking the sun. Patrick raised his eyes and saw the man with one eye. His sword was sheathed, the horned helm wedged beneath his arm. The man gazed down at him, his lips pursed.

"You saved my life," he said coldly. "For that I am thankful."

Patrick went to reply, only the man turned away before he could say anything. He picked up the twisted elf's two black swords and headed toward a small gathering of soldiers without another word.

"Charming fellow," Patrick said.

"He is one of Karak's most faithful," said Ahaesarus, watching the man as he and his mates wandered away. "It drips off him."

"Good for him," Patrick said. His vision began to get blurry. "But say, Ahaesarus, did you come to save me or let me slowly die?"

The Master Warden chuckled and placed his hands on Patrick's midsection. "To tell you the truth, I am not certain this will work," he said, his eyes peering at the spot where the gods had warred.

"Well try, anyway, or let me go."

Ahaesarus nodded and began to whisper words of prayer. His hands glowed with holy light. Patrick felt the warmth and comfort of Ashhur's healing magics course through him and leaned his head back on the soaked cobbles. He began to grow tired, but before he closed his eyes, he looked one last time at the place where Ashhur and Karak had fought, where the blood of gods had been spilled before a bolt of lightning swallowed them both, along with Jacob Eveningstar, the child of two gods.

"Ashhur, where did you go?" he asked aloud before he lost consciousness.

Chapter 52

Rachida's surviving band of sellswords tried to scale the stumpy new hillock as the winged horses approached, but the steep incline and their armor made them clumsy. Her men slid down the rocks or tumbled head over heels. Rachida herself attempted no such foolish measure. She had just seen a demon turn into a precipitous pile of rocks, elves stare up at the sky as if listening to some unheard diatribe and then half of them fall screaming to the ground, and now winged horses flew over the horizon. No, she was going to stay ready for whatever came next.

"Quester!" she shouted over the din of flapping wings and shrieking elves. "Pox Jon, Turock—get the men moving! Forget the winged horses. We have our own."

The Crimson Sword was but a few feet away, gazing undecidedly at the writhing, warping elves, and the brash young sellsword began barking orders to the others wearing Karak's armor. Pox Jon and Decker, who'd been trying—and failing—to scale the mountain, ran past her to where the few horses they had remaining lingered, held six reins per hand by others of their party. Turock and his spellcasters gave the collapsed elves as wide a berth as they could. She was impressed by the restraint they all showed, not gawking in awe at the flying horses.

But then again, the earth itself had just risen up and swallowed a demon. Dark wonders were becoming surprisingly commonplace.

The others began hustling after her, armor clanking and boots stomping the ground. Rachida waved them past, keeping a wary eye constantly on the fallen elves. There were so many, possibly more than a thousand, both males and females among them. Their bodies swelled and twisted, their skin changing color. Rachida didn't like that one bit.

She liked it even less when they stood up.

Her men were still filing past when they did so. With the new hillock creating an obstruction on one side, the cliff on the other, and so many forms packed in the two-hundred-foot area in between, the soldiers who had yet to cross the threshold stood no chance. The altered elves, their upper bodies bulky, their incisors sharp, shook their heads as if waking from a dream. That only lasted a brief moment. They roared in voices raspy and bestial and proceeded to lash out at the closest things to them—her men.

Her soldiers had weapons, whereas most of the beasts didn't, but the men were vastly outnumbered and ill prepared for the brutality of these new, savage things. The beasts leapt at their prey two, three, four at a time, biting faces, ripping at necks, bludgeoning with their fists. "No!" Rachida exclaimed. She went to draw her Twins but came away with only one. She'd forgotten that she'd given one to the Quellan who had taken charge during the demon's attack. One would have to do. "Quester—with me!" she screamed. With the shortsword in hand, she charged into the melee.

In the art of swordplay, if Moira was the gymnast, Rachida was the dancer. She flowed like water through the madness, on her toes, each part of her body moving in harmony. She spun away from greedy claws, ducked beneath snapping mouths, pirouetted around her would-be murderers. Her sword was an extension of her hand, its blade going exactly where she wished it. She flicked her wrist, severing a throat, then slid to the side, raised her free hand up, and brought her other arm around, spearing a female beast in the chest. Each time she twirled, she grabbed the collar of one of her men, shoving him toward safety. Some of her men made it; others were swallowed by the riotous horde of gray flesh.

Quester appeared by her side, the young man's forked beard colored red now, but not with dye. He was elegant in his own right, his longsword looping around, easily cutting away at the unprotected creatures. "There are too many," he called out. Strangely enough, he almost sounded gleeful about it.

"I know!" said Rachida, dipping her shoulder and stabbing upward, impaling a beastly elf through the chin.

"Retreat or die fighting?"

"Retreat," she called back.

The two of them backed away slowly, a constant flurry of motion as they kept space between them and the beasts that wanted them dead. They were soon joined by Talon Blackwolfe, who hacked away in his own special, belligerent style, his greasy, dark hair flopping about him. The three of them gathered up men as they went, until it was a group of twenty that cut their way through the homicidal host. The beasts surrounded them, pressing in on all sides. Their strength seemed to grow with each passing moment, as did their threshold for pain. Rachida slashed one across the belly, only to have it run at her again while its intestines trailed behind.

"I'm sorry, Moira," she muttered as she gutted yet another former elf.

"Get down!" she heard Turock scream.

The largest fireball Rachida had seen since Karak decimated the Temple of the Flesh soared over her head just as she ducked. It struck the ground and detonated, sending dead soldiers and flailing gray-skinned beasts tumbling into the air. The smell of scorched flesh filled her nostrils. Smoke began to choke out the space they fought in.

"Hot damn!" Turock shouted.

The beasts surrounding Rachida's pack began to thin out, when another fireball, slightly smaller this time, soared overhead, setting even more of the beasts aflame. The former elves stared at the flames, their deep-set eyes wide with fear. "Now!" Rachida ordered. With Quester in the lead, they shoved their way through those who remained. Men still died, but more of the beasts did now. A ray of lightning as thick as Rachida's body struck those off to the right, making their bodies shake and smoke and finally explode, sending more of the twisted elves over the cliff.

Finally, the beasts fell away from them. Rachida turned and ran toward the line where Turock stood with his sixteen spellcasters. The looks on each of their faces were of pure glee, Turock's in particular. The strange, red-haired man hooted as he began launching fireballs with each hand, one after the other, killing beasts and shoving the rest back.

The survivors dashed past the spellcasters and huffed their way to the other side, away from the cliff where the narrow and flat grassland spread out. Rachida glanced up. The last few winged horses descended to the peak of the new hillock and lifted off mere seconds later, a pair of elves on each of their backs. She watched them glide south, out over the ocean, and spin around, sailing back over their heads as they flew northeast. She then brought her attention to Turock. The spellcaster and his students seemed to be running out of strength, their magical attacks weaker and weaker. Not that it mattered much. Only a handful of twisted elves remained. The rest had fled around the other side of the hillock and disappeared into the forest.

When it was over, Rachida gathered her remaining men into ranks and took a rough count. Barely half of the eight hundred who had made their way south from Drake remained.

"We lost so many," she said, to which Talon dipped his head in respect.

"Fewer men, fewer greedy hands grasping for my gold," said a gleeful Quester Billings. The Crimson Sword winked at her. Rachida scowled but said nothing. A sellsword was a sellsword. He was simply living in a world Karak had built, owning the ideals Karak believed in. There would be no changing that.

She approached the spellcasters last. The group of them was gathered in a tight circle, talking enthusiastically among themselves. Rachida tapped Turock on the shoulder, and the man spun around, his eyes wild with excitement.

"Did you see that?" he exclaimed as he followed her away from his apprentices. "Did you fucking *see that*?"

Rachida nodded. "But how? I thought you said your magic was limited?"

"I know, and it was. By Karak's wilted prick, I thought I'd used up all I had fighting the demon! But it was a good thing I was spent, because had I not . . . " He trailed off.

"The fireball would have been much bigger?" Rachida asked.

"Indeed. And then who knows how many of your people would've died." The odd man laughed. "Hell, I might have blown up that mound and freed the beast again if that had happened!"

"Somehow, I do not think that likely," said Rachida.

"Probably not. However, this changes things entirely."

"How so?"

The man grinned. "Why else would magic be suddenly rendered powerful where once it was weak? My teacher, Errdroth Plentos, told me once that all magic lost potency once the brother gods came to Dezrel. So if now that magic has returned . . . "

"Then the gods no longer walk the land," she finished for him. For Rachida, the thought was exhilarating and terrifying at the same time. *Be careful what you pray for* and all. "How do you think it happened, if it did?"

"Who knows?" Turock said with a shrug. He then pointed at his fellow spellcasters. "And I don't rightly care. Just think on this,

Rachida, my wonderful slice of the heavens. Let's say the gods are gone. How many men and women do you know, in Neldar and beyond, who are practiced in the art of magic?"

She shrugged. "You, I suppose. And your students."

"Exactly," the man said with a wink as he proffered his pointed cap. "And some of the elves, of course. Which, if my grasp of numbers doesn't fail me, will make me a very, very sought-after man."

"I suppose it does."

"You just remember to save some of that gold your men keep talking about for me. I think you owe me that much."

Rachida frowned and walked away while Turock laughed, not liking that statement one bit.

An hour later, the cavalcade began the long march north. Rachida lingered behind, staring from a distance at the new hillock, the smoking divots in the earth, and the litany of corpses heaped on the ground. It was a quiet moment. She closed her eyes to pray for the souls of the dead, but suddenly realized that she didn't know to whom to pray.

"Is the great Rachida Gemcroft feeling introspective?" she heard Quester ask.

Her eyes opened. The young sellsword was beside her, the blood in his forked beard now dried. It flaked off as he ran his hand through it. The handsome man smiled deviously at her.

"Should you not be watching over my charges?" she asked him.

"I handed the reins to Blackwolfe. The man's eager. Has potential. Could make a good sellsword one day."

"Perhaps."

"Anyway, what happens with grimy Talon doesn't truly concern me. What I would really like to know is where we go from here." He laughed. "Do you wish to remain in Paradise and build a new life for yourself?"

She chuckled. "Fuck Paradise. I do not think I like it here."

That elicited a laugh from Quester as well.

"As a matter of fact," said Rachida, "I have a sudden, burning desire to march back to Neldar. Hopefully, I have someone there waiting for me, someone I haven't seen in far too long."

Moira's image flashed in her mind, her icy blue eyes, her silver hair, her slender body. Rachida felt warmth spread through her.

Quester nodded. "So we find a way around the river and head east, then?"

"No. We ride back to Conch and sail back to the Isles of Gold." She looked at her last remaining Twin, its cutting edge stained brown. "I miss my son, and I have a very special gift for my husband too."

"That, and you still need to give us our gold."

"Yes, that too."

They laughed together and turned their horses about, heading toward the rear of the convoy as it plodded over the hills.

CHAPTER 53

In the aftermath of the gods' disappearance and the deaths of the twisted elves, the people stood in shocked silence. It seemed even the dying chose to still their tongues. Laurel felt a sort of deflating in the air, as if the souls of every living being who remained on what had once been a battlefield had been stripped of their wills. Soldiers of Karak and Ashhur, Sisters of the Cloth, Wardens from the west—all simply gawked at everything around them, confused as to what they should do next.

Laurel approached the battlefield from behind, walking slowly alongside the wreckage of what had been Karak's most glorious creation. The Castle of the Lion's three towers were a heap of rubble that filled up nearly the entire courtyard. The stables to the rear of the castle were buried under a mound of gray stone. The ground had fractured, and heavy stones had begun to slide down into the earth, collapsing into the dungeons and tunnels below the castle. The thirty-foot wall was in pieces as well; only three short sections remained standing.

As Laurel placed one foot in front of the other, she scanned the ruins. Shredded bits of tapestry, pinned below the chunks of stone, flapped in the breeze. There were iron cookware and brass candleholders strewn about, crushed and useless. In places, blood seeped from below the jagged boulders—all that remained of those who had hid within the castle during the battle. Laurel hoped Zebediah and Marius, the betraying members of the Council of Twelve, were among them.

Somehow, she had a feeling they hadn't been.

King Eldrich walked to one side of her, Lyana Mori to the other. The king's hands were shaking, his eyes bulging in disbelief as he took in the scene.

"I don't believe it," he said. "She did it. Celestia banished them."

"Where did they go?" asked Lyana.

Laurel swallowed hard. "I don't know, Lyana. I don't know."

Together, the three of them crossed through the area where once the portcullis had stood. There was a rotten stench in the air. The only sign that there had once been a wall and portcullis here was a single onyx lion, its rear half pulverized. Laurel shuddered and turned her head away from the thing. Lyana's hand slipped into hers. King Eldrich cleared his throat.

"What do we do now?" he asked. His voice sounded far away.

"We keep going," she told him.

Countless eyes turned to them as the trio walked onto the bloody cobbles outside the destroyed castle wall. A group of men decked in bloodied armor stepped aside, allowing them to pass. One among them Laurel recognized—Malcolm Gregorian, the scarred former Captain of the Palace Guard. Malcolm's good eye shimmered with tears as he looked at Laurel, but there was no recognition in his gaze. The large man turned away, his massive sword strapped to his back and a pair of black blades dangling in his hands. He shook his head, looking just as lost as the men around him.

Laurel passed them by, allowing herself to patiently look upon the area where the battle had taken place. Corpses were everywhere—men, women, Wardens, and horses—grotesque reminders for those who'd survived the ordeal of what had just passed. She wondered if any of them were Pulo or Moira, or any of the other poor souls she had grown to love over the last year of her life. Whether they were or not, she knew that if they weren't disposed of soon, this area would be nigh uninhabitable. *Such a cold way to think,* she thought. It was obvious no one shared her feelings. The people simply milled about, slowly breaking out of their stupors. The wounded were treated. Wardens, themselves appearing weary and mystified, knelt before those whose injuries were most dire, seemingly without care for which god had spawned them. Laurel looked on as a soft yellow glow rose up from one of their hands. The blood-drenched Warden stared at his fingers as if shocked that this should happen. Another Warden, a towering sort who walked with his head held high, leaned over his brethren and offered reassuring words. When he stood, the comforting Warden looked Laurel's way and nodded. Laurel returned the gesture.

A great murmuring could soon be heard, a thousand whispered conversations happening at once. The survivors began gathering in small groups. It was difficult to tell who was who, what with all as drenched in blood as they were. Laurel wondered if the men out there knew one another, or if they were simply looking to the closest person to them for comfort. She shrugged and walked on.

Farther along the square, as the street leading to the South Road narrowed, Laurel found a small cluster of Sisters gathered before the front stoop of a coin lender's store. Their wrappings red and heavy, they had their arms around one another as they sobbed. Laurel held out her hand, halting Eldrich's and Lyana's progress.

"Why are we stopping?" asked the king.

Laurel put a finger to her lips and watched.

The men who walked down the road paid the Sisters no mind, wandering mindlessly toward the main throughway in a steady stream. Some tugged injured horses behind them, the only things of true value left on the battlefield. Only one individual, a woman, seemed to notice the Sisters. The woman took a pin from her hair as she weaved between the ambling men, and out fell a nest of red-blond curls. Laurel had never seen hair that color in her life aside from the poor girl who had once hung from the castle wall. *A woman from Paradise,* she thought. The red-haired woman approached the Sisters and knelt in front of them, placing her hands on the backs of the two closest to her. The Sisters turned to her, and allowed the new woman to join in their embrace.

"What are we watching?" asked Lyana.

"Healing," said Laurel.

The woman from Paradise leaned back from the embrace and faced one of the Sisters. Her head tilted to the side, and she smiled sadly. Reaching up her hands, the woman began undoing the wrappings around the Sister's head, slowly revealing a shock of auburn waves, a pair of light green eyes, a thick nose, and full lips. The girl uncovered was young, thirteen at the most. The redhead leaned forward and rustled the girl's hair before placing a gentle kiss on her forehead.

Behind the two, the rest of the Sisters began removing their wrappings as well.

"It's symbolic," she told King Eldrich.

"What is?"

"The removing of the bandages. They represent servitude. Once they come off, the allegiance to Karak ends. Look."

She pointed toward the meandering crowd. Now that the Sisters had uncovered their faces, the men drifted toward them, offering embraces and sincere words, comforting them as they would any other.

"They're allowed to care," she said. "It doesn't matter if they are from Veldaren, or Felwood, or Gronswik, or Omnmount, or even Paradise. It doesn't matter which god created them. They are hurting, they have lived though a nightmare, and they require comfort. The gods be damned."

Lyana gasped.

"I would watch your tongue, Laurel," said the king.

"Why? We have no reason to any longer."

"But we don't know where the gods went. They might come back."

To that, Laurel laughed. "You heard the goddess. They aren't coming back." She waved her arm out toward the departing masses. "And everyone knows it. We feel little because we turned our back on our god long ago. But these people? They fought for their deity, were willing to die for him. You can see the pain of loss in each of their eyes. They're alone in a world where the gods once walked among them. As are we. Faith will be given new meaning now. So will what it means to be human."

"Karak got his wish after all," whispered Lyana.

Both Laurel and the king looked at her.

The girl continued, her tone childlike and timid. "Karak always said he wanted us to be free. That he wanted us to think for ourselves and make our own way." She looked up at Laurel with pleading eyes. "Do you think he meant for this all along?"

Laurel's heart broke for her. *All she's suffered in his name, and still she loves him.*

"Who knows, Lyana?" she said. "Perhaps he did."

It was the easiest lie in the world to tell.

King Eldrich squinted and stepped off the bloodstained slate walk. "And this peace . . . do you think it will last?"

"No," Laurel replied, sidling up beside the drawn-out man and slipping her arm into his. She didn't fail to notice the way the king's breathing hitched when she did so. "The shock will pass, and life will go on. We're human. We err, we fight, we cheat, we steal, we kill. We'll do just as we've always done, only now we do it rudderless."

"And what of Paradise?" asked Eldrich. "Ashhur is gone as well, which leaves another rudderless nation in our midst, one that has been ravaged by war."

"I think Paradise is the least of your worries, my Liege. There is too much to accomplish here."

The king nodded solemnly and faced the departing mob. The weary soldiers greeted him with esteem as they walked by. "And what do I do?"

"You go among them. You talk to them. You *inspire* them. You're the king of this land, no matter who it was that named you. And with no one to pull the strings, no one can rightly call you a puppet."

"I don't have the tools, Laurel. I don't have an army. I don't even have a *castle*."

"You have something more than that. The people have known you as their king for nine years now. They recognize you as such. You must let those who would question your leadership see the real you. And as for a castle, you have the Tower Keep. It might not be as lavish as the Castle of the Lion, but perhaps that's what you require. Someplace practical. Someplace easily defensible. Someplace as ugly as the sins of the human soul. This is now a new nation, with new rules and new laws, laws that you will help inscribe. You have everything you require to become not just a king, but a *great* king."

"Not everything."

"No?"

"No," Eldrich said with a wink. "A great king needs a great queen, after all. I've heard all the Wardens' stories say so."

Lyana giggled and covered her mouth. As for Laurel, all she could do was shake her head and smile.

EPILOGUE

The cart was excruciatingly heavy. Then again, that was bound to be the case when the corpse of a twelve-foot-tall giant was sprawled atop it.

"Shouldn't you have lost some weight by now, old friend?" asked Patrick, his eyes stinging from the sweat running down his bulging forehead. He peered behind him at the corpse of Bardiya Gorgoros. The giant's skin had gone from brown to pale gray, and his gums and lips had receded, but other than that, the body was shockingly well preserved. His eyes were closed, his chin held back, as if in prayer. If anything, he appeared peaceful. Patrick turned back around, focusing instead on lugging the cart down the gentle decline. He felt tears begin to well up. "We hardly saw each other over the last twenty years, but I miss the big lug now more than ever."

Big Flick, who hauled the cart's other long handle, glanced over at him. The large young Turncloak sniffled and nodded, but said nothing.

It was early morning as the somber group of eight trudged their way from the cliff on which Bardiya had died to the rocky flatlands to the north. All were silent save the occasional sigh. Preston, Joffrey, Ryann, and the Kerrian Allay Loros walked in the lead with Warden Ahaesarus while Patrick and Big Flick hauled the cart behind them. To the rear was a second wagon, the leads of the lame horse that pulled it held by Little Flick. That second cart held a trio of corpses, those of Preston's sons, Edward and Ragnar, and Tristan Valeson, along with their paltry supplies. They had come this way to honor the dead Turncloaks, as Preston wished to bury his sons as their tradition demanded, beneath the rocky soil they once called home. Retrieving Bardiya had been Patrick's decision. The thought of allowing the man whom Ashhur had described as his most pure child to rot while animals pecked away at his corpse had made him feel ill.

Patrick grunted when his foot struck a protruding chunk of granite, sending pain flaring through his toes. He heard the horse snort behind him and cursed. He'd felt obligated to help haul the cart when they'd finally reached Bardiya's body, a final show of respect to a man he'd once called friend, but it was frustrating that the cart needed human propulsion at all. After the attack on Veldaren, horses had become a rare and valuable commodity. That they had been given this lame mare, which had been wounded during the battle, was a wonder in itself.

The three weeks since the gods disappeared from the face of Dezrel had passed by in a blur. Patrick himself had aided in clearing out the mass of corpses that filled the square where Veldaren's castle once stood. In total, nearly four thousand of Karak's and Ashhur's children had perished, along with five hundred horses. Over a hundred Wardens had also left the world for good. The number of deceased was so great that they were burned en masse, in great pyres whose flames illuminated the sky for five days straight.

After that, the process of rebuilding began. Three years of strife had ended, and yet it seemed humanity's struggles were just beginning. With no more gods to guide the way, the people were lost. They wandered the city streets with empty stares. Few talked about anything but the gods. Prayer circles began to form daily as the survivors from both sides sought comfort in those who had been raised like them. Minor scuffles broke out. Survivors leapt from the tops of the city's tallest buildings, and some wandered into the wilderness. The young human race was astray, a people without purpose, without guidance. Looking back was easier than looking forward.

Many of those from Neldar packed what they could and headed off to the various villages and townships they called home. Moira was among those who left. Ashhur's brave warriors had no such option. Food was scare, supplies scarcer. That, coupled with the long journey that was sure to face them and the uncertainty of what they would find if they ever did make it back to the former paradise across the river, forced their hand. Karak had razed much of the land, after all, and the eastern deity's beast-men now roamed free. So most settled into the strange, faraway city, pining for the life they'd once had while struggling to adapt to their new one.

Yet in the midst of hardship and blight, a slight thread of hope emerged. The king of Neldar began holding court nightly, the willowy man named Eldrich giving impassioned speeches from the steps of an ugly, imposing tower in the north of the city. Although he didn't promise that life would be easy, or that each man, woman, and child would be free from suffering, he bonded the citizens together with pledges of unity. "We will endure this together!" he would proclaim. Moods began to brighten. People went back to work, smithies, carpenters, pottery makers, cobblers, and apothecaries reopening their doors. Others began filing into the city as well, exhausted soldiers of Karak who had abandoned their god on the battlefield and braved the harrowing journey back home. The fields just outside Veldaren were tilled and prepared for the spring planting, the farmers who worked them not wanting for helping hands now that there were so many unskilled laborers living within the city limits. A semblance of order was brought back to what had once been chaos. The City Watch was re-formed, an institution that Patrick was asked to enlist in, an offer he declined. Instead, he toiled the fields along with his people, his hope being that once the crops were cultivated, he could strike off west and reunite with his family.

In the aftermath of war, he missed them more than anything, even his mother and father. Their sins against him seemed to grow less and less serious with distance, time, and hardship.

Love and forgive one another, and you will find fulfillment. He peered at the giant's corpse. Perhaps Bardiya had been right about everything all along.

"Here," said Allay Loros, his black skin glistening with sweat as he stood with hands on hips. The progression stopped.

"Here?" asked Preston. "Why?"

"Because it reminds me of home," the Kerrian said wistfully.

They had walked nearly three miles, and the cliff was far behind them. The place where they now stood was a vast meadow of swaying, knee-high grasses. To the left was a wide chasm of rushing water where the two rivers, the Gihon flowing from the northwest and the Rigon from the northeast, poured into each other. On the opposite side of the fork were the thick forests of Paradise; to the north of it, the rocky expanse of the Tinderlands. Three separate worlds, merged. *Yes,* thought Patrick. It was the perfect place for Bardiya's remains to be buried.

Shovels were retrieved from the cart, and the eight weary travelers began digging. It took nearly two hours for them to manage a hole large enough to fit Bardiya's gargantuan frame. When it was finished, the giant was gently put to rest, the hollow filled back in. Afterward, they stood around the huge mound of dirt, heads down.

"You'll be missed, Bardy," Patrick said. "I hope Ashhur is keeping you safe on the other side."

"I wish to speak," said Ahaesarus. The Warden had remained mostly silent during the length of their journey, and hearing his stern voice made Patrick twitch. "There is something I must ask you all."

"Go on," Patrick said.

Ahaesarus stepped to the edge of the burial mound. "Where will you be going from here? What plans do you have?"

Everyone stared at him as if deep in thought. None responded.

"We don't know," Patrick said finally, breaking the uncomfortable silence. "I suppose we just see what happens."

"Do you love Ashhur?" the Warden asked.

"Of course," Allay said, as if offended. "He created us."

"Yet he is gone now. How will you honor him?"

To that, none had a reply.

Ahaesarus began pacing inside the circle, looking each man in the eye as he passed him. "Ashhur spoke of love and forgiveness, of living in harmony with your fellow man, of caring for family and appreciating all life. With him now gone, who will spread his message?

"When Karak first left his children more than forty years ago, a priesthood was formed. Although the leader of that priesthood, a man named Tustlewhite, now languishes, insane, in the custody of Neldar's king, I have learned there were many more that bore the mantle. Villages throughout this kingdom have a temple; and that temple, a priest. The priest preaches, and the acolytes carry forth the message. Though they have not been heard from since Karak was banished, they will not remain that way for long. Civilization needs beliefs. They will rise up again; they will preach Karak's word. If this world is indeed free for any and all to live wherever and however they may choose, that doctrine must be balanced. Ashhur's teachings must not fade away into nothingness, lest Celestia's final condemnation come to pass."

Patrick drew his lips into a tight line. "What are you saying? That we should become priests?"

"Not in the slightest," said the Warden. "My fellow Wardens and I have talked of forming the priesthood. However, I have spoken at length with King Vaelor and his advisors over the last few weeks about many of the aspects of life I experienced on Algrahar. In particular, he was curious about the concept of a knighthood. You all may remember the stories my people told you, of an order that adhered to a strict code, pledged their lives to various kings, their duties to defend the realm and uphold the law of the land."

"The Wardens left Neldar when I was young," said Preston, "but I remember those stories well."

"Yes. They are tales of gallantry and honor, of brave men defending against invading armies and battling hell beasts. However, these men did not serve the will of Rana, but the will of man."

"The will of man?" said Big Flick, confused. "You had humans where you were?"

"No, son. On Algrahar, *we* were humankind."

"Oh."

Ahaesarus chuckled. "That is beside the point. Although these knights were indeed great warriors, they were mere peasants when compared to those who trained them. It was those who dedicated their lives to Rana's teachings—operating outside the laws of men, preaching the word of our god, upholding the holy and protecting the innocent—that were the true glory of our world. We called them paladins, their order the most trying and elite to ever be created. In fact, I was told by Ashhur long ago that he and Karak had paladins of their own at some point in the past, on some other world."

"Paladins? Never heard of them," said Patrick.

"I would think not," Ahaesarus said, placing his hand on Patrick's shoulder. "The brother deities decided the order was unnecessary. They had learned that granting men that mantle was counterproductive when the gods themselves walked the land. For if that god erred, it would be his very faithful that confronted him." The Warden pointed at the mound beneath which Bardiya was buried. "With that in mind, it is here, on the very spot where Ashhur's most faithful servant, the one who was willing to righteously defy him, has been laid to rest, that a new Citadel should be built. It is here that the paladins of Ashhur must come into being.

"You are the best there is. Preston, you and your boys have proven your dedication to Ashhur's teachings. Allay, you led your people to your god's side when most others would have sought safety. And Patrick, Ashhur told me time and again that of all his creations, you were the most beautiful. You have shown that through every waking moment of your life."

Patrick thought of his past, of all the women he had bedded, of all the men he'd killed. He thought of his doubts, of the times he'd cursed Ashhur's name when the going was rough, of the numerous occasions he had wished for his life to come to end.

"I think you overestimate me," he said.

"I think not," retorted Ahaesarus. "I think that if one man embodies all it means to be a child of Ashhur, it is you. Ashhur himself believed it, and so do I."

All grew silent. Patrick closed his eyes. *Ashhur, is this right?* He didn't expect an answer, yet he received one nonetheless. Warmth spread through his belly, extending down his arms and legs, causing his fingers and toes to tremble. He saw Ashhur's likeness in his mind, hovering over the world and smiling down on him. He saw Nessa and Corton and Bardiya and Tristan, the light surrounding them nearly blinding, their hands reaching out for him, their lips mouthing the same refrain.

You are loved.

Patrick opened his eyes and took a step onto Bardiya's burial mound. He dropped to his knees. The warmth continued to fill his deformed body. Tears streamed down his cheeks.

"I dedicate my life to you, your Grace," he said, staring at the heavens. "I will be your servant. I will protect your children. I will live my life to the fullest and show others the way. I will call others to join me, and together we will help lead the meek through Afram, until they reach the Golden Forever beyond the stars."

Allay smiled. Preston nodded firmly. Joffrey, Ryann, and Big and Little Flick slowly got on their knees, themselves looking close to tears. Hands fell on Patrick's shoulders. Ahaesarus looked down on him with pride.

"It is done," the Warden said. "You are the first."

Patrick sniffled. "I guess I am."

"And for your sacrifice, you have received your reward."

"My reward?"

Patrick yelped as he felt a sharp, momentary pain in his scalp. He rubbed the sore spot as Ahaesarus leaned over and placed something in Patrick's palm.

"Your reward."

Pinching the gift Ahaesarus had given him, Patrick raised it up to his eyes. It was a single hair, long and curly and so silver that it seemed nearly transparent in the bright sunlight. A wide smile came over Patrick's lips.

"Well, I'll be damned."

AFTERWORD

Robert

Well, this one was rough.

By all rights, it shouldn't have been. After all, when Dave and I first set out to begin this project, we already knew where this part of the story would end. It had been set up long before, documented over the many books Dave had written that took place in Dezrel. That made the outline quite simple. Battle for Mordeina? Check. Creation of the beast-men? Check. The Darakken finally being thwarted? Check. The final confrontation between Ashhur and Karak? Checkity-check-check-check.

But here's the thing: There was so much more to this far-reaching tale than just those few elements. We had multiple characters to consider, numerous locations, and the eventual drawing in of every major player. There was torment in Veldaren, fear of impending doom in Mordeina, torture in the desert of Ker, scheming in Port Lancaster, and numerous other plotlines to consider. It was a lot to consider, a lot to take in . . . and a hell of a lot to wrap up in two hundred thousand words.

That, more than anything, was the crux of why this book was so difficult. When I wrote the outline, I originally came up with eighty-six chapters, plus a prologue and an epilogue. *Eighty-six!* As it is, that's 40 percent larger than this tome is already. Some things needed to be cut, and I struggled with those decisions. I was afraid we'd end up with a half-million-word book that'd be virtually unsellable.

In the end, it was Dave who saved me from myself. He hacked and slashed at the outline, whittling the chapter count down to a reasonable fifty-three. Then, when the manuscript was finished, he slashed even more. Was it tough? Of course. There was stuff that didn't make it into the book that I absolutely adored. But you know, that's the thing with writing—sometimes your favorite bits are also the most unnecessary. For as much as Dave hates world building, his lack of sentimentality is a blessing, especially for someone like me who sometimes has trouble restraining himself.

Now, I realize that there are certain plotlines that're left rather open ended. There just wasn't room for them in this book, which happens to be the price of word-count restrictions and tight storytelling. Don't worry, we haven't forgotten about them. There are some dire things in store for Catherine, Moira, and especially Ceredon, Aully, and Kindren. We also haven't overlooked Geris Felhorn, Vulfram's children Alexander and Caleigh, or little Willa, Avila Crestwell's tiny companion. All of these characters' stories are far from over, for *Blood of Gods,* while indeed being the climax of the war between Ashhur and Karak, is actually only the midpoint of the series we had planned. There are still three more books to go—*Kings of Ruin, Prince of Beasts*, and *Queen of Lies*. When we'll actually get around to writing them, I'm not entirely sure. But they *will* be written, and that's a promise.

I of course need to thank my wife, Jess, for her constant support; Dave, for being my forever ally; and my agent, Michael Carr, for—well, just for being awesome. Thanks again to David Pomerico for hefting his way through this *looooong* three-book journey, Mark Winters for his spectacular covers, and the entire team at 47North for their unending support. I need to give a tremendous *YOU ROCK!* to Jaime Levine for stepping in and putting forth the tremendous effort to story-edit this book. This is the first Dave and I have worked with her, and the transition from our old editor was as seamless as could be. And how could I forget Jill Pellarin, who tirelessly copyedited all three of these rather hefty manuscripts and did so with undying enthusiasm?

Finally, I need to thank you, the fans, who've gone on this journey with us thus far. As much fun as it is to work on these books with Dave, it wouldn't be worth anything without your support and appreciation of the material. Just wait until you see what else we have in store!

And without further ado, I'll pass the baton to Dave . . .

David

To be fair, I don't hate world building. I'd just rather focus on characters. Just want to throw that out there before I start!

Finishing this book was bittersweet. There are moments I have in my head, long before I ever start writing a book, that I look forward to reaching, that I feel will define the novel. The ending of this book, particularly the final battle between Karak and Ashhur, I've been pondering for years now. Years. So to reach that point and to try to live up to a fraction of what I had in my head, to try to convey the sense of futility and grandeur and world-shattering decisions, well . . . that's kind of daunting. I did my best, and I hope you all found it satisfying. There's a pretty big risk of it being a deus ex machina ending, which sort of happens when you plot the history of a war solely to be history instead of an actual separate series of novels like when I first built Dezrel. But I think we earned this one.

So now the scene is done, the war is told, and looking back at all the various moments I never once imagined when I first ran this war through my head, I can only hope we hit the scale just right. This was a young world, with a young race of humankind and with gods walking among them. This should have felt different, should have carried gravitas some of my other novels never dared carry. And as much as I am proud of this series, I'm also exhausted by nearly all six hundred thousand words of it. This was a scope I'd never once tried before, and without Rob's help, it certainly never would have happened. For that, I'll forever be in his debt.

Consider this next part here for all you longtime fans: I hope you realize how much a love letter this series (and this book in particular) is for you. The creation of the paladins? The first instance of an Elholad? Kayne and Lilah becoming like they were in Old Ways? Creation of the orcs? Harruq's twin cursed blades from the Half-Orcs? The rise to power of the Trifect from Shadowdance? Yup, they're here. The war scenes from *The Weight of Blood*, the various tales Velixar told—they're all here. Speaking of Velixar, you even get to see that bastard get chopped in half and become the loveable lich he is in the rest of my books. If we could sneak in a cameo, if we could build a history for it, we did. The Breaking World is a veritable Where's Waldo of my other series, and I hope at least one or two of them put a smile on your face when you discovered them.

Rob said all the thank-you's, but I'll say them again: David, for trusting us in the first place; Michael, for listening to my pitch about this silly co-author story I'd been working on; Mark, for giving us covers far better than we deserve; and Jaime, for having to read through this behemoth multiple times with a critical eye.

But last, and as always most important, thank *you*, dear reader. We do this for you, to entertain you, to pull you out of your world and into ours. I pray your stay, despite a few dark spots, was an enjoyable one.

David Dalglish & Robert Duperre
February 25th, 2014